*At the Wall
of the Almighty*

At the Wall
of the Almighty

a novel by

Farnoosh Moshiri

INTERLINK BOOKS
An imprint of Interlink Publishing Group, Inc.
NEW YORK

First published 2000 by

INTERLINK BOOKS

An imprint of Interlink Publishing Group, Inc.
99 Seventh Avenue • Brooklyn, New York 11215 and
46 Crosby Street • Northampton, Massachusetts 01060

Library of Congress Cataloging-in-Publication Data

Moshiri, Farnoosh,
    At the wall of the almighty / by Farnoosh Moshiri.
        p.   cm.   - - (Emerging voices)
        ISBN 1-56656-315-1—(pbk.)
        1. Title.   II. Series.
PS3563.088443A88   1999
813' .54--dc21

99-21087
CIP

Cover painting by Simin Meykadeh, courtesy of the Royal Society of Fine Art,
Jordan National Gallery of Fine Arts, Amman, Jordan.

Printed and bound in Canada
10   9   8   7   6   5   4   3   2   1

To request our complete catalog,
please call us at 1-800-238-LINK or write to:
Interlink Publishing
46 Crosby Street, Northampton, MA 01060
e-mail: interpg@aol.com • website: www.interlinkbooks.com

To my mother, the memory of my father,
and the lost writers.

Contents

Acknowledgements

Without the love and support of my husband David and my son Anoosh I would not have been able to write this book. They know the depth of my gratitude. And my special thanks go to Nicole Brogdon, Mary Robison, and James Robison, whose generous support and guidance made this novel possible. I'd also like to thank the writers and professors, Daniel Stern and John Williams, for reading a chapter of this novel and encouraging me to go on.

*"Through me is the way into the doleful city; through me
the way into eternal pain; through me the way among people lost..."*
—Dante, *The Inferno*

"I alone have escaped to tell you."
—*The Book of Job*

Chapter One
With Loony Kamal

To the left and right, south and north,
the wall rises, impassable...
—Federico Garcia Lorca

In the Hallways

The bearded guard is wearing a black, long-sleeved shirt and black pants tucked into heavy military boots. He is tall and square, his beard foamy and full, his hair close-cropped. He walks in the long hallway, pulling me behind. Something in his right pocket rattles with each step: chee, chee, chee, chee... We walk with the sound of the chain.

"You are an Unbreakable now and I'm taking you to your final destination—Hall Twenty, cell number four. You'll end up at the Wall of the Almighty. If you remember and repent, you'll live. You may even get out."

I know that I'm in the hallways of El-Deen, the central prison of the Holy Republic, and I know that this guard is taking me from my solitary confinement—the Black Box—to cell number four, cell of the Unbreakables. But this is all that I know; I don't remember anything else.

"You've left your memories in the Black Box, that I understand, but how about your tongue? Did you leave that too? Say something, brother, the corridors are damn long and I'm bored," the guard says. His voice is warm and deep. It sounds familiar. I have a feeling that I've heard this voice all my life. "Have you forgotten my name?"

I nod, although his back is to me and he cannot see me nodding. For the first time I realize that there is a black leash tied to my neck and that's how he is dragging me behind. Now he pulls the leash gently and his voice becomes friendlier. He is in a good mood.

As though reading my mind, he says that the leash is because he cannot touch me. I'm not clean. If I repent and if my repentance is accepted, he'll remove the leash.

1

"But you remember *me*, don't you?" he waits for me to say something. "I'm Kamal, Loony Kamal. That's what they call me in El-Deen. Doesn't ring a bell?"

My tongue is heavy as a brick and I have no vocal cords.

"They call me Loony Kamal, because I'm a multi-talented lunatic genius. Haven't you seen me acting on the stage? Nothing rings a bell?"

Nothing rings a bell, though everything is strangely familiar: the tall gray iron doors on the right and left of the hallways, the TV sets hanging from the ceiling at each intersection, the cold cement floor and back of Kamal's head, triple layers of fat on his thick neck. This is a neck I've seen before.

The hallway is quiet. TVs off the air. The programs must have ended. There is no way to tell the time. Is it after midnight? Or afternoon nap time? When we are not close to the TVs there is no sound except this rattle coming from Kamal's pocket.

"Don't worry," he says after a few minutes, "You'll remember. It's always like this after the Black Box. Your clothes were all messed up, brother. You dirtied yourself in the Box. I hosed down you and the Box and put fresh clothes on you. You remember this part, don't you? You must have enjoyed the water. You're lucky I haven't blindfolded you. I hope La-Jay doesn't check on us with his secret cameras. I thought if I leave your eyes open, you may remember better."

When he mentions La-Jay, I realize that he is talking about the head of the facilities. But I have no image of him. I don't think I've ever seen La-Jay before. But I also remember that with his sophisticated monitoring system he always checks on different units of the prison.

"So we have to start from the beginning, huh? Like there has never been a past. I have to explain everything again. How does it sound?"

I nod and wait for him to explain. My body is unusually light, painless and relaxed. The handcuffs are tight, but they don't hurt my wrists. I'm wearing clean gray pajamas—a bit larger than my size. They smell of laundry soap. My feet are bare and the cement floor is cold. But this doesn't bother me. Kamal pulls the leash as gently as a child pulling his kite behind.

I'm a kite floating in the hallways of El-Deen.

When we turn right to a different corridor, with the color of the walls slightly lighter gray, Kamal talks about the Revolution. He says that he, son of a butcher, joined the Revolution to purge the enemies of God and the

2

Faith, carried the black flag of the Party of God and beat himself with a chain on the back until blood gushed out, smeared the blood on his face, took an oath and called himself a Devotee of the Holy Revolution. And what did *I* do in the Revolution, he asks.

I was on a wall—a tall brick wall—watching the ocean of oil, people drowning in it, I think to myself, but I cannot tell him this.

"Who was with you?" Kamal asks.

I was alone, I think again. On top of the wall. Some people were drowned and some were arrested. Black vans carried them to El-Deen. But I stayed on the wall, alone.

"Nothing rings a bell, huh?" Kamal asks and walks faster. He may be mad at me. At my silence.

Now I have the image of a monster with many heads. Not ugly at all, rather handsome, bleeding and moving in the streets. Men with black flags raise their sabers, and chop its limbs and heads. The monster moans and groans, but still moves forward. It loses more limbs and more heads until nothing remains of it. Someone must have told me this story before.

"You were on top of a wall when you got arrested," Kamal says in a strange voice. His friendly tone has turned threatening and his voice trembles a bit. "You had a big fucking flag and a shitty banner in your hands. You looked like an idiot. You could've run away and saved your butt. But you stayed up there like a pile of shit. Don't you remember?" He pulls my leash to make me move faster, as though I'm a sacrificial cow, a fat one, resisting going to the altar. "You son of a bitch! They should've shot you the same day, right at the same wall. Why do they bring an idiot like you here, to this facility? This is the University of El-Deen: The Gate of Paradise. You owe your life to the charity, generosity, and mercy of our Holy Leader. You have to pray ten times a day and thank God Almighty that you're still alive and walking with your eyes open."

Kamal is mad. I can't see his face, but I can imagine his mouth foaming and his eyes rolling like a lunatic. The three fat pillows behind his neck are crimson red. He walks faster, pulling my leash hard. I tumble and trip over.

"You are children of the devil, as our Great Leader says. Our revolutionary duty is to purge you all. Move, bastard. My time is short. I'm not at your service forever. I have work to do. It's past the midnight prayer and I'm behind my schedule. Move your fucking feet. Bigger steps, bigger, you sack of shit!"

This way I follow him and realize why he is called Loony Kamal. He takes long steps and I almost run behind him. We move for a while until all the TVs start to sing and Kamal slows down. There is a picture of a tomb on all the screens. It's an ordinary grave with a gray stone, somewhat bigger and taller than a regular grave stone. A black flag is planted above it. A deep warm voice chants the prayer. As we turn to the right and left in the long corridors, I see the same little monument and flag again and again. Kamal, much calmer now, but still mad at me, says that all this—the TV sets, super modern monitoring system, electronic doors and hidden lenses, air conditioning system and elaborate medical facilities—are "way too much" for a bunch of motherfuckers like me. He murmurs as though thinking aloud, talking to himself.

"If they'd give me these facilities to run, I wouldn't take a son of a bitch like you out of that box. I'd let you stay there till you'd gradually get buried under your own shit and puke and suffocate because of your own stink. That's what I'd do. Or I'd release a sack of cockroaches in your box to keep you company. They'd consume you little by little."

No one passes by. I notice for the first time that the corridors are empty. Kamal is quiet. I hear only the rattle, the "chee" sound. If it wasn't for the warm voice of the muezzin, chanting the prayer, I would panic at the thought that the whole world is dead and I'm left alone with Loony Kamal.

The fact that I'm not tired, sleepy, or hungry, surprises me. I'm empty, weightless, and completely without pain. Had I been in a normal condition, the tall cement walls—stretching forever and impassable—the thick iron doors and the floor, which is dark and cold, could choke me with despair. But now I look up at the windowless ceiling and realize that El-Deen doesn't even have little barred openings toward the sky and I follow my crazy guard in indifference.

I don't think that I hear any sound coming out of the closed cells. It must be either hallucination or strong imagination that makes me hear whispers, moans, and sighs. We pass each cell and it's as if a strange choral piece is performed by the ghosts inside. My heart should bleed... My heart should bleed... I think to myself.

Now Brother Kamal talks about the facilities being one of the most modern in the world. He talks about the sophisticated monitoring system and the electronic gate system. He explains how El-Deen doesn't have stairs or elevators. The floor is gently graded and without noticing we ascend or descend. But one has to be familiar with the corridors. It's easy to get lost in El-Deen. He says this as though talking to a respectable visitor.

El-Deen has seven floors above the ground and three under the ground. My final destination, Kamal repeats, is Hall Twenty, cell number four, which is located in the first floor underground, the lowest floor. There are always between twenty to thirty Unbreakables locked in this cell, unless there has been a Cleaning Up Operation, ordered by the Great Leader himself, then the cell is almost empty. The Wall of the Almighty is conveniently in the courtyard behind the Unbreakable's cell.

La-Jay, the Great Octopus, the head of the University, Father of El-Deen, lives on the seventh floor. He prays on the roof to be closer to God.

Now we slow down and Kamal shows me a blindfolded man moving himself on his butt. He is at the end of the long hall. I notice that although he is rowing with his hands to move forward, his guard is pulling him with a leash too. As we approach them I see the man's feet. They are swollen like pink balloons, ready to pop.

"This bastard was the representative of the teacher's union," Kamal explains in a low voice. "While our Great Leader had already formed the Holy Associations of Teachers, Workers, and Peasants, this son of a bitch made his own union. What do you call that, huh? Rejection of the Leader's organization. Opposition to the laws of the Holy Republic. And he's going to end up at the Wall of the Almighty. No doubt about it." He pauses a moment, as though waiting for my response, then goes on, "What is a union after all? A red organization. Look at him now! Bag of shit! He's been flogged with a cable on his feet. Believe me brother, this is worse than any other training; you can't walk for months."

"Training" rings a bell. But the bell echoes in my hollow head. I can't remember anything. Have I been "trained?" Maybe many times. Where are my wounds then?

But Kamal is still showing the teacher to me. "Look! Look how the bastard is trying to slide himself on his shitty ass. He looks like an old fucking row boat! Hey, Brother!" he calls the other guard, a shorter man with layers of fat hanging over his tight belt. The resonance of Kamal's voice in the empty hallway, in an instant flash of memory, reminds me of someone telling me a story about the monster of the well. This monster called from

5

the bottom of the deep well and his voice echoed like Kamal's: "Mmmmmmm—," the monster said. "I smell human flesh—Jinnis and Minis—the dish is fresh!"

"God bless the Holy Leader!" the fatbelly guard says, standing in front of us.

"God bless the Holy Leader and yourself, Brother!" Kamal says. "Taking the motherfucker to the Hothouse?"

"No, Brother, he is through with his interrogation. Ha-G wants to Box him again. To heal his feet." They both laugh and the guard's belly quivers. Kamal pulls my leash and the guard pulls the teacher's leash. I notice that the teacher's shaved head is bumpy and not quite round. The blindfold has covered most of his face. His lips have an unusual dark brown color. Once I knew an opium addict with such dark lips. But don't remember when.

"Come to the show!" Kamal shouts, as we walk in the opposite direction.

"I will! I've seen it three times. But I want to see it again," the guard shouts back.

At the end of this hall (Hall Twelve of the second floor, Kamal explains), he stops. The walls are a slightly lighter color now and the rooms have ordinary doors. There are no iron gates. Kamal ties my leash to a door-knob and orders me to stand and wait for him. There is a TV hanging from the ceiling between the right and left halls. Kamal spreads a kerchief on the cement floor and lays a gray square stone—a miniature grave stone—and a carnelian rosary on the kerchief. While rolling his sleeves up, he whispers something to himself. He rubs his hands and face, as though washing them. After the washing pantomime, he bends down and bows to the picture of the grave. He rises and bows again. Now he kneels down. Brother Kamal, staring at the black flag above the gray tombstone, prays his morning prayer. I lean against the door, watching him.

The Crimson Carpet

I close my eyes and see a porch facing a mountain. The mountain is so close, it scares me. It stretches from the right and left to unseen spots and up, reaching the sky. The white peak looks like a sharp, pointed nightcap; clouds around it, wrap and unwrap. There are some patches of snow here and there. But the stone skirt of the mountain is the color of iron. At dusk the skirt turns black.

Someone is praying on a crimson carpet on this porch. A woman. She is short, like a child, but stooped. She has two long white braids hanging from either side of her shrunken face. Her skin is creased and leathery, her eyes slanted, her cheekbones high. Now she wraps a large, white scarf around her head and covers her hair. The scarf is thin and on one corner a peacock is embroidered with different shades of green. The peacock's feathers are open like an umbrella. The old woman whispers and bows to the mountain, raises her hands up to the sky and mumbles something, louder this time, but in a strange language. She sits cross-legged on the carpet and prays. There is a big green peacock at the center of the carpet too. Yellow and blue flowers have grown in the crimson grass around the green peacock. She sits on the peacock's feathery umbrella, gazes at the mountain. Cries. Tears roll down and find a way through the cracks of her face. She wipes her wet face with the scarf and weeps some more. She fingers her rosary. Each big golden bead hits the other one with a click and she clicks for long moments without taking her eyes from the dark skirt of the mountain.

The air is dry and cool, clean and fragile. It's so thin it can crack and break with the slightest noise. Someone sings upstairs in a room on the roof. It's a love song: "Kiss me... Kiss me for the last time... I'm going toward my fate... " And dusk descends. Pots and pans rattle in the dimly lit kitchen. The sweet smell of saffron fills the house. A hand holds my hand, pulling me behind. I'm still staring at the old woman, who cannot hear or smell the sounds and smells of dinner—or she can, but does not care.

This hand that pulls me behind is soft and small—the size of mine and tangled in mine. We run up the steps, to the second floor and then the third. We step on the roof, which is carpeted with square tiles and turned into a terrace. There is a single room here, face to face with the mountain. We press our foreheads to the windowpane and peer inside. A young girl sits at a desk, fist under chin, a notebook open in front of her; straight black hair flows down her shoulders and sweeps the blank paper; the hair covers part of her face like a half-drawn curtain. She hasn't written anything. She gazes at the mountain, singing, "In the midst of the storm, I'm lost with the boatmen..." She sees us and with her long forefinger invites us in. We enter timidly, heads bent. She hugs us. Each of us curl under one of her arms. She smells of dust and pencil. She rubs her lips to my hair and kisses our cheeks and gives us pencils. One for each. The pencils have many tiny animal pictures on them. We press them to our chests and fly down the steps to the porch where the old woman has left her carpet. We look around to make sure she is not there, then we peep into her room and find her sitting on a cushion smoking her water-pipe. A wet cloud carries the smell of tobacco and rose water out. We tip-toe toward the carpet and sit on it, each of us on either side of the peacock. We hold hands, hold breaths, and close our eyes. The carpet takes off, floats in the thin air, landing on the white peak of the mountain.

Feeling Pain

I hear a strange voice and open my eyes. This voice does not belong to the house. It comes from the room where I'm tied to its door-knob. A wounded animal is moaning here. The sound is muffled but it's unmistakably a moan. Kamal ends his prayer, unties my leash, and pulls me behind again. I stumble and follow him, hissing to myself, "Hold her hands... hold her hands before she disappears... " Kamal, hearing me or not, stays quiet. He is calm and pensive.

On TV, a bald bearded man with round rimless glasses is giving advice to the prisoners to confess, repent, and join the Army of God. He says the Brothers who have repented and confessed their sins are now living in the comfortable wings of the sixth floor of the University, enjoying the good food and the facilities as if they are in a resort hotel. Before long, he says, they will be free to go out and serve as Devotees of the Holy Revolution.

Without turning his head, Kamal says, "What you heard coming from that room was the moaning of a red bastard: a journalist. He is being trained and re-educated for insulting the Great Leader and his revolutionary insight. The Party of God burned his office and brought him here. He's lost his vision in the Black Box. But I think the motherfucker was half blind from the beginning."

I must be alert, not get easily terrified. Kamal wants to demoralize me. Now I'm even suspicious that his choice of place to pray was intentional: he wanted me to hear the poor man's moans. Besides, while he was seemingly so absorbed in his holy ritual, how could he hear the faint noise, which I barely heard, leaning against the door? Kamal is a cunning person, a specialist, knowledgeable in his own field of work, and I shouldn't be fooled, simply because he has a bad temper or is vulgar and rude.

We reach an intersection. Brother Kamal stops and delays, as if he is thinking whether to turn right or left, or keep going straight. Here, for the first time, I realize that he is not taking me straight to my cell. He is either giving me a tour of El-Deen, or zigzagging to make me crazy. I have no doubt that the whole thing is planned in the headquarters by La-Jay and his advisors, who are sitting in the main tower watching us—Kamal and I— pass through the hallways.

Something has changed. This change might have happened after I saw the vision of the house. Or, I may have been drugged before and the effects are wearing out. I'm tired. Hundreds of aches and pains throb in my body. I'm restless and not weightless anymore. The cold artificial light of the fluorescents torments my eyes. I wish Kamal would blindfold me. My bare feet are freezing, as though the cement floor is covered with ice. The handcuffs feel heavy and get tighter and tighter with the slightest movement of my hands. Kamal stands at this intersection, debating which way to go and the bald man on TV screams, inviting the Unbelievers to the bosom of faith:

"I address you sinners, you misled, you victims of corrupt ideologies imported from the West and East. I address you students, teachers, professors, journalists, artists, politicians of the former regime. I address all of you, the deceived intelligentsia. Join the Army of God, join the Holy Party of God. God is one, His party is one, and His Army is one and here. El-Deen is your University. This is your gate to paradise. Open the gate, hold the flag, and join the heaven of God..."

Kamal turns right. I trudge behind him. My head spins and I feel like vomiting. All I hear are broken sentences from the bald man who is still screaming: "The wide-gaping mouth of hell... Be aware... You'll be cleaned and purged... Millions of fiery tongues... You'll be a heap of ash... God will blow you... " And the hallway suddenly gets crowded.

I notice several men moving on their butts, their guards pulling the leashes. Some are with crutches, some are hooded by paper bags, breathing through a hole, but there are no holes for eyes. I see a group of women in long black robes tied to one rope. A female guard, wearing the same kind of robe, carries a machine gun on her shoulder, pulling them behind. The women's faces are covered, but their eyes are out. I squint to see these eyes. Then I wonder why I am doing this. Am I looking for someone?

The Ancient Scent

Kamal is talking to me, but there are so many things to see and hear that I miss most of what he says. He is explaining that we are in the hall where the interrogations take place. The courts are here. The more we descend, he says, the darker the walls' gray color becomes. The three floors of underground have the darkest color of gray. The hopeless sinners are in the darkness of the lower floors, the repentants can enjoy lighter colors, the sixth and seventh floors have light blue and green colors and that's where the devotees and their families live. La-Jay has designed the place himself, Kamal explains.

Now there is a young man on the screen. His face is unshaven, his eyes sunken and he speaks monotonously: "— I have confessed to my sins. I have accepted the Faith. I'm working studiously for the ideological exams. I'm cooperating with the Brothers of El-Deen to find the members of the parties of devil. I'm living on the fifth floor of the University. Our lunch menu consists of chicken soup with noodles and rice, chicken breast sandwich, beef bologna sandwich with spicy pickles, feta cheese, butter, lamb stew, halva—"

Kamal stops. My knees shake; I almost pass out and melt on the floor like a soft wax. Kamal leaves me alone, but holds the end of the leash. He talks with another guard who has an older man with him. He is blindfolded and has close-cropped gray hair. I can tell that he is quite old. The corners of his lips hang down. His neck is just a pink wrinkled skin covering a big Adam's apple. He is on his hips. The soles of his feet are shredded. He has kept them awkwardly up in the air, avoiding the cement floor. While Kamal and his friend chat, the old man and I sit close to each other. Can he feel my presence? I'm tempted to stretch my arms just a bit and touch the man's hand. Both his hands are on the floor, veins popping out. I stare at them. Weren't these hands broader, fuller, and always warm? Look how they have shrunk, how only the skin is left, covering the blue veins. Does the old man know I'm sitting beside him? Can he smell me?

"—this motherfucker is the devil himself and the devil worshipers of cell four call him "Master!"" Kamal's friend is saying. He is a guard Kamal's size, another Kamal, with a big mole on his right cheek bone above his beard line.

"What surprises me, is Brother La-Jay's benevolence," Kamal tells his friend. "If I were him, I would burn this devil the first day. Why feed him from the Party's budget? This is God's money, after all."

"Well, La-Jay never loses hope. Never. Even this devil may repent," the other Kamal says.

"Where are you taking him now?" Kamal asks.

"To the Hothouse for a hot show!"

Kamal acts ignorant and asks, "What hot show?"

"Don't you know, Brother Kamal? Haven't you heard about the old man's niece? She is in the Hothouse. This devil doesn't have a daughter or a wife. They find out that his niece is in the women's ward. They take her to the Hothouse."

"Who is his niece—a whore?" Kamal lowers his voice, "I mean officially."

"A real one, Brother. She was a dancer of some sort. They have found her pictures in the Opera House. Legs naked and everything—"

"Well, have fun Brother. The old saying goes, 'the pleasure of watching is half the doing!' I'll see you after the performance. I have to talk to you about the issues we've discussed before—you get me?" Kamal says.

"I get you, Brother Kamal. Anytime."

The guard pulls the old man's leash to make him move. Now either the old man loses his control and rolls over me, or he drops himself on purpose to land on my lap. To get back to his rowing position, he has to hold on me. He finds my cuffed hands blindly and I also help him to straighten himself up. For few long seconds we hold hands. He squeezes mine as hard as he can. His hands, although bony and shrunken, are warm.

The old man had been aware of me all the time. He'd recognized me. While I couldn't tell where and when I'd seen him, he remembered me with his eyes closed. Kamal pulls the leash hard to lift me up. I stand and stumble and follow him again. Walking wearily, I raise my hands to my nose and smell the old man's ancient scent. Lotus maybe, dust. Camphor? A strange feeling of loss overcomes me. Tears burn my eyes for the first time since Kamal took me out of the Black Box.

Do I have a niece, a sister, or a wife to worry about? If the threat was meant for me, it didn't work well. My oblivion is many-folded. I don't even remember my name.

The Leader's Gaze

For a while, which seems to me longer than many days and nights, we walk quietly. Men pass by with crutches, or crawl like wounded animals. Most of them are with guards—the devotees—who pull them with black leashes; but a few walk alone, blindfolded, holding to the walls. I notice a group of women tied together by a rope sitting along the wall. I count them: seven. Ropes are tied around their necks. Two are blindfolded. They are black from head to foot. Their small yellow hands in tight handcuffs are the only human sign out of the heap of dark wide robe. The hands look like little yellow leaves grown on a fallen tree. Five of the women don't have blindfolds. I study their eyes again. They are all red. I notice a pair of older eyes, blurred by a wet milky film.

"Son!" The older woman calls Kamal. "The whole thing is a mistake. They have made a mistake. I don't know these ladies. I haven't done anything!" Her voice, muffled under the black veil, sounds older than her eyes. She must be sixty, or even more.

"Talk to the Sisters. I'm not in charge of your unit," Kamal says and drags me behind.

On TV screens the repentants' faces appear and disappear. Each reads a paragraph. Some of the voices shake. The female repentants confess and make speeches too. Some cry, unable to go on. Some read lines from the Holy Book, or quote from the Great Leader, but all the repentants praise Brother La-Jay, the Father of El-Deen, the head of the University.

The bald man comes on the screen again and explains different rules, categories, floors, foods, colors, trainings, exams, ranks, confessions, and so many other things that my head spins and I feel the nausea again. Fragments of his long speech hit my painful temples like hot bullets showering from above: "... top level repentants... names of the collaborators... pass the

12

ideological exams... identifying the devils... enjoy the green wing... private toilets... precious holy books... A middle rank repentant... some comfort... the yellow wing... the brown wing... name the names... those who resist... the unbelievers... the heathens... the blasphemers... the atheists... the reds... the blues... monarchists... materialists... Satans... those who claim... lost their memories... the Black Box... The Wall of the Almighty..."

I wish death—a sudden one, because I cannot hear one more word. I don't care much about the words, the sound is tormenting me. Either the volume is strangely and gradually rising, or my ears have become more sensitive. Finally the bald man removes his rimless glasses, rubs his tired eyes, and murmurs a prayer. His picture fades out and the portrait of the Great Leader of the Holy Revolution appears. The Leader's furrowed eyebrows and his piercing eyes stay on the screen. A military march fills the hallways and the Leader's hawklike eyes stare at me—critically.

The Loony

"I know you're tired. So am I," Kamal says. He hasn't talked to me for a while. We walk in an empty corridor again. The march changes into another one. "I'm taking you somewhere to rest. Then we'll go and eat together. How about that, huh? After dinner I'll take you to the Community Center for the show. And that's where the real surprise is. I won't talk about it anymore. You'd better see for yourself."

Kamal talks like a friend now. He promises rest, invites me to dinner and a show, as if we have a rendezvous. What is he scheming now? Should I anticipate a blast, a violent outburst, a verbal or maybe even a physical assault? The hallways are empty again and I fear Kamal. When the march ends and nothing is on the screen for few seconds, I hear the rattle of his pocket. He is carrying a chain.

Look at his neck, I tell myself. This is the thickest neck I've ever seen. And look at my neck: a swaying wire, almost breaking under the burden of my wobbling head. Look how tall he is. I'm two full heads shorter than him. His hands are twice mine, his feet in his big boots are the size of children's graves. He is a bit fat too. The three rolls of flesh behind his neck are excessive, unnecessary. If I walk faster, I can take a glimpse of his fat belly's profile.

But he is not as fat as some of the guards I've seen in the halls. He is more athletic. His thighs are muscled, twice thicker than my thighs. Who is this loony? How does a mother, a plain ordinary woman, a butcher's wife, produce such an offspring? Where have Kamal's genes come from? I picture him in a regular suit, without military boots, beardless, with longer hair. I imagine his voice to be gentler, rather soothing, his tone, polite. Would he still be scary? He can even look handsome. So it's not Kamal's size that is intimidating. He is violent and rude, moody and unpredictable, in short, a loony. I'm not scared of Kamal's body, I decide, I'm scared of his soul.

With the Metal Chair

As I'm preparing myself for Kamal's possible assault, we reach a door. This is an ordinary door at the end of a hall. Kamal fishes into his pocket and pulls a long heavy key chain out. Many keys, from the size of a nail to a dagger, dangle on the long chain. So this is Kamal's rattle, I think. He doesn't have a real chain to flog me. He unlocks the door, turns the light on, pulling me into a small room that contains a blue folding table and four blue metal chairs in the middle and a bunk bed on the left side, covered with a gray army blanket. A light-weight puffy pillow sits on one end of the bed. There are no windows anywhere. The whizzing fluorescent bulb is stronger than those in the hallways. I blink and notice a sink opposite the door. Beside the sink there is a small area hidden by a blue plastic shower curtain. This must be the toilet and shower.

Kamal empties the contents of his pockets on the table. I notice a big pocket knife and a whistle. I stare at the bed. At this moment I'm ready to give half of my life, or why half? All of it, just to be able to lie down on this bed and rest my painful head on the puffy pillow. Then I'll sleep, a long one, or rather, one without end. How long has it been since I've slept? Did I sleep in the Black Box? I can't recall.

Now Kamal ties my leash to the back of one of the blue chairs and goes toward the sink. He washes his hands and face with splashing sounds. He coughs, spits, gurgles, and dries himself with a towel. He opens a closet as though he is at home. He takes his pajamas out. They are blue and white striped, neatly ironed and folded. He takes his black shirt and pants off, wears the pajamas over his white underwear and slips under the gray blanket. I watch all this rather astonished. Is this where Kamal lives? Is this his "home?"

He hasn't said a word since we entered the room. He has tied my leash to this chair and the leash is short. I'm slightly bent over the chair. My neck is being pulled and my back is stooped. I'm in an awkward position. Is he going to sleep, leaving me in torment like this? Why doesn't he tie me to the chair in a more comfortable way? What if he is going to sleep leaving me standing on my painful feet, with my neck and back hunched like this?

But he remembers he hasn't peed. He gets out of the bed and disappears behind the blue curtain. I see his shadow and hear him peeing. He flushes the toilet and comes out. I struggle to talk, to ask him (if necessary, to beg him) to make my leash longer, so that I can straighten my back. I can manage to stand for a while, but I can't stand while my spine is cracking. The words don't come out and I realize that since the Black Box I haven't uttered a word. I'm mute.

While Kamal adjusts something on the wall—a switch maybe—I try to find a way to straighten myself up. If I do, I'll lift the chair with me. Since I don't have the strength to have a chair hanging from my neck for hours, this option seems out of the question. If I sit down, the chair will fall on me. And this is a metal chair, the kind that makes the most annoying hollow noise. In fact any slight movement will make the chair collapse. This is a torture then, I decide. He is going to sleep in front of me and prevent me from even dozing off. This is a way to break me. I'll finally collapse with the chair. I'll feel as though my head is full of broken glass and naked blades are scratching behind my eyelids. My heart will beat wildly and stop beating, will resume again and stop a moment later. I'll vomit yellow bile and crawl with the chair hanging on me. I'll beg him, "Kamal, Brother, let me sleep. Five minutes, Brother. Three minutes... I'll tell you all that I know... all I can remember. But first let me sleep... " And I'll break into sobs.

I have to decide at this very moment: either let the loony go to bed and leave me in this position (and later bear the disastrous consequences), or ask him to fix my leash and bear the consequence now.

Who said that I'm an Unbreakable? Kamal said. But does this mean I am? I cannot remember anything from the past—immediate or remote. How can I be sure that I haven't been broken one hundred times before?

15

How can I know what I have told them and what I have not? Now I'm mute, but I might have talked before. The Black Box Kamal was talking about is the Unbreakable's solitary confinement. Why have *I* been there? If I'm going toward the cell of the Unbreakables to become one, how come I've already been in the Box? Didn't he say they lock the Unbreakables in the Black Box? So this means that I've already achieved Unbreakablilty and served my time in the Box. Is this the second round then? And if this is true that Kamal is circling me around El-Deen, this round might not be the second, it might be the one hundred and second, or one million and... Crazy thoughts. Insanity. My legs' veins are bulging and burning; they are about to burst. My neck is breaking with pain. I'm confused. I feel I'm nothing but what Kamal defines and this is the utmost breakability.

There must be something to cling to, something to distract myself from the neck, spine, legs, and the damned chair. There must be something to think about, something completely different—out of El-Deen. Out. I remember that I had a vision in the hallways. But now I've forgotten it. Struggling to resurrect that vision, I close my eyes, take a deep breath and remember the little hand; it holds mine, pulls me and takes me somewhere. Out.

Grandfather's Crooked Houses

We climb the hilly street and pass the school. Both the street and the school are called New Spring. The slope becomes sharper, the hill steeper. We are weary and cold. Behind us, on top of the mountain wind whirls around the snow covered peak, white and cone-shaped like a nightcap. The nightcap becomes a salt shaker and pours white powder on our heads. I have a little paper bag in my frozen hand, a few eggs in it. My other hand is warm, tangled in my companion's. We climb and climb. On our right and left there are rows of little houses, each has a narrow yard in front and a tiny two-story building at the end of the yard. The iron gates are freshly painted. These houses look like colorful match boxes, each full of numerous children and women. In the evening, the boxes open and they fill New Spring Street like many match sticks, unless it's cold and breezy like today. Then they all stay inside, sit under one big quilt, crack sunflower hulls and chat till late.

Grandfather's three old houses are at the end of the hilly street, perpendicular to the two lines of the match box houses. They are bigger than the little houses, but much older. They don't have gates, but they have three old wooden doors with brass lion paws hanging on each of them. It's hard to say what color the doors are, because the paint has faded away a long time ago.

Grandfather's first house, the one on the left, looks like a normal house. But it's old and run down. It's square, with a brick wall around it. The wall is low, so we can see the porch from where we are, and the old woman sitting on her carpet, praying. This is a three-story house, each higher story with fewer rooms than the lower one. The first floor has four rooms, the second, two rooms and the third, just one room. The girl with long black hair who sings "Kiss me... kiss me..." is sitting in the only room of the third floor, on top of the crooked pyramid.

Grandfather's second house, the one in the middle, is not quite a normal house because it's not square; it has a triangular tendency. An ugly two-story brick house with the same low brick wall around it, this house has three rooms downstairs and two rooms up. A pyramid without head. Even from a distance you can always hear slapping and smacking, banging and slamming noises. The third house is completely triangular. This one is also surrounded by a brick wall. The smallest of all the three houses, the triangular house has only one story with two rooms. It has a triangular yard, a triangular kitchen at the end of the yard, and a toilet inside the narrow angle. There is a well in the center of the yard and it's covered with a tin lid. On windy nights the lid clatters and rattles as though the monster is moving his pots and pans.

The little hand pulls me and takes me to this house, the triangular one. Passing an old dusty fig tree grown awkwardly by the well, we climb three stone steps and stop in front of an old door. We take off our muddy shoes and enter. The humid heat of the boiling water on top of Aladdin, the kerosene heater, brushes our frozen faces. We blush and our hearts beat faster. Under the window, a woman sits in the bed, leaning her back against the wall, reading a thick book with hard brown cover. I put the eggs on the table and we both run toward her. She takes us into her bed; we curl in the hollows of her thin waist. When our cold toes touch her hot legs under the thick quilt, we breath deeply and hold it in our chests. She closes her book and looks outside. Her large blue eyes shine in the room's dim light like a pair of magic lanterns. Staring at the hilly street and the wooden gate of the school at the foot of the hill—as if she is seeing them for the first time—, she starts her story with her deep and distanced voice.

The kettle whizzes on the burning head of Aladdin, the shadows of dusk fall everywhere and she goes on: "—and the monster of the well said, 'Hmmmmmm... I smell human flesh... Jinnis and Minis... the dish is fresh!'"

The Burning Voice

"I need to take my nap now." Kamal takes me out of the triangular house. He slips under the woolen blanket and pulls it up under his chin. "It gets chilly here. Oh, I forgot the radio. I can't go to sleep without it." He lifts himself up and presses a button on the wall. The room fills with a loud lamenting voice, reproachful and begging, trembling with anger and moaning with pain. Kamal rolls and turns his back to me, curls, pulling the blanket over his head. I stay silent. It's too late to say anything.

"I beseech you, the Devotees of the Last Holy One," the voice screams, "I beseech you and demand. I beseech you and command: throw the blasphemers, the servants of the East and West, the disciples of the Satan, in the flaming trash can of the history! Let them burn alive! Let them frizzle! For now is *our* time! Time of the Great Holy Revolution. The World Revolution. The Revolution promised by the God Almighty and the Last Holy One. Be aware! Be aware that the Absent One is here, now residing among you, watching you and waiting for you. He waits to see how you purify the earth and begin his Holy Reign: the last government on earth, the government of God!"

In spite of the radio's deafening sound, Kamal falls asleep. I hear him snoring. His nostrils must be congested. He snorts. I'm left alone in the middle of the room. Now the leash feels shorter and tighter. The burning voice showers me from above, from the the hidden speakers, like sharp needles. "Hold the hand! Hold the hand so that you won't fall!" I hiss to myself and hold the soft hand. "Pull me... pull me out!" I tell my companion and the voice shouts, "Be aware of His presence!" But I'm already out.

Sahar

In New Spring dusk is short. Night falls fast and the shadow of the mountain covers the neighborhood. When it's dark, we don't want to go out. There are no street lights and the desert behind the three houses, the cemetery, and the multi-level tenant house are scary. On winter nights we hear wolves howling in the desert.

Grandfather rubs his black skull-cap on his itching bald head, slams shut the heavy *Book of the Kings* and looks around at his large family. We all sit in a circle, on the carpeted floor, under a huge quilt, leaning against big cushions and pillows. At the center of our circle, under the quilt, there is a small table and under it charcoal is burning in a brazier. We sit side by side, the quilt up to our waists. The room smells of woodsmoke.

Grandfather just read a few verses of an epic: The story of Rostam, the hero, and the dragon. How Rostam slew the seven headed, seventy-meter long dragon and how his faithful horse, Rakhsh, helped him to fly out of the magic land.

Grand-Lady is here, but absent. Her white scarf with a green peacock embroidered on the corner is loose on her shoulder. Her thin snow white hair, showing her pink skull, is divided in two parts and braided in long thin braids, hanging on her breastless chest. She murmurs something in her weird language and clicks the large beads of her rosary.

Mother reads her thick brown book, her pale face stony like cold marble. Aunty Zari knits a long scarf for her husband who is abroad. The scarf is striped with narrow lines of blue and white. Her son, Kami, plays with the ball of yarn.

Aunty Hoori, her notebook on her lap, stares at the window, weaving and unweaving the tip of her long hair, weaving and unweaving verses in her head.

Maman, after peeling oranges and mandarins, opens a few ripe red pomegranates and patiently takes the ruby seeds out. She squints her eyes and smacks her tongue. Her mouth waters. The room fills with the sour-bitter smell of winter fruits. Maman pours the red juicy seeds in a big glass bowl and adds a dash of salt and a bit of wild marjoram and puts the bowl of glittering fruit jewels on top of the quilted table.

Uncle Musa's son, Cyrus, comes in the room and brings a freezing draft with him. His eyes are wet, his snot running down his lips. He sits beside Kami and tries to grab the ball of yarn. His parents are in their own house— the one in the middle— and we vaguely hear them through the wall. They are fighting again. Uncle Musa yells, Aunty Shamsi cries, a dish breaks, a door bangs and Cyrus, grinding his teeth, pulls the ball of yarn toward himself. Kami smacks him; he cries and screams and they both pull the ball. They take the scarf out of Aunty Zari's hands, take the needles out and fight with the long sharp weapons. Aunty Zari slaps her son and takes the needles back. Kami cries.

Aunty Hoori leaves the room and slams the door. Maman calls after her, screaming that the room on the roof is freezing cold, she'll get sick. The boys holler louder. Grandfather raises his deep voice, Maman raises her thin voice and Grand-Lady weeps. Someone's hand hits the bowl of the pomegranate seeds. The seeds spill. Like a stream of blood, pomegranate juice runs over all the forty patches of Maman's handmade quilt. She hits herself, claws her red face and cries. The hot room boils and explodes.

Mother keeps reading her hard covered book, her face remains expressionless. She never raises her large blue eyes.

A little hand squeezes my hand. We hold our breath and watch the fight. I pull myself closer to my companion.

Outside, dusk has already colored the air indgo-blue and in a minute darkness will fall from top of Mount Alborz. The winter has begun. There is no snow yet, but all the signs of it. When the room gets quieter we hear the whistle of the north wind, Saba, dashing around the skirt of the mountain.

"Now let me see which of my grandchildren is the bravest of all?" Grandfather distracts us from the incident. "Poor Uncle Massi is hungry in the tenant house and his soup is getting cold here. Who can take Uncle's soup to him?"

A dead silence hangs in the room. Kami and Cyrus wipe their tears and shrink under the quilt. Grandfather looks at us with his small watery eyes under the dirty lenses of his round spectacles. We stare back at his dotted face. Fifty-five measle marks—we have counted them many times, while sitting on his lap. What does he mean by looking at us like this? Does he expect one of us to go? Can't we go together at least? And why should *we* go in the first place? Did *we* fight? And why now that outside is pitch black. Couldn't we take the soup when it was still light?

I expect my companion to volunteer. Grandfather knows very well that this little creature with massive bushy hair is the bravest of all. But my companion stares at Grandfather and says nothing. The silence gets embarrassing. All the eyes are on us. Kami and Cyrus have completely disappeared under the quilt. I hear myself saying, "I'll go!" I say this to save my companion. I pull myself out of the warm quilt. Mother makes me wear a thick overcoat, a scarf around my neck and a woolen hat pulled down above my eyes. Maman hands me the warm pan of soup. I step out.

Standing on the cold porch, I look at the darkness. The mountain and the night are one. My heart beats in my ears and bangs against my chest. Saba whistles and whirls around the white cap of the mountain and the wolves howl in the graveyard. I leave the house, but stand at the door looking around. Am *I* the bravest now? I know well that I'm not and I don't want to be.

A long shadow with a shiny moving spot in its center, climbs the hilly street. It's a man with a flashlight. He aims the light at my face, barking at me, "What are you doing out, you little brat? Go in before I smack your dirty ass. Son of a Godless bastard! In! I said, in!"

I recognize Sheikh Ahmad, our neighbor, coming back from his evening prayer. He yells at me, curses my father, and calls him names: "Bloody red— Satan worshipers—," he curses the rest of my family, and goes toward his house, the first match box on the left, the closest to our houses. He holds the flash light with his only hand and aims it at the keyhole. "God only knows who these people are," he grumbles, "Jews? Fire worshipers? Disciples of the devil, or what? They don't pray, they don't go to the mosque, they don't fast, they don't give charity, they don't wear veils, and their children are loose like stray dogs. Black plague on them. They contaminate the neighborhood." He finds the keyhole and I turn behind the house where the vacant land, the desert, is. I can still hear him hollering in his yard, calling both of his wives, "Women!" He yells, "turn the goddamn lights on when I come home."

Cautiously, I take few steps, but keep looking at the cemetery on my left. "Ooooooooooo," the wolves bay, as though they are in pain. What if their pain is simply hunger? What if they eat me up? The moment I decide to give up and return to the house, a warm hand grabs my hand. "I'll go with you. I sneaked out to go with you!"

Someone screams from inside the house, "Sahar, Sahar... Where did you go?"

But we hold hands and run through the desert.

Sahar, Mother, and I

"Sahar... Sahar ..." I whisper and open my eyes. "Hold my hand, Sahar! I'm falling. If I fall, the chair will fall with me and we'll wake Kamal up. He may kill us if we don't let him sleep."

I try to straighten my back. My spine is painful. But any twitch moves the metal chair. Maybe I should untie the leash with my cuffed hands. But the slightest movement of my hands will tighten the handcuffs. The swollen veins of my calves itch and burn. What if I gently lift the chair up with my cuffed hands, lie down on the floor and rest the chair on my chest? I can even take a nap with the chair on me. But what if Kamal wakes up and finds me sleeping? Or what if La-Jay, watching me all this time with his secret cameras, rings the emergency alarm and awakens Kamal? I fear Kamal, I fear the secret cameras, and I fear the words of the long speech pouring out of the speakers. Each word stretches long, turns into a snake, slithers toward me and stings my painful back. I fear myself and the flood of the reminiscences filling my head, washing me from inside, leaving me lonely and barren.

"Sahar... Sahar..." I hiss as if she is hiding behind the shower curtain. "Sahar... I remember you... you're my twin... hold my hand!"

Kamal snores peacefully and I try to resurrect Sahar's face. Her big black eyes come to life first: wet and shiny, little stars flickering in the large irises, long eyelashes, thick, rough, bushy hair, wild when it's short, sticking up like she has been hit by the thunder. Mother has to wet and brush her hair and force it to settle on her little scalp. It gets tangled again. Mother gets restless. Maman comes to her rescue. She brings her large wide-teethed wooden comb, sits on the stone steps of the triangular porch, holds Sahar between her fat thighs, and works on the massive hair. She tells Mother, "You don't have patience Pari! Patience. Look! I untangled it! If you don't cut it short like she is electrocuted, we'll always keep it in braids and it'll be easier to handle. God has given this girl too much hair!"

When it's combed and dried and pulled out of her face with a satin ribbon, Sahar's hair shines in the sun. It's light brown and dark brown, the color of chestnuts and walnuts mixed in a bowl. Some strands above the forehead are raisin-gold. Sometimes when we lie down on Grand-Lady's Turkman carpet, on either side of the green peacock, the warm sun shines on us and we whisper not to wake people up from their afternoon nap; sometimes when she yawns and suddenly falls asleep, I watch her hair. I even gently touch the strands: the darker ones, the lighter ones, the golden ones. Nobody has Sahar's hair.

Nobody has Mother's blue eyes, neither of us have. We have our father's eyes. Our father is on top of the wall, above the old radio, in a brass frame. He is sitting next to Mother: Mother in lacy blue wedding dress, paper flowers hanging on her curls, Father in black suit and a bow tie, tip of his white kerchief sticking out of his pocket. Mother's lips are tight, but Father's smile is wide. His teeth are large and white.

Our bed is opposite the big radio on the other side of the triangular room, where the dark narrow angle is. In the red glow flashing out of Aladdin, we look at this picture before we go to sleep. Mother is on the other side of the curtain, in her bed, under the window. She turns the pages of her thick brown book, glancing at the dark window as though waiting for someone to come. But the window pane reflects her own face.

The Multi-Level Tenant House

Kamal rolls and sleeps flat on his back. He snores differently now, inhales with a slight hiss, but whistles when he exhales. His lips twitch, as though he is having a conversation with someone. His square face, his creased forehead, his cheek bones, everything about him is familiar. Who does he resemble?

The long speech on the radio finally ends and the drums and cymbals of a military march shake the room. I wish he had turned the volume lower. How can he sleep like this?

I move my feet, turn and twist my ankles, careful not to pull the chair. I bend and unbend my fingers. They look thick and swollen. The handcuffs have gotten tighter. If my hands were not cuffed I could untie the leash and lie down for a minute. Then I would tie it back before Kamal wakes up. But let's not think about the impossible and let's not think about how much time has passed and how much is left. Kamal may sleep forever. I may faint.

I'm grateful. This is what I repeat now: grateful, grateful, grateful. I could be hanging from my testicles! I could be trapped in a sack of cockroaches; I could be in a much worse condition. I'm grateful. If this is a torture, it's ridiculously simple, yes simple, but how effective! I'm gradually being crushed under the burden of myself. They want me to feel that my body is an obstacle to my comfort. I'm grateful, yet in pain. I have to distract myself. The Hindu hermits sit on nails, don't they? And they don't feel the pain. I need to concentrate on something else, someone else. Out. Out of here and now.

I split my legs, anchor my weight and make sure that I will not collapse. I close my eyes. At first I feel dizzy, but then it gets better. The march has changed into a slower one; this music is even relaxing. A wall, a tall brick wall stretches itself up under my eyelids. It appears without any effort and I let it stay. I look at it in the darkness of my head. This is an impassable wall, extended from the right and left to the unseen horizons and up into the dark sky. But I can see the bricks very well—light and dark brown separated by thin lines of fresh yellow mortar. Yes, the wall is new and the mortar is fresh.

Sahar squeezes my hand and we both tilt our heads back to see the top; the top is blurred and blended into the fast moving black clouds. We hold our breath and listen. Someone up there is still building the wall, making it taller. Swoosh, swoosh... dump... He spreads the mortar and dumps a brick—again and again.

"This is Ali the Bricklayer," Sahar says, "and this is the wall of El-Deen."

"What is he doing here, so late?" I ask her, as though she knows everything.

"He is laying bricks on top of bricks, making the wall taller. Father is behind the wall."

"Have we ever seen him, Sahar?"

"We have. But we can't remember. We were newly born. I'm sure he bent over our little bed and smiled at us. They took him to El-Deen on our Name Day."

"Why?" I ask.

"They said he and his friends wanted to kill the Monarch."

"Is this true?"

"I don't know. Mother says he wanted to get the Monarch's money and give it to the people of Faithland."

"To build houses," I say.

"To smash their cardboard shelters and build real houses," she says.

"Ali the Bricklayer lives in Faithland too. Why does he make the wall taller, then?" I ask.

"He is a bricklayer. What can he do? This is his job."

Swoosh, swoosh... Dump! Swoosh, swoosh... Dump! Ali dumps a brick on top of a brick.

"Sahar, let's go now. Mother will get mad at us."

"Let's watch a little bit more. Maybe he'll come down and we can talk to him. Up there he can see the ironwoods and the white building. Maybe he can tell us all about them. Maybe he can see the prisoners. What if he can see Father? Let's stay."

"Sahar, when Mother gets mad, she beats us up. Let's go. Look at the black clouds! It's going to rain and we don't have our raincoats on."

"One more minute. Let me call him—A—l—i—" But the mighty north wind, Saba, takes Sahar's voice somewhere else, somewhere in the cemetery. Large rain drops fall on our bare heads. It showers now, faster and faster. Soaking wet, we run in the desert all the way to the tenant house. We push the squeaky old door open and stand inside the yard, back to the door, under the eaves. The yard is deserted. All the tenants have run into their hovels. Some have left their kerosene burners outside. We watch the rain pouring into the round pool in the middle of the yard. Rain drops make a hundred circles in the dark, smelly water.

On the right is Uncle Massi's room, the same size as the tenant's hovels. The small barred window on the wall sheds a yellow light. He is awake. Should we knock on Uncle's door and go in? Will he recognize us and give us shelter until the rain stops? Or as usual, will he ask who we are and what our names are? We run to Uncle's window, hold the iron bars and look inside. He is sitting on his bamboo spread in the middle of the room writing his poetry on a low table. His pen has a long ostrich feather and his paper is a long roll. His hair is shaggy and long, down to his shoulders, his face is bony and thin. He lifts his eyes, looking at the window. His eyes roll and show the white. We may be scaring him. We'd better leave him alone.

How about Ali's hovel, the one on the left? His wife Zahra must still be working in the public bath. Their children must be alone. Maybe we can sneak into their hovel and wait till the rain stops?

But someone from the other side of the pool waves his hands and calls us.

25

We run toward him. This is Bashi, the janitor of the New Spring Elementary and High School. He has only three teeth in his mouth, two on the upper jaw and one on the lower; they are long, yellow and slimy. His voice is hoarse and he smells of cheap tobacco, odor of dung. Before we can run away from him, he pulls our hands and takes us into his hovel.

The janitor's place is the size of one man lying down. There is a worn out mat on the floor and a kerosene lantern on the shelf. We notice an old brass trumpet standing beside the lantern. We've heard that Bashi plays trumpet in the Holy shows; in the schoolyard he blows it to call children to class. Wind whistles, the weak flame flickers and goes out. The room smells of urine, sweat, and Bashi's tobacco. Dung. Our stomachs turn. In the semi-dark, the ugly janitor forces a few sticky sugar candies into our palms, smacks our butts and pushes us out of his hovel. We throw the candies in the pool and run next door, to Hassan the Gardener's room. But a big lock is hanging on the door. Hassan and his wife Zeinab, the laundry woman of the neighborhood, are not home. We run under the rain, holding our hands tightly, trying not to lose each other.

The rain lashes our wet backs. We descend the endless stone steps of the first yard and find ourselves in the second yard. We know that the lower we go in Grandfather's multi-level tenant house, the closer we get to Faithland, the neighborhood of the thieves, murderers, and hooligans.

The same round, contaminated pool and the same kind of hovels are around the second yard, only worse, run down, half ruined. We know that an old paralyzed woman, who's maybe one hundred years old, lives in one of the hovels. Our cleaning woman Ziba, half of her face burned, lives in this level too. But her door is locked. The lame man who helps Grandfather fix up the hovels is not home either. We don't know the other tenants and we don't stop.

"Sahar, don't go further down, let's climb the steps up. Mother has forbidden us to get near Faithland. Let's go back."

She pulls me behind, we descend the stone steps and find ourselves in the third yard: the same pool, the same hovels, only worse. We know that some pickpockets and gamblers live in this yard and Grandfather wants to get rid of them, but he can't. Salman the Brainless, the famous pimp and the head of Faithland Hooligans, supports them and Grandfather is scared of him. Salman himself is friends with Sheikh Ahmad, our one-armed neighbor.

26

Grandfather avoids the sheikh too. There is a rumor that the sheikh has connections with the Monarch's secret police and since our father is in El-Deen, he can cause more trouble for us.

We run toward the big gate of the third yard. If we get out of this gate we are in the main street of Faithland, which is only a narrow alley with a smelly gutter in the middle. This gutter is Faithland's sewer, which runs over the ground. We can walk close to the walls of the shabby grocery store and the smelly butcher shop, pass the mosque, run faster when we get to the whore house, turn right, and walk half a mile, and find ourselves behind the walls of our three houses.

The alley of Faithland has turned into a river of mud now. A flood is flowing down the steep street and it's impossible to set foot in it. We decide to go back inside the tenant house, climb the steps and get out through the small squeaky door. But the big gate is locked behind us. We are stuck here. Pressing our backs against the gate, we shiver and bite our lips not to weep aloud. The tin and cardboard houses across the street with the dim candle lights flickering in them look like many witches' lanterns. What if the hooligans pull us in their shelter, kill us, and cook a juicy soup with us? There are all kinds of rumors about Faithland. They kidnap the children of New Spring and sell them to Arab Caliphs, Maman says. If they are pretty, they end up in the harems; if ugly, they become slaves. First they put the child in a burlap sack, tie the top tight and pretend it's a sack of potatoes and send it out of the country.

Sahar squeezes my hand so hard that it hurts. We finally break into sobs. But the gate of the yard opens and someone pulls us in. He is tall and square, the tallest person we've ever seen. He holds each of us under one of his arms, as if we are two small honeydew melons. Splash, splash, splash, he dashes up the stone steps, passing the second yard with two long steps, climbing the steps again and taking us to a hovel in the first yard. He dumps us on the bamboo mat of his hovel. In the light and shade of the two candles burning on the shelf, we recognize Ali the Bricklayer.

His forehead is creased and his wide face sun-tanned, the color of well-cooked brick. Ali dries his wet hair with a towel, smiling at us. His wife, Zahra, dries us with her veil, which smells of woodsmoke and the dampness of the public bath. We know her and feel at home with her. Every Thursday, Zahra washes us in the dark chamber of the public bath. She is the only person beside Mother, Maman, and our aunts who has seen us naked. She gives us hot lentil soup, which we don't want to eat, but she insists. Timidly, we look around the small hovel and find four or five little children against the wall. They are all cramped under one shabby blanket, sleeping. We smell a strange, pleasant odor in the hovel. Fresh mortar.

The moment Ali lays us down on the porch of our triangular house, Mother slaps our cheeks and kicks us inside the room. We hear her saying thank you to Ali, giving him a tip. We run to the darkest angle of the room; we duck on the floor, shivering, hiding our heads inside our arms. When Mother gets mad she likes to slap the back of our heads, our cheeks, and our butts. But for some reason she always beats Sahar harder. She is only five minutes older than I am, but Mother thinks she is the one responsible for both. The whites of Mother's eyes are streaked with blood and the blue is dark and foggy like a stormy sea. She gives me two mild slaps which still hurt and one hard blow on Sahar's head. Sahar flies to the foot of Aladdin. Now a spank for me and a burning slap on Sahar's ear. She hits us while shouting: "... fatherless miserable brats... wish they would chop you into pieces in Faithland... woe to me... a widow and not a widow... curse on me... plague and black death on me... Why did I bring you to this world?... He'll never come out. Do you hear me? Never! Never! Never! Never!" She pulls the wedding picture off the wall and bang bang bang hits it on the hot metal surface of the burning Aladdin.

In the Arms of the Chair

With the last bang I collapse. The chair falls over me and we roll on the floor right at the foot of Kamal's bed. He jumps, startled, sitting in his bed, blank. Plague on me, I whisper. He was dreaming and I've interrupted his dream; I'd better pretend that I've passed out. He may have mercy on a fainted person. Now he turns his head in confusion and sees me on the floor with the chair on my chest. The next thing is punches and slaps all over my body. He doesn't even untie me from the chair. He beats me and the chair together. With each blow the metal legs pierce my stomach, but I feel a strange sense of security with the chair tied to me. Now that I can't protect myself with my arms and hands, the chair is somehow protecting me. It's as though I'm not alone in the room, beaten to half-death by a crazy foaming beast. The chair is with me, attached to me, hugging me with its four legs like a strange metal animal. A buzzer buzzes loudly. Kamal leaves the chair and me alone and disappears behind the shower curtain.

The buzzer saved me. Was it La-Jay in the Main Tower, watching us all the time, signalling to Kamal that he was overdoing it? Or Kamal's alarm clock buzzing to wake him up? Anyway, this was a heavenly sound. Kamal would have killed me.

I lie on the floor remembering my daydream, hallucination, or whatever it was. It couldn't have possibly been a dream. How could I have slept on my feet, with my back bent forward? I'm confused. Was it Mother who beat me up or Kamal? Where is Sahar? Did she crawl under the bed or pack her little bundle to leave the house forever?

Now I'm on my back, what I desired. But hundreds of needles pierce my muscles and my ribs throb. My jaw might be broken; it hurts when I try to move it. There is a constant ring in my ears, it sounds like the reverberating resonance of an emergency drill. My mouth is dry like an abandoned well, but I can taste the metallic taste of blood on my tongue. Now my mouth is full but I cannot swallow the blood. If one drop slips down my throat I will throw my bowels up. I wish I could spit it out, but I can't get my lips together. I have no lips, but two large livers hanging from my chin. I can feel this without being able to touch my face.

The chair is still over me, crooked and miserable, like myself. Its four metal legs hug me tight on my chest and neck. "Oh chair," I whisper, "dear friend—" And when I hear Kamal flushing the toilet, I panic, because he will separate me from my companion. I'll be alone again, single, naked, with no arms around me. I'll be alone with my wounds and flooding memories. He is going to step out now, take the chair off my body and force me to stand up. He is going to drag me along the hallways again. Tears bubble in my eyes and roll down my cheeks, slipping into my ears. I caress the cold legs of the chair with the tip of my swollen fingers. I caress the chair like a lover, a mother, a twin.

Kamal steps out of the blue curtain but doesn't pay attention to me. He rolls his thick neck in front of the mirror and makes crackling sounds. He throws his arms up. A little exercise. He must be doing more than this to have such muscles, I think. Now, as though knowing what I'm thinking about, he flexes the muscle of his right arm and touches the stiff contraction, which looks like a little mountain. He is either showing off or threatening me. I close my eyes not to see him. To hell with Kamal. Black death on him.

Sahar Escapes

Sahar left once. With a ridiculous little bundle. She took some bread and cheese and the broken picture frame containing our smiling father. She didn't take money or anything else. That was the summer before we went to school. Mother beat us again because we went to the wall of El-Deen, close to the bridge, where we could see the gate on the other side, and the watchdog of the prison growling in the ditch. I hid under the bed for hours, hiccuping; Sahar left.

Nobody noticed until dinner, when Mother pulled me out and dragged me to Grandfather's. We all sat on the floor around the table cloth to eat and Sahar was not there. "Sahar... Sahar... Sahar..." thin and thick voices, worried and alarming voices, desperate voices echoed in the neighborhood. Maman ran to the tenant house, bare-headed, with her house slippers. Sahar was not there. Grandfather searched his dark room, his little storage room—where he hung paper money in colorful purses from the ceiling—and all the little holes and storage places in all the three houses. Uncle Musa went on top of the roofs and looked inside the chimneys. Nobody ate. Mother roamed in the rooms of the three houses for a while, calling Sahar's name in a low and confused voice. Then, pale in the face, she dropped on the bed, hid her head under the pillow, and stayed motionless.

Dusk became thicker and the mountain, taller. Uncle Musa, at last, took me, Kami, and Cyrus into his car and we drove down the hilly New Spring Street. We sat on the back seat of Uncle's small orange DeCave, which looked like a lady bug. The car made a strange clank clank clank; we turned into the Old North Road, and drove toward the south, the center of the city. We passed the New Spring Public Bath, Daryani Grocery Store, Rad and Rad Real Estate and got further and further away from our houses. It was early evening, the windows were down, and summer smells filled the car. People were still out. The vendors in the sidewalks were fanning salted ears of corns over burning charcoal. Some sold salted fresh walnuts, swimming in tin buckets. The neon lights twinkled. Kami and Cyrus looked around quietly. They knew that Sahar was lost, but they were happy to be out.

I whispered to myself like a lunatic. My heart beat inside my ears, my face burned. What if we never find her? What if Sahar is gone forever? But I had a deeper wound in my heart, a wound nobody could understand. Why didn't she take me? This made me cry. I hid my face in my hands and wept aloud.

"You're a man!" Uncle Musa said, "Aren't you? Huh? If not, then what's that hanging between your legs? Stop crying and help me find your sister." The back of Uncle's head, and his kinky balding hair was exactly like Grandfather's. His voice too. But Grandfather never became mad and beat anybody. Uncle Musa did. He beat up his wife Aunty Shamsi every day. We could hear Aunty through the wall, "Stop... stop... for God's sake, stop!" Uncle Musa, Mother, and Aunty Zari had weak nerves, Grandfather always said. They had taken after their wretched mother, Lady-King, who abandoned them when they were little. Uncle Massi had completely taken after Lady-King, not just a little bit, *completely*, Grandfather stressed. Uncle Massi didn't just have weak nerves, he was totally crazy. But Aunty Hoori never became mad. She was from a different mother; she was Maman's daughter.

I knew that Uncle Musa could get mad in a second, yell at me, or slap me, so I stopped crying.

"You look at the right sidewalk, I look at the left. I'm sure she is walking down this road. Or is she that stupid to go to Faithland, huh? If she's gone there, she is already finished."

I bit my lower lip with my new sharp teeth when Uncle said, "she is already finished." I bit it so hard blood bubbled out.

I wasn't sure if Uncle wanted an answer. Sahar wasn't stupid, I thought. She was brave. Sahar was the bravest and I always admired her. Many and many times we talked about running away: while sitting at the well, dropping pebbles in, listening to hear the splash and the echo of the splash, imagining the Monster sleeping in a dark damp corner; while lying on Grand-Lady's carpet—when everybody was taking a nap—looking at the peak of the mountain—the white nightcap; while whispering under our warm quilt, watching the dancing flames in the hot glass belly of Aladdin; while lying down on Grandfather's roof in hot summer nights, looking at the sky, trying to find the five stars that looked like a kite. We talked about running away, especially after each beating. But I never took it seriously. It was a play game for me, imaginary. But Sahar believed it and did it without me. Maybe she thought I would be scared. Wouldn't I? I would, but I'd still follow her. Didn't I follow her down the steps of the tenant house that horrible rainy night that we got stuck in Faithland's flood? "Sahar, I'd have come with you ..." I sniffled, whispered, and looked at the right sidewalk.

The sidewalks were almost deserted now. Darkness fell from the top of Mount Alborz like a sudden shadow. Kami fell asleep and Cyrus, Uncle Musa's son, said that he was hungry. Uncle told him to shut up and sit back. I watched the people passing by. I didn't see any children at all.

Clank, clank, clank, Uncle's orange DeCave coughed and spat, rolling down the road. We reached the movie theater: Moulin Rouge. The red neon light flashed the strange name in French alphabet. A giant windmill made of red lights slowly turned around. The box office was closed, because people were already inside. I looked at the pictures of the movie stars: half-naked men and women kissing, cowboys shooting the Indians, fat men wrestling... Under the pictures, on the steps of the theater, Sahar sat, her hair thunder struck, her little bundle between her thin legs. She munched on a cucumber, red light flashing on her amused face.

Kamal's Dream

"Here, wash your face, brother. I'm sorry for everything; you just hit my weak point. Ever since I was a child, if I wake up like this, with a loud noise or something, I go mad. My poor mother, may God bless her soul, would tip-toe to my room and whisper her beads into my ear to wake me. She would say a prayer to chase the jinnis and devils away. Aaaaaahhhoooooooh—" Kamal yawns, "—but what a dream, boy! What a dream... you just woke me up right in the middle of it."

Kamal has combed his beard, made his bed, and prayed his prayer and is putting the kerchief and rosary in his pocket. Now he wants me to wash my face. He removes the handcuffs, lifts me up and takes me to the sink. I rub my wrists under the warm water, feeling a pleasant pain. I wish he wouldn't handcuff me anymore.

I feel his presence close to me, behind my back. Like some oversized people, Kamal hisses when he breaths. I hear this and feel his warm breath on my neck. I don't dare to look in the mirror. I know he is watching me. Now he talks as if I'm his closest friend and we are getting ready to go out together. Beating a person almost to death and a minute later talking to him with trust and compassion—this goes beyond any kind of torture technique; this is madness.

"You know what I was dreaming about?" he pauses, waiting for me to say something. He goes to a closet and takes some clothes out. "Here, put these on... clean shirt and pants. You got yourself all bloody, brother. How can we go to the Community Center like this? Didn't I tell you about the show and the concert? Here, come, sit on this chair, your knees are shaking. While you're buttoning up your shirt let me tell you what I dreamed. I have to get it off my chest. My mother used to say, 'Tell me what you dreamed about, son, get it off your chest.'"

Kamal sighs and sits opposite me at the folding table. I try hard to button my shirt. My fingers are numb; I miss the buttonholes. This is not a pajama shirt, it's a snow white, starched-collar dress shirt. It's not new, but it's washed and ironed.

"There was this vast desert, like the Holy Desert," Kamal says in a low voice, staring at a spot behind my back on the wall. "Oh brother, how can I put this in words?" He rubs his forehead and eyes and tries again. "It was vast as hell itself, or as heaven; I couldn't tell, and a strange yellow light glowed everywhere. I was standing in the middle of this desert. Alone. I was thirsty, very thirsty, like the Second Holy One, the Thirsty One, the Martyred One. I was dying of thirst." He stops here, pauses and raises his voice, "Suddenly I saw the water in the distance and I trudged toward it." Kamal stretches his arm forward and shows me the water, and I try hard to place my shaking legs inside the pants—also cleaned and ironed.

"I walked and walked and walked," Kamal says, "I ran. But the more I ran, the more the water moved away... I realized that the whole thing was a mirage," he sighs and pauses. "There was no water. All was fake—the reflection of the glowing light. I sat there in the desert, crying. I cried and cried. I called all the Holy Ones by their names, the twelve of them. When I got to the Last Holy One, the Twelfth One, the Absent One, the Promised One, thunder struck and a green light appeared in the horizon."

33

Kamal bulges his eyes. I move slightly back. "I stood up." He gets up now and acts out the rest of the scene. "I stood up slowly, because I didn't want to disturb the green light. I stared at the horizon and waited." He holds his palm over his eyebrows and squints. "From the middle of the green light, a magnificent white horse appeared, a handsome man on it. It was Him: The Last Holy One, the Absent One, the Promised One. He was on His holy horse and a green halo circled around His head." Kamal moves back; he is as white as a ghost, his lips shaking. "He was coming toward me, me... Kamal, the worthless slave of God, the servant of His Revolution, His devotee, His ransom. He came to me. I kneeled and kissed his feet." Kamal kneels now and kisses the cement floor. "He touched my head with His holy hand and told me to get up. He said, 'Kamal, my son, rise from the dust and raise your head. I have something for you...' I stood up and raised my head..."

Kamal has moved toward the sink now and I have to move my chair to see him. I hesitate, then turn slightly toward him. But he doesn't seem to be aware of me anymore. He is in a trance. He goes on: "The halo around His head was so shiny that my human eyes could not stand the glow. I rubbed my eyes and barely saw his thin handsome mustache and his shiny black beard. His eyes... Oh may God have mercy on me... I can't describe the eyes. They were dark green like the bottom of the sea and piercing like Arabian daggers. He stretched his arm toward me and offered a golden cup. It was big and heavy, a Holy Grail, and it was full of fresh Water." He pauses here and I feel that this is the climax of his dream; I better not stir. My pants are halfway up on my knees and I don't dare pull them up.

Kamal goes on: "'Here Kamal,' the Holy One uttered my worthless name, 'I know that you are thirsty and I know that you are a faithful servant of God. Here, drink! This is the Water of Life, the Holy Water of Immortality. Drink and you will never perish. Accept this as a reward for your services.' I took the Holy Grail and brought it close to my dry lips. The moment I tilted it to drink the Holy Water of Immortality... BANG!" Kamal jumps and with an abrupt movement aims his index finger at my temple, as though he wants to shoot me on the spot. "You bastard, you devil worshiper, you motherfucker, you woke me up with your stupid collapse. If the buzzer hadn't stopped me, I would have chopped you into one hundred pieces and thrown your dirty flesh to the watchdog of El-Deen."

I sit motionless. He may kill me. He has revised his dream and recreated the whole incident. Now his emotions are stronger than when he beat me up. So I hold my breath and don't stir; my pants are sliding down my knees.

"Don't sit there like a bag of shit. Get up, we're late. Here, get this towel and dry your sweat." Kamal is not friendly anymore, he talks sulkingly, but there is no danger of beating.

The black pants and white shirt are exactly my size. Isn't this Kamal's room? Why should he have clothes my size in his closet? He is a giant of a man, three full heads taller than me. This clothes cannot possibly belong to him. And why did he offer fresh clothes to me? There were blood stains on the pajamas, but I could still wear them. Where is he taking me? Is it true that he is taking me to the Community Center to watch a show? Or is this another El-Deenian term? Maybe the Community Center is a public chamber where they torture the prisoners together.

I take the towel to the sink and look in the mirror for the first time. I don't recognize myself. Nothing rings a bell. I don't know this thin jaundiced face; I don't know these wandering eyes, lost behind the fogs at the bottom of sunken purple sockets.

Marching with Kamal

Trudging behind Kamal in fresh shirt and pants but still barefoot, I look at the back of his head and the three layers of fat. I feel sorry for this giant but I don't quite understand why. Kamal has strange dark thoughts, dreams, delusions. Now he walks sluggishly, absorbed in his thoughts. He is sulking. He doesn't pull the leash. I ruined his holy dream. Didn't let him drink the Water of Immortality. This must have proven to him that I'm connected to devil and woke him up on purpose. He hasn't said a word. The silence of the corridors is heavy. I haven't seen any TV sets hanging from the ceilings. I wish Kamal would pull the leash—just a little—that would be a way of talking. But he has forgotten me. I try to remember the memories I recalled in Kamal's room, but they have all thinned away, evaporated, gone. I feel lonely.

"Brother—" I hear my weak voice, a stranger's voice. "Brother," I repeat, louder. "How far—are we—?" I can't continue. These are the first words I utter. It's as though I have never talked before. I have to concentrate hard to be able to put the words in their right place.

I anticipate an explosion, but in a sulking tone he says, "First of all, don't call me Brother, because you have not repented yet. Secondly, we are not going straight to the Community Center, we have a couple of errands to do before the show, so you better move faster. I'm behind my schedule. I'm very busy and these are the most important days of my life. You'll see for yourself. I'm not telling you now. But first we have to eat something; I'm starving. How about you?"

"Nauseous," I say.

"What you need is meat, brother, you need some protein. Boy, you look like a ghost." He turns his head and takes a half glance at me. We walk a few steps and he is quiet again. Now he says, "How about a kabob? On top of rice, with some fresh onions and yogurt? How does that sound?"

I don't answer anymore. He must be playing with me. I don't remember the last time I ate. Before the Box? Or after?

All of a sudden the hidden speakers tremble with a military march. This is a familiar music. Without much effort I recognize the National Anthem. The male singer sings in an angry tone. The song is about the greatness of the Leader. The choir of women repeat a refrain in a weird language. The angry man says, "God is the greatest, the Leader is great. The enemy must know that we are the great roaring waves... We are born of the great sea... We are the sea of the great faith... We are the faith of the great..." and so on. The screaming and lamenting sisters, who are not aloud to sing solo, repeat their gibberish refrain: "Anja, anja, za za za... Anja, anja, za za za..."

Kamal hums the song and gradually widens his steps. He stamps the floor like a soldier. Chee, chee, chee, chee... Rattle, rattle, rattle, rattle... His key chain emphasizes the rhythm. He marches with the music and drags me behind. I'm forced to take longer steps and march barefoot.

Leashed, shrunken, and wobbly, I follow Kamal's robust frame in the hallways of El-Deen. Whoever is watching us in the secret cameras must be laughing at this sight.

In Grandfather's Darkroom

"One, two, three, four. One, two, three, four—" Sahar leads. Kami, Cyrus, and I stamp our bare feet on the brick floor of the triangular yard and follow her.

We are the army of the Giantess, Mother Alborz, the good benevolent supporter of the victims. We are going to attack the Monster, El-Deen, who has eaten up many people. We want to go inside the stomach of the monster, which is a maze, and take Father and other prisoners out.

"Keep your voice down, or I'll make you black and blue!" Mother sticks her head out, pulls in and slams the window.

"One, two, three, four—" We march in the middle yard. It's bigger and there is no well in it. We can play better. The fig tree of this yard has a thicker trunk and we can hide behind it, pretending we are hiding behind the ironwoods of El-Deen.

"Attack!" Sahar screams. We holler and climb the steps, rushing into Aunty Zari's living room, which suddenly turns into the Monster's belly. But before we can fight with El-Deen, Aunty Zari appears at the door. She has a belt in her hand. She is as tall as a man and very thin. Her eyes are strangely green, color of muddy green marbles.

"Out! Or I'll lash your butts, you bastards. I'm trying to get some sleep in this goddamn hot afternoon. Out! I said. Not you, sucker." She grabs her son's belt and lifts him up in the air like a dead mouse. Kami cries and starts to beg.

"No... Mother, please... I didn't scream... I didn't make noise... It was Sahar... not me... "

We dash out and through the small door between the yards, step in Grandfather's house. We resume. Mother and Aunty Zari are in the army of the Monster, we decide. But Maman, Aunty Hoori, and Grandfather are with the Giantess. We argue about Grand-Lady. Sahar and I want to cast her in the army of the Giantess, but Cyrus insists that she is mean. We decide to leave her out for now.

"One, two, three, four—" Sahar marches in front, we follow.

"Come up and sleep, Cyrus, or I'll tell your father tonight!" Aunty Shamsi calls her son in a voice as skinny as herself. She bends over the railings of the middle house's balcony. She has many pink plastic rollers on her head, sharp pins sticking out. She looks like a hedgehog. "Come up, I said!" Cyrus leaves, his lips hanging.

The game is murdered. Our army lost. Sahar and I sit on the steps staring at the green fountain, not knowing what to do the rest of the long hot afternoon. But the old wooden door of the house squeaks and Grandfather steps in.

Under each arm he has a large, round watermelon. He is sweating. Big drops roll down his forehead, linger in the little pock-holes of his measle marks and drip on his white shirt. This is when he comes back from his office, Rad and Rad Real Estate. Uncle Musa must have gotten off from his Insurance Company job and taken his father's place for the rest of the day.

"I'm a real estate man in the morning, a photographer in the afternoon, a pharmacist in the evening, and a poet at night."

"Which one do you like better, Grandfather?" Sahar asks, rolling one of the watermelons on the brick floor toward the steps.

"The poet." Grandfather squats at the small square fountain, washing his hands and face. "I like the poet the best and don't have enough time for him."

"Grandfather," Sahar calls again.

"Hmm..."

"Do you want to be the General of the Army of the Giantess?"

"Oh, with pleasure. I have some experience in this field too. You know that I've been a soldier once. A soldier on a horse! That's how I came to this country. I was a Cossack. I galloped and galloped all the way from Russia to here. I liked it here. I galloped back to Russia and brought my little mother."

"That's why Grand-Lady speaks a weird language?" I ask.

"That's why."

"Wow!" We both clap and follow him up the steps and into his room. Here it's cool and dark. Maman is lying down on the carpeted floor under the old round mirror on the shelf—her wedding mirror. A light flowery veil, which she uses only when she goes to the tenant house, shrouds her fat body.

"Sh sh sh—" Grandfather holds his index finger on his big nose and tip toes to the small room on the right. We follow him. "Let's go to my dark room. Maman is sleeping here."

"You don't take a nap, Grandfather?" I ask.

"No. If I do, I will stay up all night and look at the stars. Then I'll want to buy a telescope and do some astronomy."

"Why is it so dark here, Grandfather?" I ask.

"Because of the pictures. Let me draw the curtains now. I don't have any wet pictures today. Ahan. That's better. Well. Tell me about your army."

We tell him. Sahar does most of the talking and I nod in approval and Grandfather listens while cutting and trimming some pictures and examining others hanging on a thread like Maman's laundry. Once he opens his storage room just a crack and we see all the purses hanging from the ceiling. We know that they are full of money and he keeps them like this because of the rats.

"You got to be careful, kids, not to talk about your army to anyone. There are all sorts of bad people around. If they hear any such thing, then we'll all be in trouble," Grandfather says, his eyes on his work.

"Sheikh Ahmad, for example," Sahar says.

"For example," Grandfather says briefly.

"Now look at my beautiful daughters!" Grandfather places the enlarged picture of Mother and her sisters on the shelf and himself steps back to watch. They are sitting stiff on a bench, their hands clasped on their laps in front of a cashmere curtain which hangs in Grand-Lady's room. They don't look alike, but strangely they do.

"Pari, your mother, the oldest, is my mermaid. How can the black and white portrait show her beautiful blue eyes?" He looks at Mother's picture with fascination. "She resembles her poor mother Lady-King. She was a princess. A beauty."

"Mother is not pretty," Sahar says.

"She is not?" Grandfather asks surprisingly.

"No," Sahar answers.

"What do you think, son?" he asks me.

"Sometimes she is, sometimes she is not," I say.

"Hmmm…" Grandfather ponders for few seconds. "How about my second daughter, Zari, my golden one? The picture cannot show the unique color of her eyes, sometimes blue, sometimes green, depending on what she wears. Tall and slender like a young oak, shiny yellow hair. Isn't she beautiful?"

"The same with her," Sahar says.

"Not pretty?" Grandfather asks.

"No!" she says.

"Sometimes," I say. "When she doesn't beat Kami up; when she calls us in and shows us her wedding album."

"Hmmm… the wedding album…" Grandfather repeats. "Kami's father will never come back. We have to find Aunty Zari another husband," he says more to himself.

"You want to find Mother another husband too?" Sahar asks.

"I don't think so. Her situation is rather difficult. Your father may come back, or may not."

"He will," I say.

"Let's hope," he says and then, "Your Baba-Mirza has written a letter to the Prime Minister. We're all waiting to see what will happen. Okay, enough of this now. Let's look at our picture. What do you think about my third daughter, Hoori, my angel? Isn't she a beauty?" Grandfather asks with fascination.

"She is," Sahar says briefly.

"The black and white picture makes her even more beautiful, doesn't it?" Grandfather says. "Look at the contrast between her large black eyes and her light face. Look at her Roman nose. A goddess!"

"But she looks unhappy," Sahar says.

"Oh, she is too young to be unhappy. She'll be happy when we find her a handsome husband," Grandfather says and cleans up the table.

Outside, the end of the afternoon nap is announced by Maman who calls everybody for tea and lemon. She draws the curtains back, allowing the white peak of Mount Alborz to reflect in her wedding mirror. We all sit on the carpet, in Grandfather's cool shady room and drink hot tea in thin gold-rimmed glasses. We squeeze a slice of lemon in our tea to flavor it. We fill our mouths with large sugar cubes.

The Flying Inmate

The march ended a while ago and Kamal is sluggish again. Remembering the lemon-flavored tea makes me thirsty. I want this walking to end. I want to drink something and go to bed. That's all I want. I don't care much for food, not even a bed. Just to be able to lay my body horizontally on the floor, any floor, for an hour or two. Is this too much to ask? I'm suspecting that the whole thing is a trick to wear me out and make me weak and vulnerable. To find my cracking point, to break me, by not letting me rest.

The walls are darker now. Kamal is going to get mad at me if I ask where we are. Didn't he say we need to stop and eat something? Isn't he hungry? I debate. At last I decide to wait until the end of this hall. If he turns into another endless corridor, then I'll ask.

This is the end of the hallway and Kamal, as if knowing where he is heading now, turns to the right. He has gotten himself together again and his key chain sings the chee song: Chee... Chee... Chee... Chee... One, two, three, four... I count four steps, then I talk.

"Brother," I say. I have forgotten he has warned me not to call him "Brother."

"Hmmm..." he roars with his mouth closed. He doesn't even turn to look at me. But it seems he too has forgotten I'm not supposed to call him Brother.

"Are we—er—er—" I don't dare.

"What the hell is this?" he groans. "Are we what? Are we fucked up? Is this what you want to ask?" Kamal bursts and then, "Yes, we're fucked up, if you want to know!"

What does he mean? Is he complaining about something? The length of the corridors? Are we fucked up because we are tired and hungry and we don't reach the goddamn cafeteria? Anyway, I insist. I need to know where in El-Deen I am. I need to locate myself. This keeps me sane.

"Are we underground?" I ask.

I have not heard Kamal's laughter before. He has smirked or smiled a few times, chuckled with other guards, but nothing like this. He bursts into a hysterical laughter. It scares me. It's loud and gets louder, too. The echo of his horse laugh in the empty corridor is like the resonance of the monster's voice in the bottom of the cold well. Kamal uses all the variations of ha ha ha: "He he he... ho ho ho... hoo hoo hoo..." He snorts and makes snarling sounds with his nose and throat. He laughs as if he is gurgling water, inhaling something into his nose or coughing his lungs out. Now I'm worried. For myself of course, not for him. What if he passes out here and leaves me alone? What am I supposed to do then? Where can I possibly go? We have turned so many times to the right and left that it's impossible for me to find Kamal's room again. Now I wish I were tied to the chair. How homely the room was. It had a human smell.

Kamal stops now, wipes his tears and snot with a black-and-white-checkered kerchief and gasps. "Sorry brother. Once in a while it happens that I laugh like this. Once in a long while. I can't control it. It's like the devil is doing this to me. The way you asked 'Are we underground?' sounded so funny. Very funny. Haven't I explained all this before? Have you forgotten? Did I beat you up hard? Did you lose your immediate memory too?"

I don't know what to say. I don't quite understand what he means by losing my immediate memory. And I don't see anything funny in asking if we are underground. Something is wrong with Kamal. I panic again. We are strolling very slowly now. In this corridor there are no doors and no TVs. It's a strange place. There are large windows on top of the walls, covered with heavy metal screens. The rooms, or whatever is behind the windows, are dark. It's hard to guess if there are people inside the rooms or if they are vacant. The whole thing makes me miss the regular hallways with the iron doors of the cells. What if Kamal suddenly jumps on me? Are the secret cameras installed in this hall too? I hope so.

"This is all because of the Black Box," Kamal says, still strolling, "this memory thing. And by the way, I have to take you to the Clinic for this matter. After all, this is what we need here: Memory. This is the whole point. What are you good for without your memories, huh? Maybe I shouldn't have beaten you up like that. You remember where I'm taking you, don't you?"

I nod.

"Where?" he asks.

"To eat," I say. "But I'm not hungry, I'm thirsty." And I crave the warm lemon tea again. All my insides, from my dry mouth down to my abdomen throb with an increasing desire for a cup of lemon tea and a lump of sugar.

"That's beside the point, brother. I'm talking about serious matters now. I'm talking about your final destination, not a few errands we have on the way. I'm taking you to Hall Twenty, cell number four, the dead end. You know that if someone ends up there, no repentance will be accepted. If you want to repent, you've got to do it before that cell. Understood? Carved in your head?"

I nod.

"Now. That hall is three levels under the ground level. You see, El-Deen is built by the foreign architects. Although we are a self-sufficient nation, the Great Leader of our Holy Revolution believes that we can use foreign technology and put it at the service of our Faith. This building is one example. You see, before the Revolution, El-Deen was much smaller. We rebuilt it. We hired specialists to reconstruct the old El-Deen."

I wish Kamal would walk faster. The increasing thirst, nausea, and fatigue distract me. He is in a talkative mood now, explaining things about El-Deen that in a normal situation I would eagerly listen to. Who has access to this incredible information, after all? I noticed before that other guards barely even talk to their prisoners while dragging them around. Kamal talks about La-Jay, who was a prisoner himself, in the Monarch's time. He spent all his life in El-Deen, in a cell on the seventh floor where now his room is. On the first day of the Revolution when people opened the gates of El-Deen and the prisoners stepped out, La-Jay stayed in. He became the head of the facilities.

El-Deen used to have windows, Kamal says. In the Monarch's time, the windows were covered by black curtains, nailed to the walls. From the outside, the prison looked like a white monster with many black eyes. La-Jay blocked the windows when he became the head of the facilities. Now El-Deen is a blind monster, Kamal says. Why did La-Jay block the windows? Kamal asks and begins to answer his own question.

I cannot talk. I'm too tired, so I miss most of what he says. All I want is to drink a lemon tea and lie down. The hallway is endless. On top of both walls, near the ceiling, the windows are covered with thick screens. I've lost my memories and reveries, all evaporated. The physical necessities are tolling like huge bells in my body—dominating and overwhelming. I'm throbbing all over. I can hear the sound of many pulses in me. These are the alarm sounds, the sirens, warning me I may collapse. I'm conscious of my tongue, which is the largest part of my body now. It's the size of a thick wall, made of dry, sun-baked bricks. Kamal talks and talks and doesn't even pull the leash. He is taking his time. This is conspiracy, I think. He is torturing me and this thirst may be my cracking point. This is where I break and repent—for a sip of water.

Why seal the windows? Because La-Jay witnessed an inmate jumping out, Kamal goes on. This was before the Revolution, when he was a prisoner in a cell on the seventh floor. He swears, that means La-Jay swears, that the inmate didn't fall down, he grew wings and flew to the north, where Russia is. The flying inmate was a red, of course, and his wings were red too. So, when La-Jay became the director of the facilities, the head of the University, the Father of El-Deen, he sealed the windows to prevent the Satan worshipers from flying to the north.

43

"Can I endure?" I hiss to myself. "Help me to endure—"

"Weary, huh? You want to stop? Lie down?" Kamal asks me, as though it's up to me to decide. If I say yes or even nod, he will make me walk more. I stay quiet. But my knees shake. "Here, let me take you to this room. You look terrible. Your eyes are rolling inward. You're almost fainting. Here you can lie down a bit."

In the Hothouse

Kamal takes his key chain out and opens a door. We step in a dark room, one of the rooms with screened windows. He turns the light on. This is a different light. Yellow. A large bulb hangs at the end of a wire. The room is small and almost empty. A wooden bench is all I can see. This is good enough for me, I think. I expected worse. I'm grateful. So it's time for me to rest, to lay my painful back on this bench.

"Brother, I thought while your body is so tired and beat, it's not good for your health to eat a big meal. Here is a private sauna. I'll leave you alone to enjoy your rest. Meanwhile, I'll go to the kitchen to order us a special dish. Okay? You don't need to do anything, just relax. I'll adjust the heater."

I notice that the walls are padded with a thick quilt-like material. This is the Hothouse. I have a feeling that either someone has told me about this place or I have been here before. The heat gradually increases and gets to a level that can kill. I look at my shirt, buttoned to my neck and my pants in which I already feel warm. Can I take my cloths off?

"No, brother, don't even think about taking your cloths off. You are being watched after all. Have some respect for poor Brother La-Jay, who has been observing every single stupid movement of yours for so many hours. Sit!" he orders me. "Didn't I make you stand half-bent with your leash tied to the chair in that room? Didn't I beat you up? Haven't you walked all day? Haven't you lost that tiny bit of memory left for you to play with? So why are you standing here like a sack of shit? Sit! I'll turn the radio on in case you feel lonely and bored."

With a tiny little key, one of the many hanging off his chain, he opens a small gray box on the wall and adjusts some switches. He locks the box. A sudden wave of heat descends from above like a thick woolen blanket.

At the same time, a tired monotonous voice fills the room from all four sides like a semi-liquid glue. The voice slithers and creeps into my ears. I sit on the bench and feel drowned in the dark waters of a murky pool—one of the pools of the multi-level tenant house—in a hot summer afternoon when the thick water almost boils under the sun. The stink of the green pool makes my stomach turn. My whole insides come up to my mouth and slip down again. The voice of the man is too loud, deafening, and the heat flows in waves. Each wave is hotter than the previous one. Kamal winks at me with his red-veined eye, before disappearing behind the thick, padded door.

I'm on my back at last. Ripped off my shirt. The man with the gluey voice is saying that under unusual circumstances, such as battlefields, remote deserts, or prisons of the enemies of God, when a man of Faith does not have access to his women, he is allowed to masturbate. Saying this, he stretches his voice in a seductive way, as if he is doing it right there in the radio station.

"—We are the successors of that Holy One and we can add necessary chapters to his book of laws. You may ask, can anything in the world substitute for your beloved women? For your legal wives and your temporary concubines? Here, I want to give you assurance that in emergency situations, bear in mind, in unusual emergency circumstances, the Handbook of Sexual Laws allows you to do the act of self-satisfaction, or in other words, maaaasturrrrrbaaaaaation. This is legal, permissible, and completely understandable and can undoubtedly be a substitute for your wives, your concubines, or your young male companions."

Now, as though he has done the job and is zipping up his fly, he continues in a tired voice, "My next sermon, Brothers, will be about the sweet subject of pederasty. I'll throw some light on it. Don't miss it, dear Brothers, next week at the same time. God is the greatest! The Leader is Great! Death to the blasphemers! Long live the Holy Republic!"

A wild march fills the Hothouse. All the drums, trumpets, and cymbals of the world play together and attack my painful head from all four corners of the room. For a moment, I think my end has arrived. They are killing me with this loud noise. The heat, I think, can make me unconscious and this is not so bad. I will gladly faint in peace. Then I won't hear the horrible march.

Covering my ears with my hands I realize that I'm soaking wet. I touch my head, my face, the white shirt—they are wet with sweat. I'm dehydrated. There is no saliva left in my mouth. This is the way they want to kill me. But why kill me? Don't they want some information? How can I give it to them if they destroy me like this? But what information? I honestly cannot remember a thing.

I look at the ceiling. La-Jay must be watching me. Isn't he tired of this? Am I such an important person? I'm tempted to talk to him, tell him I cannot remember anything and I'm not lying. But this is ridiculous. I won't talk to the hidden lenses. This is what they want me to do. To beg for forgiveness. To repent. No, I won't. Since I don't remember anything, I'm innocent; the moment I remember, I'll take responsibility for my deeds. And in a courtroom, not on the bench of a torture chamber.

At last her name comes to me like a shooting star flashing in a dark sky. "Take me. Hold my hand and take me out, Sahar." I whisper her name and feel a strange joy, the joy of remembering this word—Sahar: dawn.

Picnic at the Ditch

This is our desert, a vacant land on the left side of Grandfather's three houses. It stretches all the way to the walls of El-Deen. The New Spring Cemetery is on the left and the multi-level tenant house on the right. Faithland is down there, at the bottom of the hill, behind the main gate of the tenant house. Faithland is a slum, a long muddy alley with beaten houses and shelters on both sides. From above, it looks like an infected wound.

We hold hands and walk in the desert. We are going to have a picnic at the wall of El-Deen. It's either a weekend or a national holiday. We have packed some bread, cheese, mixed nuts, and one fresh cucumber in a bundle. Sahar has hung the bundle at the end of a stick. We take turns carrying the stick on our shoulders, pretending to be travelers—pilgrims. We walk in the desert to get to the wall.

There is no grass, no dandelions, wild flowers, weeds or berry bushes here. This is a barren desert and nothing grows in it except thorns. We have new shoes on, so it must be new year, or our birthday. We shouldn't have worn our new shoes in the desert. We'll get in trouble for this. There are

46

some big stones, lizards, and dangerous snakes hidden behind them. We are not scared of them. We are not scared of anything, Sahar says.

It's a long walk—takes one full hour. Last time we stole Uncle Musa's watch and took it with us to see how long it takes to get to the wall: one full hour. We pass the long mud and clay wall of the tenant house. Uncle Massi is sitting on top of the wall, swinging his long hairy legs, enjoying the sun. He doesn't recognize us. He splits sunflower seeds with his front teeth and spits the hulls out. We pass the cemetery. From where we are we just see the biggest gravestones. Most of the graves are naked, or the stones are so small and worn out that we can't see them from the distance. Mother Alborz is watching us from behind. She is our protector. She sends her son Saba, who is very friendly, in the spring to cool us with a caressing breeze.

When we finally see the wall, it's as though we see it for the first time. It always feels like this. We stop, hold our breath and just look. How thick and tall it is! How it rises to the heavens and stretches to unseen spots from the either side. But there is a ditch between us and the wall. This was a river before, Grandfather has told us. Dried up and turned into a garbage ditch, it's full of broken bottles and smelly trash now. On such a sunny spring day, this is the worst place to have a picnic. But we have to be here. We have promised to eat close to Father on the holidays, when he is lonely and bored.

So, spreading our cloth on the dust, we sit at the ditch munching our food in silence. We constantly watch the wall. We take turns biting the fresh cucumber. Although the wall is tall, we can see the top of the ironwoods. We know that there is a big garden there and a seven story building behind the trees. We know that in one of the floors, in one of the cells, Father is sitting or lying down thinking about us, sleeping and dreaming or daydreaming us. (We have no idea at this time that he might be hanging from the ceiling, lying under electroshock, or screaming while his nails are being pulled out. We imagine him having a normal life, only locked in the belly of El-Deen.) We even feel that *we* are locked out from his world and he is where he has to be, because El-Deen is where all the good people are. Men and women who did something to change the bad things in the world.

Mother says so. Whenever she feels well enough to talk with us we crawl into her bed and each turn into a ball under her armpits. She slams her heavy brown book and talks in her low voice: "There are good people in El-Deen who wanted to change the bad things in the world." Then we ask

47

questions like "What bad things?" although we know some of them. We just enjoy making Mother talk. Her voice is low and deep; it's not high pitched like most of the other women. It's not skinny like Aunty Shamsi's. She says, "Faithland for example—." And this repeats every once in a while when she is not sad or angry or very quiet.

Father couldn't sit in a room, relax, and think about us. I realize this on the wooden bench of the Hothouse and feel his pains inside myself. I hug my wet body and break into sobs. A sudden urge torments me, a wild uncontrollable desire to lay my head between my father's neck and shoulder and only once, for the last time in my life, cry hard and loud. I whisper deliriously, "Father, Father—how did you endure all this?" and I weep. "Sahar, hold my hand and take me out. I don't want to look at the wall anymore. Sahar take me—I'm crying and I shouldn't be crying so loud. Sahar, take me—I don't want them to see me like this—the lenses, Sahar— the secret lenses in the pads of the wall—"

I hear a cymbal and sense the end.

In the Cafeteria

The smell of butter, charcoaled meat, onion, and garlic wakes me up. Before I realize where I am, my stomach cramps. A ball takes shape down inside my intestines. It moves up toward my throat and stops for a second. I open my eyes and see Kamal's face, wavy and blurred. His cheeks look chubbier and are constantly moving, as though he is chewing something hard. We are at a table, Kamal and I, and he has a plate full of rice, kabob, and tomatoes in front of him. The rice steams and looks like a mountain. Kamal pours salt, pepper, and sumac like a colorful rain shower on the peak. At the same time, he chews the meat. He bites on the raw onion, stuffs his mouth with pickled garlic, and finally washes them down with a big sip of his cold yogurt drink.

I turn my head to the right and left and see more Kamals, many of them, sitting at the tables doing the same thing. Some of them have prisoners with them. They lay their heads on the tables or sit erect in stupor, gazing at the vacant space. None of them eat. All have leashes, the leashes tied to the guards' chairs.

My leash is tied to Kamal's chair and again I'm slightly bent forward and cannot sit straight. Other prisoners are not bent. So this is Kamal's special way to harass me. I realize that El-Deen's training regulations don't say that whenever you tie your prisoner's leash somewhere, do it in a way that his back is awkwardly bent. This is what Kamal and only Kamal does. Look how relatively comfortable other inmates are. They may be starving to death or feeling cramps and nausea, but at least their necks are not pulled like mine. "Bastard!" I curse.

He has noticed I've gained consciousness, but hasn't looked at me. He must have been starving. Eats like a pig. He doesn't use the silver. Grabs a piece of bread, dips it in the white mountain, fills it with rice, claws a piece of kabob with the same bread and shoves the huge sandwich in his mouth. Now a bite of onion, several cloves of garlic, and a big sip of the white drink to wash the big bite down.

The ball expands in my throat; it becomes softer and fills my mouth and nostrils. I press my hands—still cuffed—to my mouth and turn my head away as much as I can. But the leash pulls me toward Kamal and my effort to keep myself at a good distance from him and his plate remains useless. Although the leash chokes me, I turn my head to the left, but I face another Kamal, sitting at a table, right beside me, working on a big juicy charcoaled tomato. He smashes the tomato, mixes the juice with the rice and stuffs his mouth with a fistful of the dripping red rice. He eats with his hands too. Now he licks his fingers, one by one, and makes a smacking sound. The whole cafeteria spins now—fast, as if I'm on a carousel and a crazy person has increased the speed to torture me and himself is standing there laughing. I try to see who this bastard, this crazy carousel man is. He has a white turban on his head and a black caftan on his shoulder. He has only one arm; the left sleeve of his caftan is empty.

The ball is inside my head now and is turning into a volcano. The eruption will happen any second. I know this, because all the bells, alarm sirens, buzzers, and emergency drills are tolling, buzzing and ringing in my ears.

If I wasn't spinning with such unbelievable speed, I could probably manage to tell Kamal that I need to use the bathroom. He would or would not listen to me. If he would, fine; if not, he couldn't blame me later for the disaster. But how can I talk on such a crazy carousel? And the one-armed mad sheikh is winding the metal handle again. Again and again.

I hear myself groaning like a volcano. The groan is inside my head and throat first, but then becomes audible. With another unsuccessful attempt, I try to turn my head away from Kamal, but instead, I pull his chair closer to myself. I erupt on him and his food.

The ball, which was gradually deluding and expanding, finding a way out of my body, turns into a yellowish lava and gushes out of my mouth and nose. The bile showers on Kamal and his mountain of rice. I feel pain and relief and vaguely see all the numerous Kamals getting up and coming toward me. "Take me out!" I call soundlessly and a little hand pulls me off the carousel.

Chapter Two
In the Clinic

Whether it happened so or not I do not know;
but if you think about it you can see that it is true.
—The Lakota (Sioux) prophet, Black Elk

Doctor Halal

White, white, white, white. I open my eyes to the white. The ceiling, the sheet over my naked body, the walls around me, the metal stool, a big bulb flashing its blinding light—all white. I turn my head to the right: a white door, to the left: a white curtain. This is the Clinic, the white room. But why is a curtain hanging here? Didn't Kamal say there were no windows in El-Deen?

Where is Kamal? What happened to the show? Why am I naked? I try to move my arms and touch my face. My right arm is strapped to the bed and there is a cord connected to my left arm. The needle hurts. I follow the cord, a bottle hangs up there, almost full of a transparent liquid.

So I was dehydrated in the Hothouse and they're trying to save me. They need me. I'm important to them and they have to keep me alive. I haven't talked yet. I'm alive. Resting. I haven't said anything. But what? Something about the Revolution. Me in the Revolution. That's why I'm here and that's why they've strapped me naked to this bed and are trying to keep me alive.

This much I can remember. What else? Kamal. I remember him. And his nickname too: Loony Kamal. I smile. He is proud to be called Loony. Who is he? Where has he come from? A Devotee of the Revolution, a Revolutionary Guard, son of a butcher. Son of a bitch!

Now white tides wash me away. They pour out of this blinding bulb and cover me all over. It's not unpleasant. I enjoy the tides. There is an abyss down there, at the end of the bed. That's the abyss of oblivion. And these tides coming out of the bulb are waves of memory.

A big tide crawls over me and covers my head. I try to breathe, but I can't. I feel like I'm under the water, suffocating. I pull myself out, hold my head up and scream, "Sahar! I remember you. I remember you as I remember myself." Then I close my mouth. Did I scream her name, or I only think I screamed? I better make sure my lips are tight. I better talk inside my head. "Sahar," I say inside my head, "Why don't you come and take me out? Like you always did? Why is your absence so long, so endless, Sahar?"

I break into a sob as if someone is dead. I cry for a long time, unable to remember anything else. I'm not aware of La-Jay's secret cameras. I show weakness. I crack. I even hear myself cracking. The sound is like a dried piece of stale bread crunching under someone's foot. Crunch! Aha... This is my cracking point! I hiss to myself. What an Unbreakable hero! A piece of stale bread turned into crumbs, powder, dust. My face is wet with tears and saliva and I'm not able to dry myself. "Thousands of years," I mumble, "thousands of years in El-Deen, and I have finally cracked." The white waves stop running over me. I'm being pulled toward the abyss of oblivion. It sucks me into itself like a dark womb. I scream with horror when I fall in the abyss.

Here I hear her voice. She is in pain, moaning, calling me. I can only help her if I remember my name. She calls me again, but I can't hear well. Her voice echoes in the abyss. The echo doesn't let me hear my name. I pull myself up. I'll die if I stay in this vacant dark. I slip in the white light again and struggle to find myself. Where am I? When did I get lost? Do I really want to find myself again? "Holy Mary, Mother of God... pray for us sinners, now and at the hour of our death. Amen!"

"Are you a Catholic?"

A white, featureless face hangs over me, partly covered with eyeglasses, partly with a white cloth. The man's hands are as cold as his stethoscope.

"Are you a Catholic?"

I try to shake my head.

"No?"

I want to say no, but I can't. I just shake my head.

"You were praying just now."

I keep shaking my head.

"Don't you remember?"

I'm not a Catholic. I try to say this, but I can't. I wish he would leave me alone. I wish he would stop asking questions.

He removes the cloth covering his mouth. Unstraps my right arm and shakes my hand. "My name is Doctor Halal," he smiles. His eyes are magnified behind the thick lenses. His beard is carefully trimmed around the chin and his cheeks are shaved. "Very interesting," he says, looking at a clipboard. "Not a Catholic and whispering a Catholic prayer. Low blood pressure. Doesn't respond well to 25 mg. I'll add more."

I try to look around. He seems to be talking to someone. But I can't see anyone else in the room. He holds my wrist; counts my pulse. He shook my hand earlier, didn't he? He doesn't mind touching me.

"Are you hot?" he asks.

I shake my head.

"Are you cold?"

I shake my head.

"Can you talk?"

I shake my head again.

"But you were whispering earlier," he says.

A little winged thing flies around the room. It is a miniature man, or some weird creature with a pair of orange wings. I follow it. Sits on the white curtain. It is very little, the size of a nightingale, a newborn nightingale, with funny fuzzy fur. But its wings are complete. I can't see its face, only its wings which are glowing orange.

"You need to talk to us," Doctor Halal says. "Tell us what you see and hear. Is anything bothering you now? Why are you looking at the window? I'll use the dome for the first part and strap him, but I'll remove the dome and unstrap him for the second part." He says this to the empty room again.

He pulls the needle out and straps my arm to the bed. He prepares an injection.

"In the Women's Unit I used electroshock combined with C system." This is a man's voice. I search for him, but he is not in the room.

"We can't use electroshock on this patient," Halal says while examining the amount of the liquid in the syringe. "I'll explain why in the meeting." He talks to me now: "This will help you to have vivid and colorful dreams, my friend. The heavy burden will lift. You'll become light and happy. Do you hear me?"

I nod.

"Doctor," a female voice says. "Professor W in his last seminar pointed out to the importance of complete sensory deprivation and electroshock as a way to—" I try to locate the female voice, but I can't.

"Professor Z does not agree with Doctor W, Sister. We can't wait for the foreign advisors to resolve their scientific differences. Vital security matters are at stake. The Great Leader of our Holy Revolution has set a deadline for this procedure," Halal says in a dry serious tone.

The female voice says, "The Great Leader and Brother La-Jay have not been pleased with the results of the latest tests. They are time consuming, Doctor. We have hundreds of patients on the waiting list."

"If you don't mind Sister, we will wait until this afternoon to talk about these issues in the meeting. I'd rather not discuss our differences while the patient is still fully conscious." He holds the syringe in front of the big bulb. The liquid is colorless in the half-full syringe. "Now I'm going to place these white goggles over your eyes. It's like a dome. You can leave your eyes open and look at the dome. It's a small movie screen. I want you to tell us what you see. Just talk like you're whispering to yourself; we can hear you. Do you understand? Are you comfortable? You can ask questions if you like, anything."

I look at the orange nightingale for the last time. It's still on the curtain. It has panicked. Cannot move. I hear its heartbeat. It throbs under my left thumb. I feel the warmth of its body. It can die any moment. This baby bird can die any moment if it doesn't find a way out.

The white dome covers my eyes. The world is white. A needle pierces my right arm. It stings a little. They drugged me, I think. They have drugged me before too, and now more. That was not enough. Who are they? Maybe I'm not in El-Deen. Maybe the whole thing is a dream. I had a car accident and I'm in a hospital. Doctor Halal is a good doctor. He is kind. I noticed how cautiously he injected me, delicately, like a loving nurse who doesn't want to hurt the patient. He can't be from El-Deen. El-Deen was a bad dream, a nightmare. I'm out. Something has happened to me. Maybe in the Revolution. When they started to shoot. When we all ducked. When we all lay down on the ground. When the tanks moved toward us. When the machine guns fired at us. Maybe I was there. The Black Friday. They called it the Black Friday because we all died. They ran over us with the tanks. They smashed us. Flat skins on the bloody asphalt. They shot those of us who had climbed the trees. We fell down like red leaves or the red feathers of a dead bird. If I was there, I must be dead now.

But I wasn't there. I was somewhere else—a different part of the city. I was on a wall waving a flag and holding a banner. I made a speech earlier. Then the flood came, the flood of oil. It drowned the people. I stayed there alone. My flag and banner fell down in the ocean of oil. I heard the sirens, then the ships' horns. They were getting ready to carry the barrels of oil. I was there, not in the Black Friday, but on the wall. I didn't get killed. I saw it all. Nothing remained unseen. They came with their black flags. Some had machine guns, some clubs, some even swords and scimitars. I remember I thought at the moment, "They have looted the museum and taken the ancient weapons." They took the women to the black vans. They took Sahar. I saw her for the last time. They dragged her on the ground, which was wet with oil. Her white dress and white scarf were soiled. This was the beginning of the flood. Later the level of oil raised—it reached almost halfway up the wall. The people who were drowning gulped the oil. I can still hear the strange sound : "Guloop... Guloop... Guloop..." This is the way they gulped the oil and drowned. The smell of oil is in my nostrils. Forever.

But this makes me even more confused. Where am I? Did the Doctor leave? They mentioned The Great Leader and La-Jay. I must be in El-Deen, then. If they keep me here and don't take me anywhere else, it won't be so bad. My body is relaxed. Has never been so relaxed before. I have no pain. No twitch. No sting. No throb. No discomfort. I've never been so fully and completely without pain in my life.

But I don't see anything on this screen. I'd better close my eyes and rest. My body is numb; I can't move it. My lips are big, swollen. He wants me to talk. Am I talking? Am I telling him all this?

I hear the nightingale. It is talking to me. Telling me what to tell Halal. I trust it. I trust the poor newborn nightingale. I trust the chick. I can't see it, but I know that it's sitting on my chest now. I feel its light weight. It tells me to tell this to Halal: "Where have you been trained, bastard? Who are Z and W, bastard? What are you trying to do, bastard? I won't leak. I won't crack. You better keep this in your rotten head, bastard. I won't say what you want me to say, bastard." The bird insists that I add a "bastard" at the end of each sentence. But what I'm not quite sure about is whether I'm really talking or the whole thing is in my head. I try to scream, "Bastards!" But I don't hear anything. I don't feel anything either. I'm deprived of anger or hatred. I just repeat what the nightingale wants me to repeat. These are the bird's words, not mine.

The Earthquake

Something is on the screen. But I'm not sure if my eyes are open. They are not my eyes anymore. Nothing is mine. My arms, legs, body—they are all separated from me. These eyes—mine or not, open or closed—see something. I see a bright red triangle and we are inside it: Sahar, Mother and I. We are all small. We perfectly fit in the red triangle. Everything is as it always is in our triangular room. Sahar and I share a bed at our angle and Mother is on her bed at the window, between the two angles, opposite us. The curtain separates us. Our little glass-belly heater, Aladdin, is burning in the center of our triangular space. Its glow is unusually bright. But it's the same old Aladdin, a little shorter than Sahar and I. Fiery tongues move crazily inside it. Aladdin doesn't have legs. The bottom part is a pot, full of kerosene.

We look at Mother reading on her bed. It's a strange feeling. We see her, but we are her too. We are each other and we are her. We are all one. We know what she is dreaming about. We are her, dreaming her dream. We dream our dreams and hers.

Our dream is about Grand-Lady's Turkman carpet. We are sitting on it. The green peacock and all the flowers around it are strangely bright. They are luminous. The design is so alive that it scares us. What if the huge peacock comes to life? We hold hands and sit on the peacock's open umbrella. Sahar calls the north wind. She says something like, "Sa... ba...," stretching the word. I can see the word "Saba," a little ball of fur going toward the mountain until it reaches the top, when we suddenly hear a grumbling. The mountain responds to us. Sahar says, "Mother Alborz is talking to us." We are scared, but enjoy our dream.

Now Saba, the north wind, comes. It's shapeless, or it has a strange undefinable shape. It's made of air, but we can see it. We can somehow recognize its chubby cheeks and laughing eyes. It dashes toward us. Sahar screams, "Lift the carpet up!" And Saba lifts the carpet up. Now we float in the air. We hold hands not to fall. The carpet is flat in the air. We are on Saba's shoulders and we trust him. He is not mean now, although we know that he can be mean. This is not his mean season. It's spring. The winter has ended. The clouds are very white, transparent, lacy, and white. They feel wet and we drink them. We are thirsty. Saba takes us to the top of the mountain, on his mother's nightcap and the carpet lands.

We stand up and look at the world. We are happy to be alive. All the hills and valleys, all the deserts and fields, all the cities, towns, and villages which from this height look like colorful patches on Maman's handmade quilt—all and all are radiant, alive, dear, and very close to us. They are us. We feel one with the world. We feel like throwing ourselves down, dissolving in the air, becoming the air, landing on a rock, becoming part of the rock. Pain doesn't mean anything. Death has no bad meaning. Death means turning into something else and we want it. Let us turn into a rock or a piece of fluffy cloud. Let us become a tree. Let us be part of that little lake. We hold hands and fly. Saba plays with us while we float. Sometimes he places himself under us to prevent us from falling too fast, and sometimes he pushes us forward or just tickles us like a little naughty child. We fall in the lake and submerge. It takes us forever to get down. We land at the bottom of the lake and see the glow of the greenest weeds. A school of fish pass by, and we see the glitter of the golden gills. And all this time we hold each other's hands.

Now we slip into the deep, dark well in the middle of our yard. We don't fall into it, but slip on the wet mossy wall and land in the water at the bottom of the well. The water is only ankle deep. We know that we are dreaming Mother's dream now and this dream is not as pleasant as ours. This is a dark dream. We feel fear and excitement. We are scared of the creature that is about to appear and excited to see him. It's a male. We know him forever and we don't know him at all. Our inside has a funny sensation. It throbs, squeezes, sucks something in. But that thing is nothing. Nothing is there to be sucked in, just the sensation, the excitement of the creature coming. Our heart beats like drums in our ears. He appears. Hairy, head to foot, much bigger than us, ugly, but desirable. He is scary and not scary at the same time. We scream and try to run away, but we can't. We want to climb the wet slippery wall of the well, but it's impossible. We're trapped here and the monster is approaching.

"Mmmmm..." he makes such a sound. "I smell human flesh... Jinnis and Minis, the dish is fresh..." His voice echoes in the hollow well. "Who are you?" he asks us.

"Pari—" we say.

"You're too skinny for me Pari, I have to keep you here, feed you, and make you fat." He grabs us and lays us on a wet mat in a corner. He takes a big knife out and cuts one slice of his thick thigh. He offers his flesh to us.

Meanwhile on the mat, we are lying on our back, shivering with fear and excitement. The monster sits next to us, feeding us his bloody flesh. The taste is unbelievably delicious. We've never had such a meat before. We chew slowly to prolong the pleasure. We shake and throb. We wriggle. The monster chops another piece and another, until he is thin. Not a monster anymore. He becomes our size and crawls toward us.

Sahar and I scream in our bed. The whole triangle shakes and jerks. We are panicked. What if the sides get closer to one another and smash us in between? It's the feeling of earthquake now. It's horizontal. We rock back and forth. We hold hands not to fall apart. The earth rocks, and we panic, but enjoy the movement. We want the quake to stop and we don't want it to stop.

Grandfather picks up the Aladdin and it shrinks into a shining lantern. The lantern has a strange glow. It lights all the street. We are out now. Everybody is out. This is New Spring Street. Along either side of the street, in front of the colorful match-box houses, from the top of the hilly street, where our three houses are, down to the school, the neighbors spread their blankets or set up their folding beds. We sleep in front of our houses, but not too close. The earth, meanwhile, shakes. Sahar and I enjoy the cradle. We lay down in our bed and look at the orange sky. We have never seen such a sky before, glowing with a phosphorous light.

Grand-Lady is lying on our right. She is on her Turkman carpet. Her long thin braids brush the ground. They are unusual. They have life of their own. Her braids wriggle like snakes. They slither and slide. They crawl up her body and curl on her chest, waiting. Grand-Lady's snake-braids glow a luminous orange color.

Grandfather brings his daguerreotype out, setting it in front of his house, perpendicular to the two rows of the people lying down or sitting in the street. His bald head disappears inside the black box and appears again. Maman stands beside him and holds her big round wedding mirror in front of the Aladdin—now a strange lantern. Everywhere becomes bright as a sunny afternoon. Sahar and I stare into the mirror. This is the same old mirror as in Grandfather's room, but it looks bigger and more beautiful. In the mirror, we see Mount Alborz, roaring like hundreds of lions, her white nightcap shaking when she roars.

We panic. We have never been so close to death. Death is not pleasant now; it means fading away, becoming nothing. It's an eternal interruption that will force us to leave. Death is on top of Mother Alborz and is going to fall down like a huge black shadow, covering us all. Death is everywhere, under us in the dark earth, groaning. It's beside us, sitting on Grand-Lady's bony chest.

We search for Mother. She is just leaving the triangular house. She is coming toward us. A real mermaid. Her body glows in the incandescent light. Her blue eyes are larger and glossier and send out aqua beams. We are her and we are scared of her. She is approaching us. We panic. We are approaching us in her body and we are shivering with fear. She is death. We look into the mirror to find something there and escape the death.

Grandfather shoots a picture. Bang. It sounds like a toy gun. Smoke rises from his black box. Because of the sound of the toy gun, the mirror cracks into many pieces. But Maman, as though frozen, stands still, holding the broken mirror close to the lantern.

All the women bite their lips and slap their cheeks. "The mirror broke, the mirror broke," they murmur. "It's a bad omen. A very bad omen!"

The earth rocks gently and pleasantly now and the snakes on Grand-Lady's chest fall asleep. A man stands on his bed, his black robe waving in the breeze. He raises his right arm to the sky, his left sleeve is empty. He prays. The sound of his prayer mixes with the whistle of the wind. We see the north wind, Saba, taking off from the top of his mother's shoulder, dashing down toward us. He has the same shapeless shape we saw in our dream, puffy cheeks, a ball of air. All the lanterns flicker. All the men and women rise up and face the mountain to pray. The one-armed man says, "God is great!" and the people repeat the same thing. The big black flag on top of the one-armed man's roof shakes in the wind and makes an alarming sound, a sound like flapping wings. The flag turns into a huge bat and flutters its wings repeatedly. The bat hovers over our heads, over Sahar and me, over our family.

Our family doesn't pray.

The bells toll in the distance. These are Santa Zita's bells. In a few months, we have to start our first grade in Santa Zita Catholic School. Mother has already enrolled us. Aunty Zari is sewing black uniforms for us. Ding dong: a big one tolls. Clang! Clang! This is the huge one—the one that hangs in a tower. Ding, ding ding, ding: these are the little brass bells the nuns shake all the time. Now they all chime together, scary and fascinating. We hold our breaths and listen.

For a split second—which is an eternity—all the bells stop, the wind's whistle stops, the mountain's roar stops, the earth's groan stops, the prayers and whispers and quarrels stop, and a thick, heavy, many-folded silence falls on the earth like a gigantic book. In a split second, Sahar and I feel the burden of death, heavy and pleasant, relieving and everlasting. A tiny little bird, the color of the orange of the sky, not bigger than a nightingale chick, sits on Grandfather's black camera and sings with a human voice, "Hoori! Hoori! Hoori! Hoori!" And that's all it repeats. Maman turns toward the house and holds the cracked mirror up toward the only room on the roof. Hoori's picture reflects in all the broken pieces. The waterfall of her black hair hides half of her face, the marble of her neck glistens in the light and her little fist holds her delicate chin up. Sahar holds my hand, and we pick the glowing Aladdin up and step inside the mirror.

"Hoori... Hoori... Hoori... are you a goddess or a woman?" the orange bird sings. "Are you made of the same material as the others, or are you made of unknown stuff? Not air and water, dust and fire, but things unknown to us. Where have you brought this beauty from, Hoori? Why are you sitting in the only room on top of the roof waiting for the building to shake like a hammock in the wind? Don't you know that it will crumble and fall? Why do you want to descend, to go down with mud and mortar? Why do you want to collapse, to mix and mingle with the cloud of dust? Why do you want to embrace the dark shadow, Hoori?" the orange bird says and takes us on his small but strong wings to Hoori's room on top of the roof. "Hoori... Hoori... Hoori... " the ominous bird, the bird of death, sings, and takes us into Hoori's dream. We lift the black curtain of her hair to see what we have never seen before, what has always been hidden under her hair, what must be half of her face. We lift the black curtain and half of Hoori's face is the moon, as white as white marble, glistening, radiant, stony hard, cold as ice, smooth as water, solid as rock, the beautiful half moon, half of Hoori's face.

"Oh Sahar, what strange things happen in this world! Hold my hand, Sahar, for I'm scared of death. Aunty Hoori is destined to die and this half moon will become full one day. Sahar, how can I describe this unbearable joy to you? The joy of not being alone in this strange world? You are with me and holding my hand all the time and this gives me a warm feeling. Sahar, what would I do without you? Sahar, this joy that I just described is turning into fear now, the fear of losing the joy. This is what Hoori feels all the time: fear, fear, fear, fear, and to end the fear, she plans to escape. To die."

Sahar and I step out of the mirror. Everybody is sleeping along the street. The cradle-like movement of the earth and the lullaby of the orange nightingale who sits on the black camera singing, "Hoori, Hoori, Hoori...." have put everyone to sleep. We look at Grandfather, snoring peacefully under a blanket. His bald brown head shines in our lantern's light. For a split second we share his dream. His little storage room is full of rats. The fat gray animals are climbing the ropes, jumping on the money purses. They are chewing them—the purses and the paper money. We scream, hitting our bald head. We fight with the rats, but they bite us, trying to chew our hands. The rats eat up all the money and rush to the dark room. They eat up our pictures too. They devour our three daughters: Zari, Pari, and Hoori. We run out of Grandfather's dream, before the rats eat us alive.

Sahar holds my hand and says, "Let's get out of here before we fall into Grand-Lady's dream and die again." She pulls me toward the desert, *our* desert. We pass by Maman, who still holds the broken mirror, pressing it tightly to her large breasts. "Can she ever rest?" we ask. "Can she lie down and sleep?" Her eyes are closed. She must be sleeping on her legs. We run fast as the wind, so as not to fall into the dark hole of Maman's dream. The hole is a kitchen, as dark as a grave, where hundreds of pots and pans boil with tar black soup.

The Poet-Prophet

In the desert, we walk as if we are weightless and don't feel the thorns and the sharp stones. The gentle quake is pleasant and soothing. Sahar holds up the lantern to light our path, but the sky is not as dark as it should be on such a night.

It's crimson red and the horizon, the end of the desert, where the earth and the sky touch, is burning with yellow and red, as though on fire.

Uncle Massi's deep voice echoes in the desert: "Beware and be anxious about your life. See how the earth is opening to swallow you up? It is swallowing your hovels. Where do you want to live? What do you want to eat? Is there any justice in this universe?"

Uncle Massi is leading the tenants from the crumbling multi-level house to the cemetery. A bottle of vodka in his hand, he takes long steps and big sips while rushing toward the graves. His shabby robe and dusty, tangled hair wave in the wind. He yells with passion and rage: "Judge! For it's your right to judge! Why don't you open your eyes to see how other people live?" And the poor tenants follow him like a flock of sheep. "Oh, you sinners! Oh you wretched flock of God!" Uncle jumps on the tallest gravestone and waves his arms in the air. "Why should you build your houses on the sand and they build theirs on the rock? Are their houses falling down? No. Yours are! So Judge! Judge! Judge and Judge! Where is the justice?"

The crowd sits around him and listens to him. Sahar and I hide behind a tall gravestone and feel Uncle Massi's agony. Our blood boils and our heart bounces up and down. We want to tear our chest apart and take our crazy heart out, but we can't. This is what Uncle must be feeling now.

"I'm Massi-Alla, your poet-prophet. Beware of the false prophets and listen to the real one. Faithland is turning into ashes, New Spring may even collapse, but the Alleys of Heaven, up on the solid rocks of Alborz, will never shake. The White Marble Palace of the Monarch will never shake. There will not be any peace on this earth unless you build your houses on solid rocks as they do. There will not be any peace on this earth unless *you* restore the peace! You! Not them. Twenty and five—This is my premonition. Twenty and five! This is my prophecy! Twenty and five years from now, the Alleys of Heaven will fall into the dark pit of Faithland and Faithland will rise and celebrate a New Spring! Lie now on the earth, for the earth is your mother. If it opens, it will embrace you in her warm womb, if it lets you live, then live and rise for justice, for it's for you to judge!"

Uncle drinks half of his vodka with one breath and says, "Now I'm going to recite my elegy. As you can see, I haven't written it down, it's coming to me right here and now. Lie down, close your eyes and enjoy the song of God: 'We who have piled sorrow upon the heap of sorrow... will rise tomorrow...'"

Saba blows Uncle's voice away as Sahar and I run out of the cemetery to reach the wall.

The air smells of burned wood. It's not unpleasant and reminds us of when Maman cooks a big amount of rice on a heap of firewood. But this smoke is a thousand times more. We hear the crackling sounds. Our eyes burn. We stop and try to find out where we are. Saba blows the cloud of smoke away and we see Faithland down at the bottom of the hill, burning. The people, the size of ants, run out of the cardboard houses, scream and squeak.

Sahar and I remember that once Cyrus, Uncle Mussa's son, trapped some ants in a match box and burned the box. The sizzling ants ran around in agony and climbed on each other. That's how the people of Faithland look now. Sahar and I feel the agony of the ants, of the people down in the smoking pot. Our skin burns, shrinks, and blisters. We scream with pain and run through the smoke.

The wall rises in front of us, reaching the radiant crimson sky. It's a tall wall, impassable, stretched from the either side to unseen spots. There is a ditch between us and the wall, deep and full of broken bottles. We sit and hold hands staring at the wall. The whole world is motionless and the silence is deep. Now a "swoosh" is heard, as though someone is sliding a flat metal tool on a smooth surface. "Swoosh, swoosh," and a "Dump!" Someone drops something on the smoothened surface. We hear more: "Swoosh, swoosh, dump! Swoosh, swoosh, dump!" The sound repeats forever. We raise our heads. On top of the wall, his head in the orange mist, stands Ali the Bricklayer, laying brick on top of the brick, raising the wall. We watch him for a while, then Sahar says that we should ask Ali to take us inside the prison. I disagree. We argue for a while. Sahar wins. "Don't you want to see Father?" she says and I'm convinced.

Father. Lonely Father, injured Father, Father of the broken frame on the wall, Father of white teeth and bright smile. Father of long nights of longing inside the small triangular house. Father, how tall are you? We've only seen your torso in the wedding picture. You must be handsome. Father, our absent hero. You have to tell us how you wanted to kill the Monarch. Where did you get such courage? Are you a human, Father, or are you Rostam the Dragon Killer, the hero of *The Book of the Kings*. Are you the tall, strong, brave Rostam who chopped off all the heads of the beast?

"Yes Sahar, let's call Ali the Bricklayer and ask him, beg him to take us in—inside El-Deen. Ali works here. He knows the guards. It's not impossible. He likes us. He saved us from the flood, didn't he? He will take us in and we will visit Father, but Mother will never know, or we'll be dead."

In the White Tent

"One, two, three—" Sahar counts and calls, "Saaa... baaa!" The dust of the desert whirls and rises up, the tall trees of El-Deen shake behind the wall, the leaves fly to the south like migrant birds. Sahar and I hug each other tight. The naughty son of Alborz can lift us up. Saba with his shapeless shape appears, bigger than ever. We tell him what we want and before long, Ali the Bricklayer is floating in the air like a kite. He lands on the ground and sits with us. Saba pulls Sahar's hair, hides under my shirt and tickles me and at last whistles a loud whistle and disappears.

We tell Ali the Bricklayer that our father has been inside El-Deen since we were born. He says he knows. We tell him that we want to visit him and hug him and smell him and see if he looks and smells the way he does in our dreams. Ali says he knows this. We tell Ali that he is the only person who can take us in. He says he knows this too and that's why he is here.

He tucks us under his long arms like two little honeydew melons and takes long giantlike steps, walking along the ditch. He reaches a bridge we have never seen before. While passing the wooden bridge, we hear a dog barking under us. The further we go, the louder the bark becomes. When we reach the other side, we turn and see the ugliest and dirtiest dog in the world.

"This is El-Deen's watch dog, Afreet. She is always under the bridge. If a prisoner finds his way out, she tears him apart," Ali explains.

Afreet is covered with mud and blood and we can smell her horrible odor. Saliva hangs from her sharp fangs and her red tongue moves like a hungry snake. She barks her throat out and runs restlessly around herself, chasing her own tail. The ditch now seems more like a river of blood and Afreet is knee deep in it.

Ali steps in a dirt-covered pathway and in a short while we reach El-Deen's giant wooden gate, which rises high into the sky. In a small booth on the right, a soldier dozes off on his legs. Ali lays us down cautiously, as though we are really melons and he doesn't want to break us. He talks to the soldier and in a few seconds the gate opens a crack. Three more soldiers, their guns aiming at us, step out of the garden. The first soldier talks to them and this takes a while. Sahar and I hold hands all the time and look at the dark garden from between the soldiers' legs. Our hearts jump in our throats, ready to pop out of our mouths. We wish we hadn't come.

"These trees are more than two thousand years old. They were here when the first people came to this land and called it their country," Ali the Bricklayer says as he leads us through a narrow pathway surrounded by tall ironwoods. One of the soldiers walks in front of us and two, behind. "El-Deen's Ironwoods," Ali continues, "are as strong as iron. Look how red the branches are. It's as if they are nourished by blood; it runs in their veins."

Sahar and I look around and tilt our heads back to see the top branches. They are like monstrous rhubarbs. We have seen Maman chopping rhubarbs to make a sour stew. "Come! Come, faster!" Ali orders us, "People say that these trees are enchanted and if you look at them for too long, you won't be able to stop looking at them. You'll become stiff and numb like statues. Come! Move!"

We reach a big white tent in the middle of the garden. The soldiers lead us in and there we see an old wooden rectangular table. One of the soldiers lifts Sahar up and puts her on the table. He does the same with me. Then he stares at us and laughs. His front teeth are slimy and broken. All the soldiers leave, except the slimy toothed one. Ali tells us that we have to wait for our father, because it takes a while to bring him from his cell. Sahar asks where the prison is. Ali says, it's way inside the garden. It's a tall, white, seven-story building with many black patches on it. The patches are the curtained windows.

The soldier says, "The monster with many eyes!" And makes a scary face and roars. He shows his yellow broken teeth. Now he laughs again, pleased that he has scared us. I ask in which part of the building our father is. The soldier says in the basement, under the ground. Sahar and I keep quiet, a lump growing in our throats, but the nightingale sings somewhere inside us.

"Father, Father, poor Father—" the nightingale cries in our chest. "Buried under the ground for seven years... no window to the enchanted ironwoods—"

"What's wrong?" Ali asks.

We tell him we didn't know our father was under the ground. Ali laughs and says it doesn't make any difference anyway, for the windows of El-Deen are all blocked. Sahar thinks for a moment and tells Ali that if the trees of the garden are enchanted and if anyone who looks at them will freeze like a statue, then why has the Monarch sealed the windows? Isn't it better for him to have frozen prisoners who can never run away? Ali and the slimy-toothed soldier laugh and admire Sahar's wisdom.

The soldier, still chuckling, says, "No, it wouldn't be better for His Majesty, Our Young Beloved Monarch, to have all the windows unveiled. Once, long ago something happened in El-Deen which alarmed the Old Monarch, his Majesty's benevolent father. The Young Monarch doesn't want such an incident to happen in his time."

He tells us the story of a young doctor who was the prisoner of the Old Monarch. He and fifty-two of his followers wanted a Worker's Revolution in this country, exactly like the one that was happening then, in Russia, not far away. All the fifty-three were sentenced to death, but this one, the doctor, who was their leader and the bravest of all, one night broke the window of his cell on the seventh floor and threw himself out. He didn't fall on the ground, he flew away, instead, like a bird in the sky. The soldier swears that his father—who was a guard at that time—swears that he saw the flying doctor with his own eyes. His wings were red and enormous and he headed toward the north, to Russia, where Lenin led the Worker's Revolution.

We are both quiet now, thinking. We have a vague feeling that we have heard this story somewhere before. But now the two soldiers who'd left us appear at the entrance of the tent. They step in and stand on the either side of the opening. A third soldier comes in dragging a little man with a leash. The leashed man is hand-cuffed, but still the soldier pulls him like a goat. They approach the table on which Sahar and I are standing. The soldiers make a circle around us and let the man stand alone, facing us. Ali the Bricklayer stays outside the circle, lighting a cigarette.

The little man's leash hangs like a long necktie. The lump which was choking us for a while melts in our throats and we both cry loud and hard, sniffling and wiping our runny noses with the back of our hands. The nightingale flutters and makes strange noises in our chest. The little man cannot hug us. He just stands there looking at us with his red wet eyes, behind the thickest lenses we have ever seen. His left lense has a diagonal crack.

We hear Ali's voice from behind the wall of the soldiers, "Hug your father! He can't hug you, his hands are cuffed."

We both hug the little man, lay our heads on his shoulders, in the hollow space between the big sharp bone and the thin pale neck; we smell the familiar smell of sweet sweat and bitter tobacco. He whispers our names: "Pari..." he calls Mother first. "Sahar..." he whispers in Sahar's ear.

But before I can hear the third name, my own, Afreet the bloody watch dog of the ditch breaks inside the tent. I hide under the wooden table while the soldiers take Father away and Ali tucks Sahar under his long arm and runs out of El-Deen. I run in the enchanted garden, Afreet chasing me and barking like hundreds of hungry wolves. As she rubs her dirty muzzle on my calf, I tear the white sheet and throw myself off the bed.

The Window

I'm naked and alone on the cold floor. I'm not sure what I have said aloud and what has remained inside my head; but I know well that they are all watching me from somewhere.

I look around the Clinic, gazing at the white curtain, but I don't see the nightingale. I sit on the white cot and remember everything. My dreams were vivid and colorful as Doctor Halal promised. But do I feel light and happy? I shiver, feeling the emptiness of loss. Where is she? I call her. I want her to be with me the way she used to be. I want her to whisper in my ears, tell me what to do, hold my hand and feel the same feelings. I want her in a way I have never wanted anything or anyone before. I cry and mumble senseless words. "A boat... send me a boat..." I repeat and weep. "I'll drown without her."

But something strange happens. I feel I'm stepping outside my body, looking at myself from distance. I see a thin wire of a man, pale, and miserable, bent on the verge of breaking. A feeble twig of a willow tree. I stop weeping.

Nobody comes to see me, to inquire about the test, to dig up my memories, ask me questions. They keep me waiting. This is the worst part.

I want to go out—anywhere. I want to walk with Kamal again. I remember Kamal and break into sobs. I remember his warm breath on my neck, when I was looking in the mirror and he was standing behind me talking about his dream. "Kamal! Kamal! Brother—" I call. "Come and take me with you—."

I look at the window again. The thick white curtain puzzles me. Didn't they say the curtains were black, nailed to the walls? But that was in my dream. I sit, face to the window, and debate. My bare legs hang from the cot like a puppet's lifeless legs. I'm made of rags, filled with cotton balls. I'm a puppet, the puppeteer gone. I stare at the curtain, trying to find out whether there is light or dark outside. The curtain is too thick. When was the last time I saw the sky? I don't remember.

The time passes. I'm wasting it. They will come any moment to inject more drugs, or drag me out. I'm losing the only opportunity to get out of here and find Sahar. I'm a coward. A puppet. They'll break me sooner or later. Or maybe they have done it to some extent. The watch dog of El-Deen attacked the tent and Father never whispered my name. Afreet the bloody dog saved me. Had Father uttered my name, I would have shouted it aloud. Halal would be here now, even La-Jay; they would congratulate me for remembering my name—first name, then last. They could look for my address, my family, relatives, sister. Sahar. They would bring her here, to the women's unit. They would train her.

But now I'm safe. No name was uttered. That's why they are not here, they're disappointed. They may even fire Doctor Halal and hire someone else with better methods. Electroshock, one doctor said. Maybe they have a meeting now. They are fighting over the most effective methods. I shouldn't waste time. At least I can open the window and see what is out side.
The temptation to go toward the curtain, draw it back, and open the window is now ten times—a hundred times—more than before. My heart beats in the upper part of my chest. I gasp and chew my lips, not to utter meaningless sounds. I have this urge to moan, to whine, to cry like an animal.

What is the most horrible thing they can do to me if they catch me touching the window? Hang me from my testicles? I'll pass out, I won't stay conscious to endure the pain. The real torture is what they are doing to me now. Sitting me in front of a window, leaving me with the vivid scenes of my dream. They can't possibly be neglecting me. They're watching me and this is also part of the experiment. They are laughing at me, ridiculing me. They have starved me so that I look ridiculously thin. They have taken my clothes off and they are laughing at my body. Even Rostam, the Dragon Killer, would have looked miserable if they had starved him, tortured him, drugged him, and stripped him... But the poet didn't let this happen: Rakhsh, the winged horse, appears and carries the hero out of the trouble. In real life, there is no poet to invent a winged horse for me. I'm here alone, naked, wounded... and I have no horse.

Who has written my life so dull and dry? How come I cannot get out? Nothing is going to happen. What if this takes until eternity? Who am I anyway? Do I exist?

How about Sahar? Does Sahar exist, or I have made her up? Or what if I'm real and she is real too and she is here now? What if all this time Sahar has been here in El-Deen, in the women's unit, at times very close to me. Didn't I see the black van taking her when I was on top of the wall and the flood of oil was drowning the people? Black vans all end up at El-Deen.

Sahar is here. She is wearing a white gown. I can't picture her in a black veil. It must be white, like the dress she had on when they took her in the van. She is wearing a big thin scarf around her head. Isn't this Grand-Lady's peacock embroidered scarf? Haven't I seen this scarf here in El-Deen somewhere? She is head to foot white, shrouded.

They drag her into this room, the way they pulled her to the black van. There are two guards, both Kamal's size. She is pale. Her eyes are larger than ever and as usual stars twinkle in them. They lay her on this cot and move me to that metal stool. I sit there naked and shiver. I shiver because I feel what Sahar feels.

They tear her shroud off and touch her body. She screams. They stuff her scarf into her mouth. I want to scream. But I'm voiceless. Bubbles come out of my mouth. I'm a fish a second before being swallowed by a whale. They rub Sahar's body. Their fingers are dirty and calloused. I scream and bubble out all the air in my lungs. I weep with no tears. I tear my chest and take my little heart out. A dead fish's heart, cold and bloodless.

One of the Kamals lies over her with all his clothes on. He opens his fly. She screams. I drop my cold heart on the floor and stamp on it. I kick it, smash it, tear it into one hundred pieces. I kill the orange nightingale who lived in my chest all this time, all my life. I look at the curtained window for the last time. No, the horse is not coming. I never had a horse and will not have. I'm not Rostam. I'm not an Unbreakable. I'm a cheap candle. I melt fast. I'm becoming a heap of wax on the floor. The janitors of El-Deen will clean me off tomorrow.

I crawl. Like an insect—not a scorpion, a worthless thin-legged spider. I slither in a slimy way like a mass of liquid wax. I touch my body. I'm still alive. My face is wet with tears. "Sahar..." I whisper and look up at the cot. But the cot is empty. I pull myself up and stand. My knees tremble. I take baby steps toward the window. I stand for a few seconds staring at the thick, white curtain. I don't think. I'm not anxious. I feel relaxed. Empty inside and relaxed.

I hold the rope and pull it gently. The white curtain slides from the middle to the right and left. It slides more. It reveals a window with clean transparent glasses. "The only window in El-Deen," I whisper. I look through the clear glass. No gleam of light. I see myself. I hold both hands to the either side of my face and press my forehead to the window pane. I see the brick wall, thick and impassable. I raise my head up. The wall has stretched up into the unseen sky, the right and left lost in infinity. I stay for a long time and stare at the wall. I wait for something to happen and it happens. It's a sound. It comes from far away—the top of the wall. The sound is like sliding a trowel on a smooth surface. It goes like, swoosh... swoosh... then, Dump! And that's a brick dumped on the soft and wet mortar. Swoosh... swoosh... Dump! Swoosh... swoosh... Dump! Someone is up there, laying brick on top of brick, raising the wall.

A throbbing nerve stretches the corner of my lips. I smile and whisper in a voice coming from a distant past, "Sahar, can you hear this?"

Massages and More Walking

Instead of one, three Kamals appear. Two of them beat me up. One just stands in a corner, watching. I receive punches and slaps, but they don't hurt much. The one standing there with my clothes hanging on his arm must be *my* Kamal, the loony. The beaters take turn now. One has a big black mole above his beard line and he kicks me in the stomach with his right knee. The other, a big, but amazingly brisk, guard gives me a knife-sharp back hand on the cheek and they both leave the room. This last blow throws me at the foot of the standing Kamal. I lie on my back motionless.

Now I start to feel the stings and twinges. My face burns, expanding like an enormous sun. But why? For drawing the curtain back? Or is this their way to counteract the effects of the drug? What happened to Doctor Halal? Is this the way they treat his guinea pig? And he lets them do this? He must be a powerless son of a bitch to allow these monsters to beat his patient up. What if I've lost all of my memories? All that I resurrected under such an elaborate scientific method. Where is Halal now to see what they've done to me?

"Get up!" Kamal orders and stretches his arm toward me. I hold his hand and pull myself up. He is touching me!

"Here, your clothes—fresh from El-Deen's laundry room." He hands me the black pants and white shirt. They are cleaned and ironed. I can smell the dampness of steam on them. Who has ironed my shirt? A woman?

The thought that a woman might have touched my shirt stirs my emotions. Tears burn my eyes. Maman's image with her sunken eyes and enormous breasts comes to mind. She is sitting on the floor in the middle of her room, a white sheet spread in front of her, a pile of damp clothes beside her. With a big ugly iron, which has a steaming hole on its head, she is ironing Grandfather's shirts, Aunty Hoori's school uniforms, Grand-Lady's kerchiefs and scarves, and endless sheets and pillowcases and mantlepieces. She feeds the steaming monster with more water, wets her finger-tip, touches the monster's burning body to see if it's hot enough and when she hears the whizzzz sound and her finger burns, starts to iron. Sweat bubbles on her short, creased forehead and the corners of her smiling lips droop.

"Can I try?" Sahar asks.

"You'll burn yourself and the clothes too; this damn thing is old and heavy. I've told your grandfather one hundred times that I need a lighter iron, the new kind. He keeps forgetting."

"Please, Maman, just a little bit. I won't burn anything," Sahar pleads.

"No is no, my dear. Children shouldn't touch this," Maman says. So, we just sit and stare at her motions. Each ball of ugly, wrinkled shirt turns into a new shirt, each mass of shapeless sheet turns into a starched and folded sheet. Maman's work is a miracle.

And then the image of Zeinab fills my head—the laundry woman of

71

our neighborhood, Hassan the Gardener's wife. All I remember of Zeinab is her long braids, which she always tied up at the back of her neck when she squatted in our yard in front of a large round brass tub. I remember her odor too, which was the odor of all the tenants of the multi-level house. Something rotten and moldy, something stale. Must and old sweat. Zeinab's stale odor was always mixed with the sharp smell of laundry soap. And now I see her hands too, white and wrinkled from too many washings. Shrunken.

Sahar and I squat on the other side of Zeinab's washing tub, watching her. "Can I touch the suds?" Sahar asks. "Can my brother touch the suds too?" she asks for me. We hold puffy suds in our palms and blow them toward the sun. Many rainbow colored bubbles float in the air.

Mother neither does the laundry, nor the ironing. Our uniforms are always wrinkled, our sheets are not starched and folded, like Maman's. Doing the laundry needs strength. Mother is too weak, too thin, can never squat for hours and press and wring and stretch and roll and tap and beat the large white sheets, or even our small shirts. Zeinab can, Maman can, Mother cannot. So, Zeinab comes once a week, every Thursday, does the laundry, hangs them on a long line along the wall of the triangular yard and leaves. The clothes get dry and stiff like cardboard and we wear them without ironing them.

I have a strange feeling that I've seen all these women just very recently, maybe only a few minutes ago, but I can't think where. I stand here in the middle of the Clinic puzzled and confused, the clean shirt in my hand.

"Hurry up now," Kamal snaps his finger in front of my nose. "It's late! And next time don't mess up your clothes!" he says with a mother's reproachful tone.

This is him, Kamal. No doubt. I feel an immense joy. I gasp while putting my clothes on. I'm alive. I survived. He is here. In a minute I'll be in the hallways again and we'll talk. I was drowning, but I saw a boat. I'll cling to it and pull myself up. Kamal is my boat. I survived. Now I want to get out of this clinic as soon as possible. My hands shake. The button holes might be shrunken. I can't button my shirt. Or, is it my hands?

Kamal pulls the leash out of his pocket and ties me. I want to find a word. I want to talk to him and tell him how happy I am. But I can't. Is this still the effects of the drug? I can't find a word. I can't utter one.

"Remember your leash, huh?" Kamal says. "Let's go! Ha-G is waiting for you. We're already late." He grabs my face in his hand and turns it to the right and left, checking it under the blinding light of the big bulb. "These boys massaged you a bit too much. But, it's an incredible job. No blood. No blue and purple." He forces my mouth to open as if I'm a horse. He checks my teeth. "Everything is in its place. I can't do it this way, this clean. They're specialists."

He pulls my leash and we leave the Clinic. The hallway is stretched from the right and left. Kamal doesn't linger, but turns right. The cement floor is cold and I'm barefoot again. A chill runs through my bones. I shiver. The doors on either side are ordinary gray doors and the color of the wall is medium gray. I hear Kamal's key chain rattling in his pocket and I feel secure. Let it rattle, I think. I still try to find a word, any word. I try to remember something from our past. Kamal and I. What were the things we did together, or planned to do? We need something to talk about. I feel I haven't talked to anyone for a long long time.

To be able to talk, I speed up and stay only half a step behind him. He is the same Kamal, has a serious look on his face. I hear the slight whistle of his breathing.

"Kamal!" I hear myself.

"Hmm," he says. He doesn't sound unfriendly.

"Brother, what happened to your dream? Did you dream the desert again?"

There is a long pause. Now he says, "You know something? There are a few things I want to mention to you, bastard!" His voice is full of controlled rage. "First of all, don't you ever dare calling me 'Brother' again. Unless you repent for all of your sins and move to the sixth floor, where all the repentants are. Second: don't you ever dare ask me a personal question, like have I dreamed or not? Even my mother—may God bless her soul— wouldn't dare asking me what I dreamed about. Third: yes, the dream came back to me and let me tell you that this time there was no motherfucker to interrupt me."

"Did you drink then? The water of immortality—." There must be something wrong with me to keep asking questions. Do I want him to beat me up? Didn't I get enough?

He pauses and I anticipate a sharp slap, a kick, or the choking pressure of the leash, but he sighs instead, and talks in a sad tone: "No. I didn't drink the Holy Water of Immortality. The Holy One kept the golden Grail close to my dry lips and even tilted it with His holy hand. But he didn't tilt enough for me to drink the water. I've come to the conclusion that I'm not meant to drink the Holy Water and become immortal now. The time is not ripe. Maybe I have to serve the Holy Revolution and the Great Leader some more and try to please the Last Holy One. Otherwise, why didn't he tilt the cup more? Why didn't he want me to wet my dry lips? There is a reason: it's not meant!" He sighs and doesn't talk anymore.

We walk at a slow pace for a while. I don't dare break Kamal's silence. He is not pulling my leash anymore. The leash hangs off me like a long, ridiculous tie sweeping the floor. I think about the way Kamal talked to me and feel happy that I've gained his trust. But then I resent myself for needing Kamal's trust. Who is he anyway? More than a prison guard? He may even be a torturer, or an executioner; he may eventually execute me. I decide not to talk to him anymore.

There are no TV sets hanging in these hallways to amuse me. So I look at the back of Kamal's head, his thick neck, overlapping pillowy flesh hanging on it, his wide muscled shoulders, the extra layer of fat around his waist, bursting in his tight black shirt and then his strong legs, thick and long, each a moving tree trunk. He walks sluggishly. He must be thinking about the Last Holy One: His radiant face, His large green eyes, framed with thick black lashes, His tangled eyebrows, His thin mustache—a black penciled line above his delicate lips—His green turban, emerald green satin robe.

The Holy One is holding the golden Grail for Kamal and Kamal can smell the faint scent of rosewater on His long and bony fingers. How clean and well-trimmed His nails are—oval shaped, shiny, as though manicured. There is a huge emerald ring on the index finger of the Holy One's right hand. The gem shimmers and glitters in an unusual, magical way. It reflects the desert's blue sky and its beholder's green eyes. The green gem stretches and expands forever like an endless ocean in front of Kamal's eyes. Maybe that's why he can't drink the water. He is blinded by the emerald. The Holy One tilts the cup, a bit more... more... but not a drop is meant to moisten Kamal's cracked lips. Is this the blinding gem preventing him from drinking? Next time when he dreams he has to close his eyes or use dark sunglasses, he thinks. Or, maybe the cup is empty. Would the Last Holy One, the Absent

One, the Promised One, do this to him? Trick him? Offer him an empty Grail?

Kamal keeps thinking and I read his thoughts. Should I take him out of the dreamland? If he keeps daydreaming, he'll lose his way and we may never get to Ha-G—whoever he is. "What happened to the show?" I ask.

"The show is still on. You missed the opening night, but you may make it for the second night. It all depends on you and Ha-G."

I realize that twenty-four hours have passed since he took me out of the Black Box; I feel much better about everything. To be able to keep track of time is a blessing, it maintains my sanity. I don't want to float in nothingness; I want to know how long one chamber takes and how many hours have passed, although I can never know if there is any end.

Kamal is reserved, doesn't say anything more. He is not willing to converse. So I keep quiet and walk one step behind him, like his shadow, trying to think about the Clinic. How am I supposed to face this Ha-G without knowing what I've done in the Clinic? For some reason my mind censors this.

"You are anxious now, huh?" Kamal says without looking at me. "You wonder where you're going. I can relieve your anxiety. You are going to report on your dreams. Everybody does this after the Clinic. Ha-G the Shit Mouth, El-Deen's Head Interrogator, is waiting for you. Doctor Halal is there too. Remember him? The head doctor of the facilities? They are both important arms of the Great Octopus—La-Jay. I've told you this, haven't I? La-Jay is called the Great Octopus and he has eight 'arms' which run El-Deen. One arm is Halal, one is Ha-G. The rest? You may get to know them. I cannot reveal their names. I myself don't know a couple of them up to this day. They may be 'underground arms.' I'm not an arm of the Great Octopus, I'm just a worthless Devotee of the Revolution. Loony Kamal." He chuckles. His last words are sarcastic. He ridicules himself. I don't say anything with the hope that he may talk more.

"No. Not yet—" he says, as though continuing his thoughts. "I have to serve more. Devote myself. Sacrifice. The Great Octopus sometimes cuts off one arm and takes another. The bad arm is thrown in front of the watch dog of El-Deen. That easy. He gets rid of the rotten arm.

"That would be an honor for me. To become one of the arms of the Great Octopus. I'm still young. I haven't had much time to serve the Holy

Revolution. But I will."

Kamal's voice is sad, low and hollow, and himself humble and soft. I feel sorry for him. His ambition doesn't seem dark to me. Nothing about him seems dark. Tears burn my eyes and I feel ashamed. Now I reproach myself: "Look at our Unbreakable hero! Crying for his motherfucking torturer! Have they made you crazy here? Are you crying because this loony has not been able to drink the goddamn water of immortality (and in his dream too!) and become one of the horrible arms of the head torturer, the god/devil of the facilities, the blood sucking La-Jay?" I straighten my steps.

A Thin Man with a Goatee

While I walk firmly, trying not to talk to Kamal, we reach a corridor with a TV set hanging from the ceiling. After a long time, I see the gray tomb and hear the drums and cymbals of a military march. I feel vaguely delighted. This is something else, other than Kamal. It doesn't take me long to remember the famous national anthem. Angry men shout, "God is the greatest, the Leader is great! The enemy must know that we are the sea of the great Faith—" And the screaming women repeat a weird gibberish refrain: "Anja, anja, za za za—"

From the opposite side of the hallway, a guard and an inmate approach. It seems a very long time since I last saw another inmate. I feel joy and sorrow at the same time. I squint to see them better. The prisoner is a thin, bald man with a goatee. I'm surprised that they have let him keep his sharp pointed beard. He is tall and wiry, a long elastic thing bent forward like a bow. He has a blindfold and his guard pulls him fast. Barefoot, with wounded toes, he tries to walk on his heels. When they get closer, I notice that blood has dried on his toes. They slow down.

"Where are you taking this clown?" the guard addresses Kamal, pointing to me. He is short and thickly muscled, like a weight lifter. He is the only short devotee I've seen in El-Deen, but he looks as strong as any tall one.

"To visit Ha-G," Kamal says. "It's time for this bastard to remember what he has to remember and then decide whether he wants to become a Brother or stay a Comrade." Is Kamal hostile again? Or is he acting tough to assure his colleague that he hates me enough? Now he asks the other one,

"Where are you taking this motherfucker? Let me see—I know him. Isn't he the loony blasphemer who claims to be the Last Holy One?"

"That's him!" the other guard says. "He is in the Psychiatric Wing. I'm just taking him for a walk. You know, they don't have much space to move over there. We may stop for a second at Sultan's, too, to get him a nice haircut." He bursts into wild laughter, grabs the man's bald head in his fist like a cantaloupe and rubs it violently. Gold teeth shine in the weightlifter's mouth.

Kamal laughs too, but not from the bottom of his heart.

"The haircut might help him remember who he really is," the guard says. "Then maybe a sauna, or a sauna and a massage. Both are good for his shingles. Look how his back is breaking of pain." He slaps the man's back, "Stand straight, bastard! Don't bend!" And to Kamal, "He can't. His spine is getting soft, as soft as his brain. What a pity!"

"What if he doesn't remember who he really is?" Kamal asks.

"Then back home to the Psychiatric Wing. His friends will be waiting for him. His two companions, Akir and Nakir, will lick his toes to death. But you know Brother, they're not gluttons, they'll nibble on him gradually, one toe a day. See how they're chewed up by those shameless cannibals?" He shakes his head in regret.

The inmate has a blindfold on and cannot see the guard, so all this acting must be for me. Are they hinting about *my* future? Telling me if I don't cooperate, I'll end up where this poor man is?

Kamal interrupts my thoughts. "Does he still claim to be the Last Holy One?" His question sounds real. He is wondering. I know when Kamal is not acting.

"He still claims to be Him. The motherfucker is so messed up here," the weight lifter knocks on his temple, "that he doesn't understand the Last Holy One is the Absent One and cannot be present unless it's the end of the world. Follow me?"

Kamal nods. But he looks lost and confused.

"Anyway Brother, let's go. We have a long walk to Sultan's. God bless the Holy Leader!"

"God bless the Holy Leader and yourself!" Kamal says mechanically.

I turn back to see the bald, stooped man for the last time. He walks on his heels, holding up his bleeding toes. Although this man's flesh is being eaten up every day, inch by inch, by two cannibals, he still claims to be the Last Holy One. Doesn't he deserve to be called an Unbreakable? Who am I? Who do I claim to be? Nothing. No one.

"You admire him, huh?" Kamal asks.

I decide not to answer. He must be playing a trick on me. I can't trust Kamal. Don't I know how real the Last Holy One is for Kamal? Don't I know that he dreams of him every single time he sleeps and envisions him in the endless corridors of El-Deen while walking with me? That He appears to him with His green emerald eyes and thin mustache above His delicate lips, a halo around His head? Don't I know how dear is the Holy One to Kamal? And now this bald, ugly, stooped man claims to be Him and Kamal is asking me if I admire this sight of misery.

Yes, I tell myself, I admire the fake Last Holy One and deeply envy him. He knows who he is and is insisting on it. They are torturing him to death, but he repeats the same thing: "I'm the Last Holy One, the Absent One." Oh, yes Kamal, yes Brother, I admire him. He is Rostam who conquers without his horse. An ugly Rostam, crooked, thin, vulnerable, bleeding, but unbending. He is a magic bow that bends to the last degree, but doesn't break. Yes, I admire the holy man of El-Deen, who has been reduced to a wire but is unbreakable. I say all this to myself and nothing to Kamal.

Termite of My Mind

A guard drags a man on, a leash around his waist, his torso in a burlap sack, his old hands hanging out—dry, yellow maple leaves. The two guards exchange their greetings and pray for their leader, the Revolution, and Brother La-Jay. I know the guard, he is the one with a big mole above his beard line. I have seen him before, more than once, but cannot remember when and where.

The guards stop to talk. I already know the pattern of their conversation. It's always partly to demoralize us and partly to exchange information. The sacked man melts on the floor, and I stand by, gazing at his strange hands.

"This devil has not repented yet?" Kamal asks.

"No. He watched his niece in the Hothouse, but is mute as a wall."

"So, the old devil saw it?" Kamal asks.

"Watched to the end."

"Maybe he is in shock or something," Kamal says, acting concerned.

"Only the devil knows. He was trembling like the dick of an old ass. Now I'm taking him back to the cell of the Unbreakables. His disciples must have missed him."

"Good! I'll take this one to Ha-G. His feet are itching." Kamal laughs and the moled guard joins in.

We resume walking. I'm all immersed in myself. A new pain is waiting for me—a horrible one. Will I endure, or will I break? Hasn't this little man endured? Hasn't he endured more than this? Hasn't he watched his niece being tortured? And the Last Holy One—hasn't he been whipped on his stooped back, his bleeding feet? Then I will endure.

"Did you remember him?" Kamal asks.

"Who?"

"The Master. The bag of shit. Haven't I told you that they call him Master in the cell number four?"

He may have told me, but I can't remember. All I can see in my mind is the man's old hands floating in the wind.

"You're thinking hard, huh?" Kamal says.

"I can't remember."

"This fucking Clinic didn't do shit!" he says with clenched teeth. "What a pity! What a waste of time and money. First-rate doctors, the latest scientific crap, Western technology, all wasted. You're getting worse and worse, brother. What did you dream in the Clinic, huh?"

"I don't remember."

"Think harder. You'd better practice a little before we get to Ha-G's room. He is not the most civil person you'll meet. His nickname is 'Shit Mouth.' Get it? He is far from being refined. I'm an angel compared to him. So, come on... leak! What did you dream about?"

"The earthquake," I say, the first thing which comes to my mind.

"What about it?" Kamal asks.

"Faithland burned. The cardboard houses. The tin houses."

"Faithland? Where the hell is that?"

"A neighborhood off of the Old North Road. A poor neighborhood."

"It sounds familiar. Who was there in your dream? Come on! Friends,

79

family?"

I've never seen Kamal like this before. He is nervous and pushy. Does he really have to do this?

"Family," I say.

"Family who? Name them."

"Grandparents. Aunts and Uncles. Cousins. Mother," I say and picture them after a long time, since I saw them in the Clinic.

"Father?" Kamal asks.

"He was not there."

"Brothers and sisters?" he asks again.

"I don't have brothers and sisters," I lie.

"No?" he stops and looks into my eyes.

"No," I say firmly.

He grabs the leash close to my neck, pulls me toward himself and lifts me up in the air. The leash tightens on my Adam's apple while he holds me above the floor for a long minute and stares into my eyes. His eyes are large and bulged out, with red veins running through the white. His irises are dark with anger, his pupils move restlessly. He gasps more than ever and I smell his breath, a bitter smell of wild weeds. He talks into my face, teeth clenched, voice muffled:

"You son of a fucking bitch! You devil! Traitor! Liar! Bastard! Enemy of the people and the Holy Revolution! No brothers and sisters, huh? You lie to *me*? To Loony Kamal? Open your deaf ears now: I don't mind what La-Jay says anymore, I'm going to kill you right here, because I'm sick and tired of you!"

I'm hanging on the leash, choking. But somewhere deep inside I'm happy that the end is finally coming. If he kills me right here in the middle of this gray vacant hall, no one will hear me screaming. I knew that I couldn't lie to Kamal, I was avoiding it all the time. But how could I tell the truth about Sahar? Maybe this is all they want from me. Maybe *she* is the one they want, not me. Maybe she is the leader of the women's movement, a journalist, a teacher, or who knows? A guerrilla fighter somewhere in the depth of the jungles of the North. Maybe they're after her and I'm just an unfortunate brother who is arrested because of his revolutionary sister. Or, she may be somewhere in El-Deen now—already arrested, tortured, raped. But not broken. An Unbreakable. They want to use me to break her, to destroy her. They want me to repent and appear on the screen and force her to watch me saying something like, "Sahar, sister, I found the Faith, the light, the path to heaven in this Holy University; repent and join me. Happiness is in repentance. Trust our Holy Father, La-Jay, trust your warden sisters and your devotee brothers. Join us, Sahar. Let's pray together for the Holy Leader of our Revolution. Let's pray that He lives a long life, long enough for the World Revolution. Long live the the Last Holy One! the Absent One, the Promised One! Long Live His Holy Revolution! Long live El-Deen, the Gate of Paradise!"

Kamal doesn't kill me. He leaves me alone and we walk. He needs me. But this possibility, the possibility of Sahar being here, becomes the termite of my mind, chews me from inside. I can't hide in the dark folds of my oblivion anymore. If she is all they want, I'll never have peace. I won't enjoy my namelessness.

"Come this way!" Kamal pulls the leash hard, as though forcing a wild donkey to move. "This way, to the left. You are not ready to see Ha-G, yet. He can wait. I'll tell the Shit Mouth to change your appointment. Here, this is where you have to go."

He stops at a door, pulls his heavy key-chain out and searches for a key. He finds it, opens the door, but immediately pulls back and says, "Oh, sorry Brothers. I didn't know the room was occupied. We'll wait here." He closes the door gently, not to make a noise. Now, he sits on the floor and pulls my leash to force me to sit next to him. We both lean back against the wall, beside the door. He stretches his legs out. I'm not sure if I'm allowed to do the same thing. I do it anyway. I stretch my tired legs out and relax. He doesn't say anything.

Ali the Bricklayer's Son

This hallway is like the one the Clinic was in. I wonder if we are still on the same floor. Gray walls and ordinary blue-gray iron doors on either side. It's quiet here, except the muffled sounds of smacking or clapping coming out of the room.

"They are working on a patient." Kamal points his head to the door. "This is the Freezer. I guess the guy's heart has stopped or something. They're pumping it hard, the way my mother used to beat the dirty blankets in a washing tub." He shakes his head and smiles, looking straight ahead at the opposite wall, not at me. "She'd bend on the tub, press both of her hands on the blanket, then stretch up. Bend again, push and press—again and again. She would beat and slap the blanket so much until the dirt came out. May God bless her soul, she was a strong woman. Strong and hard working," he sighs. "You know, she was my father's second wife. His first wife was a sickly woman who worked in a public bath. She washed the women—a disgusting job. Anyway, She died of consumption or something when my father was in jail." Kamal sighs and continues, still looking straight ahead at the wall. I can smell the grassy odor of his mouth. "My father took part in the First Revolt against the Damned Monarch and got in trouble. When he came out after a few years, his wife was dead and his children were all either dead, or lost, or something. They were poor, you know, very poor. My father was a bricklayer." He pauses, as if waiting for me to say something, but he doesn't look at me. Now he continues in the same strange, withdrawn tone. "They say that when my father got released, and saw that his wife and children were dead, he lost his mind for a while. You know what I mean? He went totally blank." He knocks on his shaved head. "He forgot who he was and what his name was. No offense, brother! I know you have forgotten your name too, but my father's case was different." He looks at me for the first time. There is no malice in his eyes. His pupils are resting and the red veins are gone. "Then nobody knows how he recovered. He recovered with a new name and a new job and never remembered what his old identity was.

"In his new life, my father worked with a butcher in the central bazaar and learned all there was to learn about butchery. He saved some money, bought a business, married for the second time, became rich, and had five children—I'm the first one. Then he went to the pilgrimage, visited the House of God, and grew a large stomach and a bushy beard. He is alive, big, and healthy like a bull—may God add to his life. He is proud of me. He comes here often to visit me. He is La-Jay's close friend, you know. They were cellmates up there on the seventh floor in the Damned Monarch's time.

"If it wasn't for my father's reputation, I wouldn't have the honor to serve in El-Deen. The competition was tough among the devotees, very tough. La-Jay needed good recommendations." Kamal stops talking, plunges into a deep thought, keeping me in suspense. I almost hold my breath.

The whole thing sounds strange to me. It's as if Kamal's story has something to do with me.

"Well, I don't know why I'm telling you all this. I saw these nurses hitting the man's heart, remembered my mother washing her blankets in the tub and one memory lead to another. Yes, they're pumping the guy's heart. It's frozen or something."

"Kamal!" I call him gently.

"Hmmm?"

"Does your father remember his first life?"

"No. Why should he? All there was, was misery. He lived in a hovel with a sick wife and five children."

"There were several of those hovels around the yard, a black pool was in the middle. The water was slimy."

"How do you know?" Kamal asks with genuine surprise.

"I was there. This was a multi-level tenant house."

"Bullshit! You don't belong to—. Are you telling me that you're coming from a poor family? We have to talk about this, brother. This doesn't make sense to me."

Kamal is confused. I'm confused too. Do I know his father? Is there another tenant house exactly like Grandfather's? And another bricklayer and washing woman living in a hovel with five children? Maybe. But if Kamal's bricklayer father is Ali the Bricklayer, how could he become a rich butcher and a fanatic after his mental disease? But why not? He could have become anything and he became a butcher. Now, is it possible that Kamal, the Loony, my cruel guard, my bald monster, my torturer and possible executioner, be Ali the Bricklayer's son?

Sometimes I thought that I loved Ali. Sahar and I admired him. He was manly. He never looked poor or miserable. He always paid his rent on time, never begged Grandfather for a loan, never got drunk like other tenants, and no one in our three houses ever gave him and his family old clothes. Once, or twice when Mother tipped him for a service he'd done, she felt embarrassed. Ali saved us from the flood when we got stuck in Faithland; he fed us and warmed us in his little hovel, he tucked us under his arms and took us home. He took us to El-Deen to visit our father. He did more, much more. He taught us how to lead a revolt, on a flying carpet!

Am I going out of my mind? Is Ali only a figment of my imagination, a recurring character of my dreams, or is he real? Did he exist? Does he still?

Hero of my dreams, or a real man, I loved Ali as a child and cannot believe that his offspring would be a ruthless bastard. This Loony is such a hard-hearted animal that after all the time we had together—the hallways and doors, lefts and rights, ups and downs—he almost choked me to death with the leash. And he meant it too.

The Dull Knife

I'm hot but I shiver. The hallway is warm, too warm. I want to imagine the cold to prepare myself for the Freezer, but I can't. How can I, when I'm sweating and want to rip my shirt off? Kamal unbuttons the two top buttons of his black shirt, takes his black-and-white-checkered handkerchief out and wipes his forehead. He shoves the handkerchief back in his pocket, takes his pocketknife out, pulls a smaller blade out and starts to clean the filth from under his nails. He is quiet and pensive. Completely in himself. His breath hisses when he inhales.

Now all I think about is the Freezer, the chamber I'm about to enter: the low temprature, zero, sub-zero. Cold. I remember the Old North Road area, where I lived all my childhood, was the coldest part of the city. It was on the skirt of the mountain where it snowed a lot. Four or five months a year the hills and mountain skirts were white. Even in the summer when we all sat in Grandfather's terrace, ate fresh cucumbers, and chatted, the north wind blew and brought the smell and taste of the snow to us. Now I'm about to enter a room as cold as the top of Mount Alborz, the white peak, the nightcap.

Kamal dozes off, his knife open on his lap. If my hands were not cuffed I could grab the knife in a split second and cut his throat open, like a goat's, or rather, a fatted bull's. But the blade is small, probably dull, and my hands are cuffed. Besides, is it right to kill him? They'll come and get me, maybe shoot me on the spot. I don't know how much Kamal is worth, how much I—which of us is worth more? Killing him wouldn't solve anything. I'd be in more trouble and the burden of a murder on my conscience too.

No, even if the blade was the biggest and my hands were not cuffed, I wouldn't kill Kamal. I could not.

Once Grandfather wanted to kill a chicken for a holiday lunch. As usual he made it into a show; he became the leader of an important operation. It was as though a battle were going on and he, the General of the Cossacks, wanted to know which one of his soldiers was brave enough to enter the enemy zone.

"Let's see which one of my brave grandchildren can come and help me with this chicken? I need a real strong person to hold its neck while I cut it." He was squatting at the square pool in the first yard. The chicken was pecking greedily at every piece of trash in the yard, unaware of its doom. Sahar, Kami, Cyrus, and I were all in the porch hiding behind our mothers. We hadn't seen chicken-killing before. We didn't want this. Once a year, when Sheikh Ahmad killed a sheep in the sidewalk at the edge of the gutter, our mother forbade us to go outside and watch. We didn't know why Grandfather, so different than Sheikh Ahmad, was about to do the same thing to a miserable chicken.

"I'm waiting. Who is coming to help me? Who is the bravest?"

Of course everyone knew that Sahar was the bravest and the boldest. Didn't she run away from the house all alone by herself? But now she was quiet, shying away, hanging on Maman's skirt. And Maman was laughing, the kind of laugh that made her big breasts quiver like mountains of jelly and showed her red gum, where a few teeth were missing.

"Leave the children alone, man, and do it yourself. It's getting late."

I had never seen Grandfather so disappointed. He bent his head, obeyed his wife, and didn't call us anymore. He chased the hen around the yard, grabbed it and took it to the pool. He pressed its dangling neck to the stone edge of the pool and took the knife. This was a kitchen knife, one of Maman's. The chicken screamed, wriggled, kicked, and ran away finally. Grandfather chased it, panting and cursing. He took it back and laid its miserable neck on the stone again. He looked up at the porch, but didn't say anything.

Uncle Musa was not home and no other man was around. This is a man's job, I thought. He needs a man. I ran down the steps and squatted beside Grandfather. He looked at me and his dark pock-marked face beamed. He showed me how I was supposed to grab the neck. I held the thin, wobbling neck tightly and closed my eyes. It was warm and throbbing. I felt Sahar's gaze on my back. Was she crying? Grandfather started the cutting.

Half-opening my eyes, I saw the blood on my hand. It was warm and gooey. I had never seen so much blood before. My stomach turned. The knife was dull and Grandfather had to saw the neck over and over. It was only half-cut, hanging, and the animal was constantly crying and kicking. Grandfather asked for another knife. Maman ran to the kitchen and brought a bigger one. All this time, I held the half-hanging neck, the pulsing neck in my hand. I pressed my teeth so hard that my jaw hurt. My insides were about to come up to my mouth. The smell of the chicken was worse than the smell of the Faithland sewer. The next knife split the rest of the neck in two. More blood gushed out, dripping from my hands. The headless chicken kicked stubbornly without being able to cry, and died in Grandfather's hands.

Grandfather and I washed right there at the faucet. Then I ran to our house to throw up in the toilet. In our triangular room, I sat in the darkest corner, behind our bed, shivering. I sat there alone and cried for myself and my fake bravery. Soon, I felt Sahar's presence beside me, and heard her hiccups.

No, I couldn't kill Kamal. Look at him now, snoring, just like when he slept in his own room the other day. He has rolled my leash around his left wrist, but not in a way to make me uncomfortable. His neck is hanging. He has a triple chin now, though normally he has a double. The upper part of his cheeks where there is no beard looks rosy and soft—a baby's cheeks. Sweat drops boil on his forehead. His armpits are wet.

Why should he go through all this torment with me? His father visits him once a week, as if Kamal is himself a prisoner. Kamal, the Devotee of the Holy Revolution, the Revolutionary Guard, prisoner of his Faith.

The Winter of the Snowman

In the closed room the nurses pump the inmate's heart for a long time. They keep me waiting to weaken my nerves. They're trying to scare me. They must know that I can't stand the cold, that I shiver miserably and get sick easily—high fevers. All my childhood I lived in a cold place and was sick of cold. I hated the cold and the cold tormented me.

The winter of our first grade comes to my mind. After the earthquake. The coldest winter. Grandfather said it was the coldest in twenty-five years.

That winter many things happened to us—all bad. So bad that I remember almost all the details.

The worst was the school. Every single morning, Sahar and I woke up in the dark, washed our hands and faces with freezing well water that Mother poured in our red palms, and changed into our black and while uniforms. We got dressed close to the glass belly of Aladdin, drank hot tea, had a bite of bread and cheese, and left the triangular house. Our cousins and Aunty Hoori were still in a deep sleep when we left. All of them rolled down the hill to the New Spring Elementary and High School, but Sahar and I went to Santa Zita, far away, almost at the end of the Old North Road, at the edge of the Alleys of Heaven—the rich people's neighborhood.

Santa Zita was only a few blocks away from the Monarch's White Marble Palace. Mother wanted us to get a better education. New Spring School was for ordinary children, she believed; it was below us. Her children should go to a private school to become something. Grandfather paid our heavy tuition for six whole years.

So, every single morning, we awoke in the dark, washed and dressed and wore woolen jackets and thick heavy coats, woolen handwoven scarves and sheepskin hats with earflaps. We left the house like two little balls of fur and walked a long distance to get to the road where the schoolbus came. We held hands and walked through the twilight.

We walked all the length of New Spring Street, passed the bridge over the frozen Old North River, reaching the New Spring Public Bath. Every single day, passing the bridge we thought, "Oh, what an ugly river and what a gloomy bridge this is!" The frozen water down below was dark and contaminated; the bridge was a ruin.

Most of the days we saw Sheikh Ahmad coming out of the bathhouse with rosy cheeks and a wet beard. As little as we were, we knew that an early morning bath meant that the sheikh had slept with his wives last night. He was up early for ablution. He frowned at us and crossed his fiery eyes.

We waited for the green light and went to the other side of the road where the bus stop was. In better days, the snowflakes danced and whirled around our heads; in worse days, hail beat us and stoned the naked maple trees. I shivered and hopped up and down to keep myself warm. Sahar was stronger. Many times she wrapped her own scarf around my face to make me warm. While waiting for the bus, which one day was early and the next day very late, we amused ourselves.

We opened our mouths, looked at the sky and waited for the dancing snowflakes to land on our tongues. When it wasn't snowing and a white sun was out, we stared at its pale glow for a long time, then looked around and saw dark shadows of everything, strangely long, stretching to the entrance of the public bath.

Finally the old bus arrived, full of sleepy children who all looked alike, all balls of fur. There were no seats for us, so we hung on the poles like the carcasses of the sheep hanging from the hooks of a butcher shop. The old bus made jangling sounds each time its wheels fell in the puddles and holes and by the time we got to school, we were already tired. The fat Superior Nun, our principle, Sor Piera, made us clasp our palms and pray in the stuffy cafeteria : "O Holy Mary, Mother of God, pray for us sinners, now and at the time of our death!"

One afternoon, when we came back home, a fat snowman was waiting for us in front of our three houses. Kami and Cyrus, who always got home two hours earlier, had made the snowman and were doing the last touch-ups. Mother allowed us to stay out and play only if we kept our boots clean and didn't bring mud and slush home. We added more snow to the snowman's belly and made him into a fat man.

Aunty Zari came out, tall and confused, with the old ugly clothes she wore one on top of the other, all hanging off her. She wrapped the blue and white striped scarf around the snowman's neck. This was the scarf she had woven for Kami's father, but had never sent it abroad. She didn't have her husband's address.

Maman came out in her house-slippers, her big breasts hopping up and down, quivering. She put a long broom in the snowman's right hand and laughed with delight. Some of her teeth were missing and the rest were very yellow, but it felt good to watch her laugh. She closed her small eyes, bent her head back, and laughed until she cried. Our mother in her blue-green heavy coat, a blue scarf around her head, brought the old bucket and hung it from the snowman's left hand. She smiled faintly, and her large blue eyes looked sad and tired. She went back to her triangular room to read.

Grandfather climbed the hill, ankles deep in the soft and fluffy snow, his cane in one hand, an oval-shaped watermelon under one arm. He saw the snowman and his pock-marked face opened up. He took his sheepskin

Cossack hat off and put it on the fat man's head.

This was the happiest moment of the whole winter. Sahar and I hugged each other and looked around to see if everybody was as happy as we were. But Grand-Lady, sitting in her porch on the Turkman carpet, wrapped in a black shawl, was crying again. Lately she spent all her time on the porch, no matter how cold the weather was. She gazed at the mountain, muttered something and cried.

Grandfather believed that something was happening to Grand-Lady's brain and nothing could be done about it. He said old age was exactly like infancy. Grand-Lady cried and nobody knew why, like when a baby cried and nobody knew the reason.

We looked up at the terrace to see if Aunty Hoori had seen our snowman. She was behind the window, her long black hair covering half of her face, the other half stony and motionless. Could she see the snowman? Wasn't she excited?

Uncle Musa and his wife, Aunty Shamsi, were inside their house quarreling. Uncle's voice was vaguely audible, "Bla bla bla—"

"Bla... b... l...a—" Aunty's thin and desperate voice answered in mumbles.

Sheikh Ahmad and his two wives watched us from the crack of their curtain. The sheikh's white-turbaned head was in the middle, the wives' black-scarfed heads on either side; the sheikh, frowning, the wives sighing with envy.

Mother called us in. We had homework to do, three times more than our cousins, and soon it would be dinner time. We all had to go to Grandfather's house, sit around the long white cloth, and eat the dinner feast that Maman had prepared for everyone. An hour and a half before the other school kids, we were in bed, ready to wake up in the dark.

In the Freezer

The door opens. Two bearded men in white gowns push a gurney out. Kamal puts his knife back in his pocket, stands up and pulls my leash. The inmate is covered with a white sheet, but the top of his head is out. This head is small and has dark bushy hair. Tangled. My knees buckle under my weight.

89

My blood freezes. I look at the shape of the body. It's small, the size of a child, thin and short. Can this be a man? This is more like a woman, a small woman, with disheveled hair. The nurses push the gurney along the hallway and soon disappear somewhere in the depth of El-Deen.

Maybe the whole thing is a set-up, to scare me, break me right here, even before I enter the Freezer. They may expect me to say, "Hey, Brother Kamal, I can't really tolerate the cold. What is it exactly you want to know? I'm willing to talk. Although I don't remember what I have done that has been harmful to your Holy Republic, still I can repent. I'll just repent the life I've lived. Will this do? So, cancel this Freezer part. Take me to the Shit Mouth. I can tolerate whipping better than the cold. At least the room temperature will be normal. Huh? Should we talk?"

And Kamal will probably say, "Ahan! This is a good boy! A real little brother! Let's go to the Shit Mouth and start your interrogation. You may not need the whipping at all. You may remember your siblings."

"Siblings?" I'll repeat with surprise, "What siblings?"

"Your sister, that's what I mean," Kamal will say.

"What sister? I already said I don't have a sister."

"So, you don't want to cooperate. You're wasting my time. Go in. Inside the Freezer. Hurry up before I lose my temper." And I rush inside the Freezer, for two reasons, one: I can't say anything about Sahar. Two: I don't want Kamal to lose his temper.

"Hey, move brother, don't waste my time." Kamal pushes me inside the room. "It's late. I haven't eaten anything for hours. I'm starving. I'll leave you here, grab a bite, then come back and pick you up for your interrogation. If your visit with the Shit Mouth goes well, I'll take you to the show. As a matter of fact, the performance is always better on the second night. Last night, everybody was panicky. Oh, boy, La-Jay was sitting there in the front row, watching with the same attention he watches you guys in his tower. He comes every night. Every single night of the show. He loves it. Take your clothes off, I'll bring them back."

He talks nonstop. The nap has helped him. He has regained his energy. He babbles constantly while helping me take my shirt and pants off. I look around and don't see anything. No bed, no stool, nothing—a bare room. Four white walls and a white-washed floor, that's all. There isn't even a bulb hanging from the ceiling like in the Hothouse. How cozy and roomy the

Hothouse was, with that yellow bulb, wooden bench, and padded wall. Here, the light comes from everywhere; I can't find its source. It's a blinding light, a reflection of snow in the north pole. The room is like the inside of an ice cube, or under the surface of a glacier. I'm dumb. What can I say? What do they want me to do here? Sit? Lie down? Stand still?

I'm completely naked and this is the first time that Kamal sees me like this. But I don't care. Maybe I have been naked before too. Didn't he take me out of the coffin, the Black Box? Didn't he wash me with a hose? Hosed me down, as he said? So, he has seen my nakedness. He has washed my shit off.

The cold pierces my bones. When Kamal talks, his mouth steams. He hangs my clothes on his arm and moves toward the door. He is still talking about the damn show, as if he is not about to leave me alone inside an ice cube to freeze.

"I'm sure tonight everybody will be more relaxed. I hope you can make it. You know, El-Deen's stage is unique! I'm not joking. It's the best, even better than the Damned Monarch's Opera House. The one we turned into the Central Holy Hall.

"El-Deen didn't have a stage. La-Jay built it. Of course, he invited a committee of theatrical consultants to decide about the details. You'll see for yourself—if you make it. Let me not ruin your surprise. Well, I have to go now, before I catch cold here. I'll see you." He winks at me, closes the door and I hear the lock's click.

I'm in the center of the white room, naked. Nothing is around to look at, touch, hold, think about, like, or despise. Total emptiness, vacancy. I choke with despair when I remember the old metal chair. We got beaten up together. How fortunate I was then, with that thing close to me, hugging me like an animal. Or, the loud speakers in the Hothouse, attacking me with the lusty voice of the horny sermonizer, and the instruments in the Clinic, the metal stool, the bulb, the window, the white curtain.

Why have they left me with nothing here? It's cold, but the temperature doesn't bother me as much as the worry does. My throat hurts. I can't swallow. What if I'm getting sick? Bronchitis? Pneumonia? Why does my throat hurt? How long should I stay here? La-Jay is watching me.

I look up at the ceiling to find something. Nothing. They have deprived me of a traditional prison, the familiar dungeon, the jail, the dreadful, but familiar. A place where you can struggle to keep the roaches away, find a dry

91

spot to sit, count the cracks on the wall, or follow the silhouettes on the ceiling. You find a twig, you draw a picture on the floor: A heart with an arrow piercing it. You scratch the date under it. There is nothing here to count, to fight with, to change into something else. Nothing to do anything to, anything with. I hug myself and shiver. I can't cry. I want to call Sahar but her name freezes inside my head, becomes something abstract, white, just a name, meaning dawn, but indicating nothing, neither the real dawn, nor the girl. I shiver.

I look at my body. What a nakedness! Not like the day I was born, when I was linked to her. She slipped out, and after a few minutes, I did. This nakedness is not like when I went to the public bath, either. I was a little boy then, among all the naked women. The image slips away like soap suds in the drainage. This is not like when I was naked and a woman descended on me, as heavy as the earth itself. My body was warm and wet and she smelled of lotus. Her long hair covered me like a dark blanket. But I don't remember more. Who was she and when or where did this happen?

How meaningless is my nakedness now.

I touch my head: short, prickly, close-cropped hair, recently trimmed; I can't remember when. I touch my face: bony. My neck: thin. My arms: long. I slide my hands over my chest and count my ribs. My genitals are empty skins, my legs, shaky twigs. I stare at my yellow feet. When did I trim my toenails? Or did they? Who has trimmed my toenails? Do I possess myself anymore, or do they own me from head to foot?

My kneels buckle soon and I sit. I keep hugging myself or rubbing my hands on my skin, letting the blood circulate. I get tired and lay my head on my kneecaps. My teeth rattle. I have to be careful not to bite my tongue. I hold my chin in my palm. No use—my jaws are shaking badly. The bastards are going to break me here and this is my cracking point—the cold, the goddamn cold. I'm not Unbreakable. Kamal gave me a false pride when he said he was taking me to the Unbreakables' cell. He gave me a false pride, only to take it away from me in the most humiliating way. I'm powerless, incapable of doing anything for myself, to myself. Can I commit suicide? Bang my head to the wall? I can't even do this. I don't have the strength.

But they are not going to freeze me to death. Didn't they pump the inmate's heart to keep him or her alive? They won't let me die. I'm important for them. For some reason, some unknown reason, they need me. So why are they freezing my memories? How can I remember anything? If I remember, if I concentrate on a memory, then I will survive. If not, I'll die. They want me to survive and remember. I want to survive too. I don't want to die. Not now. Not before I know where Sahar is.

But what can I remember? The winter. The hard winter of the first grade: sliding down the hill with Sahar, long walks to the bus stop. Santa Zita, the stuffy cafeteria, Sor Piera, making us pray. The National Anthem. The Catholic Anthem. Long lines, walking to class. Nobody runs or plays during the recess. Lines. Lines all the time. Lines of black-and-white-clothed girls and boys. Lines of the nuns—black and white. The schoolyard, black and white.

Santa Zita

Santa Zita has white walls, but is black inside. The nuns don't like light. Like a bride sitting in the middle of a big, square yard, this white marble building is shiny and bright—beautiful outside, but dark inside. In the yard, pine trees are shadowy and tall. Stretching along the walls, they surround the white building. White marble benches sit under the black pines. Black and white children walk or play quietly in the playground. If someone shouts or laughs loud, Sor Piera appears on her long white balcony, spots the child, tolls her heavy bell, or throws it in the yard, aiming at the noisy child.

Sahar and I sit quietly on a marble bench under a black pine and eat fresh medlar with our inky fingers, unless Tatyana is there and wants to walk with us.

"What a sweet bird are you, nightingale! What a tiny sweet bird!" Tatyana sings in her thin girlish voice—but low, very low, so that no one can hear her except us. She holds our hands and we roam around the big yard. When we reach a nun, Tatyana stops humming, bends her head and says, "Veni Santus Spiritus!" The nun faintly smiles and nods. Now she resumes again, "What a sweet bird are you, nightingale!"

This is our recess time, when Tatyana is not up there in the convent, praying. We know that she is always either in the dark seclusion of one of the seventh floor cells, talking to God, or helping in the kitchen, preparing dinner for the nuns. We know that although her parents, the Polish immigrants, love her and want her to go home, she wants to live in the convent. Tatyana wants to become a nun. Her parents disagree, they want to take her out of the convent, but they can't. Tatyana has sought refuge in the convent and the Catholic Church wants her to marry the invisible God. Her parents want her to marry a real man—a fat Polish wine maker and ham seller—, have children, and live a normal life. But they can't take her out, because she is eighteen and can decide for herself.

We know that Tatyana is in love with her god, although she sings about this little nightingale all the time when she roams around the schoolyard. We know that one of these days the Sisters are going to cut Tatyana's long golden hair and make her the bride of God.

Sahar and I are up to her waist when we walk. We look at her and admire her white oval face, her large blue eyes, her thin blond eyebrows. We admire her long golden hair, flowing straight, without a wave to the small of her back. "May I touch your hair, Tatyana?" Sahar says. She nods. We sit on a bench. Sahar puts her hand on top of Tatyana's head and slides it down to her waist. "May my brother touch too?" Tatyana smiles and nods. I put my inky hand on her hair and do the same thing, only I make the pleasure longer. I linger and take a long ride down the yellow waterfall.

Tatyana is the sun, we decide, or an angel fallen from the heaven. How can a girl be so beautiful? We wonder. She is even more beautiful than Lady-King, our real Grandmother whose yellowish picture is between Mother's brown book. Lady-King had long golden hair and large blue eyes, too. But she was short. Tatyana is slim and tall like a young willow tree. Lady-King is gray now, dead between the folds of the heavy book. Tatyana is fresh and glows with life. We are in love with Tatyana, we decide.

Tatyana's story is in the newspapers this winter. Nobody knows if the church is going to win or the parents. At home, Grandfather and Mother talk about Tatyana when we all sit under the warm quilt in Grand-Lady's room. They read the newspaper and argue. Grandfather believes that the girl is crazy. Why does she want to lock herself up in a dark convent for the rest of her life? There are so many things to enjoy in this life. Mother says this is what she wants, why don't they leave her alone? She is in love with her god, let her be. Why should she marry a fat smelly ham seller? "I would do the same thing if I were Tatyana," Mother says. "I would prefer the handsome god to the smelly man."

Sahar and I are proud that we walk with the famous Tatyana under the pines and share our medlars with her on the marble bench.

Tatyana is lost for a while. We are lonely at recess time. Every single day we sit on the bench opposite the entrance of the building and stare at the door. Or, we look up at the rooms of the seventh floor, hoping to see the tall shadow of Tatyana passing by. But she is lost. Even the newspapers don't write about her anymore.

Tatyana, the Bride of God

I stretch my legs out and rub them as hard as I can. My fingers are numb. My nose hurts and feels separate from the rest of my body. I'll die here if I don't remember more. I'll die if my brain stops working. I have to plunge more, deeper and deeper into the frozen layers of the past, or I'll freeze here, on the surface of this glacier. But first I have to move a little—I have to.

I try to get on my legs and walk around. I trip and fall, get up again and try to walk—now fast. I repeat her name: "Taty... yana... Taty... yana..." and walk faster and faster. I run around the room and make her name into a chant. I repeat and run. I hold the winter of the first grade in my head so that I won't freeze. I walk slower now and take a deep breath. I sneeze: once, twice, many times. My nose runs. Nothing to clean myself. I rub my nose with the back of my hand. It runs again. I sit and rub my chest. "Tatyana... Where are you now?" I whisper. "Are you alive? Do you somehow know that I'm thinking of you? The little boy who adored you, who had a twin sister and they both loved you. You used to walk with them in the recess time. Do you remember, wherever you are? Sahar! What do you think? Does Tatyana remember us?"

A wet March. Tatyana is lost for quite a while. Sahar plans a dangerous operation. We are sitting in Santa Zita's stuffy cafeteria doing our homework. It's pouring outside. The teacher has written a line with black ink on top of our writing pads: "From the cradle to the grave, seek knowledge!" and we have to copy it down to the bottom of the page. The purpose is to imitate the teacher's handwriting, to write as nice and neat as her. Sahar and I share a little ink bottle and are each holding a sharpened reed pen. Our hands are inky. We have smeared the ink on our white shirts, our cheeks, our mouths and noses too. We finish the page. Our handwriting is sloppy and dirty. Mine is worse. We can't concentrate.

Some of the girls are knitting. Boys are making paper airplanes. No one can walk or talk aloud. The Sisters are pacing, brass bells in hands, heavy key chains hanging on their waists, guarding the cafeteria. Sahar and I sit at the end of a long white table, pushed to the wall. We blow on our writings to dry them, close the pads and put them in our school bags. Nothing else to do. We look at the rain, hitting the windowpanes. The cafeteria is in the basement and the windows are on top of the walls. Outside is as dark as dusk. We both sigh and think about the bright days of the past, walking in the yard with Tatyana.

"Let's go and find her," Sahar whispers.

"But where?"

She points to the ceiling. "Up on the seventh floor. They must have locked her up there," she says.

"How do you know?" I ask.

"I know. I have a feeling that she is up there," and she points to the ceiling again.

"But we can't leave the cafeteria. The Sisters are everywhere," I say.

"We can't pee in our pants, can we? I'll tell Sor Mavella that I need to use the bathroom, you go and ask Sor Maria. These two Sisters are nicer. Then I'll wait for you at the end of the hall, behind the broken organ. I'll count to five hundred, if you don't show up, then I know that you can't get out; I'll come back."

"Sahar, what if they catch us? Do you know what they'll do to us?"

"What? They'll kick us out of this school. Then Mother has to enroll us in the New Spring Elementary. And that's what we always wanted. We'll go to school with Kami, Cyrus, and Aunty Hoori."

"It's easy to say. I can't."

"Don't you want to see Tatyana?"

"I want," I say. "But Mother will punish us. She will send one of us to Baba Mirza's house."

"No, she won't. She knows that we get sick without each other. She hates it when we are sick. Haven't you seen how she cries and asks Maman to help her? She won't separate us."

I'm quiet. Sahar waits for a few minutes then gets up.

"I'm going to use the bathroom," she says and pulls herself out of the tight space between the table and the bench.

"Sahar, don't!"

"I'll wait for you behind the organ," she whispers and leaves.

"Wait!" I call. But she is already saying something to Sor Mavella. The short, chubby sister strokes Sahar's bushy hair with her coarse hand and lets her leave the cafeteria. At the door, Sahar stops, looks at me and winks. Her large black eyes twinkle. I sit restlessly, chewing my inky nails and breathing heavily. Then my stomach cramps and I feel that I really need to use the restroom.

We climb the endless steps and pass through the long dark corridors. We climb again and pass more halls. All the floors are the same, the rooms the same—dark gray walls, light gray doors, darker than a hospital, as dark as a prison.

After the fourth floor, the rooms are not classrooms anymore; Santa Zita becomes a convent. We have never been beyond the fourth floor, nobody is allowed to go there except the nuns. We don't waste time opening all the doors. We go straight to the seventh floor where the cells are and open one door after the other. The little cubicles, the size of Uncle Massi's room, but clean and dark, are all empty. The Sisters are working downstairs. Tatyana is nowhere to be found. Sahar's lips droop. I know what this means; she is on the verge of crying.

"Sahar!" I whisper. There is another door at the very end of the hall. A black door. Should we open that too?

She nods. We hold hands and tip-toe to the dark end of the corridor. This door is not gray like all the other doors, it's black, a white cross hanging on it. First, we lay our ears on the cold wood, but don't hear anything. Now we turn the door knob and step in the dark. The aroma of burned wax is strong. This is a small room, only a bit larger than the cells, and not quite empty. There is a crimson velvet curtain, thick and heavy, hanging in front of the window, blinding the light and a crimson carpet laying on the floor. A gigantic black cross is on the wall, a human-size Christ nailed on it. The marble statue is as big as a real man and fake blood drips from where the hands and feet are nailed to the cross. Tatyana is lying on the crimson carpet on her stomach, perpendicular to the cross. She is wearing a long blue lace gown. Her arms are stretched to the sides and a wedding band shines in her thin finger. We can't see her face, her head is turned away from us. This head is small and round, yellow and bald, like a little raw cantaloupe. Tatyana's long golden hair is gone. She is the bride of God.

Punishment

Standing on one leg, flamingo-like, between a giant statue of Mary and a tall file cabinet, we looked at the window and saw the rain changing into hail and the hail into snow, and the snow into blizzard. Within a few minutes, the dark pines wore white robes. We stood there on one leg, in Sor Piera's office, hugging our folders tightly, shivering. When the fat principal left the room, we changed our legs. We didn't talk. I didn't blame Sahar. She didn't look at me. But I could hear her sniffling. Crying silently.

We waited forever. We knew how hard it was for Mother to get out of her warm bed, put her heavy brown book aside and get ready. She was always slow, very slow. She had to put on her nicest clothes for Santa Zita. This was the rich people's school—Mother couldn't come with her old clothes. So, she had to wear her blue-green *de piece*, brush her thick brunette hair carefully, put on some cheek powder and pink lipstick, wear her long blue heavy coat, her woolen blue scarf, her rubber boots (she didn't have leather boots), her little artificial leather gloves and walk all the way up New Spring Street in the mud and slush to Old North Road. There, she had to stand in the cold, wait for a taxi, and bargain over the tip with the drivers.

But Mother came sooner than we thought, disheveled, in her plain gray skirt and old blue sweater. No pink lipstick, no artificial leather gloves.

Sor Peira and Mother both agreed that we were getting out of control: bad. Mother wept and complained about her loneliness—"a widow and not a widow," her favorite phrase. Sor Piera was impressed. She knew that our father was locked up—but this never made her kinder to us. Maybe she thought our father was a thief, a crook. But when Mother said, "a widow and not a widow" and wept, Sor Piera's tone changed. She smiled. Her fat face opened up. Her little round eyes hid beneath the puffy sacks under her eyes. She offered Mother her snow white handkerchief, ironed and folded in four by the Sisters of the laundry room. A little black cross was embroidered in the corner of the kerchief. Mother accepted her offer and wiped her eyes off, but didn't blow her nose. Sor Piera said that Mother had very beautiful blue eyes. She shouldn't cry and make them red. Then she preached about how being a widow was what God wants, and maybe tomorrow He'd change His will. Mother nodded. She thanked Sor Piera for her kindness. She complained some more about us: we didn't listen to her, we mingled with people we shouldn't. She even mentioned that last summer Sahar ran away from the house. She said that Sahar was the planner; I, the follower; Sahar, the shepherd, I, the sheep. Sor Piera seconded with many nods.

The Superior Nun laughed. We saw two gold teeth in her mouth: one above, one below. The rest were yellow and crooked. She complained about us too. We talked in classes, we laughed in the cafeteria, we didn't say "Veni Santus Spiritos" when we saw a Sister, and our teacher had complained that our homework was dirty and sloppy.

But at the end, Mother Superior forgave us. She gave us another chance, but on one condition: that Mother should punish us severely, so that this won't happen again.

"I'll leave it to you, my dear. Punish them at home. I want to see them changed. This is a first-class private school, not the poor people's neighorhood school. I won't tolerate bad behavior here. Understood?" She said the last sentence to us. Her thick eyebrows were tangled now.

Mother stood up and said, "I promise, Mother. They will change, if not, I'll send them to a boarding school."

Walking toward the door, Sor Piera said, "They're suspended for a week. Send them next week. And I want to see that they're changed. I want to see they respect the Sisters, they study, and they don't put their nose in everything."

Mother thanked the fat nun, shook her hand, wanted to hug her, but Sor Piera didn't come closer. Mother cried some more at the door and she needed to blow her nose in Sor Piera's handkerchief, which she finally did, taking the kerchief with her. We left.

Outside, Mother didn't hold our hands as she always did. Sahar and I didn't hold hands either. We walked, ankle deep in snow, behind Mother, who took long steps down the road, stopping now and then to see if a bus or a taxi would arrive.

At home, without uttering a word, Mother slapped Sahar soundlessly and locked her up in the small kitchen, which was separate from the house, in the narrow angle of the triangular yard. While she was packing a few things for me to take me to Baba Mirza's house, Maman rushed in the room, barehead, blushed, and panting.

"Pari, Pari, Grand-Lady is lost!" she clawed her red cheeks and chewed her lips. "We've searched all the house—she is nowhere. She has disappeared like a drop of water in the dry earth."

"She'll be found," Mother said briefly in a cold tone. "I have to take this brat to his grandfather's house," she added with the same tone. "I can't take it anymore!"

Mother told her stepmother the whole story of our violation of school rules, her visit with Sor Piera and her promise to punish us severly and our suspension for a week. Then she dragged me toward the door like a sack of potatoes. Maman insisted that Mother should forgive us this time, but Mother didn't change her mind.

Maman was so confused about Grand-Lady's disappearance that she forgot to ask where Sahar was.

Outside where the snowman was standing, Uncle Musa, Grandfather, and two tenants, Bashi the Janitor and Hassan the Gardener, were having a conference. They were deciding to make three search groups, one going down the hill toward Old North Road, one behind the houses to Faithland, the third toward the Old North River.

When Mother and I passed the frozen bridge of New Spring Street, we saw Uncle's orange DeCave sliding down the snowy path, in search of Grand-Lady. I heard the usual clang clang of the car and the extra rattle tattle of the chains, now tied to the two rear wheels of the old car. Kami and Cyrus both in the warm back seat, happy to be out sight-seeing, waved to me and stuck their tongues out.

When I saw them, I remembered the summer afternoon we searched for Sahar. My throat began to grip and my temples pulsed loudly inside my head. It was cold, I had left my woolen hat at school. My ears burned and my nose felt like a piece of ice separate from my face. Although I was in torment, I thought about Sahar, crying inside my throat. She must be sitting on the cold platform of the dark kitchen now listening to the rats rustling in the empty cabinets. She must be tracing the path of a large cockroach on the wall. I was not doing better than her, but shortly, I'd be in Tuba's living room sipping hot tea. Oh, how thirsty I was. Mother had forgotten to give us our afternoon tea and snack—or, was this part of our punishment? We hadn't had lunch either. During lunch-time, we had been standing on one foot in the corner of Sor Piera's room.

While waiting for a taxi in front of the New Spring Public Bath, another blizzard dashed around the mountain. We turned our backs to Alborz and shivered like naked trees. My teeth rattled uncontrollably. Mother Alborz was sending her wild son, Saba, to punish me. At this moment my only hope was that no taxi would arrive and Mother would change her mind and take me back home. At home, I'd beg her to release Sahar from the freezing kitchen. If she wouldn't listen to me, I'd sneak out of the house, go to Grandfather's and tell him that Sahar was dying in the cold. He would convince Mother to take her out.

Saba, meanwhile, whistled and flogged the passers-by. He beat Mother too. She hunched her back, bent like she was stabbed in her stomach. I saw the way her face cracked and broke like pale blue glass. Her lantern-like eyes died out. I felt her pain in the bones of my face. I wanted to die of guilt for taking my dear mother out of her warm bed and into the cruel blizzard. She was dear to me when the wind stabbed her, but she didn't stay dear for long.

Now I blamed her. She was spiteful. We could've been home where Sahar and I would have curled under the thick quilt on either side of her. She would've slammed her book shut and told us the story of the Monster of the Well. Or, she could've left the book open, shuffled the pages and found her mother's picture there. A yellow picture with two horizontal cracks and one vertical: Lady-King. A little woman in a white lace wedding dress in front of the photographer's cashmere curtain. Her hair, loose, falling down to the ground. Then Mother would've sighed and said, "My mother was a child bride—."

Or, Mother would have closed the book gently as if it were a dear breakable object, looking out the window, at white, empty New Spring Street, and told us the story of our father falling in love with her when she was fifteen.

"I had two thick braids hanging on my shoulders, stretching down to my belly. I had a stack of high school books in my arms. I loved to read and went to a bookstore opposite the university campus to spend my allowance money on Russian novels. Your father was a university student. He saw me between the shelves, without me seeing him. One day I had too many books to carry in my arms. I dropped them in the sidewalk, where I was waiting for the bus. He helped me pick them up. He carried the books to the bus. Then he rode with me all the way up Old North Road. He walked with me along New Spring Street and saw me home. Then he carried my books, rode the bus with me, and saw me home every afternoon. After less than a month he came with his father, your Baba Mirza, to propose."

"How did Grandfather like Father, when he saw him first? " Sahar and I would've asked a question, even though we already knew the answer.

"He liked the way your father drank his tea. Maman brought some tea. It was hot and your father was thirsty. He poured the hot tea in the saucer and drank from the saucer. This wasn't the way one should drink tea at a formal occasion, you know, but your grandfather liked it. After your father left he told me, 'This young man of yours is down to earth. He is educated, but not pompous. You'll be happy with him—poor, but happy!'" This is what your grandfather said and it was true. We married and we rented a little room on top of the same bookstore. We were poor, but happy. And this lasted until you two were born and that's when there were shootings and screamings and the stamping of the soldiers' boots around the campus."

"They took him to El-Deen on our Name Day—a week after we were born."

"Yes, they broke in one night. We were sitting in bed reading this book. They took him out of the bed, handcuffed and blindfolded him and dragged him out. We couldn't even kiss for the last time. I haven't seen him for seven years now, but I keep reading the book."

"What is it about, Mother?"

"It's about a river. A revolution. Love."

Had we stayed home, the fat heater, Aladdin, would have whizzed, hot tea would've steamed on its glowing head, and Sahar and I would've stayed under Mother's warm quilt, thinking about Father, quietly.

But how different everything was—Sahar, locked up in the dark corner of the triangular kitchen, and I, bent under the slashes of the wild wind. Saba hit me in the face. But I didn't hide anymore. I stood there, facing the wind and the sharp icicles—Saba's daggers. I let them cut and pierce my burning skin. I deserved it. Mother didn't beat me at home, she beat Sahar. So, it was my turn now. Poor Sahar, are you crying in the dark kitchen now?

Are the roaches climbing your legs? Are the rats chewing your hair? Sahar, poor poor sister. All this and more for the love of the beautiful Tatyana, the bald Sister Tatyana.

At Baba Mirza's

When we reached Baba Mirza's apartment on top of the toystore, Mother grabbed my hand for the first time and pulled me up the stairs. Oh, how badly I wanted to stand there for a while and look at the toystore's showcase: the dancing clowns and winding monkeys playing cymbals, a train whistling and running on a track, passing little houses and real-looking people.

The moment Tuba opened the door, Mother burst into tears. I thought she was crying because of the cold. We never found a taxi. We took the bus. After getting off in the middle of the crowded downtown, we still had to walk a long distance to get to Baba's street. It was getting dark. We passed the shops, their neon lights winking in the twilight, but Mother never slowed down to look at the windows. She didn't hold my hand. I almost ran behind her, sniffling through my nose all the way. Not once did she turn to look at me, to see that I didn't have a hat on.

Now, her face was weary and pale, aged, skeletal. Her blue eyes were dim and blurred. Tuba hugged her and kissed her three times on the cheeks. Baba stroked my wet hair with his big shaky hand. His hand smelled of his cologne, a sharp pleasant smell, grassy and strong. He mumbled gibberish, meaningless sounds like, "Ay, Ay, Ay," or, "Hay, hi, hi," meaning, "Where have you been all this time?"

Baba Mirza, my father's father, was a man who never talked. He either made sounds or uttered verses of poetry. Now, we stood in their small, stuffy sitting room and he said, "Hay, hay, hay, hay..." and took me to the big smoky kerosene heater.

"I'm desperate, Baba... I don't know what to do with them. They're getting out of control. And they're only seven. How can I raise them without a father? How long can I stay a widow and not a widow? Waiting, waiting, waiting and waiting...until when?" Mother said something like this, cried and blew her nose in Sor Piera's handkerchief.

Tuba rubbed Mother's shoulders and said, "Calm down Pari, calm down. Everything is going to be all right. Mirza visited the Prime Minister, his former classmate, the other day. They have your husband's file on top of the stack. The Prime Minister said, didn't he, Mirza?" And she fastened her little black eyes, framed in thick eyeliner, on Baba.

I was sure that Baba wouldn't say anything. He'd either make a "Hay, hi, hi..." sound followed by a sigh, meaning "What a grief!" or an appropriate verse. I was right. He didn't say a word. He just nodded when Tuba asked him for the second time, "Didn't the Prime Minister assure you about the file?"

I pictured Baba in the Prime Minister's office, sitting, or standing on the other side of the wide shiny desk, trying to say something about his son— seven years in prison, without a trial—but remaining speechless.

"I don't have any hope, Baba. It's seven years now. I'm losing my mind. I'm aging. I'm wasting away..." Mother sobbed.

"Hmmmmm..." was all that Baba said.

Taking the china coffee cups out of the old oak cabinet, Tuba said, "Why don't you go to a class, a school or something? Make yourself busy, dear. Anyone would go out of her mind, living on top of that mountain, surrounded by prisons and cemeteries. Come to this part of the town, take a sewing class, a language class or something. You can stay here overnight if your class is in the evening. Huh Mirza? What do you think?"

Baba nodded in approval.

I sat under the round table, surrounded by their legs, my woolen heavy coat still on. My frozen ears and nose thawing, water running down my nostrils. I tried not to sniffle and not to stir. I tried to hold my breath to be able to sit there forever and listen to them. I was hoping that they'd forget me, ignore me, and never mention me.

Tuba's feet were little children's feet. She had on pair of white socks and red velvet slippers. Now she had taken her slippers off and was moving her short toes while advising Mother to take a class. Baba had dress shoes on, brown and neatly polished. Beneath the table, it smelled of Baba's shoe polish. He was always formal, wore dress shoes, trousers and dress shirt at home. When he went out, he wore a narrow gray tie with diagonal brown stripes, a vest, and a suit jacket. He used cologne everyday. He was all dressed up even when he went to buy bread and cigarettes. He had a brown derby hat, too, the same color as his three piece suit.

Now Baba's long legs were awkwardly bent under the table. He knew I was there and he didn't want to kick me. He knew I was ashamed and that was why I was hiding, but he didn't know what to say to make me feel better.

Baba Mirza and Tuba like me, I thought. I watched their strange feet. Whatever Mother says, they'll still like me. He is my father's father, how can he not love me?

"Have your coffee, Pari, I want to see your cup. Let's see what the coffee grounds say."

The sharp bitter aroma of Turkish coffee filled the room. I heard the clicks of the little china cups. I knew that Tuba was a fortune teller, a real one. She told people's fortunes and made some extra money. Living in the middle of the town with high rent was costly and Baba's pension was not enough. But the old couple loved downtown, which was full of color and sound, so Tuba read coffee cups behind a beaded curtain.

"Don't you want to come up and join us? I have some hot tea and butter cookies for you," Tuba called to me.

"Leave him alone, Tuba," Mother said. "You don't need to offer him anything. He is not here to visit, he is here to be punished. Not that your place is bad—."

"I know, I know. You separate him from his sister, to punish them. Poor things. Must be hard," Tuba sighed.

"Ay, Ay, Ay, Ay..." This time Baba meant, "Alas... regret, shame—" or something along these lines.

"Not even tea, then?" Tuba asked again.

Mother didn't answer and I never came out. I couldn't wait until she finished her coffee and left. All I wanted was to sleep. It had been a very long day—a long, long day. I couldn't believe that the Tatyana operation had happened this very day. It seemed like ages ago.

"I can see a dark lump at the bottom of your cup, Pari," Tuba said with her husky, mysterious voice, "the sign of grief. I don't see a road, the roads are closed now. The mirrors are dark, too, the candles, blown out. But here, look, I see something here! A man... but not a man... He has some kind of horn on top of his head. A long tail too. Or, maybe it's not a tail. Oh, God forbid! What a long thing, if it's a thing! This is a monster, Pari. A big heavy, hairy monster. Strange! He has opened his arms wanting to hug someone. Not to kill, but to hug. Now press your index finger here, at the bottom of the cup.

Here, where the dark lump is. Let me see. Do it harder, dear, destroy the lump. Ahan, finally—this is what I was waiting for: a bird, a messenger, a pigeon maybe, bringing good news. All the grief will end. Happiness will come. But avoid that monster!" she laughed, shriek-like. Her large breasts shook the table and the china cups hopped and danced.

Sitting on the rug, under the table, I chewed all my ten nails, envisioning the horned, tailed monster, chasing Mother to kidnap her and take her to the bottom of the dark well.

The Fever

Who knows who Tuba was or where she came from? Mother's family didn't like her. They said she used to be a "bar woman." But Mother herself never said this. She liked the way Tuba gave her practical advice and then told her fortune in her husky voice. Sahar and I liked our step-grandmother a lot. She was unlike any other woman we knew. She was old, but she wasn't old; she wore shimmering red blouses, wide colorful skirts, and danced in front of men. She drank vodka with the men and laughed loud and hard.

Some believed that Tuba was a Jew, a Gypsy-Jew. Baba fell in love with her when he was a lonely middle-aged widower roaming the bars to kill the long hours of the night. Baba Mirza and Tuba were the happiest couple anyone had ever seen. They were lovers.

Now holding my face cupped in her palms, she pressed her short chubby fingers on my cheeks to open my mouth. Tuba poured the cold watermelon juice into my throat. Through the blurred curtain of mist I saw her long crimson nails and three large rings on her fingers.

"Take this deary, take it. This will bring the temperature down." She gave me another sip of the sweet juice. "What bad luck Mirza, what fucking bad luck. The minute his mother left he got sick and his temperature rose. Did you find your hat? It's on the coat-tree. Cover your neck with that woolen scarf. His mother has not gotten home yet. Call his uncle and tell him to come and take the child to a doctor."

I heard Baba mumbling something and rustling through the pile of clothes on the hanger. He had to go out in the freezing cold, walk one block to the public phone to make the phone call. I felt sorry for him. He was old and heavy. Not that he was fat, but he was big and had long, thick, hefty legs. Baba's hair was all white, and his hands were always shaking.

Grandfather was older than Baba Mirza, but was in better shape. Mother always said that Grandfather was in such good shape because he took long walks and lived on the mountain skirts. Baba seldom left his apartment. He read all day or listened to the radio and smoked one pack of cigarettes a day. He and Tuba drank vodka every night.

When dusk fell on the tall buildings of downtown, Tuba prepared a colorful dish of cutlets and fried vegetables, and filled the crystal pitcher with ice-cold vodka, lemon slices floating in it. They both sat by the window where they could admire the flaming geraniums and watch the dusk. They drank, smoked, and listened to music. Tuba danced and Baba recited poetry until midnight. This way, they partied together every night. They seldom had company. Once in a while maybe, Uncle Yahya, Baba's brother, who lived alone like a hermit a few blocks from them, joined the old couple.

I had ruined the party tonight. Without this lousy fever I could've enjoyed their company. I would've sat and watched my step-grandmother dancing. I had seen Tuba dancing before and nothing was more beautiful than her whirling skirt. She was short and chubby and had a double chin, but when she danced she didn't look ugly. Sahar and I thought that our gypsy step-grandmother didn't have bones in her body, because when she bent her back toward the floor and wriggled her shoulders and waved her hips, her curly hair swept the floor. She smiled and winked at us when she danced.

Now I was in bed—on the couch in fact—under the window, next to the red geraniums on the window sill—Tuba's famous geraniums that bloomed all year round. My head was as heavy as an iron ball, a time bomb ticking inside. My eyes, the other side of my eyeballs, inside my head, were burning like they were on fire. I touched my eyelids to kill the fire, but I couldn't. I tried to swallow my saliva, but my throat was blocked like a thick wall. "Sahar," I whispered, "Did you see Tatyana's head? Sahar, where are you now? Are the rats eating you?" And I cried, tears rolling down my burning face.

"Did you call, Mirza?"

Baba was back. He said that the heavy snow had blocked Old North Road and there was no way Uncle Musa could come and get me that night. Besides, there was a commotion going on in my grandfather's house.

Grand-Lady who had been lost, was found now. She was fine, but the young girl, Hoori, was ill. Baba Mirza said that Grandfather advised that the best thing was to wrap me in a blanket and let me sweat. This would bring the temperature down.

Tuba sighed, cursed, and complained. She called the Holy Ones for help and roamed around the room.

"What wretchedness, what misfortune! What if the boy dies here? I've never had a child, how am I supposed to handle this? Wrap him? He is burning already. Does this make sense? Give me the woolen blanket, Mirza; I'll do whatever his quack grandfather says."

They wrapped me neck to foot in a thick woolen blanket. It looked like camel's skin, light brown. For a while I envisioned being a camel, a little camel. I didn't moan or whisper Sahar's name. My eyes bulged out and became larger like camel's eyes. My chin grew bigger and bigger. My nostrils widened and I breathed easier.

"I'm a camel, Sahar, look! I'm on a green green grass, no, on a yellow yellow sand. I'm thirsty, but there is no water in this desert. Sahar, give me some water!"

Tuba heard me saying "water," opened my mouth and dripped cold water in my throat.

"I saw the black lump in Pari's cup, didn't I, Mirza? Why on earth did I let the child stay? What if he dies here? How am I able to witness a child's death?"

"Let me go and get my brother, Tuba. He knows more than you and me." Baba's voice was sad and desperate. This was the first complete sentence he had uttered tonight. This meant that he was decisive. He knew what he was doing. I heard him looking for his derby and overcoat again.

"You want to call Yahya?" Tuba asked. "Now that you're going out again, why don't you call a doctor? There's a dentist two blocks down the street."

"It's too late now, he's gone. Yahya knows how to handle this. He knows more than you and me." And he left before Tuba could say anything else.

Uncle Yahya

Like a snail my body is frozen in a curl. I can't move anymore, and I don't want to. I feel warmer this way. I plunged deep into the past and I want to go there again. Why did I come back? Maybe I heard something and I thought Kamal was back. Kamal, you bastard! Are you trying to kill me like this? I'm not going to die, brother! I almost died when I was seven, but I survived. I'll survive again. I won't die now. Not this way. I'd rather be executed than die like a worm on the surface of a glacier. I'm an Unbreakable, you bastard! I refuse to die!

With my burning breath, I blow into my palms. Do I have fever? I press my hands to my face and block the cold and light. I stay behind the dark wall of my palms.

When Uncle Yahya came, I was still a camel, a quiet, lonely camel. Although I wanted to rip off my woolen skin and step out, camelhood amused me very much. The woolen skin burned me, it was too thick; but I liked being a camel and wished my skin wouldn't burn me so I could stay a camel forever. I stretched my long wooly neck to see who was approaching. I fastened my large bulging eyes on Uncle Yahya. He was blurry.

Uncle Yahya was a little man, just a bit taller than a child. Baba Mirza was three full heads taller than him. Uncle had small bones, Baba, large bones; Uncle almost didn't have shoulders, Baba was wide-shouldered. But in some ways they were the same. They were both quiet, so quiet that one would think they were shy. They were talking now, the three of them, as though on the other side of a tunnel. I heard Uncle Yahya's voice for the first time in my life. He had never talked in front of us.

We used to see Uncle Yahya once a year, at New Year's family gatherings, but we never heard him talking. He was even quieter than his brother. At least Baba Mirza said, "Hay, hay, hay..." or mumbled a line, but Uncle's lips were completely sealed. Our mother's family said Uncle Yahya was a bit crazy. Once he was an oil worker in the south, an activist and organizer, but since the failure of the First Revolt, he hadn't worked. He lived on a small pension and biked around the town all day.

Now he was giving directions to Tuba and Baba in his gentle and polite tone: "Would you please hold his legs, Tuba? I'll hold his shoulders. We're going to take him to the shower. Brother, you turn the water on, lukewarm. I have his legs—are you ready Tuba?"

They lifted me up in the air and took me to the small bathroom. There was a shower over a hole in the ground. The hole was the toilet. This bathroom was the size of a person standing up. Baba Mirza and Tuba, living in the middle of downtown, never used a public bath. They showered at home. I was thinking about the inconvenience of such a bathroom when suddenly Uncle Yahya held me under the running water. I tried to scream, but I couldn't. I felt I was drowning in the depths of an ocean. In agony, I could not ask for help.

"Now wrap a light sheet around him," Uncle Yahya said.

The next minute I was wrapped in a thin white sheet, up in the air again, and back to the couch. I had chills. My teeth rattled, but the clouds were removed. After a long time I saw Tuba's crimson lips, stretching with a wide smile.

Uncle Yahya's face was thin and gray. He had a prickly beard; he hadn't shaved for few days. Uncle's bony nose was a bit bent down, his forehead was wide and deeply lined, his gray hair, full, combed upward. If Uncle's hair was black, his face fuller and shaved, a thin moustache lined above his lip and his forehead was smooth and lineless, if his eyes were shiny and not dim and lifeless, he would be Father in his wedding picture. But Uncle Yahya was shrunken and burned. All the juice of life had been sucked out of him long time ago. He sat beside me and looked into my eyes. He smiled. His teeth were yellow. He didn't talk, just looked at me. We stared at each other for a long time.

Gazing into the depths of Uncle Yahya's quiet eyes, I wished Sahar was with me. I was not looking at Uncle Yahya, I was looking at Father. I struggled to take one of my arms out of the sheet. I did and stretched my hand toward Uncle, almost touching his prickly face. I whispered, "Father—." I think he heard me, because he pulled me toward himself and embraced me—tightly, so tightly that it hurt. No one had ever hugged me like this before. I wished the embrace would never end.

Now I heard his soothing voice in my ear, "It's all right son, everything is all right—."

They sat around the round table close to me, their voices muffled, coming from the other side of a tunnel again. I smelled sweet lemons. Baba peeled them one by one, and Tuba cut them in four and squeezed them with a juice squeezer. They were talking about my family. Tuba was doing all the talking. Baba mumbled, now and then, throwing in a word, but Uncle stayed quiet.

"His grandfather Rad said that the old woman was lost all day. Just imagine!" Tuba said, smacking her tongue. Fresh sweet lemon made her mouth water. "Ninety-something years old, lost. They found her at the river, on a pile of snow. One of Rad's tenants saw something moving down there at the frozen river. It was her, Grand-Lady."

"Hey, hey, hey, hey..." Baba Mirza said, "I aged and I aged, then the oblivion reigned—" he mumbled.

"But when Mirza called for the second time to say that the boy was better," Tuba continued, "his Uncle Musa said that the old woman was fine, but the girl had swallowed rat poison or something. I think the black lump in Pari's cup was the sign of all this."

"Childish... infantile—" Baba said. "A love affair, maybe—who knows? Hey, hey hey...."

"They are strange people, these Rads!" Tuba squeezed another lemon. "Who would take a child out of the house in the blizzard, bareheaded, hungry and thirsty, separating him from his twin sister, to punish him?"

The rest of their conversation was lost somewhere in the long dark tunnel—just scattered words reached me. The image of Aunty Hoori and Sahar, the rats of the kitchen and the rat poison all mixed up in my head and I felt dizzy and nauseated.

"I'll lift him... some lemon juice... open, deary... "

"He is falling asleep."

"He is not as hot as he was."

"That blanket would kill him."

"We can wait... juice... later..."

"But lemon... gets bitter..."

"Oh, watch out! He is throwing up!"

I'm Cold, I'm Cold!

"Hey, Sahar!" I whisper inside my head. "Are you still there?" The triangular yard is dark and I'm behind the kitchen door. I knock on the iron door, and it makes a hollow metallic sound like wind playing with tin cans in the street. "Sahar! Open the door from inside. You can open it from *inside*, dummy. Didn't you know that?" Sahar doesn't answer. She must be dead in there. I move out of the yard.

In the empty street, the snowman is standing, exactly the way we dressed it, with Grandfather's sheepskin hat and Maman's broom. But his button eyes are bleeding. I go closer to make sure. Yes. Blood is dripping down his button eyes. I look around to see if anyone is awake. The neighborhood is dead. On the roof of Sheikh Ahmad's house, where a black flag always waves in the wind, a bat sits. I know that the flag has turned into the bat.

Scared of the bat, I open the old door of the second house and step in. Downstairs, Aunty Zari is sleeping in her wide iron-barred bed, wearing her blue lace wedding gown; her face is chalk white. Has she powdered her face, or is she dead too? I look to find her son Kami, but I can't. I tip-toe upstairs to tell Uncle Musa and Aunty Shamsi that Aunty Zari is dead, but they are not in their room. I climb the steps further up and find myself on the roof. Uncle Musa and his wife are busy doing something in the dark. Meanwhile they quarrel in a whisper. I hide in the shadows close to them and see that they are pulling Kami and Cyrus out of the chimney. First they pull Kami out. He is covered with soot, and then, their own son, Cyrus, black from head to foot.

"Bla, bla, bla..." Uncle scolds Aunty.

"Bla... bla..." Aunty defends herself.

I'm not surprised at what I see. I know that Kami and Cyrus always play around the chimneys. I forget about Aunty Zari's death altogether, jump the short wall, entering Grandfather's terrace. I hear the "whip" sound of Uncle Musa's belt, Slash, slash, slash, he flogs the boys in the dark.

I approach Hoori's room. I've heard that she has swallowed rat poison, but she has survived. I want to visit her and see for myself that she is alive. I press my forehead to the window pane, the way Sahar and I always do, and peek into Hoori's room. Her dim blue night light is on. She is hanging from the ceiling with a rope, her black hair covering half of her face like a dark cloud, the other half cold and white like a half moon. I scream and run down the steps and rush to the porch. Grand-Lady is sitting on her Turkman carpet, talking to the mountain in her weird language, crying. I sit beside her and wait for Saba, the north wind, to come and lift the carpet up. I know this will happen.

Saba takes us up in the sky, but when I turn my head, instead of Grand-Lady, Sahar is sitting on the other side of the green peacock. I feel an immense joy and hold her hand. We both laugh. The carpet rises high and flies toward Alborz, turns around the peak of the mountain, but doesn't land there. It returns to New Spring and flies over the desert; it reaches El-Deen and passes over the wall, over hundreds of the ironwoods. Even in the dark moonless night, we can see the red trees glowing with crimson light.

The carpet lands on the roof of El-Deen. We sit there, waiting. We know that any moment Father will come. He comes. He appears out of the shadows of the roof. He looks exactly like Uncle Yahya—his beard, prickly, his hair, gray, his face, bony and long. He has gray pajamas on. He sits on the carpet between Sahar and I. We hold his hands and wait for Saba to lift the carpet up. But there is no wind, not even a faint breeze. We sit and sit for a long time. What if the guards come? What if we're never able to leave the roof of El-Deen? I smell tar and tell Sahar that they must be working on this roof. But as I say this we are not on the roof anymore, we're in Grandfather's dark room.

Grandfather wears his gray photographer's gown. He is developing pictures. The lights come on and we see Grandfather's pock-marked face. He holds a wet picture in his hand. This is Mother's picture. He says, "Look how beautiful she is! I have to print many of these and put them on all the walls."

"Why?" we ask.

"Because your mother is lost."

Sahar and I break into a sob. Suddenly we realize that we've lost our father too. That we have neither a father nor a mother. That we are orphans in this world. We sob so hard and loud that we wake everybody up.

A big warm hand held my hand. I squeezed it and whispered, "Sahar, Father is still here." I grabbed the hand so it wouldn't slip away.

"Tuba, we can give him the lemon juice now, he is awake." I heard Uncle Yahya's voice. Then I heard the shuffle of cards.

"Your turn, Mirza. Go ahead, deal while I'm giving the child some juice. Thank God he is not as hot as before."

A thin female voice sang a sad song on the radio. She complained about her lover: "I drag my long skirt behind... For you're unkind, unkind... Oh, you're so unkind..."

The cool lemonade slipped down my throat. I smiled at Tuba's blurry face. She squeezed her scarlet lips forward in the shape of a rose bud and kissed me in the air. Now I looked at Uncle Yahya's face and smiled at him. He smiled back.

"Get more sleep son. You'll be fine in the morning," Uncle said.

"Don't go," I murmured.

"I won't," he assured me.

At that moment I decided not to leave Uncle Yahya. Ever. He could become my father, our father. I was sure that Sahar would feel the same way.

"I drag my long skirt be - hind... " the woman stretched her voice.

Tuba said, "Rummy! I won again."

"Ay, ay, ay, ay," Baba replied and thought of a verse: "Is it possible to open the brothels' gates tonight? Is it possible to untangle my tangled luck?"

Tuba sent Baba to bed and Uncle Yahya home. Uncle kissed me on the forehead and promised to come back the next morning to visit me. Tuba turned the lights out and slept on the floor at the foot of the couch. Now I was feeling cold, needing my camel skin again, but I didn't want to wake Tuba up. I could hear her snoring like a man. Through the white transparent curtain, red and blue flashes of neon light lit and unlit the room.

I shivered and thought about the three houses. What was going on there? Was Sahar still in the kitchen? Was Hoori in the hospital or lying down in her room? Was Grand-Lady out on the porch? How did Mother get back home if the roads were blocked? What if she is lost? I closed my eyes and still saw the red and blue flash on my eyelids, the neon lights of the toy store under Baba's apartment. How lonely the toys must feel every night, I thought. They had to wait a long long time until the owner opened the store again, wound them, and made them move. How lonely the miniature city around the train track was. How lonely I was, lonelier than the toys.

"Oh, I'm cold. I'm cold. I'm cold—" I cried. I needed my camel skin. So badly. After that high fever, Tuba never covered me again. And I couldn't get up and find it, because everywhere was so dark, so lonely and dark.

Grandfather's Shadow

Aware that I'm curved in a snail position, I come back again. The piercing cold brings me back. There is no shell to hide in, no tree bark or dry leaf to crawl under. I'm cold. I blow into my blue hands and rub my face. I weep, then stop and cry inside my throat. Kamal wants to see me crying. They may be watching me now. I'm an Unbreakable—I won't show them my tears.

The only way to survive is to return. Let me plunge into the deep ice again. Let me go back to my neighborhood. Tuba's house is dead tonight. I can hear the hiss of the snow and see the flashes of blue and red neon. This will go on for a while, until my fever rises again and all the lights come on.

I was absent from New Spring when the snow damaged the tenants' hovels. Mother never came home that night and Sahar stayed in the kitchen until dawn. How can I recall a scene I've never lived? Can I remember an unlived memory and live it in revery? Can I step into that cold night and spend the long hours with my grandfather? He must be roaming around, checking on his tenants. I might be able to tell him that Sahar is locked up. But I have to go there as Grandfather's shadow, and shadows don't talk. Let me just see and hear without being seen and heard.

Grandfather wears his long Cossack sheepskin overcoat, salt-and-pepper Russian fur hat and the tall military leather boots he always wears, winter after winter. There is no need for a lantern tonight, it's a bright night. The sky mirrors the white earth and reflects the light. The snow freezes as the night moves on.

Grandfather sneaks out of the house. Maman tells him not to go out. She warns him of his killing arthritis pains. She says he should wait until morning, "What can possibly be fixed tonight?"

But Grandfather is restless. How can he sleep after all that has happened? His mother escaped and got lost in the snow. True, she's been found, safe and sound, but the whole thing was more than a shock. And this can happen again.

Then his youngest daughter, Hoori, swallowed rat poison. Is she in love? Does she have a problem, a secret, a grief she can't share? Why should a fifteen-year-old attempt suicide? True, he washed her insides on time. But the whole thing is too much for him to understand. Can this happen again?

His tenant house collapsed. Isn't this ugly multi-level tenant house a burden on his old shoulders? Isn't he carrying hell on his back? He's known for a while now that this property is not a business for him, doesn't bring profit. Just trouble. Isn't he satisfying his sense of leadership, then? Isn't he playing the stupid role of a prophet and his flock? A king and his kingdom? He charges some rent from these poor people—which, as little as it is, is still too much—and his conscience is always heavy with guilt. So, he gives them free medicine, cures their children, takes free photographs for their birth certificates or school files. They bring their problems to him, ask him to be their judge when they fight over the single water tap in the yard, or the public restroom they all have to share. He plays the just king. He enjoys being the Big Father.

Now their roofs have collapsed. And they expect miracles. He can't afford to fix all the roofs. The whole place is in ruins, it needs to be dumped and rebuilt. He can't possibly afford it. And he can't perform miracles. He is no prophet. He's no king. He has his own problems at home. His mother and his three husbandless daughters are all going crazy, not to speak of his lunatic son, Massi.

I drag myself behind Grandfather like his shadow. He looks at the sky and the fast movement of the clouds. The moon seems too far tonight; it lights the world only when the clouds are apart. The moon is a small, inaccessible glass marble.

The snow crunches under Grandfather's boots. His cane slips on frozen stones. Now he thinks of my mother and us. He knows that Pari hasn't come back home. She took her little son into exile—to punish him, to separate him from his twin sister. Horrible. Worrisome, he thinks. Why so cruel? What is happening to her? Year after year of waiting for her husband to come out of the jail is driving her crazy. Why punish the little ones?

The roads are closed. Pari can't come back home. Where can she sleep? What if something happens to her? Now, Maman says come to bed and get some sleep. How can one possibly sleep tonight?

He walks, ankle-deep in dry snow. It crunches under his feet. I walk behind him. I'm naked and I feel the cold in the marrow of my bones. We approach the tenant house. Grandfather opens the old squeaky door and enters the courtyard. I slide behind him like the tail of his Cossack skirt. The first thing he does is check on Uncle Massi. He knocks, but Uncle doesn't answer. He opens the door and steps in; I walk behind him. Uncle sits cross-legged on his bamboo spread, writing on a long roll of paper. His feather pen scratches the paper. A small electric burner is in a corner, a pot of tea boiling on it. A clay jar of water is in the other corner.

"Is everything all right here?" Grandfather asks.

Uncle Massi raises his head and looks deep into his father's eyes as though trying to recognize him. He bends his head and writes again.

"Roads are closed," Grandfather says. "Pari hasn't come home. Hoori took rat poison. Thank God, I washed her insides and it worked. Grand-Lady was lost. They found her at the frozen river. The roofs have collapsed —."

Uncle doesn't respond.

"Thank God your room is fine."

Uncle Massi is quiet.

Grandfather looks around the room and sees the pictures of naked movie stars on the walls and feels embarrassed.

Now he says something like, "I can see that you work a lot. You don't want to show me your poems?"

Uncle doesn't answer, doesn't even raise his head. Grandfather sighs and turns to go out. "It's useless," he murmurs. "Hopeless..."

But before he leaves the room, Uncle calls him: "Mother?"

"What did you call me, son?" Grandfather turns, startled.

"Mother, would you please read this elegy? It's about Father's death."

Grandfather takes the roll of paper and looks at it. I peek over his arm to see Uncle's cursive handwriting. Uncle bursts into a wild laughter. The more Grandfather unrolls the paper, the louder Uncle laughs. All Grandfather and I can see are meaningless marks, pre-school scribbles. Not a word, not a single word is on the long roll of paper. There are only crooked lines, dots, weird signs, and marks. Grandfather leaves the room immediately and I follow him. We hear Uncle shrieking in his cell-like room.

I'm cold. I'm cold. I'm cold. I move closer to Grandfather to feel the warmth of his sheepskin coat. I smell the sheep. Why can't I slip under his overcoat and stay there? Because I'm his shadow. A shadow is always separate from the body. I must shiver, then.

The yard of the tenant house is dark. I listen to the heavy silence and the crackling sound of the snow under Grandfather's feet and cane. I want to say, "Grandfather, why don't you go and save Sahar first? Don't you know that she is dying in the dark triangular kitchen?" But I can't. Shadows don't talk.

In the first yard, Bashi the Janitor, Hassan the Gardener, and the one-legged man, called "the Lame," squat on the ground. The yard is swept of snow, but still Grandfather has to be careful about the patches of ice and slippery mud. I shake and move behind him, my soles burning.

We get closer to the tenants. There is a burlap sack, the kind used to store rice or potatoes. Bashi and the Lame hold the open mouth of the sack, while Hassan the Gardener tries to fit something inside. Oh, it's a frozen body, as stiff and slippery as the frozen calves hanging on butcher's hook. But this is the body of a woman. Her feet are small like a little girl's. The three men push her into the sack, wrap a rope around the neck, and tie it tight. The bundle is ready.

They notice Grandfather. Bashi, the oldest of Grandfather's tenants and always acting as their representative, wipes his tears with his dirty hands and says, "Doctor Rad, sir, this is our life. This is how your tenants live, sir! Look at this. This was a woman yesterday and a block of ice now. We're turning into something else here." Now he points to the lower yards and says, "Down there, a woman turned into charcoal. She burned today. And there, in that frozen pool, we caught a baby who had turned into a frozen frog." He sighs and looks at the sky. I look too. The clouds move fast, gather and spread; they cast a dark shadow, then open, letting the moon shine. "This is what He wants for us," Bashi says. "This is His will. Our lot!"

Grandfather looks at the sky too. "Who?" he asks.

"The Almighty," Bashi says.

"Oh," Grandfather says, "him..."

I stare at Bashi's ugly face, wrinkled and dark, only three long teeth in his mouth. I can smell dung on him, the cheap tobacco he chews and smokes. How can he feel compassion for the dead woman? Does he have feelings at all?

"This is not your lot, you ignorant sheep!" A deep voice echoes in the yard. We turn around and see Uncle Massi standing at his door, his long hair waving in the breeze. The dim light inside his room has cast a halo around his slender body. He looks not at us, but at the distance, far beyond the three yards. He looks into the thick darkness, where Faithland is.

"There, my people! They need you there! Beyond the wide gate, where the road is. The Holy Ones and Mary are buried there in the snow. Come with me! Follow me—I'm your poet-prophet, Massi-Alla! Follow me down the stone steps of the Hell. They need us down there!"

Uncle Massi holds the skirt of his long robe and dashes down the steps, without the fear of ice. The Lame and Hassan the Gardener follow him in haste. Bashi stays with Grandfather, who cautiously puts the tip of his cane where there is no ice and descends. I slide behind him.

"When he was born, thirty something years ago, Bashi, I was a Minister in a southern town," Grandfather tells his old tenant, as they descend the frozen steps. "I had a little church. I even believed that I had a mission on this earth. I was chosen to bring the New Christianity into this land. That's why I named him Massi, short for Messiah." Grandfather pauses to find a secure spot for the tip of his cane. Bashi helps him, supporting his left arm, but slips himself now and then. "My older one, Musa, was born when I was a Jew. That's why he bears the name of the prophet of the Jews. And when did I become a Jew? That was in Russia when I was a Cossack in the Don area. There was a bloody war there and I was in the war. A Jewish doctor in the army taught me how to make medicine and cure diseases. I loved my master so much that I converted to his religion. But my mother always had her own faith and will always hold to it. As long as I can remember, she's fasted one month out of the year and prayed five times a day on her Turkman carpet facing the House of God."

We reach the second yard. It is exactly like the first, with a frozen round pool in the middle and hovels around it. Some of the hovels are no more than a heap of mud and snow. We hear faint moans from somewhere in the dark, but we don't linger, we descend the slippery steps again.

"And what about now, sir?" Bashi asks Grandfather. "What are you now? Are the rumors true... that you are a fire worshiper?"

Grandfather laughs. He stops so that he won't fall down, then laughs from the bottom of his heart. "A fire worshiper? Who has made up this nonsense? I believe the one-armed sheikh spreads this horseshit around. Do you know why I closed my church in the south and moved to this neighborhood? Because I dreamed of the Almighty one night. He came to me as Zoroaster, our ancient prophet. He told me to move to the capital city and find a neighborhood close to Mount Alborz and convert to the last religion. So I did. How could I ignore God? Now what is the last religion, janitor?"

Bashi stops, pauses, looks at the heavens and says, "Our own Holy Faith, sir. The Faith of our prophet, the last one, the jewel of them all."

"Right. So I returned to my mother's faith. Meanwhile, I lost my first wife who bore me four children: two sons and two daughters. How I lost her is a heartbreaking story itself and needs another chapter. I married my second wife. I waited and waited for a son, so I could call him by the name of the last prophet, but all she has brought me so far is one daughter. I named her Hoori, Angel of God. Now tell me, janitor, does this mean that I'm a fire worshiper?"

"Do you pray, sir?—if you'll allow me to stick my nose into your private life," Bashi asks with false timidity.

"Now that everybody else's nose is, yours can be as well. I do pray, Bashi, and a lot. More than five times a day. I meditate in my own way. Every night I talk to the moon, to the stars. I may even buy a telescope to be able to communicate better."

"But how about fasting, charity, pilgrimage, and the rest of the duties?"

"I fast in my own way, more than one month a year and I don't overeat when it's time to break the fast. I'm not rich enough to go on pilgrimage, and charity—don't I pay charity, Bashi? Why should *you* doubt this? Haven't I helped my tenants with low rent, free medicine, free house visits, free photographs, and more? Don't you call these charity?"

"Yes, sir, you're very generous, sir," Bashi says hypocritically, "but how about helping the House of God?"

"I won't drop anything in the sheikh's purse. It's not the purse of God. God doesn't have a purse. He hates money."

As we step into the third yard, which is darker, unswept, and almost all in ruins, a shriek echoes in the white night. This strange cry is not quite human. It's birdlike, something no one has heard before:

"Ash on my head! Ash and dirt on my head! Oh, you unbelievers! Did you see how my little baby turned black? Did you see how my jewel died? Oooh, oooh, oooh, oooh... My luck is tangled and it never opens. My destiny is dark. Ali, Ali, Ali, Ali, where are you to see the flesh of your body, the sight of your eyes, blue and black? He is gone, gone, gone, gone... My baby is gone!"

I recognize Zahra, Ali the Bricklayer's wife, squatting on the floor of the third yard, bare-headed. She clenches a fistful of her hair and pulls it out, beats on her flat chest as hard as she can. Women squat around her and as she wails, they rock back and forth, weep and moan—her chorus.

"Sir," Bashi whispers in Grandfather's ear, "This is the bricklayer's wife, her baby fell in the frozen pool. I took it out with my own hands. What a sight, sir, what a sight."

Grandfather approaches Zahra and stands behind her. He faintly touches her with the tip of his cane, "Stop this, woman! Can you bring your baby back to life? All you're doing now is neglecting your other children. Get up and put them to bed. It's cold here and it's late. Get up! Take care of the other ones. How many do you have? Six? Seven? Eight? You'll forget this one."

"We don't need you here!" Zahra screams and jumps to her feet. Her hair is standing up, as if she had been struck by thunder. Bashi holds her arms from behind; he thinks that Zahra wants to attack Grandfather. "Go, go back to your warm house!" Zahra screams. "Come when the rent is due. Or, we'll send it to you like we always do. Go! You don't have a heart, old man. No heart!"

"Bite your tongue, Zahra!" Bashi orders the woman. "Don't be disrespectful! Hasn't Doctor given you free medicine? Hasn't he treated your children for worms? Where can you find such a landlord? Huh? *You* tell me. Where? Now get up and collect your children."

"My room has collapsed, Doctor sir," an old woman says. She has no teeth at all and her jaws rest on one another after each syllable like an accordion. "Thank God I wasn't in it! I was making a fire outside to warm my hands. You see, we can't have a burner inside. A woman caught fire this morning."

"Sir, Doctor sir, wait!" a tenant pushes his way through the thick wall of the tenants and approaches Grandfather. "Where are my wife and children supposed to sleep tonight? My room is full of snow." He talks with a villager's accent.

"Move back! I said, move back!" Bashi orders the crowd.

"Give us some blankets—" a man says.

"Water... the pipe is frozen. We need water to make some hot tea," another man says.

"Give us some kerosene, sir! You can't leave us freezing here!"

"Move back, let us pass!" Bashi screams.

"Nene is cold, Nene is cold... The hundred-year-old woman calls like an owl. She is lying on the frozen brick floor of the courtyard against the wall of her fallen hut.

Grandfather passes through the crowd and limps toward the gate. He moves his hands to chase the tenants away, as if he is chasing flies. "Tomorrow! Tomorrow we'll talk!" he says. "What can I do tonight? Get some blankets from the mosque! Wake the lazy sheikh up! Isn't he the representative of God? Let him answer for Him. Did *I* send the snow or did God? Huh? Why are you all quiet now? Move back! Let me go!"

I take a last glance. The women collect Zahra's five children, who are wailing on the ground, or dozing off in different corners of the yard, all wrapped in rags. Bashi approaches Zahra, who has spread herself on the frozen mud again, plucking at her hair; he lifts her and leads her to her hovel. She stumbles and murmurs her husband's name, "Ali, Ali..."

The old janitor opens the wooden gate.

"How did this happen?" Grandfather asks. "I mean the child, the baby."

"Zahra was at work, sir. You know that she works in the public bath until late at night. It's a nasty job, sir. Twelve hours a day in the dark bathhouse. They say she has some kind of skin disease. Anyway, her husband, Ali the Bricklayer, was at a construction site. He hasn't come back home yet. He must have gotten stuck somewhere in the snow. You know that the roads are closed. The older girl was supposed to take care of the little ones, but she is only five years old..."

Grandfather looks at the sky, follows the movement of the clouds and stays quiet. I follow him in the deep snow. We walk in the middle of the alley where it's safer. Some of the walls have collapsed. I'm waist-deep in snow. I use my arms to breast-stroke.

Uncle Massi, Hassan, and the Lame are three dark spots on the surface of the white road.

"Send the homeless tenants to Faithland," Grandfather tells Bashi. "I can't afford to fix the rooms now. I'm broke. I have to make some money first, then fix the rooms. Send them to Faithland to find themselves a place. When the rooms are fixed they can come back."

"But where in Faithland can they go, sir? Look around yourself sir. You are *in* Faithland. Is anything left of it? Where are the houses, huh? The tin houses, the cardboard shelters are all gone, sir. Covered with snow and gone.

Where are the people, sir, huh? All buried. All gone!"

We look to our right and left and all we see are big piles, hills of snow. This is the main alley of Faithland, where Sahar and I were trapped in the flood one day. Bashi is right—all the hovels and tin houses are buried.

Grandfather is quiet. His tall boots are deep in the snow; his cane doesn't help much. I shiver and follow. I breast-stroke behind him. The small round moon comes out now and lights the land.

After a long silence Grandfather says, "Bashi, you know what?"

"What sir?"

"I'll sell the property; I can't do miracles. I'll sell it with the people in it. Let someone else carry the burden. Do you think I'm making money off of this tenant house?"

The janitor is quiet. But then he says, "Rely on God's mercy, sir; whatever He wants. Surrender yourself to Him." And he sighs. "If He came in your dreams once, He may come again. Surrender to Him."

"Come and see for yourself, you sinners! Come and see!" This is Uncle Massi's voice, deep and loud. He has seen us and he's waving his arms, calling us. "Didn't I warn you when the earth was shaking like a cradle last summer? Didn't I tell you if you didn't rise up, if you didn't raise your voice, more miseries were to come? Didn't your poet-prophet warn you?"

Grandfather and Bashi rush to where Uncle Massi, Hassan, and the Lame are. Grandfather slips several times and Bashi holds him up. We reach a tall mound of snow.

"Do you know what this mountain is?" Uncle asks. "Look up! What do you see? The sign of God. What else do you see? The man of God. Now, can you guess what this mountain is? It's the House of God!" And he laughs.

We look up. The top of the green minaret sticks out of the mountain. The torso of a bearded man is out too. He is hugging the minaret with one arm, his only arm. The man is either completely frozen, or freezing now. His beard is made of icicles; he is himself a snowman.

"This is not the whole thing, come! Come forward, follow me." Massi moves his long arms and calls us to go further up. There is another mountain here. Smaller, a hill. "Shh, shh, shh..." He holds his finger on his nose. "Shh, shh... listen! This little mountain talks!"

We all listen and in the frozen silence we hear a thin voice chirping like a wounded sparrow. The voice says, "Oooooooooo... Oooooo... He...lp...

123

Ooooo... He...lp!"

"Give me your shovel!" Grandfather orders Hassan the Gardener. He grabs the shovel and jabs it into the pile of snow. He pierces several spots. The voice says, "Ouch!" And a bare leg pops out. This is a woman's leg—white as ivory. And now a bare arm, now a head. In a second, a naked woman pulls herself out and stands on the pile of snow like some kind of marble statue. A large black mole sits above her left nipple. All the men bend their heads and close their eyes. Bashi murmurs, "O Holy Ones, we repent of our sins!"

"This is Mariam the Big Mole," Hassan the Gardener murmurs and immediately blushes.

"Didn't I tell you the real sight is here?" Uncle Massi says and chuckles. "That was your heavenly house and this is your earthly one. Now which one do you want to save first, the sheikh or the whore?" And he laughs again.

"Help! Help!" Mariam cries.

"Why don't you help her, then?" Uncle Massi cries. "Haven't you seen a naked woman in your life? Come, my poor sister, come. Let me lend you my old robe. You're a hundred times baptized in this snow. You're purged of your sins!"

Massi, brisk as a young lad, climbs the mound and shrouds his long robe around the woman. He lifts her up in his arms and brings her down the hill. Hassan and the Lame overcome their shock and rush to the God's House to see if the sheikh is still alive. They stumble in the snow, slip on the ice and trip over the piles and mounds. Bashi and Grandfather dig more bodies out of the whore house. More and more thin voices chirp and naked legs pop out. Meanwhile, Massi carries Mariam in his arms and rushes toward the tenant house. He sings loud and strong, "Twenty and five! Twenty and five! The end will come!"

Grandfather and I leave the tenants to tend to their miseries and the miseries of the frozen ones. Walking the rest of the alley, we turn right and find ourselves behind the triangular house. Here, Grandfather stops and listens. He hears someone weeping. He pushes the old wooden door, stepping in the dark yard. He cups his right hand around his ear, listening more. The moon is out now and the tall silhouette of the ugly triangular house has fallen on the white yard. He listens and I shiver in my invisibility. "Yes, Grandfather, yes! She is here. Go to the end of the yard, the narrowest angle of all the angles, the darkest, the loneliest. She is there in the abandoned kitchen."

Grandfather goes toward the kitchen and presses his ear to the cold iron door. "Sahar, are you in here? It's Grandfather. Are you here?"

Sahar weeps, but doesn't answer. Grandfather unbuttons his long heavy coat and fishes in his pocket. He takes a key chain out and examines the keys under the moonlight.

"Sahar, I'm taking you out, dear. Let me find the key. Your mother has not come back yet. I'm sure she is worried to death for you. She must have gotten stuck in the snow somewhere. Do you hear me, girl? Now I'm trying to find the extra key to this damn kitchen. Say something, deary. It's Grandfather. So many things happened today that nobody thought of you. I should've thought of you, sweetheart. I'm getting old and dumb. I forget a lot."

Sahar's faint voice says, "Grandfather—" and she weeps again.

"Good girl! I always knew that you were the bravest of all. You're not scared of the roaches, are you? They're just bunch of ugly little creatures." He finds a brass clover-shaped key and slides it into the key hole. "And the rats... believe me, they're better than some humans." The iron door opens with the sound of a cymbal.

Grandfather carries Sahar in his arms and we go out. He sits on the thick frozen feet of the snowman and places Sahar on his left knee. I make myself comfortable on his right knee. Grandfather wraps the left side of his sheepskin coat around Sahar; I slide myself under the fold of the right side. Sahar does not weep anymore, but makes hiccup sounds and thin moans in between. Under the moonlight, I can see that she is pale and her face has many red scars. Her bushy hair has been chewed on by the rats.

"It's strange, Sahar, very strange. I feel that your brother is sitting on my lap too. I even feel his heartbeat."

Sahar bursts into a loud sob. Grandfather wipes her face with his big rough hand and says, "Oh, no. He is safe and sound. Only maybe too warm for such a cold night. He has a little bit of a fever tonight. Your Baba Mirza called earlier. Poor clumsy man didn't know how to handle a fever. And his gypsy wife is no good either. I told him to wrap your brother in a thick blanket and let him sweat. He'll be fine. Tomorrow, we'll go and get him. Don't cry, my sugar, all is finished. Now, tell me what was this punishment for, huh? How did you two hurt your mother this time?"

"We didn't hurt her. She hurt us." Sahar says, hiccuping. "We wanted to find Tatyana," she weeps again.

"The Polish girl?"

"Yes. And she is not beautiful anymore. She is bald," Sahar wails and shivers. I shiver with her.

"So finally she became a nun!" Grandfather says. "And you two brave ones went to find her."

"Mother Superior called Mother," Sahar says between hiccups.

"And you got in a serious trouble, huh?"

"She is mean. We hate her, we hate her, we hate her!" Sahar lays her head on Grandfather's shoulder and sobs. I lay my head on his other shoulder and weep quietly.

"Shh... shh... shh..." Grandfather whispers. "Your mother is not mean. She is alone. Very alone."

As though someone has splashed a bucket full of melted silver on the sky, it suddenly glows. The dark lavender of the clouds becomes a translucent gray. I peek through Grandfather's coat and see the dawn. This light is here to stay. Sahar and I feel better now.

When Sheikh Ahmad's sickly rooster jumps on the roof, beside the black flag, and sings the song of dawn with his scratchy voice, Mother appears at the bottom of the hill. Her long blue-green overcoat is soiled, her curly dark hair disheveled, her blue eyes dim and dull. She climbs the hilly street toward us, heavy and slow, as though climbing out of a dark well where a monster dwells.

Like a Dirty Blanket

Off with this thick sheet. Off with the shirt. Off off! I'm hot. I'm a burning furnace. I'm rising dough in the baker's oven. I sit naked on the couch and weep. Tuba snores and then she doesn't snore. When she doesn't, I hear another sound. I stop weeping and peek through the lace curtain. I want to see where the neon lights have gone. Why is everywhere so dark? I want to listen to this strange sound: swoosh... pause, swoosh... pause again. I listen some more. This is a familiar sound, I have heard it before. Now someone dumps a heavy weight on a soft surface: swoosh, again. I press my forehead to the cold windowpane. It's dark. What happened to the blue and red neon lights? If it's dawn, where are the vendors, shopkeepers, flower sellers, thieves, and pickpockets? What happened to the busy downtown? It's dark and all I can see through the dark is a brick wall. It's thick and impassible, stretched all the way to the right and left. I tilt my head back to see the sky, but the wall stretches infinitely up, as though there is no sky.

"Sahar!" I whisper. "Ali is here. He is working on the wall. That's why he wasn't home when his baby turned into a frog." I listen some more, then I say, "Sahar, I was there on Grandfather's lap too. Didn't you feel me? Didn't you hear me breathing?" And again, "Sahar, did the roaches bite you? The rats chew all your hair? Did they chew your white ribbon? Sahar, it's hot under Grandfather's sheepskin coat. It's hot, hot, hot, hot." And I sob louder, very loud.

The lights come on. Tuba screams, stumbles, bumps into objects and calls her husband: "Mirza, get up! Get up! His fever has gone up again. We shouldn't have let Yahya leave. Get up! We have to shower him again."

I'm floating in the air. Tuba and Baba carry me, but I don't see them. I'm all wrapped in a hot blinding light. I scream when the cold water hits my burning body; I feel that I can't breathe anymore. The end has come, the end has finally come and you are not here, Uncle Yahya. The end has come, Sahar. Bye bye."

"Slap his chest, slap! Ahan. This is the way my mother used to wash her dirty blankets in a tub. Slap! Slap! Slap!"

Two strong hands, many strong hands, hit my chest. I recognize Kamal's voice, distinct and clear, loud and anxious, among the hubble-bubble of confused sounds, "Slap harder, Brothers! I need him alive!"

127

Chapter Three
Ha-G Interrogates

Not remembering is at a certain point necessary
to make the story this one and not another...
—Italo Calvino, t-Zero

In the Garden, on the Gurney

Gallop and gallop and gallop—the white horse circles around the clay dust arena. I saw his eyes, didn't I? They were large and wet, dark rings framed them, made him look wicked, evil. When the tall, stiff valet lifted us up and put us on the horse, I saw the eyes. But then it was too late. We were already sitting on the hard saddle.

"I don't want to ride on this horse," Sahar whispers in my ear. But it's too late. Gallop and gallop and gallop—fast around the clay dust arena. I've grabbed the reins tight. The valet told me to hold the reins tight and pull them when I want to stop the horse. Now, I have them, I want to pull them, but they slip out of my hands. My hands are sweaty and the leather reins slip. I can't pull. I lose control and sway back and forth. Sahar holds me tight and sways with me. She screams.

"Name?" someone asks with a throaty voice. Sahar's voice melts away. This cannot be the valet who is waving to us now, his voice lost in the wind. The valet screams something but we cannot hear. Saba, the north wind, sucks his voice in and holds it in his fat cheeks. But, this other voice, this throaty voice, repeats: "Name? Name? Name? Name?"

"I don't remember," I tell him.

"Brother, start with the other questions. He can't remember his name. We're working on this."

This voice is familiar. It's different than the first one. It sounds calmer, friendlier. I try to open my eyes to see whose voice is this. I find myself on a gurney, naked, under a white sheet. Opposite my gurney sits a small desk with a little man behind it. I can see a few strands of greasy hair sticking to his scalp. His back is hunched. The hunch is big, as if the man is hiding a bundle under his black shirt. Maybe he is not really hunched, the hunch is artificial—pieces of rags stuck inside his shirt to make him look uglier than he is—to scare me. I cannot see the man's eyes. The strong light of a projector blinds me. Oh, now I know. Ha-G—Ha-G, the Shit Mouth. Didn't Kamal warn me about this man? One of the strongest arms of the Great Octopus?

On the right side of Ha-G, a tall man sits, partly in shadow. He is wearing a white gown. I know him. I recognize him from his clean-trimmed beard, thick lenses and polite way of talking. This is Doctor Halal, who injected me in the Clinic. Behind him, further in the shadow, two people are sitting, their heads inside brown paper bags. There are two holes in their hoods to look through.

Sahar screams in my head and holds me tight around the waist. I can't find the reins; they have slipped from my hands. If I bend down to find them, Sahar and I will fall. The white horse is galloping fast, faster even, around the clay dust arena. He circles the same circle again and again and again, as if gone mad.

I look at the two hooded figures in the shadow. Who are they? Sahar? La-Jay, The Great Octopus in disguise, observing my interrogation? Witnessing my fall?

"Sahar!" I scream in my head. "Hold me tight!" But Saba is wild today, blows my voice away. I mutter again, "Are you there, Sahar? Have they put you inside a bag? Do you know that I'm here on this bed trying hard not to let you fall? Do you remember the white horse? Do you remember the fall?

"This is the last time bastard! What is your goddamn name? Speak up or I'll fuck you right here!" the Shit Mouth cries.

"I... can... not... remember," I say. But I'm not sure I've uttered the words.

"What? I can't hear a word. Louder, or I'll pull that thing out of your vein and you're done, finished. Do you hear me? Louder!"

I look at my right arm; the thin glassy hose is bringing a transparent fluid into my vein. I don't want to die. Not before her.

"Try to remember my friend. You *can* remember if you want to." This is Halal. It's soothing to hear a calm tone. "Why are you torturing yourself?

Look what you've done to yourself! The moment you tell us your name, we'll let you rest. Don't you think you need to rest? To eat? To drink? We can't feed you through your veins anymore. You will die like this. Do you want to die?" He pauses and I know that he is watching my facial expression. My eyes are closed, but I feel that he is approaching the gurney.

"Do you want to die?" He repeats, now very close to me.

I try to shake my head, say no, but I'm not sure if my head is moving. Has he added something to the colorless liquid? Why is my tongue so heavy, my muscles numb?

"Do you hear me?"

I nod.

"You will die if you don't remember. Is it worth it? You are young. You have a long life ahead of you. There are probably people outside worried to death for you. Everybody has a family. You are torturing *them*! Yes, that's what you're doing. You are selfish! Do you think you are protecting someone? No, my friend, you are destroying the same person you think you are protecting. Now, do you remember your name?"

The horse neighs and rises up on his hind legs. Sahar screams, "No!"

"No!" I tell Halal.

"Bullshit!" Ha-G hollers and bangs his fist on the desk. "He is playing with us, Doctor. I'm afraid I don't have patience anymore. I'm tired of this. Your methods don't work, Brother. Let me handle this."

"Ha-G, sir, I don't think he is lying or playing with us. This can happen. Amnesia. He needs to be under my attention. He is not ready for the interrogations yet. He needs medical attention. There is a knot inside his head, a big dark knot. We need time to open it."

"Nonsense! The motherfucker is hiding his name and you talk about a big dark knot! I'm sick and tired of this, Doctor, and I'm going to report this mess to the higher authorities. Now, if you allow me, I'll make him remember his goddamn name. Lift me up!" Ha-G screams and immediately two guards from either side of the room rush toward him. He screams again, his voice breaks, becomes squeaky, "Lift me up from this goddamn chair, motherfuckers!"

"But Ha-G, sir," Halal tries to control himself, "how can we work on this case together, while we have different views and approaches?"

"Don't bullshit me with your approaches, Brother. A prisoner who is the enemy of the Faith and the Holy Revolution doesn't need your caressing approaches, Doctor, he needs punishment; this is the alphabet of the Holy Interrogation. This was the practice at the time of our Holy Ones, and is the practice of our Holy Republic. Go and study the texts, Doctor. You have immersed yourself in Western books. Lift me up, I said!"

My heart pounds wildly. I feel like a prey tangled in a trap. Every single part of my body is woven with the net and the hunter is approaching. For the first time I look around the room and study my situation. I see a dozen guards, the Devotees of the Holy Revolution, armed with machine guns, standing against the walls. Am I so dangerous? Or are they here for the people in the paper bags? I try to look at all the devotees' faces to find Kamal. I have a vain hope, a childish fantasy, that Kamal is going to save me exactly one instant before Ha-G starts the torture. These guards all look alike and have the same kind of uniform—black shirts and pants tucked in military boots. Their heads are shaved and they are all tall, very tall, but none of them is *my* Kamal.

They've lifted Ha-G. He is just a torso without the lower part. His black collarless shirt is tucked in a dark gray purse. He must be very light. A small head, a thin, crooked torso and two arms that look longer than normal; this is all Ha-G is. I imagine his hunch under the shirt to be like a turtle's shell, rough and calloused. They bring him to my gurney and for the first time I see his turtle face. Red-veined, bulging eyes, fat flat nose, and almost no chin. Is he human? I wonder. Although I'm shocked to see such features, something in my hollow memory signals that I've seen this man before. But seeing him even for the tenth time is a shocking experience.

Now I start to doubt that I'm in a real prison. Is El-Deen real? Where have they found a shell-backed man with turtle features to interrogate the inmates? Is he a devotee? A clergy? A crazy half-sheikh without a turban? Where has the other half of his body gone?

"Lift his shitty head up for me!" Ha-G orders.

A third guard rushes to the gurney, grabs my head with both hands, lifts it up and holds it in front of Ha-G's face. His long knotty fingers hurt my skull. Ha-G slaps me several times with all his might. His hand is strangely wide and flat, as though made for slapping.

"Who did you work with?" he asks. His face is too close to me and I feel the odor of his mouth. It's a strange musty smell, sour and bitter and very sharp.

The odor of old cheese or long forgotten vomit on an unwashed shirt. He blows a heavy wave of breath onto my face and says, "Name the organization!"

"There is no organization," I say. Or I think that these words come out of my mouth.

"Where were you arrested? You can remember this one, can't you?"

I stay quiet. I'm thinking hard to remember where they found me. Haven't I remembered this many times before? Or, maybe Kamal told me. Once I knew where I was arrested, but now I'm blank. Ha-Ge, fed up with my silence, slaps me again. My head is still in the guards' hands, and is shrinking like a squeezed pomegranate. The guard's knotty fingers are taking my juice out.

"I ask you one more time, motherfucker, where did they arrest you? We know this, because *we* arrested you. I just want you to talk, bastard! You don't even remember this?"

"No," I say and release my breath. I'd held it for a while, so as not to breathe in Ha-G's odor.

But before I can breathe again, he shoots out from between the two guards like a cannonball and slaps me with the back of his left hand. A large ring on his third finger tears my nose and blood gushes out. I recognize the Great Leader's picture carved on the gold-rimmed carnelian ring. Everything turns around my head and I see millions of black dots swimming in the air. Shit Mouth's saliva, like a shower of venom, pours on my face and this is so nauseating that I forget about the pain and the thick dark blood dripping from my nose. I close my eyes and cry, tearless and soundless—a lonely cry.

"You bastard, devil, son of a whore, you worthless insect, I'll make you lick my ass, you motherfucker! Are you playing with me? With *me*? Do you remember who am I, or have you forgotten this too? I am Ha-G, the Shit Mouth, the Head Trainer of the University, the Angel of the Gate of Paradise! The strongest arm of our Father, La-Jay. No one is stamped with damnation or salvation without passing through my gate! You want to go to heaven? I'm the doorman. You want to dive in the pit of hell? I'm the watchman, sitting in the box, issuing your bloody ticket! Do you know me now, bastard? I'm the Head Interrogator, the Great Leader's Special Advisor, a veteran of the Holy War! Do you think I was born with half of my body in a sack, bastard? I sacrificed it to the Last Holy One, the Absent One, in the battlegrounds. I sacrificed it to the Holy War!

"Now, I'll show you," Ha-G goes on, "I'll do something that makes you wish for death. But then I won't let you die. Do you hear me? I won't let you die, bastard! Bring that miserable sight here! That bag of shit! They have to look at each other face to face and tell me stories. Take me to my desk now! And bring me a hot tea, my throat hurts."

The guard drops my head and runs toward the end of the room where the hooded people are. While Ha-G's two guards sit him down, the one who was holding me drags one of the hooded people with a leash. This person is shrouded in a white gown, from the shoulders down to the floor. The gown even covers his or her hands and feet. This inmate is small, shorter than me.

My heart hammers against my chest. I feel like throwing up. What are they planning to do? Is this her? They want to unmask her and force her to witness my torture. Or, make me witness her being tortured. But why? What do they want? My name? If this is Sahar, she may have told them my name. Or, may not. She may have resisted.

But, is Sahar small? Smaller than me? When was the last time I saw her? Where did I see her? Does she exist, or is she just a figment of my imagination? What if she doesn't exist, has never existed, and I have made her up to survive in El-Deen? But, what if she exists? She is my twin, here in El-Deen, in the same room, at the foot of my gurney, head in brown paper bag, body in a long white gown.

No, I don't want to see her. Not here, not now. I have to leave. I must leave. I'll make myself go. I'll manage to go before they take the hood off. Shit Mouth screams something I can't understand and the room spins around my head. I'm on the white horse again.

The False Rakhsh

Gallop and gallop and gallop—we are still turning in a wide circle around the clay dust arena. I don't have the reins in my hands. Sahar is holding onto me and I'm pressing my thighs to the horse's moist body. It's life and death. I have to keep us, both of us, on the crazy horse until he finally stops. If we fall, we'll die.

The horse has all the power, I have none. He runs fast now, makes us shake and sway. He slows down, neighs, and lifts his front legs up. When he gallops again, slower, we see Mother sitting on the terrace. Saba blows Mother's French perfume onto our face. Sahar screams, "Mother, help!" But she can't hear us. Saba mischievously takes her voice somewhere else. Mother laughs and waves to us. She is happy, because she's having a good time and we're riding General Nasri's favorite horse.

The horse passes the tall, skinny valet. Now, he is laughing too, yelling something in the wind and shaking his hands. The horse neighs again, this time louder and longer; he rises up on his hind legs and bends the big knuckles of his front legs. Sahar screams and slips off the horse. We fall. I hear Mother screaming in the terrace. The valet rushes toward us, helps us get up. Our new clothes are all red with clay dust, but neither of us is injured. The horse gasps, staring at us with hatred, as though he is mad that we're still alive. The black rim around his eyes, his wide nostrils shivering furiously, his long forehead divided by his snow white mane, all look evil to me. This is an evil horse, Sahar. Watch out!

We walk. Our knees shake, our thighs throb, our hip bones hurt and the cloudless sky spins around our heads. But, we're alive. We shake the dust off our clothes. What a pity—these were our special clothes for the party, all light-colored. Sahar's puffy chiffon skirt is stained with red clay and my white starched shirt and blue pants are dirty, too. Sahar's pink satin ribbon is lost and her wild hair stands up as if she's just been electrocuted. My red bow-tie hangs miserably from my neck.

Mother stands in the terrace, looking at us. She makes sure we're not injured and sits down again, sipping her drink. She sits with General Nasri, his wife, and his brother-in-law, Prince Amir Khan. Mother wears a gorgeous turquoise dress that Aunty Zari made specially for this occasion.

"He is a naughty horse, isn't he?" the valet says. His long face resembles the horse's. "His name is Rakhsh. He's an Arabian horse, a gift from the Amir of Bahrain to the General."

"How come he doesn't have an Arabian name?" Sahar asks. Her tone is bitter and challenging. "Rakhsh was Rostam's horse and he was a red horse, a very kind horse too," Sahar says.

"Whose horse?" the valet asks, while drying the horse's sweaty back with a large towel.

"Rostam's horse. Rostam was the strongest ancient hero. He could lift the White Monster up with one hand or chop off the seven heads of the dragon. Whenever Rostam was in trouble, his horse Rakhsh would come out of the ocean, fly to him and save him. Haven't you heard about him?" Sahar says reproachfully. "It's even in the school books."

"No, I haven't. This one can't fly!" The valet laughs and slaps the horse's fat butt. "And I'm sure his master is no monster killer. He can barely lift a child up!" he laughs more and leans his head toward the General.

We turn toward the terrace to take a closer look at our host. He is standing now, looking into binoculars, pointing at the mountain range on the north side of the building. He hands the binoculars to Mother. He is a short man, just a bit taller than us, maybe up to the valet's chest. But he owns the green castle and the stable full of horses and the multi-level garden, so it doesn't matter if he's short. Our grandfather is tall and strong, but owns three crooked houses and doesn't own the multi-level tenant house, the beggar house, anymore. Salman the Brainless, the tallest and strongest of all men, doesn't own anything, except a rusty chain and a knife.

The Multi-Level Garden

"Passed out?" I hear Doctor Halal at the other end of a long tunnel.

"The son of a bitch is pretending..." Ha-G shouts.

"Let me examine him." Halal approaches me.

Sahar and I hold hands and walk toward the castle. Halal's cold fingers lift my eyelids. He says something. I can't hear anymore. I'm going to stay with you, Sahar, I tell her. Let's go and sit in the garden.

"His eyes have rolled in, sir. He is not quite conscious. We have to postpone this."

"This is a fucking trick—"

"Sir—"

They slap me. But no matter what, I'm going to stay with Sahar. We hold hands and walk toward the garden. Our knees buckle and our thighs throb. It feels funny to walk. Mother laughs in the terrace, we look up to see her. She is sipping a pink drink with a crystal straw in the tallest glass we've ever seen. Mother's blue eyes are turquoise now, the color of her dress.

She has set her hair, lifted it up in a turban-shaped *chignon*.

Since she has started going to the beauty school, Mother's hair is always set. We haven't seen her naturally curly hair for a while now. But, this turban they've made for her is too big and makes her look like an ancient Egyptian queen. She looks so different. She is not pale and tired-looking anymore. She is not frowning or complaining, but laughing. A beautiful, carefree queen.

"I won't postpone this interrogation!"

"I've no choice, sir, but to report this to our medical advisors. This is unheard of. You can't interrogate a corpse, sir!"

"I will!"

More shouts. I can hear them. I'm aware of them. I know that Halal and Ha-G are fighting over me. But I don't want to follow this. No matter who wins, I'm going to stay in the garden with Sahar.

"Sahar, the man is a real prince. Did you see how Mother warned us in the car to behave ourselves?" Look at his white suit. And he is big too, much taller than Grandfather."

"The same size as Salman the Brainless," Sahar says.

"Or the Monster of the Well."

"I will ask for a special meeting with Brother La-Jay and the medical advisors!"

"You can ask for one hundred meetings, Doctor—I don't care! What I'm going to do, is purge! And I have the power to do it. The Great Leader is on my side! I'm going to throw you and your advisors out of the Holy University!"

"For your information, sir, I visited His Holiness last week. He supports me and the advisors."

The Prince has a thin moustache that he fingers all the time. He twirls the ends, smooths the prickly hair, pulls and plays with it. He looks at Mother instead of looking at the mountain that the General is fervently lecturing about. The Prince is smoking something thick and smelly, bigger than Uncle Musa's cigarettes, and much bigger than Bashi's dung-smelling papers that look crooked and yellow. This one has a nice scent. The breeze carries it all the way down to the red-brick pathway we're walking on.

Now the Prince talks with that thick stick between his teeth. No one notices us passing under the terrace, or maybe Mother does, but she ignores us because our clothes are not clean anymore. She didn't introduce us to the hosts when our clothes were clean; now she definitely won't.

We wonder where our friends are—Moni, Mina and Minoo—the General's son and daughters. We walk to the south side of the building to find them. Here, a large marble deck looks over the multi-level garden. Children play in the first level. Their laughter and screams blend with the chirping of many birds flying around the willows.

"Sahar, why did we go to the arena at all? We should've come here from the beginning. Look how beautiful everything is!"

"Because Mother wanted us to ride the General's horse. A big deal! That mean, ugly horse has stolen Rakhsh's name," Sahar says.

"Mother has been here many times, Sahar. Hasn't she? She has seen everything before."

"Mrs. General likes Mother. That's why she invites her here."

"Mother wants to finish her beauty school and open a Salon around here! I heard her saying this to Maman," I say.

A door slams.

"Take this miserable sight away. Put the hood back. We won't cancel the interrogation. We'll just take a break! Dial Brother La-Jay's number for me and give me another hot tea."

Ah, they're going to leave me alone, Sahar. A break. Did you see how it worked? Just staying with you. All the time. This is what I have to do here. Stay with you all through. This is not a trick, Sahar, because you are real and you're really with me, aren't you? Now, let's talk more. About Mother. Let's leave this turtle alone. Let him call Brother La-Jay. Let him have his tea.

"Well, why does Mrs. General like Mother? Mother is a poor woman. Today I realized that Mother is poor, that we're all poor!"

"She is pretty," Sahar says.

"Oh, yes. Especially with this turquoise dress. Did you notice how her eyes have become turquoise too? She smells so good that I want to hug her and stay like that for a long time."

"She is pretty. That's why General Nasri's driver comes and picks her up," Sahar says.

"I know."

Glasses clink in the terrace above us. We look up and see a group of men and women standing, facing the garden, drinking and laughing. A woman laughs louder than everyone—a shriek of joy. The children scream and run through the bushes. The nurses follow them. The birds chirp and hide inside the willow branches. The breeze brings the sweet scent of saffron. We hear china dishes clanking. Behind us, across the deck, white uniformed waiters walk in haste; they carry large silver trays.

The room is quiet. Everybody must have left. I won't open my eyes again. Someone might be standing at my side. They took the hooded person away. I better go back to where I was and find out why the General's driver comes once a week and takes mother to the green castle.

When the gray-haired, gloomy-faced chauffeur drives the long black car up the hill, parks it in front of Sheikh Ahmad's match-box house, gets out to open the rear door for Mother, Sahar and I shrink and melt from shame behind the window of the triangular room. Maman, our aunts, the sheikh's wives, and all the other neighbors shrink and melt behind their windows, too. We all want this large black ship to go away. It goes away but takes Mother with it to the Alleys of Heaven—not far from the Monarch's White Marble Palace—to General Nasri's Green Marble Castle.

Sahar and I sit on the first step of the deck and watch the kids playing in the first yard, but we keep thinking about this: why does Mother come here? And now she brings us too—to this garden party. We've never been to a garden party before, or to any party except family gatherings—informal ones in Grand-Lady's room, under the quilt, or formal ones in Grandfather's room, on rented chairs.

Mother borrowed some money from Grandfather to buy us new clothes. She borrowed money for her turquoise dress too, promising that she'll not only pay that back, but pay more, help the whole family, help Grandfather to repair the three falling houses. She went to the corner fabric shop, the one next to Daryani Grocery Store, and bought herself this silky turquoise material and asked Aunty Zari to make her a dress. She promised her sister she would pay her later.

For weeks, Mother was excited and talkative. She called us to her bed and just like old times she hugged us, telling us stories about this castle. She described the multi-level garden many times, before we came here. Mother didn't talk about anything else. She didn't talk about Father and how they fell in love. For a long time now, she hasn't talked about Father, not since she cried in Baba-Mirza's house and said that she was a widow and not a widow.

And now we're on the deck of the castle, sitting on the step, watching the garden. There are so many things to watch. Things we've never seen before.

More than a dozen children play. One of them is the wolf and has to chase the others—the sheep. They all scream and run away to hide behind the trees. The wolf touches one and then the one touched becomes the wolf. Two ladies in blue uniforms stand at the bottom of the steps and watch the kids. Now and then they say something in a foreign language. They don't let the children touch the flowers or get close to the big pool. The flowers are all roses and they are the darkest red, almost black. The pool is neither round nor rectangular, but natural looking, like a lake. Five white swans and one black swan skid lightly over the glassy water. Weeping willows bend down around the pool, as though watching themselves in a mirror.

In the second level of the garden, we see bright red tulips, another lake-like pool and more weeping willows, swaying in the breeze. In the third level, the flowers are white. Mother has told us before that they are Arabian Jasmines. Their scent is stronger than any other flower. On the third level, there is a lake, with rare fish, General Nasri's treasure, but we cannot see them from here. We are dying to go down to all the levels and see these marvels, but we can't pass through the children and the nurses without being noticed. Besides, maybe it's forbidden to go to the lower levels.

Mother has told us that a stream, a branch of the Old North River, passes behind the rows of jasmines at the end of the third level, finds a way out through the wall, and joins the mother river behind the castle. The mother river pierces the mountain, rolls over many stones, flows inside tunnels, and finally reaches the sea.

"Can you believe that this stream is a branch of the same river that we always see? The one we walk over on its ugly bridge?" Sahar asks me.

140

"In our neighborhood, the river is dirty and the bridge is broken," I add.

"When the river passes Faithland, it gets even dirtier and uglier," Sahar says.

"The ditch at the wall of El-Deen is the worst part of the river. That's where Afreet the watchdog of prison lives, ankle deep in blood. But here, Sahar, here is like—I don't know what it's like, because I haven't seen anything like this before."

"I know."

We are quiet for a while, watching the boys and girls run around the trees and chirp like the birds above.

"He kissed her hand when we came in, the big Prince," I start again.

"Kind of long too. In front of everybody," Sahar says.

"Mother is prettier than all the rich women here."

"So?" Sahar looks at me. Her eyes shine in the sunlight. The green of the willows, the blue of the cloudless sky, the golden light of the day, all reflect in her glittering chestnut irises, making them hazy and wavy.

"Did you see how the big Prince was staring at her?" I ask.

"So?" She repeats again. She is mad.

We keep quiet and watch the children. Now they are in two groups pulling a rope from both sides, the blue uniformed nurses supervising their game. The nurses keep shouting something like, "Alle... Alle..." It seems that all of the children can understand this language. Moni, the oldest of the General's children is the first one in the right hand team. Mina, his sister, is the leader of the left hand team. Moni is few years older than Sahar and I. Mina is the same age as us. Minoo, the youngest of all, is in the kindergarten. Mina's team falls down on the marble floor and screams. For a second we see a colorful pile wriggling on the light green marble, laughing and screaming.

"Some of these kids are in my ballet class," Sahar says.

Madame Aida's School of Ballet

One warm afternoon in May, almost at the end of the first grade, Mother came to Santa Zita and told us not to get on the schoolbus, she was taking us somewhere. She was all dressed up in her olive green *deux piece,* a bit too thick for the May weather. The girls of the hairdressing school had set her hair like a tower on top of her head. She had high heels on and looked very tall. But we were tired and very hungry—we didn't want to go anywhere, except home where we could eat our usual snack, bread and cheese with sweet hot tea, and play in the street with Cyrus, Kami, and Sheikh Ahmad's sons. But Mother held our hands and made us walk along the shady sidewalk of Old North Road. We were going toward the north, toward the rich people's neighborhood, the Alleys of Heaven.

"Where are we going, Mother?" Sahar asked.

"To Madame Aida's," she said briefly.

Sahar and I didn't ask who Madame Aida was, because Mother was in one of her quiet moods. She was far away, and didn't want us to bring her back. Whenever she had the thick book on her lap, sitting in bed behind the window of the triangular room, staring at the empty street, she was like this. Even if we asked something, she didn't answer.

We looked at the houses on our right side. They were very different than the houses in our neighborhood. Were they houses, or schools? Each of them was the size of Santa Zita, but much nicer. Most of the gates were open. A shady road between the glossy green boxes took the large cars to the tall, wide buildings. There were long walls protecting the gardens, climbing vines covering them and purple jasmines hanging over the top, peeking into the street.

"How many rooms do these houses have, Mother?" Sahar asked.

"At least fifteen rooms," Mother said.

"How many rooms does the Monarch's Palace have?" she asked again.

"At least one hundred rooms."

Sahar sighed. We turned right to an alley, where we couldn't see the sky anymore because of the branches of the locust trees clenching their twigs together, making a dome above us. There was no need to read the sign of the street. This was the main alley of the Alleys of Heaven.

Mother stopped at a three-story brick apartment. A soft melody dripped down from the third floor. We looked up and saw an open window in a little semi-circle balcony, full of star jasmines and geraniums. The scent of the tiny star-shaped flowers made us drunk and dizzy; the smooth music was dreamy. Mother pushed the door gently and we entered a small, very nicely furnished waiting room. A few women were sitting, some reading magazines, some chatting in whispers. The fat leather armchairs were inviting. In the middle of the low glass table a big crystal bowl full of candies winked at us. We couldn't take our eyes off it. But there were more things to see.

On the walls, beautiful women were flying in white puffy dresses, their arms wide open, their legs stretched out as much as their arms; they flew with four wings. Men too—legs lifted up touching their ears, or in flight with four wings.

None of the ladies in the waiting room looked like Mother, or like any of the women we knew. Their hairdos were big, like oversized cabbages on top of their heads. Their faces were painted with green and red powders. Their perfumes were too strong. We stood there in our dusty black and white uniforms, and our mother in her best dress, which was very plain compared to what these women had on. We stood there paralyzed.

A lady who was smoking a long cigarette, her smoke smelling of mint chewing gum, said, "Who do you want to see?"

"Madame Aida," Mother said.

"Are you sure? This is a dance class," the woman said, studying mother from head to foot.

"I know," Mother said and tried to smile.

"She's teaching upstairs," the woman said and looked at her magazine again.

We stood there, not knowing what to do. There was no place to sit. Some of the women were still staring at us, and some ignored us.

"I'll make room for you here, come and sit!" a short woman with big orange hair said. "I'm Mrs. General Nasri. My daughter Mina is taking her ballet lesson upstairs. Come and sit here."

We all crowded beside Mrs. General on the leather loveseat and she started to talk to Mother, nonstop, about herself (the only daughter of the former Prime Minister), her husband, the General (the right-hand military advisor of His Majesty), her recent trip to Europe, her shopping in London, her vacation in the South of France, her children's Swiss nurses who brought them to the dance class, but one was on vacation and the other was sick, and how hard it was for her to take them here twice a week, although the driver drove (she never did, she hated it), and so forth. Then she stopped and asked questions from Mother.

"Where are you from?" She asked.

"Here," Mother said and forced herself to smile.

"You don't mean you live in the Alleys of Heaven, do you?"

"No, we live in New Spring, it's further down the road."

"Oh!" she said and all the other women studied us again.

"Where did you hear about Madame?" she asked.

"From herself," Mother said.

Now every single woman, puzzled and confused, scrutinized Mother's face all over again.

"Oh, you're Madame's friend?" Mrs. General asked.

"She comes to the Academy of Hair Design. I've trimmed and set her hair several times."

"Oh, you're a hairdresser!" Mrs. General said.

"I'm going to be," Mother said bashfully. The women squeezed their lips and turned back to their magazines. "I told Madame about my twins." Mother continued, "I told her I wanted them to learn to dance. She said bring them to my class. She gave me her address."

"Do you know that she is the best? The most expensive? I wonder why she goes to the hairdressing school to fix her hair? We have several European salons around here," Mrs. General said with genuine wonder.

"She is stingy!" The woman with the long cigarette said in a hush and pressed her cigarette butt in a crystal ashtray. "Haven't you heard? She is famous for that. She doesn't want to spend money. I guess they don't charge in those hairdressing schools, do they?" she asked Mother.

"No. It's free," Mother said.

"She was a poor Russian immigrant when she opened this place," Mrs. General said. "But she was the best. She used to be the Prima Ballerina in Moscow, then she fell and broke her shin. And that was it. The end of her career! That's her on the wall, can you believe it?" She pointed to the picture of the beautiful girl flying in fluffy dress. "She is the best ballet teacher in the capital. And her tuition is high too. I wonder why she doesn't go to a decent beauty salon." Now she hushed her voice more and added, "Do you know that even the little princess comes here to take ballet lessons?

"Really?" Mother asked.

"Yes. His Majesty's youngest. Her nurse and two body guards bring her twice a week. She is not here today, otherwise, they wouldn't let you in. They would check identification."

"Oh..." Mother blushed.

All this time, Sahar and I were listening with one ear to this conversation and the other to the smooth music, which now and then would muffle or stop with Madame's harsh voice from a room upstairs commenting, or counting, or banging her stick on the wooden floor.

Now the music stopped and didn't start again. In a minute Madame Aida descended the steps. She was an old woman, short and overweight, thick around the hip and thighs, with a painted shrunken face. She had a red dress on, showing her short muscular calves, which were lined with blue knotty veins. She limped and leaned on her walking stick. Sahar and I instantly looked at the flying girl on the wall and back at the lame Madame. She ignored all the women and came straight to Mother, greeted her in a funny accent, locked Mother's hands in her crooked fingers, said how happy she was to see her and the twins, and took us upstairs.

In the large room on the third floor, surrounded by mirrors, Sahar and I stood half-naked and Madame Aida examined our bodies—mainly our legs. Like a Mongol buying a good horse, she looked at Sahar's body with a satisfactory smile. She didn't like me because I was too shy, I hunched and bent my neck, staring at my toes all the time. I almost peed in my shorts when she examined my legs with her rough crooked fingers.

She accepted Sahar into her first level. She said she liked her long neck and her boldness, the way she smiled and stared into her eyes; Sahar was graceful and she was going to make her into a dancer, "a real one," Madame emphasized.

That's how we were separated for the first time—Sahar and I. Every Monday and Wednesday, Mother appeared in the schoolyard and took Sahar with her. I rode the bus alone, crying in my throat all the way to the New Spring stop.

Lunch under the Chandeliers

Moni comes. Sweat drops glow on his flat forehead. He apologizes for leaving us alone. He talks like a grown up, like a gentleman. He says,

"Pardon me..." all the time. He invites us to lunch. Passing under the round terrace, he explains how the architects designed their small castle. If anyone chose to sit in the east part of the terrace, he would see the green pasture, stretched beyond the clay dust arena, to infinity. This is where Mother was sitting with the General's family. The west part of the terrace, Moni says, is called the Sunset Terrace, one can watch the sun setting behind Mount Alborz's white peak. The north part was designed for those who want peace and tranquillity, so it faces the Old North River, which flows calmly and constantly in its stone bed. The south terrace faces the multi-level garden, the black swans, roses, tulips, Arabian Jasmines.

"What is that tall tower?" Sahar asks, pointing to a turquoise minaret glowing in the distance in the middle of the green meadow.

"That's the family mausoleum. We'll all be buried there. It's scary. But it's a fun tower, it moves."

"Does it really move?" I ask.

"Yes. Father had the architects build it after the famous moving minaret in Esfahan. If you stand on the roof of the tower and walk to the right and left, the tower sways."

"Wow!" Sahar and I say, staring at the glittering minaret.

"You have the biggest house we've ever seen, Moni," I say.

"You know, our house is the fourth or the fifth best after His Majesty's White Marble Palace. I wish it was the second best. I don't like it here. It's boring," he says. "We don't have a private beach."

"But the sea is just behind the mountain," Sahar says. She knows this from our geography book. The biggest lake of the world, Caspian, which is called a sea for this reason, is north of Mount Alborz.

"I know," Moni says. "Our father says he would spend millions to bring the sea here if he could, but Mount Alborz is too heavy to be moved."

"Mother Alborz is a strong giantess!" Sahar says. She looks at me and winks.

"Why do you call it 'Mother Alborz?'" Moni asks. "Why giantess?"

"My brother and I think that Alborz is a woman. The strongest of all. Our uncle believes that she will shake and destroy the whole world after twenty-five years."

"Who is your uncle?" Moni asks, fascinated.

"A poet-prophet," Sahar says and winks at me again.

"Where is he now?"

"In his cell, in the multi-level tenant house."

Moni is puzzled, but he is too polite to ask more. We've made a full round of the castle and we're back on the deck again. Moni stops at the open glass doors of the large hall and we see that all the tables are set for lunch. The hall looks like a big, fancy restaurant. Moni looks up at the huge chandelier with hundreds of candles burning in crystal holders and says, "If Mother Alborz shakes, our house will be the first one to get smashed under the avalanche." He is completely under Sahar's spell.

"Do you remember the last earthquake?" I ask him.

"Which earthquake?" Moni asks.

"Last year, the end of spring. Do you remember?"

"Oh, that. We were in Europe then. The servants told us that the horses broke loose. But nothing happened to our house."

"Faithland was destroyed. Turned into dust," Sahar says.

"Where is Faithland?"

"We'll show you if you come to our house to visit," Sahar says.

"I'd like to see your house," Moni says.

"It's a triangle," Sahar says.

"Really?"

"Really," we both say.

"How many rooms do you have?"

"Two," we say.

"Strange!" he says. "I'd really like to see it."

We eat at a long table—one of the many tables set in the dinning hall. This one is for the children. Mother doesn't need to come and help us. The nurses and waiters do. We look around. Men and women eat, chat, and clink their crystal glasses, drinking wine. On top of the white tablecloths, roses and tulips from the garden are arranged; the huge chandelier above our heads is heavy with hundreds of tear-shaped crystals reflecting the rainbow colors of women's dresses. The women laugh and gossip, show off their jewelry, and fill their dishes with jewel-like food. The food shines like rare gems: golden saffron rice, emerald herbal rice, glittering desserts, rare fruits, stuffed turkey, leg of a lamb, fish fillet, and large black drops of caviar.

Mother sits at the next table, between the Prince and the fat orange-haired Princess, his mother. The old princess looks exactly like her daughter,

Mrs. General, but bigger and much older. She has a half crown full of diamonds on her thin, puffed up orange hair. She looks at Mother all the time and with her hoarse voice, an old man's voice, admires her loudly. "Isn't she a beauty?" And she strokes Mother's bare shoulder.

Now and then Mother turns to look at us. She smiles once or twice. Sahar and I can't tell whether she is happy or not. She may be embarrassed, squeezed between the Prince and his Mother. She may be wishing she were sitting at the children's table, eating with us. She may even be wishing she were home, eating in Grand-Lady's room, on the floor around the table cloth, with Cyrus and Kami nagging and Aunty Zari slapping them. But no, she is one of them now; no one can tell she is from New Spring and she lives in a two-room, falling triangular house. She eats like them, talks like them, smiles like them, but looks more beautiful than them. We hear whispers about her, comments, questions, tales.

"They say she is a princess, a relative of His Majesty's mother."

"Where has she been all this time?"

"She has lived in Italy all her life."

"Oh, that's where Amir Khan has met her!"

"Definitely!"

"Good match!"

"You think so?"

"Why not?"

"Haven't you heard the rumors?"

"What?"

"The Prince. He can't marry!"

"But why? I've always wondered though. He is getting old—"

"It's a long story, I'll tell you some other time—."

In the Pink Room

Feeling ice cold fingers on my eyelids, I murmur, "Don't lift my eyelids... no, let me be..."

"I'm going to make it easier for you to dream." I hear a whisper and open my eyes. Doctor Halal's face is very close to me; he whispers in my ear. I glance around. The room is empty.

"I'll do my best not to let Ha-G whip you. We won't get anywhere with physical punishment. Relax, don't squeeze your hand." He injects something into my vein, but I don't even see the syringe.

Footsteps. Many of them. Gallop of a herd of horses. Doors slam, chairs squeak, guns click.

"So he's up again! Back to life!" I hear Ha-G.

I have to escape. Why did Halal lift my eyelids? Why did he bring me back? This time Ha-G won't have mercy on me. I close my eyes and wait for Halal's drug to work. But I don't feel any difference. What if he has tricked me? What if there was no drug in the syringe? Then I'll be awake and alert and Ha-G will whip me. "Itching sole," Kamal once said. They'll whip me on my soles.

"Ha-G, sir, I just talked to Brother La-Jay—"

"I talked to Brother La-Jay too," Ha-G interrupts him.

"I think we better sit here and meet before starting the interrogation again," Halal says.

"I don't see why we need a meeting. Brother La-Jay wants the process to go on," Ha-G says.

"Yes sir, but he assured me that I can go on with my approach—"

"This is ridiculous!" Ha-G says.

"We need to compromise. The patient has gained consciousness and will become even more alert if we give him few more minutes," Halal says.

"Only a few minutes then. I have other work to do too. We start in fifteen minutes." Ha-G screams at the guards: "Stay outside, we are having a meeting! Bring that bag of shit for the interrogation."

Again the gallop of a herd. The guards leave. Halal and Ha-G sit at the either side of the desk and talk. I know that Halal is using all his might to prolong the meeting. He is waiting for the drug to affect me.

I close my eyes and wait for fantastic images, but all I can see is General Nasri's multi-level garden. For some reason, this is the only image. Sahar and I are running down the marble steps to the jasmines and up to the roses, up and down again, many and many times.

Now we join the children and get barefoot to step in the stream and walk on the slippery stones. The water is ice cold, we scream. We feed the swans of the first lake and watch the glittering fish of the third lake. Fish as thin as paper, as red as blood, fish with butterfly wings, fish with rainbow patterns, armed with long saws.

We run around the round terrace many times, looking at the changing scenery: mountain, river, pasture, garden, mountain, river, pasture, garden. We pass behind Mother and the prince, who are watching the lonely peak of Alborz in the Sunset Terrace.

We wade in the second lake, which doesn't have fish and swans and is made for wading. We splash water at children we don't even know. We laugh with them and they think we are one of them. The nurses dry us and give us fresh clothes. Meanwhile the grown-ups rest in their rooms to get ready for the evening party. The children will have dinner and will watch a movie in the media room before going to bed. We are staying in the castle tonight, leaving midday tomorrow.

Mother doesn't come to say goodnight.

In which room of the castle is Mother resting? Is she alone? Is she thinking about us at all? Doesn't she want to come and see us and say goodnight to us? She wants to, but is too shy to ask. Or, maybe she doesn't want to see us, she thinks that we are fine and we are having fun.

Thinking about all this, Sahar and I sit in the silence of the pink room on our beds. We are sharing the bedroom with Moni and Mina. This is Mina's bedroom and everything is pink in it. The nurse comes with towels and helps us take a bubble bath. The bubbles are pink and smell of strawberry bubble gum. We haven't taken a bath before, only a shower in the public bath, but we don't say we haven't. The nurse gives us pink pajamas to wear and tucks us under the pink sheets. Even in bed with all the lights except the pink night light turned out, we wait for Mother to come and say goodnight.

This is a bunk bed and Sahar is on top. She bends over me and whispers, "She didn't come."

"No."

"Do you miss her?"

"Yes."

"Me too."

Mina falls asleep immediately, but Moni turns and twists in his bed. "If the mountain shakes," he says, "We'll get smashed, won't we?"

"It won't shake now," Sahar says, "My uncle says twenty-five years from now. You won't be here, then."

"I'll live in France. I hate it here." And then he keeps quiet.

"Is everything real?" I hear Sahar's voice from above.

"It's real," I say.

"Do you know what Mother is going to do now?" She asks.

"Get ready for the party," I say.

"They call it soiree here. Do you like Prince Amir Khan?" She lowers her voice.

"No," I whisper.

"Doesn't he look familiar to you?" she asks.

"I don't think we've seen him anywhere before. But he looks familiar, very familiar."

We are silent for a while, listening to the soft snores of Mina and Moni, listening to the tick-tock of a clock somewhere in the room, and seeing images of the swans, horses, flowers, food, fish, and hundreds of tear-shaped crystals hanging from a chandelier, reflecting a rainbow of colors.

The Blank Face

"So, he looks familiar, huh? Good. You're starting to put your shit together. Where have you seen him before?"

This sharp odor, invading my face, is Ha-G's smell.

"I asked, where have you seen him?"

"In General Nasri's house."

"Which General?" he asks.

"Nasri," I repeat.

"Who the hell is General Nasri, Doctor?" He turns his head toward Halal, who must be sitting at the desk. My eyes are closed, but I can tell he has turned his head, because the odor is removed.

"He was one of the Damned Monarch's military advisors, Brother, executed in the first week of the Revolution," Halal explains.

"Have you seen this person in General Nasri's house, did you say?" The smell of rotten cheese attacks me again.

"Yes."

"When? he asks. "Before the Revolution, or after?"

"I was seven and a half, just before the First Revolt happened."

"Seven and a half? Which First Revolt? Are you crazy, or are you playing with me, you son of a fucking bitch!" He showers my face with spittle.

"Who is he?" he asks.

"Prince Amir Khan," I say.

"Who?"

"Prince—"

He hits me across the mouth to shut me up. "Fool! You shit-brain, rotten fool!" He turns his head away. "He is playing with us, Doctor. Don't be fooled by his miserable sight. He planned all this when he was supposedly unconscious. He has made up a shitty drama for us. He was thinking, Doctor, scheming, making up an absurd story about a damned General and a fucking prince. *You* are responsible, Doctor, for this shit! For stopping the Holy Interrogation, when it could have gotten somewhere!"

"Ha-G, sir, he lost his consciousness and we had to wait. But the point is, sir, we can't overdo this. He is talking nonsense now, incoherent. His system is not functioning."

"Bullshit! Crap! I'll take this case to the highest Revolutionary Committee. You're defending a Satan Worshiper, an enemy of the Almighty and His Holy Revolution. I'll take you to the court, Doctor, I'll fight with you! Lift his head up!" Someone lifts my head up and holds it close to his. "Now you! Open your damned eyes and look at me!"

I try to open my eyes, but I can't. My eyelids have stuck together; they are as heavy as metal sheets.

"Open your goddamn eyes, I ordered!" He shouts into my face.

With much effort I open my eyelids a crack. I just want him to stop talking, stop breathing. His breath is now a wind, blowing and hitting tons of human waste into my face.

"Look at this miserable sight now! This bag of shit! We'll start from the beginning. Who is this person?" He points to a ghost sitting on a high stool, close to my gurney. The ghost is wearing a white gown, down to the floor, but the face is unveiled.

In a flash, I remember the two hooded people in the first part of the interrogation. This must be the same person. Or, maybe it's the other one.

"Another moment of delay, and I'll pull your needles out. No food. I'll let you rot here." I notice that a guard is holding the Shit Mouth up in the air, like a diapered baby. "Look carefully and answer my question.

Who is this miserable sight?"

I look at the person on the stool; I see a ghost again. A white-robed ghost. The face is chalk white. No features.

"Who do you see?"

"It's blank," I murmur.

"What do you mean by blank? Hold his head higher."

The guard pushes my head forward.

"No features," I repeat.

"No features?"

"No," I say.

"So, how come you said he was familiar?"

"The Prince was—" I murmur again.

"Which prince?"

"Amir Khan—"

"Where is he?"

"In General Nasri's house. There is a soirée tonight—"

"The General again, the bullshit again. You're playing with me, huh?" He stretches his long arm and grabs my neck. He repeats crazily, "Huh? Huh? Huh? Huh?" My head wobbles on my neck like the hollow head of a plastic doll.

"Are you really crazy, or you want to drive *me* crazy? No bastard, you don't know me yet. I'll make you talk! Pull all the needles out!" He screams. "Let's see if he really wants to die! I'll come back after my midday prayer and I'll bring my cable with me. Leave him here. Maximum security. No one is allowed to get near the gurney. Understood? Take me out; fast!"

The guard who holds my head up drops it. Someone rushes to the gurney, pulls all the needles out and rolls the IV away, to a distant corner of the room. Two guards drag the robed inmate out and above the loud noises of stamping boots, slamming doors and dragging chairs, I hear Ha-G's voice, now from distance: "You have over-drugged him, Doctor, you have made him crazy. Your experiments aren't worth shit! He is useless now. Empty as a bag of farts. I'll take this case to the Revolutionary Committee! I'll take you to the Holy Court!"

The Soirée

The pink clock strikes three times. It's a clown's face, with large eyes and a red open mouth. With each tick tock, the large eyes look to the right and left and a long, red tongue sticks out, slipping back into the mouth again. Sahar and I hold our breath and wish the stupid clock would stop ticking loudly so that we would be able to hear more of the music outside.

This music is soft and dreamy, unlike any other tune we've heard before. It's not exactly like the soft music of the ballet class, nor is it the kind of music Aunty Zari listens to on the radio when she is sewing. It's a mixture of ballet music and the strange music that Baba Mirza's wife, Tuba, dances to. The other unusual thing is the neigh of horses, coming from all four directions. The guests must be riding the General's horses at night.

Making sure that our roommates are in a deep sleep, we both get out of our beds and tip-toe to the pink curtain. Mina and Moni snore like bear cubs. Mina, the eight-year-old, sucks her thumb with munching sounds.

"Let's draw the curtain back," Sahar whispers.

"They will punish us—"

"Who? I don't think they punish children here," Sahar says.

"How about Mother? When we go home—"

"Nobody will notice. We'll just draw the curtain a little bit to see the garden. This room is facing the front terrace, where the multi-level garden is."

"Is this where their party is?" I ask.

"Yes! Fortunately!" She giggles. "We can see the whole thing!" In the darkness of the room, I see stars twinkling in Sahar's glossy eyes.

We draw the pink velvet curtain back, just enough to place our faces in the crack and hide our bodies behind the folds. The wide deck is glittering with phosphorous light, as though many moons are shining all at once. Indeed, down in the first level of the garden—the black rose level—several moons are glowing on the green surface of the marble floor. Further down, on the second and the third levels, more moons cast a bluish light. Some of the moons are large and some small, but on all of them, half-naked dancers whirl and twist with the strange music.

The dancers, all young girls, wear something like green moss or seaweed, which barely covers their breasts and private parts. With each twist and turn, the moss, or seaweed, slips away and shows the nakedness to the guests who are sitting or standing around the large deck, watching the girls.

The guests are the same men and women we saw today, but now wearing even more elaborate clothes. They sip from their crystal glasses, moving and wriggling with the music. But they all have black half-masks on so only the tips of their noses and their lips are out. The large moons on the marble floor and the mossy girls dancing on them are so fascinating that we don't pay attention to the people. We hardly bother to look for our mother either, who must be dressed and masked, standing among the crowd. We fix our eyes on the dancing.

Suddenly the music becomes faster and the girls pull the moss off, throwing it all in the water. They strip naked. At this point, some of the men take off their clothes and join the girls on the moons. Each man picks a girl, and they disappear behind the willows or jump in the glassy fountains.

Horses are everywhere. They move gracefully in all the three levels of the garden, stamping on the flowers. Some naked guests disappear with naked horses, some with a horse and a naked girl. Sahar and I rub our eyes to make sure everything is real.

"Look!" Sahar almost screams, "Mother!"

Now that most of the guests are behind the trees and the rose bushes, or wading in the water, the deck is deserted, and we can see Mother and Prince Amir Khan, sitting on a bench, whispering and sipping their drinks. They both have half-black masks on. Mother is wearing a glittering gown, sapphire-blue, the color of the darkest moment of twilight. The dress is tight around her thin waist and open wide at the neck, showing her marble white shoulders. Her hair is designed in the shape of a big blossom, a fantastic flower on the top of her head, which makes her look much taller than she is. She has scarlet red lipstick on. Amir Khan's chubby hand is on her bare shoulder and his thin prickly moustache almost rubs her ear.

Now Amir Khan gets up, holds Mother's hand and they walk toward the marble steps. They take measured steps in slow motion, gracefully, like a king and a queen, heading toward their throne for Coronation. They descend the steps, reaching the largest moon on the marble floor. Amir Khan and Mother stand in the middle of the moon, as though they are in the spotlight. We notice again how tall and square the prince is. Mother in the long, blue gown (which we now see has a small sweeping tail behind it) is like a little mermaid in the arms of the Monster of the Well.

Sahar sighs and says, "The woman whose name means mermaid, turns into a real mermaid."

"She is not a good match for our Father," I say. "Father is short."

"He wasn't that short," Sahar says. "He has shrunken in El-Deen."

"Father will shrink to nothing," I swallow a lump of tears.

Suddenly the large moon turns red and becomes a glowing crimson spot light. The "Emperor Waltz" fills the whole castle. Like a blue feather in the whirlwind, Mother's prince leads her whirling around the red moon. After the waltz, the red moon slowly slips away and opens like the hot lid of a large furnace. Prince Amir Khan leads Mother down into the ground. We don't see any steps; they just slip inside the ground and vanish as though melting in the burning flames. The red lid slips back again and turns into the pale moon.

Sahar and I are speechless for a while, then I mumble: "Sahar, did you see that?"

"Yes," she whispers. She has held her breath in her chest. "He *is* the Monster of the Well. That's why he looked so familiar."

"What will happen to Mother now?" I ask.

"Nothing bad. He is in love with her. He will cut his own flesh and feed her."

"To make her chubby; to eat her later," I add.

"Exactly the same way as in Mother's fairy tale. But listen!" Sahar says. "We have to go out now. Nobody will see us."

"But where?"

"To the end of the garden, the wall."

"Why?"

"Someone is waiting for us," Sahar says.

"Who?"

"You'll see! Come!"

She pulls me behind. As we leave the pink room in our pink pajamas, I look at the pink clown clock and its moving eyes for the last time, but I have a feeling that I'll see this strange clock again. The large eyes look to the right and the left, make a tick and a tock, and finally stare at me. A red tongue sticks out, making a face. It's as though the clown is ridiculing me for something that I haven't done yet, but which I'll definitely do.

The hour is four.

In the halls and chambers of the Green Marble Castle, there is a strange smell, an aroma of something sweet burning. Like when Maman makes fig jam and she gets busy with other work and her jam burns, sticking to the bottom of the pan. But this is not quite the smell, it's more bitter, much more bitter.

Instead of going out to the garden, we follow the smell, which rises from downstairs, from the basement of the castle. There is a wide marble spiral stairway in the left corner of the big dining hall. We hold hands, walk barefoot on the cold marble and descend. Here we see a hall bigger than the one upstairs, with a different design.

The place looks more like the interior of a Caliph's harem. The floor is covered with many colorful carpets, each a masterpiece of the craft. On the walls there are ancient miniatures in golden frames. One of them is a large panel showing almond-eyed, half-drunk Saghis with dagger eyebrows serving wine in turquoise jars to lazy-looking, lovesick men with black mustaches, who lean on one arm under the tree of life.

Handmade pottery is everywhere, peacock feathers in some, exotic flowers in the others. We see a fantastic collection of ancient armory—pieces displayed on the shelves of a huge oak cabinet, or protected by glass boxes, with little locks on them (because of a rare emerald or a large ruby on the handle of a dagger, or an ancient king's inscription on a sharp, golden blade.)

At the far right side of the hall, comfortable mats and cushions are on the carpeted floor. General Nasri and several men and women lean and recline on the cushions, or they lie down, smoking a long pipe we've never seen before. The pipe is not anything like Grand-Lady's water-pipe. A red spot burns at the tip of a long stick, which they pass from hand to hand. The smell of burning jam is strong here and makes us nauseous. The smokers, wrapped in a thick fog, moan, whisper, or murmur imperceptible things. A small three-leveled fountain made of glistening blue and green tiles is just beside them and water slips smoothly from one level to another, playing a soft, uneven music.

"Let's go up, Sahar. I'm getting dizzy. What if we faint and they find us here," I say.

"Look!" Sahar says. "Look up! The moons!"

I raise my head and see the moons on the ceiling. The same moons that were on the garden floor, now design the basement ceiling.

"We are under the garden," Sahar says.

"Where is the largest moon, the one Mother and the Prince slipped under?" I ask.

"I can't see it here," Sahar says. "Look at all these rooms around the hall. The red moon may be on the ceiling of one of these rooms."

"You don't want to open all the doors, Sahar?" I say, reading her mind.

"I do. Let me see... One, two, three... four... There are seven. Don't worry, follow me. These people are so drunk with this smoke that they won't see us. Let's find our mother," she says.

"Sahar, why did we come out of the pink bedroom, huh? Didn't you say we had to go to the end of the garden, that someone was waiting for us?"

"Yes, I did. But you see, it's always like this. We plan to do something, and other things happen. Do you remember our journeys in the desert? We wanted to reach the wall of El-Deen, but before that we had to stop at the tenant house and things happened there."

"Okay, don't waste the time now. It's almost morning. The guests or the servants will wake up and see us. What is it exactly you want to do?"

"I want to open all seven doors and find our mother."

The Seven Chambers

We open the first door. It's dark inside, but we recognize a large bed in the middle of the room and a moon on the ceiling, but without that phosphorous glare. The moon and the bed are linked with a slide—the kind that we find in any playground. A naked man is lying on the bed moaning; he is tangled in numerous clumps of green moss, trapped in a mossy net. He moves his arms and legs faintly, but there is no hope he can untangle himself. He moans weakly, "Untangle my tangles! Untangle me, girls!" But there are no girls around. All there is, is darkness, like the very bottom of the sea. The man is trapped in seaweed, and the mermaids, gone.

As we open the second door a crack, a blinding light hits our eyes. Again, we see a large bed and a moon above it. This one still shines and throws a strong light on the bed. A slide links the moon and the bed. At the right side of the room, a tall pale woman in a black nightgown sits in front of the large mirror of a dressing table. Her back is to us; she cannot see us, so we linger a bit to see her better. She takes her black mask off; her eyes are half closed, as though she isn't quite awake. She starts to pull long black pins out of her hair. She does this slowly and meticulously, for a long time. How many pins has she used in her hair? Although we are bored, we don't leave, we cannot leave. Under a strange spell, we are condemned to watch the scene.

Now the tall woman lifts her arms up, holds the big puffy hair on top of her head and removes it like a hat. Instantly, she becomes short and shrunken and her head looks very small. Her natural hair—a few strands of greasy, yellowed hair—are sticking to her little skull. Sahar steps back with fear and disgust and holds on to me. The woman puts some green cream all over her face and smooths it around like a mask. Her painted red lips stay in the middle of her green face like a large blood stain.

Opposite the dressing table a door opens and a short, bald man with a big belly steps out. He has satin purple pajamas on. The woman sees him in the mirror and with the strangest voice we've ever heard—a voice that cracks, like an old person's, but is very authoritative, orders:

"Go and change your purple pajamas, Fuful! I'm not feeling well tonight."

"You should've joined the dancers in the garden, my precious. Then I'd have followed you and taken you behind the weeping willows," the man says. His voice is thin as a child's; he giggles into his palms.

"Shut up, you fool, and leave me alone! You were dying to undress and jump on those girls, you bastard!" The woman says and smears a handful of green cream on her wrinkled neck.

"But I didn't, did I?" Fuful says. "I slid down with you, instead. Why? Huh? Because I love you, Malekeh! You are my queen, my beauty." He approaches the woman, kneels down and puts his bald head on the woman's lap. "My eternal love!"

Malekeh grabs the few strands behind the man's head and lifts the bald head up; she takes a fistful of the green cream and smears it on Fuful's face. Now in a thick seductive voice, she says, "If you really mean it, change those silly purple pajamas and wear your green ones, the alligator green."

The man tries to get up, but she says, "No, no, don't get up! Crawl on your little tummy for me."

Fuful crawls on his big belly like an obedient alligator. He turns toward the bathroom, stretching both arms forward. He opens and closes his arms vertically as if they are alligator's lips, making a weird sound as if he is biting the sea animals, chewing them and finding them delicious: "Snap, snap... hum hum hum... yum yum! Snap, snap... hum hum hum... yum yum..."

We don't stay more to see the alligator green pajamas and the rest of the ritual; we close the door and open the third one.

Here, an old man, tall and thin, almost a skeleton, with snow white hair, lies naked on a large bed—the same kind of bed linked to a slide. The moon above still casts some light, but is getting dimmer and dimmer. The old man's body is yellow, calloused, and creased; it is cracked and wrinkled like an old piece of leather. Two naked dancers tie a rope around him as though he is their hostage. But he talks to them in a friendly tone, giving instructions:

"Don't pull it too tight, girls! That's better. It's a bit tight on my neck, though. Aha... fine. Don't forget, I may beg you to stop, but you don't pay any attention to what I'm telling you. Now, you can start!"

The girls, who still have some moss around their breasts and hips, take long peacock feathers out of big vases and tickle the old man on his feet, armpits, neck and all his sensitive parts. He is tied tightly and cannot move, so he makes funny but at the same time horrible noises. First, he laughs, then he moans and begs, and finally he shrieks:

"Ahhhh... Ha ha ha ha... Oooooy... Eh eh eh eh... NOT THERE! STOP! Mmmmm... STOP! THIS IS AN ORDER!" But the girls don't stop.

What surprises us the most is the girls' complete lack of expression. Their faces are blank and stony as if they're doing this because they have to and there is no fun or joy in it. They don't smile. As beautiful as they look, they are lifeless as ghosts.

"Stop! I beg you, stop! Didn't I say just a little bit? Ahhhh... NOT THERE, YOU ARE KILLING ME! STOP IT, I SAID! Do you know who I am? Do you know who you are tick... Ooo00y... ling?"

The girls keep tickling the old man mercilessly. He shakes and jerks like a fish in a net having the last convulsions before death.

"Do you want to see him dying, Sahar?" I whisper in her ear.

"No. It's horrible. I wish I knew why he wanted to be tortured. Let's go, we have more doors to open."

In the fourth room on a large bed under the moon, at the foot of the slide, an old obese woman sits, half naked. Her face has a strange resemblance to a hen's, but it's heavily made-up and now all the reds, blacks, blues and browns run down with her tears. Her legs are wide open and she has a large tray of food between them. Two moss-covered dancers feed her with an extra large spoon. She cries and chews the food, making chuckling sounds. Before gulping one spoonful down, the second fills her mouth. The dancers have lifeless, mechanical expressions on their faces. The fat, old lady tries to say something, but she cannot. She is filled up to her throat with food.

"She is going to burst! Let's get out of here," I whisper.

But before we leave the room, the woman rolls on the bed and lands on her fours like a gigantic chicken. Her enormous ass faces the door. The dancers pull her huge panties down and reveal the white mountains of her behind. They take an enema bag, fill it with food and pump it into her body. With each pump the monsteress screams, but we can't tell whether this is a cry of joy, or shriek of pain.

Sahar covers her mouth tightly with both hands. She feels sick.

"Let's go, Sahar. She is going to burst any second. Let's go."

We tip-toe out and before the door completely shuts behind us, we hear the explosion. The chicken woman bursts like a balloon and her insides fly in the air. We hear something hard hitting the door, but we don't linger to see whether it's a tooth or a gizzard.

Mother is not in the fifth room either. On the large bed we see a pile of naked people, one on top of another. They must have slid down the same slide and landed on each other. These men and woman are half or completely naked, some are wet from wading in the fountain, some are muddy from laying down behind the trees and bushes, some are covered with blue and green bruises from where the horses have kicked them, all are drunk, not quite conscious. They moan, drool and vomit, and only a few struggle faintly to pull themselves out.

Two naked dancers are on duty here. They try to pull the legs or arms out and rescue these people from the pile of human mess. But as though the pile is sticky, or the limbs are too heavy, the girls don't get anywhere and the pile keeps moving and wriggling like a mound of worms.

Now all I want from Sahar is to let us go. "Sahar, it's getting late. The sun will rise any moment and the servants will get up." I beg her to leave the rooms alone and let us go to the garden. But she doesn't listen to me.

"We still have two rooms left. Mother must be in one of these two."

We open the sixth door and Mother is here. The first thought that comes to our mind is: how come Mother is not in the seventh room? Seventh is always the last, the final, where the answer is hidden. So how come she is in the sixth room?

This bed is different from the others; it's a round rotating bed, the size of the big moon on the ceiling. A red slide links the moon to the bed. Mother is still in her twilight blue gown, but she doesn't have her mask on. She sits in the center of the bed on a scarlet velvet cover, leaning on her right hand. Like the glittering tale of a reptile, the long extension of her gown is curved around her on the bed. The flower wig on top of her hair is removed and her natural hair, thick and bushy, hangs over her shoulders. The bed turns around, so slowly that we can study her from all angles. She is a goddess in deep thought.

The bathroom door opens and Amir Khan enters. He is naked. Sahar and I hug each other tightly and hold our breath. Amir Khan is even taller and bigger without his suit on. Long black hair hangs from his chest, arms, legs, and even his back. Long hair hangs between his legs. He goes toward a small table in the corner of the room and puts a record on the gramophone. This is a very sad song, the kind we've heard in movies. The male singer sings, soft and dreamy, about the moon, about his lover and this last visit and then separation, forever.

The Prince opens a drawer and takes a big knife (more like a machete) out and approaches Mother who is constantly turning and now her back is toward us.

"He's going to kill her!" I almost scream, but immediately cover my mouth.

"No, wait!" Sahar whispers. Her voice is calm, as if she knows the story to the end. But she is shaking.

"Pari! My beauty!" Amir Khan's deep voice fills the room and even echoes as though they are inside a well. "Are you human or a mermaid? Speak to me!"

The bed has turned now and we can see Mother's face.

"Are you the same man I dream about whenever I try to remember my husband's face?" Mother asks with a little girl's voice.

"Yes dear, I'm the same man... the same!" Amir Khan replies.

"Are you the same man who opens the flood in my stomach, filling my whole body, when I dream I'm on a swing and the swing swings back and forth?" Mother asks. The bed rotates; we see her elegant profile.

"Yes, Pari, I'm the same man," replies Prince Amir Khan.

"So come and fill me with your enormous body! Pull me out of my mermaid shell, turn me into a woman!" she almost begs.

The music has now reached its peak and the singer is saying something about an April rose.

But Amir Khan doesn't climb into the bed to take Mother out of her mermaid shell, instead, he says, "You are so thin, so fragile, so unreal, so breakable that I cannot touch you. I have to feed you with my own flesh, my dear, and make you plump!"

"Oh!" Mother almost cries. "Not now? Then when?"

"When you have enough flesh, so that I can eat you!"

"You don't mean eating me as food?" Mother asks.

"No, I mean eating you as a girl!" the prince says and puts the machete on his thick thigh and cuts one fat chunk. The blood gushes out and sprinkles everywhere. With one hand, he puts the warm flesh on a plate, while holding his wound closed with the other hand. He sits on the bed and orders, "Come! Hurry up, lick the wound!"

"Lick?" Mother asks.

"Yes, lick... your saliva will stop the bleeding. Didn't you know that?"

Mother bends her head, licking the oval-shaped wound on Amir Khan's thigh. The blood stops gushing out. Amir Khan pours some salt and pepper on the piece of flesh, which looks like a round steak, and gives it to Mother.

"Eat this!" he orders.

She eats the warm raw flesh without a word, blood dripping from the corner of her lips.

The bed keeps turning. Amir Khan lies down and puts his head on Mother's lap. He is weak and tired and needs to rest, but before falling asleep, he says, "Pari, can you smooth my hair and untangle my locks?"

"Sure, dear, but which hair? On your head, or your body?"

"Start from my head. I feel like my skull is itching. Isn't this funny? It's like hundreds of lice are living in my hair. My body itches too. Can you do this favor for me?" he asks tenderly.

"I'll do anything for you, anything!" And she starts to scratch, to stroke, and to untangle Prince Amir Khan's bushy hair.

We stay long enough to see how Mother picks a small lice, squeezes it between her manicured fingernails, and with an expression of victory, searches for the next one. Amir Khan's snores start from low volume and become louder and louder. The bed keeps rotating and the record player keeps repeating the same song over and over again: "The moon is yellow and our love is like an... April rose... April rose... April rose..."

We close the door behind us and sit right there on the floor. We feel exhausted.

"Well?"

"Did you see how Mother's fairy tale came to life?" Sahar asks.

"What's going to happen now? Is she coming back home with us? Can she?" I ask.

"No," Sahar says. "She can't. She has to stay here on that bed for seven days and seven nights. When the Monster of the Well—excuse me, Prince Amir Khan—is through with feeding her his flesh, then—"

"Then what?" I ask.

"I'm not sure. The story says that the Monster eats her, but I don't think such a thing happens in real life."

"Real life? Sahar, do you call this real life?"

"Get up now! It's almost dawn. We have to rush to the end of the garden, someone is waiting for us," she says.

"Wait, Sahar!" I scream, because she is already at the foot of the marble steps. "Wait!" I call again.

"What is it?" she stops.

"How about the seventh door? The last one?"

"Does it matter anymore? We found Mother in the sixth room and the mission is over," she says.

"But it's just one more room. I want to see what is in the seventh room," I insist.

"Okay, let's see," she agrees. We hold hands and stand in front of the seventh door, each waiting for the other one to open the door. This time I do.

There is no furniture except one wooden chair in the center of the vacant room. A boy in white tuxedo and black bow tie—costumed like a waiter in the castle—is sitting on it. His legs are open and he is concentrating hard on keeping a yo-yo moving up and down between his legs. He is a child, only a few years older than us, though his face is old, yellow.

"Hey!" Sahar says.

The boy raises his head, his yo-yo hanging suspended.

"Who are you?" Sahar asks.

"Saboor. A servant. They call me Saboor the Servant," the boy replies lifelessly. He barely moves his old wrinkled lips.

"Why are you doing this?" Sahar asks. "You should be sleeping now."

"I don't sleep at nights," Saboor says. "I have to sit here and wait for orders. These lights tell me which room needs something." And he shows a switchboard on the wall with many bulbs on it.

"You mean, when the guests need something they push a button, you see the light and rush to their room?" Sahar asks.

"Yes. I get them what they need. It's not always food. Different things. My job is to find it—bring it immediately—whatever it is," Saboor says.

"For example what?" Sahar asks.

"Tonight room number two wanted a live alligator, number three, ostrich feather, number four, enema, number six, an Arabian dagger—"

"Did you really find these things?" I interrupt him.

"Yes." He winds the thread around his yo-yo to start again.

"Why do you yo-yo all the time?" Sahar asks.

"To keep from falling asleep. I've tried different ways, but this is the best. Once, I cut my finger and poured salt and pepper on the wound, but still I fell asleep."

"What do they do to you, if you fall asleep?" Sahar asks.

"Whip my feet... then I have to do my job walking on my hands."

"Who whips you? General Nasri?" Sahar asks with hesitance.

"I can't talk—" Saboor says.

"But this doesn't happen all the time, does it? They don't have such big parties—soirées—every night. It's just once in a while," Sahar says.

"I'm on duty every night. If not a soirée, something else. Mrs. General's poker parties upstairs, the General's opium parties down here—" he says.

"But they don't call you that much, do they?" Sahar asks.

"They do. They want impossible things, things I'm not able to find."

"More impossible than a live alligator?" Sahar asks.

"More impossible," Saboor says sadly. "Milk of hen, breath of man..."

Sahar doesn't say anything more. We stand there watching Saboor with his yo-yo, fixing his red, burning eyes on the round, yellow disk that rolls down, comes up, rolls down, comes up, and he does this forever. But before we close the door behind us, Sahar sticks her head in again, as if she can't leave without saying the last words to Saboor.

"Hey! They're all asleep or passed out now, the night is over, go and get some sleep."

Saboor doesn't raise his head or his yo-yo will stop. But, while moving his arm up and down, with a faint voice he says, "The trash and the leftover food, the vomit and the shit... I have to clean them all..."

We close the door, hold each other's hands, and turn our backs to the lazy drinking men and the half-naked Saghis in the Persian miniature. Without even looking at our right and left, we climb the spiral marble steps to the first floor. Neither of us wants to see the sight of the General and his guests again, but we hear their moans and groans and smell the thick bittersweet opium smoke rising up in a cloud. We step out of the large dining hall, finding ourselves on the south deck. A tender breeze brushes our faces as dawn descends.

Ali's Secret and Riddle

We feel Saba's presence, blowing gently between the locks of our disheveled hair. The sky is lavender—the color of Mother's nightgown—but now it turns to silver, and in a second to a milky color; in its glow we recognize General Nasri's multi-level garden, all in ruins.

The tall black roses are smashed, the shy tulips withered, and the white petals of the Arabian jasmines are all scattered miserably around, showing the naked bushes. The glistening mirrorlike water of the lake is dull and gray. No swans swim gracefully.

As we descend the marble steps and walk toward the end of the garden where the stream runs along the wall, we almost trip over the carcass of a black swan. It lies on the marble floor with wide open wings and a long, crooked neck. We cover our mouths not to scream; we move on.

Now and then between the willows, we see a naked leg of a woman or a muddy head of a man. We see Mrs. General's body, short and chubby, curled between the four legs of Rakhsh, the white Arabian horse we rode on yesterday morning. Rakhsh himself looks dead or asleep, laying motionless head to head with Mrs. General. But there is someone else too, who is almost completely under the heavy horse. We recognize General Nasri's tall valet, lying naked under the horse and the woman, his yellow, bony legs and his long, thin head sticking out.

We find panties, neckties, broken mirrors, eyeglasses, false eyelashes, black masks, pieces of clothing, and earrings on the floor of the garden. There are red stains all over the marble steps, but we can't figure whether they are blood stains or lipstick marks. The horses are all gone, but the smell of horse sweat mixed with the odor of human discharge and expensive perfumes are all in the air. The last sights we see are the rare fish of General Nasri, lying flat around the third lake, their scales shining like false rainbows in the morning sun.

"Can you believe all this?" Sahar asks.

"Now I can believe anything, Sahar. Don't look around, go straight to the end of the garden."

The stream still flows in its eternal stone bed, steady and quiet, as though nothing has happened, as though it is still yesterday and the flowers are alive, the swans are proud, and the fish are happy in the cool crystal water. Time doesn't mean anything to the flowing stream, and yet, time means everything. We sit here and look at the wall on the other side of the stream. It's a tall brick wall, exactly the same as El-Deen's wall. We don't say a word; we don't sigh. Silence, total silence, is what we need, and total silence is here, because even the birds don't fly over General Nasri's garden today. Saba has stopped playing with our hair; he has kept his breath inside his cheeks, sulking somewhere inside the drooping leaves of the willows.

Now we hear the old familiar sound, the ancient sound of swoosh, swoosh... dump! Swoosh, swoosh... dump!"

"This is Ali the Bricklayer," I whisper, "laying brick on top of brick."

"He is waiting for us," Sahar says.

"Why?" I ask. "Why is Ali waiting for us?"

"He wants to tell us why he is doing this. He wants us to ask him, 'Ali, why do you lay brick on top of brick and make the walls taller and taller?'"

Saba knows his job. He lifts Ali up and brings him down. We see how

Ali floats like a kite and lands at the stream. He sits with us like once before at the garbage ditch behind El-Deen's wall. His eyes are red from sleeplessness, his hands and face, muddy; he smells of clay and mortar.

"Ali, why do you lay brick on top of brick and make the walls taller and taller?" Sahar asks.

"This is a curse," Ali says, "an eternal damnation. And today I've called you here to reveal my secret to you."

"Why today of all days?" I ask.

"Because today is the day of the First Revolt. This revolt is important enough to be registered in the thick book of our history. The next one will be the real Revolution, which will happen twenty years from now. Today is like a rehearsal for that Revolution."

"Are we in it? In this rehearsal?" Sahar asks.

"You will lead it," Ali replies.

"We?!" we scream.

"Yes. But before that I have to reveal my secret to you. I have promised myself to reveal this secret to the leaders of the First Revolt and ask their advice."

Now Ali fills his big fists with the stream water and washes his face. He takes more fistfuls of fresh water and drinks out of his cupped palms. "You see," he looks at us the same way he did long ago when he talked about the enchanted trees of El-Deen. "The ancient kings have cursed me to be a bricklayer all my life—and my life is very long, longer than anyone can endure. I have to make the walls, all the walls, taller than they are, as tall as they can get, or make new walls and make them tall. Now, if I ever stop doing this, if I ever stop being a bricklayer, I have two other choices: the first one is death. I'll fall down from the tallest wall that I've made. The second choice is to stay alive, but have a different identity, become someone else, someone different than myself, maybe even opposite myself, a stranger to myself and those who know me. Now, what should I do? I'm asking you two, the leaders of the First Revolt—which option should I choose? Raising the walls? Changing into someone else? Or death?"

"Raise the walls and stay alive!" Sahar screams, but suddenly changes her mind and cries, "No, don't raise the walls anymore! It's gloomy, it's dark!"

"Stay alive and become someone else!" I scream. But in an instant I imagine that Ali might change into an evil person and I yell from the bottom of my lungs, "No! Don't become someone else; die!"

"No, don't die, raise the walls!" Sahar says, but then immediately, "No don't raise the walls, stay alive and become someone else!"

"No, Ali, stay yourself, you are good. To hell with the walls, raise the walls!" I cry.

"No, no, no, no! I hate the walls!" Sahar screams hysterically.

We can go on forever, but Ali stops us, laughs so that all the creases of his suntanned forehead open. He says: "You, see, my little leaders, it's not as easy as you thought. You don't need to give me the answer right now. I have time, plenty of time. Now go ahead and get started with your revolt. People are waiting for you. You'll think about me and my life later, after your work is done. I can wait."

"How are we going to start the revolt?" Sahar asks.

"You have to ask Saba to help you. With Grand-Lady's carpet we will bring all the revolutionaries here," Ali says.

"Here?" we ask.

"Yes, to fight with these people. They're not fit to be our rulers," Ali says.

"But these people are already half-dead, they won't fight!" I say.

Ali laughs and says, "You think so? Wait and see how they'll defend themselves and their property. Now go ahead and start. The time is ripe."

We whistle for Saba and give him instructions and in a blink of an eye, Grand-Lady's crimson carpet is here. We sit on the either side of the green peacock and Ali sits on its tail. Our worry is how to fit all the people we need on the small carpet, but Ali assures us that the magic carpet will expand and get larger than its normal size.

The Four Precipices of Oblivion

We glide in the morning sky. Wet clouds lick our faces and playful birds follow us, circling our heads. Alborz is tall and white, her long skirt stretching forever. Below, the Old North River roars and crawls toward the sea, its eternal home. General Nasri's green marble castle and similar castles and mansions of the Alleys of Heaven are now behind us as we get closer and closer to our own neighborhood—New Spring.

169

But while we are still above Alborz, before reaching the three houses of Grandfather, we see a gray one-story building in a precipice between two steep hills. We have never seen this building before, because it is completely hidden in the folds of Alborz's giant skirt. Saba, sensing our curiosity, lowers the carpet, giving us a chance to take a close look at the ugly flat-roofed building.

Now, we see many shaved heads, behind the windows and in the courtyard. Men and women wear gray robes. Bald and pale, they lift their arms to the sky to wave to us. Some laugh and some sit in a corner doing nothing. Some catch the air in their fists or fight with an invisible person. Some cannot wave to us, they don't have arms—their arms are inside their gray robes and the robes are tied tightly around their bodies. Some cry, as though suffering from an intolerable pain; some laugh almost to death from an unbearable joy. Some dance in the dust, kicking their filthy feet in the dirt, spinning in an endless circle; some mourn over an empty grave, weeping without tears. Some hold the air in their arms, rocking a baby; some rock themselves like a baby. The morning has just arrived here in this ugly place. A scream of agony and a violent horselaugh shake our carpet. Ali tells Saba to lift the vessel up.

"Don't linger here anymore; you saw the asylum," Ali says.

"Ali, we've lived in this neighborhood all our lives and never knew such a place existed," Sahar says.

"Nobody wants to know about the asylum. That's why they've built it in the first precipice," Ali explains.

"The first precipice?" we ask.

"There are four of them. They're called the Four Precipices of Oblivion, because people want to forget about the residents of these places."

"Where are the other three?" Sahar asks.

"Do you want to take a look at them? There, on your right, behind the peak of that hill, that's the second one. It's even worse than the first one; there is almost no building. Can you see? It looks like a big opening at the bottom of the precipice. There are four tall brick walls around a big hole. *I* have made those walls. Long ago. They have resisted rain and snow, storm and even avalanche. This is the leprosarium."

The carpet is above the big hole, the deep opening in the precipice. Although the hole is between the two steep hills, still a tall wall protects it.

170

Men, women, and children, naked or half-naked, their bodies covered with large black sores, are smiling at us and waving their hands. Some don't have lips to smile, but their eyes smile. Many don't have hands to wave, so they wave their feet. A few are without feet or hands—they sway their bodies. Some don't have a body, they're just a head, the head moves.

"Are they human?" Sahar asks.

"They used to be. The disease is chewing them up. Many of them are almost completely chewed to the bone, and some still have long days and nights to endure," Ali says.

"What do they eat?" I ask.

"Once a week, the Queen comes above the precipice with her helicopter and her servants throw the leftovers of the white Marble Palace in the hole. They get good food. They are grateful and love their queen," Ali says.

"Let's go, Saba," Sahar orders the north wind. "I don't want to see anymore."

"Where is the third precipice, Ali?" I ask.

"The third one is worse than the second. We'll get there in a minute."

We are quiet. The carpet moves like a wave. If it wasn't for the ugly precipices, we could enjoy this ride. This is what Sahar and I always dreamed about: riding on Grand-Lady's Turkman carpet, gliding over Alborz. Last time we sat on the carpet, it just shook a little and dumped us on the porch again. Now, it's floating in the air, like a crimson heron, piercing the clouds, finding its way through the steep peaks of the hills. Yes, we could enjoy this ride, if the Four Precipices of Oblivion were not here.

"Here, look! Between these two hills. This is the third one," Ali breaks the silence.

Saba lowers the carpet and we see another opening at the bottom of a precipice. This one is deeper in the ground and its tall walls are made of tin. The hole looks like a big tin box, without a lid. Again, men, women, and children look up at us, but no one smiles or waves a hand. We look carefully to see sores or other signs of a disease, but these people look healthy and normal. They are soiled from head to foot and covered with rags. Some of them are half-naked, but others wear layers and layers of dirty rags. Men sit in groups, playing with something like marbles or coins. Now and then, they shout at each other or get into physical fight. The women sit in the dust, leaning against the tin wall; they take the lice out of their children's hair or scratch their calloused skins with long, broken nails.

"This looks like Faithland," Sahar says.

"Only walled and separated from the neighborhoods," I add.

"What is this place, Ali?" we ask.

"This is the beggar-house. Once in a while they collect the beggars and bring them here," Ali says.

"Does the Queen feed them too?" Sahar asks.

"No, the Queen doesn't encourage begging. She thinks they must work. She hates them and they hate her too."

"What if there is no work for them?" Sahar asks. "Like the one-legged man in the tenant house who lost his leg and his job in the sugar factory?" Sahar asks.

"When there is no job they become pickpockets or drug dealers," Ali says. "When they cannot fill their stomachs with illegal jobs, they become beggars."

"Can these beggars get out of this tin box at all?" I ask.

"No. Once they're caught and put in the box, they have to stay here until they die. The dead open the space for the newcomers. It's an endless process. More and more beggars fill the streets of the city, more and more are collected and dumped here, and more and more die here, opening the space for more beggars. But how serious the government is about collecting them depends on their day-to-day policies. For example, at the time of the Great Coronation, when they had foreign guests coming to our country, they collected almost all the beggars. They even collected some of the vagabonds and homeless people who were not begging. This hole was packed full with these wretched people. They died of hunger or got leprosy and were sent to the Second Precipice. Some went crazy and were sent to the First Precipice. A few killed each other, and were thrown in the Fourth Precipice—the Precipice of the Criminals," Ali explains.

We are quiet again. The beggars are indifferent to us. No one waves. We pass.

Ali continues, "The Precipice of the Criminals is the last one, worse than all the others."

"Nothing is worse than the beggar-house," Sahar says quietly. She is in deep thought.

"Why do you think so?" Ali asks.

"I think this is where our real grandmother was, unless there is another beggar-house, a better one somewhere," she says.

"No, that's it. I know about your grandmother; everybody knows. Her name was Lady-King. They called her, Lady-Beggar here," Ali says.

"She died here," I say.

"I know," Ali says. "She died of grief. Because she was a real princess once."

"They should have sent her to the First Precipice. She was crazy, not a beggar," I say.

Now Ali raises his thick eyebrows, creases his forehead, and looks deep into my eyes. He says, "Son, the miseries of these four precipices are so much alike that most of the time it's hard to decide in which precipice the person really belongs. Do you think these beggars down there are all sane, or free of crime? Or the people with leprosy, are they sane? Do you think the lunatics are not beggars, or the criminals are not insane?" Ali sighs and turns his head toward the peak of the mountain, as though looking for something.

"But Ali, the people beyond these steep hills, the people living in their comfortable houses are also insane and most of them are criminals," Sahar says. "We see so many of them everyday. We saw some of them in General Nasri's castle."

"But they haven't turned into beggars, have they? That's why they can enjoy their freedom. The moment they lose their possessions, they end up here," Ali says.

"Let's go to our neighborhood and see who wants to join us for the First Revolt. Let's move fast, and forget about the precipices," Sahar says.

"So, you want to forget about them too!" Ali laughs, "Didn't I tell you? This is the quality of the precipices: oblivion. But, look at your right now. I don't want you to miss the strangest of all. Can you see that huge cage, hanging between the two hills? It's wrapped in a thick fog. Let's get closer. Can you see now? At the bottom of the precipice, there is a lake. They say its water is poisonous. If the criminals attempt to escape from the cage, they'll fall into the poisonous lake and nothing will be left of them except their bones."

Now our carpet is closer to the huge cage and we see how it is suspended between the sky and the lake. Men and woman, barred from each other, sit or stand in the cage. If someone walks, the prison moves and everybody curses.

"Can't they ever move?" I ask Ali.

"They can. But the cage is made in such a way that with the slightest movement, it tilts to one side, like a see-saw, and they think that they are falling into the poisonous lake. This is the way the government is punishing them. These prisoners don't need guards or wardens, they sit, or stand quietly forever and dream about their previous crimes, or all the crimes they could have committed, but didn't have a chance to. They are not doing that bad. They have rich imaginations that help them survive," Ali says.

"I wonder why they want to survive at all," Sahar says bitterly.

"Everybody wants to survive," Ali says. "That's the law of life."

"Are these criminals ever sent to the other precipices?" Sahar asks.

"Yes, once in a while one of them runs out of imagination and can no longer plan a new crime in his mind, then he loses his mind and does something dangerous, like—"

"Like what? " Sahar interrupts him.

"Like committing a real crime. He attacks someone and of course the cage moves like a see-saw and all of the inmates scream and holler. Then a helicopter comes, opens the lid of the cage, sends a rope, a hook, and a straight jacket down, and the other criminals straight jacket the rebellious one. They hang him on the hook and send him up. The helicopter, takes the inmate to the First Precipice—the asylum—and sends him down."

"Does this happen frequently?" I ask.

"No. For two reasons: first, the criminals' imagination is amazingly rich. Their dreams of crimes are sometimes so long and complicated that they don't even want to interrupt their dreams for their ration of food (which is a piece of bread and a sip of water) dropped down every day. Second, they are not willing to be moved to the asylum; they don't like it there."

"I think the asylum is a better place," Sahar says. "It has a building, better food, and people who laugh and play. They waved to us, do you remember? They were not as miserable as the people of the other three precipices."

"These criminals are scared of the lunatics," Ali says. "The lunatics are noisy and irritable—they don't let the criminals dream. No torture is harder for these inmates than not being able to dream. Besides, they somehow like this state of suspension. It's exciting, very close to the way they've lived in the free world."

Saba is still; the carpet is flat and stiff, as if on solid ground. The north wind doesn't take us closer to the poisonous lake and the suspended cage. We cannot see the faces. But the moment our carpet begins to move again, a loud noise like the roaring of wild beasts echoes in the mountain. We turn and see the huge suspended cage, rocking like a barred see-saw. An inmate—a woman—runs up and down the cage, shouting curse words, imperceptible.

"She has run out of dreams," Sahar says.

"Let's move faster, Saba, we don't want to see them falling in the lake. Saba, please, move toward our neighborhood," I beg.

Saba blows under the carpet, raises us up and pushes us into the clouds. The sound of the wind fills our ears and the screams of the inhabitants of the cage fade away. We are quiet for a while and happy that we are getting distanced from the Four Precipices of Oblivion. But, Saba slows down as if knowing Ali's intention.

"Don't you want to take a look at El-Deen, from above?" Ali asks.

"El-Deen?" I ask. I realize that for a while now I haven't thought about the monster and our father inside.

"The Four Precipices of Oblivion are just four ugly sores on Mother Alborz's rough body," Ali says. "They are meant to be hidden and forgotten. But, El-Deen is not a pimple or a sore; El-Deen is a monster, it's huge, it's meant to be visible. El-Deen is a constant remembrance, a symbol, a lesson. El-Deen does not contain the poor, the criminal, the insane, or the deformed. It contains the beautiful, the sane, the whole—those who are capable of thinking constructively about a way out of human miseries."

Ali keeps quiet and sinks into a deep thought. We don't know what to say. We are not sure if we have understood what he just said. Do we really want to see El-Deen from above? What if we see our father under unbearable torture? We want his image, the image of him in the white tent shedding tears on our feverish faces, to last forever. We don't want to see him while the torturer is pulling his nails out, or shoving the bottle of boiling water into his intestines.

"No, Ali, we don't want to see El-Deen. Let's go to our neighborhood," we say.

He doesn't insist. We just see the white eyeless beast, the blind giant from the distance, tall and proud, as strong as Alborz, as cruel as her, stretched up into the morning mist behind the hills and valleys, cliffs and precipices. We don't get close to the monster.

A View of the Family from Above

Grandfather's three crooked houses have no roof. We can see all the family. It's the weekend and everybody is home except us. The triangular house is cold and empty. Sahar and I are up here in the sky and our mother is in the green castle of General Nasri, in the sixth room of the basement, where her monster-prince is still sleeping on her lap, while she sorts through his thick hair, looking for lice.

Who can we recruit in the middle house? Uncle Musa? He has probably had a big fight with Aunty Shamsi, and has even slapped her bony cheeks. The fight must be over now because Uncle is sulking in a corner smoking a cigarette, and chewing the hanging tip of his moustache. Kami has escaped to the balcony with a match box and is busy burning the ants. Aunty Shamsi is putting her things in a small handbag to leave. She talks to herself and sniffles.

"Shamsi, you better go back to your parents. He doesn't need you here. Go before a strong wind blows you away, or a hard rain washes you off!"

"Look at Aunty Shamsi," Sahar says. "She is so thin and little that she wears Kami's clothes all the time; and why is she talking to herself?"

"Because she doesn't have anybody else to talk to," Ali says.

"She wants to leave her family and go to her parents," I say.

"As you can see, your poor Aunt has shrunk into a child again. That's why she needs her parents now," Ali says.

"Is there anybody who can help us in the First Revolt?" Sahar asks.

"See for yourself," Ali says. "Look at your Uncle. He has beaten his wife and is smoking—daydreaming, probably planning to get out of this house and find something fun to do—away from his family. Your cousin is burning the poor ants out of spite. Do you need these people?" Ali asks.

"I don't thing so," I say. "But how about Aunty Zari?"

Aunty Zari and her son, Cyrus are on the porch. Cyrus has done something vicious again and Aunty is punishing him. His arms are stretched forward and his mother is whipping his palms with a willow twig. He screams and Aunty Zari whips harder and says something from between her clenched teeth, something that we cannot quite understand. All we hear are scattered words: "Plague—black death—devil—"

"Live them alone," we say. "Let's move."

In the first house, Grandfather's house, Grand-Lady is packing to leave. This is her second attempt to run away. She is planning to walk through the desert, pass the river, reach the mountain, and drop herself on the first flat rock, and die there. Now she is wrapping her water-pipe carefully in a big scarf, her prayer stone and carnelian rosary in a small kerchief. She puts her little embroidered vest on, hides her two long, white braids inside her thin, white scarf and she is ready to leave. But there is one thing left to do. She has to roll up her little Turkman carpet and take it with her. How can she leave without it? She looks for her carpet around the room, but cannot find it. She steps on the porch and looks around. It's not there, either. Saba, as though knowing what is going on, moves the carpet behind a thick cloud.

Maman, our step-grandmother, has squatted with a burlap rag in her hands, scrubbing the soot covered floor of the kitchen. Rats jump and play around her. She wipes her sweaty forehead with her sleeve and chases the rats away. "Shoo, shoo, shoo!" she screams and curses the naughty animals.

In his lab, Grandfather calculates his income with an old abacus. Since he has sold the multi-level tenant house to Sheikh Ahmad, his business in Rad and Rad Real Estate has become very slow. So he does this all the time: click, click... click... and more clicks. He writes something on the paper, stacks the money and ties the stack with a rubber band. Gets up on his stiff legs, goes to the little dark storage room, puts the stack in the purses hanging from the ceiling with strings and returns to his table, counting more money and making more clicks on the abacus. Grandfather's herbs and drugs have gathered dust, he doesn't make medicine anymore. His pictures are forgotten too. His camera is broken; he hasn't developed new pictures for a long while.

Ali says nothing. We leave Grandfather alone to stoop over his accounting work.

Saba lifts the carpet up above Hoori's room. This is the only room on the roof. Planning to build a complete apartment on the roof, Grandfather started the project, but never finished it. This one room stayed alone for

Hoori to occupy it and enjoy the view of the woods of the Alleys of Heaven, the castles, the golden domes, and the turquoise minarets.

On this sunny midsummer day, Hoori hasn't opened her window to look at the view. She sits in the dark room with the curtains drawn, staring at the wall, searching in the foggy corners of her confused mind for a way to die. Images like a slide show come to her mind, click, and change. How about falling down from the roof and smashing like a rotten tomato on the sidewalk? How about inhaling gas? Head in the oven, doors and window sealed. Hanging from a rope? Face dark purple, pee dripping from the pants. Cyanide? Insides on fire, throwing up black bile. Veins cut? staring at the two streams of blood running out of the body. Or, the Japanese style? *hara-kiri*? kneeling on the floor, dagger in hand, body and dagger one?

The images come and go, making her heart beat faster. Her stony moon-white face twitches, her dark eyes widen with fright. She smiles a moment, frowns the next, chooses an image but doesn't like it, clicks to another one.

"Ali, let's take Aunty Hoori with us and save her from this agony," Sahar says. "She is young, she can change. She can help our Revolt."

"To be young is not enough," Ali says. "To be selfless is what we seek. Look at your Aunt. Look how she is obsessed with herself. All she thinks about is her own life which she insists should end right now. Do you really want to try and call her to join us?"

We stay quiet. Ali repeats again: "Do you? Let's try, so that you know what I mean."

The carpet is above Hoori's room now, standing flat like a roof. We drop a rope down and call her:

"Aunty Hoori, hey... It's us, look up!"

Hoori looks up and sees us on the carpet, but she is not surprised.

"Do you want to join us for the First Revolt of the people? We are taking the tenants too. Do you want to come?" Sahar asks.

Hoori gets up and touches the rope. She caresses it like it is a dear thing. Sahar and I are happy that she is touching the rope, thinking about our suggestion.

"Ali, she is holding the rope. She wants to come up. Let's help her climb," I say.

"Do you think she wants to come up?" Ali asks. "Wait and see what she is planning to do with the rope. Look! She is making a loop, and she knows well how to do it too. Now she is tightening the loop around her neck..."

"She is hanging herself with our rope!" Sahar screams.

"Didn't I tell you she cannot think about anything outside herself—outside her life and death?" Ali says.

"She is going to die, Ali. Do something!" we beg.

"Throw the rope down," Ali orders.

"But if we give her the rope, she will hang herself," Sahar says.

"She will, but they will save her this time too. She is not meant to die now, not before she is eighteen and all alone in a small dormitory room in a remote city," Ali says prophetically.

We leave our rope for Aunty Hoori to get busy preparing her second unsuccessful suicide. We head toward the multi-level tenant house.

Summer is the best season for the poor tenants. They can sit outside their hovels, enjoy the sun and chat. They can sleep in the yard instead of cramping inside the dark hovels. They can wash, cook, and eat in the yard. Everybody is here except Uncle Massi who is in his room with his wife. Since Uncle rescued Mariam the Big Mole last winter from under the heap of snow and took her into his hovel, he is the happiest man of the tenant house. They married under the pressure of Sheikh Ahmad who raised hell about a man and a woman staying in one room without the wedding prayers.

So, Uncle Massi and Mariam the Big Mole live in Uncle's cell-like hovel, which does not have room for two people sleeping side by side. People say they sleep on top of each other.

Since there is no roof, we look into Uncle's room.

"How can they sleep like this, Ali? Look at them! And they sleep too much too! It's almost noon now!" Sahar says.

"Let them enjoy their slumber. You're too young to understand certain things. Your uncle has never had a woman in his life. Now he has one. This is enough reason for sleeping this way day and night. But we don't need them for the First Revolt, do we?"

"We definitely don't!" Sahar says, "but I don't think Uncle Massi wants to be left out of this. Have you forgotten how he was leading the people at the night of the earthquake?" Sahar asks.

"He will mislead the people, if he wakes up," Ali says.

179

Now Ali takes an advising tone. He sticks his long forefinger out, moves it in front of our faces, and says, "Avoid three types of people in any revolution, my children: the lunatic, the religious, and the crook; they mislead your masses. I hope your crazy uncle won't get up," he says in a whisper.

The First Revolt

As the carpet lands in the first yard, the tenants gather around it. They have been waiting for us. Children touch the carpet, looking at the green peacock with admiration. Grown-ups ask questions like, "Does it feel good to float in the sky?" Or, "How high can this fly? As high as an airplane?"

Zahra, Ali the Bricklayer's wife, brings hot, fresh tea in small glass cups with sugar cubes on the side. We sit on the carpet, sip the tea and talk about the First Revolt. Sahar and I notice that Ali pulls himself back, leaving the leadership to us. We explain to the tenants that the goal is to land in General Nasri's castle, occupy it, move forward on the carpet toward the white Marble Palace of the Monarch, and surround it.

We talk about the chants, songs, and slogans that we need to sing and shout up there. As we fly toward our destination, other people will join us. We will stop in the courtyards of the factories and poor neighborhoods; we will stop for the university students and peasants; we will gather at least one million in front of the Monarch's castle. This will make him panic. He may even leave the Marble Palace with his private airplane. He may leave the country. Our first success will inspire other revolutionary groups; they will join us and our numbers will grow.

The next stage of the Revolt will be capturing El-Deen. From the Monarch's Palace, we will move to the edge of Alborz's skirt, to El-Deen. We will surround the prison and kill Afreet the blood-sucking watch-dog of the ditch. We will open the heavy gates and free the prisoners. The inmates who are the real revolutionaries and have planned their dream revolution for many and many years in the dark corners of their cells will take over the rest of the revolt. Violence is not our goal and we won't use it, we tell the tenants, unless the enemy uses it to defeat us.

The meeting takes several hours and Zahra brings many trays of hot tea.

We drink and discuss. Bashi the Janitor suggests that we should take some weapons with us, just in case, to defend ourselves. Everyone agrees and brings something from their hovels. Hassan the Gardener brings his shovel; the Lame says his crutches are enough; Bashi cannot find anything so he brings his old trumpet, the one he uses in the schoolyard to call children to class; Zahra, Ziba, and Zeinab grab their rusty kitchen knives and sooty frying pans and bring a few tin containers of kerosene too. As we sit on the carpet ready to fly, Sahar and I notice that Grand-Lady's small Turkman carpet expands to make space for all.

Ali the Bricklayer hands a flag to Sahar and a banner to me. We try hard to read what is written in blood red on the white banner, but we cannot. We stand and raise our arms up; the tenants look at us and the flag and the banner, waving gently in the evening breeze. They smile with admiration and delight.

It's twilight when Saba smoothly lifts the carpet. We have planned to fly over the second and the third yards and then circle over Faithland to see who wants to join us. But before we completely take off, Uncle Massi flings his door open and appears in the frame. His brown robe hangs on his naked body, his long hair waving in the breeze. He shouts:

"You sinners! You traitors to your poet-prophet! You rotten flock, behold! Heading toward the Revolution without your Leader?" He grabs the long stick that he has been using as a cane, calls his wife, and as brisk as a cat jumps on the carpet. "Mariam!" he shouts, "Come and join me in my first mission. I'm leading my flock to restore justice in the world!"

Mariam the Big Mole, her curly black hair disheveled, her eyes puffed from too much sleep, half-naked, revealing the big mole on her left nipple, rushes out, screaming, "Not without me, Massi my love!" And pulls herself up on the carpet.

We recruit some of the hard-working tenants of the second yard, but we don't let the gamblers and pickpockets sit on the carpet. Hassan the Gardener chases them away with his shovel. In Faithland, Saba is careful not to land on the messy ground; he lifts it half a meter above the gutter of urine and excrement. A few construction workers with their hammers and axes climb up; a few vendors leave their donkeys in the street and join. As we want to take off, we hear a loud holler from the end of the main alley. Now we hear the rattle of chains and clanks of iron balls. This is Salman the

Brainless's gang—the crooks of Faithland. Salman, bigger than ever, with two large skeletons and a few long-tongued serpents tattooed on his chest and thick arms, shakes a heavy chain above his head, runs, and gasps and hollers with his hoarse voice: "I'll smash those who start a revolution without me! I'll wrap this chain around them, and squeeze their juice out!"

The crooks draw blades, butcher knives, and chains and hold the cold weapons on our thin necks. Uncle Massi wants to confront them, but they kick him under his chin and throw him in Mariam the Big Mole's lap. Ali holds his forehead and covers his face, sinking into despair. The carpet takes off with Salman the Brainless and his gang chanting a gang song. Salman says, "Am I the strongest?" The crooks say, "Oh, I am!" Salman says, "Can I fuck them?" The crooks say, "Oh, I can!" Salman: "Thirsty for blood?" The gang: "Oh, we are!" Salman: "Hungry like a bull?" The gang: "Oh, we are!" And then all together, they raise their hoarse voices and sing: "So, we're going to tease them, fuck them, smash them, and squeeze them... for the day has come!"

The moment we get above Hoori's room, she hangs herself and kicks the chair off. The muffled sound of the chair startles Maman in the kitchen. She feels a sharp pain inside her chest and rushes up into her daughter's room where she unties the rope, brings her down and calls for help. Our carpet moves on and we don't see how Grandfather leaves the stacks of paper money on the table for the rats to feed on and rushes toward the scene.

As small as a little old tortoise, Grand-Lady rolls on her tiny feet, with her bundle in her hand. In the blur of the dusk, she walks toward the mountain, where she thinks she should die. Sahar and I look at her from above the clouds and feel despair. But Ali who is sitting behind us, whispers in our ears that we shouldn't be worried for our great grandmother because she won't die on a flat rock tonight. They will find her two days after the First Revolt, unconscious, but alive, and Grandfather will cure her with his famous potion of seven boiled herbs.

Saba blows his breath out in a long sigh under the carpet and as our vessel escalates someone screams, "Wait for me, children, wait for me! How can you leave without me, huh? Don't you need God's blessing in such a moment? Don't you care about your religious duties? Have you prayed? Have you chased Satan away? Has anybody poured water on the dirt and chanted over beads to cancel the bad omen?"

This is Sheikh Ahmad, the one-armed frowny muezzin whose left leg froze in the last snow when he got buried on top of the minaret. Now he limps and runs, holding his long robe with one hand. He trips and falls, gets up and runs again. He reaches under the carpet and begs us to take him with us. We order Saba to go higher and leave the one-armed, one-legged sheikh behind, but it's too late. Salman the Brainless drops his chain down and the sheikh climbs it up with unusual skill.

Uncle Massi says, "This bastard hypocrite is going to ruin my mission. It's not a long time since he was licking the Monarch's ass! Now he wants to join the poor people's revolution!"

Sheikh Ahmad says something in Arabic with many "kh" sounds that we don't understand, but we guess must be curse words. Then the sheikh turns to Uncle and says, "You better keep quiet and cover your sinful wife. I take refuge in God. What a sight! Cover yourself sister, before it's too late!"

When Sheikh Ahmad realizes that Uncle Massi and Mariam the Big Mole don't pay any attention to him, and that Mariam's left breast is still hanging out, so that her mole shows even bigger than normal, he grabs Mariam's skirt and pulls it up to cover her naked breast; but instead, he leaves her round belly and white thighs out. The tenants laugh and the crooks whistle and clap. Ali shakes his head in regret and his eyes fill with gloom. The carpet rises smoothly, while the sheikh's two wives appear at the door of their house with bowls of water in their hands. Looking up at us, they sprinkle some water on the ground, and murmur prayers under their lips to cancel the bad omen and burst the devil's eyes.

Sahar and I do not understand Ali's gloom. Although Uncle, Salman, and the sheikh, the three types of people Ali warned us against, found their way on the carpet, we can still win the Revolt. We feel a choking joy in our bodies and souls. We will break the gate of El-Deen and set our father free. There is no end to our happiness. The carpet moves in the smoothest motion on top of the clouds, as if on the white surf of a vast sea. Sahar and I stand up, raise our flag and banner, and invite everybody to sing with us. In the purest blue of the twilight, when the sky is azure and the sun is spreading its thin orange net over the world, we sing, "Arise, you prisoners of starvation! Arise you wretched of the earth—"

But as the tenants start to sing with us, Sheikh Ahmad screams, "Stop! Stop this double blasphemy!" He tries to get up on his feet, but being without one arm and lame in one leg makes it hard for him, so he shouts, "Stop, I said, you sinners! Don't you know that music intoxicates you? Leads you to inactivity? Don't you know that singing is sin, especially for women? Let's all get up and pray! No words are more appropriate at this moment than the words of God! Rise you sinners! If you all rise, the carpet will be steady. If only some of you rise, we will all fall. What does this mean? Unity! Unity for God's cause! That's what this holy vessel is teaching us! Look at me now—I'm struggling to stand up, but I can't. The holy carpet is telling me that I cannot stand up alone. All of my brothers and sisters must rise too. Rise now and see the miracle! Rise now and pray! Face the Holy Land!"

All the passengers of the carpet—even the crooks, even Mariam the Big Mole—obey the sheikh and rise to their feet to pray. Sahar and I have the same thought: the cunning sheikh is drawing our people to his side. Now he is calling our carpet the holy vessel! What should we do?

Only two people have not risen up to pray: Ali the Bricklayer, who sits at the end of the carpet on the tip of the peacock's tale, plunged in deep thought, remote, and inaccessible, and Uncle Massi, opposite him, playing with the curls of his long hair, watching the sheikh with a sarcastic smile.

In the dark blue sky of this summer night, the silver scythe of the moon and a single red star glow not far away in the horizon. Sheikh Ahmad stands apart from the masses, in front of them, and calls out in Arabic, "There is no god, except God!" And everybody repeats the same thing. Women are behind the men, standing separately in the last row. Mariam the Big Mole, using her skirt as a scarf, repeats, "There is no god—," kneeling down on the carpet, bowing to the crescent moon, her fat, naked butt sticking up, aiming at the sky.

Our carpet, now called Sheikh Ahmad's holy vessel, expands as we stop in the dark courtyards of the factories, inviting the sleepy workers of the last shifts, or as we land in the gloomy alleys of the shanty house neighborhoods, recruiting the tenants. Young men and women of the university campuses carrying their colorful banners and flags join us. They chant their student song: "Move forward, the army of the youth!" The peasants carry their hay forks and rakes. With their dark, calloused hands they shake our hands, and then sit on the carpet.

While passing over the center of the city—the intersection of the four major roads—we see a little man in the deserted streets of late night on an old squeaky bicycle. He bikes toward the Old North Road.

"This is Uncle Yahya, Father's uncle!" Sahar screams.

We tell Saba to lower the carpet.

"Uncle Yahya! It's us!"

He looks up and waves at us without showing any surprise at the sight of a huge carpet, now covering the whole sky, carrying thousands of people.

"Uncle, join us for the First Revolt!" we both shout.

"That's where I'm heading. I'll join you there. This is what I've been waiting for all my life. Long Live the Revolution!" Old Uncle Yahya shouts, waves his fist, and almost loses his balance on the old bike.

"Don't you want to sit on the carpet?" Sahar asks.

"I better not. I'll get sick up there and besides, I'm used to my bike. Good luck children. I'll see you at the end of Old North Road!" He pedals fast and whistles the tune of our song, now forbidden on the carpet.

As he pedals up hill to join the revolt, Uncle Yahya's shrunken body swims in his old gray suit, three sizes larger than him. This small stooped body looks like Father's when we last visited him inside the white tent of El-Deen.

Now the sheikh decides that we can chant slogans only if they are not blasphemous and do not have music.

The workers chant: "Workers, workers united! The monarchy defeated!"

The tenants of Faithland and other shanty towns chant: "Homeless, homeless united! The rich landlord defeated!"

The peasants chant: "Peasants, peasants united! The landowners defeated!"

The students chant: "All the forces united! The monarchy defeated!"

And all together, "Death to the monarchy! Death to the monarchy!"

The gigantic vessel glides over the thin web of clouds and the city below shakes with our chants. The lights flicker inside the houses and the many closed eyes of the city open. People gather on the roofs to look at the sky and see the largest carpet of the world carrying a million people to the Monarch's castle. But the sheikh, fearing that the slogans may get out of his control, screams with his squeaky voice, "God is the only leader!" And many repeat, "God is the only leader!" He screams, "Our party is the party of God!"

And many repeat the same thing.

Salman the Brainless and his gang, in competition with Sheikh Ahmad, rise to shout *their* slogans: "We're going to fuck them and tease them, smash them and squeeze them, for the time has come...."

We reach General Nasri's green marble castle—a standing ballerina with a white tutu around its waist—now in deep sleep. The carpet lands on the eastside pasture where Sahar and I rode Rakhsh, the white horse, this morning. We all step out. There is a moment of silence and confusion. People look at each other, not knowing what to do, or where to go. Uncle Massi climbs the moving minaret—the blue-tiled tower of Nasri's crypt— and addresses the people. His voice is deeper and stronger than ever and echoes in the silent night. For a split second Sahar and I doubt our uncle's insanity. He looks majestic, like a prophet, his robe and dark hair waving in the breeze:

"Behold, my people! The thick darkness of your night is ripped apart now, but not for long. The oppressors will bend low to you, but not for long. They will offer you gold and precious stones, but alas, not for long. Behold! Darkness shall fall again and cover the earth. I can see the violence, devastation, and destruction in the black horizon of the east. The sun shall be no more. Behold and behold—"

Swaying on the moving minaret, Uncle Massi talks to the people who raise their heads, and stare at him, listening to him with open mouths.

"Who is this man discouraging the masses?" A worker asks angrily.

"He is a lunatic, I know him. And his father is a landlord too!" A tenant says.

"Pull him down! Pull the crazy bastard down!" several people shout. The crooks of Faithland push and prod the people violently and run toward the minaret. Salman the Brainless cries like a beast:

"Let's chop him to pieces right here!"

Salman's men try to climb the minaret, but the tiles are slippery, they can't reach the top. Uncle stands in the small balcony of the minaret, which is swaying to the right and left, making his speech, now even more agitatedly. He raises his voice above the murmur of the crowd:

"Your hands will be defiled with blood. Brother will kill brother, father, son! Behold and rise! Cry loud and spare not! Lift up your voice like a trumpet—"

Now Bashi the Janitor, hearing the word "trumpet," blows in his trumpet, which like the muffled sound of a pirate ship, breaks the dense darkness of the night and hits the stone wall of the mountain. Uncle goes on, "—for this is the day of the First Revolt and blood must run in the endless bed of this old river!" And he points to the Old North River on the right side of the pasture.

Sahar and I look for Ali the Bricklayer, but we cannot find him. He has vanished. Weren't we supposed to be the organizers and leaders of this revolt? Didn't Ali hand the flag and the banner to us? No one can see our flag and banner now.

Now one of the students calls everybody's attention. Like an acrobat, he stands on the shoulders of his friends with his legs apart: "Listen to me friends! Let's not waste the time. Let's start a riot and put an end to this misery. These people who are sleeping and dreaming their opium dreams in this castle cannot hear our harmonious breathing—the breath of a million. These people are our enemies. We plow the prairies, build the cities, dig the mines and lay the railway tracks, but they take the crops and the buildings and the treasures and the wealth. We stand in the cold and the sun, starving, while they lie in bed and eat themselves to death. We toil, they rest; we produce, they consume; we suffer, they enjoy! Let's unite now! Break their power and gain our freedom! To the castle!" he cries.

"To the castle!" everyone cries.

"Long live the Revolution!" a worker cries.

"Long live the Revolution!" the crowd responds.

A bullet is shot in the air, stopping the agitated mob from running toward the castle. Heads turn to search for the man; eyes stop on Sheikh Ahmad who stands erect on Rakhsh, General Nasri's Arabian horse. The Sheikh's robe has stretched into a black flag, his only arm is up in the sky holding a revolver, aiming at the heavens.

"Brothers and Sisters! This is the voice of the Almighty pouring out of my humble mouth. Don't let the poisonous teeth of that hellish serpent shoot venom in your brains. His is a Satanic ideology, which stings you and sickens you forever. Don't fall into this spider-web of imported thoughts. The time has come to cleanse and purify our revolution once and for all from Satanic influences. God plowed the earth, not us! God built the cities, not us! God laid the train tracks, not us! The mines are God's, the crops are

God's, and we belong to Him! This is the Revolution of God! And we are from the Party of God! Cleanse and purify your party! Get rid of the blasphemers!"

With the last cry, Rakhsh neighs and rises on his rear hoofs, but the Sheikh, like a toy soldier sticking to a toy horse, remains erect. Salman the Brainless's gang leads the mob. They attack the students, rip off the speaker's shirt and beat him with sticks and clubs. Now they attack the rest of the people. They beat up whoever is younger, whoever wears colorful clothes—the ones who carry flags and banners. The shower of clubs and stones, pots and pans, punches and kicks fall from every direction on the unprotected heads and bodies of the students.

Someone cries, "Stop killing your brothers and sisters! The enemy is in the castle!"

Someone else cries, "Let's kill them all at once and purify the Army of God!"

A woman cries, "Help, help! Rape, rape!"

Children whine.

Several bullets are shot and all the horses of General Nasri neigh in the pasture, galloping toward the people.

Someone calls, "Light! Give me a light!"

A torch brightens the pasture, then more torches appear and we see the sleepy faces of the hosts and guests, all in bathrobes and pajamas.

"What are you doing on my property?" General Nasri, shorter than a little boy, appears on the east terrace. His voice is trembling, his gray hair sticking up. A group of his guests—all old and puffed up—stand behind him.

"This is the Holy Army of God," Sheikh Ahmad says, stepping forward. "Repent, or you and your rotten friends will be stoned in the main square of the city."

"We are the representatives of the workers, peasants, and students. We are here to confiscate your property and arrest you!" says the leader of the students, now bloody and wounded.

"I am Massi-Alla, the Poet-Prophet, behold! And before my flock occupies the rooms and chambers, prepare the castle for us, for we shall sojourn in thy house. We are tired," Uncle Massi says.

"Pull your shitty pants up and go get us some gold and jewelry. I need your wallets too—I mean all of your motherfucking wallets! I'm Salman the Brainless, the head motherfucker of all the motherfucking slums!"

The General whispers something in his valet's ear. He and other servants run inside the house. Mrs. General, who has just arrived gasping and wrapping herself in a silk gown, says, "Gentlemen! Please make yourselves comfortable. The servants will bring you whatever you want. I'll serve champagne to everybody! Why don't you come in, it's chilly out there."

Salman the Brainless screams, "The lady says come in! It's gonna be a party, friends! Let's go in!" And before the General's servants can do anything, the flood of people breaks loose and flows through the large glass doors of the green marble castle. The spacious dining hall with the huge chandelier, still glowing with hundreds of candle-shaped bulbs, is full of people. The rest of the crowd fill the multi-level garden, and all the terraces around the house. The servants bring some precious objects and lay them on the floor. Among them, Sahar and I recognize the big panel of the Persian miniature—the picture of the almond-eyed Saghis serving wine to lazy, sleepy men.

Among the hubble bubble of the crowd, pops and bangs and wheezes and splashes of hundreds of champaign bottles, Sahar whispers into my ear, "What will happen now? Will they get something and leave? This is not what we planned to do."

"Things are out of our hands now. Ali has disappeared and you and I cannot do anything without his support."

"Ali knew this from the beginning," Sahar says. "He knew that the revolt was doomed to fail. I just hope everything ends up peacefully and nobody gets hurt."

"Look, Sahar! Look at crazy Uncle Massi, sitting on top of the chandelier!"

"Sin, sin, sin, sin! Cursed is a man who trusts the owners of the castles. Cursed is a man who makes peace with them. You shrubs of the desert, you thorns and dusts of the earth, how can you take a piece of diamond, a sip of wine, and forgive your oppressors?" Uncle cries.

While trying to sit on the other side of the chandelier, Sheikh Ahmad calls to people: "God and the Holy Ones order you to confiscate all the mobile and immobile properties of this house in favor of the Army of the Holy Revolution."

Now both Uncle and the sheikh are on the hot bulbs of the chandelier, swaying to the right and left, each making his own speech. People look at them confused.

"All for the Holy Army—" Sheikh screams.

"Sin and treason—sin and treason—deadly diseases will fall on you!" Uncle cries.

"Confiscate the properties for the poor masses—" A student calls from a corner.

"Shut the mouth of that blasphemer!" Sheikh calls from top of the chandelier, where he is now wrestling with Uncle Massi.

"Attack!" Salman the Brainless shouts. "Let's con-fixate everything!"

The mob rushes into the rooms of the castle. Many fall and get smashed under the galloping feet, screaming with pain, while others holler with excitement. Someone blows into a trumpet. This is Bashi, the old janitor, standing on a table, blowing in his rusty trumpet and moving his erect penis up and down in the direction of Mrs. General Nasri, who screams and faints. Sheikh Ahmad and Uncle are still wrestling on the hot bulbs. The chandelier swings now and makes crackling sounds.

Pulling his pajamas up, General Nasri climbs a table. He tries to shout with his nasal voice, "Ladies and gentlemen of the aristocracy! It's time to get armed! Long live the Monarchy!"

"Get all the bows and arrows, spears and swords, our honor is at stake!" says the thin old man who wanted to be tickled last night.

In a minute, the General and his guests are all armed with the antique armory and a bloody battle begins. The masses, half-naked and barefoot, with sticks, stones, pots, and pans and the aristocrats, shielded and hooded, with two-thousand-year-old rusted spears and swords, fight with each other—one to one, three to one, one to four.

Among the crowd I recognize Malekeh, the tall wigged queen and her short bald alligator lover, now wearing silk alligator-green pajamas. They are fighting with Hassan the Gardener and his wife who are armed with a rusty kitchen knife and gardening scissors.

On top of a table, the old mountainous woman of the fourth room, the one who was fed from both ends, stands like a thick tower of fat with a huge bow and arrow in her hands. This antique bow and arrow could have been from the battle of Alexander the Great and Darius, the King of Kings.

She aims at Bashi's penis, which is still erect and dancing in all directions. But the arrow misses the aim and instead pierces a royal guest and a pauper, stitching them together. The old princess, Mrs. General's orange-wigged, half-crowned mother, is now connected by the lower abdomen to Anvar the Hanging Snot, one of Salman's ruthless collaborators.

I search the crowd to see if I can find our mother and Prince Amir Khan, but I can't. My heart starts to pound violently and my mouth dries up. For the first time since the beginning of the Revolt, I feel panicky. I turn to Sahar, I need to talk to her. I need her more than ever. But she is not beside me anymore.

"Sahar! Sahar! Where are you?" I call her in the midst of the chaos and look around. I run downstairs, to the carpeted hall where last night we opened seven doors to find our mother. Maybe Sahar has taken refuge here. Now I think of Mother again. What if they kill her? What if they kill Sahar too? I rush to the sixth door and open it wide. I freeze at the sight.

Time has had a different pace here. Time has passed in a strange pace. The round bed still turns and the record player plays the same song: "The moon is yellow... and our love is like an April rose... April rose... April rose..." Mother wears the same sapphire blue gown, with her hair, loose on her shoulders. Prince Amir Khan lies on her lap, and Mother searches his hair, picking the lice, one by one, squeezing them between her sharp nails, smiling with victory. But one thing has changed. The prince is thinner, much thinner now and Mother, chubbier, rounder. There are several oval shaped wounds on the prince's body where the flesh is missing. Mother is not pale anymore: her cheeks are red and there are blood stains on her chin.

I stare at them, paralyzed, wishing Sahar was here with me. Amir Khan gets up gently and moves toward the table. He is so thin that his penis looks larger than normal. Mother has cleaned and trimmed the long hairs hanging off his thighs and I can see his private parts clearly. He picks up the knife, moves toward the bed and says, "Pari, my mermaid, my love. Today is the end of the long longing. It's the seventh day and I have to feed you for the last time, with the last part of my body. Then you'll be mine. We will live together, forever, and ever after!"

"Amir, my love! I can't eat anymore... please! Can't we just leave now? Am I not chubby enough? Don't I fill your arms? Won't you enjoy me now? I'm afraid that you'll make yourself weak. I want you to be strong and robust

191

as the first day that I saw you."

"Why do you want me to be strong? Won't you love me if I'm not square and robust anymore?" Amir Khan asks.

"Oh, I'll love you even if you're weak as a child. I'll love you even if you're thin as a needle!"

"That's my Pari! Now, eat this last piece of my flesh!" the prince says in his most tender tone.

Amir Khan's penis is standing up now. It's horizontal in the air like the bull's horn. He lays the knife at the end of the horn. Mother screams.

"Oh, no! Not that! No, no, no, no!" And she weeps hysterically.

It's too late now. The prince has chopped the horn off and is laying it in a plate. He offers it to Mother who covers her eyes.

"Here, eat this while it's hot! But first, lick my wound. I'm bleeding."

I don't stay longer to see the rest. I murmur, "Sahar, Sahar... you missed this one... you missed it... you missed it... Where have you gone?" And I weep.

I remember the last room, the seventh room, where the yo-yo boy named Saboor waited for the orders. Sahar might be here, might have come here to hide. I open the door; Saboor is still sitting on his stool, staring at his yo-yo; it slips down, comes up, slips down and rolls all the way up again.

"Saboor, do you remember me?"

"I do," he says without stopping the yo-yo.

"Have you seen my sister?" I ask.

"I haven't," he says.

"Do you know what is happening upstairs? They are killing each other. Get out of here. You are free now. I don't think your master will survive."

Saboor raises his head for a split second and looks at me with his red eyes. But he doesn't say anything. He just keeps his yo-yo going. I close the door and lean my back against the wall to think. A large square spot on the wall is brighter than the rest. This is where the Persian miniature was. The oak cabinet and the glass boxes displaying the ancient armory are all broken and empty. What should I do now? Sahar is lost. Ali the Bricklayer is lost. Mother is lost. Grand-Lady's Turkman carpet is now a useless holy vessel, too large to take me home.

What shall I do?

I look at the silk mats and cushions, the long hand-carved pipes, the cold ashes left behind by the opium smokers, all scattered on the carpet. I stare at the water, still gurgling in the fountain, singing an uneven tune. How come no one comes down? Is this part of the house a dream, and the rest reality? Is everything a dream? Is everything reality? Where is Sahar? Was she a dream and now vanished? Have I always been so lonely, so completely lonely?

I climb the stairs and find myself in a quiet battlefield. The war is over. The people of the carpet and the residents of the castle lie down side by side on the green marble floor. Some are dead, some moan with pain, breathing their last breaths.

But up there, on top of the chandelier, Uncle Massi and Sheikh Ahmad still wrestle, spending their last drops of energy to kill each other. The ceiling has a big fissure and I hear crackling noises. Suddenly a cloud of dust descends and with a huge bang the crystal chandelier falls on the marble floor with Uncle and the sheikh still on it. Hundreds of crystal particles and broken bulbs cover the floor and shower the dead and the living. The sheikh and Uncle get up and run out. I follow them, because I know where they are heading. They want to fling themselves on the carpet and escape. With each step, shards tear my flesh and small particles of crystal pierce the soles of my feet, but I run and scream.

"Wait! Wait for me! Take me with you. I want to go home!" I run on the glass toward the south deck, where the multi-level garden is. Here, I see a multi-level battlefield. Blood runs down the marble steps; the garden is covered with corpses.

Sheikh Ahmad runs and Uncle Massi chases him. I run on my bleeding soles to the pasture where the carpet lays still, as large as a vessel, for a million people. The green peacock on the carpet looks like a gigantic dragon among monstrous flowers.

From the direction of the moving minaret, Mariam the Big Mole runs toward Uncle Massi, crying with joy, "Massi, my love! I found you finally. Let's go back home. Let's go to our little room, lie down and rest."

She approaches Massi with open arms, but a bullet pierces her left breast; she falls across the tail of the peacock. Uncle kneels down, lifts Mariam's body up in his arms, looking at the wound. It's a big hole right on the black mole. Through the hole he sees Sheikh Ahmad hiding a revolver under his robe. Uncle doesn't attack the sheikh; he sits cross-legged on the peacock's tail, holding Mariam's head in his arms. He mutters something, slowly, then quickly, in a whisper, then loud. He mutters a crazy song: "A hole, a hole... a hole on the mole..."

Sheikh Ahmad tries to raise the carpet, but he cannot. He murmurs prayers, whispers over beads, but the carpet stays still. He sees me for the first time standing outside the carpet with my bleeding feet.

"Hey boy! You little brat! I'm talking to you! Move this goddamn carpet, soon! Isn't this carpet yours? Then move it, let's get out of here before the Monarch's army arrives."

So now this is not the sheikh's holy vessel anymore, but *my* carpet. His worthless life is in my hands. I can play with him. I can make him pee in his pants. I can keep him waiting until the Monarch's army arrives. Then they'll unwrap his turban from his head and use it as a rope. They'll hang him by his turban from the sharp peak of this moving minaret. I'll stand here and watch him shaking like a worm, vibrating his only arm and his crippled leg, like a miserable spider stuck in his own web.

But I don't. I want my uncle to take his bride home and sing her his crazy song.

I call, "Saba! Sa - ba! Lift the carpet and take them home!"

I don't want to go home with them; not without Sahar. Did I come alone, to go alone? So I tell the north wind to take them home.

Saba swishes from the top of his mother's peak, now hidden in a dark cloud. The carpet instantly shrinks to its normal size and stays flat as it takes to the air. But before it glides high in the sky, Salman the Brainless runs out of the castle, screaming for the carpet to stop. His arms are full of loot. "Wait for me! I'm still alive! Wait for me!"

He reaches the carpet, throwing the objects up first. Golden Candle holders, hand-carved silver picture frames, heavy necklaces, mink coats and other precious and semi-precious objects cover the carpet. Salman jumps, holding the stiff edge of the carpet, pulling himself up. He sits safe and sound on a crimson flower; dries his sweaty forehead with his tattooed arm. But as the carpet lifts itself higher and glides, one of Salman's objects rolls to the edge and falls down right at my feet. It is the pink clown-clock of the pink room—the children's room. It lands with a *ding*, facing up, its large eyes looking at me. But the clown's eyes don't move to the right and left anymore; they are fixed, staring into my eyes. The hands of the clock are missing and don't show the time. The red tongue sticks out and goes back in, making a face at me. Then the cheeks of the clown-clock swell and swell and fart in my face.

It must be dawn, but as Uncle Massi predicted, there is no sun. It's darker than a black night. That silver scythe of the moon and the red star are gone. I turn to go to the garden, but I hear a faint noise—no, a whistle. Someone is whistling, moving closer and closer. From behind the minaret, I see the small figure of Uncle Yahya, pedaling toward the castle. He whistles the tune of "Arise, you prisoners of starvation!" He has come to join the First Revolt.

I don't want to see the old man. I don't want to see his face. And I don't want him to see me lonely and miserable. As Uncle approaches in the dark, I vanish into the willow trees. The soles of my feet bleed as I run. I trip over the still warm corpses of the children, men, and horses. I trip over Moni's small corpse. Was it yesterday when he was playing tug of war with the other children, supervised by their Swiss nurses?

I get up and trip again, leaving a trail of blood behind me. I run down the marble steps toward the wall of the garden. I sit here at the stream, plunging my burning feet in the water, which is already red. I look at the wall. I know Ali is here. He was here all the time, laying brick on top of brick, raising the wall. I hold my breath and listen. I hear his trowel smoothing the mortar, swoosh, swoosh, swoosh... He dumps a brick and again, swoosh, swoosh, swoosh... I whisper as if there are thousands of ghosts around and I don't want to wake them up. I whisper, "Sahar, can you hear this?"

Suddenly, I decide what Ali's decision should be. He asked us yesterday to help him choose one of the three options: raising the wall, changing into someone else, or dying. I have found the answer for him. I gather all my strength, curve my palms around my mouth and scream into the hollow night, "Die, Ali, Die!"

Many smaller and skinnier voices repeat, "Die, die, die, die..."

Ali the Bricklayer falls down from the high wall and lands at my feet. His scalp cracks open like a fresh round honeydew melon and his brain slips out like yellow seeds. I gather the warm slippery brain of Ali the Wall Raiser, Ali the Wise, inside the bowl of my cold hands and mount the steps.

I pass the castle, once a ballerina, now beaten and raped—an ugly whore. I head toward the pasture and as I walk in the dark, I hear crackling sounds behind me; I turn for a last glimps and I see tall flames stretching upward, lighting the tar black sky. In the shadows of the flames, I see a girl running naked with a torch in her hand. She runs on the tips of her toes, light and easy. As she circles the round building and throws more flames to the burning castle, she laments in a strange way, making bird sounds— sounds unheard from humans.

"Ooooy... Ooooy... Ooooy! Ooooy... Ooooy... Ooooy!" She sings like an owl.

There is no star to follow, no bird to trace. Everything is black except the sudden orange flashes from behind. I walk along the Old North River, its red waves slapping the rocks, moving forward and foaming red. I hear the muffled gallops of a horse, then its neighing. I look around. The neigh comes from the direction of the horizon, beyond me, from the dark. I squint my eyes and see a white spot in the far distance. Now it gets closer to me, galloping, it passes me, dashing through the dark like the wind. This is Rakhsh, the false Rakhsh, taking Sahar with him. I see his large eyes framed with wide black rings. I see Sahar's hair disheveled in the wind. I cry out, "Sahar, where is he taking you?"

Thirty Lashes

"Twenty-five, twenty-six, twenty-seven—"

Someone is calling these numbers between the sounds of swish... swish... swish... But my feet do not burn anymore. I open my eyes and look down to see if I have feet at all. I find myself strapped to a gurney, no sheet covering me. The first face I recognize is the turtle face of Ha-G the Shit Mouth. His bodyguard holds him like a baby again. Ha-G whips my feet with a long cable as his guard counts.

"Twenty-nine, thirty...." Ha-G stops. "Take me close to him!" He orders. "I woke him up!"

Ha-G's guard carries him to the side of my bed, lifting him up very close to my face. I hold my breath so as not to smell his rotten odor.

"Now tell me who this Ali is—you were whispering his name all the time," Ha-G demands.

I raise my head, looking at my hands. They are both tied to the gurney.

"Why are you looking at your hands?" he asks.

"The brain... the warm brain..." I murmur and burst into tears.

"Are you fooling me again, you motherfucker? Who is Ali, huh?" Ha-G grunts.

"A... bricklayer... he was..." I mutter.

"Where? Where was he a bricklayer?" he asks, showering me with saliva.

"In Faithland and everywhere. Did I lose your brain... Ali?" I lift my head again and look at my empty hands.

"Ha-G, sir, the patient is not in a good shape. We may lose him this way." I recognize Doctor Halal's voice. "He has already given us a lot of information. Everything is on this tape. Give me some time to analyze his hallucinations, sir. Let him rest now."

"Rest, rest, rest, rest! This is all you keep saying, Doctor, as if we're running a hotel here. He has rested enough and I'm aware that you have helped him to rest more—with your various injections and whatnot. But enough is enough: he either answers my questions or goes to hell where he belongs."

"But sir! I have to analyze this tape, to put his muttering together. Please give me at least twenty-four hours. I'll submit my report tomorrow at this time, sir!" Halal says politely.

"Okay, Doctor. Tomorrow at this time. Tomorrow you and I will talk about this bastard's crazy delirium. You'd better provide a complete analysis for me, otherwise I'll report you to the Revolutionary Committee. But before you take him away, let me ask him one more question, this one just for my own curiosity. This is the last thing the bastard mumbled. Lift his rotten head up for me!" He orders the guards.

Two guards from somewhere behind me lift my head and shoulders in such a rough way that my spine hurts. Ha-G, with his bulged-out eyes, stares into my eyes. His pupils move fast, and restlessly, like a lunatic's.

"Now tell me one thing and then get your shit out of here. Who is Sahar? Huh? A woman, a horse, or what?

"Sahar is dawn," I say, "the end of darkness, when the sun comes out. Daylight trapped in night. Oh, poor poor child..." I weep again, "Where did the horse take you?"

"Send him to the Psychiatric Wing until tomorrow night. That's where he belongs. I'll continue the interrogations after I hear Brother Halal's report. Take him now!"

The Shit Mouth's special bodyguard carries his hunched torso out. I look at them and the way the guard waddles. The gray sack at the end of Ha-G's crooked body looks like the dirty diaper of a grotesque baby, a diaper full of excrement. His long arms hang from either side like cobras with wide flat heads. I lay my head down, waiting for the clicks of guns, gallops of boots, and squeaks of metal chairs to end. All the armed devotees follow Ha-G out. Doctor Halal picks up his tape recorder and folders and leaves without glancing back at me. The room is empty now, but I still feel the presence of one person. I can hear him approaching me.

"Hey brother, look how small the world is! You and me again, me and you! Let me open these straps and let you breath. Then we'll head toward the halls, huh?"

I look at Kamal's fleshy face, bending over me to unstrap the leather belt around my chest. He winks at me. I laugh and cry.

Chapter Four

In the Psychiatric Wing

*To be able to see straight, without overlooking
the twists, turns, and zigzags of reality...*
—Vladimir Ilych Lenin

Debating Kamal

What does remain of a dream? Scattered images, insignificant, at times absurd; if meaningful, unsayable.

Kamal wants to know what I dreamed about while Ha-G was interrogating me. All I can tell him is: a lunatic on a moving minaret, a gloomy bricklayer on top of a wall, a cunning sheikh and a cruel crook on a flying carpet; all I can say is: the wall, the river of blood, and the white horse. He insists, and all I remember is a barefoot girl burning a marble castle with a torch, someone's hair, disheveled, lost in the wind.

But what is this loss I'm feeling? This failure? This remorse? I'm Rostam after killing my own son by mistake; I'm Spartacus after defeat. But I cannot say this to Kamal. He won't understand. He won his revolution, I lost mine.

Now I'm on my butt, using my hands as oars, moving forward in the long hallways like a boat. I'm careful not to scrub the soles of my feet against the cold cement. My soles are swollen like small pink balloons. The skin will peel off in a day or two. If I'm careful enough and avoid the floor, there won't be much pain. But if my feet touch the cement, even a gentle touch, thousands of shards of broken glass sting my flesh, tearing it and running up into my veins.

Kamal has leashed me again, but doesn't pull the leash. He holds the end of the long scarf, walking one step ahead of me. I have slowed him down. I remember how fast he used to walk.

From below, where I'm sitting and sliding myself on the floor, Kamal looks even bigger. He has the same black shirt on, the same pants tucked into his huge boots. His hair is close cropped, almost shaved, but his beard is long, longer than the first day; he hasn't trimmed it. I cannot see all of his face, but I can study his profile, which looks different, shadowy, stretched. He must have lost some weight. He walks with an even pace—preoccupied. His heavy key chain rattles in his pocket.

"Is the show still on?" I ask him.

"It's on," he answers briefly.

"How... are... you?" I ask.

"Me?" He turns to look into my eyes, then laughs, but not happily. I notice that his forehead is creased—more than before.

"I'm fine! Tomorrow is my wedding!"

"Congratulations! I'm happy for you!"

I find myself excited. This surprises me. Feeling lighter, I row fast and slide on my butt.

"But I don't care!" Kamal says.

"You don't?"

"No. I'm not prepared for marriage. I haven't had the Holy Water of Immortality, yet."

"It didn't happen?" I ask him. "The Holy One didn't come to your dream anymore?"

"He came, but it didn't happen."

We are at an intersection now. He stops, looks around to see if anyone is coming, then pulls me to a corner out of the lense field and squats in front of me.

"Take off your shirt and sit on it. I'll pull the sleeves, you'll have a free ride. No more rowing brother, your hands must be tired."

Once more he looks around and helps me to take my shirt off. He pulls me up and spreads the shirt under me. He takes the leash off my neck, ties it to the long sleeves and pulls me behind. It's like I'm sitting on a sled, Sahar pulling me across the snow. We turn left. The cement floor and the walls lighten. As we proceed, they turn grayish white and then as white as fresh snow.

"This is the Psychiatric Wing, brother. I'm sorry you ended up here. You could have easily avoided this. Right now, you'd be sleeping on a real bed on the sixth floor, enjoying your sweet dreams. You could repent, get re-educated and go home before long. Is it so hard to repent?" He turns and looks at me. He has widened his eyes into full circles. I feel that he is asking this frankly. He is really wondering.

"Kamal, is it easy for you to deny the Last Holy One? All of the Holy Ones? Your revolution, your government, your Great Leader? Is it easy for you, Kamal?"

I don't know what is getting into me. I'm talking the way I've never talked before. I'm calling him Kamal, no more "Brother" or any other title.

He thinks for a moment, then says, "It's different, brother, it's different! My beliefs are right, yours are wrong! You see the difference?"

"But you don't even know what my beliefs are, do you? Have I said anything, yet?"

"Not yet!"

"You just assume that I have certain wrong beliefs, don't you?" Either I'm out of my mind, or this is *me* pulling out of the fog now that the drugs are wearing off.

"So you're denying them, huh?" he asks.

"Denying what?"

"Your beliefs," he says.

"I'm not denying anything; I'm just saying there is nothing to deny and no reason to repent."

"You're a Godless bastard and everybody knows this. You even look like one!"

Kamal's logic, or lack of logic amazes me. This is a dangerous game, but I go on.

"Even if we assume that I'm what you're calling me, I don't think I should repent. Have you ever thought about this, Kamal? That you're up there, holding the leash, forcing me to say, 'yes'—what if I was up there and pulling you behind? Would you say 'yes' to me? Would you deny your Holy Ones?"

With a brisk movement, Kamal pulls the leash, the sleeve, and the shirt and makes me roll over the cold cement. I land on my burning feet.

"You son of a bitch! Don't you ever dare talk about our Holy Ones. Get up now! I said get up! You have to walk on your goddam feet. To hell with you, devil worshiper. What are you talking me into? Denying my faith? The Holy Ones? The Great Leader of the Holy Revolution? You bastard motherfucker, how dare you compare your intoxicating ideas—as our Great

Leader says—to our heavenly ones?"

He ties the leash tightly around my neck, like the first day, and foams at the mouth. I'm on my feet, ready to walk on the cold cement, which turns quickly to hot coal as I take the first step.

The Psychiatric Wing is quite a long wing. White, windowless doors are on the right and left; lenses—the hidden eyes of La-Jay—are installed at each intersection; TV screens hang on the walls, each showing different angles of the cells. The inmates are wearing something white (straightjackets?). I can't see much, only white shadows, barely moving. It may be night-time; they may be sleeping. Are these cells full? I ask myself. So many out of their minds?

Now that Kamal is taking me to my temporary cell to lodge with the lunatics, I feel the sanest I've ever felt before. I feel that I can tolerate the pain almost as proud and erect as an Unbreakable. Still I cannot remember my name or my immediate past, but I know who Kamal is, and I know that I'm not his kin. Kamal is nothing to me; he is all that I'm not. I congratulate myself for this much sanity. Kamal is my torturer, I'm his prisoner—the line is clear.

Rattle and rattle and rattle. The key chain hops in Kamal's pocket. He is walking fast to speed me along. I'm on burning coal now. On fire.

Fire-Wednesday, 1

"Jump, jump, jump! Don't be scared! You *can* jump. Fire won't catch you!" Sahar's voice calls.

From the foot of the hill where New Spring Elementary and High School stand, up to the top, where Grandfather's three houses are, the street is in flames. Heaps of firewood are burning in a long row every two meters. All the neighbors—children and adults—are jumping over the flames. The last flame, the one closest to our houses, is the tallest. Nobody, not even tall men, can jump this high. To leap over this, means to pass through fire.

Sahar wants me to jump over the tallest. We've done all, except this one. I don't want to pass through fire. I'll burn.

"Hey, come on, jump! Don't be scared!" she insists.

"No, I don't want to. This one is very tall. What if my pants catch fire? What if I land in the middle of the flames? I'm not good at high jumping," I say.

"Look at me. it's easy..." she says and runs toward the tall flame.

With her red skirt and yellow shirt, with her thick hair—now much longer and tied tightly with a ribbon in a ponytail—she runs like a little ball of fire, stretches her legs wide apart in a *grand jeté*, and flies above the flames, landing on the other side, safe and sound, laughing with joy.

Everybody claps for her.

"My brave girl!" Grandfather shouts and takes a picture of her. "She's going to be the first woman astronaut!"

"I'll make them honey and hot milk every morning," Maman tells Grandfather. "These two are not as tall as they should be. Look at Kami and Cyrus, praise God, since they've gone to military school, they've become as tall as you!" Maman knocks on the wooden door.

Kami and Cyrus are setting off firecrackers with Sheikh Ahmad's sons. Hearing Maman, they stretch their backs to look even taller.

The air smells of gunpowder. Thousands of little sparkles glow in the sky. On the horizon, colorful balls explode into a million stars. There are fireworks in the City Park.

Now Sahar approaches me—short and slight, thin and light, her ponytail hopping and swaying as she walks. "Did you see? It's easy, I told you! Fire won't catch you if you're a good person. Now I'm going to say the words."

She checks her distance, runs again, and while leaping through the fire, screams, "My yellow be yours, your red be mine!" Gasping, she runs toward me. "Now I won't get sick this year. Jump! For my sake! I don't want you to get sick. Tell the fire that you're changing your yellow with its red."

But I don't jump. The fire is tall for me. If I jump and fall into the flames, Sheikh Ahmad's wives—all four of them, the two old wives, and the two new ones—will laugh at me. I can see how they're looking at me and giggling. Standing at the gate of their yard, they're all wearing black veils from head to foot. They're watching me with one eye, peeking from a small opening in their veils. They point their henna-red fingers at me and whisper into each other's ears. They smell of cheap rose-water and I smell their smell in spite of all the smoke and gunpowder in the air.

Now Sheikh Ahmad comes out of the house, his thin black clergy robe—his house robe—hanging on his shoulders. He shoos his wives in. "In, in, in, in! Quick! Don't you have anything better to do? Are you watching these Godless fire worshipers? These blasphemers? In... shoo! shoo! It's time for the evening prayer." He sweeps the air with his only hand and limps behind his women, leading the chicken into their coop.

Mother, sitting on the front steps of Grandfather's house between Maman and Aunty Zari, watches us for a long time, then says, "This girl doesn't know fear, she may burn herself."

Mother doesn't mention me. I look at her new hair and hate the way she has shaped it into a thick yellow boa curled on top of her head. I hate her red slippery dress too. It's too tight on her round hips and large breasts and too open on her neck. She is not thin like in the old times anymore. Although I stare at her eyes—two large blue fish, penciled all around—she still doesn't see me. She is watching Sahar.

"Sahar should've been born a boy. She doesn't know fear!" she says.

"God makes mistakes too," Maman says with a sigh.

"My Kami has become tall like his father," Aunty Zari says and sighs. "Do you remember Kami's father? Do you remember how tall he was?"

"Let's go up and watch the fireworks from the roof!" Maman says and gets up. She doesn't want Aunty Zari to talk about the husband she married and lost fifteen years ago. She doesn't want her to poison the festive evening.

Maman is not in the kitchen tonight; she is taking the night off. It's Fire-Wednesday, the last Wednesday of the year, and everybody should be out until dusk, leaping over fire and pouring their pain, sickness, and misery into the ashes, taking life from the fire.

Even Grand-Lady is out. She is wearing her red velvet vest, covering her hair with her thin white muslin scarf, a peacock embroidered on one corner. Grandfather lifts his little mother, holding her like a baby in his arms. He passes her gently over a small flame and wishes her long life. Grand-Lady mumbles something in a language nobody understands.

Now we all go inside Grandfather's house. In the largest room—Grandfather's room—big bowls of mixed nuts, all kinds of melons, pomegranates, citrus fruits, and pastries design the tables. We all sit around the room—adults on the wooden Polish chairs, rented specially for Fire-Wednesday, children on the carpeted floor. Grand-Lady sits on a cushion, leaning against an embroidered recliner, smoking her water-pipe.

I sit cross-legged next to Sahar, in front of a plate full of mixed nuts. Sahar cracks pistachios with her thumbs, takes the salty seeds out, eats a couple and offers me one. I chew the tasty seeds and watch my family. I count them to see who is missing: Aunty Hoori and Aunty Shamsi are missing. Aunty Hoori's large picture is on the bracket next to Maman's wedding mirror. Sorrow waves in her almond-shaped gazelle eyes. Maman wipes her tears off when she lights two tall candles on the either side of her oval mirror.

"Read Hoori's poems for us!" Maman asks Grandfather in a pleading tone. But Grandfather ignores her.

We know that Aunty Hoori is studying at a university far away in the south. She sends her poetry to Grandfather. Maman says, "At least read her last letter to us. It's not just for you, it's for us too!" Grandfather, leafing through *The Book of the Kings*, trying to find an appropriate epic to recite, shakes his head and sighs.

Uncle Musa stays only for a short time and leaves. Since Aunty Shamsi has left him to live with her parents, Uncle is having an affair with his blond secretary. We all know where he is going, but we don't say anything.

Now I watch Aunty Zari's lanky body, folding on the chair like a half-empty, sitting scarecrow. She blinks ten times more than a normal person. Sewing is ruining her eyes. Now she is the neighborhood's dressmaker. While thinking about Kami's father, she stitches from morning to night.

Next to Aunty Zari, Mother sits. She cuts the juicy flesh of a chunk of watermelon in smaller pieces, placing the bites in her mouth carefully, so she doesn't wet and smear her lipstick. Mother's breasts, her upper belly, and her lower belly form three smooth, slippery, red hills on her body. Ever since she has opened a beauty salon in the Alleys of Heaven, she is calling herself Marie. Her salon's name is "Salon Marie."

Mother gets mad if someone calls her Pari. She gets mad if we call her Mother. She doesn't want to be Pari or Mother anymore. And this happened two years ago, around the First Revolt, when she suddenly changed from a thin, pale brunette to a chubby, red-cheeked blond. She finished her School of Cosmetology, framed her diploma, and opened a beauty salon—Salon Marie.

"Can we call you Mother like before?" Sahar and I asked.

"No more Mother, do you understand? Call me Marie. Everybody knows me by this name now."

We stopped calling her altogether.

"—Now Siavoosh, the Persian prince, has to gallop his horse through the tall flame. He must prove his innocence to the king—" Grandfather is telling us the introduction to the story of Siavoosh, preparing us for the epic he is about to recite. But I stay in my own world, watching everybody and eating pistachio seeds absentmindedly. I have heard this story before.

Now I remember the day that Sahar, Maman, Aunty Zari, and I crowded in Mother's small car to go and visit her new place. We knew that this was Mother's Salon and she was going to open it tomorrow. Mother was going to live here. She was going to leave us with Maman and Grandfather and live by herself in this fancy apartment. Sahar was excited about our new life in Grandfather's house. "Maman is fun," Sahar said. "She will let us do whatever we want." Sahar didn't seem to mind about Mother leaving.

We sat in the backseat of Mother's red car. It smelled of rubber. I watched the back of my mother's head and counted the many hair pins that pierced her large tomato-shaped chignon. I wasn't happy about living in Grandfather's house.

In Salon Marie, Sahar and I sat under all the six blow driers and posed in front of the large mirrors. Mother's beauty salon smelled of fresh paint and plastic. The largest room was where the blow driers and mirrors were. Two assistants were supposed to help Mother every day. She was going to live in the two other rooms. Sahar and I stood in her little semi-circle balcony, surrounded by the tall locusts of the Alleys of Heaven and listened to hundreds of birds chirping. Mother had already filled the balcony with blood-red geraniums.

Back home we stood in the middle of the triangular room among the old furniture and many boxes piled up in the room. Mother was not taking anything with her. She bought new furniture for her place. She even left her thick brown book behind, the book she and Father were reading ten years ago, when Father was arrested. Before we left the triangular room, I looked at a white square on the dirty wall. Mother's wedding picture was packed forever, Father's smile buried in the box.

Now Maman is our mother. Sahar has occupied Hoori's room on the roof and my room is right below hers, on the second floor. My room used to be Uncle Massi's room when he was a child and he wasn't as crazy as he is now.

Every night Sahar hops up and down and practices her *jeté* and *changement*, then taps her feet three times on the floor, meaning time to sleep. Then she taps once, meaning goodnight. I climb the chair and knock my ruler three times on the ceiling, meaning goodnight, then once, meaning I love you.

Sahar and I sleep in separate rooms now. We may not think the same thoughts anymore, but we still dream the same dreams.

Confession in the Dark

Kamal stops, knocking on a white door. Three times. The door opens; I squint to see the white shadow against the blinding light.

"Brother Nurse, this patient must stay in room eleven. Straightjacket him!" Kamal says.

Brother Nurse must have been dozing off; he rubs his red eyes and takes us in. He is a short Brother, with a thin prickly beard, small mousy eyes, and sickly yellow face. His face is full of pock-marks. It's a long while since Brother Nurse has been in the sunlight.

In the middle of the white room, there is a square table and four chairs. I take a quick glance at a refrigerator, a cot covered with a white sheet, a hospital table full of drugs, syringes, and instruments, and a TV screen high on the wall showing the interior of different cells. This is the nurse's room, where he lives, works, eats. He opens a closet and takes out a white straightjacket.

I'm standing on my bleeding feet.

Kamal whispers something in the nurse's ear; the nurse nods and prepares an injection. Now he takes off all of my clothes, stabs my right hip with the needle of a big syringe, and wraps me in the wide white cloth. Then he ties the long laces around me tightly. My hip burns and stings, but I can't rub it.

"How is everything here, Brother?" Kamal asks the nurse. "I haven't been in this wing for a while!"

"Crowded! That's what it is. With the Holy War going on, more and more Godless bastards sneak into the ranks of the Holy Army and get messed up here." He points to his head. "Then they end up in my wing. Because you know, you can't bear the fire pouring down on your head unless you believe in the Holy War and the Holy Ones. I've been there myself; it's crazy, Brother." Now he rubs his eyes, and then his whole face, in a circular motion, either to concentrate, or to chase a bad image out of his head. He goes on: "One moment you look at the sky and you think it's fireworks, and a moment later, all the stars shower the earth and dig huge holes in the ground. You look around and what do you see? Arms, legs, teeth, and toes... all scattered around you. You touch yourself to see if you're still here. Yes, you're here, but why are you here? What a fucking life is this? You've got to have faith in the Last Holy One to be able to continue," the nurse says. He drops himself on the white metal chair, exhausted. "I spent a whole year at the Holy Front. I'm grateful they sent me here and gave me this job. Very grateful."

"You're right, Brother," Kamal says. "Faith in the Last Holy One—that's what we need. That's our foundation, our reason to live and fight the enemies. By the way, how is that bastard doing? That loony blasphemer of room eleven?" Kamal asks.

"That lanky devil? Crazier than ever. He is my midnight show, Brother." The nurse laughs with delight. "I just sit here, fix the screen on him, and watch him all night. He lectures, takes short naps, lectures again, paces around the room with an air—one hand on his waist, one, moving above his head—like Napoleon or something. He lectures that poor boy, Saboor, and tells long stories for the two cannibals, Akir and Nakir. He has tamed the cannibals and this is something I need to report. They're no good anymore."

"Does he still claim to be—" Kamal hesitates. He doesn't want to utter the name of the Holy One.

"Oh, more than before," the nurse says. "He says, one day we will all know about him, but then it'll be too late. He says he is the Absent One who is present here just for a short time, to test us. If we don't recognize him, he'll disappear again and the world will end with him. A real loony, I'm telling you. But not dangerous. He is my late night movie!" He repeats again and chuckles. "But we have another one—"

Kamal is in a deep thought and cannot hear the nurse anymore.

I'm standing on my bleeding feet. The laces of the straightjacket are tied so tightly that blood cannot circulate in my arms. If Kamal doesn't take me out, I'll collapse.

"Brother Nurse," Kamal finally says. "Can the patient and I talk for a minute, before we lock him up in eleven? I'd appreciate it. You can take a short walk in the corridor and stretch your legs a bit; you must be tired sitting alone watching these loonies all the time. I just need to do a short interrogation."

Brother Nurse is hesitant. It seems that no guard has ever asked him such a thing before. But on the other hand, he knows Kamal and trusts him. He lingers and rubs his face.

Kamal says, "If you're worried for your patients, I'll watch the screen for you while I'm interrogating."

The Nurse feels better, goes toward the door, but comes back again, heads toward the old yellowish refrigerator, takes a large red apple, polishes it with his white gown, and leaves the room. I hear his first bite.

Kamal sits me on a chair, turns the blinding lights out and sits opposite me at the small folding table. The room is dark. What is he cooking now? Is this a new trick? I've learned enough about El-Deen to know that Kamal has no authority to interrogate me. My heart pounds so loudly that I fear the loony may hear it. He is quiet for a few long seconds, I hear his breathing. There is no window, no source of light. In total darkness, we're both blindfolded.

As I'm feeling the warmth of Kamal's gigantic body from the other side of the table and listening to the hiss of his breathing, which always make me think that he is gasping for air, he starts. His voice is calm and soothing; his breath is rusty and bitter, with the odor of grass and weeds, but it's not revolting.

"Brother!" He pauses, waiting for me to respond.

"Yes."

"May God forgive me for what I did in the hallways. It was against the Holy Laws. A trainee who is whipped with cable on his feet, is allowed to move on his butt. I forced you to walk, and fast too. Forgive me."

My heart throbs under my Adam's apple. What is this? I've seen Kamal's human side before and it's always an introduction to his most savage mood.

"I have problems, brother. Difficulties. I don't have anybody to talk to.

I asked the Brothers to send me to the Holy Front to serve in the Holy War, but they didn't accept my request. They need me here. I was hoping to get martyred there and join Him in the Heaven and get rid of this lousy life." Kamal sighs. His breath trembles. "I don't know where to start from. You seem to me like an understanding person. Godless, all right, but understanding. You're well-read. Maybe you've read in your books about people who are not happy with their lives. You see, tomorrow is my wedding and I don't want to marry. She is a nice girl, my own relative, a second cousin. She works here too, in the women's ward. We both make good money. La-Jay will give us a nice room on the seventh floor where he and his eight hands and top level devotees live. It's a large room with a bathroom and even a little kitchen. All the Brothers envy me, but I'm not happy. You see, I like her, but I haven't seen her since she was six years old. After age six, she went under the veil and avoided the company of men. I have seen her from a distance, veiled. Her round face was out, but that was not enough. How could I read her mind in her face? Her soul was veiled from me, brother."

Kamal sighs, makes a few tsk, tsk sounds with his tongue and goes on, "They say she trains the women. You see, I have no problem with that. Everybody does it here; it's for the Great Leader and the Holy Revolution. But for my wife—I, myself, have not hurt anybody and am not willing to do that. Yes, I know what you want to say. I tied you to that chair, beat you up several times—but that's all. I didn't whip you, brother. I hope you were conscious enough to see that.

"You know, my problem, I guess, is that she tortures. In the real sense, I mean. Hot bottles and other instruments for the girls. I don't know how and when she became like this, under her black veil. That's why I believe women should stay home, cook, and raise the kids. You let women go out and do the men's job, they do it excessively; they go too far. She is a head trainer now—her heart is made of stone, harder than a man's."

"Do you *have* to marry her?" I ask Kamal cautiously.

"I have to. It's an annual group wedding. Every year ten male and ten female devotees get married in El-Deen. La-Jay himself reads the prayers and weds them. There is a ceremony on the stage of the Community Center. It's tomorrow night—ten couples. La-Jay thinks he is doing me a favor, matching me with my cousin. She is a tough girl. She could be good for the Holy Front." He pauses, listens and says, "The nurse is back. I can hear his footsteps. There is one more thing, brother. I want to ask you a favor." Kamal talks fast and broken. "Watch the Last Holy One for me. I mean the crazy man. When I come to get you tomorrow, I want you to tell me who he really is. And I pray to God that you survive in eleven. There are two loony repentants, Akir and Nakir, who may get wild. This is very important to me, to know about the crazy man. Do you get me? Very important. I have strange dreams lately. In my last dream," Kamal gasps, continuing in a whisper, "He tilted the Holy Grail as usual and the moment I was going to drink the Holy Water of Immortality, He whispered in my ears: 'Kamal, my son, I'm not Absent anymore. Find me if you can, then you'll drink the Water of Immortality!'"

In the deep darkness of the room, I hear Kamal weeping. I want to stretch my arm and hold his big hand, but I have no arms. All I have is words.

"Don't cry, Brother," I hear myself whispering, "I'll find out who the man is."

The nurse's key turns in the hole and Kamal jumps up and turns the lights on. He wipes his tears and as the nurse enters he fakes an authoritative voice: "Remember my last words, bastard! Now move and let us lock you up in eleven." And to the nurse he says, "May God protect you, Brother Nurse. I watched the screen for you. Your loonies are all sound asleep."

Number Eleven

Number eleven is as bright and hot as noon in desert. The strong light adds to the heat. I can hardly keep my eyes open. I blink, squint, and look around, wriggling in my straightjacket, trying to loosen it up. I won't be able to move my arms if the cannibals jump on me. But there is total silence. Nothing stirs.

Gradually I recognize a small cell, white walls, a TV set hanging from the ceiling showing white flakes. Two men lie down side by side against the right wall beside the door, their heads inside black paper bags. They're not wearing straightjackets; instead, they have on black shirts and pants like the devotees. These two men look strangely alike: their arms and legs, torsos, and hips are exactly the same size. They must be Akir and Nakir, the cannibals.

Against the wall opposite the door a boy sits in a box—an ordinary carton box. The boy's head is tilted on his chest, his arms hang out loosely. He looks like a puppet made of scraps of garments, with a cotton-filled head and soft, cotton-filled arms.

The Last Holy One sits against the third wall. I recognize him from his long, stooped torso and his bald head. I remember I saw him once in the hallways walking on his bleeding feet. He is not straightjacketed either. He hugs his long legs inside the curls of his arms and his bald head is drooped on his knees. Sweat bubbles on his scalp. He snores.

I sit leaning against the fourth wall, watching them. This is the first time (as far as I can remember) that I have had cell-mates. A vague joy tickles my heart. Ha-G wanted to punish me by sending me to the Psychiatric Wing, but I'm happier here—happier than ever. There are people to watch, to listen to, to talk to. But what if the two crazy repentants, the twin cannibals, torture me to death? Even Kamal was worried about this. He wished me luck surviving.

I stretch my legs out. My feet burn. The wounds throb and twinge. The straightjacket is tight and blood doesn't circulate very well in my arms. Both my arms are asleep. Now I think that with all these pains and this blinding light and the tormenting heat and the possibility of the hooded twins attacking me any second, I won't be able to sleep. I'll miss the opportunity to rest and get my energy back for tomorrow—the second interrogation. This time, Shit Mouth is not going to give up on me. Still, I have to stay awake and alert, to watch the sleeping cannibals.

I think about Kamal and the strange scene in the darkness of the nurse's room. His gloom, his creased forehead, and his voice, almost unreal when he talked so gently, like a friend, convinced me more than ever that he was related to Ali the Bricklayer. Could Kamal be Ali's son? If he takes me to his wedding tomorrow I'll find out. I'm sure that Ali the Bricklayer, who is a wealthy butcher now, will come to his son's wedding. But it all depends on tonight—if I survive—and tomorrow—if Ha-G doesn't kill me on that gurney. I have to stay sane and alive to go to Kamal's wedding and see Ali the Bricklayer changed into a butcher.

But didn't I ask Ali to die?

It was at the end of the First Revolt, when the night lingered and the corpses covered the earth and the earth stopped breathing. It was then, when the girl burned the castle and the white horse, the false Rakhsh, took Sahar away. I screamed at the foot of the tall wall, asking Ali to die. He listened to me and threw himself down. His skull cracked open right at my feet and his brain slipped out. I took the warm brain in my palms and carried it with me.

Then how did Ali the Bricklayer, Ali the Wall Raiser, Ali the Wise, change into someone else—into a butcher? Was that a dream? What is reality, then? If all that was dream, then Sahar is not lost. The false Rakhsh didn't take her away. She stayed with me. She lived with me for many more years. When did I lose her?

I close my eyes and seek darkness, but everything is still bright. In the hot, hollow vacuum of my head behind my red eyelids, I search for her. When did I lose you, Sahar? I repeat this again and again. I still had you when I landed on the fire, on the eve of Fire-Wednesday, right before the New Year.

Fire-Wednesday, 2

"Don't be scared, jump! You *can* jump. Fire can't catch you!" Sahar's voice echoes in my burning head.

I run all the way downhill, to where the school is, and then uphill, wide-legged and awkward as a giraffe; I run toward the row of the burning firewood. I don't have my shoes on. With each step I land on the small heaps of fire. The family and neighbors step back and watch me. Four pairs of black eyes—the eyes of the sheikh's wives—stare at me from behind the thick curtain of their room. I run toward the last flame, the tallest. With each step I land on burning flames, approaching the big fire.

Sahar screams, "Don't be scared. You can! You can! Say the words!"

As I open my mouth to tell the fire that my yellow belongs to it and its red belongs to me, I land right in the middle of the tall flame. A long, wet tongue licks me all over. With a quick whizz sound my hair instantly turns into ashes. But my feet burn the most. Grandfather and Uncle Musa pull me out and kill the fire on me. My red shirt turns into black ashes; it powders and falls. Some laugh, and some bite their lips. Kami and Cyrus horselaugh with their hoarse voices. I hear people saying, "He failed! Failed the test!

Good for nothing!" Sheikh Ahmad's wives smile and drop the curtain. Mother disappears inside the house, her painted face squeezed into a shrunken mask. "Imbecile!" she murmurs.

Everybody leaves the street. The game is over. The sun sinks behind Alborz and night falls on the city. It's time to eat, drink and tell tales. No one stays in the dark, except for those who want old gypsies to tell their fortune in the shadows of the walls, or the little gluttons who hide under their grandmothers' veils and beat a spoon on a pot at every single door for some sugar plum candy or mixed nuts. The crackling of the firecrackers and explosions from the fireworks get fainter and fainter and finally die. The glowing stars above the city sink behind the mountain like falling stars.

"Don't cry! Are you crying for the burns, or what?" Sahar holds my hand.

"Not the burns, Sahar, not the burns. I didn't pass through the fire—I failed—" I weep.

Sahar lays my head on her shoulder and strokes my half-burned hair. "You didn't fail, you didn't!" she says. "This was just a game—for fun. It's Fire-Wednesday, dummy, it's not anything serious! There are other things in life, real hard, real dangerous. You won't fail in them."

"I'm not as strong as you, Sahar, and you know it. Everybody knows it." I weep some more.

"Don't cry! I'll be with you forever. I'll be your stronger part, then we won't fail!"

"Will we be Unbreakable?" I ask.

"Unbreakable!" she echoes.

Now she pulls my hand and takes me to the desert.

"Where are you taking me, Sahar? My feet burn, my shirt has turned into ashes, I'm cold, I can't walk. It's dark too. I'm scared. Let's go in, sit with the family and listen to Grandfather's stories."

"It's a long time since we have journeyed through the desert," Sahar says. "It's a long time since we've been to El-Deen's wall."

"But now? In this dark? While everybody is sitting in Grandfather's room, eating and drinking? Why now?"

"It's now that Father needs us to be close to him. The New Year is coming, but Father doesn't have a celebration. This is the loneliest time of the year for him," Sahar says, holding my hand tightly, pulling me behind.

I keep quiet and follow her. The rough sand, thorn bushes, and sharp stones tear up my burned feet. I bleed and Sahar drags me behind. She walks faster and faster, without noticing my pain.

The desert is one huge shadow, the shadow of the mountain. Mother Alborz is tall and black to our right, casting her heavy silhouette on all the neighborhoods of the Old North Road. We reach the tenant house. The old wooden door is open as usual, and swinging with a squeaking sound. Sahar pulls me in.

For a long time, since the failed First Revolt, we lost interest in the tenant house and its residents. Some of the tenants, like Hassan the Gardener, and the Lame, are in the Fourth Precipice of Oblivion—the cage of the criminals. The court decided that their revolt was criminal and not political. So they're locked in the moving cage between the two cliffs. Zahra, Ali the Bricklayer's wife, served two years in the cage and was released. Some of the participants of the First Revolt (Bashi the Janitor among them) are in El-Deen. Some were released after the initial interrogations (Uncle Massi among them) and some were never arrested (Sheikh Ahmad and Salman the Brainless among them). One of the rebels, however, disappeared from the face of the earth: Ali the Bricklayer.

Ali has been missing for two years. Zahra, his wife, has started to wash the women at the public bath again. But she has lost most of her customers. Ladies of New Spring don't want a criminal, fresh from the Fourth Precipice, scrubbing their skin. But our family still calls her. Now, she is quiet most of the time, her eyes wandering. She murmurs to herself. While she was imprisoned, other women of the tenant house took care of her children, but last winter her four-year-old son died of pneumonia. She lost her second child to the cold winter of Old North Road.

Now, on the eve of Fire-Wednesday, Zahra, the washing woman of our public bath, is squatting in front of her hovel, sipping her hot, dark tea. Her three fatherless children roll in the dust around her. She is taking one evening off before working all day tomorrow. Tomorrow will be the day before New Year, the busiest time of her job. Tomorrow she will wash the people all day long, from four in the morning, until ten at night, when the manager—the master of the baths—turns the huge furnace off, hangs the red towels on the roof, and closes the bath with a double lock.

"How are you, Zahra?" Sahar squats in front of her.

215

"Ay, ay, ay, ay." That's all she says.

"Ali will be back, Zahra, I'm sure he will!" Sahar says, assuring the woman.

"Whatever *He* wants!" Is all Zahra says and turns her eyes up, toward the dark sky.

Sahar pays a visit to all the widows of the three yards. She squats in front of them, says something in sympathy, then drags me behind.

"Sahar, you're not going to see Uncle Massi, are you? They say he is the worst he has ever been," I warn her. "Why are we doing this, Sahar?"

"Have you forgotten that these steps are all part of our journey? We have to pay visits to these wretched people and then go to the wall. It's time to renew our vow." Without waiting for me to respond, she knocks on Uncle's door.

Uncle doesn't open his door. Sahar pushes it open, pulling me behind.

"Who are you?" Uncle Massi asks. He sits cross-legged on his old bamboo spread, now shredded into sharp sticks and straw. He is writing on a lap-desk with a feather pen. Since his wife, Mariam the Big Mole, was shot in the First Revolt, Uncle hasn't left his room. He hasn't talked to people, hasn't preached to the neighbors, hasn't claimed to be their poet-prophet, and hasn't sat on the wall of the tenant house drinking vodka and cracking sunflower seeds.

"We're your sister's children," Sahar says. "Pari's..."

"A hole... a hole..." he murmers, writing on his long role of paper. "A hole in her mole..."

Sahar and I look at each other and then look around the cell-like room. We still remember when these walls were covered with pictures of Western movie stars. But that was before Mariam. Now the walls are designed with something else. We have to look carefully to recognize the scraps and pieces of a red-checkered dress. A sleeve is hanging here, a piece of a skirt nailed there. The material is pale and dusty—yellowing. Uncle himself has a worn-out red-checkered bandana around his forehead. This must have been Mariam's belt. We feel Mariam the Big Mole's smell around, a sweet and sour smell, the smell of camphor, rosewater, dust, and sweat. We stare at Uncle Massi, his cursive and his walls. Without raising his head, he writes, "Why the mole? Why the mole?"

We leave.

"What happened, Sahar? Why did that revolt fail?" I trudge behind her in the dark. I'm on my bleeding feet; I trip on the thorns and stumble on the rocks. "Did you hear Zahra's silence, Sahar? Did you see our uncle, crazier than ever? And what happened to Ali the Bricklayer?"

"It's not easy to wrestle with giants. It's not easy to destroy the monsters," Sahar says. "Twenty and Five... no, in less than twenty and five, the earth will grumble and Alborz will roar!" She says this and her face glows in the dark night. Sahar's large eyes look larger and glossier and her hair (gone wild again) curls in a dark cloud around her small face. I look at my twin, at her strange ageless appearance, and I fear for both her and myself.

"Twenty and five years," I murmur.

"Now, less," she says.

We reach the wide ditch surrounding El-Deen. The ditch is now half filled with blood. The tall shadow of the wall leans heavily on us and the ironwoods hide in the dark. We hold hands and look deep into each other's eyes. Slow and clear, into the dark starless night, Sahar recites:

"Here, in the midst of this deep night, at the end of this dark year, in the eve of this last Wednesday, the Wednesday of fire and fear, when the strongest are cruel, Mother Alborz is blind, El-Deen the monster of the Monarch is merciless, chewing our father in his large mouth over and over, forever. In the midst of such a night, we, the twins of our ever-changing mermaid mother and our shrinking, imprisoned father, we, the inseparable, unbreakable twins of the Old North Road, swear to grow up and stop the evil and put an end to human misery. In less than twenty-five years!"

Now we get up and run along the ditch, toward the moving bridge where Ali the Bricklayer took us once, in the now remote past. We reach the bridge, under which Afreet, the watchdog of El-Deen, barks all night long.

"Run, run, run! Run to the gate!" Sahar screams. She is on the other side of the bridge.

I run, but my burning feet don't carry me much further. I run and I'm still on the moving bridge. Afreet jumps to reach me. I can feel her wet mouth on my legs. My knees tremble and I hear the pink blisters on my soles bursting one by one, like little balloons. I fall over my face, unable to get up. Sahar's voice is lost among the ironwoods, and I'm motionless, lying on the suspended bridge.

I know who is biting me on my foot, pulling me down into the ditch of blood. The bitch, Afreet, the she-dog of El-Deen doesn't tear me up at once. She pulls me down in the bloody mud. My body sinks and only my head and feet stay out. She licks my wounded soles and tongues my blisters, nibbling on my shredded skin. I scream and with each scream swallow a mouthful of mud and blood. I try to call Sahar, but my mouth is full.

Ilych, the Last Holy One

I scream with horror. Under the blinding light of room eleven, two long tongues sticking out of holes of black paper bags, are licking my wounded feet. Akir and Nakir, the hooded cannibals of the Psychiatric Wing, are nibbling on me.

"Stop this! I order you to stop!" A deep authoritative voice commands.

I find the tall, thin figure of the Last Holy One above my head, ordering the identical hooded repentants to move back. He is wearing a white shirt with an old black vest over it, a chain hanging loosely between the middle button and the left pocket. This must be a pocket watch, I think. To possess a vest and a pocket watch and to be able to order the torturers around—who is this man?

Akir and Nakir crawl back and sit against their wall, sulking. The Last Holy One offers his right hand to shake my hand. He realizes that I'm straightjacketed.

"Oh, what a shame! What a shame! Let me unjacket you, comrade!" He kneels down, gently lifts my body, helps me sit, and starts to untie the long white laces. Meanwhile, in a low, almost murmuring tone, which gets louder as he continues his speech, he whispers into my ear, "Most of the people in El-Deen either believe that I'm the Last Holy One, the Absent One, or they have doubts about me. They let me wear my vest and carry my watch—." He stops untangling me, takes an old rusty watch out of his vest pocket, clicks it open and looks at it admiringly and talks to himself. "It's half-past five now: dawn. The TV program will start in a few minutes. We have to prepare for the counter-anthem." For a second he loses track of his thoughts and then again, "This watch—look comrade! This is a historical watch. A witness to the dialectical process of class struggle. It should be in a showcase in a museum, but it's hanging on me because it's my old companion."

Now, as he works on my laces and continues his speech, his voice gets louder. He shouts into my ear, "This dear watch was with me on December 1895, in cell number 193 in St. Petersburg's central prison. I lead the workers' strikes then. It was with me on July 1900, when I crossed the Russian frontier to start an All-Party underground newspaper, *Iskra*. It was with me when I was suffering from inflammation of the nerves, screaming from intolerable pain, and preparing for an All-Party Congress, working day and night on reports, resolutions, speeches, and so on and so forth. It was with me in bloody 1905, in the moonlit December of 1907, when I crossed the frozen Finnish channel." He sits on his knees, and, leaving me tangled for a minute, he holds the watch dramatically in front of his face, raises his voice, and says, "This watch, this old friend, was ticking and tocking in my pocket, on my abdomen, when the ice cracked open under my feet like my Party itself! And finally my comrade watch was with me when I arrived at the Tsar's station in the Vyborg district, where thousands of Bolshevik workers and soldiers greeted me."

With an abrupt movement, he unfastens my last tie, and, as if freeing me from the fetters of oppression, throws the large white cloth away with a grand gesture, gets on his legs and tries to stand as erect as possible (I realize how hard and painful it is for him to stretch his stooped back). He continues, now in a high pitched scream, "And it was with me, and was ticking, and was tocking in my pocket, on my abdomen, when I climbed the soot-covered tower of the factory, struck like thunder and cried, '**Comrades! We do not need Bourgeois Democracy... All Power to the Soviets!**' And thousands of caps and berets flew in the sky."

He offers his right hand to me, gasps and introduces himself, "I'm Vladimir Ilych Lenin. You are my friend and comrade, so call me Ilych for short."

I swallow my saliva—or rather do the act of swallowing. No saliva is left in my mouth. I mumble, "But, I thought—you—were—the Last Holy One..."

Lenin kneels down and whispers into my ear, "I'm fooling them, comrade! I'm fooling them all. From the top of the pyramid to the bottom. One of these days they will crown me with their biggest turban and take me to their Great Leader. There is a conflict between the devotees now. And I have to mention here: the devotees belong to

219

different strata of the petit-bourgeoisie. Some are absolutely convinced that I'm the Absent One, appearing here and now to observe them and test them and this is the end of the world, and some have serious doubts about my identity (petit-bourgeois conservatism, comrade!). This second group—apparently stronger—believes that they should keep me here for a while and make sure of who I really am. But, in any case, they have given me certain privileges, as you can see. My vest, my watch, and my chamber pot." With a victorious smile, Ilych points to a small, yellow, chipped, chamber pot, enamelled, with a crooked handle on the side.

"I pee in it. I'm the only unrepentant prisoner who has the privilege of a private pee-pot!" He laughs, a gay and healthy laughter, like a carefree normal person. "Now before the voice of the reaction fills the room," he points to the TV screen hanging from the ceiling, "let me introduce these comrades to you. These two fellows are Akir and Nakir. That's what the authorities call them. Some religious names perhaps, angels of death or something. I don't think they're brothers, they've just had identical lives, identical destinies, and thus, identical forms. For, you know, my friend, it's the content that brings about the appropriate form. Form follows content. But can a form create a content? Dialectically it should, but don't we need a dominating pole? In the case of these identical creatures," he gestures to Akir and Nakir, "what is dominant? The content or the form? As you can see, their clothes and hoods are the same color, but this is because the authorities want them to look alike. Maybe the angels of death were twins or something. Their identical sizes must be a coincidence. We should never underestimate the role of coincidence in history, comrade. I've been observing these phenomena for a while now. A very long time. They never talk, but they like to lick!" he laughs loudly again. "They lick blood. The guards take them to different cells to let them work on the wounds of the tortured inmates. But their eternal home is here. Here is where they dwell. If I hadn't stopped them earlier, they would have eaten up your feet. It's sad, isn't it? This is not a bad dream, comrade—this is the objective reality!"

Now Ilych paces up and down the cell, playing with the sharp tip of his goatee. He continues, "This is where liberal bourgeoisie leads us. The struggle of a liberal for freedom is half-hearted, friend. Their property, status, and class interests are tied up with the social order they want to fight.

Thus, in the face of hardships, like imprisonment and medieval torture, they easily compromise—and what a compromise! They repent and become instruments of torture. They change identity and finally, as you can see, become feet-eaters. There is no limitation, comrade, to what liberal bourgeoisie can become." He sighs, walks toward the still-sulking twins, and smiles at them. "But these fellows are good boys. They respect me and listen to me. Although I'm not sure why. For, at the bottom of their hearts, they neither believe in Lenin, nor in the Last Holy One."

I make myself comfortable and lean my naked back against the warm wall. I know that the Last Holy One, or Ilych, can talk forever. But I'm so thirsty for conversation that I bear the constant twinges on my feet and listen to him with the utmost attention.

"This little chap, Saboor, is our brave thirteen-year-old warrior from the unholy battlefields of El-Deen. He has serious problems with the lower part of his body, but is happy and extremely optimistic about the future of the working class and the upper part of himself, which functions pretty well. Saboor is my dearest companion in this cell. I'm planning to send him to Gorky when we are out of here. I want Maxim to help him to write the story of his life."

I look at Saboor's jaundiced, motionless face and his distant gaze, empty of hope. He is awake and staring at us, his thin arms hanging from either side of the box. I stretch my arm to shake his hand, but he doesn't move.

"Saboor! Our comrade wants to shake your hand," Ilych says.

Puppet-like, Saboor extends his right arm and I shake his cold hand. The sensation gives me a shiver right to the marrow of my bones. I feel as if holding the hand of a long-dead corpse.

"Saboor," I murmur. "Haven't I seen you somewhere before? Didn't you use to have a yo-yo?"

He is silent, motionless as though deaf. The Last Holy One talks instead of him.

"Maybe you have seen him in the 1905 Revolution, comrade. He was even younger then, busy making dynamite at home and burning pictures of the Tsar in the streets."

"He used to live in a castle," I say. "Saboor, the Servant! That's what his name was! He used to stay up all night, on call, in case the aristocrats needed something. To prevent himself from falling asleep, he played with a yo-yo.

But that was at the time of the First Revolt—more than twenty-five years ago. That child must be a man now. Saboor!" I repeat his name again. "Didn't you ever grow up? And what happened to your legs?" I ask in vain, because he remains a statue.

"Nothing is wrong with Saboor's legs," Ilych says. "He sits in a box, because he cannot control his discharge—neither his pee-pee, nor his poo-poo. This happened in the Russo-Japanese War, the war that fattened European imperialism. Saboor sacrificed part of his nervous system to imperialism. Now he shits on the world!" Ilych paces the cell in deep thought.

Meanwhile, a picture appears on the TV screen, the picture of the Great Leader of the Holy Revolution. His eyebrows are tangled in a deep frown and his eyes pierce whoever dares to look him in the eye. The loud Holy Anthem fills the cell. The choir of Brothers repeats, "God is Great! The Leader is Great! The enemy must know that we are the great roaring waves—" and so forth.

The Last Holy One calls out, "Akir, Nakir, Saboor! Are you all ready?" He explains to me, "Every morning, in order to resist the sound of reaction, we sing louder than them, we sing *our* anthem, the anthem of the masses of the world. Join us, comrade, but you don't need to march with your injured feet."

I slide myself toward Saboor's box to sit next to him. But an unpleasant odor, the smell of rot, hits my nose; I move back. Ilych, Akir, and Nakir, make a line and march around the small cell, singing, "Arise, you prisoners of starvation! Arise, you wretched of the earth!" Saboor's colorless lips move, but no voice rises. Akir and Nakir have hoarse, ear-tearing voices. The closer the Holy Anthem rises to its peak, the harder Ilych and the hooded twins stamp on the cement floor, screaming from the bottom of their lungs. The sound of the Holy Song and the noises of the marchers are so unbearable that I cover my ears and hope for the end of this double anthem. "Is this a madhouse?" I murmur to myself. I remember that this *is* a madhouse and I smile in my new misery.

Now the wrathful picture of the Leader leaves the TV screen, a tomb appears, and a deep voice recites the morning prayer. The door opens and Kamal appears in the frame. He looks gray and dull, his eyes sunken, his forehead creased with many lines, and his lips hang over his long beard.

The marchers are quiet now. Akir and Nakir crawl back to their wall and sit side by side. The Last Holy One, exhausted by the march, moves to his wall, sits, hugs his legs, and stares at Kamal, piercingly. Saboor's cotton-filled body droops again. He dozes off in his box. With his index finger, Kamal motions me to go out. I leave the cell; he locks the door behind me and takes me to a corner without a hidden lense. He squats, motions me to squat, and whispers in my ear:

"I have a good news for you, brother. Ha-G and Halal fought over you for two hours early this morning. After Ha-G read Halal's report, he immediately rejected it. Ha-G wanted the interrogation to start at seven today. But, Halal called the Headquarters and talked to La-Jay for fifteen minutes. He even talked to one of the advisors in a foreign language. Ten minutes later, La-Jay called Ha-G and they talked for another fifteen minutes. At the end of their conversation, Ha-G, as mad as a rabid dog, left the room—I mean was carried out of the room. I'd never seen the hunchback this mad before. Halal sat there with his files and reports, waiting. Fifteen minutes later, instead of Ha-G, a messenger came and said that the interrogation was postponed to another time, but Ha-G is going to take the case to the highest Holy Revolutionary Court. I was there all the time, brother, to see what your destiny would be."

Kamal lays his heavy hand on my bare shoulder and says, "Halal has won for now, but only God knows what will happen later. Congratulations, brother. You won't see the Shit Mouth for a while, which means less pain and stress. In the hands of Halal, all that can happen to you is lots of sleep, more dreams and too much relaxation. Besides, you'll spend more time with me. I'll finally take you to the Community Center tonight. You'll watch the performance and the group wedding. *My* wedding, Brother, *my* wedding." He sighs and a shadow passes over his face.

There is a long silence. Kamal stands up and helps me to get on my feet. I feel that he is hesitant to take me back to the cell; there is more to say. I hear the end of the morning prayer coming from the TV set that hangs from the ceiling. A Western military march follows. From the corner of my eye I see the picture of the tomb fading into a black flag that waves in the wind. Now the Soldiers of God march in files toward the Holy Battlefields in the South. The child-soldiers stamp their feet in the last row, carrying flags bigger than themselves. The Sisters march at a distance. They are long, dark shadows, black ghosts, machine guns against their shapeless shoulders.

Gloom draws a dark curtain on Kamal's face. He mumbles and says, "Now, what news do *you* have for me? Did you talk to the man? Did he talk to you? Did you find out who he is?"

What can I tell Kamal? That the man is not the Last Holy One, that he is fooling them all and he thinks he is Vladimir Ilych Lenin? What will happen to Kamal, then? I have a strong feeling that he has built up hopes that the crazy man in room eleven is the Last Holy One, appearing on earth to test them—all of them—but particularly, Kamal, because he is the chosen one. If I disappoint Kamal, he will lose hope forever. And for a monster like him, losing hope is the most dangerous thing. If I lie to him, he will drink the Holy Water of Immortality in his dream; he will become happy. Why shouldn't I make him happy? Why shouldn't I help Kamal to become a better person? But I need more time. I need to talk to Ilych first, see if he wants to go this far in his game and contact Kamal as the Promised One.

"What have you found out, brother? Huh? Time is short. I have to go. There is an inmate in the Black Box—I have to walk him back to his cell. Hurry up!"

"Kamal," I whisper, "I'm still not sure who he really is. But he is an unusual person, a natural leader, a genius maybe. I need a little more time; give me more time, Brother."

"You'll have it, brother. Stay here until evening. But evening is your deadline. When I come back to pick you up, I want a simple yes or no. Understood? What you just said warms my heart. These qualities match the Last Holy One's: leadership, genius. They match."

Kamal thinks for a second, a smile frozen on his face. He is daydreaming. Now, suddenly carried away by his emotions, he says, "Oh, brother! You don't know what this means to me. If he really is the Promised One, then I can demand the Holy Water of Immortality right here. Why in my dream, and not in reality? Oh, brother, I can drink it before my wedding. But if not—if the man is not Him—." Kamal's eyes instantly fill with red veins and his teeth clench. I step back, for the possibility of an assault. But, he continues with the same self pitying tone, "—I won't be able to go through that group wedding tonight. How am I supposed to have intercourse with my bride, while the holy desire for the Absent One is undermining my human desires? Do you get me?" He stares at me strangely. He wants me to nod or show some sign of understanding. "His image, His handsome face, His green emerald eyes, His thin moustache, the dark curl of His holy hair, hanging out of his soft silk turban... Oh, brother, I won't be able to wed any woman!"

Now I have no doubt that Kamal wants me to assure him that the crazy man is the Last Holy One in disguise. He is in love with the image of the Holy One and cannot become happy without his recognition.

The Attack of Shingles

Ilych is moaning when I enter the cell. He is embracing his thin torso with his long arms, rocking himself back and forth, groaning. He is in pain.

I sit beside him on the floor and look at him. His yellow face is squeezed like a dried plum. He tries to stretch his back. Sharp hairs of his goatee stand up erect. On TV, the announcer of the military film is shouting agitating slogans: "Join the Holy Army of God! Purchase a piece of land in the Heaven of God!"

Ilych howls now, rolling on the floor, scratching the hard cement with his nails, biting his lips. He is wet with sweat, writhing and rolling as though wrestling with an invisible monster. I watch him for a minute and decide that he is not acting. He is suffering from an agonizing pain.

Not knowing what to do, I turn to Saboor and find him snoring. I turn to Akir and Nakir and ask, "Is he sick? Can we do something for him?"

They both shake their paper-bagged heads, meaning, no.

"Is there anything I can do for you?" I ask Ilych. He stops rolling and looks at me with eyes full of tears.

"This is an attack of shingles. They call it holy fire, too. It's a disease! What an appropriate name: holy fire!" He wipes his tears with the back of his hands. "It's an inflammation of the nerve terminals of back and chest. I've had this nervous ailment since 1902, when we were establishing a united Party with a single program and constitution. They treat me with iodine here, which gives me unbearable pain. I'm sorry, comrade! I should have informed you before. These friends know that they can't do anything for my pain, so they go on with their routine. It will pass, though, the pain I mean.

It's already better. A few attacks everyday, then exhaustion. It seems that the pain is lessening. I have to empty myself. This helps, takes the iodine out of my system." He crawls toward his enamel pee-pot, kneels in front of it, opens his fly and aims the hot, jetting urine at the middle of the pot.

"You may excuse me, comrade! I have to do this. I'm sure they have given me this pot for my disease—not for anything else. Not that I'm privileged! Maybe I'm totally wrong about having privileges here. This is a rotten cell, after all, isn't it?" He pees for a long time and fills the pot. "Rotten! And in the Psychiatric Wing too! I've never been so humiliated. Siberia was different. Much different. Sometimes I doubt their recognition and respect. What privilege? Huh? Do you call this a privilege?" He pauses, waiting for me to answer.

"I think it's a privilege to have that pot. What do others do when they need to empty themselves?" I ask, thinking about my own possible needs, not being able to remember the last time I peed.

"The nurse comes and gets them. He takes them to the toilet in the hall. Saboor doesn't need one. He pees in his box. They simply change the box everyday. Now he has a picture of corn oil on his box, yesterday he was sitting in a box of Darjeeling tea, imported from India. So, you think that this is a privilege, huh? To pee here, whenever I want? And my pocket watch. This certainly is a privilege." He clicks his watch open and with a childish joy stares at it. "It's half past seven, Kremlin time. It's my nap time. I take a short nap after my morning holy fire to accumulate energy for my afternoon one, which is more severe. They give me more iodine with lunch." He lies down against the left wall, puts his hands together, places them under his cheek, and closes his eyes.

The announcer is still screaming, "Brothers and Sisters! The warriors of the Holy Front invite you to join the War of God! This is the battle of Virtue against Vice! And there is a reward for each warrior! If you stay in this world, you'll be rewarded with the honor of visiting the Holy Leader in His Holy Balcony. You'll have the honor of kissing His Holy Ring! But if you're more fortunate, you'll retire from this earthly world and your reward will be the honor of visiting the Last Holy One, the Twelfth One, the Absent One, the Promised One, in the Holy Garden of Heaven! Rush and enroll, before the ranks are full. Procrastination will cause regret—"

Before I can hear the rest, Ilych opens his eyes and says, "I was wrong, comrade. They don't believe I'm the Last Holy One. The ignorants want to get killed, go up there, and see Him. I'm here, am I not? Why then does nobody take me out? Why does nobody kiss my hands? I was wrong. It was all illusion, sheer subjectivity! There's no privilege, none."

"Brother," I mumble, but I realize that he is a comrade. "Comrade," I say, "There is someone—one of them—who is very much interested to know if you really are the Holy One. He wants me to find this out for him. You were not wrong. You have made an impact."

Ilych sits up and looks at me.

"A follower? A real follower? Who is he?" But he doesn't let me speak. He is excited, keeps talking. "This means that I can still lead. I can attract the masses. They like me. I'm not forgotten. There is someone who thinks about me, wants to see me... "

"What should I tell him?" I ask. "That you are the Last Holy One? Then he will request the Holy Water of Immortality. He has these dreams, recurring dreams about you—I mean about the Last Holy One—giving him the Holy Grail. But each time he wants to drink it, the Holy One takes the cup away and tells him that he is not ready to become immortal. Not yet."

"Humm..." Ilych thinks and plays with the tip of his sharp beard. "Hmm... interesting. He wants his dream to actualize. He wants the Holy Water in real life. Illusion can never take the place of the reality—the objective reality. The proof of the pudding, Marx says, is in the eating. He wants to drink it. That's the proof for him. 'If you exist, Mr. Last Holy One,' our friend reasons with his man, 'give me a sip of your water in real life—if not, you do not exist!' This chap is a materialist by nature. He doesn't want the illusion of the Holy One and the Water, he wants *the* Holy One and *the* Water. He wants the pudding!" Ilych says, stares at a vacant spot in the air and rubs his beard. "Hmm... Tell him I'm Him! The Absent One! The Promised One! And I'll provide him the Water of Life! I will satisfy him, comrade, I'll make him Immortal!"

A cymbal clangs at the end of the military march, highlighting Ilych's brave decision. He retires to his wall and lies down again, hands under his cheek. He looks as innocent as a little child, but before long, he gets the chills and starts to shake. His teeth rattle.

"Can you do me a favor, comrade?" he asks.

I nod.

"Can you cover me with your straightjacket? These chills come after the holy fire."

I cover the curved, skeletal body of the Last Holy One with my straightjacket and tuck the sides under him. He falls asleep in a second. I look at his face: no trace of agony. He looks relaxed and relieved. I look around and find Saboor sleeping in his smelly box, his head drooped on his chest, his boneless arms spread wide apart, his hands covering the pictures of vegetable oil. The twin black angels, Akir and Nakir, have fallen asleep, too—hooded head to hooded head.

Confession of the Female Repentant

The programs of The Holy Republic's National TV are interrupted by El-Deen's special: "Confession of the Repentants." A female repentant addresses the brothers and sisters, inviting them to the faith. Fully covered in black, she is just a small circle in the middle of the screen. Her voice is mechanical and monotonous:

"Freedom is where the Holy Faith is! Our Republic is the promised Heaven on earth. His Holiness of the hot Holy Desert mentioned in His last Commandment that—" and she recites several lines from one of the Holy Texts by heart, to prove her points and to show that she has passed the ideological exams.

I can't focus on the small talking circle on the screen. Now that everybody is asleep and the commotion is over, my feet sting and a severe fatigue fills my veins. I think about the hours I've spent in the Psychiatric Wing and it seems to me that I've spent a lifetime here. I feel that I'm part of cell eleven and the crazy games of it—crazy indeed. This game of the Last Holy One and Kamal is the most dangerous of all.

What if the whole thing is a scheme to make me confess? What if Kamal is acting out a role and the Last Holy One is not Ilych, but an agent of El-Deen—a repentant—acting as Lenin to make me talk? But I haven't said a word about myself, have I? Ilych was so absorbed in his two personalities that he forgot to ask who I was, or what my name was. Did I say his two personalities? Let me not forget that he is neither of them. His real self is a third one, now hidden behind the two. Who is he? Or, who was he when he was himself? I don't have a clue to answer this.

Although I'm not unhappy in the company of Ilych (and even the harmless twins and Saboor) a tormenting thought prevents me from relaxing: What if they change me too? What if I forget why I'm here, and where I'm heading to? I'm myself and nobody else, I repeat. I'm here because either I took part in the Revolution to change the Monarch's government, or because they think that I was involved in the Revolution, and I was not. In any case—in the Revolution, or not—I'm not on the side of La-Jay, Ha-G, Halal, or even Kamal, who has made friends with me recently. I'm not on the side of the Last Holy One, either, for he is lost in his insanity, and I'm still sane. My destination? I can still remember, cell four, Hall Twenty, third floor underground—the cell of the Unbreakables. That's where I belong. Here, this wing, is only one stage in my long journey and although I feel the deepest compassion for my suffering companion, Ilych, I have to leave him here tonight and continue. The moment I reach the cell of the Unbreakables, I can go crazy, or die. But I'm not allowed to break now.

I sigh with relief and lie on my stomach to let the soles of my burning feet stay up in the air. The cement floor is warm and I don't have a shirt on. I feel like lying on the warm marble platform of a public bath. After such a long time, I am actually feeling a pleasant sensation. My body is relaxing now; only my feet are throbbing. The monotonous voice of the female repentant pours down from the ceiling like a dark lullaby. I become weightless. I float. I ascend. Through dark air, I enter a gloomy heaven. With each fragment of the woman's confession, my body moves forward into a soft black cloud, opens it and enters into yet thicker darkness. The voice showers me like a warm rain.

"I have seen Heaven in El-Deen. I have experienced the transcendental cleansing of guilt. I have apologized and repented. I have begged for pardon, begged for indulgence, expressed my regret. I have fallen down on my knees, flagellated myself, accepted the Holy Veil willingly and voluntarily. I have kissed the Holy Ring on the finger of the merciful Father of the Repentants, Brother La-Jay, Head of the Holy University. I have seen heaven in El-Deen. I have—"

From behind a thick black cloud, Sahar's face, white as a full moon, appears. But I notice that this is not her whole face, just a small circle in the middle. A black veil is covering her forehead from above her eyebrows, circling her cheeks down to the lower lip. Her large eyes, small nose, thick and pale lips are out, the rest is darkness. I sit up and shake myself. I rub my eyes to remove the image. Suddenly, the horrible thought comes to me that the woman confessing up there is Sahar. I look at the TV screen, but I don't find any resemblance between Sahar's face in the black clouds and the face on the TV screen. This one has a bony nose, thin lips and eyes a bit slanted. She is not Sahar.

"Sahar, Sahar..." I whisper. "Are you here in El-Deen? Have you repented? Did you break?" I swallow a painful lump in my throat and lie down again, this time on my back. I stare at the slanted eyes of the woman, trying to remember the last time I remembered Sahar or dreamed about her. Wasn't it last night in the same cell? It feels like I haven't thought about her for days now. How meaningless time is in El-Deen.

The cement floor is getting warmer. My heels burn. I turn over again and lay my face on the hot floor. Is this heat intentional? Are they torturing the lunatics too? The female repentant is gone and a military march is playing. It must be midday, ten o'clock or so. What does outside look like now? What if it's spring—before the New Year? If it's spring, then the sun must be out. The March sun.

The Public Bath

"This is the last time you can come to the baths with us," Maman says. "Starting the new year, you must go with your grandfather. You're becoming a man!"

In the brightest day of March, we walk on the long narrow sidewalk of New Spring Street carrying our bundles of fresh clothes. The snow is melting under the bridge of the Old North River and as we walk quietly, we hear the little thawing noises and big rushing sounds of many narrow rivulets that are anxious to join the mother river.

In our bundles, carefully arranged by Maman, we have towels, brushes, combs, good smelling soaps, soft and rough loofahs and plenty of delicious snacks—leftovers from last night, Fire-Wednesday. Maman is wearing her brown scarf, long skirt, woolen stockings and rubber boots. She moves her heavy body along the side walk, avoiding the slush and patches of melting snow.

Although we're not walking fast, she gasps for breath.

Sahar and I hold hands, walking behind her. The sidewalk is narrow and Maman is fat. Sahar is taller than me now. Nobody can tell we're twins. She is wearing the same yellow and red outfit from last night. She still smells of burned firewood. Her hair is pulled back, tied with a red ribbon; her ponytail swings behind her. When Maman says this is the last time I can go to the baths with them, I turn and look at Sahar, as though seeing her for the last time. She turns to me. For a second my heart leaves my body and cold air fills my veins.

First they separated our rooms, now we can't go to the baths together; next year we'll go to different schools. The distance between us grows wider and wider. I look at Sahar, missing her while she is still here. I miss her so much my mouth tastes bitter. I know that this taste will stay with me forever.

The stars do not twinkle in Sahar's large eyes: tears sparkle instead. She is thinking my thoughts.

Humming the "Blue Danube" to herself, Aunty Zari walks a few steps behind us. In the white light of the day, she looks oddly pretty, but not young anymore. Diagonal lines cross both sides of her face; they stretch from her temples to the corners of her fast-blinking eyes. Two curved lines form a parentheses around her still young lips. Since her son, Kami, has gone to military boarding school, Aunty Zari sews peacefully from dawn to night. She has become calm and quiet, serene—all inside herself.

Now she is wearing old, shabby clothes again, one layer on top of another, but everything is blue and green, the color of her eyes. Aunty Zari with her tall lanky body, her ugly outfit, her beautiful green eyes, her smooth light brown hair, the color of fresh dates, the strange lines on her face and the way she hums the waltz in her throat (the notes hit a stiff lump and crack before becoming a tune) is a mixture of young and old, beautiful and ugly. Sahar and I love her and fear her.

Our aunt behind, our big gasping step-grandmother in front, we feel secure, but lonely. These women are close to us, but not as close as a mother. Sahar cannot bear the silence, so she talks.

"Why isn't Mother coming to the Public Bath with us anymore?" Sahar asks Maman, although she knows well why Mother is not coming.

"She has a private bathroom in her apartment now," Maman says. "Why should she go through all this trouble? The Public Bath is for the poor ones, for us who live in old houses without a shower. Your mother is an affluent lady now," she sighs.

"How affluent?" Sahar asks.

"Well, compare her to all of us. She has her own car, hasn't she? A car ten times better than Uncle Musa's. She has her own business—may God bless her business—she is doing better than all of her brothers and sisters, isn't she? She is making more money than your Uncle Musa makes in the Insurance Company." She gasps, pauses and finally says, "She has a kitchen with white tiles and a white refrigerator, white gas stove, and white cabinets." She sighs again.

"I don't like her apartment," Sahar says.

"I like it," Maman says. "I'd give up half my life to cook in that white kitchen. I would. I swear to my God!"

"Is Aunty Hoori coming for the New Year, Maman?" Sahar asks.

"She hasn't written a word since autumn. She may come, or, she may not," Maman says as if talking to herself.

"She writes poems," Sahar says. "Just imagine! I saw them in the newspaper, Grandfather showed me," she says with excitement. "I wish I could become like her," Sahar says.

"My little girl was never happy here," Maman says. "And I don't think she is happy there. I have a feeling. But I wonder why?" Maman stops walking and turns to look at Sahar. She wants to talk more, but as if realizing that we are only children and she shouldn't talk about serious matters with us, she keeps quiet.

New Spring Street ends when we reach the Old North Road. The Public Bath is on the right corner, next to Grandfather's real estate office. The waiting room is full of people, but we have reserved our private chamber for the early morning. Still we have to sit and wait until the chamber is cleaned. There are mirrors all around. The hall looks infinite. We all sit in one row. Maman takes out her knitting.

If we talk here, our voice will echo and everybody will hear us. The ceiling is high. People will see us too; the walls are made of mirrors. So we sit quietly and watch ourselves in the opposite mirror. Maman has frowned. Her arms are moving mechanically, knitting a red jacket. She may be thinking about Hoori, trying to imagine her lonely room in the girls' dormitory. We know that the jacket will be Hoori's. Everything that Maman knits belongs

232

to Hoori. She folds them, packs them in a box, lays rose petals in the folds, and sends them along with lots of nuts and homemade pastries. Grandfather keeps telling Maman that the weather is warm in the south, that Hoori doesn't need all these woolen clothes, but still she starts another knitting project, weaves her thoughts, her worries, her fears, and her love into each and every single knot.

We look at Aunty Zari in the mirror. Her soft yellow hands lie limp on her lap. Her lifeless blue-green eyes are wide, staring at herself. These eyes, which normally blink hundred times more than other eyes, are still now. The "Blue Danube" is dead in Aunty Zari's throat.

Sahar and I are quiet, holding hands. We look at people and talk to each other without using words. "Look how happy everybody is! Tomorrow is the New Year!" Sahar's eyes tell me.

"Yes, I can see. Nobody is missing in their families," I answer her by looking at her eyes in the mirror.

"Many are missing in ours." I know she is saying this, because the corner of her lips droop.

"Mother is in her marble bath in the Alleys of Heaven," I tell her.

Her eyes sparkle, telling me, "The Monster of the Well is with her."

"Father is in El-Deen," I tell her by staring long and deep into her eyes.

"Do they know it's New Year in El-Deen?" She suddenly asks out loud.

"No," I close my eyes. "They don't keep track of time."

"Thirty-nine—not here?" The Master of the Baths calls. "Then, forty! And forty-one!" He is a skinny man. His shirt buttons are open, fuzzy hair sticks out from his chest, a red towel hangs on his shoulder. When a chamber door opens, steam floats in the hall and clouds the mirrors. The Master of the Baths wipes off the mirrors with his red towel.

We carry our bundles down a long corridor with chambers on either side. Iron doors, like the doors of prison cells, open to small, mirrored dressing rooms with platforms to sit on and hooks for towels on the wall. Another iron door links the dressing room to the washing area.

Sahar and I take our clothes off, tip-toe to the second iron door, and open it cautiously. We don't like it when it makes a loud noise like a cymbal. The washing area has a tiled platform on the left and a shower on the right. A small brass tub sits under the dripping hot and cold taps. The ceiling, like the ceiling of the waiting hall, is high. A single eye-window is up there; the opaque glass is covered with steam. This window opens to the roof of the baths, where many towels hang on the lines, swaying with the northern breeze, but now it is shut and blurred with steam. We cannot see the infinite blue sky of March. Sahar and I descend two steps, entering the washroom. We take a shower and sit on the white-tiled platform, waiting for Zahra, our washing woman, to come.

Maman's body is a wonder. It's a land to discover. All she is wearing is a white cotton panty. Her skin is yellow-white, the color of ivory. She is only heavy from the waist down. Her breasts are young and large, her neck and shoulders lineless, full, and smooth. Her torso is not fat at all. But she has wide hips, a swollen belly and very thick thighs. Fat and flesh fold and wrinkle and overlap on Maman's thighs. "These are the reason she can't walk fast," I always tell Sahar. And Sahar says, "Maman is fat because she never walks. She is trapped in her small kitchen, turning around herself, the rats turning around her."

Big and beautiful like a monument, the goddess of the kitchen, Maman sits on the platform, unbraiding her long braids. This will take her a long time, a very long time. She has to use her special soap, which is called "mud" and looks like a piece of dried mud too. But her mud soap cleans and shines her hair better than our scented shampoos. She has to comb her hair with her wide-toothed wooden comb. She has to divide her kinky hair into two long braids, and wrap them like ropes around her head until the next bath, when it's time to untangle them again.

Aunty Zari's body is melting like a yellow wax candle. She is lanky and bony, and the thin layer of flesh on her hips is soft, loose, and empty. Her skin covers her body like a thin yellow nylon, not quite stretched, wrinkled like some women's stockings. She has no muscles, no breasts. She is as flat and yellow as Maman's kitchen board.

Sahar has grown up. On her chest, once exactly like mine, two hard little breasts are sprouting, the size of half lemons. These days, while playing together, if I hit her chest accidentally, she screams with pain and scolds me. She is opening a red, ripe pomegranate now, taking the ruby colored jewels out and putting them in a bowl for us to eat. Her hands are red with the juice, her mouth has watered. I'm staring at her. My heart fills with love and grief. If Grandfather's camera were here, I'd take a picture of Sahar and make the moment eternal.

Sahar's wet skin shines like olives, her thick hair drips and sticks to her shoulders, her long eyelashes are wet like when she cries, her half-lemon breasts are like black rose buds. This is the last time I see my twin naked.

The iron door opens with a loud cymbal clang. Zahra enters. Cymbals announce the entrance of a queen, but now this skeleton, this brown sack of bones, this breastless woman with empty skin hanging on her chest, enters. This is Ali the Bricklayer's wife, the washing woman of the public bath. In a moment she will scrub our body with the roughest loofah, rubbing away all the dead skin. We enjoy when she rubs our backs where our fingernails can never reach. We shower and our skin shines like newborn babies after their first bath.

Zahra scrubs Maman's skin and they chat. Sahar and I are ready to leave, but we linger and play with the water in the brass tub. We remember how we used to sit in the little tub when we were very small. Both of us would fit in it. We'd sit opposite each other, pretending we were in a boat.

"Sahar, have I ever told you that I'm scared of the public bath?"

"No. But I knew," she says.

"Did you?"

"Of course. You're afraid that you'll get trapped here."

"Yes, exactly. What if both iron doors get locked? What if I yell and scream, but nobody hears me?"

"And the walls are slimy and slippery," Sahar says, "impossible to climb."

"What if I'm trapped here for a long time and my body gets soggy from too much humidity? What if I lose weight and my skin hangs on my bones like Zahra's? Or if nobody ever notices that I'm dying here."

"I know. I always knew your fear," she says.

Exercise, Toilet, Mass Prayer, and Lunch

She always knew. Even though I wouldn't tell her. So, she must know now—wherever she is, if she's alive—she must know where I am.

Unable to sleep, I sit up and lean against the wall. One of the hooded repentants has slept on top of the other one. The one under is vertical, the one over, horizontal. They've made a black cross. The Last Holy One snores, moaning at intervals. A familiar face appears on the TV screen—a thin face with tiny eyes, a dirty, prickly beard, and pock-marked cheeks. He is the nurse whose room is down the hall. He addresses the inmates, or the patients of the Psychiatric Wing:

"Brothers of the Psychiatric Wing, get ready for your prayer, restroom, and lunch. Patients of cells 8, 12, 13, and 17, get ready for your shots. Patients of cells 10 and 15—." He keeps announcing.

My friends all wake up as if the nurse's voice is their alarm clock. The Last Holy One stares at me for a long moment, trying to remember me. He looks lost and empty. Akir and Nakir are up on their feet, fixing their paper bags. The black bags are twisted, the eyes and mouth holes in the back. Saboor is motionless—not a word, not a yawn, only his eyes wide open.

At last the Last Holy One says in a hoarse voice, "The ability to see straight without overlooking the twists, turns, and zigzags of reality, this is what Marxism teaches!"

I'm not sure if he is talking to me, but I look at him and listen attentively.

"I told them and warned them," he continues, "that comrade Stalin has concentrated enormous power in his hands. And I'm not sure he always knows how to use this power. That's what I told them. He is rude, I said. Too rude. I proposed to the comrades to find a way to remove Stalin from that position, appoint another man who is more patient, more loyal, more polite and more attentive to comrades. Less capricious." He sighs and rubs his goatee. "It's all past now. Past. It's lunch-time. Do I know you, comrade?" he asks me.

"Yes. We had a conversation," I say.

"About?"

"About—"

I don't know what to say. I decide to remind him of our last conversation, the one which concerns me the most. What if Kamal comes and the Last Holy One doesn't remember anything?

"We talked about a man, a prison guard, who is interested in the Last Holy One and you agreed not to disappoint him," I say cautiously, for the fear of his denial.

"Oh that!" He cheers up. "Now I remember. The Holy Water of

Immortality! That's what this young man wants, this victim of ignorance and reaction. And I will give it to him. But, still, I cannot recall your name. Have I introduced myself?" He extends his hand to me, "I'm Vladimir Ilych Lenin. And you?"

"I have forgotten my name. That's why I'm here."

"Oh! Yes, of course. They don't believe you, huh? They think you're crazy? This happened to Mr. Turniphead, too. I'll tell you his story after lunch. As a matter of fact, I dreamed about him today. Yes, I definitely did. I always do. I dreamed about Mr. Turniphead and his journey in search of his name. Remind me to tell you this story. Now, comrades, it's exercise time!" He lifts himself up, straightens his stooped back as much as he can, and stands in a line with Akir and Nakir, facing Saboor.

"Don't you join us? If we don't exercise a little, we will rot here. Get up Mr. Turniphead! Quick!" he orders me.

"My feet are injured. I can't stand up," I say, hoping he remembers my wounds. But he has forgotten all about me. I'm a new person for him and he constantly calls me Mr. Turniphead.

"Your feet are injured, comrade Turniphead? Oh, that's too bad. So, you can exercise like Saboor, just the arms. One, two, one, two... slower now, onnnne, ttwwooo. A-h-a, that's better."

They stretch their arms up, open them sideways and repeat this several times. Saboor in the box stretches his rubber arms up and opens them, each time hitting the sides of the box, where pictures of the vegetable oil cans are. Now the Last Holy One starts doing jumping jacks. Akir and Nakir do the same thing, breathing fast and noisily inside their hoods. Saboor and I, unable to jump, just do the arms. The door opens and the nurse comes in.

"Restroom time! Hurry up! Make a line." Akir and Nakir immediately make a line, but the Last Holy One doesn't join them. "Bring your chamber pot and rinse it," the nurse orders the Last Holy One.

"The Holy Ones don't pee, my son. The pot is empty," he lies.

"Hey, you!" The nurse addresses Saboor, "We're out of empty boxes now, they're going to bring some from the kitchen this evening. Wait until then."

"Didn't I tell you to stand in the line?" the nurse asks me.

"I can't stand," I say. "My feet feel numb."

"Then move on your butt."

The nurse takes a long black leash out of his pocket, ties it tightly around my neck, then around Akir's neck and finally around Nakir's. He ties us to one another, holds the end of the leash, and walks in front of us. He leads us to the end of the hall, where the restroom is. I row fast, moving on my butt. If I don't, the people ahead of me will pull the leash and I'll roll over and make them trip and fall on each other.

The nurse doesn't unleash us to pee. The door stays open while Akir pees and we, connected to him, wait outside. The leash, now tighter on our necks, is choking us. Nakir goes next; Akir and I are almost strangled. And finally it's my turn. Now I have to stand up. While resting all morning, my wounds' condition has changed from burning and throbbing to a strange numbness. Large blisters are forming on the surface of my soles and if I stand on my feet, they will burst.

"Hurry up! It's late. We want to catch up with the mass prayer. Get up!" the nurse orders.

I get up and roll on my heels. Akir, Nakir, and the nurse stay behind me at the door. I stand in front of the metal toilet bowl and wait. I cannot pee. I must have peed on the bed of the Clinic, or during the interrogation. Maybe they had spread a plastic sheet under me, not to wet the bed. But I cannot remember when was the last time I stood in a toilet and peed like a grown up man.

"Come out now, you're making us late for the prayers. If you can't pee, then you don't need to force yourself." He pulls the leash and takes me out of the restroom. I trip over Nakir and fall on the floor. I row back to the cell.

In the cell the nurse has the injections ready for me and Saboor. This time in our arms and with the same syringe. He injects fast, the way he did in his room, without rubbing alcohol on the spot. Now he warns us that he'll watch us from his room.

"Make a line for the mass prayer and pray. No cheating today. You have to do the whole thing, from the start to the end. If you cheat, you won't get lunch." He threatens us. "And you!" he yells at me, "Get up! It's midday prayer; I'll watch you in my room, if you don't pray, I'll send you back to Ha-G for more lashes on your blisters."

At last he leaves, slams the door, and locks it. I get up on my numb feet and feel the large blisters squeezing under my weight like soft, tiny mushrooms. But there is no pain.

I stand in a row beside the Last Holy One, facing the TV. I murmur in his ear, "I don't know how to pray."

"I don't know either," he says. "Nobody can hear the words you're murmuring. Just bend down and get up like the man is doing on the screen. Usually at this time I compose my lectures. For some reason, I can concentrate very well."

There is a sheikh on the screen, his back to us, praying. Numerous men, some in ordinary clothes, some in the black outfit of the devotees, stand in rows behind him. Veiled women stand separately in rows, following the sheikh's movements. He bends, we bend; he stands erect, head up toward the sky, we do the same; he kneels down, we do, and so on. Meanwhile, the Last Holy One murmurs to himself, "One: A transfer of state power to the bourgeoisie cannot happen peacefully, as the Menshevik leaders hoped. Two: The country is passing from the first stage of revolution—which, owing to the insufficient class-consciousness and organization of the proletariat, placed power in the hands of the bourgeoisie—to its second stage, which must place power in the hands of the proletariat and poorest sections of the peasants. Three: An end to the impermissible, illusion-breeding demand—"

At the end of the prayer, the sheikh says, "God is the greatest; the Leader is great; death to the Blasphemers!" Ilych murmurs, "We shall now proceed to construct the socialist order!" The sheikh says, "Amen!" Ilych says, "Amen!"

The nurse comes with a big round tray. Like a professional waiter, he carries it on the palm of his right hand, shoulder-level. The tray contains five plastic bowls of soup. Inside, a few leaves of parsley swim in piss colored water. Five small paper cups stand, half-filled with water. Akir, Nakir, and Saboor start immediately. Plastic spoon after plastic spoon they swallow the yellow water. They make all kinds of munching and choking noises with their mouth, as though eating a heavenly dish.

"Eat, comrade! Eat!" Ilych orders me. "It's not as thick and rich as the stew Mr. Turniphead's wife was supposed to cook for him, but it's not that bad either."

"I've been fed through IV for a while, it's hard for me to eat," I say.

"Have a sip of water first. You need water. Your intestines must be dry," Ilych says, sipping the last drops of his soup from the bowl. Now he takes a white kerchief out of his vest's pocket and wipes his greasy lips and beard.

He leans back against the wall and starts in good humor, "Now, I'm going to tell you the story of Mr. Turniphead. You may identify with him." He turns to Saboor, who concentrates on carrying a spoonful of soup from his bowl without spilling a drop. The bowl sits on the floor, half a meter away from his wide open mouth. "You can enjoy this story too, comrade Saboor. You are not quite aware of your name and identity either."

I empty the paper cup first. Lukewarm water slips down my dry throat. Now slowly, I start eating my soup. It's too salty, but I like the parsley leaves. I keep a leaf of parsley in my mouth, trying to recall its sharp grassy taste. This one is tasteless.

Ilych rubs the pointed tip of his goatee and starts his story.

A Caucasian Folk Tale

"This is a Caucasian story, comrades. My Tartar father heard it from his Azari grandmother, and the Azari grandmother of my father heard the story from her grandmother, who was from the city of Hamedan, somewhere in Persia. We call our story a Caucasian story, for simplicity. Nobody knows who told the story to the woman in Hamedan two centuries ago, and where that person herself was from.

"In any case, whenever I'm imprisoned—in St. Petersburg, Siberia, or El-Deen—I recall this tale and have recurring dreams about it. The way I'm going to tell you the story may not be exactly the way my father told me when I was little and living in our house in Simbrisk. It may not be quite the way my father's Azari grandmother told him either, when he visited her every summer in Baku. Most probably this version is very different than the Hamedani version of my great-great-great-grandmother, too. This is my version, the version of my recurring dreams, mixed with recollections of my father's version, which I'm sure has traces of the original (if there is an original!) Hamedani version.

"Imagine somewhere in the general vicinity of Caucasus—a town not far from the Caspian Sea. The time? When the means of transportation were horses and carriages for the well-to-do and a pair of strong legs for the poor. The roads? Muddy. Caravansaries every few miles. Wheat fields between the towns. Schools, in open air. Teachers, the Mullahs. Text books, only the Holy Book.

Public baths, everywhere—for the wayfarers to wash out the dust. Vendors, selling salted turnips, walnuts or steamed beets in the bazaars. Bazaars, wherever a few vendors spread their goods. Kings, more accessible, some of them even disguised as beggars, walking the streets to see how their people lived. Some offered their daughters to poor, but brave men, because they were not particular about the purity of blood. Princesses, looking for men with wisdom and good heart, not gold and good looks. Foods, richer, greasier, and plentier. Butchers, important figures in society—big, robust, smelly, and strong. And so on and so forth.

"Now this husband and wife, Mr. and Mrs. Turniphead lived in the capital city, which itself was not much of a city by today's industrial standards. This was just a town, only a bit bigger than smaller towns. The couple belonged to the lowest strata of the middle class—hand-to-mouth. They had a small house, not quite in good shape. The man worked hard. He worked in the Marriage and Divorce Office as a copier and his fingers were always inky. The woman was a housewife. No children. (The tale doesn't tell us why they didn't have children.)

"But all of this is beside the point. The point is that Mr. Turniphead loved his wife dearly. Very dearly, indeed. Whatever she desired, he did his best to provide for her. The wife, I imagine, was slightly older than him, chubby, full-breasted, rather square, smart, capricious, cunning, flirt, fun-loving, talkative, thoughtless. At times quite mean. Mr. Turniphead was simply simple, small, honest, honorable, trustful, truthful, thankful for everything, thoughtful, but not enough doubtful, not quite made for this world. On the whole, a fool!

"Now one beautiful morning in March—a weekend maybe, for Mr. Turniphead was happy to be home—Mrs. Turniphead stayed in bed quite a while, then lazily got out of the bed and dragged herself to the small kitchen where Mr. Turniphead was making a special breakfast of fried heart and liver of lamb for her. She dumped her hefty body on the chair and said in a spoiled voice, 'I'm craving lamb stew today. I even dreamed of lamb stew last night.'

"Mr. Turniphead said, 'No problem, my dear, we'll cook a good one for lunch.'

"'We can't!' she said.

"'Why not?'

"'Because we don't know how many red beans and how many split peas we need to cook with the meat.'

"'We don't?'

"'No, we don't,' she said. 'And I'm craving this stew so bad that I may get sick. I suspect I'm pregnant, or something!' she wept.

"Mr. Turniphead dropped the frying pan and went pale in the face. He stuttered, 'P... p... preg...nant?'

"'Maybe,' she said, and wiped her tears off.

"'How can we find out how many red beans and how many split peas we need for this stew? We definitely need to make this dish right away!' the good-hearted husband said.

"'The only way to know is to ask the chef of Deezee, the famous caravanserai in Hamedan, the man who has a reputation for his lamb stews,' she said.

"'But, Hamedan is almost a thousand miles away from here,' the husband said.

"'I know,' she said.

"'Isn't there anyone here who can tell us how many red beans and how many split peas we need?' he asked.

"'No. My mother, who died last year, knew.' She burst into tears again, remembering her dead mother.

"'I'll go, then,' he said.

"'Oh, no!' she screamed.

"'I have to go. It's for your health!' he said.

"'You will?' she asked.

"'Oh, yes. I'll go to Hamedan, to that caravanserai, and I'll ask the cook how many red beans and how many split peas we need. I'd better get ready before the sun gets warm.'

"'Oh, my dear dear husband. I cannot believe how much you love me. I'll fetch your winter boots, the roads may be muddy. And Hamedan is way up north, the ground may be covered with snow. Your heavy boots are sturdier. It's an awful long walk,' she said worriedly.

"'Very long, indeed. Almost a thousand parasangs! Only God knows when I'll get there,' he said as he prepared for his trip. He wore his heavy winter boots and warm felt hat. His wife gave him a cane, made him a bundle of snacks— some mountain bread, some cheese, some fresh mint, and parsley, some walnuts, and a canteen of water. She kissed him on both cheeks and said farewell.

"'What will you do without me, my dear?' he asked, setting foot on the dusty road.

"'I'll sit here behind this window and wait for you. I won't even move!' Mrs. Turniphead said. 'I won't open the door to anyone except you, my dear.'"

Ilych stretches out his legs, scratches his bald head and turns to Akir and Nakir, "Have I told you this story before?"

They nod with their big heads.

"And you're still interested?"

They nod again.

"How about you, comrade Saboor?" Ilych turns to the boy in the box, but Saboor is fast asleep, his head wobbling on his chest, his arms out of the box, hands flat on the floor.

"Our young warrior Saboor is asleep. I wanted him to hear this story. It could make him talk. In old times, these folk tales used to have therapeutic effects. People would listen to them and experience catharsis. Now back to our story. Our hero, Turniphead, had a long dusty road ahead of him— endlessly stretching toward the north where Hamedan was. There were infinite wheat fields on his left, and scattered houses, blue minarets, and black chimneys of public baths, on his right. The more he walked, the fewer the number of the houses, minarets, and chimneys became, until there was nothing but patches of shapeless shadows belonging to the past behind him.

"Now, all our hero thought about was the future: how many red beans, and how many split peas? This was the question, the quest. He didn't care about the present: the farmers throwing seeds in the fields, the mourners burying their dead, or the drummers leading the procession of a village wedding. Mr. Turniphead did not care about the past either: the man he was, the job he had, the house he lived in, and so on. He even forgot his beloved wife; all he thought about was the beans and the peas—and how many of each.

"To make a long story short—because the afternoon attack of my shingles will happen around three-thirty—" Ilych clicks his pocket watch open, looks at it, clicks it close, and continues—"Our hero reached Hamedan in a cold dusk, when the color of the houses, stray dogs, snow-covered trees, and domes of the mosques were all gray and black as ash and soot.

"He asked a few passers-by who were rushing home to escape the chilly evening wind, where 'Deezee,' the famous caravanserai was, and they showed him. He got there without any difficulty and asked for the chef. When he appeared behind the counter with a big kitchen knife in one hand and a leg of a lamb in another, his mustache greased and curved up, our hero said, 'You must pardon me, honorable chef, for interrupting your work. I've come a long way from the capital city, at my wife's request, I suppose, but I'm not quite sure now... anyway, to ask your eminence, how many red beans, and how many split peas, do we need to make a lamb stew? Because I think, or rather my wife thinks, that the proportions are crucial...'

"The chef stared at him stonily, like he had never seen such a phenomenon before. Then he laughed, loud and hard, a horselaugh that attracted all the costumers' attention. Mr. Turniphead, of course, felt extremely self-conscious and bent his head in shame. The chef raised his voice so that everybody could hear him and said: 'So, you've come all the way to Hamedan to ask how many read beans and how many split peas you need in your stew?' And he laughed again and all the customers laughed with him, loudly and harshly. 'Well, I think I shouldn't disappoint you then, because in the whole kingdom, only I know how to make a lamb stew, and as a matter of fact, I'm making one now, for these hungry gentlemen.' And he shook the leg of the lamb in front of Mr. Turniphead's nose.

"'For a successful lamb stew,' the chef said in a professional tone, 'you need to add one handful of red beans and half a handful of split peas to your meat and chopped onions. Did you get me? One handful of the first one and half of the second one. Your wife is right: more of this or less of that, less of this one and more of that, will ruin your stew!' And he winked at the audience.

"Our hero thanked the chef one hundred times, bowed, and walked backwards, until he found himself in the cold, dark street, ankle deep in slush and mud. Now he regreted leaving. Why didn't he stay there and spend the night in one of the cozy rooms of the caravanserai? He could even taste the steaming stew. Tomorrow, before sunrise, he could head toward the capital. But, it was too late now—he had closed the door behind him and could still hear the people laughing at him. The chef's horselaugh was louder than everybody's. No, there was no way for him to go back, rest, eat, and sleep.

"So Mr. Turniphead walked along the narrow alleys of Hamedan, thinking how meaningful the name of this town was. Hamedan meant one-who-knows-everything! And people here knew everything. This was the city of knowledge, people were knowing and generous, although they seemed to be a little harsh to strangers. Mr. Turniphead thought that he had traveled all the way to learn something. But, to learn what? He tested himself—to learn about the amount of beans and peas. How much? He tested himself again—one handful of red beans, and half a handful of split peas. He smiled and sighed in relief. He remembered the recipe, and nothing mattered anymore. Tomorrow he would start walking toward his home, where his beloved wife was still sitting behind the window, waiting for him.

"He walked and reflected and all he thought about was the future; the past was vanished, the present was of no importance. His wife, the steaming stew in the middle of the kitchen table, and possibly a little cradle in the corner, a tiny bundle burping in it. His heart skipped with joy."

To accompany Ilych's Caucasian tale, the TV shows a religious contest in which the participants chant different passages of the Holy Text. They're either prison guards or the repentants of the sixth floor. They sing the Holy Text with an emotional and nostalgic air. Some have warm voices. Some lose control, weep, and stop singing.

Akir and Nakir have lain down on the hot floor, hands under the paper-bagged heads, waiting for the rest of the story. Saboor snores. Ilych sips water from his paper cup and continues:

"At last Turniphead reached a public bath. Of course, all the roads in the Middle East end in public baths. An oil lamp was hanging from the awning, its flame flickering with the cold breeze. In old times, my friends, public baths were open twenty-four hours. They were the warmest places in the freezing winters of Caucasus for lonely travelers to pay a black coin and sleep the whole night on the hot tiled platform beside the steaming pool.

"So Mr. Turniphead paid a coin and entered. He washed himself in the soothing warm water of the pool and lay down on the floor beside a few homeless people who were already snoring. All our hero repeated to himself before he drifted into the whirlwind of sleep was, 'One handful, half a handful—' so as not to forget the right amount of beans and peas.

"Before the cold sun of Hamedan shone above the blue minaret, even before the muezzin, the killer of sleep, sang the song of God from the bottom of his lungs atop the turquoise tower, Mr. Turniphead was on the road, taking long and fast steps toward the capital, repeating, 'One handful, half a handful...'"

"Don't fall asleep my friends," Ilych tells us, "the exciting parts are to come!"

One of the hooded twins has laid his head on the belly of the other; they have formed a big black cross.

"The sun came up," Ilych said, "and our hero was passing a village outside Hamedan. The farmers were throwing seeds and singing a gay song in their native dialect. Turniphead, who was also full of joy (the joy of going back home), unaware of the present and unaware of the farmers, screamed his line in the cool empty space: 'One handful, half a handful!'

"Suddenly, strong mustached farmers ran toward him and started to beat him up—some with big fists, some long spades, and some heavy shovels. Shocked and panicked, crying with pain, our poor man asked, 'Why? What have I done? Why are you beating me?'

"The farmers said, 'You bastard, son of a bitch! Are you suggesting that we are throwing one handful of seeds to harvest only half a handful? Huh? Is this what you were shouting?'

"'No, my dear men. I swear to Allah that this is not what I meant. I wasn't talking about your seeds or harvest. I was repeating the amount of beans and peas in my wife's lamb stew; believe me, good men, that's all I was saying in order not to forget them after such a long trip!'

"Believing him or not, the farmers pulled him up on his feet again, offered him some water and bread, walking with him a few steps. The oldest of them held his arm, whispering in his ear, 'Son, if you want to be secure in your long trip and get to your wife safe and sound, you have to repeat, "One becomes one thousand, one becomes one thousand!" Which means you give one seed to the earth and you harvest a thousand. Do you understand? If not, other farmers will beat you to death! So what is it you say?'

"Mr. Turniphead thought for a second and said, 'One becomes one thousand!'

"'Good man! Now off you go, we have work to do here!' the old farmer said, pushing him to the road.

"Turniphead limped and repeated, 'One becomes one thousand...' unable to think about anything else.

"In the next village, a funeral procession was approaching the graveyard. Our hero was taking tired steps, trudging along the right side of the road. He was repeating absently, 'One becomes one thousand... One becomes one thousand...' All of a sudden the four men who were carrying the casket dropped the heavy container and attacked Mr. Turniphead from four sides. Their assault was even more violent than the farmers'. They beat him almost to death. He, with a faint voice, as though calling from the bottom of a deep well, begged, 'Don't! Please, don't! What have I done to deserve these beatings? I'm a harmless man. Please, stop! I apologize if I have offended anybody—.'

"The men stopped beating and barked at him with their foaming mouths, 'You motherfucker! You come to the public cemetery and tell the mournful people who are about to bury their dear one, that this death is not enough and one thousand more will follow? Huh? Is this what you're suggesting? Isn't one enough for us? Should we lose a thousand?' And before Turniphead was able to say anything, they beat him some more. He screamed, 'Stop, my good fellows, I never intended to imply this. What I meant was the harvest—the seeds. I didn't see you. I didn't know here was a cemetery. Believe me!'

"Believing him or not, the black-robed, mustached mourners told him, 'What you have to do is to recite the prayer of dead. This is a big cemetery and you will pass other processions too. Do you know the prayer, or not?' Mr. Turniphead nodded. 'Good! Now go on your way and repeat it and have some respect for the dead and their mourners. Say, "We came from Allah and we'll return to him. Amen!" Right? Go now! We have to bury our poor father.'"

"You see how it is, comrade?" Ilych narrows his eyes and addresses me in a pensive tone. "This is life, my friend! Isn't it? You're set to do something, but before you know you find yourself doing something else. Doesn't this sound familiar? That's why Marxism teaches us the ability to see straight without overlooking the twists, turns, and zigzags of reality! Well, it took humanity thousands of years to learn this. But have we learned finally? Even we, the designers of the first proletarian revolution, have not learned this simple fact. This is a question to think about, comrade. We have to criticize ourselves for our frequent turnipheadedness, wavering of principles, losing the right path, blurring the realities, and all and all, weaknesses.

"Now back to our wretched fellow who is left in the middle of the road. It was a warm afternoon and the further Mr. Turniphead distanced himself from Hamedan and approached his city, the air became warmer. He was thirsty and hungry, dragging himself along the dirt road, repeating, 'We came from Allah and we'll return to Him. Amen!'

"Now in this village, there was a wedding party. The surna players and drummers were walking ahead of the happy procession. Little girls with white gowns and fresh flowers and handsome boys with embroidered vests followed them, dancing. The groom's friends were carrying the white-veiled bride on their shoulders—she was sitting on a pannier like an ancient queen. The rose-cheeked groom, fresh from the bath, walked with his brothers, following the pannier, joking and laughing. The older relatives walked slowly, some carrying flowers, some throwing rice and sugar and star jasmines on the bride's vehicle. The whole village was on top of the flat roofs, watching and clapping.

"Mr. Turniphead, unaware of the present, oblivious of the past and the future, only concentrating on his prayer, stepped in the middle of the procession, almost hit the bride's pannier, and sang the prayer of the dead—loud and from the bottom of his lungs, 'We came from Allah and we'll return to him. Amen!'

"As you can guess, my friends, the young brothers and friends of the groom attacked him even more savagely than the previous mourners and farmers—for life and the living are more important than death and the dead, even though people pretend to privilege the second. So punches and slaps, kicks and spit balls showered our hero's head. While he tried to protect his face from merciless blows, he begged, 'What have I said now? Huh? What have I done?'

"The rose-watered, thick-mustached men said, 'Bastard! You must either be crazy, or the spirit of death on earth! We are celebrating a joyful wedding and you, son of a bitch, suddenly pop in out of nowhere and recite the prayer of dead; you even try to knock over the bride's pannier. Who are you anyway, huh? We've never seen you around here. You may be Satan himself. Look at your dusty, raggedy clothes, your torn-up boots, your dirty face. Beat him some more, brothers!'

"'No! Please! Stop! I'm just a traveler, going back to where I've come from—' (but he could not think where was the place he had come from), 'and I was just repeating what they told me to repeat in the neighboring village. What should I do now, good fellows?'

"The young men gave him a tambourine, telling him to beat on it and sing the wedding song. They told him that this was a happy day in this village and in other villages too. Was there a better day than this mild sunny spring day to get married? 'Besides,' they advised him, 'keep your head up! why are you bending your head down like a mourner! Head up! Aha!'

"So, Mr. Turniphead, injured, but with raised head, beat on the tambourine, hopped along the dirt road like a happy frog and sang, 'Tom tom taram, tom tom tom! Tom tom taram, tom tom tom!' He repeated this again and again—rather mechanically—unaware of the present, the past, and the future. The reason and the function of the tambourine and the tune itself were lost to him."

Ilych's back is tired. He gets up and tries to pace up and down the cell while telling us the rest of the story. The chanters chant endlessly in the TV contest, Akir and Nakir are still lying in the shape of a cross, waiting for the rest of the story, and Saboor snores.

"As I mentioned before," Ilych says, robbing his beard and pacing in front of me, "this story belongs to the times when schools were outdoors and the students sat on the sidewalks in front of a mosque. The mullah with a long stick in his hand—an instrument of punishment—taught the little boys reading, writing, grammar, and even arithmetic, all from the Holy Book. Bear in mind that girls were not allowed to have an education in the feudal society.

"Well, as you may suspect, our poor, bloody, broken, oblivious, head-to-the-sky, dancing hero, beat on his tambourine, hopped like a circus monkey, stepped over the Holy Books, and sang, 'Tom tom taram, tom tom tom!' and received the lashes of the mullah's stiff stick on his butt and back. He also received hard punches from the little boys, who either knowing exactly where they should beat, or not knowing the sensitivity of the spot, punched where they could reach, smashing the poor man's balls.

"'Stop! For Allah's sake, stop!' Turniphead shrieked and begged.

"'For Allah's sake?' The Mullah asked. 'You devil! You blasphemer! You sinner! Beat him more and take him into the mosque for interrogation!'

"'No, please! I'm innocent! They forced me to do this! They said there were weddings everywhere, I didn't even feel like singing and dancing. All I want is to go back home.' Home? He thought for a second, but couldn't remember anything about it.

"Believing him or not, seeing his miserable sight, the mullah and his disciples let him go, but before he set his foot on the road, the sheikh whispered in his ear:

"'Son, whenever you see a piece of paper lying on the ground, take it, roll it, and find a hole somewhere and stick the paper in that hole. Do you know why? Because, this worthless piece of paper may be a page of the Holy Book, or a sacred prayer. Even if it's just a piece of trash, there's no harm, you'll help cleaning up God's earth. Now bend your head down to see what's under your feet. Walk carefully, and look for papers. Go now, we are behind in our spelling class!'

"The twists, turns, and zigzags of reality, twisted, turned, and zigzaged our hero. Indeed, he now looked more like a zigzag than a man. He entered the public bath of the next village to wash his wounds, rest, get himself together, and possibly eat. In the course of the journey, he had lost his coins, his bundle of food, canteen, and even the bread the farmers gave him.

"The washing area of this public bath was rather busy. Some men were wading in the pool, some pouring buckets of water on themselves, the workers of the bath were massaging the customers, and some were simply sleeping on the warm tiled floor. And this was what our hero desired. But before he lay down, he saw a piece of paper. Maybe it was a wrapper of henna or hair remover. It was thicker than a piece of paper, it was rather a piece of cardboard. Anyway, Turniphead remembering the mullah's advice, picked the paper, rolled it carefully, and looked for a hole. The washing area was dim; he couldn't see. He looked around; there was no hole. A large man was lying on his belly, snoring like a bear. He was tattooed all over his enormous body—dragons and all kinds of reptiles. Turniphead, again unaware of what and where and who, shoved the rolled cardboard into the man's tattooed ass.

"Excuse me, dear comrades, but this is exactly the way my father, his Azari grandmother, and the Hamedani grandmother of the Azari grandmother—and God only knows how many generations before that old woman—have told the tale: yes, lost and confused, sleepless, and fatigued, Mr. Turniphead either mistook the hole on the white and blue butt with a hole on the tiled platform, or he lost his judgment and knew that this couldn't possibly be an ordinary lifeless hole, but still shoved the stiff roll into it. The consequence? Well, guess for yourself. The large man and the workers and massagers of the bath, who were even bigger than the tattooed man, beat our fellow near to death, kicking him out into the street, in the middle of a muddy gutter."

Ilych sighs and sits down again. Feeling dizzy and fighting with sleep, I lie on my side, resting my head on my hand, looking at him. He stares at a spot on the wall as if looking out a window.

"Back on the road again. Turniphead was not far from home. The fields on the right side, and the houses, minarets, and the baths on the left looked very familiar. He almost mechanically found his way through the crooked alleys of his neighborhood and stopped at the door of his house. It was dusk, when there was no color except the dim gray of the sky. But Turniphead was not aware of the time and season. He was sick, exhausted, and lost. He needed to eat and sleep. But why had all this happened? He asked himself. Oh, the stew. He still remembered. The damn lamb stew! He went to Hamedan to ask how many red beans and how many split peas they needed to put in the pot.

"How many then? One handful of red beans and half a handful of split peas. He smiled. He hadn't forgotten the recipe in spite of all that happened to him. He knocked on the door and waited a while. His wife had waited behind the kitchen window all that time, he thought. Poor woman had stared at the dirt road day and night, counting the stars, waiting and waiting. Now he was home with the recipe.

"Finally he heard her approaching. She asked from the other side of the thick wooden door, 'Who is it?'

"The overjoyed husband answered, 'It's me!'

"The wife asked, 'Me who? Introduce yourself, I'm not supposed to open the door to strangers.'"

"Now let's pause here, comrades," Ilych says, "and listen to the heartbeat of the poor man. Had his voice changed? Had his beloved wife forgotten him? Why was she interrogating him? Why didn't she open the door right away and embrace him? Well, the truth of the matter was, Mrs.

Turniphead had a guest inside the house and couldn't open the door. She didn't expect her husband to be back so soon. She miscalculated the time it took to walk to Hamedan and back. Her guest was the butcher of the neighborhood, the one who always brought meat to the door. In the absence of Mr. Turniphead, she invited the butcher over once or twice, they chatted a little, laughed, flirted, or maybe even more. Who knows? Now the butcher was inside. Where in the house, and in what position? We do not know and that's beside the point. What matters now is that Mrs. Turniphead could not open the door to her husband.

"'Introduce yourself!' she went on.

"Mr. Turniphead said, 'I'm your husband and I'm back from Hamedan. I brought the recipe of the lamb stew. Will you open the door now? I'm a bit tired.'

"There was a moment of silence, then the woman said, 'Your voice does not sound like my husband's voice. His voice was soft and gentle, and yours is rough and scratchy.'

"Turniphead said, 'I'm him, your husband, believe me. We need only one handful of red beans and half a handful of split peas in our stew. Now open the door, I can't stand on my legs anymore. And I'm thirsty!'

"The wife asked, 'Well, if you're really my husband, and you're back from Hamedan, what is your name?'

"Well, my dear friends, this must be the climax of our tale. There was a pause. Our hero touched his steaming forehead, rubbed his eyes, his long beard (he didn't have a beard before) and thought hard to remember his name. But he could not. He was blank. Blank as a piece of white paper. All he could remember, all his painful head contained, was one handful, half a handful, and nothing more. The cruel woman double-locked the door and said, 'You're not my husband, go away. If you are, go find your name. I can't open the door to strangers!' And she left to join the greasy, fat-smelling butcher.

"Mr. Turniphead lingered a bit and turned back. He walked aimlessly in the dark blue alleys of the city. He passed the vendors, who were closing up their day-time merchandise to open their night-time commodities. A muezzin chanted the prayer of the evening on top of the tall minaret and invited people to the mosque. He passed the tired donkeys, dragging the carriages behind them, hungry and thirsty, dreaming vaguely of a pile of hay and a bucket of water. Turniphead's eyes burned. He wiped the tears off. The sight of the tired donkeys made him cry. How lonely they were. How labored and lonely!

"What was his goddamn name? When did he forget it? At what stage of his long journey did he lose his name? Did he know it when he was still in Hamedan? Or, did he lose it after the beatings? But it didn't matter now. What mattered was if he didn't find it, he wouldn't be able to go home—ever.

"He reached a public bath. This one was in the center of the town, the best bath of the capital. He went in, but not in the washing area. After that last beating he prefered to avoid people. What if he lost his mind, rolled up another piece of paper and stuck in it in someone's ass? He climbed the steps and went to the roof to rest there under the naked sky.

"He stood on the roof and looked at the city. It was a spring evening, indigo blue. All the city lights flickered like precious gems in the dark depth of the Caliph's treasure box. He wanted to sleep. Maybe all he needed was a deep sleep and he would remember his name in the morning. When was the last time he slept? He couldn't remember. He took his dusty jacket off, spread it on the sand, took his pants off too, and rolled them into a pillow; he curled up like a baby, and fell asleep.

"Now down there on the sidewalk, the vendors were selling snacks to the customers of the baths. Large, red pomegranates, fresh, slim cucumbers, and Lebanese oranges for those who went in, and steaming beets, boiling beans, and salted turnips for those who came out. They all called loud to attract attention. The vendor who called loudest and advertised his merchandise most aggressively was the one who got the most business. This was the law of the market—the louder the vendor, the better the vendor.

"Bear in mind, comrades," Ilych says stretching his painful legs out with an "ouch!" and moving his butt on the hard cement to make himself more comfortable, "bear in mind that we're talking about the feudal economy. Capitalism was not introduced into the eastern parts of the world yet. The vendors were peasants, in fact, who brought their products to the city to sell. The system was monarchy—there was a big king, who was the king of kings, and there were Amirs, or in today's terminology, governors, chosen by the king. Amirs were from noble families and lived in castles and possessed acres and acres of land. In fact, Amirs were the main landowners of the region. Their European equals in middle ages were vassals, dukes and, so forth.

If you are interested in the subject, you can look at Engels' *Peasant Wars*.

"Anyway, I had to present a little introduction and social background for the scene to come. When the Amir's page passed by on a horse with a big megaphone in his hand, our hero was in a deep sleep.

"'Citizens!' yelled the page in the megaphone. 'Brothers and Sisters! Our beloved princess has lost her precious diamond ring—a gift from the Queen of Queens. This happened in the public bath where she was wading this morning. Whoever finds the ring will become His Majesty's son in-law.'

"Now, don't be surprised, my friends. It was very common for the Amir's royal family to go the public bath for wading and massage. Some of the mornings when his majesty, or his family, craved a good hot bath and a massage, the owner of the bath chased all the people out, cleaned and disinfected the whole area, and made the public bath into a private one for the Amir or his family. Sometimes the Amir attended the baths with his viziers; they held their conferences in the steaming pool; sometimes his wife went there with her friends to gossip and wade. But frequently the little princess attended with her maids and classmates to play. That morning, the princess had been there and she had lost her diamond ring.

"My analysis of this irrational proposal of offering the beautiful fourteen year old princess to whoever finds the ring is this, my friends: I think the ring itself was of political significance—a gift from the Queen of Queens. Each time the Amir and his family attended the balls or ceremonies of the Royal Palace, the ring should've glittered on the princess's finger, for the Queen checked on it. If the ring was missing, the Queen felt offended and this could even endanger Amir's position. Besides, offering their daughter to a commoner was a common practice, a political device, to deceive the masses, suggesting, 'Look how close our links with the people!' And in the old times it worked, too. People could be more easily deceived than now. But all of this is beside the point, comrades. The point is, when this announcement was made, our hero was in a deep sleep on top of the bath's roof and could not hear it.

"What our poor man heard and what made him jump up in shock, then joy, then amazement, and finally ecstasy, was what one of our vendors shouted. The salted turnip seller who hadn't had as much business as the hot beets seller, or the boiled beans merchant, took a deep breath and screamed from the bottom of his lungs, 'Turnip head! Turnip head! Salted turnip head!'

"Well, as you can easily guess, our oblivious hero, hearing his lost last name, was shocked, then amazed at the cunning games of destiny, and finally felt an uncontrollable ecstasy. Naked, among the hanging towels, on the dark roof of the public bath, our man danced and threw his arms and legs out, singing with joy, 'I found it! I found it!' just as Archimedes screamed 'I found it,' and danced naked when he discovered the law of floating objects in the public bath."

Akir and Nakir, tired of lying in the same position for so long, break the black cross, turn on their sides and rest their hooded heads on their hands. Saboor is still in a deep sleep and the participants of the chanting contest are in the middle of their sad songs. Ilych sighs and says, "Yes, comrades, we cannot underestimate the important role of coincidence in our lives. Coincidence is the only threat to dialectical materialism! When coincidence dances, dialectics become lame. If the princess had not lost her ring, if the Amir's page had not announced what he announced when our hero was in the depth of his sleep, if he could've heard the announcement, he wouldn't have screamed, 'I found it!' And this horrible incident would not have happened.

"As you can guess for yourself, when he jumped up and down and screamed what he screamed, the royal guards of Amir rushed to the roof in a second to see who had found the ring.

"'Where is it? Where is it?'

"'Where is what?' our wretched man asked.

"'The ring, the ring.'

"'Which ring?' he asked innocently.

"'The Princess's ring. Show it immediately!'

"'Which princess? Which ring?' he asked absentmindedly.

"'What did you just find?' the guards asked, now kicking and slapping him.

"'I found my name. That's what I found. Thanks to the turnip seller. Now I can go home!'

"The guards, now positive that the half-naked man was either crazy, or making fun of them, or both, gave him a massage (in El-Deen's terminology) the likes of which he had never even received from the former farmers, the gloomy mourners, the joyous wedders, and the serious mullah and his pupils. To make a long story short, he spat out a couple of broken teeth, threw up blood, grabbed his tattered coat and pants in his hand, and descended the steps. He headed toward his house. Although he was bleeding and in agony, he knew his name, and his wife would open the door. His mouth was full of blood, he had lost two teeth, but he was happy. He knocked.

"Now, inside the bedroom, someone was snoring loudly and roughly. Turniphead could hear it from behind the closed door. He knocked again—louder. The snore stopped. His wife trudged toward the door. He thought how his poor wife's snore had changed while he was away. Loneliness, sitting behind the kitchen window day and night, had changed her too. He felt sorry for her.

"Mrs. Turniphead, sleepy and cranky, said from behind the door, 'Who is it, at this time of the night?'

"'It's me, your husband! Open the door!'

"'My husband? This is you again, with your rough voice. You even whistle when you pronounce an *s*. You must be a toothless vagabond. Go away!'

"'Didn't you say find your name and come back? Well, I found it!'

"'Well, what is your name, if you claim to be my husband?'

"'Turniphead!'

"'Oh, Turnip dear, it's you?' she said, but kept the door shut.

"'Yes, dear, it's me. Do you believe me now?'

"'Yes dear, I believe you. Did you ask about the red beans and split peas for the lamb stew? I'm still dreaming about it every night.'

"'Yes, I did. Now, open the door!'

"'First you tell me how many beans and peas we need, then I'll open the door,' she said.

"Now our hero paused. How many red beans and how many split peas? The night was as still as the vacant hollow inside his head. He had forgotten. He knew it the first time he came to this door, but then he didn't know his name. Now, he knew his name and didn't know this. This! The whole purpose, the question, the quest, lost! Lost? Had he lost what he suffered to gain? Had he lost the fruit of his endeavors? Didn't he endure? Didn't he endeavor to find out how much of this and how much of that, to be able to come back home and tell his wife, to be able

256

to cook the damn thing and eat the rotten stew and put an end to all the miseries? Didn't he? So, how much then? Huh? HOW MUCH?

"'How many?' the wife asked, yawning a long yawn.

"'How many?' he echoed.

"'Yes, how many? Did you ask the chef?'

"'I guess I did. But it was a long time ago.'

"'Then how many?' she asked.

"'I don't remember.'

"'Then go back and ask him again, Turniphead, and don't come back without the recipe. I'm sick and tired of waiting for this goddamn stew!' she double-locked the door, banged the bedroom door, and before long two snores, one louder and one lower, were heard in the street.

"Mr. Turniphead looked at the eastern sky and saw the light of the false dawn. When the sun rose, the heat would make it difficult to travel. He better set off before the muezzin's first call. He headed toward the road of Hamedan, the city of all knowing people, to ask the chef of Deezee, the famous caravanserai, how many red beans and how many split peas they needed to make a good lamb stew.

"He had a long road ahead of him, endlessly stretching forward to the north. Infinite fields of wheat were on his left side and scattered houses, blue minarets, and black chimneys of public baths were on his right. The more he walked, the fewer the number of the houses, minarets, and chimneys became, until there was nothing, but patches of shapeless shadows behind him, belonging to the past... "

I rub my eyes to make sure I'm still awake. Akir and Nakir have fallen asleep, breathing with difficulty inside their black paper bags. Saboor has just waken up.

"Ha, you're up finally!" Ilych says, "Saboor, the hard-working hero of the proletariat! You missed the first trip of our hero, Mr. Turniphead, but now listen to the second one. As I mentioned before, this may help you to remember who you are. Your turnipheadedness, my young friend, has progressed terribly! Listen now, this is exactly where you fell asleep and missed the rest of the story. Our hero is now thinking about the future, unaware of the present and the past. Only the future: how many red beans, and how many split peas? This is the question and the quest!"

The announcer of the chanting contest introduces the winner—a young repentant, heavy-bearded and proud. He wins a sacred rosary and a praying stone that has been blessed by the Great Leader of the Holy Revolution. But the faces on the TV screen are blurred and Ilych's voice comes from inside a tunnel. I try to fix my eyes on Akir and Nakir, but their paper bags stretch long and reach the ceiling, or expand from the sides and fill the whole room. Saboor's thin arms grow and turn into a pair of limp snakes slithering lazily on the floor. Ilych's face looks thinner and longer but a second later, wider and flatter. His voice sounds like a bad tape. I touch my face to make sure my features are in place. It takes a long time to check all my features. They are here, but somehow feel bigger. I try to bend my knees, but I can't. I don't have any control over my legs, which feel separate from my body. I lean back against the wall, closing my eyes. It must be the injection from that bastard nurse.

Ilych is talking to me and I like to be able to hear him. I hold my cold face in my hands so that it doesn't expand like a lump of dough on a baker's board. I try to concentrate.

Ilych asks, "Do you think, comrade, that Mr. Turniphead will learn a bit more on his second trip and a tiny grain more on his third until finally he'll learn what he should? I believe he will. This is what Marxism teaches me, my friend. This is simply the way history moves; this is evolution. Human beings learn—but bit by bit—a tiny little bit after each trip to Hamedan, which contains all the miseries that you're aware of. We learn, but after great suffering. This may look circular to you and it is, but each circle becomes wider than the previous one, until at the end we reach the almost straight line; I say almost, because of all the curves and zigzags of the reality. Well, you know what I mean, don't you?

"Now, my dear Saboor, where have we been? It was a cold dusk in Hamedan, when the color of the houses, the snow-covered trees, the stray dogs, the domes of the mosques, and the passers-by, were all black and gray as soot and ash..."

Sahar's Dance

"Sahar, what if we get trapped here in this chamber and the iron door locks?"

"What a thought! Why?"

"What if Maman turns into stone, Aunty Zari melts like a soap, the floor opens and swallows you, and I stay here, trapped, alone... the doors locked... the ceiling high... the walls slippery... ? Huh, Sahar? What if?" The minute I utter the last word, the iron door bangs like a cymbal. I run toward it, push it and beat on it. It's locked. "Sahar! Didn't I tell you? We're trapped in here!"

I turn to Maman to tell her we are trapped in the chamber of the public bath. Her arms are up on top of her head to massage her scalp with the washing mud, she is frozen in this position. The suds, which were running down her long curly hair are frozen too. I stretch my arms and touch her hair: it's made of stone. I touch her breasts, stone, her big belly, stone, the fatty ridges of her enormous thighs, stone. Maman has turned into a statue!

"Sahar, can you see this? But look! Look at Aunty Zari, she is melting! Hold her, Sahar. Don't let her disappear!"

I try to hold on to my aunt's soft, slippery body, but she melts in my hands, turning to yellow suds and bubbles. Some of the bubbles rise up, glide through the air for a moment, and burst silently. Vanishing. Aunty Zari slips down the tiled platform and slides toward the dark drain.

The drain is a hole on the floor under the shower head. It gets wider and wider, the size of a well's mouth. Now it sucks everything in. I hold on to Maman's stony body so as not to get sucked down the drain. Now the dark hole pulls Sahar's slim body toward itself. She slips down the platform and into the drain. I run to follow her, but the hole gets smaller and smaller, turning into a little drain which doesn't suck anymore.

"Sahar!" I weep. "Sahar!" I repeat.

I'm left alone. The iron door is locked. Maman is stone. Aunty Zari is bursting bubbles. Sahar is under the ground. The eye-window on the ceiling is high; the tiled walls are slippery. I sit on the platform and look around. The leftovers of the pomegranates are still in the bowl, shining like rubies. Only a few minutes ago, Sahar was munching them hungrily, clucking her tongue. I raise my head. Behind the opaque window, the sky is turning indigo. It's dusk.

Like a spider, I crawl on the tiled wall, but I slip down. I crawl again; I slip down. Again and again I crawl and return to the cold platform. I sit close to Maman, the only human shape in the chamber. I lean against her statue, staring at the pomegranate seeds. The shower still runs. I look at the drain. I look at the window on the ceiling. I crawl again toward the slippery wall and climb it. I hook my nails to the narrow mortared lines between the tiles. I hook my toenails, too, and climb like a scorpion. When I reach the ceiling, I bounce and throw myself toward the glass. Like a trapped bat, I thrust and hit the opaque window with my head. I break it and land on the roof.

Red towels hang on the clotheslines. I find my way through the maze of the large red towels. I reach the edge of the roof, and look at the town. This is a small town with crooked narrow alleys covered with dirt and dust; there is no asphalt. Donkeys carry people around. Men wear felt hats, women, colorful scarves. Vendors are down on the sidewalk selling everything. One shouts, "Cucumbers! Slim, firm cucumbers!" The other one yells, even louder, "Hot steaming beets! Fresh beets, I have!"

I smell turnips and beets. I inhale the grassy scent of fresh cucumbers. There is a tall minaret in the middle of the town, an old mullah standing on it, chanting prayers. The turquoise dome of the mosque glitters in the twilight blue. Smoke rises up from soot-covered chimneys and the smell of fresh food rises over the town. The roofs are all flat, the buildings, short, the alleys, narrow. Dust hangs in the air, and the smell of dung and wet hay mixes with the aroma of lamb stew.

I know this town and I do not. I walk on the roof, almost tripping over something. It's a man, sleeping half-naked. He has made his coat into a mattress, his pants into a pillow. He is curled into himself like a fetus. I squat beside him and look at his face. This is Uncle Yahya, Father's uncle. I shake him.

"Uncle Yahya! Uncle Yahya!" I scream with joy, "Wake up! It's me, your nephew's son! I need your help, Uncle! Wake up!"

He wakes up and rubs his eyes, staring at me.

"Uncle Yahya!"

"My name is not Uncle Yahya," he says.

"Who are you, then?" I ask.

"That's the whole point!" He rubs his eyes and yawns. "The whole point is this!"

"What?" I ask impatiently.

"I've forgotten my name. That's why I'm here, on top of this roof and not in my warm bed."

"Why have you forgotten your name?"

"Oh, it's a very long story, son. I'm sure you've heard it before."

I think for a second, then I say, "I've heard only one story in my life which had something to do with forgetting names, and a lunatic told it to me."

"And what was that? How did it start?" the man asks.

"Oh, it was a long story about a man who leaves his house to go to Hamedan—"

"—to inquire how many red beans and split peas he needs for a lamb stew," he says.

"That's right!"

"That's me!" he says.

"You? Are you him?"

"That's right. I'm him. And now I'm almost at the end of my story—well, if you can call it an end!—the part where I'm sleeping on the roof of the baths and the vender calls from the sidewalk, and suddenly I find my name and—"

"—you jump up and down and dance and sing like an idiot or that philosopher: 'I found it! I found it!'" I say.

"Yes, and the guards beat me, thinking that I've found the diamond ring," he says.

"Did you say now is right before the vendor calls your name?" I ask.

"It's just a few minutes before the turnip seller yells, 'Turnip!'"

"Listen, Mr. Turniphead. I'm going to change your destiny for good. You resemble my Uncle Yahya a lot. He looked exactly like my father and my father has been locked up for twelve years now, since I was born. I love you, because you look like them. I want to change your destiny!"

"How?" he asks.

"Before the vendor calls, 'turnip,' we'll leave."

"What do you mean?" he asks.

"I'm new here, I don't know anybody in this town. I want you to be my guide and take me to the town with you. I'm looking for my twin sister."

"Are you sure she is here?"

"She must be. I was down there in that bath chamber with my step-grandmother, my aunt, and my sister. Suddenly the earth opened and swallowed her. You may help me find her. My Uncle Yahya would."

"And how will this change my destiny?" he asks, looking very puzzled.

"We'll avoid the coincidence. I myself am a coincidence in your life, but I'm a good one. We'll avoid the bad one. Now the vendor will call your name, but you won't be here to sing and dance. You'll never get beaten up or lose your teeth."

"And never go to my house again," he says.

"And your wife won't send you back to Hamedan," I say.

"Let's go." He gets up, putting his clothes on. "You don't have anything on," he tells me. "Here, wear my coat. It's ragged from my long journeys, but it will cover you."

My friend's coat hangs down to my ankles. We descend the back steps of the public bath and step onto the street. Here, a bicycle leans against the wall. Turniphead goes toward it, as if this is his bicycle. He acts more and more like Uncle Yahya. His back is almost stooped now, his hair gray. He sits. I sit behind him and curl my arms around his waist. He pedals in the dark alleys. The moment we turn into the third alley, we hear the faint voice of the vendor calling, "Turnips, I have! Salted turnips!" My friend sighs with relief.

We turn right and left many times in the narrow dirt alleys. We pass the open windows of the houses and smell the strong scent of fried parsley and coriander. Biking down the hilly streets, we see more turquoise domes, minarets, flat roofs, and smoking chimneys. We see little children jump rope, play hide-n-seek, and wrestle in the dirt, until the dusk deepens and mothers call them in. We reach another hilly street. My friend pedals with difficulty. He is out of breath. We get down. The slope is too sharp. We reach a school, then turn left. This part of the hilly street is steeper. We climb. I notice that the ground is paved here. We walk on asphalt. The houses on our right and left are different from the houses we saw before. They are small identical houses with colorful iron doors and little yards in front, perpendicular to three awkward houses at the end of the street. The first house is square, the second one something between square and triangular, and the third one, completely triangular. I look around and search for the horizon, but there is none. We are surrounded by a gigantic mountain, ink blue in the deep dusk.

"This is the New Spring neighborhood, and that house with all the lights on is where I live—my grandfather's house!" I look at Mr. Turniphead who is completely Uncle Yahya now. "There must be a New Year party at

Grandfather's house! Do you want to join us, Uncle Yahya?"

"No, son," he says with Uncle Yahya's voice. "I have to bike around the city, and it's getting late."

I ask him what Sahar and I always wanted to ask and we never did: "Why do you always bike around the city, Uncle?"

"To see the people. I like to see the people," he says.

"People think that you're crazy!" I tell him.

"I know. But I think that they're crazy! The world is a big crazy house!" he says and chuckles.

Now we are at the door of Grandfather's house. I hear a gay rhythmic music. A dance tune.

"Come in Uncle, please! Everybody is here," I insist.

"It's getting late, son," he repeats. He gets on his bike and turns to go.

"Hey, wait!" I call after him. He stops and turns to look at me.

"Just in case... if you should end up in that little town again, with the dirt alleys and turquoise domes—" I hesitate for a moment, not quite sure whether I should mention this or not. "—if you ever end up at the door of that house again, will you remember your name?"

"I do. My name is Turniphead," he says.

"And how many red beans and split peas?" I test him.

"One fistful of red beans and half a fistful of split peas," he says.

"Good luck, Uncle. And thank you for the ride!" I wave to him. His bicycle rolls down the hill. I keep looking at him until he disappears behind the wall of New Spring Elementary and High-school. I know I'll never see him again.

I climb the wall and reach the windowsill. The double windows are wide open. I sit here in the dark and peek into the bright room. This is the same traditional New Year party that repeats year after year, forever and ever after. Grandfather, as the oldest of his large extended family, accepts visitors on the first day of the New Year. I'm sure since early morning people have come and gone, paying visits, and now in the evening, only the close relatives have stayed for an intimate party.

Uncle Musa is adding more vodka to the men's glasses. Grandfather and Baba-Mirza play backgammon.

"Double six!" Baba-Mirza says and recites half a line of an epic: "Bring what's remained of your manhood, Doctor Rad!"

"Six and five!" Grandfather says. He responds with a different verse: "Now sit by the stream and watch your life passing by, dear Mirza!"

Tuba, in red satin, henna-red hair, and crimson lipstick, reads Mother's coffee cup. Mother wears turquoise again, like old times. Her blonde hair, now a shade lighter, is set in a big bun on top of her head. Her large blue eyes with wide blue lines around them are a pair of restless fish.

"Your New Year's cup is bright, Pari! Look at this corner," she points her long red fingernail into the cup. "This is money! More money, my dear! I don't see anything dark, except this part of the cup... there is a man... he's kind of stooped... He's either old, or... wounded..." Tuba stops.

"Wounded?" Mother asks. "Then what? Is this bad, Tuba?" she asks anxiously.

"It depends," Tuba says mysteriously. "It all depends!"

"What depends?" Mother asks.

"Go and wash the cup! Rinse it well, it's finished. I'm done. Let's dance now. Let's celebrate! What happened to this music?"

Drums start a playful tune. Now strings interfere and make a whirlwind. As Maman enters with a tray full of teacups and sugar cubes, Tuba kicks off her shoes and dances. Everybody stops what they're doing and watches Tuba the dancer, Tuba the fortune teller, Tuba the gypsy-Jew. She whirls, moving her shoulders, whirls again and twists her hips. The skirt of her red satin dress wraps and unwraps around her muscled calves. Now she holds Maman's hand, pulls her to the middle of the room, and invites her to dance with her. But Maman is no dancer, she is shy.

"No, no, my rice is burning, I have to rush to the kitchen!" Maman says, blushing.

But everybody insists: "Dance, Maman! Dance, dance, dance!"

She is forced to join Tuba. Her face and neck are blushed, she bites her lips. She cannot wriggle herself like Tuba; her butt and thighs are too fat. She opens her arms and moves her hands around, as if she is stirring eggs in a bowl.

Now Tuba, whirling and wriggling, pulls Mother in the circle. She joins and does her neck dance. She lifts her penciled eyebrows one at a time and moves her neck to the right and left. The door opens and Aunty Zari appears in the frame, her long blue wedding dress down to the floor. She does waltz steps, stiff-legged, swinging back and forth, back and forth.

The men sitting around the room clap and whistle. They laugh and point to the dancers and tease each other. Grandfather drains the vodka from his shotglass. He burns, groans, and wipes his lips with the back of his hand.

"Where have you found this gypsy woman, Mirza? Knock on wood, she dances like a girl!" Grandfather says.

"Love appeared and set fire to the universe!" Baba-Mirza recites half a line of a poem as an answer. He's already drunk.

Right at the moment when the strings stop playing and the drummer thumps on the smooth skin of the drum, Sahar appears out of nowhere. The women make a circle around her and let her dance in the middle. Sahar's dark hair, which brushes her shoulders, is not as wild as before. Mother has treated her hair with a special creme for the New Year's party. Now Sahar's hair glistens like black silk. A few curls bounce up and down, here and there. Her lemon breasts shake under her tight yellow blouse. Her short red skirt opens like the petals of a tulip as she whirls. She stamps the floor, lifting her arms and brushing her hair up, letting it fall, and brushing it up again.

Now Sahar tip-toes toward Grand-Lady, who sits cross-legged on her Turkman carpet, clapping hard. Pulling Grand-Lady's white peacock embroidered scarf off her old shoulders, Sahar playfully whirls it in the air like a cloud of white smoke. She makes a veil with the scarf, covers her face teasingly, showing only her eyes, then uncovers herself and does the eyebrow dance.

Sahar choreographs a whole new performance. She mixes all her balletic steps with the movements of this ancient dance. With her yellow and red outfit and with Grand-Lady's white scarf, she creates a living flame in the middle of Grandfather's room. Men in excitement clap, snap their fingers, laugh with joy, admiring Sahar's dance. Women in the circle surround her like an aging chorus of a weird tragedy; they praise Sahar's growing beauty, weeping inside their throats for their own lost youth.

I hear noises behind me in the dark street. From where I'm sitting on the windowsill, I turn and see Sheikh Ahmad running out of his house like a lunatic, his four wives following him.

"Leave them alone, sir! Leave them alone! For God's sake, it's New Year," the women beg.

"This is intolerable! I can't take it anymore. I called El-Deen to send a van. Sin, blasphemy, lechery, and corruption." He holds the skirt of his robe in his only hand. "This is what this family is all about. I'll put and end to it now!" He runs toward our house.

"Leave them alone, sir. Let them be!" The women beg.

"They drink, they dance, they worship fire, they never pray, never pay a penny to the mosque, and now their crazy music is taking over the neighborhood. God-fearing people are praying tonight."

A black van pulls up the hill, and five machine-gunned guards jump out.

The sheikh says, "There, that's the house of devil! Go in and see for yourselves! I won't set my foot there. It's not clean. You go, Brothers, see what's going on."

Two huge, bearded guards break the door and rush into the yard. In a second they are in Grandfather's room. Sahar has knelt down, shaking her shoulders, doing the back bend. Grand-Lady's scarf is stretched up in her hands. She looks like a dying flame. The guards pull her up, wrap the scarf around her head like a veil and handcuff her. They prod her out of the room. The needle screams on the disk and makes a scratching sound. The music dies. Everybody freezes as if time has stopped. The guards push Sahar into the dark mouth of the black van and join her from the open doors on either side. They speed down the hill.

I drop myself off the window sill and run behind the van. I call her in the dark, "Sahar! Sahar! Where are they taking you?"

"They are taking her to El-Deen," Sheikh Ahmad says. "That's where she belongs. She has to be re-educated! Trained!"

"Sahar!" I weep, turning behind Grandfather's three houses, where the desert is. I pass the multi-level tenant house, thinking that I hear Uncle Massi's voice, weeping in his grave-room and murmuring, "Her mole! Her mole—" But I have to go on. There is no time to stop, no time to spare.

I trudge in the dark desert, on thorns, on snake holes, on lizards dashing away. Tripping over the rocks, I pull myself up, and trudge on. I fall, and pull myself up again. I pass the dark Faithland; I reach the ditch. I sit here, facing the wall of El-Deen. No bundle of food to spread and feast on. No Sahar to whisper to. I sit here motionless, unaware of the present, the past, or the future. I sit and wait.

Swoosh... swoosh... dump! Swoosh... swoosh... dump!

"He is alive!" I whisper. "Is he alive?"

Swoosh, swoosh... dump! Ali the Bricklayer builds the wall, as if saying, "Yes, I'm alive!"

"Sahar, can you hear this?"

No answer comes. I weep in the dark.

The Immortal

"Now our hero has a long road ahead, endlessly stretched forward toward the north, where Hamedan is.... Why Saboor? Why? Are you crying, son? "

I hear Ilych's voice and realize that my strange journey is over. Mr. Turniphead's second journey is over too, but Ilych is sending him to Hamedan again, for the third time. Saboor cries soundlessly in his box, tears rolling down his yellow face. Akir and Nakir who have listened to the story for the second time, join in weeping. But they cry noisily. They sniffle and cough inside their paper bags, making strange gurgling sounds.

A picture of a tomb appears on the TV screen and someone chants a mourning song for the Third Holy One, who was martyred, hungry and thirsty, more than one thousand years ago in the Holy desert.

Sahar's image, her last dance, the dance of fire, comes to my mind again. I see her red skirt, folding and unfolding like petals of a red tulip. I found her and lost her again. A big lump grows in my throat and breaks. I join in the mass weeping. I hold my forehead in my hand and weep like an orphan. But the grave disappears from the screen and the mourning song ends. Now the rhythmic National Anthem fills the cell, loud and forceful. Brothers and Sisters and Child Soldiers march with their machine guns, singing, "—We are the roaring sea—." Stamping their booted feet, erect and angry, they roar and rush toward the Holy Front to be martyred. Their leaders hold up gigantic pictures of the frowning Leader.

"That's enough now!" Ilych screams. "Enough of tears! Get up! It's time for our anti-anthem. If we let the venom of bitter despair poison us, we will never taste the sweet flavor of victory! That's exactly what the enemy wants: to break us with despair, with negative thoughts, gnawing doubts, pessimism, illusion, and what-not. They want to weaken our willpower, to deprive us of the ability to see straight, to make us overlook the twists and turns and zigzags of objective reality. They want us MAD, comrades! But we are the sanest, aren't we? Now get up and sing the joyful song!"

All of us, except Saboor, rise and sing, "Arise, you prisoners of starvation! Arise, you wretched of the world!" We stamp our feet on the cement floor and when the anthem reaches its peak, we raise our voices to cover it.

Like a lunatic, I stand in the middle of the cell, hitting my blistered soles on the hot floor, singing from the bottom of my lungs. Ilych, Akir, and Nakir march in single file around me, singing and saluting. Saboor screams in his box, "Inter... national! Inter... national!"

Now the cell door clangs open and Kamal appears in the frame, staring at us. The anthem and the anti-anthem end, but Ilych immediately bends as if he is shot in the stomach. He rolls on the floor, hollers with pain and kicks his legs in the air and against the wall. I know that this is the second attack of his shingles. We move back and make a room for him to wrestle with the demon.

Kamal slowly approaches to lift him, but I tell him that we have to wait until he recovers.

"He's being contacted," Kamal says, his eyes fixed on Ilych.

"Contacted?" I ask.

"By Him!" Kamal points to the ceiling.

"It's his shingles, the holy fire," I explain.

"The holy fire..." Kamal echoes me. "I know. I've had the privilege of experiencing the holy fire before. This Man is the Last Holy One and He has contacted me," he points to Ilych. "Now He is being contacted by Him," he says, pointing to the ceiling again. "When They contact you, your whole body burns. It's like a powerful wave of electricity, running through your veins. I know it!" He stares at Ilych with love and admiration.

Ilych, meanwhile, rolls on the floor, making snarling sounds. He utters confused fragments of something like a speech. He whispers now and shouts a second later. He tries to get up, but collapses heavily on the cement.

"Plans... charts... schemes... but without an organization.... an objective condition... degree of class consciousness... immediate and complete emancipation... theoretical victory of Marxism..."

Kamal listens to all this carefully and tries to grasp the hidden meaning of them. He sits on the floor, like all of us, waiting for the holy fire to die. The attack of shingles pass and Ilych stops kicking and jerking. He sits back, leaning against the wall, gasping. He is wet with sweat, his eyes are blurred.

He is blank for a moment and doesn't see us. When he sees us, his gaze fixes on Kamal. I'm not sure if he remembers anything about him. But he acts differently now; he is not Ilych, he is the Last Holy One.

"Are you here to see me, son?" He asks Kamal, hypnotizing him.

Kamal, like a schoolboy, gets on his feet and says, "Yes, sir!"

"On the matter of the H.W. I?" The Last Holy One asks.

Kamal hesitates a moment, thinking hard to solve the riddle. His broad, fleshy face is red and squeezed with mental pressure. His whole life depends on this. What if he is not able to solve it? He is not. He asks, "H. W. I, sir?" like a student who has forgotten his line.

"Yes," The Last Holy One says. "Are you here to take it?"

"Take" is a clue. Kamal solves the riddle: H. W. I means the Holy Water of Immortality. He says, "Yes, sir. I'm here to take it."

Now I realize that Kamal didn't even ask me if this man was the real Last Holy One. The moment he entered the cell, he knew what he wanted. Kamal wanted immortality, here and now.

"I assume that you've seen me, son—I mean in your dreams," the Last Holy One says.

"Yes, sir!" Kamal says timidly.

"I brought the Holy Grail to your lips. I tilted it, but not enough to let you drink it."

"Exactly, sir!"

"Help me rise now!"

Kamal holds Ilych's arms and lifts him up.

"In a minute, you'll become immortal!" Ilych says.

Akir, Nakir, and Saboor watch a show they have never watched before. They hold their breaths not to miss a thing. While the Last Holy One trudges to the corner of the cell with difficulty, Kamal stretches his tall body to hang my straightjacket on the security lense. He wants to turn the TV off, but he realizes that there are no switches on the set.

Coincidentaly, the most appropriate program is on: slides and music. To fill the gap between two religious programs, they show nature scenes and play harmless music. Now we see the floating of puffy clouds, the swaying of willow trees, the flight of many swans, and the glow of a glittering lake with a funeral music playing over the slides.

Ilych turns to us, holding his chipped enamel pee-pot. There is a mischievous smile on his face that only I can read. He addresses Kamal: "Here, my son, take this and drink it to the last sip!" He pauses and then says, "Don't stop in the middle, don't waste one drop of the Holy Water of Immortality. All with one breath!"

Kamal holds the rather heavy chamber pot, grabs both handles and gulp gulp gulp, drinks the golden water to the last drop, wiping his mouth with his sleeve.

"You are immortal now, my son, and we name you Kamal the Immortal!"

The hooded twins make a sound like "Hurrah" or "Hoola" inside their hoods, and Saboor claps with his puppet hands and laughs with joy. Ilych, the Last Holy One of the Psychiatric Wing, jumps on the shoulders of Akir and Nakir like an acrobat, raises his voice dramatically, lifts his right arm in the air and screams, "We do not need bourgeois democracy... All power to the Soviets!"

The twins take off their hoods, throw them to the ceiling and scream, "Bee beep hurrah!" and Kamal collapses—either from ecstasy, or nausea, or both.

Chapter Five

The Holy Show

I'm like a flag unfurled facing far horizons.
I sense the oncoming winds through which I must survive...
—Rilke

Kamal the Actor

Kamal leads me through the dark. My hands are cuffed, my feet burning. I stumble and trip over people who sit in rows on a steep cement floor. Right by the stage, behind the tall chain links, Kamal sits me in the first row. The cement is cold.

He whispers into my ear, "I have to leave you here for now. Watch the show and enjoy yourself. I'll get you after the show and the wedding. Don't talk to anybody. The devotees and the repentants are everywhere. And don't touch the fence, it's electrified." Before I can ask him how long I'm supposed to stay in the dark, Kamal disappears.

I'm among hundreds of beating hearts, but I feel as lonely as a man on a desert island. These are my fellow inmates, in pain like me, lost in oblivion, bent under the burden of memories. Why do I feel so alone, then? Why do I want Kamal to stay with me, to hold my leash, and tell me what to do? "You bastard!" I curse him under my breath. "You son of a bitch!" I chew my lips with anger.

I look around in the dark to distract myself from Kamal. A searchlight, a thick column of blinding light rotating around the sitting area, passes over the inmates. Suddenly the small round stage glows; strong rays of blinding light pour from the high ceiling, invade the shadows. The stage is bare.

I can see the inmates now. Seeing them, strangely, strengthens my other senses. I hear the thumping of their hearts, the pulsing of their wounds, the twinging of their burning blisters. Once in a while, I hear a muffled moan. I smell the odor of their sweat. They stir around me like a dark sea.

What if this calm sea is hiding a tornado in its dense depths? What if all of us, handcuffed and wounded as we are, move like a whirlwind and in our

271

circular movement, rise and ascend, pierce the ceiling and jet out, pierce the other ceiling above this and the next one and the next, reach the last ceiling (if there is a last one) and like an outburst of lava break the final obstacle, release ourselves, spread in the fresh air of the outside like particles of fire, particles of a burning sun. I daydream as the long thick beam of the searchlight passes over us, illuminating our faces for a second, before leaving us in dark.

Now I can see the whole auditorium. The square stage in the center, surrounded by chainlinks, is like a boxing arena. The stage is lower than the level of the sloped sitting area which is cemented, chairless and enormous—a round hill, built for more than a thousand. While some of the guards pace back and forth between the aisles, the inmates and the rest of the guards sit on the bare floor.

Following the searchlight, I recognize the women's section on my left. It's hard to see them; they're all wearing black veils, showing only a small part of their faces—a round circle in the middle. Black veiled Sisters holding machine guns pace up and down the aisles. I follow the column of light as it passes over bandages wrapped around wounded heads, patches on damaged eyes, thick beards covering thin faces. I know that the shrunken, beardless faces belong to the inmates who have not repented yet. Some have thick mustaches, hanging over their sealed lips. I look at bloodshot eyes, red from sleeplessness or long hours of weeping. I see shaved heads bent over sharp kneecaps. I stare at a one legged man, his empty trouser leg pinned on to his chest. As the light moves, my eyes move with the light, but I don't find a familiar face.

The Unbreakables must be here. What if I'm sitting among them?

On my isolated island, I hear the slightest sounds, and smell the faintest smells of this dense human sea. I hear a muffled "Hoo... hoo... hoo..." Someone somewhere is weeping.

After several rounds, the light leads me to the section opposite the stage. There I recognize the authorities sitting on large cushions behind the chainlinks. I notice Doctor Halal's face, his thick lenses reflecting the strong light like a pair of laser beams. Ha-G's small, hunched torso sits in his big bodyguard's lap. The guard sits cross-legged, holding the Head Interrogator's diapered butt in his broad hands the way one would hold a newborn baby. On Ha-G's left side a white-turbaned sheikh sits; I squint to see him better.

His arms are hidden under his robe. In the same row there are more bearded men whom I cannot recognize.

Now the whole auditorium rises to its feet and shouts, "God is the Greatest! God is the Greatest! Our Leader is Great! Our Father is Great!" I hear a guard shouting from behind me, "Rise, bastard! Rise for our Holy Father!" He can not be addressing me, because I am standing up. I didn't even notice when and how I automatically stood up. The guard is shouting at an inmate who has either fallen asleep or passed out. I hear slaps and kicks and clicks of machine guns and the crowd is still shouting slogans, "Death to the infidels, unbelievers, blasphemers! Death to the West and East!" And now more fervently, hitting their chests with their fists, they chant, "Neither West nor East, only the Holy Republic!" and again, "God is the Greatest!"

The man who aroused these fervent slogans waves at the crowd and sits on a cushion between Ha-G and the white-turbaned sheikh. He looks plain, doesn't have a large beard, but prickly hair covers his face—one week-old growth; he is wearing a gray business suit, his white shirt buttoned up to his neck. His thin black hair is combed back. The only unusual detail about him is a round scar on his left cheek, something like a stamp, now half hidden under his large, dark sunglasses.

As the Father of El-Deen, the Great Octopus, the head of the Holy University, sits on his cushion, the auditorium lights go out. An old man— short, stooped, shabby, and dirty—steps onto the stage carrying a bucket of water and a long broom. He leans the broom upside down against the fence and lays the bucket beside it. Then ties a rope across the stage, hangs plastic grapes and wine leaves on the rope and disappears in the dark.

Where have I seen this old man? I close my eyes, reviewing the hallways of El-Deen, the chambers I've been in, but I don't find him. I must have seen him outside. But at this moment I can't remember anything beyond El-Deen.

Now from either side of the stage, musicians enter. They are all old men, carrying their instruments along with small stools. One of them is the same shabby man, carrying an old trumpet in his hand. There is another old man, the oldest of all—in his nineties maybe—who sits on his stool, placing his drum between his legs. The band of old men play the Holy Republic's National Anthem; the crowd rises. I get up, realizing how for the past half-hour or so these sights and sounds have overwhelmed me. I've almost forgotten my throbbing blisters, now wet with infectious discharge. I've almost forgotten my friend Ilych and his anti-anthem. Now I miss him. I whisper, "Arise, you prisoners of starvation! Arise, you wretched of the earth—" in the memory of Ilych and feel a choking lump in my throat. I wipe my tears with my cuffed hands and stop singing. I listen to the old men's poor performance, the angry choir of devotees and repentants.

"Sing bastard! Sing or I'll shoot you!"

A cold current runs through my spine. This is a thick voice coming from behind my head as if addressing me. But it's not. I hear slaps and punches, then muffled moans, curse words, and at last clicks of several guns. The huge black sea stirs, a storm building deep inside.

Someone from the top rows shouts, "Leave him alone. He can't sing! Can't you see he has lost all his teeth?"

"Shut up, or I'll shoot you on the spot!" The guard yells back.

"Shoot me! Shoot me! Why don't you shoot me, then?" the inmate shouts with a hoarse voice, then he weeps. Someone must be holding his mouth because his voice is muffled, but still it's loud enough to be heard. He cries and mumbles, "This man's mouth is full of blood and the bastard wants him to sing! And sing what? That how the Great Leader—"

Behind my back, many inmates hush their friend. The anthem goes on and I imagine that the man's friends finally shut his mouth tight before he could finish his last sentence. The anthem ends and the slogans rise in an uproar—the same slogans we shouted only a few minutes ago. Now La-Jay waves his hands and we all sit down. The old drummer beats on his drum, and the shabby man puts his trumpet down, and approaches the middle of the stage, facing the authorities. At first his back is to me, but as he makes his speech in a trembling voice that emerges from a toothless mouth, he turns to all four directions, addressing the audience.

"Brother La-Jay, the founder of the Holy University of El-Deen, the Gate of Paradise! Merciful father of us El-Deenians! Dear Brothers of the main headquarters! Dear foreign advisors, most honorable guests who are serving our Holy Revolution willingly and voluntarily! Dear Brothers of the Societies of the Holy Revolution! Dear Brothers and Sisters of the Holy National Guard! Dear warriors of the Holy Front, the heros of the battle of God against Satan! Honorable parents of the brides and grooms whose children will be wed and blessed after our Holy show! Dear hard-working devotees of El-Deen, the restless educators of the University! Dear repentant Brothers and Sisters! And finally dear trainees, students of the Holy University! My name is Sultan, your humble director and actor of the Holy performances. Tonight I have the pleasure of presenting to you the most popular of all our shows—" Now he raises his voice, spelling out the words with a whistle coming through his three teeth, "**The Miracles of the Eighth Holy One and His Martyrdom by Caliph Maamoon's Poisoned Grapes!**"

The ninety-year-old drummer drums and the cymbal player, a bald old man, clangs his cymbal. The stage darkens for a second and when it's lit again, Kamal stands in the center, tall and robust, turbaned and robed, his eyes highlighted by stage make-up. He is holding a walking stick.

"Kamal... Loony Kamal!" I whisper. "Kamal the Immortal!"

As Kamal paces around the stage with the help of his walking stick, pretending to be trudging on a rough road, the old, shabby Sultan, stands before the musicians, acting as the narrator of the show. With a strange sing-song tone, different than his normal shaky monotone, he whistles the words, lamenting and narrating :

"As you can see, dear ladies and gentlemen, dear Brothers and Sisters, dear God-fearing citizens, our Holy One is on a rough road. His Holiness is going on a trip from the city of Med to the city of Tus. His faithful servant, Abasel, is left behind. His Holiness is strong, young, wise, and handsome. Poor Abasel is weak, old, ugly, and stupid. Now I have the honor of acting as Abasel, the Holy One's companion. I'm going to join His Holiness on his rough journey. Now, Brothers and Sisters, sit back and relax, for the first part of our show is about to begin!"

Scene One: Visiting the Blind Barber

As the old drummer rattles, Sultan picks up his trumpet and blows into it like Israfil, the angel of God. Then he announces: "**Scene One: The Holy Trip from Med to Tus and Visiting the God-fearing Blind Barber.**" He puts on a felt hat, wraps some rags around his feet, and runs stage left to join Kamal. Now he acts as the Holy One's faithful servant, Abasel.

Abasel: (gasping) Your Holiness! Please wait for me. I'm very old, I can't catch up with you, sir!

The Holy One: We have to rush, Abasel. We can't make the good Caliph
wait. Tomorrow evening is the grand ceremony in the city of Tus.
Caliph Maamoon will introduce me as his immediate successor. Our
Holy Religion will have a chance to spread all over the world. Our
revolutionary policies will be different than Maamoon's. The good old
Caliph is passive and hasn't done anything to spread the Holy Faith. We
will expand the Faith up to the cold north, down to the hot south and
left to the mild wild west. The residents of the eastern parts are already
faithful and God-fearing, needing only revolutionary leadership!

Abasel: I don't trust this Maamoon, sir! I have a gut feeling that he has a trick
up his sleeve.

The Holy One: Oh, Abasel, Abasel! You've always been an old cynic!
Maamoon is a good and just Caliph. He has never done any harm. See
how God-fearing this man is! In spite of having a young son, he wants
me to be his successor, because he wants the Holy Lands to be ruled by
a descendent of the prophet.

Abasel: It's his young son that I fear. He is studying in Cairo. What if he
seeks revenge? What if?

Kamal and old Sultan keep circling the stage, pretending they are traveling
on an unpaved road. But the strange thing is that the young and strong
Holy One uses a walking stick, while the old and weak servant walks
without one. Now and then Abasel forgets to act old and Kamal forgets the
rough road.

From the shadows surrounding the luminous stage, another old man,
bald and a bit chubby, runs to the stage. He has a black scarf around his eyes,
the kind of scarf the guards use as a blindfold. But this one is not tied tightly;
the old man can see. As he stumbles and falls, gets up and stumbles again, I
realize that he is the same bald cymbal player, now acting the role of the
barber. He pretends to be blind. He is completely out of breath,
carrying a small briefcase in his hand.

The barber: (drops himself at the foot of the Holy One) Bless me, sir! Bless
me for I'm just a wretched, blind barber, my foot at the edge of my
grave!

The Holy One: How did you recognize me?

The barber: Oh, sir, I've been following you since you started your trip. I've been trying to catch up with you, but—may God preserve your strength—you walk too fast!

The Holy One: What can I do for you, barber?

The barber: Just bless me, sir! I don't want anything else. Just a simple blessing.

Abasel: (whispers in the barber's ear and pinches his fat belly) Ask for a miracle, stupid! A miracle for your blind eyes!

The Holy One: So, just a blessing will suffice, huh?

The Barber: (hesitant) Or, maybe... a miracle too.

The Holy One: A miracle? What kind of a miracle do you want?

Abasel: His eyes, sir! He is blind!

The Holy One: Oh, I see. You want to regain your sight. Is that right?

Abasel: Yes, sir, he wants his sight back, sir, to be able to be a barber again. How can he trim people's hair like this?

The Holy One: Abasel, will you shut up and let the man talk for himself?

Abasel: Sorry, Your Holiness. I got excited. I haven't seen a miracle for ages now!

The Holy One: Are you being sarcastic, or what? People haven't asked for one, have they? This means that our citizens are doing well without miracles.

Abasel: But this wretched man can definitely use one.

The Holy One: Come on now! Kneel down here. I'll unwrap this scarf and rub your eyelids a little bit. Okay? Let's see if it works. But wait a minute? Do you pray your daily prayers?

The barber: Oh, yes, sir! And more!

The Holy One: Do you fast in the Holy Month?

The barber: Oh, sir, for even more than a month.

The Holy One: Do you give one fifth of you income to the poor?

The barber: I *am* poor, sir.

The Holy One: Well, since you're poor, the rest of the laws don't apply to you. You can neither visit the House of God, nor join the Holy War. All right, I'm going to rub now!

While the Eighth Holy One rubs the eyelids of the poor blind barber, Abasel paces up and down the stage, wringing his hands or chewing his nails. He soliloquizes.

Abasel: What if the miracle doesn't work? His Holiness hasn't done this for a long time. It'll be very bad for his reputation. What if this man is not a barber and is in reality Caliph Maamoon's agent? What if he wants to test His Holiness and see if he really *is* the Eighth Holy One, the descendant of the prophet? I have fears. I have doubts. What if...? What if...?

Meanwhile Kamal rubs the barber's eyes. Someone sitting in my row whispers to his friend, "The most stupid show I've ever seen! They call this a play!"

In the absolute silence everybody hears him. Someone sitting right behind me rises up. He is an armed guard. He looks around to locate the inmate.

"Who was that?" He asks. No one answers. But the guard doesn't follow up on the case; he wants to see the rest of the show. He just threatens the critique. "One more word and I'll take all your unit back to the cells." He sits down and now the tip of his heavy boots pierce my lower back. I don't stir. He may change his position in a little while.

The show goes on. The barber jumps on his feet, screaming with joy, "A miracle! A miracle! I can see!" Sultan blows in his trumpet and the audience rises and roars, "Wow! Praise God!" As if a real miracle has happened.

Abasel: (aside) Thank Heaven it worked!
The Holy One: Now that you are a barber again, as good as new, trim my hair and beard. I have to visit the Caliph in a short while.
The barber: (runs joyfully to bring a stool; opens his briefcase) By all means, sir! By all means! This is an honor! An Unforgettable honor!

Kamal sits on the low stool, the barber trimming his beard with real scissors and blades. I can see Kamal's real hair falling on the stage floor. This is all amazing. The utmost unreality throughout the performance and now a real haircut! I expect my neighbor, the drama critic, to whisper something about the stupidity of the show, but he is quiet. I imagine him sitting in the dark, biting his lips.

While Kamal is having a real haircut, Sultan/Abasel sits on his stool in the orchestra and sings a lamentation about martyrdom. Although everything is fine now and none of the characters are unhappy at this moment in their stage life, the old man sings about death and sheds real tears. Maybe this song is meant to foreshadow the Holy One's eventual martyrdom, or maybe it's highlighting the general theme of martyrdom—those that have happened in the past, those happening everyday on the Holy Fronts, and the martyrdoms that will happen in the future of the Holy Republic.

Sultan opens his mouth wide to sing his lamentation. From the first row where I'm sitting, I count his teeth: one on the upper gum and two on the lower. If he had a mouth full of teeth, he wouldn't look as old as he looks. Now Bashi, the janitor of the New Spring Elementary and High School, comes to my mind. He had only three teeth too. Sahar and I tip-toed to the first yard of the tenant house to visit Uncle Massi and the rest of the poor tenants. Bashi was the one who always gave us hard candies with dirt and lint stuck to them. Sahar was scared of him and he knew that. He laughed with his toothless mouth to scare her more.

But when we were little, Bashi was an old man. Hasn't he aged then? Is he immortal too? And how has he ended up here in El-Deen? He was arrested in the First Revolt along with Ali the Bricklayer, Hassan the Gardener, and the other tenants. But they were all released a few years later. I saw some of them in our thirteenth summer, walking in the procession of the Holy Mournings, hitting themselves on the chest and back with chains. Bashi was in front of the procession blowing his old trumpet. Yes, the same trumpet!

The First Day of the Holy Mournings

The four days of the Holy Mournings. The Black Holidays. On our thirteenth summer four major incidents happened, each on a mourning day.

On the first day, Sahar and I found Ali the Bricklayer. After many years of disappearance, out of nowhere he appeared. He was disguised as the Third Holy One, the Thirsty One, the Innocent One.

We woke up early, Sahar in Hoori's old room on the roof, and I, in Uncle Massi's old room. We looked through the thick indigo dusk and heard the distant sound of drums, trumpet, and cymbal. I opened the window, and stuck my torso out. Sahar bent over the railings, her long hair hanging down.

"Hey, can you hear this?" I asked her in a whisper.

"Yes. It's coming from Faithland. The mourning procession must have started. Listen! Can you hear the chains?"

We both held our breath and heard a sound like, "Chee... chee... chee... chee... " and then a vague uproar.

"They are beating themselves... " Sahar said.

"With chains and poniards," I said.

"They're getting closer; can you hear?"

"But they never come to New Spring, they stay in Faithland."

"They're coming now! Come up. Let's watch them from up here."

I climbed the steps, joining Sahar on the roof. We leaned on the cold railings, waiting for the mourning procession to arrive. We had heard the sound of many processions from a distance, but had never seen one. Our hearts beat loud and fast like they did when we were much younger, watching something we were not allowed to: Ali the Bricklayer on top of the wall, the shanty houses of Faithland, inside Uncle Massi's room, or Sister Tatyana wedded to God.

"Sahar, they'll see you from down there. Cover your hair!"

She rushed to her room, coming back with Grand-Lady's white scarf, the one with a green peacock embroidered on the corner. Sahar's hair was now long, thick, and curly, hanging all around her like a wild jungle. She tried to hide her massive hair under the slippery scarf, but the humid morning air had puffed and curled up her hair so that it was wilder than ever and didn't stay still.

"Sahar, this scarf doesn't work, you need a thicker one, black too. These are mourning days. The mean sheikh will say something to you."

"I don't have a black scarf," Sahar said, "and I don't care about the stupid sheikh, either!"

"Look! This is him running with his limp leg to join the procession! Move back Sahar, don't let him see you!"

The one-armed sheikh held his thin black summer robe with his only hand, running, his leather slippers flapping on the asphalt. When he reached the left side of the triangular house where New Spring Street becomes a narrow alley, the Holy Procession arrived. With each hollow clash of the cymbals, more neighbors rushed out of their houses. Children ran to join the Holy One's followers. They wanted to be part of his army. Women all in black stayed in front of their doors. They had pitchers of cold water ready for the thirsty participants. But they were not allowed to join the show.

We saw Bashi the Janitor first. He had his old trumpet hanging from his neck. We hadn't seen him for years now. He was stooped and his gray prickly beard had grown long and white. Hassan the Gardener and the Lame were here too. We remembered that they all were arrested in the first revolt. Now suddenly they were all here with cymbals, swords, and scimitars.

Sheikh Ahmad became the leader of the procession. He walked in front of the group, holding a big, black flag with green Arabic calligraphy shining on it. Behind the sheikh, a carriage moved slowly, as if carrying bride and groom. Sweat and blood running down their chests and backs, torso-naked men surrounded the carriage. Two horses pulled the coach, one snow white, one jet black. The horses were decorated with beads and bells and feathers. There were no bride and groom in the carriage, but two big men, one impersonating the Third Holy One, being captured and on his way to the ditch of the execution, and the other one, sitting beside him, acting as his executioner, Shamar the Shiny Shield. Immediately, we recognized the actor playing Shamar. He was no one but Salman the Brainless, the famous hooligan of Faithland. He was wearing black, a shiny red cuirass covering his torso. He held a red shield in his left hand. He wore a red iron hood with one sharp pointed horn on top. Salman's natural scars made him mean enough for the role of the Holy One's executioner.

When the procession cut through the crowd, Salman opened his big mouth in a scary groan, making a horrifying monster roar: "Rooooaaaaaar...." Small children ran away.

Sahar and I squint, but couldn't recognize the actor playing the Third Holy One, the Thirsty One, the Innocent One. He was handcuffed with a rope. He wore a green turban, a black scarf covering his face, leaving his eyes and creased forehead out.

"Look at the Holy One's eyes!" Sahar said in whisper. "Haven't you seen him before?"

"I'm not sure. I can't see well. Look! They've stopped. They're going to act out the whole thing right here, in front of our house!"

"But why? Why don't they stay in Faithland like they do every year?" Sahar asked.

"Maybe the sheikh wants to spread the religion in this neighborhood."

"Or harass Grandfather, because he doesn't believe in all this," Sahar said.

"Look, Salman is dragging the Holy One out of the cart!" I cried.

Right under the terrace where Sahar and I were standing, people made a circle, creating a round stage. The followers of Shamar the Shiny Shield entered the stage. They lay their arms on each other's shoulders and kneeled down, bending their heads. This way they made a low wall, the wall of the ditch. Inside this man-made ditch, in the center of the circle, the Third Holy One was supposed to be martyred.

Salman the Brainless, or Shamar the Shiny Shield, dragged the Holy One into the ditch. The actors froze and Bashi the Janitor blew into his trumpet, then recited a lamentation in a sing-song tone. His three teeth made his words screech in a funny way.

As Bashi chanted his whistly lamentation, the members of the procession wailed and cried loudly. The human wall cried too. The horn-headed murderer, Shamar, pushed the Holy One down on the ground and tore off his turban and veil, throwing them away. The executioner raised his scimitar to cut off the Holy One's head. Sahar screamed, not because of the intensity of the drama, but because the unveiled Holy One turned out to be our old comrade, Ali the Bricklayer, gone and lost for years, but apparently, not forever.

"Ali is back!" I said.

"I can't believe my eyes. He is in the Holy Procession!"

"He has the main role too! The Third Holy One, the Thirsty One, the Innocent One!" I said.

"He didn't come to see us," Sahar said sighing.

"He doesn't want to be our friend anymore."

Now Bashi, the narrator of the street show, explained that the Holy One was in the desert, thirsty, and his last wish was to have a sip of water before his execution. But alas, the red blasphemer, the ruthless devil, Shamar, didn't let His Holiness have water.

As Bashi narrated the story in the middle of the round stage, Shamar held the brass bowl of water under the Holy One's nose. The moment His Holiness wanted to take a sip, Shamar threw the water into His face, then laughed his monster laugh. People stoned Shamar. But before they lost control, killing Salman, the unfortunate impersonator of evil, the cymbal clanged and Shamar brought the scimitar down. With one blow, he cut the Holy One's head. As Ali the Bricklayer, the actor of the Holy One, ran off stage, disappearing behind the carriage, someone rolled a bloody head on the ground—a fake made out of a brown paper bag.

The moment people saw the fake head, they cried loudly and screamed as if it was a real head. The chain men beat themselves on the chest and back and the women in front of their doors wailed and clawed their faces until blood ran out.

"Oh, oh! Holy One! Oh, oh, Dear One!" They all sang and beat themselves. Some got into a frenzy, taking out poniards, hitting their foreheads. Some fainted and were taken out of the procession, where women splashed water on them. The audience wept, and while the actors moved down the hill, more men joined in, taking off their shirts, beating their bare chests with their hands, hard and fast. The sound of many slaps echoed in the mountains as they disappeared behind the curve of New Spring Street.

"Oh, oh! Holy One! Oh, oh, Dear One! Dead and gone, dead and gone!" sang the neighbors who were still in front of their doors. Some repeated, "Thirsty mouth! thirsty mouth!" as they wept.

Sheikh Ahmad's four wives lamented and moaned in front of their door. The fourth one, the youngest, fainted. From top of the roof I saw her black veil in disarray and her long honey-colored hair spread on the sidewalk.

Waiting for the sun to rise from behind the giant mountain, Sahar and I listened to the distant "slap, slap, slap" of the hands on chests and the "chee, chee, chee" of the chains for a while.

"And what happened to Ali the Bricklayer, Ali the Wall Raiser, Ali the Wise?" I asked.

"The designer of the First Revolt is the Third Holy One now!" Sahar said.

"And his cause is forgotten."

The sun came up but we couldn't see it. It was a cloudy day, a dark day for the middle of summer. The air was stagnant.

As the last neighbors cleared the street, returning to their daily chores.

From the curve of the narrow alley on the left of our three houses, Uncle Massi trudged toward New Spring Street. He was all in rags, Mariam's red-checkered belt still his bandana. He was barefoot and dirty, his tangled hair now down to his waist. Uncle's voice was not his voice anymore. It had changed into the coarse voice of a person who has been sleeping in the rain and wind. His voice came from a hollow inside his head, "A hole, a hole in her mole... Why the mole? Why the mole?" He repeated.

"Most of the time he is down there in the streets," I said, "roaming around, repeating the same phrase."

"Once he was up on the walls, claiming to be the poet-prophet," Sahar said.

"We all change. Even crazy people don't stay the same," I said.

"I want everything to stay the same," Sahar said.

I held her hand to make sure she was there with me. I kept her by my side the whole day.

Scene Two: Visiting the Rude Gardener

The auditorium is a silent sea. A dark stagnant water. But I can hear the beating hearts.

Sultan, the old man—who either resembles Bashi the Janitor, is Bashi himself, or a twin I'd never known Bashi had—ends his lamentation on martyrdom, then gets up to address the audience:

"Brothers and Sisters, as you witnessed, the good grateful Godfearing barber of Med trimmed His Holiness's hair and beard, kissed his ring, and flew off like a happy bird! He gained his eyesight back, now he rushes to open his shop and fill his sack! But our Holy One must continue his way to Tus where Caliph Maamoon is waiting with a crown and a dish of fruits! So His Holiness walks like powerful Rostam while poor Abasel, His obedient servant, limps behind him like a wounded lamb."

Here, Bashi raises his shaky voice and announces as loudly as he can: "And now the second stage of His Holy One's Journey: **Scene 2: The Holy Trip from Med to Tus, Craving Grapes and Visiting the Ungrateful Gardener.**"

Kamal and Sultan as the Holy One and the old servant stroll around the stage. Kamal with a cane, old Sultan without. Meanwhile the second old man, the cymbal player who acted as the bald barber, is busy placing some cotton balls on the plastic fruits and wine leaves that hang from a rope.

The Holy One: Abasel, I'm thirsty!

Abasel: Sir, if you can just bear it for few hours more, we'll get to a village where we can eat, drink, and sleep a little bit.

The Holy One: But I'm thirsty for fruits, especially juicy grapes. And now!

Abasel: Now sir? In the middle of nowhere?

The Holy One: Look at that garden!

Abasel: Yes, I can see. But the trees are covered with snow. We're in the middle of winter now and the closer we get to Tus, the colder it becomes. No fruits, sir, I'm sorry.

The Holy One: What if I make a miracle?

Abasel: Another one?

The Holy One: Why not? Why not use my special powers for ourselves?

Abasel: Yes, indeed, sir, why not? As a matter of fact, I'm also hungry and thirsty!

The Holy One: Now I'll bring spring to this man's garden. Look at the old man, how sad he looks! No fruits, no business, no profit! This miracle will help him too.

Abasel: Definitely, sir! This is not an entirely selfish miracle, sir, go ahead! After the barber's eyesight, I have no doubt that you can make it!

The Holy One: Did you have doubts about me, Abasel?

Abasel: To tell you the truth, sir, just a tiny little bit. But it's all gone now. No doubts, sir. You're a real miracle maker! Go ahead! We talk about fruits and my mouth waters. You know that Persia has the best grapes in the world.

The Holy One: The big golden ones are the most delicious, "The King's grapes."

Abasel: I prefer the seedless ones better, the ones that are called "Ruby Grapes." They are working-class grapes and if you're not careful you may end up eating little worms and ladybugs that hide inside the clusters. But seeds mess up my digestion. Oh, sir! Make some seedless ruby grapes for your poor old Abasel! Now that we've talked about it, I'm craving them like a pregnant woman.

The Holy One: In a second, my old friend.

Kamal, as the Holy One, faces the garden (the rope with plastic grapes and cotton balls hanging on it), raises his arms, points his ten fingers to the plastic fruits and recites, "God is the greatest! Say that there is no god, except God!" While repeating this several times, the gardener takes the cotton balls off the rope and the audience roars, "Wow!" and "Praise the God!" Now the gardener jumps up joyfully, calling his wife.

The Gardener: Spring! Spring! Woman come out! Grapes! All ripe! Bring a basket, we have to take these to the bazaar and make some money today. Oh, God Almighty! I can't believe my eyes! What a sudden spring! It's a miracle!

The Holy One and Abasel: (approaching the gardener. Together) Good evening, Brother!

The Gardener: Good evening!

The Holy One: What a beautiful garden you have. Full of fruits!

The Gardener: Yes, but it wasn't like this a minute ago. Who are you?

The Holy One: Travelers. This is my servant. We're going to Tus for business. We're very hungry and thirsty.

The Gardener: Oh, I see. There is a caravanserai down the road. If you walk fast you'll make it there before dark. I have to go the the nearby village and do some business before it gets late. Woman! What happened to the basket? Hurry up!

Abasel: Hey fellow! This is the Eighth Holy One talking to you. Invite him in, wash his tired feet, and offer him some grapes!

The Gardener: The Eighth Holy One? I don't have time for jokes right now. I'm busy. If I don't hurry up and take my fruits to the village, they'll rot.

Abasel: I'm sure they will! But at least offer some fresh grapes to the Holy One.

The Gardener: Are you crazy, old man? The Holy Ones don't visit poor villagers just like this. They are busy up there in the Heaven of God. And grapes at this time of the year are as precious as jewels. I'm going to sell them and make some money. Get off my property. Now!

The Holy One: Listen, old man. Would you offer us something? Anything to eat? We won't come in. We'll sit outside your property and rest a bit.

The Gardener: All right. Let me go in and see what the woman has.

While waiting for the gardener, Sultan starts to sing again. This is either a new lamentation on the theme of martyrdom, or it's the rest of the former song.

The inmate who was weeping before weeps once more. The guards let him weep. Someone whispers, "This is boring!" His friend says, "It's better than being in the cell!" The first one says, "My legs are sleep—" Now the guard sitting behind me raises his voice, "Shut up you two! No talking!" The tips of his boots pierce my back again.

The searchlight passes over the authorities. I see a stirring of the dark bodies. Someone, a tall man, finds his way through the first aisle. Doctor Halal rises, shakes his hand, making room for him. The searchlight shifts to the women's section. I can't see the newcomer anymore.

Black head after black head, women all looking the same, one veiled woman multiplied by the hundreds. I focus on the eyes. I recognize the slanted eyes of the repentant I saw on TV before. These are the kind of eyes you never forget: Mongolian, rare. Now I see red swollen eyes, blurred eyes, without a glow. Lost. Wrinkled lids framing aging women's restless eyes, wandering around searching for their children. Now, young glossy eyes—the large and beautiful eyes of wounded gazelles. Black irises—sorrow overflowing in dark fountains. Next, the eyes that blink too fast, nervous eyes, eyes of women on the verge of insanity. And eyes that do not blink, but stare at the vacant dark, lifeless. Eternally open.

The strong beam highlights the thick eyebrows and long eyelashes. So many eyes, a collection, an exhibition, a bazaar of eyes. The eyes of El-Deen's women. Eyes that have seen enough for a lifetime.

But what am I searching for in this bazaar? Why am I rotating with the beam of this searchlight? Whose eyes am I seeking? The thick column of light moves on and leaves the eyes in the dark. I'll wait until the next round.

The light passes over the authorities again. I catch a glance of Ha-G the Shit Mouth sitting in his guard's lap, fingering his nose, then yawning. I think that I smell the foul odor of his mouth again. I shiver with fear and disgust. Now he is just a harmless bundle of pitiful flesh, sitting in his black diapers, watching a show.

The light passes over three men sitting in the second row. One is bald, one has thin yellow hair, and the third one is gray-haired, with a goatee. They look like foreigners. The beam is over the newcomer now. I recognize Ali the Bricklayer's face, now puffed with fat and flesh. His hair is white and cut short, his forehead the same creased forehead, his face covered with gray, prickly beard. Ali's wise and piercing eyes are narrower and almost lost between the cushions of his fat lids. He is sitting between Doctor Halal and La-Jay. Now he is whispering something in La-Jay's ear; they both nod and agree.

The Second Day of the Holy Mournings

The nightingales didn't sing in the branches of the old fig tree. Singing was forbidden. We stole Grand-Lady's Turkman carpet from her porch, spread it on the terrace in front of Sahar's room. Sahar tip-toed all the way down to the kitchen, brought some bread, cheese, and a pot of fresh brewed tea. Sitting on the carpet on either side of the green peacock, facing the mountain, we ate breakfast.

We waited for the nightingales to come. Waited for the sky to lighten. But the birds didn't fly today and the sky stayed dark on the second day of the Holy Mournings. Thick gray clouds covered the summer sun. There was no breeze, so the old fig tree remained still. The silence and the extreme immobility of the nature made us wonder if everything was real. We felt a vague anxiety that we couldn't describe.

From where we were sitting, if we stretched our necks a bit, we could see Grand-Lady's little body rolling around the yard. She looked more like a little bundle of dry bones, carelessly wrapped together in an old rag. If this bundle fell apart and the contents spilled out, she'd turn to dust.

Grand-Lady was ninety-two. Lately she didn't do anything except roam the house, whispering something to herself in her mixed language. She couldn't walk for months, but a few days before the Holy Mournings, she started to walk again. Maman said that this was a miracle; her mother-in-law had become young again! But Grandfather said that this was the sign of death. Grand-Lady's end had come. He said this in despair, looking at his tiny mother, sighing. Now she was moving around aimlessly, looking for something, but not sure what.

Maman broke the silence in her dark kitchen. We heard the clinks and clanks of her pots and pans. Like all the other neighbors, she cooked halva today. For Maman this was more a lifelong habit than a religious ritual.

She made a wish each time she cooked halva. We knew that all her wishes were for Hoori, her only child, who was at that southern university, way beyond the central desert, and who didn't write much. In a minute, Maman would stir the flour in hot oil, wishing Hoori would return, wishing she would never leave again. In a minute, the sweet burnt smell of fried flour, saffron, and rose-water would fill the neighborhood.

From the next house we heard Aunty Zari's scratchy music. Oblivious of the mourning days, when music was strictly forbidden, she played the "Blue Danube" on her old dusty gramophone while cutting garments on her sewing table or stitching long hems. Since her son Kami had gone to the military boarding school and she had started sewing for money, we hadn't heard Aunty Zari speak louder than a whisper. But we remembered how she used to holler at Kami, cursing him and his absent father. She was quiet now, working in peace, hemming and humming the rusty waltz.

"I hate these mourning holidays!" Sahar said. "My dance class is closed for a week! We can't walk in the streets, movie theaters are closed, everybody is locked in their houses. Prayers and lamentations everywhere. Even the sun doesn't come out!

"So you enjoy dancing now?" I asked her. "You can't live without it." It was a while since we'd talked about her dancing, a territory I was not allowed to enter.

"What a thing to say! Of course I can't live without dancing! I've been dancing for seven years now! Madame Aida believes that I'm almost ready to join the Company—the Royal Court's Dance Company!"

"This means becoming a professional," I said.

"This is what I've been trained for, dummy! Mother—oh, excuse me, Marie—has spent zillions on me!"

"I know. But are you happy?"

"Sometimes I am. Sometimes I'm not. When I dance, I enjoy it a lot. But I don't want to do just the steps my teacher wants me to do. I want to do more, be free, make up my own steps, leaps, and turns. You know what I mean?"

"Yes. Like when our teacher teaches us how to write, and I write my own poem instead of listening to him."

"Something like that. Sometimes I don't like to go to class. I want to be outside, dancing in the mountains! Last week when I was doing the

289

exercises, I looked through the window. The sun was setting. Have you ever seen the red glow through the locust branches? Anyway, instead of concentrating on my legs, I was imagining things—"

"What things?"

"I imagined the sun sinking among El-Deen's ironwoods, Father not being able to watch it. Then I imagined you—"

"Really?"

"Really. I imagined you sitting alone in your room, doing your homework. I wanted to run away from the stupid dance class and rush to you. I wanted to be with you, to walk with you in our desert. Do you remember our journeys?"

"We held hands and walked all the way to the prison wall!"

"We visited the tenant house first. Uncle Massi, Ali the Bricklayer, Zahra, Bashi—"

"We had a bundle of food and walking sticks."

"We sat by the wall of El-Deen and had a picnic at the ditch full of garbage!" she laughed. "Then we heard Ali the Bricklayer laying bricks on top of bricks, raising the wall."

"We stared at the wall for hours. Father was behind it," I said. "We swore to take him out, to take all of them out!"

"We dreamed a lot! The same dreams! Do you remember?"

"We imagined that this carpet could fly, or the mountain was a female giant!"

"Mother Alborz, and her son, Saba, the naughty north wind," she laughed.

"He helped our carpet fly. The carpet took us to the First Revolt. Were those all dreams, Sahar?"

"We dreamed about Ali the Bricklayer a lot," Sahar said.

"We loved him and respected him. He was the leader of the people's revolt!"

"Those were all games, make-believe."

"Some were and some were not," I said. "Father was real. El-Deen was and is real."

"Father is still there. It's thirteen years now. We've grown up. We don't even go to the wall anymore to visit him," Sahar said.

"He may be dead now and we don't even know it," I said.

"Baba-Mirza says the Prime Minister has promised him again. He may release him this time," Sahar said.

"But it's too late."

"No, it's not!" she almost screamed.

"Don't build your hopes, Sahar. He is dead!"

"He is not!" she raised her voice louder.

"I don't want to argue with you, Sahar. Why do you yell at me?"

"You are the one who yells!" she said and her eyes filled with tears.

"Sahar, why do you cry every time we talk about something? I don't think that *I* make you cry—"

"No, you don't. It's me," she said and now sobbed loud and hard. Her large black eyes filled with tears.

"Sahar, you're not happy," I said.

"Are you?" she asked.

"No," I said. "But I know why I'm not happy. I hate my school. You're still at Santa Zita; you don't understand what it means to go to a boys' high-school. Some of them are big!"

"Do they bother you?" she asked worriedly.

"No. They just force me to do their homework. They make fun of me. I'm too short. Quiet."

"And I'm not there to protect you!" she said, wiping her tears.

"No. But don't be worried for me, I can take care of myself. All I have to do is to do their homework every night!"

We both laughed. Sahar laughed and cried at the same time. Then she started the hiccups. Even when we were little, she hiccuped after she cried.

"Listen," she finally said. "Mother is talking about sending me to Europe."

"What?"

"She and Madame Aida are cooking something up. She wants to send me to a dance school somewhere in Europe. Madame Aida says I can. I'm good."

"What do you want?" I asked.

"I won't go without you. I'll go only if we can go together," she said. "This is my condition and I've already told Mother."

"What did she say?"

"Nothing. Just looked at me hard with her fish eyes. She looked hard

291

and long, but didn't say anything."

"Sahar, you won't go without me!" I said this, half-begging, half-ordering.

"I won't. But listen! The procession is moving again. I can hear Bashi blowing his trumpet."

We sat quietly, listening to the heartbreaking sound of Bashi's trumpet. The gray clouds moved above us in haste. The sky was windy up there, but on the earth everything was still. Now the smell of fried flour filled the terrace. We heard Maman weeping in her kitchen, sniffling, then blowing in her kerchief noisily.

"She misses Aunty Hoori," Sahar said. "Listen! The trumpet and drum are louder now. The procession is coming here."

"I don't think so. Each day they perform in a different neighborhood. Look! Sheikh Ahmad is running so he won't get behind. He wants to be the leader again and carry the big flag." I pointed out the lame sheikh to Sahar.

"Look at him! His wives are bringing his slippers. He's forgotten to wear them."

We both laughed at the mean, clumsy sheikh, but soon we stopped. The trumpet's sound was melancholic. In the Holy Play performed somewhere not far from us, the followers of Shamar the Shiny Shield pushed the Holy One inside the ditch. Now Shamar cut off the Holy One's head and people screamed with horror.

Sahar wept.

I let her weep, turned my head to leave her alone. I saw Grandfather down in the yard setting up his old daguerreotype. I wondered whose picture he wanted to take. He set a chair against the brick wall opposite the daguerreotype, stepped back, sticking his bald head under the black cloth. He adjusted the lenses, approached the chair, moved it slightly to the right, and hid under the black cloth again, repeating all these steps patiently, many times.

"Grandfather is about to take somebody's picture, Sahar. Look!"

"Leave me alone, okay?" she said angrily.

"What's the matter now?" I asked.

"Nothing."

"Don't you want to tell me?" I asked.

"This is something you won't understand."

"Why? Are we not friends anymore?"

"It has nothing to do with that, dummy. I'm a girl. You are a boy. You can't understand!" she repeated.

"Understand what?" I screamed, my voice breaking and becoming thin and then thick, until I lost it altogether.

"Don't yell anymore," Sahar said. "Your voice squeaks when you yell. You sound ridiculous," she laughed in her tears.

"*You're* ridiculous! You crazy little brat! Don't you ever laugh at me again!" I felt an increasing rage.

"I didn't laugh at you. You started it. I just said I have a problem you can't understand, but you keep sticking your nose into my life!"

"Okay. I won't stick my nose into your life anymore, Miss Superstar! Bye! I'll go to my room and shut up so that you won't hear my stupid voice." I got up, running toward the steps.

"Stop!" Sahar screamed. "Stop! I said! Don't leave me alone here. Please! I can't listen to this trumpet alone. It's scary." She wiped her tears off.

Slowly I returned and sat on the carpet. She poured me some more tea and looked deep into my eyes. My head was bent on my chest. But I felt the weight of her dark eyes. Each strand of her long eyelashes became a needle, piercing my heart.

"Every month I get these cramps under my belly. It hurts," she cried. "I think it's coming now. When it comes, I want to die."

"Sahar, don't say that!" I sat close to her, holding her hand. "Sahar, you need to see a doctor. Have you told anyone? Tell Grandfather. He is almost a doctor!" We both laughed at "almost," but soon Sahar cried again.

"I don't need a doctor. All the girls get cramps. Maman talked to me." Now she cried harder.

"Don't cry! If Maman says that all the girls get it, then don't worry!" I stroked her hand.

"I cry because Mother doesn't even know! All she thinks about is her beauty salon, her friends, parties, new wardrobes, new cars and my dance class. My dance class is the only time she notices me. I don't exist as myself, as her daughter! I'm just a little dancer. One of those ballerina pictures she has on her walls."

"What about me, then?" I asked. "I'm not even a picture on her wall. I don't exist at all."

"Poor you!" Sahar said, kissed my cheeks, wetting my face with her tears.

"Sahar, I think now I know why mother moved to the Alleys of Heaven. She wanted to be with the prince."

"And that's where most of the money comes from. My dance tuition and all..."

"So we know all this. We always knew all this. Why should you cry, then? Maman is our mother, and Grandfather, our father. Look at him now! Look at Grandfather, Sahar! He is taking Grand-Lady's picture!"

We stretched our necks, looking at the yard. The white scarf framing her wrinkled leathery face, Grand-Lady sat stiffly on the chair, posing for a picture. She stared at his son's finger, which was the only part of him out of the black cloth. Grandfather said, "Smile, Mother!" Grand-Lady stretched her lips in a big smile. This was the first, the last, and the only smile on Grand-Lady's face. Grandfather snapped his fingers in the air, something cracked like a toy gun, and a little smoke rose from top of the daguerreotype. The smile became eternal.

"I won't let you go, Sahar," I said.

"I won't go. Don't worry."

As we rose to roll Grand-Lady's carpet to take it back to her porch, a black van crawled up the hill like a giant cockroach, parking in front of our house. A tall man in a khaki uniform got out and knocked on the door. Grandfather, who was about to carry his daguerreotype in, opened the door. The man said something. Grandfather closed the door behind him and followed the man. We noticed that while Grandfather trudged toward the van, his knees buckled under him. He leaned against the car, grabbing his bald head with both hands as if it were a ripe fruit about to fall from an old tree. The man stayed motionless. His clean-shaved face was made of stone.

Now Maman opened the door and stepped out. Grandfather tried to get her to go back in, but she insisted on staying out; she wanted to see what was hiding inside the van. Sahar and I bent over the railings, holding our breaths. The trumpet, the drum, and now and then the metallic bang of the cymbal were the only sounds in the world. Uncle Musa came out of the middle house wearing a thick houserobe in this heat, chewing the cold pipe that had recently replaced his nice-smelling cigarettes. He was holding a newspaper in his hand. They all gathered around the van, waiting for the uniformed man to open the rear door. When the man raised the big black iron door, it made an annoying sound. Now a coffin slid down and landed on the asphalt. At the same time the middle house's door flung open and Aunty Zari, sewing scissors still in her hands, rushed out, shrieking, "Is this my Kami? Have they shot him at that military school?" Uncle Musa took the scissors from his sister, grabbed her shoulders and shook her hard while whispering something in her ear. She screamed, "Oh, no! Hoori! Little sister!" and when she mentioned Hoori's name, Maman, who had been paralyzed for the last few minutes, dropped herself on the coffin and banged on the wood. Now she took her scarf off her head and threw it away. She clenched her thick gray hair with both fists, pulling hard, as if to yank it out. Grandfather and Uncle Musa tried hard to hold her back, but stronger than two men now, Maman thrust herself on the coffin again and punched the wooden lid. She knocked and banged and slapped the lid as if the devil were chasing her; she urged the resident of the wooden box to open the door and let her in.

Most of the neighbors were out now. Sheikh Ahmad's wives stood at their door in a straight line, wiping their tears with the corner of their black veils. The whole scene was happening in a round stage where yesterday the martyrdom of the Third Holy One was performed. On today's stage, Maman was the main actor. Her long gray braids were loose, the braids she washed every Thursday in the public bath with washing-mud, the braids I'd watched being woven and unwoven every single week of my life. Now she wanted to be hairless. As if her hair were her life, she wanted to pluck it out and throw it away. Her strong rooted hair didn't come out easily, so she snatched the scissors from Uncle Musa's hand and before anyone could stop her, cut both her braids from the roots. Now she crawled on the coffin, hugged it tightly, and refused to be moved.

People already in black for the Holy Mourning circled around our family and wept. One of the sheikh's wives, the same one who had fainted after seeing the execution of the Holy One, fainted again.

"Aunty Hoori is in the casket," Sahar said coldly. "I knew that something was going to happen. I had this feeling since early morning. Oh, it's flowing! The blood, the damn blood is flowing." She grabbed her belly tightly, rushing into her room.

"Sahar! Stay with me. Sahar, don't leave me alone here!"

A Dish of Onions

Abasel ends the lamentation on the theme of martyrdom and the play goes on. Those inmates who had rested their heads on their knees, dozing, wake up to watch the rest of the show. The search light moves over the authorities and I catch a glimpse of Ali the Bricklayer wiping his tears. Now as the beam moves over the inmates and the guards, I see more people wiping their eyes. Sultan's sad song has been a tear-jerker. But now the old man, in cheerful tone and light movement (much too light for his age), continues acting the part of Abasel, the Holy One's faithful companion.

Abasel: He is coming, sir! The gardener is coming! I can see a tray in his
    hands. It sure took him a long time to bring something for us to eat.
The Holy One: I hope they're grapes!
Abasel: Anything, sir! Anything juicy and rich! Hunger and thirst are killing
    me. I'm an old man after all.
The Holy One: Here he comes. I see something green on the tray. It must be
    a cluster of Kings' Grapes. But the old man's face is not friendly, Abasel.
Abasel: To hell with his face, sir! Let's eat his grapes!

Now the gardener paces twice around the stage to indicate the distance and approaches the Holy One and Abasel. Rude and frowning, he shoves the tray into Abasel's chest.

The Gardener: Here! Eat and leave! You made me late. Now I won't have
    enough time to pick all of my grapes and go to the village.
Abasel: But this is an onion!
The Gardener: This is all we have. Onions are good for travelers. Nutritious
and juicy. If you want some water, there is a well behind the wall.
Abasel: All these ripe fruits hanging on your trees and you offer the Holy One
    an onion? And with the muddy skins on it?
The Gardener: Get up, you crazy man and leave my property, or I'll kick you
and your Holy One out. I have four strong boys inside; do you want me to call
them?
Abasel: (to the Holy One) sir! It's time to take action. We need another miracle.
    Immediately! Teach this rude old man a lesson he will never forget!

The Holy One: Should I bring the winter back?

Abasel: Just bring the winter back, sir? If I were you, I'd burn his damned garden! This ungrateful fool insulted you the way even your enemies don't.

The Holy One: I guess you're right, Abasel. I have to undo what I've done and burn the whole garden up!

In front of the gardener's wide eyes, the Holy One recites a prayer and spring turns into winter. This time Abasel lays the cotton balls back on the plastic fruits. The faithful audience roar, "Wow!" like a many-headed monster. The gardener, seeing the miracle with his own eyes, drops to the ground at the foot of the Holy One, begging for forgiveness. But it's too late. The Holy One points his ten fingers to the garden while Abasel draws a match and burns the shabby broom standing in the corner stage. The gardener screams "Fire! Fire! My garden is on fire!" and begs the Holy One to stop it. But Kamal and Sultan have already left the old man's property and are walking around the stage. The gardener, crying loud and hard, grabs the bucket of water, throwing it on the flaming broom, killing the fire.

I notice that some people in the audience laugh at the gardener and enjoy watching his misery. The guard sitting behind me mumbles curse words, "You ungrateful bastard! You deserve this!" Now Sultan addresses the audience:

"Well, dear Brothers and Sisters! As you just witnessed, our honorable Holy One punished the greedy, foolish gardener and resumed his Holy journey—hungry and thirsty. His old faithful servant, Abasel, dragged himself behind His Holiness without saying a word. Right outside the city of Tus, near the thick woods, they met a hunter who was chasing a deer. The next miracle of the Holy One occurs when His Holiness communicates with the pregnant deer. Sit back and enjoy!"

Scene Three: Visiting the Bold Hunter

In a sing-song voice, Sultan announces: "**Scene Three: The Holy Trip from Med to Tus, Visiting the Impatient Deer Hunter and Reading the Mind of the Poor Pregnant Deer.**"

On his four legs, a boy acting as a deer enters the stage. He makes one round of fast gallop and stops facing the authorities, then he turns, facing the opposite side where I'm sitting. His resemblance to Saboor is amazing— Saboor the servant, the sleepless butler, Saboor in the box, the buttless boy of the Psychiatric Wing. He is thin like the two Saboors, with a yellow jaundiced face, awkward long arms, and a long wobbly neck. I remember how as a butler and a buttless inmate in the box the poor boy's neck wobbled on his shoulders when he dozed off.

But this boy on all fours cannot be Saboor. Saboor of the Psychiatric Wing could not possibly leave his box. Didn't the Last Holy One tell me that the poor boy couldn't control his bladder and bowels, that he constantly emptied himself in the box? And I believed the crazy man. Maybe Saboor was not dirtying his box, maybe he sat there simply because he is insane. This boy must be Saboor in the skin of a deer. So the insane Saboor who sits in a box all day, impersonates a pregnant deer at night.

Now a young man, tall and square like most of the prison guards, enters the stage as the hunter. He carries a toy bow and arrow. He chases the deer, aiming at him. He pulls the bow and shoots, pulls again and shoots. But none of the arrows hit the galloping deer.

Kamal enters the stage as the Eighth Holy One and the conflict begins.

The Holy One: Stop!

The hunter: Who are you to stop me? And how dare you? Look, my prey is running away.

The Holy One: Let her go, good man, she is pregnant! She wants to go behind the bushes and give birth to her babies. She says you can hunt her after she gives birth to her babies.

The hunter: How can you tell what she thinks?

Abasel: This is His Holiness, the Eighth Holy One, the Young Martyred One!

The hunter: He is?

Abasel: If not, how could he read the deer's mind?

The hunter: (bows, pays respect, and moves a few steps back.) I'll sit here and wait for the deer to give birth and come back. Then I'll hunt her. You may forgive me, sir, but I'm a hunter and this is the way I earn my living. I have a hunting license, sir—you can check it if you don't trust me!

The Holy One: No license needed, young man. I understand everything.
    You'll have your deer in a few minutes! We'll sit here, waiting with
you. To make the long waiting short, my old servant Abasel will chant a
    lamentation for us.
Abasel: On the theme of martyrdom, sir, because it will happen at the end
of   this play.

Kamal, Sultan, and the young guard sit on the floor. Saboor disappears on
his fours. Sultan starts to sing again. His song is either the rest of the old
one, or another similar song. As the song starts, I notice that some of the
guards and repentants weep in the dark auditorium and blow their noses.
The searchlight turns around and around.

   I follow the light again, searching. Ali the Bricklayer holds his creased
forehead in his wide palm, either weeping or dozing off. Ha-G the Shit
Mouth is completely asleep. He has laid his big head on his guard's
shoulder like a deformed baby, probably snoring into the man's ear. Next
to him, La-Jay has an unusually stiff posture. Since the beginning of the
show, I haven't noticed him moving. The dark sunglasses conceal most of
his facial expressions. Halal has turned his back to the stage and is
whispering something in one of the advisor's ears.

   I review the exhibition of eyes in the women's section. I search for one
unique pair, which I cannot find.

   What was unique about Sahar's eyes? Even in the days of despair, in
the midst of pain and grief, there were twinkling spots in the depth of her
black irises. These flickers gave her an expression of playfulness, as if death
itself was not serious enough. The stars in Sahar's eyes had drawn their
constant glow from life itself. They were not the kind of stars that would
ever fall. Even in El-Deen.

   Now each time the beam passes over the women, I search for Sahar's
eyes. It's a game, a painful play, a gloomy pastime that I amuse myself with
at every interval. The name of the game: In whose eyes is life laughing? Or,
whose eyes are laughing at life? I'm looking for those playful eyes!

The Third Day of the Holy Mournings

Early morning our women wore black for Hoori's funeral. But Maman's mourning dress didn't fit her anymore. Sahar and I sat on the steps opposite the open door of Grandfather's room, watching the women struggling to zip up Maman's old black dress. Tuba, who had come at dawn with Baba-Mirza and Uncle Yahya for the funeral had knelt on the floor, sweating. She was trying to pull Maman's zipper up. The dress was old, from when Maman was young and one of her relatives had died. Since then, no one had died. Maman had grown fat and the dress had shrunk in the trunk. The once black crepe material was a wrinkled, yellowish gray now, and the starched lace collar was rolled inside. Finally Tuba gave up, rose to her feet, sighing and shaking her head in disappointment. Mother suggested that Maman could wear her usual, comfortable house dress, covering herself with a black veil.

All the while Maman was a piece of lifeless flesh. Grandfather had given her a strong tranquilizer plus his special potion of seven boiled herbs. Both Maman's eyes and mouth were half open and every few minutes a strange sound came out of her throat. Something like a snore, a lion's groan, or a shriek, muffled in the lungs and emerging as a strange faint sound.

We all walked toward New Spring Cemetery. It was hot, but there was no sun. Thick clouds covered the sky like layers of dirty blankets. Grandfather, Uncle Musa, Baba-Mirza, and Uncle Yahya walked in front, all sweating in their dark suits. Grandfather and Uncle Musa didn't wear hats, and the back of their heads and necks looked alike. Uncle Musa was losing his hair, too. The narrow margin of thin curls around his scalp was graying. On both men's brown foreheads and necks, sweat bubbled. Baba-Mirza and Uncle Yahya, his brother, were wearing derbies, identical brown, as though the brothers had bought them together. Baba-Mirza was tall and square, even a bit taller than Grandfather, and his brother was short and shrunken, standing only up to his shoulder. Sand and hot pebbles made cracking sounds under the old men's polished shoes.

Mother and Aunty Zari were holding Maman's arms. Tuba, too fashionable for a New Spring funeral, wore a short silk black dress that showed her muscled calves, a little velvet black hat tilted on her red hair. She wore her usual make-up, only with a lighter shade of lipstick.

Mother wore a black scarf, so it was hard to guess what color her hair was.

Her face looked stony, motionless, and without a wrinkle. We watched her as if watching a woman we've seen all our life at a distance, but never close enough to be able to touch her. Aunty Zari was in a long black dress that hung off her like a monk's robe. She dragged her stiff legs behind like a tall ghost.

Maman's knees buckled and jerked and she let out a weird groan now and then. A few neighbors joined the procession. Sheikh Ahmad's four wives, head to foot in black veils, walked behind us. They cried loud and hard, as if Hoori had been their own sister or daughter. The Sheikh's fourth wife, the one who fainted while watching the Holy Procession and fainted again when the black van brought Hoori's corpse, passed out in the arms of the other wives, who pulled her up, slapping her face to bring her back.

Grand-Lady was not with us. Since dawn, knowing that something was wrong (because nobody brought her breakfast in a tray, or helped her to use the bathroom) she walked around the house, picking up her belongings. She collected her things in several bundles, stacked the bundles in the dark corner of her room. She even emptied her water-pipe, wrapped it in a white sheet, and lay it on top of the stack. The last thing she took was her Turkman carpet, which she rolled up, laying it beside the pile. When we left the house to go to the cemetery, Grand-Lady left too, but she took the opposite route. As we trudged sluggishly toward the New Spring Cemetery, as brisk as a young girl, our great-grandmother ran toward the mountain skirts.

The procession reached the tenant house. Here we stopped, waiting for Hoori to join us. Last night Grandfather and Uncle Musa had carried her coffin to the tenant house to let Maman rest a while. Otherwise, she constantly dropped herself on the box, hugging it tightly, then beating it violently. But after they took the coffin away, she rested in peace. Maman remained still until dawn.

Now two tenants, two young night-shift workers from the sugar factory, brought the coffin out on their shoulders. Although all the tenants were Sheikh Ahmad's tenants (Grandfather had sold the multi-level house to him), they still paid respects to Grandfather and ran his errands. We didn't see any of the old tenants—Bashi the Janitor, Hassan the Gardener, and Ali the Bricklayer must have left earlier for the third day of the Holy Show. Only their wives joined the procession. But Ali's wife, Zahra, Maman's old companion, was not there. She had died last year when Ali was in prison.

Ziba, Hassan's wife, the laundry woman, and Zeinab the cleaning woman cried hard and loud inside their ragged veils.

When Maman saw the black coffin, the tranquilizer and the seven herbs suddenly lost their effects and the old loud shriek that was muffled in her lungs found a way out. She let out a lion's groan, dropping herself on the box to hug and kiss, scratch and beat it with all her might. The loose, black veil slipped off her body, laying flat on the dust, revealing Maman's housedress— an old, pale, white cotton shift with small purple flowers, the front part yellowed by many oil spots. Like an owl she screamed, "Hoori, Hoori, Hoori!"

The women were not strong enough to lift her up. Grandfather and Uncle Musa held Maman's arms, pulling her back from the coffin. They held her up in the air. She resisted setting her feet down on the ground. They carried her in the air, like a heavy sack, all the way to the cemetery.

The grave was open and ready. As we approached we saw someone sitting at the edge of the hole staring into the hollow ditch. This was Uncle Massi, his hair loose around his body, his red-checkered bandana tied around his forehead. Half-naked and half-conscious, he was squatting at the graveside. When he saw us, he rose, moving a few steps back as if panicked. But when the workers lay the coffin down, he ran toward it, throwing himself on the hard wood, banging the lid with his fists.

"Come out! Come out, I say!" He beat harder. "Come out, I'm your poet-prophet. I order you to come out!" He stood up and looked at the sky, making a fist and shouting at the fast moving clouds, "Nobody dares to die here!"

Grandfather whispered something to the workers and they grabbed Uncle Massi's arms, holding him back. Tame as a lamb, he hunched into his rags and moved back.

Uncle Musa opened the coffin, taking the corpse out. Aunty Hoori was wound in a white shroud. Nothing of her was out, but we could recognize the curve of her thin waist. Uncle Musa lifted his sister up in the air as though she were a baby in many folds of a white sheet. Maman passed out and missed the rest. Sheikh Ahmad's fourth wife passed out too, but came back when the other wives slapped her face. Grandfather began to cry. This was the first time we'd ever seen him crying. With his thumb and forefinger he held the arch of his big bony nose as if holding a mouse by its tail.

He closed his eyes; three or four times his head jerked back and forth, then he removed his fingers from his nose and dried his tears with a big, white kerchief. He didn't cry anymore. Women wailed and moaned, some beat their chests and mumbled things to God and the Holy Ones. Mother stared at her sister's corpse with her dry blue eyes and murmured, "Finally!"

Silence fell upon us. No one wailed, no one sniffled, coughed, or even breathed. No one said anything more. We all stared at the small body with the curve of thin waist as Uncle Musa lay it in the cold hole. But now Uncle Massi freed himself like an arrow, thrusting forward.

"Wait! I can do a miracle! Let me bring her back to life! I'm your poet-prophet! Have faith in me! Let me do a miracle!" He said the last sentence in a pleading tone.

A poor sheikh, one of Faithland's miserable beggars who always sat in front of the mosque with a brass bowl to collect a few black coins, appeared out of nowhere, starting to chant the prayer of death. Grandfather and Uncle Musa hadn't invited a sheikh to pray. This one either had come on his own to earn some money, or the God-fearing tenants had invited him. He squatted at the edge of the grave, held one hand around his mouth, singing in a bad voice. He had no teeth at all and when he opened his mouth wide to chant, we saw his small tongue vibrating in the middle of his dark dry throat.

The sounds of the trumpet, drum, and cymbal of the Holy Procession came from Faithland's direction, covering the poor sheikh's faint death chant. Uncle Musa paid him some coins, dismissing him. The procession got closer. We heard the slap, slap, slap... of the wide hands and the bare chests, but we didn't hear the chains yet. Grandfather poured the first shovel of dust on Hoori's body and then the other men poured more. When they poured the hot, dry dirt on the white bundle, men and women wept in unison.

A cold current rushed down from my heart to my toes. I turned to Sahar for the first time since we left the house and looked at her eyes. I wanted to record this moment in my memory. I wanted to include Sahar in the picture. She was standing beside me at the edge of the grave, staring at the dust that now almost covered Aunty Hoori's shrouded body. Small tides slowly overlapped the dark pool of Sahar's eyes, taking the shape of tear drops, rolling down her face. But when she turned to me, I saw the sparkles in them, the stars, which said everything was not serious after all! I smiled at her and looked around to see if anyone had seen me smiling. No one. Whoever was here at that moment at the edge of that grave was deaf, dumb, and blind, drowned in the dark bottoms of grief.

On the way back, the music of the Holy Procession accompanied us. Maman never came back to, but lay on the stretcher the neighbors had made from her large, black veil. Two workers held either side of the stretcher, carrying Maman's heavy body home.

Sahar and I left the weeping women in Grandfather's room. They sat around Maman on the carpeted floor, sprinkling water on her and massaging her shoulders. We didn't join the men, either, who went to Uncle Musa's house for a drink of cold lemonade. Instead we snuck into Grand-Lady's room, which was quiet and dark and smelled of tobacco, rose-water, and sheepskin. We looked at the stack of our great-grandmother's bundles in the corner of the room and her Turkman carpet rolled up beside the pile. We were both quiet and could hear our rapid breathing. We didn't need to talk. We knew that we were there to see, smell, and touch our childhood, to say farewell to it. We knew that we were there to see the past for the last time and leave it behind, on top of Grand-Lady's pile.

When we left the room and stood on the porch, facing the mountain, we breathed deeply. Our breath quivered when we exhaled, as if we'd been relieved of a horrible burden, or had realized that everything had just been a bad dream. The huge mountain was there, dark and gray, blocking the horizon. We stood facing it, listening to Maman calling "Hoori, Hoori, Hoori..." like an owl, listening to the trumpet and drum of the Holy Procession. When the cymbal banged, Shamar the Shiny Shield cut the head of the Third Holy One and blood gushed out of hundred bare foreheads. We heard the chains beating the bloody shoulders, "Chee, chee, chee, chee..." the chains sang while men and women roared, "Oh, oh, Holy One, oh, oh, Dear One! Dead and gone! Dead and gone!"

Sahar and I stood there staring at the mountain, imagining Grand-Lady somewhere in the folds of Alborz's skirt, spreading herself on a big rock like an old eagle, kissing it and whispering to it in her strange language. We imagined her lying there, her head on the cold stone, smiling, the second smile of her life, not at her son's daguerreotype, but at the mountain, saying "Thank You, Mother Alborz! For calling me and receiving me!"

We imagined this as we looked at the sky of the third day of the Holy Mournings, a sky as dark as a moonless night.

The Hunter Learns His Lesson

The moment Sultan's chant ends, the young hunter jumps to his feet, pacing the stage restlessly. The interval has ended and the actors are back in their roles. Those in the audience who were asleep wake up to watch.

The Hunter: So where did this deer go? It's been a while. What if she is not coming back?

The Holy One: Be patient, my friend. The deer will be back. Giving birth to two babies at once is not that easy.

Abasel: And she is all alone by herself too. No one to help her out!

The Hunter: I've wasted my time. It's already twilight and I won't be able to hunt anything in the dark. What if the deer won't show up? Then how will I go home tonight? What will I tell my wife and children?

The Holy One: Be patient, my friend! Sit down and let's talk while we're waiting.

The Hunter: I'm sorry Your Holiness, but I can't sit at this moment. What if the damn deer doesn't show up? Who will feed my hungry family?

Abasel: When the Holy One tells you to sit down, sit down. Don't be disrespectful!

The Hunter: You shut up, stupid old man! Who are you to tell me what to do and what not to do? Why did I trust you people from the beginning? How do I know that this man is really the Eighth Holy One?

Abasel: Didn't you see, he read the deer's mind?

The Hunter: I'm not sure that he did. He just said that the deer was pregnant. Anybody could see that! Then he said the deer says she will give birth to her babies and come back. He made this up so that I lose my prey.

The Holy One: (shaking his head in disappointment) Why should I want you to lose your prey, brother? I'm your friend. I didn't want you to kill an innocent deer who had two little babies in her belly. I thought if you really had to hunt this deer, at least you should let her babies live.

305

The Hunter: You see? Didn't I say you planned all this to save the deer? A deer who runs away from the scene of hunting will never come back again, unless she is a stupid deer. And that four-legged animal didn't look stupid to me.

Abasel: (aside) To tell you the truth, I'm also worried about this. What if the deer doesn't show up? What if this strong hunter in the middle of this wilderness cuts our throats from ear to ear, while we have only a short distance left to reach Tus and put the crown on our heads? What if we never get to Tus? What if? What if?

The Hunter: This is the end of my patience! (he draws a dagger out of his belt) You, bastard, are not a Holy One. And you, old man, are the stupidest wrinkled creature I've ever seen in my whole life! I'm going to cut your throats from ear to ear!

Abasel: Help! Help! Somebody help!

At this point, Saboor the deer runs in on all fours, carrying two small stuffed animals with his teeth. He drops the toys at the feet of the Holy One. The hunter steps back and places the dagger in his belt. Suddenly the deer starts to talk. I recognize Saboor's thin voice.

The Deer: Your Holiness, let me kiss Your Holy Feet. You let me give birth to my babies in peace and quiet.

The Hunter: (aside) What? The deer talks? So, this man *is* the Holy One! Oh, damnation! What have I done? How can I undo what I did?

The Holy One: Dear deer, you don't need to kiss my feet. Leave your little ones here with us and go with this hungry hunter to your doom. Keep your promise, poor animal! (He wipes his tears.)

Abasel: (Weeps, aside) What a heart-breaking scene! This wretched mother has to leave her babies here and offer her milk-filled breasts to this cruel hunter's arrow.

I hear many guards and repentants weeping or sniffling in the dark. The guard sitting behind me shakes as he sobs. I can feel this from the way the tips of his boots pierce my lower back. The actors and musicians on the stage all cry. The hunter cries harder than everyone, blowing his nose in a black- and-white-checkered handkerchief. The show almost stops for all this weeping.

An inmate sitting somewhere on my right says, "Absolutely stupid!" He doesn't even try to lower his voice. "They don't know anything about theater! This is unbelievably absurd!" Several guards hush him; he keeps quiet.

To stretch the melodrama, the deer kisses and sniffs her babies, shedding real tears. The searchlight passes over the authorities and I see Ha-G the Shit Mouth, El-Deen's ruthless interrogator, sobbing in his guard's arms. La-Jay, on the other hand, is calm and motionless. It's impossible to say what goes on behind his dark glasses. The foreign advisors look around astonished. Ali the Bricklayer, is bending, holding his forehead in his big palm.

The Deer: Here, I dedicate my babies to You, Your Holiness! Take good care of them and don't leave them alone in this jungle! Farewell! (She kneels down in front of the hunter and opens her arms wide, ready to receive the arrow.)

The Hunter: Go, wretched deer! Go and take your babies somewhere safe, for I may change my mind if hunger forces me to. Go! I spare your life. And you old man, I apologize for my rudeness. Your Holiness, I'm speechless, I don't know how to beg Your pardon. Can You forgive me? Can You forget my arrogance now that I spared the deer's life? (He kneels in front of the Holy One, bends his head.)

The Holy One: Get up, my friend! You don't need to be worried. You have a good heart and you're a God-fearing man. Be more patient in your life and serve your God, who is Compassionate and Merciful. Sacrifice your next prey to His Holy Mosque in the city of Tus. Here, take this purse of money, go and buy your family some food and keep the rest for your children's needs. These are gold coins, my friend—you can even start a business and stop hunting poor animals!

As the hunter kisses the Holy One's hands and runs off with the purse of gold, Saboor the Deer lifts her babies with her teeth, running off to the opposite side. Now Kamal and Sultan as the Eighth Holy One and his servant Abasel resume their journey by pacing around the stage. After one round, Kamal leaves the stage, and Sultan stands in the center, addressing the audience.

Scene Four, Part One: Ajooza and His Son, Omar

"Brothers and Sisters! Dear El-Deenians! I'm sure that so far you've enjoyed our show and now you're longing to see the last scene, the most exciting one. Be patient, for our actors are changing. In a minute, we'll be in two spots at the same time. You'll witness two shows at once. One will happen in the house of the mean old woman, Ajooza, Caliph Maamoon's secret agent who trains her stupid son, Omar, to trick the Holy One and create a scandal; the other scene will take place in the court of Maamoon, where our Holy One sits as an honorable guest waiting for his coronation. But let me not tell you more. Sit back and enjoy your Holy Show! **Scene Four: The End of the Eighth Holy One's Journey from Med to Tus and Martyrdom by Caliph Maamoon's Poisoned Grapes.**"

Kamal enters, wearing a green satin robe and a silk black turban. The other guard, who acted as the hunter, now acts as Maamoon, the Arab Caliph, wearing a false gray beard, a hanging gray mustache, a fancy robe, and crimson turban. Kamal and the guard hold either side of a curtain, hanging it on the same rope that held the plastic fruits in the gardener's scene. This curtain is like a tapestry, a picture of lions, leopards, and tigers roaming in a jungle. Maamoon sits on a stool in front of the curtain and the Holy One sits on another, next to him.

Now Sultan enters with a stool and a dish full of plastic grapes. He uses the stool as a table and places the fruits on it. Now like a faithful dog, he sits on the floor at the foot of the Holy One.

On the right side of the stage, the old man who acted as the barber and the gardener wears a long shabby gray wig and a scarf over the wig. He is already wearing a woman's dress over his shirt and pants. He impersonates an old woman. Saboor enters and lies on the floor at the foot of the old woman. As the old woman and the boy start acting on the right side of the stage, Caliph Maamoon and the Holy One soundlessly converse on the left side. They nod, laugh, frown, point forefingers to the sky, asking God to be their witness, and so on. But the spotlight is on the woman and her son.

Ajooza: (takes a white sheet and wraps it around Omar like a shroud) You're dead now. Do you understand? And this is your shroud. You're ready to go to your grave. But I hear that the Eighth Holy One, the Young Martyred One, the successor of the Caliph, is in town for His Coronation. So, I'll take your corpse there to the palace and beg the Holy One to recite the Prayer of the Dead for you. Now in the middle of the prayer, I'll kick your ass like this! (she kicks Saboor's butt)

Omar: Ouch! Not too hard, Mother!

Ajooza: I'll kick you; that's your cue. It means that you have to get up, unwrap the shroud and say, "I'm alive!" Then, I'll make a fuss that if the Holy One is a real Holy One, how come he recites the Prayer of the Dead for a person who is still alive. Then the other people, Maamoon's agents, will make a big commotion, the Caliph will cancel the coronation, and call the investigation. Understood?

Omar: Yes, Mother.

Ajooza: Now, what is it you must do?

Omar: After the kick I'll get up.

Ajooza: Now, let's practice. Ready?

Omar: Yes, Mother.

Ajooza: "Yes, Mother," my ass! You're supposed to be dead. Omar?

Omar: Yes, Mother.

Ajooza: Didn't I just tell you don't answer? You're dead now, I'm taking you to the palace. All right, pretend we are in the palace. The Holy One recites the prayer: "Bla, bla, bla, bla—" (she kicks him, but he doesn't move). Why don't you move, then, bastard? Didn't I tell you to get up and unwrap the shroud?

Omar: I thought you said I'm dead.

Ajooza: You're dead at first, but then in the middle of the prayer you come back to life, so that we can accuse the Holy One of praying for a live person. Understood?

Omar: Oh, yes.

Ajooza: Now let's start from the beginning. Ready? (Omar doesn't answer. She is happy. She kicks him in the butt and he gets up and unwraps the shroud.)

Omar: I'm alive!

Ajooza: Why did you get up, you stupid bastard?

Omar: Didn't you say get up after the kick?

Ajooza: This kick was to test you to see if you're dead. This was your first kick, the real kick is in the middle of the prayer. Understood, you blockhead?

Omar: I'm confused, Mother (he cries); do we have to do this? And to the descendent of the Prophet!

Ajooza: You shut up and don't interfere. Caliph Maamoon has promised me gold coins and a house in a good neighborhood. Besides, he is my Caliph, I have to obey his orders. Now let's practice more. I didn't know you were so dumb! No wonder they kicked you out of school in second grade! Are you ready now? (Omar is not sure whether to answer or not. Finally he decides not to.) Get up, Omar, and have some apple! It's juicy, I've just brought it from the Bazaar.

Omar: Where are they? Where are the apples, Mother?

Ajooza: (beats him up) You stupid, dumb-ass, bastard, son of a whore! That was a trick to see if you can act dead. (She beats him up some more.) You idiot, blockhead, good for nothing!

While poor Saboor is being beaten up realistically by the old man disguised as the old woman, the guards, the repentants and the authorities laugh with delight, enjoying the farce. My right-hand neighbor whispers to his friend, "He's torturing the boy on the stage! I know him; he is one of the head torturers in Hall Seven."

The more the audience laughs, the harder the actor/torturer beats the boy. We hear the slaps, punches, and kicks, and Saboor's faint, muffled moan. The inmates who are sitting around me get restless. I sense a movement, a hidden tornado again, building in the depths of the dark sea. The searchlight moves over the heads of the authorities and I see that Ha-G the Shit Mouth is shaking with hysterical laughter. Ali the Bricklayer has grabbed his chin in his big hand—I cannot tell whether he is laughing or not. For the first time I see a faint smile on La-Jay's stony face.

It seems that either the old man, encouraged by the audience, is stretching the comic effect to get more laughter, or as is his habit as a torturer, he is prolonging an otherwise short scene. One of the inmates, maybe the same one who defended the toothless prisoner earlier, gets up and shouts, "Stop this beating! You're killing the boy!" The machine guns click; the guard behind me stirs, removing the sharp tips of his boots from my painful back. Some inmates hush their friend and urge him to keep quiet, but some others join the complainer.

"Why is he beating the boy?" one says.

"Stop him! This is not a torture chamber!"

"Look! He is jumping on the boy's chest! He'll die!"

"Stop the show! Stop this stupid show!" several inmates holler.

The murmurs turn into an uproar. In the women's section, on my left, several women get up and shout, "Stop beating the boy!" The commotion reaches to the point that the guards all stand up, aiming their machine guns at the inmates. But before a disaster happens in the community center, someone shoots one bullet and everybody freezes. The actors on the stage freeze too.

My jaws rattle. I hold them with my cuffed hands so as not to bite my tongue. I look at the authorities' section. La-Jay, who is up on his feet, puts the revolver back in his pocket in slow motion. Someone shouts, "God is the greatest!" And many hoarse voices roar, "God is the greatest!" The same person shouts, "Long Live the Holy Leader!" And the guards shout, "Long Live the Holy Leader!" The voice shouts, "Death to the blasphemers and unbelievers!" "Death to the blasphemers and unbelievers," the faithful shout. Then the auditorium shakes with the resonance of one word, "La-Jay! La-Jay! La-Jay! La-Jay!—" They repeat and repeat and some even beat their chests in frenzy, as they chant, until the Head of the University, the Father of El-Deen raises his right hand and invites everyone to silence.

The Fourth Day of the Holy Mournings

Chee, chee, chee, chee, men beat their bare shoulders with chains all through the night. At dawn on the fourth day of the Holy Mournings, the darkest of all dawns, the army of the devil defeated the army of God. Shamar the Shiny Shield won.

From evening to dawn, shopkeepers, residents of the tin houses, gang members, hooligans, street people, beggar-sheikhs, and other ranks of underdogs, either performed the show or watched the performance. Women cooked halva in the dark kitchens. As they poured the flour into boiling oil, the smell of death filled the neighborhood. All through the night, women served platefuls of the hot gooey dough to the sweaty mourners.

311

Shamar the Shiny Shield cut the dear head of the Third Holy One, the Thirsty One, many times, in many performances, in many man-made ditches.

The heat was intolerable. I woke up wet, soaking with sweat, disturbed by a strange feeling of loss. I knew that I'd dreamed about something, about many things, but now there was a hollow in my head. For a few minutes, I didn't know where I was. I smelled burnt halva and I remembered myself, but still not my dreams. From the distance I heard people crying, "Oh, oh, Holy One! Oh, oh, Dear One! Dead and gone, dead and gone—" I remembered Hoori, her open grave, her small shrouded body, the curve of her waist. I remembered Grand-Lady's bundles, stacked in the corner of her room, her body carved on a rock, far away on the skirt of Mount Alborz. I opened my window, looking out in the dark. I knew that the moon, maybe the full moon, was somewhere behind the clouds. But the clouds were too thick. The fig tree was still. I stepped out and sat on the steps. Grandfather with his old lantern was roaming the yard. He took a few steps, stopped, stared at something and walked again. Now he went toward the porch, climbed the steps, opened Grand-Lady's room, entered, but didn't stay long. Coming out he stood with his back toward me, facing the mountain. He bent on the railing, folded in two; his once broad shoulders were so stooped that he looked like a hunchback. His body shook.

I climbed the narrow stairway, stepping on the roof where Sahar's solitary room was—Hoori's old room. My sister's light was on, but she was not there. On the wall opposite her bed she had a tall poster of a dark man in a black beret, rifle on his shoulder, piercing your eyes with his eyes. On the wall above her bed, she had a poster of a male dancer, leaping high in the air, his legs opened and his delicate arms curved above his handsome head. The guerrilla fighter and the dancer looked in different directions: the first one, to the south where Faithland was, the second one to the north, the Alleys of Heaven.

The terrace was dark. I couldn't find Sahar. I sat by her door and leaned back against the brick wall. I could neither see the mountain, nor the hidden moon. The whole world was one thick cloud, dark as the burnt halva that smelled of death. This smell rose to the roof, filling me with hunger and despair.

"I can't sleep tonight." Sahar came toward me through the dark. She was barefoot, wearing a long, white gown, her wild hair down. A ghost.

"I can't either. I slept a little. Had a bad dream."

"Me too," Sahar said, sitting next to me, hugging her knees. "We were both here, you and me, sitting in the dark," she said. "It was close to dawn. We were waiting for it, for the dawn, but it wouldn't come. The clouds were too thick and the sun wouldn't shine. Then a storm started. I said, 'Hey, this is Saba, our friend. He's back to visit us!' But Saba was wild and violent, whirling, twisting, roaring, and sweeping everything away. He picked everything up. Picked us up too. We were in the air, but it wasn't fun at all. I was gulping mouthfuls of dusty air, suffocating. It was as if I were inside a grave, with them pouring dust on me and my mouth open. I was still alive! I wanted to scream and call you, but I couldn't. Then I saw both of us floating in the space like astronauts. We saw Grand-Lady's carpet flying by itself. We tried hard to reach it. First you reached the carpet, you hung on it and pulled yourself up. Then you helped me to sit on it. The moment we sat on the peacock, we were in peace. The wind stopped for us, but it was stormy all around."

"Sahar, let me tell you the rest," I told her. "The Turkman carpet rose and took us over the brown skirt of Mother Alborz. We saw Grand-Lady. She was a picture on a flat rock, as if she were carved there and no wind or rain, no snow or avalanche could wipe her away. I said, 'Sahar, she became part of the mountain—.' Then we passed over El-Deen. It was a huge white building with many black windows, a giant with many eyes, all the eyes shut. We passed over the ironwoods. I told you, 'Look! They're really red like the day Ali the Bricklayer took us to visit Father. Ali said blood was running in the trees' veins!'

"Then the carpet took us over the Alleys of Heaven. We peeked into Madame Aida's School of Ballet and saw you there. You were dancing to the saddest music we'd ever heard. Your body was so loose, you could curl and twist like a snake. You could leap and fly like a falcon, Sahar! We left you alone to dance your lonely dance in the mirrored room and moved to Mother's apartment, not far from the School of Ballet. We hovered over her balcony, filled with red geraniums, tall and wild, not like any other geraniums we'd seen in real life. We peeked into her apartment through her transparent lace curtains and saw her packing her things. The place was almost vacant and the tall blow dryers and empty mirrors were the only things left of Salon Marie. Mother was leaving."

"The carpet took us to Santa Zita," Sahar said. "The storm bent the strong pine trees, tearing up the volleyball nets. In the middle of the dark schoolyard, we saw Sister Tatyana standing alone in her black gown. Tatyana pulled off her scarf and threw it in the air. But she wasn't bald, her heavy golden hair waved in the wind. She danced a whirling kind of dance, so beautiful that we both cried. Then we left Tatyana among the pines and moved on—"

"—Along Old North Road, Sahar," I told her, "coming down toward the New Spring neighborhood, we saw a little man biking in the dark, his bike swaying with the wind. You screamed from the top of the carpet, 'Uncle Yahya! Uncle Yahya! Do you want a ride?' He saw us, smiled, and said, 'No, thank you, I'll feel sick up there. Besides, I'm faster on my bike. I'm rushing to your neighborhood, because someone is coming.' We asked him, 'Who is coming, Uncle?' But he didn't tell us. He biked faster against the wind.

"When we reached New Spring," Sahar said, "and we passed over the roof of the public bath where the many red towels were hanging in the wind, you told me, 'Sahar, once I lost you here in one of the chambers of this bath.' I said, 'I don't remember.' Then our carpet moved to the curve of New Spring street where the school building is. Here, we saw Mother. Her hair was her old hair, wavy and black, long in two thick braids like when she was only a high school girl who gave birth to us. She was climbing the hill, carrying only a small suitcase. With her girlish body in her turquoise blue dress she approached the triangular house, opened the door, and stepped in. Through the cobwebbed window, we saw that she went to the triangular room, and hung her broken wedding picture on the wall. She sat under the picture, staring at the door."

"Sahar," I called her. "Then the storm in my dream became wilder than ever. Sheikh Ahmad's black flag on top of his roof turned into a bat and flew toward us; his robe turned into black wings and he became a gigantic raven with long sharp beaks, but on our carpet, we were safe, Sahar. We were sitting on either side of the peacock and not even a breeze disturbed our peace. Our carpet lay still in the air as though on the solid floor. We both saw him coming at the same time and we gasped. We couldn't say a word to each other. Father, with much effort, climbed the hilly street against the wind. The wind pushed him back like a falling wall, but he wrestled with it, trudging toward the triangular house. Father was short and shrunken, Sahar, wrinkled and gray. He was even more gray than we saw him last in the white tent of El-Deen. One of the lenses of his glasses was cracked, he was wearing a wrinkled pair of pants and a gray shirt. His shoes were old and too big for him. He stood in front of Grandfather's house, pausing for a second as if trying to remember something, then he turned right and headed toward the triangular house where our mother was waiting for him. Saba seemed to bring his sigh to us: 'Ahhhhh!'"

Sahar and I felt a faint breeze on our faces. The first breeze in four days. We rose and walked through the dark toward the railings. We heard the slow rustle of the fig tree. Within a second, the breeze turned to a wind and the clouds became purple, moving hastily toward the mountain peak. Papers, scraps of rags, leaves, and feathers rose up, floating in the air. The wind became a storm in a second. Somewhere not far away, it rained. We smelled the wet dust mixed with the scent of halva. The oh, ohs of the mourners resonated in the mountains like ghost songs. We held hands so that the wind couldn't lift us up.

First we saw Mother, thin and girlish, her hair divided in two thick braids, climbing the hilly street. With a serious look on her face, as if she knew what she was doing, she marched against the wind, approaching the triangular house. Soon she was under the eaves and we couldn't see her, but we heard the key turning in the key hole. Suddenly hundreds of black flags filled the sky. In the light and dark of the hidden dawn, the mourners' flags looked like a flock of monstrous crows lost in the confusion of the storm. Under this ominous dark ceiling, Father pushed the wind with his palms. Like a prisoner digging a tunnel in the impassable wall, he dug his way toward his bride's house.

Scene Four, Part Two: Martyrdom

On the left side of the stage, Caliph Maamoon and the Eighth Holy One are having a conversation in a loud voice. Two attendants are standing at either side of the caliph. They're wearing black shirts and pants and black paper bag hoods like Akir and Nakir, the cannibals of the Psychiatric Wing. As I look at their skinny bodies and their weird bouncing gestures, no doubt remains for me that they *are* Akir and Nakir, the crazy repentants.

The old woman, Ajooza, drags her son behind, limping around the stage, indicating the distance between her house and the palace.

Maamoon: My honorable friend, Help yourself with food and fruits! We'll start your coronation in few minutes. (He whispers in his attendants' ears) Why is the old woman late?
The Holy One: On our way to Tus, we craved the King's Grapes.
Maamoon: (claps his hands) The King's Grapes! Soon! (he winks at the attendants, pointing to the dish of plastic grapes)
The attendants: (putting the grapes close to the Holy One) The King's Grapes, sir!

As the Eighth Holy One stretches out his arm to pick a large cluster of grapes, the old woman, Ajooza, enters the palace. She screams and whines. Makes a scene. Meanwhile, Akir and Nakir wrap Saboor/Omar in a wide shroud.

Ajooza: His Holiness! My son, my only son is dead! (She kneels in front of the Holy One, kissing his hand). But I'm so fortunate that His Holiness is here in our town! Bless him, sir! Bless his dead body so that he can enter the garden of heaven without the inevitable interrogations at the gate! He has sinned in his short life, His Holiness. I beg you to bless my poor boy's soul ! (She cries hard and loud)
The Holy One: Get up good woman! Get up Mother! I'll recite the Prayer of Death and bless his poor soul. Don't worry.

Now Akir and Nakir bring the corpse in and lay it at the feet of the Eighth Holy One who raises his arms as if performing a miracle, reciting, "There is no god except God—" and "We'll all return to Him—" Ajooza kicks Omar, but Omar does not move. She kicks again, but he remains still.

Ajooza: (in a whisper) Get up, bastard! The prayer is over! I'm kicking you son of a bitch! Get up!

The Holy One: Is something wrong, Mother? Why do you kick your dead son?

Maamoon: What are you doing, you stupid woman? Kicking your dead son? (He kicks Omar angrily) Get up you bastard, before I chop your head off!

Abasel: (whispers in the Holy One's ear) I smell something, sir!

The Holy One: I can't smell anything. I don't think they've cooked a decent meal for us! Their grapes are not large, either!

Abasel: By smell, I mean a conspiracy, sir. Look how the Caliph is kicking the corpse!

The Holy One: You're right. First the mother kicked and now Maamoon! What can this mean? (to Maamoon) What does this mean, Maamoon? Why are you kicking the dead boy?

Maamoon: (angry) This dead boy must not be dead now, that's why (he jumps on him, as if he's a trampoline). He has to rise!

The Holy One: Oh, I see! So there is a conspiracy against me! He was supposed to rise so that you'd accuse me of reciting the Prayer of Death for someone alive. Is that right?

Maamoon: (bends his head in shame) Yes. This was my son's stupid scheme to get rid of you and put the crown on his empty head.

The Holy One: He knew this from the beginning (he points to the sky). So, while I was reciting the prayer, He took the boy's life.

Maamoon: You are the most humble Holy One, Your Holiness. This was *Your* miracle that took the evil boy's life; but You give all the credit to the Almighty!

Now someone sitting in the back row gets up and screams, "There is no miracle here, the boy died under torture!"

"Sh... sh... sh..." Inmates try to shut him up. But he goes on, "Yes, they killed the boy!" Several voices support him.

The machine guns click and the show stops for a few minutes. I hear movement and struggle and muffled sounds behind me in the dark and feel that the guards are taking the protestors out. Things return to normal, and the actors resume. Ajooza suddenly screams.

Ajooza: My son! My dear Omar! Dead for real! (she drops herself on the corpse)

317

While Ajooza is weeping and pulling her hair (the wig), Maamoon lies flat on his chest at the feet of the Holy One, pleading for forgiveness.

Maamoon: Forgive me, sir! I repent! The conspiracy was not my idea. I swear to the Holy Book of God! It was my bastard son's idea. He is the one who plotted this shameful scheme. He is in Cairo, sir, and wants the crown for himself. He pressured me, said that if I didn't listen to him, he'd attack Tus with a squadron of the Egyptian army.

The Holy One: I don't know what to say, Maamoon. This is very disappointing. Very!

Abasel: (whispers) Don't believe him, sir! He is lying. Don't trust him.

Maamoon: Don't listen to this old man, sir! He has lost his wits. you're generous and forgiving, gentle and manly. You're Holy and innocent. You're—

The Holy One: Cut it short, Maamoon! I'm still angry and very hungry!

Maamoon: (claps his hands) Food! I'll spread the most colorful table you've ever seen in your life, sir! (claps his hands) Food! Food!

Abasel: Sir, if I were you, I wouldn't compromise for food. Do another miracle and get rid of this traitor. Then we would have all the food, all the palace, all the kingdom, sir!

The Holy One: What kind of miracle do you mean?

Abasel: (points at the curtain) Do you see the curtain?

The Holy One: Yes. What about it?

Abasel: The picture of the animals!

The Holy One: So?

Abasel: Sir, do your masterpiece of miracles, the miracle of miracles. Bring these brutes to life and let them eat up the evil Caliph and his friends!

The Holy One: I can't.

Abasel: Why not?

The Holy One: It's hard. Do you know how much energy that takes? It's not as easy as you think.

Abasel: Look, sir! The Caliph is whispering in his attendants' ears. He is cooking up something else for you. We're in danger, sir! His bastard son may arrive too—I don't think he is in Cairo! We have neither an army, nor arms to defend ourselves. We need these lions and tigers, sir! I'm worried to death! What if—

The Holy One: All right, Abasel. Cut your whining. I'll give it a try. (He raises his arms, his fingers pointing at the curtain. He murmurs.)

Maamoon: What are you doing, Your Holiness? I ordered a stuffed lamb, buttered and saffroned rice, and fresh halva. Sir! Sir! (to Abasel) What the hell did you whisper in his ear? What is he doing staring at the curtain?

Abasel: Don't speak. He is concentrating!

Maamoon: On the curtain?

Abasel: Yes, on the curtain, you fool!

At this moment a new actor, a short man with small eyes and a pock-marked face, enters the stage with a big round tray on his right shoulder. I recognize the nurse from the Psychiatric Wing. As he lays the tray on the floor, three small people in the skins of lion, leopard, and tiger, appear from somewhere in the dark, leaping through the curtain. They run and hop on four legs, making roaring sounds. The audience cheers. Some scream, "Praise the Lord!" or "Long live the Holy One!" The show temporarily stops and the actors freeze. The whole auditorium rises and all the guards and repentants lift up their right arms and tighten their fists. They roar from the bottoms of their lungs, "Long live the Holy One!" Three times. Then, "Death to the blasphemers!" Three times.

Maamoon cries, pleads, and licks the Holy One's feet like a dog. The beasts sit around him, roaring with mouths wide open, showing their teeth.

Maamoon: Forgive me, sir! I beg you! Let me stay alive and become your servant! Let me lick your feet like an obedient dog, sir! My kingdom is yours. My crown is yours. Send the army and get rid of my bastard in Egypt. You'll defeat the Egyptian army in a minute with your miracles. Sir, let me remain your faithful feet-licking servant. Sir! I'm your humble repentant!

The Holy One: Get up Maamoon, you're disgusting! (He motions to the beasts to sit quietly. They lie down like house pets.)

Abasel: Sir, don't make a mistake here. Let the animals eat him.

The Holy One: I'm tired, Abasel. I'm tired of all this and I'm thirsty and hungry. (He sits on a stool, holding his head) This last miracle drained me, Abasel. (He gets up, grabs a cluster of grapes and puts

319

the whole thing in his mouth.)

Maamoon: No, sir, Stop! Stop! Spit out the grapes! Help, help! Call the doctor!

Abasel: (Lifts his hands and hits himself on the head) Damnation! Disaster! May the black plague take me away! The grapes are poisoned!

The Holy One: (Grabs his throat, then his stomach, and collapses.) I'm returning to you, my Lord!

Abasel: (Points to the beasts) Eat the evil Caliph! Soon! (The animals vanish through the curtain.)

Maamoon: (to his attendants) You stupid bastards, you should have removed the poisoned grapes after I repented. (Screams) Executioner! Chop their heads off!

Two big guards acting as executioners enter the stage with huge scimitars and pantomime chopping off the hooded heads of Akir and Nakir. Meanwhile, Abasel lays his Master's body flat in the center stage, weeping and chanting the lamentation song, this time on the specific theme of martyrdom of the Eighth Holy One, the Young Martyred One. The actors weep and hundreds of guards, repentants, and authorities cry in the auditorium. Like an orchestra starting a march from a low key and building to a climatic peak, the believers beat their chests with fists and palms, first low and slow, then fast and loud. When the rhythm becomes like the resonating pulse of hundreds of monsters in a dark well, they all chant, "Oh, oh, Holy One! Oh, oh, Dear One! Dead and gone, dead and gone!"

Storm in the Community Center

We are forced to beat our chests with our cuffed hands. If we don't the guards will aim the guns at our temples. I beat myself. I raise my heavy arms, hitting my fists to my bony chest. Although my wrists are pulsing with pain, I keep doing this as long as everybody else does. If I stop, one of the guards, in a moment of anger or frenzy, may shoot me. While thinking about this and beating myself mechanically, I hear someone shouting somewhere behind me.

"Beat your chest, bastard! Beat harder! Have respect for the Martyred One!"

Another voice shouts back, "Can't you see he's sick? He is vomiting blood—"

There is a commotion again, clicks of the machine guns. I feel the circular movement of the storm building up under the dark sea. Murmurs and whispers, hushes, and clicks create an atmosphere of chaos. I hear someone close to me saying, "If they shoot, they'll shoot all of us. They want to get rid of us, anyway!"

I look at my left where women are standing in the dim light. I search for Sahar again. What if one of the frantic guards machine-guns us and I never see her again? Sensing the danger, I follow the searchlight to find Sahar's eyes. I'm finally going out of my mind. Why should she be here?

The beam is on the opposite side now, where the authorities are standing, raising their fists, chanting. I spot Ali the Bricklayer's fist in the spotlight, the same fist that was raised in the First Revolt against the Monarch's injustice. The light moves on, passes over me. As if it's going to stay on me, I pose and even smile for Ali to see me from the other side of the round stage.

Now I feel that the tides move down from the top of the slope in a wavy motion. A strong tide can wash me out and push me to the heart of the electrified chain link. If the tides get stronger, I may roll down and hit the fence, becoming charcoal in a split second. The guards scream a new slogan now, "One party in the land of God: Party of God, Party of God!" They shout this and throw their angry fists to the face of the imaginary enemies, the members of the other hypothetical parties.

From the women's section, a strong alto screams, "Long live Freedom!" The auditorium freezes for a long second. Then suddenly the sea quivers, as though an earthquake has built up underground and now is shaking the roots of the earth. Hundreds of voices shout from my right and left, "Long live Freedom!" I fall on my face and let people step on me. My instincts tell me that if I stay hunched, like a porcupine, I may get kicked, but not killed. So, trying to maintain my distance from the deadly fence, I make myself into a ball and remain motionless. Now I hear several gunshots in the dark and hundreds of strong projectors suddenly flood the auditorium.

With the invasion of the lights, the sounds stop. I raise my head only slightly to see the inmates all washed in blinding light like an x-ray. They all look transparent as ghosts, naked and defenseless. Now for the first time, as clear as objects laid under huge magnifying lenses, I see many men and women in bandages, holding crutches, with arms or legs in casts, or displaying open wounds. Blue and black bruises show on swollen faces and empty sleeves are pinned to bony shoulders. "The Holy University," I murmur in delirium and watch the guards take black blindfolds out of their pockets and tie them around the prisoners' eyes. Next comes the leashes, the long black ropes they tie around their necks. I realize that there are more guards in the auditorium than I had thought—one for every two or three inmates. A deep voice shakes the speakers installed around the sitting area: "Hall by hall in a single file! Put your hands on the shoulders of the person in front of you. Evacuate the Community Center immediately. First, halls eighteen, nineteen, and twenty, cells two, three, and four, I repeat, halls eighteen, nineteen, and twenty—"

With their cuffed hands on the right shoulder of the person in front, the inmates on my side evacuate first. So they belong to halls eighteen to twenty, the maximum security zone, the Unbreakables' section. In my porcupine position, I smile and then laugh with delight. Kamal the Immortal has sat me among the Unbreakables. If I survive this commotion, my next stop will be my final one: Hall Twenty, cell number four, as Kamal has said from the beginning. I'll reach my destination. There I can relax and prepare myself for death.

I think about all this while people evacuate the auditorium. No one pays any attention to me. The guards and inmates pass by me, or even step over me without saying a word. Only one inmate stops and lingers above my body. But his guard prods him with the butt of his gun and forces him to move.

When they all leave and around me is empty, slowly, I raise my head and look at the women's section. They are standing in lines, hands on shoulders, blindfolded, and black from head to foot. There is no chance anymore to see if Sahar is here. Their eyes are hidden. The exhibition is closed. The game is over—the game of let's see in whose eyes life is laughing, or whose eyes are laughing at life.

The authorities stand still, watching the evacuation. I see all of them through the many diamond-shaped holes of the chainlinks, but I don't find La-Jay. Ha-G's guard is taking him out now. The Shit Mouth is angry, waving his long arms in the air, screaming. Ali the Bricklayer stands in the white light looking at the opposite side, our side. I try to rise, to lift my heavy cuffed hands and wave at him. I sit on my knees and smile, as though I'm posing in front of a camera. But before Ali can notice me, one of the guards kicks me with his heavy boot like an empty barrel, hurling me downhill. I roll and roll, knowing that I'm heading toward the deadly fence.

What an absurd end, I think. This is not the way I thought I would die. So I stop myself from dying. One step before the chainlinks I claw the cement floor with my nails. I stay on my stomach and close my eyes. The cold cement soothes my hot throbbing temple. No one passes here. Gradually, I feel lighter, as if the heavy burden of my body has been removed and I'm all spirit. I see myself flying over the distinct boundaries that separate one year from another. I fly backward in time; I land in the middle of our thirteenth summer.

Our Parents' Wedding

"Pose! Smile! Move closer to each other! One, two, three—," flash, click, smoke. Our parents' second wedding was eternalized in the mysterious depth of Grandfather's old daguerreotype.

Mother wore a sky-blue gown, masterfully cut and sewn by Aunty Zari, now the dressmaker of several neighborhoods. Mother's natural dark curls were adorned with fresh rosebuds—blood red. Sitting beside her, with his dark gray suit and new gray mustache, Father looked respectful and remote. Mother had bought him a pair of new eyeglasses. They were black-rimmed; the thick lenses reflected the sun. Sahar and I stood behind them. Sahar was taller, her thick long hair woven in one braid that hung down to her waist. When we posed for the picture, she lay her braid gently on her left breast. I was slightly shorter than Sahar, with a shadow of a thin mustache above my lips. My nose looked wide and awkward. We all smiled, except Father who smoked. When Grandfather clicked and took the picture, a white cloud covered Father's face forever.

Grandfather's square yard was set for our parent's second wedding. It was the end of the summer; autumn hung in the air. Everybody had almost recovered from Hoori's death and Grand-Lady's great escape. Forty-five days had past. Maman had resumed her post in the dark kitchen and now was cooking a wedding rice for fifty people. She still cried for Hoori, but only when Grandfather was not around. Sahar and I had caught her in the dark corner of the storage room, opening the old chest containing Hoori's clothes. We'd seen her smelling them one by one, moaning like a wounded animal.

The aroma of saffroned rice with lima beans, stuffed lamb, and fried herrings flavored with dill and lemon rose in the air. Maman's huge soot-covered pots of rice sat on piles of burning wood in the corner of the yard behind the fig tree. Old wooden chairs, called Polish chairs, rented from the pawn shop, sat around the yard. Fresh fruits and pastries covered small tables. The cement floor was sprinkled with water to settle the dust and cool the long day's heat. On top of tall posts planted around the small square pool, kerosene lanterns hung to light the yard at night. The musicians—an old drummer, Bashi the Janitor's friend, Bashi himself, who played trumpet for the mourning processions only a few weeks ago, and a young gypsy-looking violin player, hired by Bashi—sat on the porch on Grand-Lady's carpet, facing the yard, tuning their instruments. The neighbors and relatives filled the yard. As the endless number of children entered, they left their parents, rushing toward the pastry dishes, sweeping the sweets into their mouths and pockets at once. Uncle Musa brought more boxes of pastries, piling them up on the dishes.

This wedding was Grandfather's idea. When Father came back from El-Deen after thirteen years, nobody noticed him. Everybody was mourning for Hoori and Grand-Lady and no one except Sahar and I knew that Father and Mother were in the triangular house. We let them be. Sometimes we peeked through the dusty window, watching them. They were quiet all the time, almost motionless. Both were sitting on an old mattress under their wedding picture. Father was sometimes lying down, laying his head on Mother's lap. We saw them like this for many days. We couldn't tell if Mother hummed something or told Father one of her fairy tales, or if Father whispered anything to her.

Then gradually everybody noticed their presence in the cobwebbed house. Maman started to cook for them and Sahar and I took them the food, leaving it behind the door. Grandfather decided that the mourning should stop and a wedding must be announced. "No more crying in this house!" He said one day. "The dead will not return, but those who are alive need attention!"

One Friday evening, right before the sun set behind the sharp peak of the mountain, Grandfather told us to sprinkle water in the yard, spread Grand-Lady's carpet by the fountain, bring a cool watermelon and a sharp knife and sit there and wait for him. Sahar and I sprinkled the hot cement and lay the carpet by the fountain. The water was thick and green, covered with algae, but when we turned the jetting water on, it gurgled and splashed fresh water in the dark fountain. We sat there on Grand-Lady's carpet on either side of the peacock, setting the watermelon tray in front of us.

Grandfather, who was now perpetually hunched, his fingers crooked with arthritis, limped toward us, sat on the wide green wing of the peacock, and cut the blood-red melon. He said that the melon's red color was the sign of good luck. Then he talked to us like he used to when we were five or six and we would sneak into his dark room, asking many questions. He told us that he wanted to talk about our father. But was there anything we would like to say, before he started to talk?

"Father hasn't seen us, yet!" Sahar said. "He doesn't care for us. All he needs is Mother."

"Do you feel the same way?" Grandfather asked me.

"I feel the same way," I said.

"Anything else?" he asked.

We both stayed quiet, bent our heads, listening to the murmur of the fountain.

"Well," Grandfather said and cut the melon in several thin slices, each like a wide smile. "When someone is locked in for such a long time, not talking to anyone, not eating normal food, not sleeping normal sleep, not seeing the sunshine, not breathing the fresh air, living in the dark, lingering between fear and hope, because maybe the torturer is coming to take him, or maybe they want to set him free; when someone lives like this year in and year out, and then one day suddenly they open the iron door and tell him, 'You can go!'—well, he doesn't want to go." Grandfather stopped here and handed each of us a smiling slice of red, juicy watermelon. We bit and licked our fingers.

"They open the big gate, letting him out and he goes out and he doesn't like the sun, it's too strong for him; he hates the wind, it makes him shiver; he can't walk well, his legs are stiff; and finally when he goes home, he doesn't want the good food, the normal sleep, the fresh air. He doesn't want his family. He is still in the dark and he thinks the same dark thoughts and lingers between the same hopes and fears. He lives as if he is still in his cell. It takes him a while to recover and let the sun in and talk to people. So don't be disappointed and let your father be alone for a while." Grandfather said all this, then said nothing, just bit on the melon and with his little eyes, magnified behind his thick round glasses, stared at the jetting water stretching up toward the sky and spilling back in the pool, making many circles.

Now and then, looking at Grandfather's pock-marks, Sahar and I ate several slices and remained quiet. Fifty-five—we'd counted his dots when we were four or five. Grandfather was quiet too. He ate all the slices with a swooshing sound, then burped once he was full. At last he rose, with some effort, to go back inside, but stopped, staring at the jetting water. He said, "Out here we suffered too, didn't we? Our angel died and our mother vanished as if we'd never had a mother. But still, what your father has gone through inside that place is a thousand times more horrible than what we've gone through here. His was like a nightmare that he could never wake up from, ours is a bad dream—we'll see the sun again. Bear this in mind!"

Grandfather left us and the heavy dusk fell. Sahar and I became one with the night.

Mother and Father stayed together for forty days and nights and that's when Hoori's mourning was over and Grandfather forbade crying in his house. Women changed out of their black, except Maman, who stayed in hers for one whole year.

When it was time for us to go to the triangular house and visit our Father, Sahar and I tried to dress up. Sahar wore a white summer dress. For some reason she wrapped Grand-Lady's white scarf—the one with the picture of a peacock embroidered on one corner—around her long hair. My pants were too short, so Aunty Zari cut them and made them into a pair of nice shorts. I wore Grandfather's white shirt and tucked it in the shorts. We held hands, Sahar and I, like when we were small and headed toward the triangular house. Knocking on the triangular room's old chipped yellow door, we stood waiting. Sahar looked tall and graceful like a swan, while I felt ridiculous—a mustached ostrich.

Ah, Father, why didn't you come when I was a lovely child? My heart banged against my chest as the door cracked open.

There was some furniture in the room that Maman had brought from her house. We stood by the door, waiting. Father was sitting at the table by the window, the same window mother had looked through year after year, witnessing the seasons coming and going until she forgot what her husband looked like. Father sat, looking at the yard, at the entrance door, at New Spring street stretching down to the school's gate. So he had seen us bringing food for them. He had seen us lingering in the yard, peeking through the window to see him. He had seen us but never called us in.

Now he turned and looked at us. Magnified under the thick lenses of his new glasses, one of Father's eyes was smaller than the other. There was a long scar along his left cheek, starting from his temple running down to his thick gray mustache. Father's lips were dark purple. He smoked a thin cigarette, the kind of bad-smelling cigarette the poor tenants and the janitor smoked. His hands were shaking and the ashes fell on the table. His fingers were strangely crooked and on the tip of them there were almost no nails.

We didn't run and throw ourselves in Father's arms as we had dreamed all our lives. We didn't even smile.

Mother broke the silence: "Look how tall they've become. They're thirteen now. When they took you away, they were three days old. It was their Name Day."

Father squeezed the cigarette butt in the ashtray, then held his head in his hands, leaning his elbows on the table as if he had a bad headache. He lay his arms on the table, resting his head on his arms like he wanted to sleep. I heard Sahar's heart and read her thoughts. "Has he gone crazy?" she was thinking. "God, let him not be crazy!" she wished.

We watched Father's stooped shoulders, skin and bones, slightly quivering as if he had breathing problem. Through his thinning salt-and-pepper hair the pinkish skin of his head showed. Mother motioned to us to leave. She smiled, leading us to the door. This was the first real smile since we were in elementary school and she called us to her arms to tell us a story. In forty days Mother's face had become thin and pale. Without make-up, she looked younger and older—younger because she was as plain as a schoolgirl, older because thin lines spreading spider-like around her blue eyes and thin lips showed.

A few days after our visit, Grandfather planned the wedding. He officially announced the end of the mourning period and started to invite people.

Mother left the house to take care of her business. She rented her beauty salon, bought some decent furniture, had the workers paint and fix up the triangular house, bought herself sky-blue taffeta and had her sister make a wedding dress for her, bought father a dark gray silk suit, a red tie, and a pair of new glasses, bought Sahar and I each a pair of shiny leather shoes and a formal outfit. She decided that since Grandfather had extra rooms in his house and the triangular house was too small, Sahar and I should keep staying at our grandfather's.

So we had a pair of new parents living as our neighbors. In their wedding party we were both hosts and guests. Father never talked, never embraced us.

"Was the visit in the white tent all a dream, Sahar?" I asked her almost everyday. "Didn't he hug us, then? Didn't we put our heads on his shoulder and cry? Didn't we feel his tears wetting our faces? Or did we imagine all that?"

Leaning against the brick wall of her room, Sahar sighed but said nothing. She stared at the peak of Alborz. We were sitting on Grand-Lady's carpet, now ours, on opposite sides of the green peacock.

The second wedding was going on. Sheikh Ahmad's four wives watched the party through the crack of their bedroom's curtain. The Sheikh didn't let them join the party, but their many children ran through our yard, hanging around the pastry tables, filling their pockets with cakes and fruits.

Baba-Mirza and Grandfather sat together, drinking vodka like in the old times, exchanging verses on the theme of freedom. Baba fixed his thick-lensed spectacles and said, "As the great bard says, 'Last night at the break of the dawn, they saved me from grief.'" Grandfather didn't let him finish. He wanted to recite the second line himself: "And in the midst of the dark, they handed me the water of life!" he said. They clicked the small crystal shot-glasses, then drank in one fast sip.

Tuba danced in her red satin skirt. Her rainbow-colored silk handkerchief swayed in the air. Other women joined the dance. Aunty Zari had already drunk a few glasses of vodka and was laughing loudly. She wriggled her bony butt to the beat of the music in her old wedding dress. She had tried to mend the garment for her sister's second wedding, but not very successfully.

"Now that Pari's husband is back, mine will show up too! One of these days, one of these days!" she said, opening her arms wide like the thin wings of an old goose, twirling around.

"Sahar! Sahar! Sahar! Sahar!" the dancing women clapped and chanted, asking Sahar to join them. But she didn't want to dance. Hiding in the dark corner of Grand-Lady's room where she used to sit and smoke her water-pipe, Sahar covered her ears with her hands.

"Sahar, you don't need to hide. If you don't want to dance, don't dance!"

"I want to sneak out of here and go to the desert, to El-Deen's wall. Now!" she said.

"There's no reason anymore to go the wall," I told her. "Our father is out!"

"He is not!" she said. "He is not our father, the father we waited for, for thirteen years."

"He is. Didn't you hear what Grandfather said? He'll recover."

"He won't. I know that. Look! He's leaving the yard."

We watched Father through the window, rising slowly and leaving the party. We went out to follow him. The women had stopped calling Sahar. Maman was serving rice and lamb. Zeinab, Ziba, and other women of the tenant house were helping her.

It was dusk and dusk is always darker in the skirts of Alborz. Father entered the triangular house; we followed him at a distance. At the mouth of the well, he removed his silk suit jacket and lay it on the well's tin lid. He opened the old kitchen door and stepped in.

When Mother repaired the house, she didn't touch the remote kitchen. She left it there as it was with all the dust and cobwebs, rat-holes, and cockroaches. Now Father stepped in and locked the door from inside. Sahar and I stayed in the dark yard, waiting for him to come out. He didn't. We heard the wedding music from Grandfather's house. It was a rhythmic music, the drum invited the dancers to wriggle their bottoms, to quiver their shoulders and breasts. We heard women bursting with laughter. Tuba and Aunty Zari were drunk. Sitting on the stone step behind the kitchen door, we waited for Father to come out.

"What are you doing here?" Mother said in a hushed angry tone. The many rosebuds in her curls shivered when she talked. One fell on the brick floor like a blood drop.

"Father is inside the kitchen," Sahar said.

"I know," Mother said.

"What's he doing there?" I asked.

"Nothing!" Mother said. "He just needs to be alone!"

"Why doesn't he sit in the room, where it's clean and nice? He can turn the lights out if he wants," Sahar said.

"I don't know," Mother said. "He does this every evening. Now go back and help Maman out with the dishes! Soon!"

"Mother!" I said. And I realized that I hadn't called her this for a long time, since before she opened her beauty salon and became Marie.

"Yes," she said.

"Nothing."

And I meant it when I said "nothing." What could I tell her? I'd forgotten how to talk to her.

But Sahar had not forgotten. She had more practice talking to Mother. They'd always shared, at least, Sahar's dance. And besides, Sahar was bold, her voice didn't crack in her throat the way mine did. She didn't hate her nose or feel short.

"Mother," Sahar said, as she was turning to leave the yard.

"Yes," she stopped.

"I don't want to dance anymore!" she said.

"What?"

"I don't want to become a dancer. That's what I mean," she said.

"You *are* one," Mother said. "You've been picked among many students to be sent to Europe. Madame Aida is getting you a scholarship from the Queen's Foundation! We won't have to pay anything. Do you understand?"

"But I'm not going to Madame Aida's anymore. And I'm not going to Europe either." Sahar spoke dryly and mechanically, like someone possessed.

"You're not old enough to decide your life, Sahar," Mother said and turned to leave. "I've spent a fortune on you! Invested in you and you pick tonight, my wedding night, to torture me—" Her voice cracked, but we didn't see her face because, slamming the old wooden door, she'd already left the yard. Her perfume, a delicious scent of wild lilac, stayed behind. I bent and picked up the little red rosebud and threw it into the well.

Visiting the Wall

Sahar and I walked through our old desert between the cemetery and the long wall of the tenant house. In the new leather shoes Mother had bought us for the wedding, we walked awkwardly on the stones and thorns. We didn't have a bundle of food or a walking stick like when we were small.

We saw a shadow approaching us, then we heard clicking and clanking sounds, chain rubbing on metal. A rhythmical click, click, clank, clank, and then someone appeared out of the darknesss on a bike.

"Uncle Yahya!" Sahar screamed.

"Uncle Yahya, are you going to our parents' wedding?" we asked.

Uncle Yahya stopped, one foot on the ground. "No, I'm not going to the wedding. I'm late, I have to be somewhere."

"But where?" we asked. "Aren't you happy your nephew is released?"

"Oh, I'm happy. Very happy. But I have to go," he insisted.

"Uncle Yahya, why do you bike all the time?" I asked.

"I watch the people," he answered. "That's what I do."

"You don't get tired of it?" Sahar asked.

"No, never. It's amusing," he answered.

"Uncle Yahya, how come you're biking in this desert? There is no one to watch here," Sahar asked.

"Oh, there are many. I just saw a neighborhood down there. It's called Faithland. There are many people there living in tin boxes. Many."

"Where are you going now?" we asked.

"Up to Old North Road," he said, "to the Alleys of Heaven. I have to get there before dawn."

"But why there?" Sahar asked.

"One should go there after visiting Faithland. I saw the tin houses, now I want to see the marble castles. But it's already late and my legs are not that strong anymore. Bye!"

He pedaled in the desert, heading toward New Spring Street.

"Uncle Yahya!" Sahar screamed.

"Yes?" we heard him shouting back.

"Father doesn't talk to us!"

"I know," he said. And he said something else, but we didn't hear him. He was far away now, rolling down the steep street, turning right, then left, biking toward Old North Road.

"Didn't he act strange, Sahar?"

"Very. He was cold and remote. As though we were dreaming him."

At the wooden door of the tenant house, we lingered, pushed the door open to check on Uncle Massi. His room was dimly lit. After Hoori's death, he had started writing poetry again. We hadn't seen them to decide whether they were real poetry or just scribbles, but we'd noticed Grandfather carrying long rolls of paper to his room. There were also rumors that Uncle left his room at nights, went to Faithland, and climbed the wall of the whorehouse. He held a lantern up, preaching to the poor people who gathered around him, listening, as he claimed to be their poet-prophet like in the old times.

Sahar and I didn't know most of the tenants anymore and since our grandfather was not the owner of the multi-level house, we didn't feel free to run up and down the steps and investigate all three levels of the house. Besides, we were too old for such games. We just peeked through our uncle's window and found him sitting on his bamboo spread, writing on his lap desk. Before he saw us, we left the tenant house, heading toward El-Deen's wall.

As we walked, the last rays of the late summer sun left the sky. Alborz looked bigger, an enormous shadow, an eternal dark.

"Mother Alborz, the giantess!" I whispered.

"El-Deen, the Monster!" Sahar said.

"They're still here and they will be here forever. Even after you and I are gone," I said.

"Gone where?" Sahar asked.

"Mother is going to send you away. I know that," I said. "And when you go, I'll go."

"Where?"

"Somewhere. I may walk toward the mountain like Grand-Lady, and get lost there. Or, I may fly on the Turkman carpet and go to remote cities with blue minarets and turquoise domes."

"Don't be silly! Why are you talking like this? First I thought you were serious. But you're crazy."

"I may go where Aunty Hoori died. I want to see where exactly she cut her veins."

"Stop talking like this, please!" Sahar pleaded.

"I may die too, then you won't see me anymore!"

"But why? Why do you want to die?"

"What reason will I have to live if you leave?"

"But I won't!" Sahar said.

"You will! Mother is strong. She's always been. She'll send you away!"

"I won't go!" Sahar said stubbornly. "And don't whine about it anymore. We're at the wall. Look! Let's sit here."

We sat at the edge of the ditch, facing the wall. Alborz sent us a gentle cool breeze; this was the messenger of the north, Saba.

We sat and nothing happened. Both of us secretly wished that Ali the Bricklayer would lay brick on top of brick like he used to. We wished he would raise the wall. This was a selfish wish, a cruel one: a wish to make the past happen again. But the past was past, Father was out, and Ali was not a bricklayer anymore.

A dark silhouette approached us through the evening mist. Ali.

"Hey, Ali, it's you!" Sahar and I screamed with joy and rose to greet him. "You knew that we were here waiting for you. You showed up like in the old times! But you're not on top of the wall anymore!"

Ali, silent as the mountain, looked at us as if he didn't understand our language. He passed us, walking toward Faithland.

"That was Ali and that wasn't Ali," Sahar said.

"Didn't he say he had three choices to make?" I asked.

"To raise the wall, to die, or to change into someone else," Sahar said.

"He's made his choice, Sahar."

"Ali the Bricklayer is not Ali the Bricklayer anymore," Sahar said.

"Like Father who is not Father anymore."

"Let's go," Sahar said, running away from the wall. "I want to go back to the wedding and eat some cake!"

She vanished in the dark and I trudged after her blindly, calling, "Sahar! The day that you're not you anymore, I'll die!"

Kamal's Father

"Hey Brother! Didn't I tell you don't get close to the chainlinks? What if you'd been electrocuted here?"

Kamal's voice. Kamal the Immortal, the lead actor of the Holy Show, the impersonator of the Eighth Holy One, the Young Martyred One! I open my eyes; I smile at him. How soothing to open your eyes and see a friend, a caring friend.

I sit up, looking around. The auditorium is empty, the lights are dimming. Someone in the light room is turning the spotlights off. Now that the top of the hilly sitting area is in total darkness, it's impossible to say how far the auditorium extends. But the stage is still fully lit. There is a long table on the stage, covered with a white tablecloth and surrounded by twelve chairs. Sultan, the narrator of the show, the old toothless man who resembles Bashi the Janitor (or is Bashi himself) cleans up the stage, sweeps the floor.

"Kamal, what happened to your wedding, Brother?" I murmur.

Kamal explodes with laughter; his voice echoes in the empty auditorium like a monster's laugh in a deep cave. Someone standing behind him laughs too. He is only slightly shorter than Kamal, but square and robust like him. He is older, his hair gray and his full beard salt and pepper.

"Listen to what my little brother is saying, Father! He's always like this. He either passes out when he is supposed to be awake, or comes to life when it's better to pass out. How many times has this happened since we've been together, Brother, huh?" He is talking to me now.

They both laugh. I try to concentrate on what Kamal just said. He called the man, "Father," so this must be Ali the Bricklayer, or the former Ali, because now I'm sure that he doesn't remember anything of his Alihood.

"This is my father!" Kamal says, "I talked about him, remember? And Father, this is my friend—" He pauses, then, "my nameless friend. He has forgotten his name. But he will remember soon. This little brother helped me to become immortal and I'm indebted to him."

Former Ali wants to shake my hand, but since I have handcuffs on, he grabs my hands and squeezes them hard. A sharp pain runs toward my shoulders, but I'm happy that he likes me and doesn't mind touching me.

"I'm Abbas the Butcher, Kamal's father. Thank you for your help. Everybody outside knows that the Last Holy One, the Absent One, is in

El-Deen and they envy the El-Deenians. Believe me, brother, you're a fortunate person to be here. And I want to thank you again for making it possible for my son to be the first devotee of the Holy One. The first Immortal!" Abbas the Butcher says in Ali the Bricklayer's warm voice.

"But my little brother is a bit tired and maybe hungry too. When did you last eat, brother? In the Psychiatric Wing? So, you need some food and a long rest. Let me take you where you can relax, brother.

"Kamal!" I almost scream in the hollow theater. "Kamal, aren't you taking me to Hall Twenty, cell number four? I'm not really that tired. I'd rather go where I belong."

Kamal and his father both burst into loud horselaughs again. Kamal repeats, "Where I belong!" and slaps his legs, laughing more.

"Do you know what he's talking about, Father?"

Abbas shakes his head, meaning no.

"He's talking about the hall of the Unbreakables, the hall next to the courtyard, where the Wall of the Almighty is—the ward of the blasphemers who don't want to repent. This is the only thing my little friend wants: to become an Unbreakable! As if he is in a rush to visit the black angel. This makes me sorry for my little brother. Why shouldn't he stay alive and enjoy his life?"

Kamal's father shakes his head in real regret. He acts as if he strongly believes that I should stay alive and enjoy my life. I glance at the stage where the old man is mopping the floor and picture myself growing old in El-Deen.

"He's cleaning the wedding table down there. You passed out and missed it," Kamal says. "We were six male devotees wedded to six female devotees tonight. La-Jay recited the prayer. I'm glad Father could make it. I wish my poor mother was here."

"She saw you from heaven and she's happy," Abbas the Butcher says, while pointing to the highest spot light on the domed ceiling with his eyes.

"My bride went to the sixth floor where our new apartment is. She is waiting for me," Kamal says. "But I have to finish this damned long mission first. You, little brother, you're the longest mission I've ever had. I have to take you to—"

"Cell number four." I interrupt him.

"Oh, oh, oh!" Kamal shakes his head and moves his forefinger in front of my nose, "Don't you ever make the decisions for me, all right?"

I realize that although Kamal considers me his friend and thinks that he is indebted to me for his immortality, he still regards me as his prisoner and will never allow me to interfere with his decisions. Friend or no friend, Kamal is still my guard and I'm at his mercy. So I stay quiet, letting him unlock my handcuffs and tie the familiar black leash around my neck. I let him blindfold me.

"Okay. I opened your handcuffs so that you can crawl on the floor. Your feet are infected, you can't walk. Sorry, I have to blindfold you. Later in the hallways I'll uncover your eyes."

Now Kamal's father tells him, "Well, son I have to go now. It's late and I have a truck full of meat to deliver to the other facilities. Then I have to be at the slaughterhouse before dawn. We have to slaughter 5,000 cows this week. For the anniversary of the Great Revolution. I have to work day and night. I'll come and see you after the anniversary is over. Take a few days off if you can, stay in your new place with your bride. Good-bye and God bless you!"

"Don't make yourself tired, Father!" Kamal says, "Don't overwork!"

"Don't worry, son. My skin is rough. I have seven lives!" He laughs and then addresses me, "And you, brother, good luck to you! I hope things get better for you. Don't be stubborn, you're young and have a long happy life ahead of you. Believe me, all these imported ideologies are traps laid for our youth. Stick to our own Almighty, our Great Leader, our Holy Ones, and enjoy your life. This is advice from a man who has lived a long life!" He shakes my hand and I feel the broad, warm hand of Ali the Bricklayer holding and squeezing my cold bony hand. He holds my hand a bit longer and I feel that he's staring at me with his dark eyes as if piercing the blindfold and penetrating into my head. Does he know me, then? He turns to leave and suddenly I hear myself calling him, "Ali!" like when I was a child.

"What did you call me?"

"Aren't you Ali the Bricklayer from Faithland?" I ask.

"Don't be ridiculous, let's go!" Kamal pulls my leash.

"Kamal, I know your father. I know his former identity. Believe me!"

"Hush! Quiet! Don't act crazy here, okay? Let's go now. I can't keep my bride waiting because of your crazy delusions!" He pulls me while saying to his father, "Good-bye, Father. This little fellow is all messed up here."

Although I'm blindfolded, I know that he's knocking on his head.

Kamal pulls me in the opposite direction of his father. I hear Ali's footsteps fading away on the cement floor. In the darkness, I slide myself on my butt, following Kamal. Although he's pulling me gently, I have a fear of rolling over and hurting myself. I row with my hands, pushing myself forward. I'm surprised at the strength of my thin wrists and small hands. I wish I could remember my former life. What did I do with my hands as a free man?

Now a cool breeze sweeps my face and I sense that we've entered a new area. I row the broken boat of my body on the endless river of the cold cement. We must be in the corridors again. I know this, because Kamal lingers for a second and turns right.

Chapter 6

In Sultan's Room

...they smote me, they wounded me;
the keepers of the walls took away my mantle from me.
—Song of Songs

Rowing in the Dark

For a while we move in silence. Inside my head is as dark as my vision. Being able to see must have to do with being able to think. I have a feeling that my memories are all locked in a box inside my hollow head and the key is lost. Sliding on my butt on the cold surface of the cement floor, tormented by the locked box inside my head and tired of the endless effort of rowing and keeping my feet up, I stop. I'm tempted to remove my blindfold and look at my feet. This black scarf has deprived me of my senses. I can't feel my soles. The word gangrene pulses in a dark corner of my brain. What if I lose my legs? Why haven't they treated my infected feet? I reach the eye-band to remove it, but Kamal pulls the leash gently and murmurs, "Not now!"

My feet are my only worry. With each chee sound coming from Kamal's fat pocket, the word gangrene bounces in my head. "Chee... chee... chee..." Kamal's key chain chants. "Gangrene... gangrene..." the black furry word dances in my head.

In a sudden flash, as if finally one particle of memory has snuck out of the fat box, I see Kamal in a turban and robe in the middle of a fully lit stage. I grab this image and hold on to it. Now I remember the whole show. I decide to talk about it. This will distract me from my feet.

"You're a good actor, Kamal!" I hear myself saying. "Congratulations!"

"You're talking finally. I thought you were never going to comment on my performance," Kamal says, without turning to me.

"Most of the time I'd forget it was you acting. It was so real!"

"Hmm... So, you liked it, huh?"

"I admire you for portraying such a different personality. The Holy One is so different than you."

"A good man, huh? Merciful, innocent, not knowing what evil is. A Saint. He can't survive in this world without his cunning servant, Abasel. And even with him, he doesn't."

"He has one flaw, though," I say cautiously. "Everything about Him is holy except this—"

"What? I don't think the Holy Ones have flaws."

"I don't know about the rest of them. But this one, the Eighth Holy One, the Young Martyred One, has one human flaw."

"What?"

"He loves grapes!"

Kamal laughs his monster laugh, which echoes in the empty hallways. He pulls my leash gently and turns to the right. "What a thing to say! Is love of grapes a human flaw? I don't interpret it this way. I believe that God has destined for the Holy One to crave grapes and eat the poisoned one. He wants Him to go up there and join Him. The Holy Ones are in direct contact with God."

"How about the Immortals?" I ask Kamal.

"The Immortals? You mean human Immortals like me?" Kamal repeats my question and slows down, as though he has never thought about it before. "You're asking if the Immortals have contact with God?"

"Yes, and what is the difference between them and the Holy Ones?"

"Well, brother, I think you're gradually gaining your wisdom back. This is a wise question and dangerous to answer. Especially in the position that I'm in. You know, between you and me, I'm the first human Immortal in El-Deen and maybe even in the whole Republic. And you had the privilege of witnessing my immortalization rituals. Other than me, only three devotees have become immortals. My very close friends."

"Did you take them there too?" I ask.

"I did," Kamal says and lowers his voice. "In the intermission between the play and the group wedding, I took my friends and introduced them to the Holy One. I asked Him to make them immortal. I couldn't waste time. It was very dangerous to be the only Immortal in El-Deen."

"You mean... the possibility of... assassination?"

"Not exactly assassination, because Immortals never die. The possibility of being expelled, banished from El-Deen. We need our roots here. El-Deen is the center of the government of God. El-Deen is the heart. Word of mouth spreads through El-Deen faster than the speed of light. I needed a team, a group. How can I put it—?" He mumbles to find a word.

"A party, maybe," I suggest. "The Holy Revolutionary Party of the Immortals!"

"Exactly! Thank you, brother. And I may use this elaborate name. So I have some friends now and we're in constant contact with the Last Holy One. My friends are guarding His cell, because he is in danger too. What if the crazy Ha-G orders His execution? So he has to be protected and we need more devoted devotees."

I imagine my friend Ilych under pressure to produce the Holy Water of Immortality for an increasing number of Revolutionary Guards and I control myself not to laugh loudly.

"That's why I can't wait until I finish this mission," Kamal continues, "I mean your job. I want to join my friends. These are crucial times," he says worriedly, "so crucial that I've almost forgotten my bride!" he chuckles to himself.

"Kamal!" I call him after a short pause.

"What?"

"So much has changed for you since I first met you. Your temper has changed too." I tell him this frankly.

"Yes, brother. I'm a different person now. Not quite a human being with—with—flaws, as you put it. I'm half-holy. And this is the answer to your question, too: Immortality is a stage between humanity and holiness. And I'm in this stage now. When I achieve what I want to achieve, I'll become a Holy One. The Thirteenth One!" He says this firmly, with a deep belief.

"May I ask what is it you want to achieve?"

"I want to actualize what God, His prophet, His twelve Holy Ones, and the Great Leader of the Holy Revolution have theorized about. Under the guidance of the Last Holy One, I want to put these sacred theories into practice."

Ah, now I know! Kamal is picking up Ilych's terminology! Ilych must have lectured him about theory and practice.

"What are these sacred theories, Kamal?"

"The theories concerning the expansion of the Holy Revolution. My task is to spread the Faith all over the world," he says.

"By means of?"

"By means of the Last Holy War. This Holy War starts from here, from within El-Deen, the heart! First I have to purge the impure elements—But hush! I hear footsteps." He speeds on, pulling my leash.

Now he stops. I stumble and almost fall. The sound of footsteps stop, too. I feel the presence of more than two people.

"The ability to see straight—" Kamal says.

"—without overlooking the twists and turns—" someone says.

"—and the zigzags of reality," a third one says.

After this strange greeting, which has replaced their regular "God bless the Holy Leader," Kamal and his friends start to whisper. I can hear them well.

"Why are you here? What's going on?" Kamal asks.

"They took the Holy One," one of the guards says. "I guess they're taking Him to the Wall of the Almighty. They must be around Hall Seventeen now." The man has a lisp when he pronounces *s* sounds.

"You shouldn't have left your post," Kamal says angrily.

"They forced us," the other one says. His voice shakes. He's panicked. "Ha-G came, with five guards. They said if we didn't leave the Psychiatric Wing they'd take us to the fifth floor's West Wing, the wing where the disobedient guards are."

"Conspiracy! This is a fucking conspiracy. They're trying to undermine us. If they take the Holy One to the Wall, then they'll try to get rid of us too. Don't you see? We have to do something before it's too late," Kamal says.

"Leave your prisoner here and come with us to the headquarters," the first man, the one with the lisp, says.

"I can't leave him here in the middle of nowhere. I have to take him to Hall Twenty and finish this goddamned job," Kamal says.

"The Holy One's life, our own lives, are in danger. I'm sure they won't let the Immortals live," the one who is panicked says. "Leave this fucking piece of shit here and forget about this job, Brother Kamal."

"He is a friend," Kamal says, "I can't leave him here. They'll kill him!"

"What do you mean by 'friend'?" the man with the lisp asks.

"He is the one who connected me, connected all of us, to the Last Holy One. I'm indebted to him. His only wish is to go to cell four of Hall Twenty, and I have to fulfill his wish," Kamal says.

"He wants to go to the hall of the Unbreakables?" they both ask.

"Yes. That's where he wants to go," Kamal says.

"Then he's a fucking red. How can you trust him, Brother Kamal?" the panicked man asks.

"I'm telling you, he helped us with our immortality!" Kamal is losing his temper. "I can't leave a friend here, especially in this fucking zone, close to the Community Center and the Headquarters, by maximum security. I have to get him somewhere safe."

"But before getting to the cell of the Unbreakables he has to stay at Sultan's. Your friend definitely won't be safe there," the guard with the lisp says.

"I know. Sultan will give him a hard time. I'm trying to think of a way to take him to the Unbreakables' cell without stopping at Sultan's," Kamal says. "Then tomorrow things might change. There may be no Sultan anymore. We'll change the bastard. He's as cruel and corrupt as Ha-G."

"Talk your friend into changing his mind, Brother Kamal. Tell him about Sultan's barbershop and about what they do to the Unbreakables. Tell him about the Coffin, the weekly Cleaning-Up Operation and all. Then leave him somewhere safe and join us. We have to talk and plan," the lisping guard says. "There are more things going on in El-Deen—"

"Like what?" Kamal asks.

"Ha-G's bodyguard, the big man who carries him around—" he pauses and then goes on, "he kind of made a gesture to us. Didn't he?" he asks his friend.

"Yes, he sure did," the other one says and his voice cracks again, "He pointed to Ha-G's neck and moved his hand like a knife, showing that he was going to cut off Ha-G's head. That's what I understood."

"If they kill Ha-G, Halal will get all the power," Kamal says thoughtfully.

"Halal is a fucking fake. I don't trust him," the first guard says. "He spends most of his time with the foreign advisors, speaking languages nobody understands. Once we were all praying at the sixth floor prayer center and I was standing beside him—and as God is my witness—Halal didn't know his lines, he moved his lips, faking the words of God. I swear to all the Holy Ones!" he says, agitated.

"Fake or no fake, through Halal we can climb up the ladder and get to La-Jay," Kamal tells his friends. "Without Halal, it's impossible to get to the

Headquarters. When we get up there, then we'll think about him and his foreign advisors. But we have to talk about all this tonight. I'll join you before midnight. Wait for me in the rest area of the first floor," Kamal says.

"What about the Last Holy One?" The guard with shaky voice asks.

"Unfortunately we can't do anything to stop the bastards from taking the Holy One to the Wall," Kamal says. "I think this is God's will. He wants His favorite Holy One back in heaven and He is calling him to His Wall. What we have to do is to save ourselves. We are not Holy Ones, Brothers, we're only in the first stages of our immortality. But the future of the Holy Revolution is in our hands. True, they can't kill us, but they can banish us, send us somewhere in the middle of the desert. Then the Holy Revolution will fail, the world will end. Be brave, Brothers, you are Immortals! May God protect you!" Kamal says, pulling my leash to make me move.

"May God protect you, Brother Kamal! See you before midnight!" they both say.

While Kamal and I are gradually gaining distance from the two guards, I hear a faint moan and then dry coughs. Now the coughs sound like the wheeze of a horrible whistle. The sound is definitely coming from infected lungs. I realize that all this time the two guards had a prisoner with them.

"The bastard got pneumonia in the Freezer," I hear the lisping guard saying. "I'm going to drop him right here in this room and get rid of him."

"But no one is working here. He'll die," the other guard says.

"Then let him die," the first one says. "I don't have time to take him all the way down to the interrogation room," the first one says.

"Ha-G is waiting for him there," the other one says.

"Let him wait. He gave me this assignment at the last minute to chase me away from the Psychiatric Wing. I won't do it. I'll just leave this son of a bitch here in this empty room," he says.

"Who is he, anyway?"

"He is a clown, that's what he is," the first guard, the one with the lisp says.

"What clown? Who?" his friend asks.

"Don't you know him? He is the filmmaker. The one who made a comedy that made fun of the Holy Republic. He acted the role of the Big Sheikh, himself. A real clown!" he says.

"Oh, now I know. That was the first year of the Revolution, right? When everybody was free to do whatever shit they wanted to do. I saw his movie. You could easily figure out that by the Big Sheikh, he meant the Great Leader."

"That's why he's been here all these years," the first guard says.

"And he hasn't repented yet?"

"No. La-Jay even proposed to him the management of El-Deen's film department. He rejected it," he says.

"Let the bastard die, then. This way you serve him. Because eventually either Ha-G will kill him, or Halal will drive him crazy with his drugs."

Kamal turns left to a different corridor and the guards' voices fade away. I hear the filmmaker's whistling coughs from far away.

Kamal walks slowly, almost lets go of the leash. His key chain doesn't sing the chee song. I know that he is preoccupied. There is a chaos in his head. Should I talk? Ask him if we've passed the maximum security zone? If at least he could remove my blindfold?

I decide not to talk now. In the dark I row for a while, thinking about the filmmaker. I don't remember such a film. I'm not sure if I was free at that time. Did I ever go to the movies?

What a phenomenon, I think. To make a film, to act in it and to spend the rest of your life in El-Deen. To refuse to repent, when you know that if you repent, they'll give you a nice room on the sixth floor, they'll let you run the film department, they'll give you a wife, one of those sophisticated female repentants—maybe a former actress, a script writer, or something. But you reject all this. You want to die. And you will. You'll die on a cold gurney in a dark deserted room—a chamber no longer used. You'll have a high fever first, then the chills, fever again, chills. You will cough, you will spit blood. You'll almost throw your lungs up. You'll roll in your phlegm and blood. You'll scream for help and you'll die alone. No one will hear you; all the rooms are empty around you. You'll die—all for a comedy, a film you made to mock the "Big Sheikh."

I was in the freezer too, but I didn't get pneumonia. My immune system is good. The last thing I ate was in cell eleven, a watery soup, yellowish, with a few parsley leaves swimming in it. Ilych told me to eat it and I did. I haven't eaten anything since. I haven't peed or emptied my bowels either. And I'm still moving. Although not on my feet. My feet are injured. Ha-G whipped me.

One hundred lashes. But my soles don't hurt. I wish they would. But I'm grateful that I can breathe. Breathing is the most important thing. There is no whistle, no extra sound in my lungs. I never cough. Few days ago three guards beat me hard. But I don't feel the pain anymore. I was drugged. They have drugged me ever since Kamal took me out of the Black Box. I remember the Clinic, where Doctor Halal told me that I was going to have colorful dreams. They drugged me on the interrogation bed. Halal sneaked in the room and injected something without Ha-G knowing. They must have mixed something in my soup too. Maybe they're drugging me all the time and that's why my feet are numb. They drug me because they want me to move—the moment they want me to stop, they'll stop drugging me, then I will collapse and feel all the pains in the marrow of my bones. That will be my cracking point. I'll crack. I'll break. I'll leak. I'll remember. I'll confess. I'll repent.

My destiny is in Kamal's hands. He said he'll take me to cell four. He will skip Sultan's room. This room must be the last station they take the stubborn prisoners. Sultan is cruel, they said. They want to change him after their coup. Or, did they say all this to frighten me?

Who is Sultan? Didn't the narrator of Holy Show introduce himself as Sultan? Is he the same man? The man who resembles Bashi the Janitor? The man with three long slimy teeth in front? The man who sang many lamentations on the theme of martyrdom and whistled through his teeth? I'm worried now. What if he jumps on my chest the way they did on poor Saboor's chest? What if he breaks my bones? On one hand I want to get to cell number four as soon as possible, and on the other, I wish Kamal could hide me somewhere safe, succeed in his coup d'etat and let me out. But out where? To do what?

No, I want to become an Unbreakable and go to the Wall.

Then why am I so concerned about my health? Why do I test to see if my lungs are clear, or my feet better? So I want to live. Or I want to live without pain until the moment of death. Pain. It's pain that I'm scared of, not death. Isn't this the main reason why they torture us? Many of us could become heroes if they'd just kill us, without torture. Pain breaks the prisoners. Haven't I read somewhere about Socrates and Galileo? Socrates drank the hemlock and died heroically. They showed the instruments of torture to Galileo and he repented. Galileo would have died heroically had they just handed him the poison.

The Unbreakables of Hall Twenty are called Unbreakables because they've passed through the chambers of pain without breaking.

"Let me remove your blindfold," Kamal calls me from the other side of a dark tunnel. "We are out of the maximum security zone."

We stop. Kamal unties the black scarf. I see his face in the corridor's blinding light. He has aged since the last time I looked at him carefully. Now he resembles Ali the Bricklayer more. I smile at him. I like him. We have a history together. Ups and downs. Good moments and bad moments. Ridiculous moments. Horrible ones. Sad moments. We have hated each other. Raged. I've lived a life with Kamal.

Now he stands in front of me. I haven't lost him yet. I'm not alone. So I smile like a child. A child sitting on the floor waiting for the grown up to lift him up. Kamal has grown. I have shrunk. He smiles back. I feel that any instant he is going to lift me up in his arms like a parent, a big brother, and kiss my cheeks. But he doesn't. He just looks at me. My eyes burn with tears.

"We are something, brother. You and me!" he says when we resume moving, now side by side. He walks slowly to let me row and slide my butt on the cement. "This has never happened to me before. It must be you. The way you are. You are good, brother! That's all I can say. Good. I learned to be good walking these goddamned hallways with you. You didn't do anything in particular, but you were good and now I find myself becoming more and more like you and less like I was before, when I was called the Loony Kamal. You remember?"

I nod, but I don't say anything. I let him talk.

"Maybe it's because you listen a lot. I don't like talkers. I like listeners. You know what I mean?" he sighs.

"Are you unhappy?" I ask.

"I don't remember the last time I was happy. But I wouldn't even bother thinking about it. I just was. Without knowing anything. For example this is one of your qualities. You ask me how I feel. Then you make me think about myself. Am I happy or not? When I was the loony, I wouldn't care. Now I do. To answer your question, I must say, no, I'm not happy, brother. Not a bit."

"We all change, Kamal. Many times in our lives. If I could remember my past, I would tell you about the changes in myself and the people I knew.

Just think about your father, he was a bricklayer once—"

"Oh, this shit again! This pisses me off, brother. This bricklayer crap. Just forget the fucking business and close the damned case. I have more important things on my mind and one of them is you. What to do with you."

I keep quiet for a while to let Kamal calm down. I row with the rhythm of "chee"—the key chain hopping in his pocket. I look at the dark gray walls. Didn't Kamal once say, the more we descend in El-Deen, the darker the walls will get? We must be somewhere underground now. There are TV sets at each intersection, but the picture of the gray tomb is fixed and the sounds are off.

"Every now and then, they lock up the Unbreakables in coffins," Kamal breaks the silence. "There, in total darkness, silence, and immobility, they lose their minds. Most of them become mentally fucked up. They no longer know who they are, confusing their illusions with reality. Besides, every few weeks there is what La-Jay calls a Cleaning up Operation. The order comes from the Great Leader himself."

"I know, Kamal. I remember you told me this before."

"I don't want you to die, brother."

"I don't want to live in El-Deen."

"I may become an influential authority in El-Deen, one of the arms of the Great Octopus, or who knows—? I may release you!" he says this last sentence in a very low whisper, but without turning his back to me.

"I don't have anywhere to go," I say.

"Bullshit! You must have family, friends, neighbors," Kamal says.

"I don't remember anything, Kamal."

"You will. Once you're out, you'll find your way home."

"What if I don't? Or what if I don't have anyone anymore?"

"You want to die because you have lost your memory, huh?" Kamal asks this looking straight ahead of him, for the secret cameras are everywhere.

"I want to join the Unbreakables. I want to be one. This is the way I fight," I say.

"Fight with who?"

"With El-Deen."

"But do you think you will win anything?"

"I may die, but I won't lose. I'll lose if you free me against my will."

"Okay then, I won't free you. I'll take you somewhere safe on the sixth floor, until the day you want to leave. How about that?"

"You're kind to me, Brother, but this is not what I want. If I stay on the sixth floor, El-Deen will change me."

"How?"

"It will turn me into a repentant who clangs cymbals in the Holy Shows."

"You want to die!" Kamal says angrily.

"I've lost my revolution."

"Then fuck you! And fuck me for wasting my time on a lunatic like you. You're a stubborn godless bastard! You talk like this because you still believe in your sinful beliefs. And you're fooling me with your shitty philosophy because you think that I'm just an ignoramus motherfucker that you can talk me into taking you to cell number four to be with your fucking comrades and die with them. That's what you wanted from the very beginning, what you still want! And I think you remember more than what you claim. I especially think that you remember your beliefs very well. Because I don't think people forget what they believe in," Kamal says all this in one breath and sounds loony like the first day.

"You're angry at me."

"You bet I am. Now stop here. I have to pray. Let me tie your leash to this door knob. Rest your arms and hands. Your palms are red and swollen, brother. Too much rowing on this fucking frozen sea! You don't have soles either. No palms, no soles. How are we going to move you the rest of the way?"

This is an intersection with a TV set hanging from the ceiling showing the picture of the gray tomb. Now a muezzin is chanting the late night prayer. On the screen the picture of the tomb changes to the blue-green tiles of a dome. This must be some holy place. I lean back against the door I'm tied to. The leash is a bit short, pulling me up. But if I sit straight, it won't choke me. My palms burn. The skin is coming off. But I don't feel my feet. I have no feet.

Kamal spreads his kerchief, sets his carnelian rosary and sacred stone and bows to the blue tomb. I hear him mumbling his prayer. I've seen him in this position many times before. I close my eyes and in spite of my stretched spine; I feel relaxed. Little beetles start to move inside my brain. But the feeling is not unpleasant. They scratch my red eyelids with their tiny wire legs. Friendly beetles, friendly beetles—and everything goes dark.

At the Murky Water

We stand at the murky water to see you go. All the family is here except Father. You know that since his release, Father has never left the house. You know that all day he sits behind the window and smokes and all evening he locks himself up in the dark kitchen behind the house. Naked. So Father is not here, but we all are.

There are other families too, seeing other passengers go. Holding their suitcases tightly, they step in the dark water and pass. We see them safely reach the other side, a foggy shore. The water is shallow. Knee-deep. People step in the shallow water and splash, splash, splash, reach the foggy shore.

You have a little red bag, shaped like an oval box. Mother bought you this so that you look like a movie star. When you open the lid to get something, I see your face in an oval mirror. You don't see me. The shore is dark.

It's so dark that I can barely see who is kissing you good-bye. I recognize Maman, holding you longer than everyone. She cries and calls you Hoori.

I stand here out of the circle of the family and think about my feet. I know that you're going to step into the murky water and reach the other side and this means that I won't see you anymore. I want to follow you. But my feet are injured. I can't wet all these bursting blisters. They will hurt. I can't stand pain, Sahar, and you know this. I can't follow you. So I let you go.

I'm the last person you embrace. My heart pounds in my throat. You look into my eyes and I search for your little stars, the ones that always shine in your irises. But your eyes are dull and stagnant like this strange night, like this murky water. You don't smile. We hug coldly, the way we've never hugged before. We don't kiss and you walk slowly toward the water. You step in it and I watch you lifting each foot and plunging it in the water and I hear your splashes. Then you're on the other side, lost in the fog.

I turn back to leave. Opposite the water is a wall, a thick, tall brick wall. I bend my head back to see the top. It's way up into the depths of the indigo sky. But I see—or think that I see Ali the Bricklayer, the size of an ant, laying brick on top of brick. Swoosh, swoosh... dump! Swoosh, swoosh... dump!

Now someone says, "Come with me!"

I turn and see Uncle Yahya with his bicycle. I ask, "Where do you want to take me?"

He says, "You're not going back to New Spring anymore, are you?"

I say, "No, I won't. I've sworn if she leaves, I won't go home ever again."

"Come with me, then. Sit behind me and hold me tight."

"But where are we going?"

"We'll ride on the bike and watch the people. I may take you to the south with me."

"Where Hoori died?" I ask.

But we are on a familiar road, unpaved. On the right there are turquoise domes, public baths with red towels hanging on the roofs, clay huts, and tall minarets, sleepy muezzins chanting the evening prayer on the top. On the left are vast fields of wheat, glowing like gold in the dark and light of the blue dusk.

"Uncle Yahya, this is not the south road, this is the road to Hamedan. I know this road. I've been here before. Where are you taking me?"

"Son, we're going to Hamedan to ask the cook of the caravanserai about the amount of red beans and split peas in a good lamb stew. Your mother is waiting for the recipe."

I bend forward and look at him. This is not Uncle Yahya, this is Father. I say, "Father, you're talking!" I feel an immense joy, but this doesn't last. Now I feel panicked.

"Father, don't go to Hamedan! The journey has no end. You'll forget the amount of peas and beans and finally you'll forget your name too. Don't go!"

Father is deaf. He pedals on the rough road. The bike bumps up and down, bouncing over the pebbles and stones. Now I lay the right side of my face on his shoulder, gazing into the swaying stalks of wheat. A cold breeze sweeps my face and tears run down my cheeks. The breeze becomes a strong wind and my tears run faster. I shake and shiver, weeping in the wind.

"Why are you crying, son?" he asks.

"Didn't you see how she left? She left forever and you and I have started a journey with no end!"

Hanging on Kamal's Shoulder

"Don't cry, brother, we're close to your destination. Get up!"

I open my eyes and see Kamal's face. He is blowing into my face.

"This is the way my poor mother used to wake me up. She'd blow on my face. Softly though."

I touch my face to see if it's wet. It's not. I've cried without tears. Kamal unties my leash, lifts me up with a brisk movement, and lays me like an empty sack on his right shoulder. Now he resumes walking, as fast as he can.

"So she left, huh?" he asks.

My head hanging down Kamal's shoulder, suddenly fills with blood. Did I dream aloud? Did I call Sahar's name? What does Kamal mean by, "So she left?" Does he know who she was?

"You have doubts about me, don't you?" I hear him saying. "You're wondering why you trusted me, why you accepted my friendship, huh? It's a bit scary. How human beings don't have any solid thing to stick to. This doubt, doubt about everything and everybody around, is a major human flaw. And you know why? Because the whole damn shit, the whole fucking life is just a fog, a smoke. It's fucking unreal. Nothing is solid for you human beings. Because you are mortal. Believe me, brother. It's all because of mortality."

Kamal's steps are firm and soldierlike. His key chain bounces in his pocket next to my ear. My head is hanging down so close to his fat waist that I can smell his sour sweat.

"Why should you be scared of me now?" he says after a pause. "Huh? What are you scared of? Death! *Your* death, or *hers.* It doesn't matter. You don't trust me because you want to protect her. She is mortal. For us immortals it's different. We are not scared of death anymore. Life is not fucking fog and smoke. Everything is solid. We trust. We are not insecure. Now imagine how it is for the Holy Ones! They're at peace. They may look stupid to you, because they trust, but they're not stupid. They're peaceful. Death does not exist for them. And imagine God Almighty! How things are for Him? Imperceptible!"

Now he keeps quiet for a few minutes and walks with the same military pace, hugging my legs. Chee, chee, chee, chee... My lifeless arms and my heavy head dangle with the sound.

He is carrying me on his shoulder because he is late. He is carrying me because he has an important meeting at midnight. He is immortal now and wants to plan a coup d'etat. He is not carrying me because I don't have soles and palms to row on the cement, or because he loves me dearly. He may even hate my guts. He may even volunteer to perform my execution himself.

He may tie the rope around my neck, or aim the gun at my heart. He is carrying me like a sacrificial calf on his shoulder. He is carrying me to the altar where he may chop my head and shed my blood in front of the gigantic picture of his great leader. He hates my guts because I don't think like him. He hates my guts because I carried the flag and the banner of a wrong revolution.

"This is not the first time I'm thinking about all this shit," Kamal says. I used this analysis for my acting. First I had a hard time figuring out how a Holy One must behave. Then I thought about the opposites, the human beings. How *they* behave. How insecure they are. And how secure the Holy Ones are. Then I got the role! You saw it for yourself. Remember?"

I don't answer him. I haven't spoken a word yet. My heart, pressing against Kamal's back, beating on Kamal's heart, is aching. I can't wipe Sahar's image from my mind. If she was true and not a figment of my imagination, she left when we were sixteen. Mother sent her away to become a principal dancer and I never went back to my childhood neighborhood. I haven't seen my twin ever since, although I've searched for her in every dark corner of my dreams.

Now we reach the end of the corridor. Kamal turns right and while my head is hanging down on his back, I see a TV set upside down on the wall between the right and left hallways. A close up of Uncle Massi is on the screen. Upside down.

I burst out without knowing what I'm doing. "Kamal, stop! My uncle!"

Kamal stops, lays me down on the floor, jerks and shakes his shoulder to exercise it. Now he squints, looking at the picture. We both listen for a minute. The man is reciting an ode. He is praising the Great Leader of the Holy Revolution. His hair is long and Messiah-like, but all gray. His beard is bushy and down to his belly. He doesn't have a turban or a bandana around his head, but he is wearing a robe, a sheikh's black robe.

"This is not your uncle or anyone's uncle, brother. This is Sheikh Massi-Alla Nadeem El-Ommat, the Poet Laureate of the Holy Republic. I've seen him many times on TV and once from very close. When my devotee friends and I had the honor of visiting the Great Leader under His holy balcony, this poet was up there. He was the only one on the balcony with the Leader besides the Leader's son. I remember that he recited a long elegy. He is the most popular and respected poet of the Republic now."

I talk no more. Why should I insist that this is my crazy uncle? They can easily trace me back and find my folks. But I can't take my eyes away from the screen. Seeing Uncle Massi reminds me of New Spring, Grandfather's three houses, the tenant house, Faithland, Sahar, Mother. But they all move in my head in a fast whirlwind, no particular image stops to rest. I can't hold on to anything or anyone.

Hey Uncle Massi, I talk to my crazy uncle in my head, how did you get up there from your humble grave-room in the tenant house? What happened to your beloved Mariam's bandana you always wore around your head? Did you forget her?

"Let's go, brother. We don't have time to waste."

Kamal lifts me up and this time, hangs me on his left shoulder. As he walks away from the TV set, I try to look at Uncle Massi's upside down picture. He has a long roll of paper on the desk, the kind of paper Grandfather used to buy for him. He unrolls it as he reads the lines. Kamal turns right again and I can't see Uncle anymore, but his deep and now a bit hoarse voice echoes in the empty hallways, "Twenty and five passed and thee arrived/ We were ill and crippled, blind and deprived! Thy halo shimmers as thou riseth/ My eyes go dark though I am the wisest!" He stretches the last rhyming words to create a powerful effect as he used to do when he was a crazy poet climbing the walls.

This proves that when Sahar left, I didn't go back to New Spring. Many things happened and I was not there. Uncle Massi kept writing his nonsense poetry, gave up the idea of being the people's poet-prophet, and joined the Holy Republic. Apparently, he became their Poet Laureate.

He is an important man now. Stands on the Holy Balcony with the Great Leader. He recites long elegies without the fear of boring the Leader and many sheikhs. He wears a new robe and combs his hair and beard for his own program on the Republic's TV. He is the Poet Laureate. He is my uncle. Can't he get me out? Uncle Massi getting me out is different than Kamal setting me free. If Uncle frees me, I stay myself. If Kamal frees me I have to repent. Sell my soul.

What if Uncle Massi says that he doesn't know me, that he has never seen me before? What if he denies that my sister and I took him food in a little pan in cold, dark winter nights when the wolves howled on the hills?

Or, what if he says, yes this man is my nephew, but he is contaminated by corrupt ideologies and he has a twin sister who is even more contaminated because she is a dancer. Their father was in El-Deen at the time of the Monarch and was a stubborn red bastard under the influence of the Satanic ideology of the Northern neighbor. He lost his mind in El-Deen, while his wife, the twins' mother, lived a shameful life in the bosom of aristocracy, the Alleys of Heaven, the image of hell on earth.

Kamal's voice coming from above and behind, startles me, "This is Hall Eighteen, brother," My left ear is pressed against his shoulder blade, so I hear the resonance of his voice in his chest, "two more halls to number twenty. A short walk to cell four." And in a low voice, he adds, "I'm telling you for the last time, brother! Don't go there. I can open one of these rooms, leave you here for now and pick you up after the coup. I have a feeling, a premonition, that we will succeed. This corruption cannot go on in El-Deen. El-Deen is the Holy University, the University of God, and must be purged of its corrupt elements. Ha-G and his group must go. I will succeed, brother. Let me leave you here in this room," he stops in front of a door, taking his key chain out.

"No!" I almost scream. "Don't lock me up here, Kamal! I beg you! Take me to cell four, Brother! You have promised me!"

Kamal lays me down, pushes me against the wall and grabs my collar. For a split second I sense danger. I feel as if a heavy wall is collapsing on me. What if all this time, he was acting and this is yet another chamber he wants to force me to enter? But it seems that first he is going to slap me while I'm pressed against the wall. He wants to teach me a lesson. Is Kamal the same loony Kamal? Has he always been loony and I was deceived?

"Brother," he whispers this onto my face, while still holding my collar tightly, almost choking me, "before entering their cells, the Unbreakables have to stop at Sultan's room. Some of them never come out of this room. You get me? I don't want to scare you, but this man's nickname is Asscracker."

"Can't you take me straight to cell four?" I mumble.

"They'll see me in the cameras. Sultan checks the halls and cells too. He knows when someone enters his hall. There is no way to skip his room. Besides, Sultan issues the numbers. You can't enter the Unbreakables' cell without a number. So, I'm telling you for the last time, if you want to

355

become an Unbreakable, you'll have to deal with the Asscracker!" He says this and releases my collar. Sweat runs down from behind his ears, melting in his shirt collar.

Is he really concerned about me?

Let me not forget that Kamal is a Devotee of the Holy Revolution, El-Deen's guard, one of La-Jay's favorites. He may be using a classic method to break me. He acts friendly and even shows worry for me, to gain my trust. Kamal is frightening me about the tortures that the ruthless Sultan is planning for me. He wants me to change my mind just a few steps away from the Unbreakable's cell. Did I go through all those chambers just to end up in another chamber?

On the other hand, Sultan exists. Sultan the Asscracker. He is going to break my ass, jump on my back and smash my spine. He is going to smash my bones, the way they did Saboor's on the stage. But if he really kills the Unbreakables, then how come the cells of Hall Twenty are full? I still remember when at the beginning of our journey, Kamal said, there were twenty to thirty prisoners in the cells of Hall Twenty. How did they survive Sultan? If they did, I will!

"Brother Kamal! Take me to Hall Twenty. I'm ready."

"So be it! I'll take you to the fucking hall, brother. Doubt, doubt, doubt, this is your undoing!" he says, lifts me up, and carelessly dumps me on his right shoulder. This time my head hangs close to his knees. He speeds.

Kamal's Denial

"One fistful, half a fistful, one fistful, half a fistful—" his voice echoes in the hall. The echo comes to us first, then his voice, and himself the last. Blindfolded, barefoot, handcuffed, leashed, and naked, except for a rag around his hip, Ilych appears. Kamal stops, lays me down, and pulls me back to the wall. We sit on the cold floor, watching.

We watch the Last Holy One, the Absent One, the Promised One, approaching. Two robust guards are in front of him, one pulling the leash, the other, holding an M-16. Two are on either side of him pointing the barrels at his temples, two are behind him piercing his naked back with the cold muzzles of their guns. The Holy One is in their circle chanting in a carefree way, as though he is on his way back from Hamedan, before all the disasters, repeating the recipe of the lamb stew, not to forget it, dreaming of the hot, rich soup and his fat wife.

"One fistful, half a fistful—" he almost sings. His spine is stooped from the constant pains of the "holy fire," the Shingles. His goatee stretches longer, all gray.

"Ilych!" I scream. Kamal pinches my arm to make me quiet. But it's too late. The guards hear us. Ilych hears too. They stop.

"I'm not Ilych, my name is Turniphead. Turniphead from Caucasia," Ilych says.

"Why is your prisoner not blindfolded, Brother?" One of the guards, the one holding the leash, says to Kamal.

"He is a repentant, a friend now. He is injured. I'm taking him to see a doctor," Kamal says.

"Still. This is Hall Eighteen. You have to blindfold him," he says.

"I will," Kamal says.

"Aren't you Kamal the Immortal?" Ilych says, stretching his long neck forward toward us, "I recognized your voice, my son!"

"My name is Kamal, but I'm not Kamal the Immortal," Kamal says briefly, trying to change his voice.

"Yes, you are Kamal the Immortal. My first disciple. My first immortal! Don't you remember the Holy Water of Immortality? Don't you remember your Holy Father, the Promised One?" he insists.

"I don't know what you're talking about," Kamal says coldly.

"What the hell are you babbling again, you lunatic bastard!" one of the guards says, hitting Ilych with his gun butt. Let's go, the Revolutionary Sisters are the fire squad today. They're waiting for you at the wall!"

"Wait! Let me see what he's trying to say," the first guard says. "Ha-G is chasing down these so called Immortals and this man must be one of them. The crazy bastard knows his name."

"Brother," the second guard says. "Everybody knows who this Brother is. Haven't you seen the Holy Show? He is the actor who plays the Eighth Holy One. Our duty now is to take the crazy man to the wall. It's getting late."

"I'm the commander of this troop, Brother Nasir, let me do what I need to do. Let's remove this bastard's blindfold and see if he really knows this devotee." With one sudden motion he removes Ilych's blindfold.

357

Now Ilych blinks fast and looks at us. But he ignores Kamal and fixes his gaze on me.

"Don't you know this guard?" the commander asks.

"I know *him*!" Ilych points his long finger to me. "He was with me when I had my vest and pocket watch. He was with me in December 1895, in cell 193 in St. Petersburg's central prison." He winks at me.

"How about this guard? You just recognized his voice," the commander points to Kamal.

"Him?" Ilych pauses. "I haven't seen him in real life. But several times I've appeared in his dreams. I held the Golden Grail, full of fresh water for him, but each time I wanted to give him a sip, he woke up and lost me. It was frustrating for both of us!"

"He is talking nonsense, Brother, we're wasting our time. Ha-G will get mad," Brother Nasir says.

"How about you, Brother Kamal?" the commander ignores his friend, "Do you know this man?"

"I already said that I don't know him, Brother," Kamal says.

"Anyway, you have to report to Ha-G's office as soon as your job is over. This man called you 'Kamal the Immortal'; we need to check your ID."

"I'll be there, Brother," Kamal says.

"You know well, Brother that if you don't report, Ha-G will issue a warrant for your arrest. Fifth floor is now overcrowded with disobedient devotees."

"I said, I will be there," Kamal repeats nervously.

"Okay. Blindfold the crazy bastard!" he orders the other guards. "You too, Brother," he addresses Kamal, "go ahead and blindfold your repentant. Hurry up now! He saw more than enough!"

While blindfolding me, I hear Kamal whisper under his breath, "Motherfuckers... sons of bitches—," prolonging tying the scarf around my head. I realize that he is waiting for the troop to pass. Now I hear the guards' footsteps taking Ilych away. When they reach down the hall, Ilych screams from the bottom of his lungs, "The ability to see straight, without overlooking the twists, turns, and zigzags of reality! Without this we're all Turnipheads! One fistful, half a fistful, one fistful, half a fistful—" Then I hear slaps and smacks on his naked skin.

Squatting on the cement floor, Kamal lets go of my blindfold and holds his head in his big hands. He moans, swaying back and forth like a mother, lamenting over her child's grave.

"Get up, Kamal! The secret cameras will see you. You are already in trouble. They want you to report. Get up, Brother. Take me to my cell then go and save yourself!" I almost beg him.

"I said I didn't know Him. I said I'd never seen Him. Him! The Last Holy One! My Master! I'm a coward. A bastard. A good for nothing. An empty sack full of air. I'm not worth immortality!"

"Don't be silly, Brother. How could you acknowledge him while they were taking him to the wall? They would take you too!"

"I should have gone with Him. Maybe that was what He wanted me to do. To keep Him company on His Heavenly Trip," Kamal says.

"First of all, you couldn't possibly join him on his heavenly trip. You are immortal, Kamal, aren't you? And what about the Holy Revolution? Who's going to save the world?" I repeat all that he's told me before to make him get up and move. "Get up, Kamal! You are responsible! You are an immortal!"

He pauses for a second and stops swaying. Then he rises and lifts me up. He has lost most of his strength—I wish I could walk or row on the floor and let him relax for a while. He hangs me on his shoulder like a heavy burden and I hear him sniffling. Kamal weeps quietly. We walk in silence for a while.

"My heart is bleeding, brother. The Revolutionary Sisters commanded by my wife are going to shoot him. She'll shoot the last bullet in the Holy One's brain. So she is not home waiting for me, after all. She has an emergency mission tonight. What a fool I am." He mimics himself, "Waiting for me!" Then he pauses for a few seconds and chuckles bitterly. "My wife! The Head Trainer of the Women's Wards, the Commander-in-Chief of the Revolutionary Sisters! And I was supposed to fuck her tonight! To hell with this fucking life!" He continues talking to himself. "Thank you, little brother! Thank you for reminding me of my mission. I became emotional and forgot where I was supposed to go. I already knew that they were going to martyr the Last Holy One, didn't I? What gave me so much pain was my denial. I had to choose between my Master and my butt, and I chose my butt."

"This happens, Kamal."

359

"Such a holy man!" He murmurs. "Such insight! The more I think about his phrase, 'The ability to see straight—' the more I believe in him. He screamed it the last moment for me. That was his last advice to me." Kamal turns left and says, partly to me, but mostly to himself, "—the twists, turns, and zigzags of reality—"

Saboor's Corpse

Two white-gowned nurses or guards in white appear from the end of the hall. They push a gurney. When they reach us, I see Saboor's naked body. Nothing is covering him. The body of a thirteen-year-old. A sack of broken bones.

"Who is this?" Kamal asks.

"Don't you recognize your fellow actor, Brother Kamal?" One of the nurses says. "This is your deer."

"What happened to him?" Kamal asks. "We need him for the show!"

"You have to find another actor, Brother. This one is finished. His ribs were broken on the stage. Don't you remember how Ajooza kicked him and the Caliph jumped on him?"

"That was the most exciting part," the other nurse says. "It was so real!"

"I've heard that Sultan wanted his actors to jump on the boy to create a real scene!" the first guard says.

"I was deep in my role," Kamal says, "otherwise I wouldn't have let this happen. Poor boy! May God bless his soul!"

"Don't ask a blessing for the soul of a fucking traitor, Brother Kamal," the first nurse says. "This child is one of the oldest trainees. But no training worked on him. They arrested him at the beginning of the Revolution with a bunch of aristocrats. He was their faithful servant."

"Didn't he work for Brother La-Jay for a while?" the second one asks.

"Brother La-Jay did him a favor. You see, he was a little boy. Brother La-Jay said, okay, come to my place on the seventh floor and live with me, I'll take care of your training myself. La-Jay liked him so much that he let him sleep in his own room. Then the boy started to act weird and talk bad behind Brother La-Jay's back. La-Jay got mad; the boy got into trouble," the first guard says.

"I remember very well," the second one says. "That's when they sent him to the Psychiatric Wing."

"Over there he insisted that he wanted to sit in a box, because he didn't have a butt. So they let him sit in a box!" the first guard chuckles.

"He was harmless though," the second guard says. "That's why they used him for the Holy Shows."

"Didn't you know all this, Brother Kamal?" the first guard asks Kamal.

"No, I didn't. All I knew was that the poor kid was a damn good actor. Where are you taking his corpse now?" Kamal asks.

"To bury him behind the wall," the first nurse says, pushing the gurney.

"God bless the Holy Leader, Brother Kamal," they both say while moving in the opposite direction.

"And yourself," Kamal says briefly.

While the two nurses move away with Saboor's gurney, I hear bits and pieces of their conversation.

"I didn't like the Holy Show... too long... I was starving to death... "

"Did you finally eat?"

"Oh, yes: roast lamb... lima beans... from the sixth floor cafeteria... my mouth still waters... Saffron and butter... rice..."

The guards' voices fade away.

Kamal's Last Advice

At the end of Hall Nineteen, Kamal blindfolds me, holds the leash in his hand, and makes me walk. My soles are still numb. I feel like I'm walking on the surface of the moon, not completely touching the floor. I baby-step with my legs open. I know that I look ridiculous. My pants are falling down too. I must have lost more weight since Kamal took me out of the Black Box. My shirt is all soiled and ripped off.

"Sultan is watching us," Kamal says from between his lips. "This is Hall Twenty, *his* hall. He knows that we're approaching. I can't talk much anymore. He may have strong listening devices. May God protect you, brother. In twenty-four hours I'll come and take you to cell number four. Let's pray to God Almighty that at that time I'll be strong enough to change the organization. And that you'll be alive."

Here he stops. There is an iron door, bigger than ordinary doors of the cells.

It's almost a gate. I glance at the rest of the hall and notice the darkest shade of gray on the walls and the cement floor. All the cells have iron doors. There are no barred windows, or any kind of openings to the hallway. Before Kamal can knock or ring, a key turns in the key hole.

"Be strong, brother!" Kamal whispers in my ear, "He's opening the door. Remember: concentrate on your soul and forget your body! Sultan is here to smash your bones, but he cannot reach your soul if you protect it. Soul, my little brother, soul!"

The gate opens.

The Asscracker's Quiz

The moment I see the old man's face, with his toothless jaws resting on one another like folds of an accordion, I remember the tenant house. This thunderstruck shaggy hair, these small eyes moving restlessly in the sockets, this prickly beard sticking out like the white hair of an old toothbrush are Bashi's. This is the janitor. I remembered how he held his ugly face between Sahar's face and mine, brushed the infectious odor of his mouth on our skins, and showered his thick saliva on us from between his three yellow teeth: "Here, take these sugar candies I brought you from school and get out of my sight!" He laughed, phlegm almost choking him; he coughed and opened our palms, shoving sticky masses of cheap hard candies into them, spraying us with his saliva. Pushing us out of his room, he spanked us and laughed some more. Sahar and I threw the candies in the dark pool, running as fast as we could.

Now this man's lipless mouth smiles at Kamal; he greets my guard with respect, and leads me in with a bow as if I'm an honorable guest. He pushes the heavy gate to close it, but Kamal sticks his big head and wide shoulders in, opening the gate a bit to send me his last message.

"Hey, little bastard! Don't forget to see the twists, turns, and the zigzags! And your soul! Your fucking soul! See you tomorrow!" He winks at me behind the old man's back, showing the sign of victory with his two raised fingers before closing the gate.

"He's koo koo! That's what he is! They call him Loony Kamal. He's rough, too! Oh, very rough! He's my most talented actor. I've left him on his own.

He doesn't need a director. Did the loony give you a damn hard time?" Sultan asks in a fatherly tone. "Make yourself comfortable now. You need rest. Sit here on my barber's chair. You bet it was a long walk! Walking in El-Deen is the best exercise. These fucking foreign advisors run in the hallways with shorts and undershirts! Just imagine, they use the hallways as racetracks! They take advantage of everything. And that sissy, that Doctor Halal, he has given these fucking strangers all sorts of privileges. Well, I better quit complaining and get to work. These are signs of the post-revolutionary syndrome, as I call it. Nothing can be perfect. We'll eventually get rid of Halal and other gigolos like him. We will purify the Great Revolution. God is on our side, isn't He?"

He doesn't wait for my answer. He comes toward me, helping me to sit on the tall chair which could be either a barber's or a dentist's chair. Humming a sad tune in his throat, he lays my head back on the small headrest, gently, like a civil barber, or a kind dentist. Now he casually straps me to the chair with three leather belts as if customers of a barbershop must always be strapped to a chair.

"You know that I'm the director of the Holy Shows and a major actor, don't you?"

I nod, but I'm not sure if it's okay to nod. Do I have to speak?

"So you've seen me on the stage."

I nod again.

"One night I act as Abasel and the next night as the barber, the gardener, and the old woman, Ajooza. I think, you saw me last night as Abasel, didn't you?"

I nod.

"Who is Abasel?" he asks quickly.

"The Holy One's companion."

"What is his other role in the show?"

"He's the narrator too," I say.

"Excellent! Now what are the other roles I play on alternate nights?"

"The barber..."

"And...?"

"The gardener..."

"And...?"

"The old woman," I say.

"Her name?"

"Ajooza."

"Fantastic! You must have been absorbed in the show. Normally the trainees don't remember anything. The play is too long and they're tired and sleepy. Besides, they have no idea that there is going to be a test about the play. So, they sleep through it and then later they are in trouble. But not you. You're a smart lad. Attentive!"

Sultan walks away from the chair, but I'm not sure if I can raise my head and look at him. I decide not to. I hear his voice from the end of the room.

"This is my room. This is where I live. I rehearse my parts and take care of the props here. You see, I'm the stage manager too. Look! Raise your head and look!"

I lift my head and for the first time notice that the room is long and narrow. At the end of it, at least four meters away from where I'm sitting, there is an old rug and a few cushions on the floor. Against the wall, the show's props are sitting in a row. I recognize the old woman's gray wig, a rusty sword, a pair of gardening scissors, several bunches of plastic grapes, a big brass tray, and a trumpet. A TV set with a much bigger screen than those in the hallways hangs from the ceiling but it's off now.

Now I hear a whisper and then the muffled sounds of slap and punch. I hear a woman moaning. But it's as if her mouth is full of cotton balls. I glance at my right and I see an opaque glass partition, a tall, long screen dividing the room in two halves. Behind this screen shadows move.

"Don't pay attention to that part of the room," Sultan says. "You see, we have a lack of space in El-Deen, or rather a lack of organization. There are many rooms empty on the other floors, and here they are using half of my room. These people are temporarily sharing my space. But, don't let this bother you. They're just interrogating a prostitute—a singer, or a dancer of some sort. Hopefully, she'll repent before morning and we'll get rid of them. Now let's ignore them and just stick to our own work."

Sultan approaches my chair. I lay my head back on the headrest and wait. My heart is pounding in my throat. What is the purpose of this long friendly introduction? Why doesn't he start torturing me? Is everything carefully planned? Even the woman?

"As you have noticed I was acting as the narrator all this time. Do you remember the narrator of the Holy Show?"

364

I nod.

"And did you notice that I was acting the narrator all this time?"

I nod, although I had no idea he was acting the narrator.

"Now I have to become Abasel, the Holy One's companion. Then, the barber, then, the gardener, and finally the old she-devil, Ajooza. I have to rehearse all these roles for tomorrow's show. You may not see Sultan at all. Sultan doesn't come out unless something disrupts the process of the rehearsal. But if Sultan comes, he'll be mad as a rabid dog. Naturally!"

He goes to the end of the room, puts on a felt hat, wraps some rags around his feet, and places his right hand on his back, hunching like an older man. He sticks his chin out and limps around the room. I recognize him now. He is Abasel, the Eighth Holy One's servant, as I saw him in the show only a few hours ago. He goes to a table at my right side and takes a big syringe out. The syringe is already filled with a milky liquid. He just puts a new needle on it and squeezes a bit out. He does all this with the skill of a nurse.

He is going to inject. This may be the kind of drug that makes me talk, kills my willpower, brings my memories back. He's trying to break me here on this chair. There may not even be a need to crack my bones. I may talk without being beaten up. I may say everything: who I am, what my name is, who my twin is, where I worked, who my friends were, why I raised the banner and flag of the Revolution—a wrong revolution, not the Holy one!

"No," I murmur. "No drugs, please!"

He slaps me twice, right and left. Hard and fast. The room spins around my head.

"This is Sultan speaking, bastard! Do you know him? Have they told you about him? Sultan the Asscracker, the most powerful arm of the Great Octopus! Do you recognize him or not? Didn't I already warn you not to interrupt the rehearsal? Didn't I say if you do, I'll get out of my role, out of the loving, caring, nursing Abasel, and become Sultan, my real fucking self? Now which one do you want to deal with? Sultan, or Abasel, huh? I'm talking to you, son of a fucking bitch!"

"Abasel," I murmur.

"Good!" He pulls my sleeve up and ties my arm with a thin hose. "My dear Holy One, this will soothe you. You are suffering from fatigue, insomnia, and amnesia. You need this to get your strength back. There will be no pain. None whatsoever."

He says this in a gentle tone, injecting the milky liquid as softly as he can in my popped out vein. Now he pushes a button and suddenly my legs raise up. He limps to the end of the chair, looking at my feet. He shakes his head in regret.

"Tch, tch, tch tch! Your holy soles are shredded, smashed. Blood and pus are running. I have to take care of this before it becomes gangrene. What a sight! What misery!" He smacks his tongue, shaking his head again.

The room spins around my head. The muffled sounds from behind the partition become clear now. They echo in my head. Sultan sits on a stool in front of my feet, sticking a Q-tip into my blisters. Is he curing me, or is this a torture? I scream with pain and my neighbor, the woman, screams too. Sultan says something I don't quite understand.

The woman screams again. It's a kind of shriek I have never heard in my life. Long nails scratching one's liver. This is the image in my head: fresh, flat, bloody liver, live liver, pulsing liver, long dirty nails, nails of a witch, nails of a monster, scratching this tender liver.

Now a red light flashes in a remote corner of my head. On, off. On, off. A prostitute. A singer or a dancer of some sort. A dancer. She is being tortured right in the same room with me, behind an opaque divider. And Sultan wants me to know it. No, he wants me to doubt it. Doubt torments more than knowing. If I doubt, I may confess. If I know, I may seal my lips.

It's her. No, it can't be her. She went abroad. We were sixteen. She never wrote to anyone. She disappeared shortly afterward. Madame Aida told Mother that Sahar has quit dancing. The government stopped her scholarship. She vanished. Neither Mother nor anyone else went to find her. Mother said she couldn't afford to go abroad. I wasn't in New Spring. I was somewhere else. Uncle Yahya wrote to me. Wrote all the news of her disappearance. The news that she was not going to the dance school anymore. No scholarship. No money. Sahar vanished in the fog of a foreign land.

If she had died, our embassy would have informed us. She didn't die. She was either lost there, or she returned. She might have come back, but never to New Spring. I was not there either. I didn't have any contact with my family. I'd made myself lost. For years. She might have searched for me, but in vain. She might have given up searching for me. I had asked Uncle Yahya not to tell anyone where I was. Uncle hadn't told my family. But where was I when I was away from home? No. This is what Sultan wants.

Now Sultan chants what he's been humming before. It's a familiar song. Abasel's mourning song on the theme of martyrdom. He keeps picking my wounds and singing. I bite my lips not to scream. The girl shouldn't hear me, whoever she is. If I scream, I'll weaken her.

"You're lucky, sir. If you feel pain, you're damn lucky! It's not gangrene! Just a little infection. Penicillin will take care of it. Ha-G hasn't done a bad job. The motherfucker knows what he's doing!" He says this, then he chants again, "Cry, Oh, believers—cry! Cry, Oh, devotees, cry for the martyrs!"

Sultan's medical instrument changes. He takes a strange-looking spoon, a crooked needle with wider tip. He pierces my blisters. I tear my lips. I taste blood.

"This is called a curette. It's a nice surgical instrument. Very well made," he murmurs more to himself. He pierces me again. The girl, as if feeling my pain screams, "No, not that!" She screams inside my head. Now I hear myself screaming, "No, not that!"

"You interrupted me, bastard! You forced me to become Sultan!" I hear this from the depth of a deep well. Say please!" Sultan orders me.

"Please!" I say.

"Please what?" he asks.

"Please stop!"

"Now repeat this," Sultan says, "I'll tell you the whole story, Sultan!"

"I tell you the whole story, Sultan!"

"I won't!" the girl shouts and cries hysterically.

"I want the whole thing, bastard, not the kind of garbage you made up in the Clinic. I don't need your fucking babyhood. I need the whole goddamn story of your fucking heroism. Understood? The banner, the flag, and the sons of bitches you worked with. The top of that brick wall. Your stupid speech. That story. Who was your leader? Who handed you the banner and the flag? Where are they?"

"Where are who? I don't remember anyone," I say frankly.

Sultan is on his feet now and he is Sultan all the time. He slaps me several times. "Sultan asks questions, not you, motherfucker! If you go on asking questions instead of answering them, Sultan will stay forever. Now which one do you want to deal with, Sultan, or Abasel?"

"Aba... sel..." I mumble.

"I won't..." the girl murmurs behind the divider. Or is she inside my head?

"Good, sir! Now repeat, my dear, 'I'll tell you the whole story, Abasel!'"

"I'll tell you the whole story, Abasel!"

"Excellent! Now I'm going to pour this soothing medicine on your soles and lay this wet towel on your hot forehead and let you relax and tell me your story. Both Sultan and Abasel love stories; no wonder they're such good actors!" He pours a cold yellow liquid on my feet. It burns, but instantly makes my feet numb. Then he lays a wet towel on my head.

I smell food. Meat. Charcoaled meat. Something like shish-kabob. The woman's trainers must be eating behind the partition. I hear them munching noisily. My bowels squeeze with nausea. The woman moans behind the opaque wall.

"You must be hungry, my Holy One, huh?" I hear Sultan from the end of the room. "You may eat after I receive the honor of hearing your story, sir. Actually, I serve my customers when I'm rehearsing the gardener. Do you remember in the play where the ungrateful gardener brought the Holy One just a raw onion? This is the part I'll rehearse today. I'll get you what you deserve. If you tell me a juicy story, I'll bring you juicy food, like what these gluttons are eating now. If you tell me garbage," he says this in Sultan's tone, "I'll make you eat garbage! Okay? Okay. Now, I'll sit on my rug and lean my tired back against these old cushions and comb Ajooza's hair for the show. Her turn will come later. I'm all ears for you, sir, all ears!"

I watch him sitting on his carpet, combing the wig like an old woman combing a child's hair. What does he want to know? What if I won't be able to put a juicy story together? He'll become Sultan, he'll use the curette—that sharp spoon—and pierce my wounds. He'll kill me gradually.

If I put a story together, he may believe it or not. If he does, he may like it or not. If he likes my story, he'll make me repent. He'll have them take me to the repentants' floor. They'll put a paper bag over my head and send me to the cells to spy on the inmates. They'll make me talk on the TV, confess to my sins, and advise others to do the same. On the repentants' floor I'll grow old and eventually they'll give me a peaceful job, a reward for my good behavior. They'll make me the cymbal player of El-Deen's band. Because the old cymbal player will be dead by that time. Then I'll clang the big cymbal between the scenes of the Holy Show and I'll doze off between the clangs.

If I resist to put a story together, or if I make a story, but fail to please Sultan, he will kill me here on his barber's chair.

"I'm all ears, sir, all ears," Sultan says in the voice of Abasel.

"Arise, you prisoners of starvation—" The Last Holy One's voice rises from behind the wall. This is his anti-anthem. But before he can go on with, "Arise, you wretched of the world," I hear the chatter of the machine guns.

"The goddamn Wall of the Almighty is right behind my room," Sultan complains. "They've executed the crazy bastard. Distracted me. Interrupted my tranquility. Shit! Now, I'm out of my role again. I have to start from the beginning." He gets up and approaches me.

"I've heard that you made friends with that son of a bitch who is on his way to hell now. Did you?"

"Ilych..." I murmur. Tears burn my eyes. If I cry for Ilych, Sultan may turn into a rabid dog, but I can't stop the tears. I don't have any control over my emotions. Words pour out of my mouth as if someone else is uttering them.

"One fistful, half a fistful," I murmur and laugh. "Poor Turniphead. Poor poor Mr. Turniphead. Good-bye. You got rid of it, you got rid of the whole thing—the journey, the caravanserai, the beatings, the beans, the peas, the repetition—" I laugh and cry, "and me. Stupid me, miserable me. I'm crying because you got rid of the whole damn thing. You're relieved, you don't exist to feel relieved or not. I'm crying for myself." I weep like an orphan at his father's grave.

"I know the story of Turniphead," Sultan says, ignoring my lamentation. "I have it here on tape, in case you want to hear it. He told me the whole thing. It was amusing, I confess. I knew this Ilych of yours better than anyone else in El-Deen. I played an important role in his final destiny. He wouldn't break. The motherfucker wouldn't break even when I changed into Ajooza and jumped on his chest. He never told me which organization he belonged to. I never discovered where he came from. But I took his mind from him." He laughs, a kind of donkey laugh I've never heard from him before.

Sultan laughs until he almost cries of laughter. "You should've seen your Ilych when first he came to El-Deen. He was a theoretician, a historian, or something. A bald-headed doctor, full of blasphemous shit. Full of Eastern and Western crap." He laughs more. "And now there is a rumor that some of these ignorant guards believe that he was the Last Holy One in disguise. He appeared here in El-Deen to test us. The man was crazy. *I* drove him crazy! I, Sultan, the Asscracker, the longest and strongest hand of the Great Octopus!"

Behind the wall, the Revolutionary Sisters sing the Anthem, "We are the great roaring waves... We're born of the great sea—" And the refrain, "Anja, anja, za za za—"

The guards on the other side of the divider munch their food. The woman weeps. Her voice is muffled again, as if they've filled her mouth with cotton balls.

"It's hard for me to go back, sit there, and become Abasel again," Sultan says. "This execution made me sick. Yes, I have to confess. I liked the man too. We spent quality time together. I couldn't catch up with his insights, of course. But we had long discussions. Especially when I was acting the patient barber. Let me become the barber now. I'm in a melancholic mood. I'm rather tender and emotional. Now that our friend is dead, I can't be cruel."

He goes to his props, covers his eyes loosely with a scarf and picks an old beaten briefcase. I hear him saying, "Besides, I don't think you have remembered your juicy story, yet. You may remember it while I'm rehearsing my barber part and trimming your hair. I wonder why they let your hair grow so long."

Now I watch him, holding the briefcase in one hand and stretching his other arm forward, approaching me. He waves his arm in the air, acting like a blind man. He comes straight to my chair and hits my feet. I scream. He stops, saying, "Who is it?"

If I want Sultan to stay the barber, the gentle and humble character of the show, I have to let him play with me. "I'm—I'm—" But I don't know how to introduce myself. Do I dare to act as the Eighth Holy One? If I say, I'm the Eighth Holy One, he may get mad and become Sultan again and use the curette on me. So I mumble, "I am—a customer."

"My customer?"

"Yes."

"But I've lost my business. I'm blind! Who are you?"

"I'm a traveler," I say, suddenly remembering the show.

"From where to where?"

"From the city of Med to the city of Tus."

"Why are you going to Tus?" he asks.

"To visit Caliph Maamoon."

"Who is with you?" he asks.

"My servant," I say and my heart beats in my throat. Sultan is leading me to the point where I'll be forced to say that I'm the Holy One.

"What is your servant's name?" he asks.

"Abasel."

"What is your name, young man?"

"My name?"

"Yes, your name!"

I pause. A long pause. He pulls his blindfold down and throws it away. He drops the briefcase and kicks it hard, screaming from the bottom of his lungs. "You stupid, fucking bastard, you ruined the rehearsal! You're wasting my time, mumbling like an idiot! Can't you say who you are and let us go on with the scene? When I ask you who are you, you have to say, 'I'm the Eighth Holy One, the Young Martyred One.' Period. Understand?"

"Yes, sir!"

"Don't 'sir' me, bastard! We don't have sirs anymore, we have Brothers, you blockhead!" Now he grabs my face in his calloused fingers, shaking my head so hard that I feel dizzy and nauseated. "Use your brain now! We'll go on with the scene! Unless you like Sultan better than the humble barber, huh? Which one do you prefer: Sultan, or the barber?"

"The barber," I say, and tears burn my eyes.

To act as he wishes. Not to be able to say no. Not to be able to say, "Neither Sultan nor the barber! I won't go on with this shit! Fuck you!" To be weak. Breakable. A toy in Sultan's hands. Drugged. Soft.

But Ilych resisted. He didn't let Sultan play with him. *He* played with Sultan. He told him the whole absurd story of Turniphead and made Sultan listen to him. But Ilych lost his mind. He didn't break; he went crazy. Where is the line, then? How can I tell if I'm still sane?

"Okay, I improvise now! These are not the actual lines. Ready?"

I don't answer, but he goes on anyway. He blindfolds himself, approaches me and says, "Is anybody here?"

"Yes," I murmur. I take part in the rehearsal again. I can't help it. Either he has drugged me, or if the milky liquid has been penicillin then I'm a

371

coward. I'm scared of him. I'm doing all he wants me to do and I'll do more.

"Who are you?" he asks.

"I'm the Eighth Holy One, the Young Martyred One, on my Holy trip from the city of Med to the City of Tus. I'm going to visit Caliph Maamoon and my servant Abasel is with me," I say in one breath.

"Oh, Your Holiness! What an honor! This is your humble servant, the blind barber of Med. I was searching for you everywhere. They said you were traveling on this road, so I came to find you," he pauses for me to say something.

"What do you want from me?" I ask.

"A miracle," he says.

"What miracle?"

"I want to see. I want to be able to open my business and make my living again," he says impatiently, showing that he doesn't like my choice of dialogue.

"I'm sick, barber, come later. I'm strapped to this chair. I can't do miracles for you! I need a miracle for myself!" someone with my voice says. This voice is so sincere that even Sultan is impressed.

"Oh, my Holiness! Let me open these fetters. This must be the devil's job, the ruthless Caliph's." He works on the straps and opens them one by one. "This is my miracle, sir, I opened you. Now I want *your* miracle! A tiny little one for your humble servant!"

I raise my arms and recall what Kamal did on the stage as the Holy One. Now I murmur meaningless words.

"Your Holiness, please pray louder so that I can enjoy the words of God."

I'm trapped. I don't know how to pray. Since I was a child I've heard people praying, but I could never learn. The heavy sounding, angry Arabic words, uttered from inside the adults' throats, were too hard for me to learn and memorize. But now Sultan wants me to recite a prayer for him. The whole purpose of the barber scene is to test whether the inmate knows how to pray.

"Your Holiness, don't keep your poor humble barber waiting. The prayer, please!"

"I can't," I say.

"Why? Aren't you the Eighth Holy One, then?"

"No!" I say and lean my head back and get ready for the blows or whatever is going to shower on me. "Soul! Your fucking soul!" I murmur Kamal's last advice to myself.

Sultan removes his blindfold, throws his briefcase to the rug, and straps me to the chair without a word. He limps behind me, pushes a button, raises the chair and starts to shave my hair with an old dull razor. Dry. All without a word. He shaves like a professional barber, but more like an army barber. He works fast and rough; he pulls my ears to shave behind them. I feel completely hairless now, but Sultan keeps shaving my bald head. The dull blades scratch my skin. I hold my breath not to scream.

Behind the opaque wall, the girl is quiet. But I see shadows moving. I hear a squeaking sound. Sultan pushes my head to the right, pressing it down to shave my neck. I see a large, dark shadow behind the screen. The shadow of the girl hanging from her feet. Her head is very close to the floor, her long hair sweeping the cement. The squeaking sound is like the sound of an old well's rusty wheel. We had an old well in our triangular house, didn't we, Sahar? We used to turn the wheel's cold handle bar to draw a full bucket of water up. Squeak, squeak, squeak—remember? What if the Monster of the Well comes up? Remember?

They turn the handlebar and raise the girl up, like a bucket. Now she is close to the ceiling. Sultan keeps shaving my bare skin. Blood crawls on my head, dripping behind my ears. Burn, burn, burn. The worst burn ever. "Sahar, are you here?" I whisper. "Is that you hanging upside down? Sahar, can you hear me?"

Sultan doesn't utter a word. I ruined his rehearsal. He dries my blood, goes behind the chair and brings something with wires hanging from it. He lays it on my head like the aluminum lid of a frying pan, I feel the cold metal on my hot scalp; wires hang on my face.

"This is Abasel speaking. I'm narrating the show. Dear gentleman! You don't need to be worried. The switch is off. But if Sultan turns it on, you'll receive a jolt of 500 volts for thirty seconds. This will give the ingredients of your brain a good shake. It will mix and blend everything in a way a good mixer and blender does with different fruits. The only accident that might possibly happen is the eyeball incident. Your eyeballs may pop out of your sockets and hang on your cheeks. Vomiting, urination, and defecation may also occur. Your skin may turn red, blistering and swelling to the point of bursting. But as I said, the switch is off now.

"I'm going to leave the mixer on your head and rest a bit. I'm an old man after all. Out of breath. My favorite show is coming on in few minutes. I watch it every week. No matter what. Meanwhile, dear sir, I'll leave this tape-recorder on your lap. I expect you to tell your story as nicely as you possibly can. Sultan wants to enjoy it later. Be sure that all the rights are reserved for him; he won't make a duplicate for Doctor Halal and his advisors. This will go into Sultan's archive—he loves stories, as I've mentioned before. Now while I'm watching my show, you feel free to talk in the recorder. Sultan is interested in your adult life. Friends and family, especially women. Jobs. Social life. I'll check on you in an hour. If the tape is not satisfactory, then the rude gardener will come and give you a few jolts with this fruit mixer. And then he'll serve you raw onions. Understood?"

I nod. Sultan leaves the small cassette-recorder on my lap and goes to his carpet. He turns on the TV, leans against his cushions, and while combing Ajooza's gray wig, stares at the screen. On screen I see the picture of the Holy Revolutionary Army marching toward the Holy Battlefields. The volume is low, but I can hear the narrator's formal epic tone and heavy metaphors agitating the nation. He raises his voice and in an old fashioned declamatory method says, "The lions of the battlefields... the brave revolutionary Brothers, their chests protecting the Holy Revolution like iron shields... the caressing wings of the Revolutionary Sisters—female eagles—smiling like the golden sun of the Holy Land. Shine! Shine! Ye stars of the Revolution—this is the way to face death! That white horse waiting in the Holy Desert to take his dear children to the Heaven of God, where the Last Holy One is standing at the gate, greeting them. Welcome! Welcome, the Holy One says, opening his embrace—"

There is more. I hear some fragments and miss the others and then a military march proceeds. The march fades out and a familiar sheikh appears on the screen. The moment I hear his voice I remember him. Once in the Hothouse I heard his whole program about masturbation. I even remember that he promised to talk about "the sweet subject of pederasty."

So this is Sultan's favorite program. He turns the volume up, makes himself comfortable, hugging Ajooza's lifeless wig. The Sheikh's tired, monotonous voice fills the room:

"As the successors of the Holy Ones, we can always add necessary chapters to the book of sexual laws. And I want to assure you, dear Brothers, that the following program has been prepared under the direct guidance of the Holy Committee of HRNT, the Holy Republic National Television, meaning under the direct supervision of the Great Leader of the Holy Revolution. Sexual intercourse in emergency circumstances is a problem that our brothers encounter everyday—"

The sheikh's slimy words roll toward me in waves. I lean my head against the pad and look at the shadow of the woman hanging behind the screen. A prostitute of some sort. A singer or a dancer. A tall woman. Or maybe the shadows cast behind opaque screens seem taller. Sahar was small. One doesn't grow much taller after age sixteen.

They have pulled the girl up and kept her close to the ceiling. Her arms are thin and long, her waist, slender. Is she naked? If she were wearing a skirt, it would hang down, covering her torso. Is she wearing pants? Is she naked and these men are watching her hang upside down? Does it matter to her that she is naked, if she is? Or is all she thinks about (if she thinks at all) the blood streaming down into her skull, filling her head?

Sahar wasn't this tall and her hair was not straight. It could never hang on her shoulders. It was wavy and wild; when it was long, it was massive and fuzzy, puffed up, never tame and loose. This is not Sahar.

So that's decided. This woman cannot be Sahar. But who am I? Scheherazade? If I don't tell a juicy story for my king, he'll give me a jolly jolt. Let's say he is exaggerating about popping eyes or bursting skin; how about mixing the ingredients of my brain? Isn't this what he did to Ilych? To all the inmates of the Psychiatric Wing?

Concentrate on your soul—soul, my little brother, soul! Kamal advised me. He meant sanity. Sanity is the road to unbreakability. If Sultan mixes up my brain, I'll break. There are different ways to break, my friend. To confess and repent, is one way; another way, is to go insane. Who is more vulnerable than a crazy person?

Let's say I tell Sultan a story. What should I keep quiet about? Names. Other people's names. Whoever I name, they'll arrest. I have to invent my own names. Invent the incidents, too. I have to control the words, because they may burst out of me like the explosion of an oil well. This drug, this milky substance—which might not have been penicillin, after all—this drug which has made me thirsty for all the waters of the world—is penetrating into the burning cracks of my brain, washing everything out with the pressure of a fireman's hose. And I'll make stories for this crooked king, staring at this shadow—which is swaying slightly like a long pendulum. The shadow of a prostitute or a singer, but not a dancer, not the shadow of my sister, not Sahar. No.

To the Land of the Beloved I Send Thee

Father spent his days behind the window of the triangular house, smoking and staring at the steep street and the two rows of the identical houses. All his nights, no matter what season of the year, he sat in the dark kitchen, naked.

Sahar left. Mother, unable to cure Father of his silence and his rituals in the dark, re-opened her beauty salon, colored her hair yellow and became "Marie" again. I left the neighborhood.

I stayed with Uncle Yahya, Father's uncle, in the only room of his dark apartment in the center of the city, where the vendors called early mornings and the drunkards sang late nights. Five years I stayed with the old man.

I sometimes rode on Uncle's bicycle around the city and watched the people. But most of the time, I stayed home reading in the dim room. The books were old and yellow, soft and smelly. I read the *Fall of the Roman Empire, What is to be Done?*, Omar Khayyam, *The Conference of the Birds*, Russian novels—all kinds of books, carrying smells of remote times, dried roses, must, the scent of lotus or a woman's perfume. Sometimes, the pages turned into powder between my fingers. Laying on my stomach on the damp floor of this dark room, I read for so many hours that tears ran down my burning eyes and my head pounded with pain.

The room had one window above my bed. The thick gray curtain, holding the dust of decades in its folds, was always drawn. There was no reason for Uncle to draw the curtain back and open the window. Outside a wall stretched from right to left, to unseen spots, the top raised high into the unseen clouds. At times I peeked through the curtain with one eye, listening to hear Ali the Bricklayer's trowel smothering the wet mortar, dumping one brick on top of another. I heard if I listened whole-heartedly. Then I whispered Sahar's name.

Dusks, suffocating dusks, when Uncle came back from his long bike trips to sit motionless in the dark, close his eyes, and contemplate all he had seen and heard, I left the apartment and walked the busy streets. I passed by the aroma of fresh baked pastry and Turkish coffee rising from cafés, the scent of gladiolas and lilies sold by old Armenian women, the odor of wet leather blowing from the vents of shoe stores, where old Armenian men hunched in dingy workshops and banged hammers on nails, making a pair of red leather shoes for a young girl, or a pair of shiny black boots for a boy. I swallowed the sounds and smells of life and work, something I'd been deprived of all my childhood in the New Spring neighborhood, where my view had been the still mountain, the silent desert, the dead cemetery, and El-Deen's wall, the end of all—the cul-de-sac.

Here, people, cars, and carts filled the luminous central avenue and the neons winked throughout the night. Here, there was hope for everyone. A loaf of bread for the beggar, a long-stemmed rose for the lover, and a cup of fresh coffee for the tired traveler; a fortune told by an old gypsy behind the beaded curtain of a small café, was a glimpse of hope for the desperate, the hopeless. The wrinkled woman dipped her crooked forefinger into the tiny cup to show a sparrow bringing a message from a lost person, or a mirror with a loved one reflected in it. If there was a black lump in the cup, if the mirrors were dark, or the doors were locked, she sighed a long sigh, stared at the customer with her charcoal black eyes, and sealed her lips.

Drunk on the odors, I swayed among the crowd and reached Baba-Mirza's small apartment, just a few blocks away from Uncle Yahya's. My grandfather and his wife Tuba lived above a toy store. I stood there and watched the toys; this was a childhood habit. The mechanical monkeys nodded endlessly, the winding bears kept clanging their little cymbals, the blonde dolls posed in their swim suits like Western movie stars, and the train, the same old miniature train, circled small toy-towns. I stared at the toys, whispering Sahar's name under my lips. All we had when we were children were long walking sticks to help us in the desert, a bundle of food to picnic on at the wall of the prison, and Grand-Lady's Turkman carpet for imaginary flights. But whenever we visited Baba-Mirza and Tuba, Mother let us look at all the toys in the toy store's showcase for a while.

Tuba served me veal cutlet and fried potatoes. The old couple drank chilled vodka in small shot glasses and put green olives in each other's mouths, removing the bitter taste of vodka with the bitter taste of olives. I drank my first shot of vodka with them on a summer night. I remember that melancholic violin and percussion music rose from their old gramophone and mixed with the scent of Tuba's star jasmines sitting on the windowsill. I went crazy. The music and smell whirled softly in the breeze, blowing from the open window. I wept.

"I want to go. For good!" I told Tuba and Baba. "I want to go to the south where once my aunt Hoori took her life."

Tuba cried. Her black eyeliner and her red cheek powder ran down her fat face. She sighed and made a Turkish coffee for me, as late as it was, so that she could read my cup.

The roads were open, she said. There was a vast desert, or maybe an ocean, but the tides were dark. I was standing on the black tide facing a woman with many bodies, but one head. Tuba cried. The bottom of my cup, she said, my heart, was as dark as the bottom of a grave. She dried her tears. "So young and so unhappy."

Baba-Mirza, aged and shrunken, his once tall and robust body hunched and shortened, listened to my fortune and remembered a line from his favorite bard, the melancholic sufi. He recited with his husky voice: "Alas! A glorious bird like thee in the dust-heap of grief/ hence to the land of the beloved I send thee!"

But then the music suddenly turned fast and rhythmic, the violin died and the percussion went mad. Tuba could not sit and cry anymore. She was a gypsy, a dancer by nature. She danced for us. I wept when I saw her red scarf whirling above her head and melting down like the flames of a dying fire. I remembered Sahar. I remembered that once when we were twelve, she danced the fire dance on a New Year's eve.

The same night I told Uncle Yahya that I wanted to leave. He didn't try to change my mind. He said he always knew that a day would come when I'd need to start my own life. And now I was old enough. My father was not about to speak and my mother, returning to the Alleys of Heaven, was not around. Since Sahar was gone, there was nothing to keep me in this city.

I packed. But before leaving, I had to visit my neighborhood for the last time. I wanted to see the places, not the people.

This was a midsummer afternoon, a time of the day when in New Spring even cats and dogs had crawled into patches of shade to doze off. Even Maman had left her kitchen for an hour to lie down and rest.

But I knew that two men were awake. Grandfather, who spent all his afternoons in his lab looking at the old yellow pictures of his mother and his three daughters, daguerreotyped many years ago, and Father, who sat behind the window of the triangular house staring at the street.

Did I care if Father saw me climbing the hilly street? Did I care about him anymore? I never forgave Father for going out of his mind when he finally came to father us. I didn't care if he suffered. Who said that crazy people suffered? The sane suffered, watching them disappear while still being present. Aren't people what they think? Father either didn't think anymore (they took out all his thoughts in El-Deen), or he thought things beyond communication, things so dark they made him speechless. Whatever the reason, we had longed for him throughout a cold, lonely childhood, longed for him to come out and father us, but when he came, he didn't. He couldn't.

Now in the height of the heat, he sat behind the dusty window watching me climb the hill. He knew why I had come to New Spring, but he stayed motionless as I passed the triangular house.

I raised my head and looked at the terrace of Grandfather's house. Sahar was not bending down to talk to me. Her long hair was not hanging on the railings like loose tendrils of a dark Ivy.

I turned behind the house, stepping into the vacant land, our childhood desert. Through my thin shirt, the heat burned my back. On my left, the gravemarkers at the cemetery melted under the sun. Hoori's body was dust now—it didn't feel the heat in the cold depths.

The old door of the tenant house was swinging as usual. I peeked in quietly and glanced at the courtyard. The odor of the round pool, the green water evaporating in the sun, turned my stomach. Two butt-naked urchins sat in the shade of a dusty tree playing with empty cans, rolling them on the ground like toy cars. They could not possibly be Zahra's and Ali the Bricklayer's children. Most of their children had died, and a couple who survived were grown ups now, pimps or pickpockets in Faithland or in the corner of the jail. A big lock was hanging on Bashi the Janitor's hovel, showing that no one was living there. Hassan the Gardener, his wife, the Lame, and all the other tenants that I had known had vanished.

I descended the stone steps, Sahar's shadow behind me. In the second yard, I saw an old woman squatting in the shade of a dusty fig tree swaying back and forth, a faint groan rising from her closed mouth. In the third yard, three young men threw dice in the shade of the third fig tree. They didn't even raise their heads to look at me. I didn't run away either, like when I was a little boy. I stayed there, watching their game, as if I were invisible. Then I opened the gate to Faithland and stood there.

Once Sahar and I were stuck in the flood here. We both shivered and cried, didn't know what to do. Ali saved us, tucked us under his arms and took us to his hovel. Once when I was with Grandfather, Faithland was buried under the snow. Uncle Massi found his love, Mariam the Big Mole that night. She was naked under the heap of snow, her bare legs out. And many more times I was here. In my dreams, in my memories, my illusions, and make-believe.

This was the gate of Faithland, the black wound of the earth. I stood here and watched the murky, infected street, the tin and cardboard houses, the puddles of standing water, the human and animal excrement steaming in the heat. I chased the flies away, millions of them, sitting on the heaps of shit, then whizzing around me to sit on me. "Twenty and Five... twenty and five ..." Uncle Massi's deep voice echoed in my head. "Faithland will rise and the Alleys of Heaven will fall... " A few more years were still left. Sahar and I had taken an oath to save these people, to open the gates of El-Deen and release the prisoners. Where did she go, then? How could I carry the flag and the banner alone?

A tired, dehydrated donkey appeared on the dusty road. Burlap sacks full of heavy honeydew melons hung from either side of the animal. The donkey-man dozed off, sitting on top of the donkey, hopping when the animal slipped on the pile of shit. Melons rolled in the filth and the donkey and the man fell in a deep puddle. The man woke up; frightened and confused, he finally remembered who he was, where he was, and what he was supposed to do. He screamed from the bottom of his lungs, "Honey I have... honeydew melon! Sweet as sugar! Honey I have! Taste it, then buy it!" He woke the neighborhood.

I sat under the sun, facing El-Deen's brick wall. Sahar's shadow beside me. I didn't see Ali the Bricklayer, the size of an ant, on top of the wall. Neither did I feel Saba around—the little north wind who lifted us up or brought Ali down.

I sat wrapped in the thick blanket of air, motionless, my vision blurred. The brick wall of El-Deen was tall and the tops of ironwoods were burning in the sun. In the hot cells of the prison there were men and women who could still remember the outside, dreaming about it, but there were many who had no image of the blue sky, green leaves, or Alborz, the giantess. The images had vanished from their heads long ago.

I dragged myself back, Alborz on my left breathing heavily, steaming in the sun, Sahar's shadow, cold and slight, on my right. I whispered her name, "Sahar..." and I found myself at Hoori's grave. I lay face down on the gravestone and stayed there for a while. The sun stung my back, but on my heart I felt the chilling cold of the depths.

"Where is the other one?" I heard a deep voice and raised my head. Uncle Massi was squatting beside me, his hair and beard, graying and long, Mariam the Big Mole's red belt still his bandana.

"Who?" I asked.

"The other you. The girl. Where is she?"

"She's gone. Didn't you know that? A long time ago. Her face is for-got-ten."

"We forget the faces, the smells too. Everything." He paused and then said, "Unless we keep something somewhere safe."

"What do you mean?"

"Something of them, in a closed box, or between the pages of a book. To keep the smell. I didn't do that. I forgot."

"You kept Mariam's belt around your head."

"This was a mistake. Her smell is gone now. Under the sun and many rains. Her face is gone too. We never took pictures."

"Then we have to forget. If they're gone, they're gone. Let's forget." I stood up, shook the dust off my pants to go.

"You're leaving," he said.

"Yes, Uncle."

"I can tell it's for good. You won't see me for a long time. Next time you see me, I'll be the poet-prophet. I'll lead the final revolt."

"I know, Uncle."

"And they'll publish my poetry and hang my pictures on the walls of the city."

"Yes."

"Or, I'll die in the revolt and get famous after my death. I'll become a martyred poet. Either way."

"Either way," I repeated. "Go home now. It's hot."

"Home?" He laughed.

Finding my way among the graves, I heard him weeping.

I reached Grandfather's house again. The yard's wooden door was open. Sneaking in, I saw the porch and Grand-Lady's Turkman carpet, as if ready for the old woman to sit on the peacock and pray. No one was in the yard. I tip-toed like a thief, climbing the steps of the porch. I rolled the carpet as gently as Sahar and I used to do after each game, tucked it under my arm, and left the house.

Walking down the hilly street, I felt the weight of Father's eyes on my back. Behind the window, through the clouds of smoke, he was looking at me. I imagined a dark red substance, a lava, moving in his head, making him see images, unspeakable, making him remember and forget, remember and forget.

"Raz is the city of roses and gas," Uncle Yahya told me when we were in a taxi going toward the bus station. "It has two faces: beautiful and ugly. I lived and worked there when I was young. I was an oil worker. I left when the worker's revolt failed. I escaped."

"Tell me more, Uncle," I urged him. "Tell me about Raz."

"Then I have to tell you from the very start—when you reach the city. At the end of your bus trip, when the long south road leaves the central desert behind and approaches the gate of Raz, you'll find an enormous arch decorated with green and blue mosaics in complicated patterns, designed by the artists of ten centuries ago. You'll see an inscription on top of the arch— a line from one of the two poets of Raz, the sufi poet, praising his ancient city's beauty.

"Now there will be a long street, lined by free pines on either side, leading you to the clock square. You'll see a circle of green grass and at the center, a clock made of red roses. A post grows out of the center of the clock, a torch burning with natural gas on top of it. This fire never dies.

"You'll stand at the Rose-Clock, watching the rotation of roses, the passage of time. But gradually you'll feel weak and dizzy. You'll raise your head and see the red sky and you'll wonder why such a strange color. Then you'll feel like fainting. The scent of roses and the odor of gas will make you sick.

"At this point, you'll feel that all that you've seen and smelled in the past few instances, have been too strong, too strange and you'll want to return to where you've come from. You'll not be aware that there will be one million more sights and scents and that you'll see and smell and you'll survive.

"Now if you turn right, the dirt road will take you to the gas part of the city. Even standing right there at the Rose-Clock Square, if you look to your right, you'll see the tall metal towers of the oil refinery and you'll hear the distant click-clacks and hums and rattles. At night, looking at this direction, you'll see hundreds of torches burning in the dark.

"From the Rose-Clock Square, if you turn left, the paved Rose Boulevard will take you to the rose city. The University of Raz is at the very end of this boulevard, at the foot of the hills, where your aunt lived for five years and took her life.

"The people of Raz frequently kill themselves. This is because of the unbearable presence of roses. Of course this doesn't mean that they don't enjoy their lives. The people of Raz are famous for seeking pleasure. They drink homemade wine in their gardens, make love on their roofs, and sit for hours in the mild sun. You'll notice all this while walking the sidewalks of Raz. You'll see people sitting, leaning their backs against the walls, enjoying the sun. You'll wonder when they do their jobs.

"This may happen to you too; it has happened to me. You'll go to the tailor to get your suit, or to the corner grocer to buy some beans. The store is empty. You look for the tailor or the grocer and find him sitting outside in the sun. You ask for your suit, or some beans. He says go and come back later, at sundown—now he is enjoying the sun. Some say that people of Raz are sluggish, but this is not the case; they take pleasure in life, they suck the marrow of it, but in a melancholic way, a way mixed with plenty of poetry and pain. Your young aunt was a poet too, wasn't she? She went to the wrong place.

"Now I have to tell you about the two poets of Raz. One of them is the sufi poet, the lover, the crazy one. His monument is a white marble gazebo surrounded by tall cedars and rose bushes. The other poet is the wise one, the one who advises and gives lessons on life. His monument is made of black marble and a stream of fresh spring water passes by his grave. Both poets were equally popular and lived seven hundred years ago.

"People of Raz don't go to mosques or churches that much. They go to these two shrines, picnic under the vine-covered lattices, and drink red wine. There is a line on the sufi's grave saying, 'If you're having wine here, spill a sip on the thirsty dirt/ It's not a sin, it's for the benefit of the dead!' and people pour some wine on the ground for their beloved poets and the rest of the dead.

"Now let me tell you what will happen if you take the right road and go to the gas city. Walking in the main alley of this part of Raz, you'll see the hovels of whores and the match-box houses of the oil workers. The smell of gas and the open sewer will make you sick. You have to watch your step not to land on piles of shit. If you raise your head to look at the windows above, framing the painted faces of women, or to watch the many torches burning like a jungle on fire, you'll step in the mess up to your knees. In the workers' district, children will be playing in the mud, and dark, greasy-faced men will be washing their hands at the public faucet at the corner of the sidewalk. The workers' wives will call you in, invite you to have a meatless stew with them.

"Let's take you back to the Rose-Clock Square again and imagine that you'll take the left road, the rose boulevard, taking you to the rose part of the city. As I said, you walk or drive along the Rose Boulevard where you'll see the largest roses of the world, each the size of a serving plate, growing in unique shades and colors on the fresh green grass. Then you'll reach the famous bazaar of the city, which will pull you inside its wide mouth. If you go in the dark, cool corridors of the bazaar, the aroma of saffron, turmeric, rose-water, and cinnamon will make you drunk. Some people believe that the bazaar enchants the newcomers and they better avoid it for a while. They may get lost in its tangled labyrinths and never find their way out.

"So you'd better pass the bazaar; leave it for later, when you're settled and more familiar with Raz. Now on either side of the Rose Boulevard there are narrow streets where the common people of Raz live in their crooked alleys, and at the end of the Rose Boulevard, beyond the University of Raz there are chains of hills that surround the city. The mansions of the affluent are built on the skirts of these green hills."

Finally the taxi stopped at the bus station's dusty garage, where people ran into each other in confusion, trying to find their buses and load their bags. While I carried my only suitcase and my carpet under my arm, Uncle bought me a ticket and squeezed a ball of paper money into my fist. He made sure that the suitcase and carpet were safely loaded on the bus's roof and my seat was a good one—behind the driver, by the window. Then he gave me a wrinkled piece of paper with two names and addresses on it. One belonged to an old man, a lodger who had been Uncle's old fellow worker at the oil fields, but was now crippled and retired, renting off his rooms, and the second belonged to another old man, an owner of a small bookstore who lived in the storage room of his shop and could offer me a job.

Before the bus took off, Uncle Yahya gave me his last piece of advice. He said, "Son, It's easy to get lost forever or die soon in this beautiful city you're heading to. Stay alive and live in both parts, see the people of both rose and gas. I won't write to you unless there is something worth writing."

"Will you write if you hear from Sahar?"

"In that case, I will." He patted me on the shoulder and left. When I was climbing the steps he came back, called to me, and said, "It'll take you eighteen hours to get to Raz and you'll travel through the central desert. Watch the desert carefully, day and night. Nothing is lonelier than the desert. It'll make you sad at first, but then you'll feel happy to leave it behind."

The bus roared and crawled on the dusty lot. I saw Uncle standing in the sidewalk, holding his palm over his eyebrows to see me better. Now, suddenly, he ran toward the bus, waved his arms to stop it and jumped up the tall steps like a young lad. He apologized to the driver and the driver pulled the emergency break and stopped. Uncle Yahya came to my seat, gasping for air. He drew a wrinkled piece of paper out of his pocket, and said, "This woman lives in a narrow cul-de-sac, called 'Safa.' Her house is the last one on the right. You'll recognize it from the orange blossoms hanging over the walls." Now he paused and said, "See if she is still there. Her name is Naz-Gol." He blushed.

"Is that all, Uncle?'

"That's all."

"No message?"

"No message. Just see if she's alive."

The Crazy Dervish

The tape clicks on my lap. I open my eyes, searching for Sultan. He has squeezed into a ball on his cushions, snoring. His shaggy hair is standing up. He looks like a porcupine.

I remember the girl, my neighbor. My eyes were closed all this time and I didn't see her. She is still hanging from her feet. Must be dying now. All the blood of her body in her head, her head full of blood, heavy, ready to burst. The last thing she said was, "I won't, I won't—." She didn't repent.

What if she is just a dummy, hanging there, behind the opaque screen. What if they have hung a dummy to scare me, to teach me a lesson? I look at the shadow carefully. It doesn't swing. I listen, she doesn't moan, whisper, or sigh. The woman is dead.

I can't see Sultan. This plate is on my head and the wires hang all around my face. I raise my arm to touch it, but I stop. What if I connect it by accident and receive an electroshock? Should I flip the tape over and continue? Should I wake Sultan? When I woke Kamal he beat me for interrupting his dream. What if Sultan keeps sleeping and leaves me waiting? I'm thirsty and I need a sip of water. My soles are starting to sting again. A good sign.

I decide to wait. Let Sultan sleep. Let the time pass. Kamal may come and save me. I'm sure that wherever he is, he is thinking of me. He may succeed in his coup and take power in El-Deen. What if he assumes full power, becomes the head of El-Deen? What if he lets me go without forcing me to repent?

"Out, little brother, out! I'm setting you free. Go!"

If Kamal sets me free, I'll go to Raz and live there forever. I'll work half time in the refinery. I'll rent a room at the end of Safa cul-de-sac—in a house surrounded by orange blossoms, with a little yard full of roses, a fountain in the middle, water gurgling day and night. Sparrows will nest in the four corners of the yard. I'll spread the Turkman carpet and sit on it without remembering whose carpet it used to be, who used to play on it, who dreamed of flying on it, who stole it when he left town for good. I'll sit on the porch and grow old.

I'll sit on the carpet and read yellow books used by many people for many years—their dried flowers, love letters, or grocery lists hidden between the pages; perfumes trapped between the words forever.

I'll eat bread. Freshly baked in the corner bakery; I'll drink plenty of water out of a cool, wet clay pot. A lady called Naz-Gol will be my landlady. She'll claim knowing me from many years ago when I was her tenant in the same house. But I won't remember her. She'll bring me a little dish of cooked cabbage and rice, the favorite dish of Razians. She'll sit with me on the carpet and talk about old times, when my uncle was her lover and lived with her in the same house. He had to leave her when the workers' revolt failed. She'll talk about my youth, when I lived there in her house and then had to escape when my life was in danger. She'll tell me that I left my carpet with her and promised to come back. She'll say that I kept my promise and I came back. She'll say all this, but I won't remember a thing.

Naz-Gol will make wine in her cellar. She'll offer me warm ruby red wine, but I won't take it. I'll avoid anything that will make me talk. Water. That's what I'll drink all the time. I'll consume all that I have in the cold clay pot, then I'll plunge myself into the fountain, holding my mouth open under the fresh jetting water. I'll wade all afternoon while my neighbors take naps. Then the honeydew melon man will come on his donkey to wake people up: "Honey I have! Honeydew melon!"

Days will pass. I'll live the life of a hermit. I'll become a dervish. But I'll lack the joy of dervishes. I won't worship anything. I won't dance. Sometimes, I'll go and sit at the tomb of the sufi poet. Dervishes will come in with their long white robes, their hairs and beards hanging down to their waists. They'll dance. They'll whirl around themselves and around the marble tomb. They'll form planets and turn around the sun. They'll chant, "Ya Hagh! Ya Hagh! Ya Hagh!" I'm the God. They'll repeat the name of God so many times that it'll change into "Ha! Ha! Ha! Ha!" They'll become one with Hagh. Then they'll throw their arms wide open in ecstasy, rip their robes, turn and turn, until they collapse. Some will faint, some will rise and dance again. Some will cry. They'll weep loud and hard from the intensity of love.

I'll sit there under a cedar and watch them with dry eyes.

I'll grow old. I'll get a pension and stay home all day and night. I won't have a radio, a television, or a music box. I'll let the birds sing for me and the jet of water hum a lullaby. I won't remember my past or plan the future.

I'll live in the present. Out of all the people of the world, there will be one person I'll know. Naz-Gol. She'll talk and I'll listen. She'll reminisce and I won't remember. She'll age as I age.

Neighbors will have no doubt that I'm crazy. Children will call me "Crazy Dervish," and throw stones at me. Once in a while, when I go out to wander in the streets, these little boys and girls will chase me, laugh and stone me. One day a little girl will throw a rose. I'll stop, pick it up, and approach the girl. All the other children will run away. The girl will stay. I'll look into her eyes and see stars twinkling.

"Why a rose?" I'll ask.

"Because I know you."

"How? For how long?"

"Forever."

"What's your name?"

"Sahar!"

I'll run away from her, go home, lock all the doors on myself and stay there until the hour of my death.

The people of Raz are more than clever—they're clairvoyant. Most of them have a sixth sense. The neighbors will spread rumors about me. They'll say in a whisper that the Crazy Dervish has spent a long time in El-Deen and that's why he lost his memory. The new head of the facility, Kamal the Immortal, released him, but the poor man cannot enjoy his life anymore.

They'll talk about me, but I won't even know, or care to know. All I'll care about will be my rose bushes, my fountain, my sparrows, my old books, the clay pot of water, and Naz-Gol, entering my room with the jingle of her bracelets. The neighbors will gossip in the curves of the narrow alleys of Raz. They'll say, "They almost killed him of thirst in El-Deen. That's why he drinks water all the time. Naz-Gol says that he has stopped touching his food. He lives on water."

I'll live on water and gradually divorce my belongings. I'll stop reading too. What do I need wisdom for? Why should I learn? So I'll put all the thick, yellow books in a burlap sack and leave the sack for the garbage man. Then I'll stop tending to my roses. I'll let them whither. Why do I need roses? I turn the jetting water off. The music of water is the pleasure of the soul. Let my soul fast as my body does. So the water in the fountain will turn murky and dark. Contaminated.

Sparrows will ruin their nests and fly away. Frogs and lizards will come, instead. Large cockroaches will crawl on my porch and rats will chew the old Turkman carpet. They'll start to chew me too. My beard and hair will grow long, and the rats will eat them bit by bit. Naz-Gol will stop visiting me. I won't even wonder whether she is dead or alive. The neighbors will shake their heads in regret. "He's not that old," they'll whisper. "Look what El-Deen has done to him!"

One night I'll die on the Turkman carpet, half-chewed by the rats. My head will be on the peacock's head, my thin, naked body, curled on its green wings. I'll die, incomplete, as I lived incomplete. Before my death I won't even dream of Sahar, my twin, my half.

The neighbors will find me. Shrunken, the size of a child. They'll bury me in the dried up flowerbed. Then they'll clean the house and rent it to someone else. The new person will plant some roses in the flowerbed. They'll grow fast. But one of the roses will be different.

There are more than two hundred kinds of roses in Raz, but this one rose bush will be the two hundredth and one. The peculiar color of the blossoms—a strange shade between purple and blue, with a tinge of orange, the color of the sky at dawn—will not be the only strange thing about the blossoms—their behavior will be the strangest. The new tenant will swear that every morning at sunrise, the blossoms whisper to each other.

The neighbors will come and keep vigil all night. They'll hold their breaths to listen. They'll decide that the roses whisper something like, "Sa..." Or "Ha...," moving and swaying even though there is no breeze. The clairvoyant people of Raz will spread the rumor that the rose bush of the last house of Safa cul-de-sac is the same Crazy Dervish who was buried there. They'll call the bush the Crazy Rose Bush. They'll explain that "Sa... ha...," which the blossoms whispers at the end of each night, is in fact "Sahar," meaning dawn. The flowers are calling the dawn and urging it to come. The people who'll keep vigil all night will report that the roses dance out of joy, out of love, they dance a dervish dance, they dance all the dances the Crazy Dervish never danced.

The last house of Safa cul-de-sac will become a visiting place. The government will buy the house and make it into a tourist spot. They'll sell tickets. People will come and hold vigil all night in the dark porch, waiting for the dawn, when the blossoms dance and sing.

I'll become immortal in the rose bush with "Sahar" on my lips.

Future generations will tell many versions of the story of the Crazy Dervish and the Crazy Rose Bush, and the real version—the story of a man who had a twin, lost her, raised the banner and the flag of a wrong revolution, was arrested, lived a long time in El-Deen, lost his memories, was released by the new head of the facility, Kamal the Immortal—will be lost forever, like a handful of dust in the autumn wind.

The Gardener

Sultan finds me in tears. I'm pitying myself, imagining what may become of me if Kamal sets me free. I may end up a miserable dervish, one who can't even dance, who doesn't know how to dance, who chants and dances only when he is not human anymore. What can a rose bush do after all?

"Crying, huh? Memories? Reminiscences? Here, eat something and fill the other side of the tape." Sultan leaves a tray on my lap. There are two raw onions in the tray with dusty skins on them.

"Water!" I murmur.

"That's all I've got, sir! There is draught in the villages of Tus. No water."

He is acting the damned part of the cruel gardener. He is wearing the gardener's felt hat. I remember how rude this character was. He won't give me water. Onions are all I will get. Can I suck the burning juice of the onions? If he'd take the skins off, I could. But now he holds the large, dirty onion in front of my mouth and orders me to bite into it.

"Here, take a big bite! This is better than water. It's water and medicine at once. You know that they take penicillin from onions. You're so lucky, sir, that we are hospitable. We're feeding you in spite of draught and famine in our village. Now eat!"

The smell of onions turns my stomach. My bowels twist. A big lump of bile moves up to my throat, filling my mouth. I swallow it, force it back, but it moves up with more pressure.

"I noticed that you have a metal hat on your head. Let me remove it, so that you can eat comfortably. You are a strange people, aren't you? Who has put this iron hood on your head? Maybe you've run away from the crazy house or something, huh? Now I'm going to peel this onion for you. What else do you want?" He improvises more lines for the gardener, while removing the pink skins of the onion for me. He draws his pocket knife, cuts the onion in four and shoves one part into my mouth. "Eat now! Chew!"

My heart beats in a funny way and the lump of bile, now a cold liquid, moves slowly up, fills my head. Sharp needles pierce my scalp, yellow water jets out of my mouth and nose. I throw up. The onion falls on my lap. My insides shake with such force that the barber's chair rattles as if in an earthquake. I want to stop the spasms, but I don't know how. I imagine a thick column of light piercing my head, entering my body with force, washing my insides clean. But more poisonous water pours out of me, fills the tray on my lap and wets my pants. Meanwhile, the gardener slaps me right and left, screaming from the bottom of his lungs.

"Stop! Stop, you ungrateful man! Is this the way you act in the house of a humble gardener? A broken, poverty-stricken gardener? Stop your shit and puke, or I'll put the mixer on your head again and plug it in. Remember the mixer, huh? This is Sultan speaking, you asshole!"

My bowels gradually stop twisting. I lay back and close my eyes. Sultan gives me a hard backhand, screaming again. "Don't sleep, bastard! Are you animal or what? First you shit in your pants, then you sleep like nothing has happened. Sit up and fill the other side of the tape. I have work to do. I can't leave my business and spend all of my precious time with you. I have to go to the town and sell some grapes. Fill this tape. It's for Sultan. And you better tell him real stories. Juicy ones. If not, Ajooza, the ruthless whore, will rip the rest of your bowels out. Understood?" He takes his gardener's felt hat off, goes to his rug, and collapses on the cushions.

After a few seconds I hear him yelling, "Hey, you pile of shit! This is Sultan talking to you! Don't waste the tape. I'm watching you and listening too. When I see that you're passing out, I'll blow my horn. Understood? So when you hear the horn it means that you have to get your shit together, and go on with your story."

I lay my head on the headrest, staring at the shadow of the woman. I decide to keep looking at her until the end. I won't think about my wet body. I won't smell my own odor. I won't blame myself for what happened. I'll repeat what she repeated, "I won't... I won't!"

The first words I murmur into the recorder are "I won't." Now I wait for the rest to come. But my memory fails. My dreams and fantasies, especially this recent daydream about the Crazy Dervish, keep interfering with real incidents. But I have to talk. I don't want to hear Sultan's horn. I don't want him to curse me anymore. A story. A juicy one. That's what I need. My lips are dry. They're cracked. The vomit has dried up on my chin. I'm thirsty. I smell myself and my bowels move again.

I won't. I won't throw up. I won't.

The City of Two Hundred Roses

I passed the central desert. I saw the sea of sand, mirages—vast, nonexistent, luminous bodies of water. I closed my eyes and drank them. I memorized the desert, carved its solitude in my mind. I passed the ruins of ancient cities. I saw the shadow of a girl in white transparent silk running with a torch between the half-ruined columns.

The bus reached the blue mosaic arch—the gate of Raz. I saw the many shades of turquoise and the inscription on top: "Welcome to the city of two hundred roses." And the lines of the sufi poet: "Hail to Raz and it's unique beauty! O Lord protect her from decay!"

I stood at the Rose-Clock and wept. The burden was heavy on my back. The weight of the sights and sounds. I stood there, looking at the moving roses showing the passage of time. I wished I hadn't come. I stood there until it became dark. I looked up and saw the orange sky. I looked at my right— hundreds of torches burned on top of metal pillars; at my left, the Rose Boulevard stretched into the city. I took a deep breath, inhaled the scent of roses mixed with the odor of gas. I turned left and stepped onto the boulevard.

When I passed the open mouth of the bazaar, I heard voices, calling me in.

"You're a sailor—on the black ocean—a gauger at night—alone with the shadows and shapes... How can you go on? Come in and rest—"

Did I mumble meaningless words? Sultan's horn blows hard. I stare at the woman behind the glass wall: "I won't!"

The house was dark. This was Khan-Baba's house. The old man was paralyzed from waist down. His wife's name was Gol-Agha. She was old, too.

But she colored her hair with henna. Her hair was orange. She had long orange braids hanging from either side of her wrinkled face. Her legs were bent like two bows, two parentheses, with nothing in between. She was almost crippled with a disease which was chewing up her bones. Their son was called Karim. He was forty years old, but acted ten.

Khan-Baba had let one of his rooms to a high school girl—a girl whose face I never saw. She was alone by her own in the city of Raz. The old couple said she was from the capital, where I was from. She had lost her virginity there. She had taken a lover, as young as she was. Her parents banished her, sent her to Raz to die, to become a prostitute, or to survive. So far she had survived, they said. Good people hoped she would survive the rest. Mean people hoped she would end up on the dirt road of the gas city, the alley of the prostitutes. She used the back door of the house. She went to school until four o'clock and sang the rest of the time.

"Come! Look! I say, come! Hey you!" Karim whispered to me. "Look into this hole!" He laughed.

I looked through the hole of the wall and I saw the girl. She undressed. Took her gray school uniform off. Her body was olive-colored, her breasts limes. She put a black-and-white-checkered summer dress on. I couldn't see her face. All I could see was her slender body, as slender as a young willow. She was a faceless girl for me and stayed faceless until the end. Now Karim pushed me away and peeked through the hole.

"She is combing her hair," he reported. "She is singing. She is lying down, she is—"

Gol-Agha and Khan-Baba sat on the porch, faced their little yard, smoking opium. At dusk, they turned the water jet on and the water spilled and splashed in the fountain. The crickets sang and the girl sang in the remotest room of the house. The sweet burnt smell of opium, the scent of orange blossoms hanging on the walls, the smell of roses blooming all year round, made me dizzy and sick. An urge grew in me to get up, walk to the kitchen and cut my veins with Gol-Agha's sharp kitchen knife. But I remembered and repeated Uncle Yahya's advice: "It's easy to get lost forever or die soon in the city of Raz. Stay alive and live in both parts of the city."

I went to the gas city. I walked along the dirt road, the Gas Street. I saw the prostitutes' two-story clay huts, the oil workers' hovels, the beggars' tin houses and cardboard shelters on the right, and a forest of derricks, catcrackers, and oil pipes on the left. Every crooked window of a clay hut framed a woman's face. The last window framed hers.

This was a girl whose face I saw every day. But I never saw her body. This was the bodyless girl. So I went to the Gas Street every day to see her. Who did she resemble? Oh, yes, the beautiful Tatyana, Sister Tatyana, the bald nun.

Then I walked all the way back to the rose city and passed the dark entrance of the bazaar. The bazaar blew its aroma out and called me into its mouth.

"You're a sailor—a gauger... You keep vigil all night—with shadows and shapes... How can you go on? why don't you come in?"

Sultan's horn. The shadow of the girl is blurred. I squint to see her better. My shirt is dry now. My pants feel like cardboard. My head pounds. I'm dying. Water! All I see is water. I stare at the shadow of the woman and the glass wall becomes a waterfall. She is a mermaid behind the curtain of water. The mermaid is moving, diving. I'm going to join her. I'm going to thrust myself into the glassy waterfall, leaving my mouth open. To be able to drink. Water.

The horn. Like in heaven. Or, do they blow it in the hell too? Sultan wants his story.

At the sufi's tomb, I sat inside the monument—the white gazebo. I sat at the poet's grave, rested my left hand on the white marble, and closed my eyes. The marble was ice cold.

A large rectangular pool was outside in the garden. I was aware of its fresh water and of the hundreds of fish wriggling under the green mirror of the surface. I was aware of the sweeping twigs of the weeping willows sipping the water. Don't drink the whole pool of water, you thirsty willows, leave some for me. Now I'm paying respect to the poet, the bard. I'll be out in a second to plunge my head in the smooth water.

"Do you want the sufi to tell your fortune, son?" A voice said. I looked up and saw a dervish. Long white robe, long white hair, long white beard.

"Which sufi do you mean? The poet, or you?"

"Wise youth!" He laughed. "Both. Both of us. Do you want me to read the poet's verse for you? I open the book, the ghazal on the right page is yours."

I didn't say "yes," but he whispered something to the book and opened it. He glanced at the page, frowned, and shut the book with a bang.

"Too bad, huh?" I laughed. "An evil fortune? Dark?"

The dervish shook his head, "No. Nothing is dark if you have faith."

"Faith in what?"

"In Hagh," he said.

"Is he God?" I asked.

"Yes and no," he said. "Mine is in me, theirs is not in them, that's why they look for him up in the sky."

"So you're in love with yourself."

"I am." He smiled. "Because Hagh is me. I'm in love with you too. And with all living things. Do you want to hear the story of Mansour the Quiltmaker?"

I didn't say "yes," but the dervish began to tell me the whole tale.

"Let me make the long story short for you, son." The old dervish leaned his bony back against the marble pillar, drew his knees close to his chest, and stared at the glow of the green pool. "A long time ago, at the time of the Arab Caliphs, Mansour the Quiltmaker, who was a poet, too, claimed to be Hagh. At first people heard him chanting something while beating the cotton balls for his quilts. The chant went like this: 'Ya Hagh! Ya Hagh!' Then they saw him walking the alleyways, screaming, 'I am Hagh! I am Hagh!' They took the news of this blasphemy to the caliph, who ordered Mansour's arrest.

"The Caliph's guards chained Mansour while he was whirling around himself and circling a tree, chanting 'I am Hagh!' They took him to the dungeon. The Caliph told him that if he repented, he would be free; if not he would be tortured to death. Then he asked Mansour, 'Now, where is Hagh?' Mansour answered, 'In me.'

"They brought him to the city's main square so that all the people could see him and learn a lesson. The Caliph ordered his torturer to chop off one of Mansour's limbs and repeat the same question.

"They chopped off one arm and asked, 'Where is Hagh?' Mansour said, 'In me.' They chopped off the second arm and asked, 'Where is Hagh?' The quiltmaker's answer was the same. Then they chopped off his legs too. Now he was a head on a torso. They asked him, 'Where is Hagh, you bastard blasphemer?' He said, 'It's here, in me!' They chopped his head off. The torso died, but the head rolled on the ground and landed at the foot of the caliph, smiling and saying, 'I am Hagh!'"

Sultan blows the horn.

"Cut the crap, bastard! You're talking nonsense again. Get your shit together if you don't want Ajooza to come. No fairy tales anymore. I don't give a damn how the stupid quiltmaker fucked himself up. Tell me your *own* story. The juicy ones, the ones with people, secret meetings, fucking banners and flags. Hurry up! Who gave you the banner and flag and sent you up the wall?"

One night a strange sound woke me up. Chep, chep, chep, chep... and then faster. I heard gasps, someone out of breath. I stepped into the dark corridor. Karim was peeping through the hole, watching the girl's headless body.

I packed and left in the middle of the night, heading toward the other old man's place, the bookseller's.

I walked in the empty streets of Raz. The air was so thin, so transparent and fragile that it brought tears to my eyes. The night was a virgin I invaded. The night was her, the headless girl.

Didn't her slender figure, her olive skin, resemble Sahar's? Could I stay in that house and witness her being raped every night? That was the end of Khan-Baba's house. Since then, every night I dreamed about saving the girl, taking her out, taking her some place where Karim's eyes wouldn't pierce her through the crack of the wall.

The gas torches of the gas city dimly lit the Rose Boulevard. I found the narrow alley and the shop. The door was open. The light was on. I knocked. No answer. I stepped into the bookstore. It was very small. Only one person could walk in the narrow space. There was a short counter that only one person could fit behind. The four walls were shelved to the ceiling and the shelves were full of books.

I knocked on another door at the end of the store, and a voice said, "Come in!" So I entered. It was a small room, a storage room: books in boxes, books falling out of boxes. A table stood in the middle, with five men sitting around it, smoking. Behind the curtain of smoke, I saw sunburned faces, thick mustaches, spectacles, pencils sitting behind ears, dark tea steaming in slim tea glasses.

"Who are you?" An old man with thick snow white hair asked.

"I'm Yahya's nephew." I showed the man the wrinkled piece of paper with Uncle's name and address on it.

"Yes, I recognize Yahya's handwriting," he said and looked at me piercingly. As if he found what he searched for in my face, he rose, extended his arm, and held my hand in his broad hand for a long moment. His grip was tight, as if he didn't want to let me go. After this long handshake suddenly he opened his arms and embraced me. I smelled ash on him. Old dust and ash. Then the rest of the men rose and embraced me. Some dried their wet eyes. Some shook their heads. They hadn't seen their friend, Yahya, for more than twenty years. They fed me and pampered me that night because of their love for my uncle.

They knew my father too. They knew that he was released but wouldn't talk. They all sighed or shook their heads in regret.

That night I realized that Uncle Yahya had been a comrade of these men. A revolt had taken place more than twenty years earlier in the oil refinery, where they were all working. It had spread all over the city and Uncle Yahya and his friends were planning to organize similar riots in other cities with the hope of a revolution. Their dream was to end the monarchy and bring about a workers' republic. But the oil workers' riot was suppressed by the Monarch's army. Many were killed or arrested. Some fled to other cities and disappeared forever. My Uncle fled to the capital in disguise, gave up the idea of the revolution, lived like a hermit, and biked the rest of his life.

The old man offered me a bed in the storage room. I stayed there and worked for him. I dusted and shelved his books from morning to evening and in the evening I left for a long walk along the Rose Boulevard. But whenever I passed the arched entrance of the bazaar, these voices called me in, "You're a sailor on the ocean of oil... a gauger... Come in!" But I remembered my uncle's advice and avoided the bazaar.

"Don't weave nonsense again. Go on with the bookstore, that's what I want. Go on! I'm talking to you, bastard! Go on!"

"I can't. I won't... I won't!"

"What?"

"Water! One sip! Losing my damned soul! Can't see straight anymore...

Can't see the twists... One sip! I beg!"

"Say 'please!'"

"Please!"

"Okay."

I feel Sultan's presence beside me. I can't see anymore. The shadow of the girl has been blurred for a while. She is drowned in the waterfall.

Sultan goes somewhere behind the barber's chair. I hear him talking to me. "Don't pass out. I'm going behind the screen to get you some water. You go on."

Kamal! Kamal! I call him inside my pounding head. How much of the twenty-four hours has passed? Or is it twenty-four years? I can't go on anymore, Brother. I can't. I'm remembering, Kamal. I'm getting close to the real thing. It's all coming to me. Haven't you won yet? Haven't you toppled El-Deen's damn government? Win and let me out! Now I want to go out. Now I remember why I fought!

"Here, take this water and drink as much as you can," Sultan says. "I got stuck back there with these two imbeciles. They ate too much and fell asleep. They kept the woman hanging for too long. She died. It's a pity. They let her die, before she repented. We are not supposed to rush the evil souls to hell. We have to purify them first. That's why we call this facility 'The University of El-Deen: the Gate of Paradise.' Do you get me? We don't want to kill the sinners and pile them up in hell. Our holy duty is to provide purified souls for heaven. Imbeciles! They'll get in trouble.

"Drink now! Why are you staring at me? And the girl was a virgin too. It's a strict order not to execute the virgins. If it's absolutely necessary to send them to the other world, their virginity must be removed first. Now these assholes ate too much, took a long nap and forgot to fuck her. I don't care! I'm not going to touch her corpse. It's not my business! You are my business. I didn't see what happened behind the screen, did I? I was busy with you and so far it hasn't been that bad. We have progressed. We're getting to the stuff that will please La-Jay. This is the sort of story that our sissy Doctor couldn't get out of you. Imbeciles! All of them. I'm the longest hand of the Great Octopus! The strongest! They call me Sultan: the King!

"Well, let's see where we are. Did you speak into this when I was back there, or did you pass out? Okay. It seems that you've wasted a lot of tape here.

Let me rewind this. The last thing you said was that the old man offered you a bed in the storage room of the bookstore and you shelved his books. Then what? But first drink this. Come on. Open your eyes and drink! This is the loving Abasel, speaking. Drink, son!"

I drink sip by sip. Once Ilych advised me to drink slowly, taking small sips. I hold the large slippery glass with my hands, sip the lukewarm tap water, and watch Sultan's face. He is fixing the tape. His face is pitiful. His skin is shrunken to yellowish paper, creased over and over and wrinkled from all directions. His jaws are folded like an old accordion. How can he speak with only three teeth? Doesn't El-Deen have a dentist? Can't he have a set of decent dentures? Or does he keep this appearance on purpose, to scare the prisoners? I watch his small irises swimming restlessly in the blood pool of his eyes and decide that he is a lunatic. Dangerous. But he is in a good mood now, humming something in his throat. He is happy because the woman is dead and the lazy guards will get into trouble. He is looking forward to seeing them in trouble. I don't think he'll beat me up.

Now he switches on the tape recorder, goes to his carpet, and turns the TV on—soundless. He sits, his ears to me, his eyes on the soldiers of the Holy War, marching in the desert. I sit quietly for a long moment, thinking about what else to say in the recorder to amuse Sultan and pass the time. My story must entertain him and at the same time sound politically important. But I have to be careful not to reveal names. Sultan blows his horn, meaning hurry up, don't waste the tape. I watch the dead body of the girl, hanging behind the glass wall. Wasn't she lucky to die before they raped her?

Naz-Gol's house was at the end of Safa cul-de-sac, a little brick house with a tiny square yard walled all around. Orange blossoms hung over the walls. The house had two rooms and a porch in front of the rooms facing the yard; the yard had a little fountain in the middle surrounded by rose bushes. The fountain was made of blue tiles and the water reflected the sky. A single jet of water sprinkled softly and gurgled day and night.

After my temporary stay in the storage room of the bookstore, I moved to Naz-Gol's where I could have a room and the whole yard to myself. The old man and Naz-Gol were good friends from way back. The old man told me that Naz-Gol had been my Uncle Yahya's lover when they were young; she never married after Yahya fled.

Naz-Gol was ageless. Old and young. If she'd been Uncle Yahya's lover, then she must be old now: how come she looked so young? Her hair was dark amber, piled in a bun behind her neck, but I saw the hair down around her shoulders too, flowing to her waist when she washed it at the fountain. Her body was round and full, her breasts, large. She was ripe and fleshy, not slender like a twig, the way Sahar, Hoori, or the headless girl were. Naz-Gol had the body of a childbearer, a mother. She had the body of Maman. Naz-Gol received me like a son. She kissed me and smelled me, saying that I had Yahya's scent on me.

So, I spent my mornings in the old man's bookstore, helping him out, slept a few hours in the afternoon, had my tea with Naz-Gol on the porch, and went to the oil refinery for the night shift. The old man found me a job on top of the tallest tank. I became a gauger.

The three of us—the old man, Naz-Gol, and I—toured the city every weekend. They showed me the rose city—two hundred varieties of roses, the tallest cedars and free pines in the world, marble shrines to the two poets, and the many turquoise domes and minarets all around the city. We never entered the bazaar.

Once we approached the gates of the university, and I saw the white dormitory building where Aunty Hoori had lived, and I urged my hosts to take me back. I was not prepared to go in. I was too involved with life to be able to think about death. Remembering Hoori would bring my childhood back, would bring Sahar back. Sahar's memory tormented me. I was happy without her for the first time in my life.

At dusk, I walked to work along the unpaved path of the Gas Street. I passed the clay houses of the prostitutes. I reached her window and slowed down to see her better: the bodyless girl. Her long light hair was the color of fresh dates, her large eyes, the color of honey. Her long graceful neck made her into a marble statue. She was motionless, framed by the crooked window. One day, she smiled at me, or maybe I thought the faint quiver at the corners of her lips was a smile. I ran toward the forest of derricks to spend my night alone on the ocean of oil, thinking of her smile. I had memorized the lines of her face, the curve of her neck. I had created her body in my mind.

In my light, disturbed afternoon naps, when I could still hear and feel everything around me—the sparrows flapping their wings by the fountain, the honeydew melon man chanting and approaching our neighborhood, Naz-Gol's anklets and bracelets jingling while she made wine in the cellar— this woman, this mixture of the bodyless girl and the faceless one, appeared to me. But she had the scent of Naz-Gol, the smell of aged red wine and lotus.

Sleeping on my Turkman carpet in the shady part of the porch, I dreamed of this woman descending on me like a cloud, covering me like a soft feather blanket. Her long hair fell on me, her breasts touched my chest, her lips lay on mine and then I couldn't breath. I wanted to move, to get up and slip into my gray overalls and go to work. I couldn't. Now the weight of the earth was on me. This woman, this mixture of the real and nonexistent, flew as light as a winged creature, landed on me and then became as heavy as the world itself. Many afternoons I struggled beneath her to set myself free. I thought in my confused dreams that she must be my end, that the woman was death and she was here to take me, to take my breath under the weight of her lotus-scented hair.

Sultan's horn.

"Hey buddy! This is pretty juicy and I'm really enjoying it—the way you put the words together and shit—but go ahead and get to the parts that La-Jay wants to hear. Finish up your story, though. Did you fuck any of your ladies or not? The prostitute, the high school girl, or the old woman? Which one did you fuck? Wrap this part for me and move on to the refinery. That's what La-Jay wants. I could go on with this. But the tape is not just for me."

One afternoon, on the way to work, I stopped at the clay hut of Gas Street and looked up at her window. A woman with a thickly-painted face took me in. She pulled me through a dark corridor, then pushed me into an empty room. A bamboo spread was on the floor, the walls were dried mud and mortar without even one layer of paint on them. In a corner, a brazier sat, cold charcoal in it. The smell of stale opium hung in the air.

"Who do you want to see?" the woman asked.

"The girl in the window frame," I answered.

"She laughed. Many women laughed. I looked around and saw more than ten women, young and middle-aged, some even quite old, piled on each other in the door frame. They all laughed hysterically.

"All the girls here are in the window frames, sugar!" the first woman said. "Which one? Which window?"

"That one!" I mumbled and pointed to the direction of her window. "The girl with golden hair!"

They all laughed again. Some beat their bare thighs, some slapped each other on bare shoulders.

"Her?" The woman asked. "She is just for display, not for fuck!" And she laughed more and they all laughed. "Her name is Naroo. She can not fuck."

"I just want to see her," I said.

"What do you mean 'just to see?' Do you know where you are?"

"I do."

"What are we?"

"Women," I said.

She laughed, they all laughed. Some almost fainted of laughter and one, an older one, neighed like an old horse. The woman dried her tears and wiped the paints off and said, " You must be joking! Are we women? What do we do here?"

They all waited for me to answer and make them laugh. I had made their day. I was the happiest moment they'd had all day.

"You live here," I said.

"Live here and what? How do we make our living?"

"You make—love—" I mumbled. They laughed at me again. Some repeated, 'Make love!' as if they'd never heard the phrase before. At last she said, "Okay, how much money do you have? You know that seeing the girls costs here. Do you know that?"

"I know."

"You are not an oil worker, or are you? You sound like a young man out of school. Are you an engineer or something?"

I shook my head.

"A plain worker?"

I nodded.

"Okay. Give me your money and go upstairs to the room on the left. She is there. But she can't fuck!" she screamed after me. "You understand?" And the women all laughed.

It was as if Naroo knew that I was going to see her. She had seen me walking into the house. She was sitting with her back to the window now, facing the door. She sat on a wheel chair, an old gray blanket covering her legs. She smiled. I smiled too and looked around to see if there was a chair. There was not. A mattress was on the floor on the bamboo spread. I stood there.

"Sit down!" she said.

"Where?" I asked.

"On the mattress."

"This is where you sleep."

"Haven't you come to sleep with me?" she asked.

"No."

"She stopped smiling. Moved her chair toward the window.

"Naroo!" I called.

"Yes."

"Don't turn your back to me. I want to see you."

"Did you pay just to see me?"

"Yes."

"You can take my blouse off. But don't remove the blanket," she said.

"I want to see your face, Naroo. Just your face."

"Why?"

"Because I dream of you and you're real in my dreams and I want to see if you're real outside my dreams too. And I'm alone. I need a friend. I had a friend all my life. But very different than you. She was dark. Her hair was not smooth and wouldn't flow down like yours. Her hair was thick and wild. We played together, grew up together. We talked a lot and often dreamed the same dreams. We even flew on a carpet." I laughed like a silly boy.

"What happened to her?"

"One day she left. She crossed the ocean. Went some place that I could never walk to."

"You could become a sailor and follow her with a ship."

"I am a sailor now. But on the ocean of oil."

She sighed. "An ocean of oil won't take you to her, won't take you anywhere."

The woman called me from behind the door. She knocked and said, "Your time is over, sir. Unless you have more money!"

I didn't. I rolled Naroo's wheelchair to her window so that she could see out and kissed her forehead. I bent and looked through the crooked porthole to see what she saw all day and night, gazing outside. Her view was the refinery: the farm of pipes, the forest of derricks, the jungle of catcrackers. Towers and the flaming torches, burning day and night. Down on the dirt road, the oil workers' path, their children were rolling in the open sewers, sliding on the mud, splashing the murky water at each other.

"Look!" I told Naroo. "Look at the top of the tallest tank—that is where I walk all night. I'm a gauger. I feel the oil running under my feet. I turn the wheels and let the oil flow. Then I turn them again and stop the flow. I have the beating heart in my hand, the beating heart of this land. I'll come more. Naroo. What kind of name is Naroo?"

"It's a Razian name. It means pomegranate."

Sultan blows the horn, lifts himself sleepily on his right elbow and says, "You left? You didn't even remove the fucking blanket to see if there was a hot pussy between her legs or not? You fucking idiot! Or, maybe you're not telling me the truth! Huh? Are you making this whole thing up?"

"No."

"Didn't the girl have anything waist down?"

"No. A few years before I met her, she'd lost half of her body in an oil well explosion."

"Aha! So I don't need her in the tape anymore. Move to your job. So, you say that's what you were. A gauger, huh? You want me to believe that a sissy like you, born with a silver spoon, turned into a gauger?"

"I wasn't born with a silver spoon."

"How were you born, then? In the slums?"

"Not far from them."

"Tell me about it."

"Don't you want to hear about Raz anymore?"

"I do. I do. Fuck your childhood. Tell those fairy tales to Halal. Tell me about the other two women."

"First I need to wash my face and wet my head. My head is burning."

"What the fuck is this now? First you needed water, now you want to wash yourself. You're getting demanding, my friend. We don't have much time left. The sun will rise shortly. I want to hear this fucking story, the women's story. Not the one you couldn't fuck, the other two. I want to see which one you finally fucked. I'll get you some water to wash, and you tell me the juicy parts, okay?"

"I will."

"But bear in mind, kid, this is not really Sultan. This is Abasel, the good-hearted Abasel, the old companion of the Eighth Holy One. And you know what? You know something about Abasel? He loves women. Yes, the dirty old bastard has loved hot pussy all his fucking life; he still does. But does he get any here? Once in a while he fucks a dead corpse, like this bitch behind the wall. But the hot pussies go to the seventh floor—if you know what I mean! Anyway, you're lucky to be dealing with poor, old, deprived Abasel now. Sultan would crack your ass for your demands. Sultan, the longest arm—the fucking king! The Asscracker!" He farts, he laughs at himself, he grumbles, and limps behind the opaque wall.

"Here, take this bottle and wash your face in this tub. I can't take you back behind the screen where the sink is. It's a mess there. The girl is still hanging upside down, blood is dripping from all her holes, and the bastards are still sleeping. While you're washing I'll fetch something for myself to eat. Then we'll start."

He drags himself behind the screen again, mumbling something. He looks tired and drained, older than when I first saw him. His back is more stooped. Sultan is not acting old. He is old.

I wash my hands and face with the water in the bottle and pour some on my head. The skin of my head burns. I glance at the girl behind the divider. All the blood of her body in her head, now dripping. The head is full, can not contain more. Blood must drip. Find a way out. "I won't—" she said, and died. She fought. Hanging upside down in El-Deen's last chamber, she fought.

I use the last drops of water and leave the small plastic tub on my lap. If Sultan doesn't remove the tub, I'll use the dirty water to wet my burning head again.

One weekend, the old man took us to the three hills. That was part of my education, he said. I had to see the hills and then see the hovels of Gas Street to store rage.

"This city is your university," the old man said. "Walk around and learn.

This is the University of Revolution."

He brought me suit and tie, because they wouldn't let us on the hills if we didn't look rich. Naz-Gol wore a black dress, long to the ground, but open on the neck and shoulders. She didn't pull her hair back in a bun, as she always did. She let it fall down, and tamed it only with one tiny pin behind her neck. I couldn't take my eyes from her. She was ageless.

In the old man's rented car, we passed the beautiful alleys of upper Raz. They reminded me of the Alleys of Heaven. The mansions and gardens looked the same. But here the trees and shrubs were different. Crawling roses with hundreds of multi-colored blossoms hung on the walls, the orange flowers covered the lattice roofs of the walkways, and pines, all kinds of pines—cypress, cedar, and juniper—trimmed by nature to perfection, stretched to the sky.

We passed the bright cafés and dim nightclubs with only one red lantern hanging on the doors. We passed the open decks and terraces, each giving out the sweet aroma of charcoaled meat and the dizzying smoke of opium. Dreamy music floated in the thin air. Tuxedoed valets opened the doors of large, dark cars, helping ladies in long gowns step out. The scent of sweet perfume rose and lingered in the air. Click click of high heel shoes, a whisper, a giggle, and the red mouth of the nightclub sucked the guests in. The next limousine arrived.

The old man said that since we had neither time nor energy to stop at several places, we'd pick one that had all the pleasures of the three hills at once. OCC, the old man suggested, the Oil Company Club, located on the peak of the second hill, contained all the varieties of entertainment.

We sat at a table by a big round pool that was lit from under the water with large moon-shaped blue lights. Jets of water sprang all around, while soft music floated in the fresh air. The crisp breeze of Raz carried the scent of two hundred kinds of roses and mixed them with ladies' perfumes before sending them up to the Club's terrace.

While the young stiff-backed waiter in white served us big chunks of sizzling shish-kabob on a flaming dish, I looked around at the men and women in dazzling clothes and jewelry, eating, clinking wine glasses, and bursting into laughter. Some of the guests with their pale hair and eyes looked like foreigners, speaking in languages I couldn't understand. On the round dance floor, surrounded by weeping willows, a few couples moved smoothly, their faces rubbing slightly, their lips almost touching.

I looked at the sky to make sure I was in Raz. It was Raz's sky— ultramarine above the rose city, fading into orange, and gradually blending into the blood crimson above the gas city. I thought about Naroo, sitting at her window now, looking at the red sky, the deserted alley, and the metallic horizon—the farm of pipes. Was Naroo real, or were these people? Were both real? How could these two worlds live side by side?

I stored rage.

"These are the oil executives," the old man said. "Those are their foreign advisors. They are here to ship our oil out. Go and walk around, son. Peek into different halls, rooms, bars, whatever there is. No one will stop you as long as you smile at them as if you know them, as if you are one of them. Meanwhile, Naz-Gol and I will sip our bitter wine and reminisce."

The horn. Sultan wants me to stop. He chews with his three front teeth, making munching sounds. He sniffs. With his mouth still full, he says, "Okay, be brief in this part. I know how those motherfuckers lived. They're all dancing in hell now. Get to the women. The ones you fucked. Which one did you finally fuck, huh? More on that." He wipes his mouth with the back of his hand and gets up to take his tray behind the screen.

"I'm thirsty," I say. "More water... and the belts hurt..." I mumble, pointing to the straps.

"Hmmm... more and more demands. Okay. Just let's hope Sultan doesn't show up, nor Ajooza, who has been waiting for her entrance for a while now. Here, you can breathe better. Let me prepare you for the juicy parts: The fuck!" He laughs, lifts the dirty water tub from my lap and unstraps me. He disappears behind the screen.

"I'm using the restroom here," he yells. "Don't say anything now. Wait for me." I hear him singing a vulgar song that is forbidden in the Holy Republic: "Open the door and let me in, Nayer! Seeing you is a deadly sin, Nayer!" He farts. "Fortunately you don't need to use the restroom. You emptied yourself right there! Yuk!" He farts again and laughs. "Bad food. Damn bad food. Gave me cramps. The motherfuckers go to the sixth floor cafeteria all the time and eat as if they're in the Oil Club, and all I have here is canned food, or stale bread and stinky cheese. I've told them one hundred times that I need a refrigerator here. Who cares? I can always call for delivery service, though, but I don't want to do that when I have an important case. Duty comes first!" He farts.

I hear the flush and then Sultan comes out with a glass of water for me. "Here, drink! These suckers are still asleep. But I want them to sleep. I want to see them punished. Bastards. They let the girl die a virgin! Imbeciles!" He grumbles and drags himself to his cushions. "I'm going to lie down here. I feel sort of weak. The cramps got to me. But I'm all ears." Now he whispers, "First the fucking scenes, okay? Then the banner and flag!" He chuckles. "I deserve some fun too, don't I? Is this life I have here?" He makes himself comfortable on his cushions, curls toward me hugging Ajooza's gray shaggy wig. He says, "I'm ready. Make sure to turn the tape off when you talk about the juicy parts. When you get to politics, turn it on again. Go on!"

In the building, I opened a double door. Men and women were gambling. I saw round tables covered with green felt, I heard the shuffling of cards and the rattling of colorful poker chips, muffled voices, sudden outbursts of laughter, then a sigh, a curse. I closed the door.

I opened the second double door: people watched a film. On the large screen a naked woman was taking off the last part of her clothing—a transparent silk stocking. I closed the door and opened the third one. Here was an indoor pool. Men and women were wading and tanning under an artificial sun. The fourth room was dark. I stepped in a red fog. The odor of alcohol and cigars turned my stomach. Half-naked girls served drinks. In the fifth room there was an eating contest—"

Sultan's horn. "Cut the crap! Enough! Are you wasting the time or what? I don't give a damn about the doors of the fucking Club. And I don't give a fuck what the suckers were doing there. Either go home and fuck the landlady, or go somewhere and fuck someone else if you want to save your fucking bald head. Did I unstrap you for nothing? Sultan is on his way, I'm warning you!"

Not knowing where I was going, I stepped into a large hall where a private party was going on. It was dark. I stood by the door and watched. On a small stage, a girl was dancing. It was a different kind of dance. I'd never seen anything like this before. She had on something like a bathing suit. A narrow top, and a tiny triangular patch in front. But she was covered from head to foot with a black transparent silk. As she moved and wriggled, she pulled the see-through veil down as if she were about to show her face, but she never did. All around her on the stage were little pieces of clothing which she kicked away with the sharp toes of her high heels as she moved. For a while she danced and played and wriggled and strolled with the two tiny pieces she had on—the narrow top and the black glittering triangular satin that covered her front. This material was shining with sequins or beads.

The hall was full of men. I didn't see any woman. They were all sitting on the edges of their seats, drinking and smoking. I was watching everything through a thick cloud of smoke. Now the music became strange. It invited the girl's hips to wriggle more. She turned her back to the hall, snapped her top open and threw the piece on the floor. The men whistled and clapped. But the girl's back was to them—they couldn't see anything except her naked back.

The girl's body was young and olive-colored, the curve of her waist, the shape of her buns, all resembled the headless girl's—Khan-Baba's tenant.

"Don't stop, sucker! Go on," Sultan says in a faint voice. "I said, go on!" He whispers and wriggles on his cushions. He clenches Ajooza's hair with his fists and repeats, "Go on! Tell me how they fucked her. Hurry up!" He begs and I hear him hitting himself, "Chep, chep, chep, chep—"

Now with a sudden turn, she exposed her breasts. They were not very large, maybe a bit bigger than Razian limes. Her nipples stood up. As she danced, her breasts quivered and she held them in her palms as if to stop them from shaking. Now she lay on the stage floor and slithered like a snake toward the men. One man, a tall, bald, middle-aged man with round rimless glasses, stood up and limped toward the stage. He lay on the floor and slithered toward the girl. He reached her and shoved rolled-up paper money into the triangular part of her silk panty. She sat and opened her legs, she caressed her thighs, lay on her back, and ran her hands over her body. She made the snake movements again. A fat man approached her and shoved more money into the satin part of her panty. He gasped for air as if he were suffocating. The girl rose, pulled the thin black veil slowly down over her face and body, pulling the glittering panty down along with the veil. But no one saw anything, because the moment the veil and the little triangular piece fell on the floor, all the lights went off and the music stopped. Men clapped and whistled. Chairs fell. Glasses broke. I left the hall.

Outside, in the carpeted hallway, I leaned against the wall and closed my eyes. I couldn't go back to the garden. I was filled with lust, shame, and rage. I was the bald man slithering like a worthless worm. He was me.

Standing there, not being able to join my friends, I reviewed the show again and again. I realized that the girl wore a pair of high heeled shoes all the time. They were red and glittering with sequins. She never took them off. Had she taken the shoes off, she would have been the same height as the high school girl in Khan-Baba's house. Was it her? Had she finally ended up here?

I went to the men's room to wash my face. "Chep, chep, chep, chep—" came from the chambers.

The old man took us home. But I didn't go in. I told Naz-Gol that I wanted to take a long walk. I walked around Khan-Baba's house. The girl's window was dark. I fought the urge to go in and make sure that the girl was still living there, that she was still in school, and still singing love songs all evening long. But I passed the house and wandered around the deserted boulevard. I found myself in the sufi's tomb. The gazebo-shaped monument was glowing like a torch in the dark garden. The seven marble pillars surrounded the poet's grave.

"Is that you, young man? Come! Come and sit with me!"

I looked around to find the voice. The white marble tombstone was gleaming under the moon-shaped light installed under the domed ceiling. I found the old dervish sitting against the seventh pillar, facing the dark garden. I approached him. He was naked. His white hair hung down to his waist.

"It's you," I said.

"It's me," he said.

"What happened to your white robe?"

"I divorced it."

"Find my fortune in the Master's book. Read a ghazal for me."

"I don't have the book of ghazals anymore."

"What happened to your book?"

"I divorced it."

"You don't have anything now?

"Nothing. No belongings."

We sat in silence for a while and watched the dark garden. It was a moonless night. Then I asked him, "Dervish, how did you divorce your desires?"

"I found true love."

I rushed to the bookstore. It was only an hour before dawn. I opened the door with my key and tip-toed to the storage room where the old man worked and slept. But the light bulbs over the big table were on. More than ten men and women stood around the table, working. I knew a few of them, but I didn't recognize most. They nodded at me and continued to work. They were cutting, pasting, folding, and packing stacks of leaflets. The tap tap tap of an old printing machine was covered by the loud, scratchy sound of a radio—some Arabian music from beyond the waters. The old man approached me, laid his hand on my shoulder and led me out.

We walked in the dark alley along the short wall of the gardens. Our footsteps echoed on the brick floor. The city was in a deep sleep.

"What's bothering you, son? Tell me!"

I inhaled the fragrant air, kept it in my lungs for a long moment, then released it and said, "How should I divorce my desires?"

"Why should you?"

"To be able to find true love."

"True love is love of justice. If you're able to sacrifice your life to bring justice in the world, if you're ready to give up your comfort to fight the oppressors, if you struggle to change the world to a better place, then you're a true lover. Let me tell you the story of Mansour the Quiltmaker, son."

"I know the story."

"But the version you've heard is wrong!"

"How?"

"When Mansour called, 'I'm Hagh,' he meant that he was the voice of justice. Hagh means the truth and the truth is justice. Why do you think the authorities chopped the quiltmaker's limbs off? Had he been a harmless crazy man claiming to be God in the alleys and bazaars, why should the caliph have felt threatened? Mansour didn't have a self, didn't know what ambition was. He didn't want anything for Mansour. He divorced his self to become the voice of Hagh—justice."

411

"I admire him. Is this how a true revolutionary must be?"

"A true one," the old man says and sighs. There is much grief in his sigh.

"Have you ever seen one or heard of one? Not in tales and myths, in real life."

"I have, son. Once in a very long while..."

We walked in silence and listened to hundreds of secret sounds all in hush, all in whisper. Raz was in a deep sleep. The ancient city was dreaming.

"And love for women?"

"What about it?"

"How does a revolutionary love?"

He laughed, loud and merrily, so deep that his eyes filled with tears and the city awoke. "With passion, son, he loves with passion!"

"I'm twenty-one—"

"I know, son. It's time. Find yourself a lover and get to work. These are crucial times. We can't wait. I want to be able to introduce you to our friends as a comrade. Let me know when you're ready."

The curve of the alleys brought us back to where we left. We stopped at the door of the bookstore and shook hands. As I turned to leave, the old man called after me.

"Avoid the dervishes, son. They're all lost."

I walked along the dark cedars of the Rose Boulevard in the last minute of the night. At the end of the boulevard, the iron gate of the University stopped me. I pushed it gently. It squeaked open for me. I walked along the short wall of boxwoods and reached the girls' dormitory—a white, one-story building. The windows to the lawn were dark. Girls were asleep. Which window had belonged to Hoori? From where had her blood dripped to the grass? I looked for a bush, a tree, something growing outside one of the rooms as I had always imagined; I couldn't find any. The lawn was empty and gray in the dusk.

I sat on the steps and let the day come. Now the reason why I moved to Raz seemed meaningless, absurd. I moved here to be where Hoori died, yet it took me months to visit her place. Now that I was here, I didn't mourn her anymore. Hoori was an obscure shadow in my foggy past and her memory didn't torment me. Sahar, who vanished like my young aunt was wrapped in a thick smoke too. Uncle Yahya never wrote to me, which meant that he hadn't heard any news of her. She was either lost in the foreign lands or returned and lost somewhere in our country. Sahar's memory was hiding somewhere in a dark corner of my confused head.

A woman came down the steps and asked me if I needed to see someone in the dorm. I said I didn't. I was lost on the campus. She showed me the way out.

I walked back home. Tip-toed to my room and lay down on my Turkman carpet. Did I fall asleep and dream of her? Or was she real? She came to me and descended on me as light as an angel first, then as heavy as earth.

There is no way to tell. But I remember the waterfall of her amber hair flowing over my face, wrapping me in the scent of lotus. I remember her burning lips, seeking mine in the dark. I remember her weight, that dear warm weight, the weight of the burning sands of the desert, now pushing me down into the hot earth to bury me forever, then sucking me back in itself, to give me life.

This was a new love.

I hear Sultan snoring. I stop. I put the bastard to sleep. Let him sleep then. He may sleep a long, deep sleep, as long and deep as death itself. And Kamal may come and take me out.

Why didn't I walk back to the poet's monument that night and talk to the dervish some more?

"What is true love, dervish?" I should have asked him. "How is it that a life-long love thins down into a shadow and hides behind the fog? How is it that now I seek a different love?"

I didn't go to the dervish; I followed the old man's advice. I buried the sufi in me, hid my love for Sahar somewhere in the dark part of my self, and joined the comrades.

I worked, loved, and lived in Raz for ten years and Uncle Yahya didn't write me a line.

One day I saw the first white strand in my hair and hot blood rushed into my heart. It was as if the door of that dark chamber had suddenly opened and Sahar had flapped her wings like a crazy sparrow.

Her hair was growing gray too.

Twenty and five, I murmured under my lips. Twenty and five had passed since we were six.

Sahar, the Revolution must be coming!

The Revolution

Slipping off the barber's chair, I approach Sultan. He is snoring. I grab the gray shabby wig and shove it into his mouth. He struggles in his sleep, jerks his arms and legs like a tortoise lying over his shell. But I press my hand on his mouth; he stops breathing. Then I pass through the opaque wall, stretch my long arms to the ceiling and untie the girl's ankles from the hook. Like a feather she lands on the floor, standing on her legs. I notice that she is transparent and her body is glassy like a fly's wing. I see through her. As she stands on her legs, the blood flows down from her head into her body, like sand in an hourglass. Her blood runs into all the veins and her heart starts to pump. She is not as tall as I imagined, just my height. We hold hands and pass through the cell's thick wall.

We step into a courtyard. A tall, brick wall is stretched around the yard. "This is the Wall of the Almighty," I tell her. "This is where they execute the prisoners." We step over the fresh blood that runs in the crack of the brick floor, gathering in small puddles. "This is Ilych's blood," I say. "He was the last one they shot."

We pass, my companion and I, like ghosts, through the Wall of the Almighty. We find ourselves in the refinery.

"Are we in Raz?" she asks with surprise. But I can't answer her. I'm confused myself. We walk over the pipes—some running parallel, some crossing. We tip-toe on a thick oil pipe. It's hot—burns our soles. We feel the oil flowing under our feet. Climbing the catcrackers, as brisk as wild cats, we ascend the derricks like children playing on monkey bars in a school yard. We stand on top of a derrick, looking at the farm of pipes. Hundreds of torches burn on metal posts. A steel jungle on fire. The horizon appears glazed under the orange sky. The incandescent orange gently blends into a darker color, becoming a crimson cloud.

We reach Gas Street. Hundreds of people are out. I see Karim there, looking around with an open mouth. I ask him what's going on. He says, "Don't you know? The Revolution has started in the capital; the Monarch has fled the country; there are revolts everywhere. The workers are rioting in the refinery and the members of the Party of God are stoning the prostitutes. I came to see the naked women stoned."

Karim points to the tallest spot in the refinery, the top of a huge tank and says, "Can you see that man? He is the gauger. He is going to turn the gauge off. He is going to stop the flow of oil."

"Who is he?" I ask. Knowing that he should be me. But I'm not there.

"He is a sailor, brother," Karim says. "A gauger is a sailor, a sailor who seeks a storm."

"What is his name?" I ask and my heart pounds in my throat like a huge drum.

But Karim melts in the crowd, disappearing like a drop in an ocean.

"What's his name?" I shout. But there are loud voices, much louder than mine, shouting slogans.

The crowd sweeps us away like flood water moving weightless twigs. It pushes us and pressures us from all sides. I hold the transparent girl's hand tightly, squeezing it to make sure that she is here and that her hand is warm and full of blood. Many times the flood takes her away, but I reach out for her hand and find her again. Then I feel warmth and joy.

We approach the prostitutes' hovels. Half-naked, disheveled, and sleepy, the women are dragged out of their huts and thrown on the dirt road. Sheikh Ahmad and Salman the Brainless are stoning them. The women roll in the dirt, screaming and moaning, begging for forgiveness. But the sheikh agitates the people to stone harder. Everybody picks a stone, hitting the women. Sheikh Ahmad and his four veiled wives throw the largest stones; they hit hard. I look at the women, the ones who laughed at me one day when I wanted to see Naroo. Now they are beyond recognition. Blood has covered them. Their laughter is dead.

I look up to see where Naroo is. The porthole is empty, Naroo is not there. I find her strapped on her wheelchair among the crowd. Any minute they'll throw her on the mud to shower her with sharp stones. I run toward her and remove the gray blanket. A pair of skinny legs, the legs of a starved child, hang from her body. I make her stand on her feeble legs. I hold her hand and we walk together.

Now Naroo's hand is in mine, but I feel that both the transparent girl and Naroo are one and the same. I don't feel my cell-mate's loss, she is here. She is Naroo. We free ourselves from the crowd and run out into the open, stopping in front of the Rose-Clock. But the clock has no hands. No one can tell what time it is. The sky of Raz is misleading. It's neither the color of day, nor night.

The streets of the rose city are empty. Everybody is in the gas section, where the Revolution is happening. I walk with Naroo, but now her legs have grown longer and stronger. She is even taller than me, holding my hand the way a woman holds a child's hand. I look up at her face and recognize Tatyana before her wedding to God. Her long golden hair shines in the incandescent light. As we walk, she hums her Polish song, "What a sweet bird are you, nightingale—What a tiny sweet bird!"

I ask her, "Tatyana, can I touch your hair?"

She smiles and says, "Yes, you can."

I run my hand over her hair. It slips as if on soft silk.

We reach Naz-Gol's house at the end of Safa cul-de-sac. She opens the door for us and takes us in. "Have you found your bride at last?" she asks in a motherly tone. I tell her about the Revolution and urge her to hide my Turkman carpet because we're all going on a long trip. Will I ever come back again? I don't find an answer.

Naz-Gol hides the carpet in a big trunk, locks it with a small key, and hangs the key around her neck. She shuts off the fountain, buries the wine bottles in the flower beds, draws the curtains, and locks the doors. Now I find myself holding Naz-Gol's hand. But I don't feel a loss. Because Naz-Gol contains Tatyana, Naroo, and the transparent girl. She wears her long, black dress and her amber hair is loose down to her waist.

We take long steps. Each step moves us many kilometers forward. We reach Khan-Baba's house. The old paralyzed man and his crippled woman are frozen on their porch like objects from a remote past. Their opium is cold on white coals that have turned to ash. We open the high school girl's door. She is sitting at her desk, her back to us, studying. But she is headless and her body naked. She wears only a pair of red, high-heeled shoes.

I lift her up, make her stand on her red shoes, and we pass through the walls, leaving the dark house. Now I'm holding the headless girl's hand in my hand, but I don't miss Naz-Gol, Tatyana, Naroo, and the transparent girl, who are all one and in her. We take long steps again and she manages to walk smoothly on her heels.

When we reach the mouth of the bazaar, we see many men being thrown out, as if the mouth of the bazaar is spitting them out. These men are carrying heavy sacks full of gold on their shoulders. They hear the uproar of the people from the distance and scatter, running off to hide their money somewhere safe.

We reach the gate of Raz. But before we pass through it, I linger to read the inscription on top of the arch—a line from the wise poet. I remember that the inscription on the other side of the arch, greeting the guests, was from the sufi poet praying that Raz would never decay. This one is from the wise poet, so it must be advice. But the line is written in an ancient handwriting I've never learned. The letters look like nails, screws, small hammers, miniature sickles, and axes.

Not able to read the advice, we leave the city. Here I realize that I've lived in Raz for ten years and have not even once visited the wise poet. I must not have needed wisdom.

Soon, we reach the ancient ruins outside the city and stop to see if the barefoot girl is still roaming among the half-ruined marble columns. "There! There!" I tell my companion. "Do you see a white shadow behind the third column? Now she is here. Do you see her shape? Look at her torch! Oh! I can see the tail of her long skirt. She disappeared behind the marble throne. She's about to set fire to the castle of the kings."

We step onto the desert.

But the desert is an ocean of hot oil; we walk, ankle-deep in the thick, greasy liquid. My feet burn and I cry of pain and agony. Half way through the ocean, I stop and my heart freezes as if I'm dead. I tell my companion, the headless girl, that I'm already missing Raz. I have a premonition that I'll never see that dear city again. She pulls me and says, "Come now! Leave everything behind! The Revolution is waiting for you!"

In the capital city, we join the millions who walk like us on the ocean of oil. Men, women, children sitting on their parents' shoulders, or wobbling in bags hanging from their mother's backs, young and old people, hand in hand, all chant one chant, all sing one song and move forward. I hold my companion's hand tightly, so as not to lose her. I turn to look at her and make sure she is with me.

I see Sahar.

"I found you, finally," I scream over the crowd's loud noise, feeling an immense joy. I don't feel the loss of the headless girl, Naz-Gol, Tatyana, Naroo, and the transparent girl. Because they're all one and now walking with Sahar's strong legs. I squeeze her hand and say, "Hey sister, how come you never wrote to anyone from where you were?"

"Because instead of going to the dance school, I joined the revolutionaries.

I was underground. Now I've returned to change the monarchy into a republic."

"Sahar, isn't this what we waited for all of our lives?"

She nods and mimics crazy Uncle Massi, "Twenty and five! Twenty and five!"

We all sing a song that starts with "Arise! Arise!" I look around and recognize Saboor, Akir and Nakir, ahead of the crowd, moving their arms like conductors of a huge orchestra, leading the choir of millions. My heart fills with joy to see Saboor alive.

I look up at people who cheer and wave colorful handkerchiefs in their porches and balconies. Tuba and Baba-Mirza standing in their small balcony wave at us. I look for Uncle Yahya, but I can't find him. Sahar finds him and says, "Look! Look where Uncle Yahya and his bike are!" We look up and find him on top of the roof of a public bath, smiling. The red towels hanging out to dry wave around him like many flags.

We, a procession of several million, reach an intersection and stop. From the right side, another procession approaches. These people look different. They're in their clean suits and ties, tailored dresses and fancy hats. They carry large pictures of the Monarch and the blue flags of the monarchy with golden crowns shining in the middle of them. I recognize General Nasri on his white horse holding an antique spear in his right hand, a shield in his left. His guests, on horses and on foot, are all armed in ancient armory. I show Sahar the old man who wanted to be tickled, the obese woman who was fed from behind, the man in alligator pajamas and his bald wife. General Nasri's Arabian horse neighs once in a while and stands on his rear legs. The General's wife walks hand in hand with the young valet. I recognize our hosts, Mina, Minoo, and Moni, grown up, but still in their pink satin pajamas, each carrying a golden crown.

Sahar shows me Uncle Musa holding a blonde's hand, marching. We see Mother, hand in hand with Prince Amir Khan, screaming, "Long live the King!" Grandfather drags Maman behind, trying to catch up with the monarchists' procession. But his legs are bad and Maman is too fat and they're left behind. He screams, "Wait for us! Wait for us!" But the aristocrats don't pay attention to him.

Cyrus and Kami, our cousins in blue military uniforms, armed to the teeth, sit side by side in a jeep, escorting the monarchists' demonstration.

Aunty Zari, in her long, pale blue wedding dress waltzes absently, not knowing where she is or what's going on. She gets in the way of horses and men. The guards push and prod her, drag her to the wall, forcing her to stay there.

Now the crowd of millions is outraged to see the aristocrats and is about to attack the carriers of blue flags. Cyrus and Kami stand up in the jeep and order the shielded, hooded National Guard to make a wall and protect the monarchists.

From the other side of the intersection, the Holy Republicans, members of the Party of God, appear. The men are all in black shirts, carrying black flags, walking ahead. The black veiled women march behind them. They carry human-size pictures of their Great Leader. Men and women chant slogans and beat their chests with chains: "One party: Party of God! One leader: Chosen by God!" I show Sahar Sheikh Ahmad, Salman the Brainless, Hasan the Gardener, the Lame, and many other tenants and hooligans of Faithland. But we don't find Bashi the Janitor.

Sahar shows me Uncle Massi.

Now all three processions reach a wall and stop. This is a tall brick wall. The crowd of millions become a silent sea. "This is the wall of El-Deen," I whisper in Sahar's ear. "Aren't we supposed to open the gate now and take Father and the other prisoners out?"

But before Sahar and I can decide what to do, those who are closer to the gate hit it with their strong bodies. We see flames here and there. People burn the Monarch's dummy and the blue flags of his dynasty. Some burn a different dummy, a thin man with a goatee in a black tuxedo and a stove-pipe hat. They move this dummy on a stick, making him dance, then they hold a torch to his tall hat and cheer when he burns. Now they burn a flag full of stars. They cheer and stamp their feet in the oil with joy. Some people wade in oil, splash it around, playing with it, as if it's a clear pool of water. People chant: "Thanks to the oilman, the oil is ours at last!"

Now Salman the Brainless drags Afreet (the bloody watch-dog of the prison) by her tail. He brings her in front of the gate, cuts her head from corner to corner. People cheer. At last the gate breaks open; the crowd parts into an alleyway for the prisoners to walk out.

The first man we see stepping out of El-Deen is La-Jay, wearing large, dark sunglasses. Almost nothing of his face is shown except a round mark on his right cheek like a large button. On La-Jay's right, we recognize Ha-G's torso in the arms of a bearded man and on his left, we see Bashi the Janitor, now nicknamed Sultan, limping one step behind. Following them several black robed sheikhs emerge.

Sheikh Ahmad and Salman the Brainless try to arouse the people by hot speeches, inviting them to join their side. Half of our crowd join the Party of God, leaving our group and running toward the Black Flaggers. Men lift La-Jay up on their shoulders, hanging rings of flowers around his neck. Uncle Massi, meanwhile, in a robe—a sheikh's robe—but without a turban, climbs a telephone post and recites an ode in praise of the Party of God. The bearded men lift Uncle up and put him on their shoulders; they hang rings of flowers around his neck and call him the Poet Laureate of the new republic.

Now another group of prisoners appear at El-Deen's gate. Ilych, tall and lanky, Father, short and shrunken, and for the first time, several pale, tired women step out in one group. Some hold crutches under their arms, some are missing an arm or an eye. They look like wounded soldiers returning from a bloody war.

I recognize my old comrade and employer, the owner of the bookstore, from his massive white hair among the crowd. He is with a heavilyy-built, tall, and athletic-looking man. The old man is moving his arms fervently, making a speech for the people who have circled around him. He invites them to join their group. The heavy-built man distributes colored flyers among people, answering their questions.

Suddenly our mother screams and leaves her prince, running toward the gate of the prison where Father is standing. She throws herself in Father's arms, sobbing hysterically.

Ilych, wearing his black vest, takes his pocket watch out, looking at it. He winks at me, as if he can see me among millions, as if he is saying, "This old, dear watch is yet witnessing another Revolution!"

The young, strong students of our procession lift Father and Ilych up and put them on their shoulders. They hang rings of flowers around their necks.

Now the tall man who was working with the old bookseller, approaches me, holding my hand, pulling me out of the crowd. He leads me to the gate of the prison. My old friend smiles at me, nodding in approval, as if saying, listen to the tall man, whatever he says is my wish, too. The tall man says,

"Here! This is the banner of our Revolution and this one is the flag. Take these and climb the wall!"

"Me?" I ask.

"Yes, you. Aren't you the gauger? The captain of the ship?"

"I'm the gauger, yes. A sailor on the sea of oil."

"I'll help you to climb the wall. It's time to lead the vessel!"

He clasps his hands, weaves his fingers together and makes a platform for me to step on. I climb the wall, the flag in one hand and the banner in the other. I look down to see his face again and I feel that I've seen this person before.

"Haven't I seen you before?" I ask from top of the wall.

"Start your speech; don't delay!"

"But haven't I seen you all my life? What's your name?"

"My name is Mansour, Mansour the Quiltmaker. Now start!"

On the wall, I raise the flag and hold the banner up. Down below the sea of people ebb and flow like the tides of an ocean.

"I'm the gauger. A sailor on the ocean of oil," I shout, addressing people, "I keep vigil all night with the shadows and shapes." My voice is loud and strong, as if it's not my voice, but belongs to many. "I've seen how our black gold flows into the tanks, fills the barrels and the barrels pile up in the ships and go far beyond the oceans to lands you've never seen. They use our black gold and raise their skyscrapers while we live in hovels and holes. I've seen Gas Street, where women—our sisters and mothers—sell their bodies to buy a loaf of bread. I've seen Faithland and the long row of tin and cardboard houses stretched along the open sewers. This must stop! I'm coming from Raz, where I turned the gauge off! No more oil flows into tanks before we form a republic!"

Millions of mouths shout: "Hail to the brave oil man! Hail to the gauger!"

I wave the flag to stop them, because I sense that time is short. "I, the gauger, your sailor, have no fear of tides. I stir and seek the storm. Death to the monarchy!"

"Death to the monarchy!" people repeat.

"Hail to the republic!"

"Hail to the republic!" people shout.

Now a voice, deeper and louder than mine, as if rising from the mouth of all the bearded men shouts from a spot higher than mine. This is Sheikh

421

Ahmad's voice coming from the top of a minaret.

"Look up you believers, you children of God, look at the sky! Your reward is there, not in the dirty oil. What is gold? Black or yellow? These are Satan's toys! Look up, for your savior is coming. And today is the last day of your desperation. The end of your agony. Heaven will be yours!"

The crowd looks up and through the darkest gray clouds of the western horizon, a carpet floats toward them. The closer the flat vessel becomes, the bigger it looks. A frowning sheikh sits cross-legged on the carpet with two men seated on either side of him. Doctor Halal is on the right and a foreigner on the left. They constantly fix the sheikh's turban, comb his beard, wrap his black robe around his shoulders and whisper into his ears. They prepare him to become the Great Leader of the Holy Revolution.

Now as all the heads tilt back and all eyes stare at him, the frowning sheikh waves a stiff hand to the people. His right eyebrow rises slightly in the suggestion of a smile. Millions roar: "Holy Leader, hail, hail! Holy Leader, hail!" And then: "The party one, the party one, the leader one, the chosen one!"

Most of the people kneel down in the oil, bow, and pray, so that only a small group still shout, "Hail to the oil man!"

There is confusion. Anarchy. Some look on top of the wall, where I'm still waving the flag; some who are hypnotized by the sight of the flying carpet and the piercing eyes of the Great Leader, kneel down and bow to him in a trance.

The tides of the dark ocean roar, boil, and bubble. They become monstrous. People strive to save themselves. They swim and struggle, scream for help. The loudest roar is heard from the mountain, as if Alborz is hollering in rage. Avalanches roll down and hit the people. Some drown and some are smashed by the gigantic rocks. Meanwhile the National Guard, led by our cousins Cyrus and Kami, shoot those who try to run into the alleys to save their lives.

The carpet descends and stops close to earth, close enough for Sheikh Ahmad, Salman the Brainless, and a group of armed hooligans to sit on it. They all surround the Great Leader, fanning him, kissing his ring, and whispering into his ears. Uncle Massi, trying to keep his balance, stands on the carpet and recites his longest ode, "Twenty and five passed, the Eastern Sun rose from the horizon of the West/ My heart breaks the prison bars of my chest."

The wide, flat carpet soars, rises higher, and takes Uncle's voice with itself.

It floats toward the peak of Alborz, where on one of the largest rocks, a house and a balcony face the whole land and wait for the Leader.

Meanwhile, down in the ocean of oil, a big transformation happens. The former National Guard changes into the Army of God and attacks the people with scimitars. To the end, though, faithful to their king, Cyrus and Kami shoot themselves in the temples, not to see the blue-uniformed, clean-shaven National Guard changing into black shirts and dark beards.

The Army of God chains Mansour the Quiltmaker, dragging him into a man-made circular stage. The hooded executioner raises his sword and chops off Mansour's limbs one by one. Each time, Mansour screams, "I'm the Hagh!" The executioner chops off all of the quiltmaker's members and his head rolls and stops at the foot of the wall on which I'm still standing. Mansour's eyes search for me, find me, and blink several times. Then his pale lips whisper, "I'm the Hagh." The head dies.

In the chaos and confusion, the members of the Party of God pull black sacks over women's heads, push them into black vans, driving the vans into El-Deen. Some black-sacked women stay in the streets and scream in darkness, but the frightened people don't get close to them.

La-Jay, calling himself "the Great Octopus" and "the Father of El-Deen" returns to the bosom of the white monster, now called "The University of El-Deen: the Gate of Paradise." Ha-G and Sultan join La-Jay to train the unfaithful and lead the infidels and blasphemers back to the road of God.

The bearded men pull Father out of Mother's arms, chain him, and drag him into the prison. They arrest Ilych and others too. Now they take all the monarchists into El-Deen. They make sure all the people who were supposed to be locked up are locked up and then they close the big iron gate and plant a black flag on top of the tower. A big, ugly dog appears out of nowhere, jumping into the ditch of blood to guard the prison and tear up whoever attempts to pass the gate. It's the same filthy dog, Afreet, coming back to life.

I see the old man of the bookstore wandering in the half-deserted street, stopping above each corpse, watching it. Although he is the only man walking and his white hair shines in the last rays of the sun, not even one armed guard notices him. As if he is invisible, he trudges toward the south road, returning to Raz, to his corner bookstore. He turns toward me, and waves to me, a sad smile, stretching his pale lips. I know that he's saying,

"We'll see each other next time, son. The next Revolution!" He walks away slowly, as if in grief. No one sees him.

I sit on top of the wall alone and watch all this. I search for Sahar, but she is lost in the chaos and confusion. Did the Black Flaggers put her in one of those sacks and take her inside El-Deen? Did the white horse of General Nasri take her away again? Did she drown in the black water? Get smashed under an avalanche? I lost her and there is no way for me to know where she is. I sit in oblivion. Who am I? Was the whole thing a dream? Did I find my name and lose it again? Did I ever find it? Does Sahar exist?

The black ocean of oil flows into gigantic barrels and the barrels roll down into ships. The streets are dry now, as if the oil has never flowed in them before. There is a vacant desert below me and I'm the only man left on top of this tall, brick wall. Have they forgotten me? I still have the banner and the flag. I cannot read the words on the banner. They're written in the ancient alphabet I've never learned. The letters look like little nails, miniature hammers, sickles, axes, and screws.

Now I hear a sound, at first faint, then stronger, coming from my right side, then my left side. Swoosh, swoosh... dump! I see Ali the Bricklayer dumping bricks on fresh mortar, raising the wall. His sun-burned face, the horizontal creases of his broad forehead, his wide shoulders, and thick neck all look very much like the man who handed me the banner and flag—the man who was chopped to pieces in front of my eyes, the quiltmaker whose name I've forgotten. Are they twins?

Ali doesn't see me. He keeps working. If I stay where I am, he will bury me under the cold mortar and hot brick. I'll become part of the wall. So I'd better move. But I can't. I stay here and listen to the swoosh, swoosh, and forget everything. The longer I sit, the more I forget. The Revolution? I can not remember. My name? Lost.

Swoosh, swoosh... dump!

Brick on wet mortar.

Swoosh, swoosh... dump!

Oblivion.

Ajooza

One, two, three, four, five, six, seven. Seven single shots behind the wall.

"'Sahar, can you hear this?" I murmur in delirium.

"I can hear the fucking shots. Yes. This means that I've overslept. This is the early-morning execution. This is the weekly Cleaning Up Operation. They hang them every Monday morning and then shoot one bullet in their brains to stop their moaning and wriggling."

Sultan puts on his grizzly gray wig in haste. He tries to get himself into a woman's dress. The wig is tilted and the dress is tight; it wrinkles around his chest and sticks to his crooked back.

"I'm late. I'm fucking late and this is all your fault. Your goddamn fault, Omar! Do you hear me?" Sultan's voice is thin and scratchy like an old woman's.

Did he call me Omar? With unusual clarity I recall the Holy Show. Sultan is acting the role of Ajooza, Caliph Maamoon's mean agent, and I'm supposed to be her son, Omar. Saboor was Omar and I remember what happened to him. If Kamal doesn't show up this minute, I'll be smashed under Ajooza's feet. She will use me as a trampoline. After all, this is Sultan's real speciality and the reason he is called the Asscracker.

"Okay, I'm ready, Omar! You know the plot already, don't you?" he says with his thin voice. "I'll wrap this white sheet around you like a shroud and you act dead. Okay? You'll be dead and ready to go to your grave. But when I'll ask the Eighth Holy One to recite the prayer of death for you, you'll have to get up and scream, 'I'm alive!' This way we'll discredit the Holy One and Maamoon will cancel the coronation. Understood?"

She doesn't wait for an answer. She pulls me off the chair and drags me by my collar on the floor. My body is numb from hours of sitting motionless. But my soles are burning again. My shirt and pants are stiff as cardboard. Ajooza wraps me hastily in a large, white sheet. She is behind schedule. In a minute, she'll start to kick and then she'll use me as her trampoline.

Kamal, if you're coming at all, come now! The effect of that fucking injection, whether it was drug, vitamin, or penicillin, is gone. Kamal, don't let me break for feeling physical pain. Come and save my soul!

"Okay, you're wrapped now, Omar! When I kick you in your belly, it

425

means that you have to get up and say, 'I'm alive!' Ready? All right. The Eighth Holy One is reciting the prayer of death for you: 'Bla bla bla—bla bla bla bl—'"

"I can't!" I hear myself screaming. Ajooza's sharp pointed shoe pierces my abdomen. I know that I have to get up and say that I'm alive. But I don't know how to do it. I'm all wrapped in a shroud and the sheet is tighter than a straightjacket. I can't get up and she keeps kicking. Now she alternates her right and left foot, kicking my right and left sides.

"You dumb-ass bastard, motherfucking pimp! Didn't I tell you to get up and scream, 'I'm alive!'? Did I, or didn't I?" She kicks me more.

"I'm alive! I'm alive! I'm alive!" I scream and roll on the floor so as not to let her jump over me. But the more I roll, the madder she becomes, trying to step on my chest. "I'm alive!" I scream and feel her high heels on my ribs.

"Stop! This is an order!"

Ajooza gets off my chest and turns to the door. She freezes.

Bloody vomit creeps out of my mouth. I can't wipe it. I struggle to stay conscious and see Kamal. He won! He won! This is all I repeat in my head and dance with joy in my tight shroud.

"The order comes from the central core of the Holy Revolutionary Party, the Party of the Immortals." Kamal says in an authoritative tone. "I'm Kamal the Immortal, the Thirteenth Holy One, the Everlasting One, the leader of the Holy Internal War. This is the warrant for your arrest, Sultan." Kamal shows Sultan a piece of paper. Sultan stares at Kamal and the two guards behind him; he is not able to move. His wig has slid and is hanging on his ear. "Open the sack, Brothers, and let Sultan see his old friend."

The guards open a burlap sack and the headless torso of Ha-G the Shit Mouth rolls out and lands at Sultan's foot. Blood has dried on the hunched torso.

"His personal bodyguard chopped his head off and joined us," Kamal says. "Ha-G was the most polluted element in El-Deen. May justice be restored after we throw him into the trashcan of history. Now, it's your turn, Sultan the Ass! Your bloody government of this filthy barbershop is over. Handcuff him, Brothers, and take him to the west wing of the fifth floor where the corrupted and disobedient elements are waiting for their trial."

"But who said I'm disobedient, Your Holiness? I'm your humble servant.

I'll do whatever you say! Our Holy Revolution needs young forces like your Holiness! I'm with you, sir!" Sultan in Ajooza's attire pleads like the old servant, Abasel. "Brother!" He goes on, "Traitors and infidels are behind this wall. Please remove the screen and see for yourself!" Sultan takes a step toward the opaque glass wall.

"Don't move! Stay here!" Kamal orders. "Brothers, go behind the screen and see what's going on!"

"They killed a virgin, sir! This is what you should call treason and disobedience. Imbeciles!"

Kamal's guards remove the screen and unhook the woman from the ceiling. They drag her corpse to the front. She is yellow. A shade of yellow I've never seen before. Shadowed by gray. Is this the color we become after death? Her face, breasts, hips, and thighs are covered with patches of purple and blue. Her hair is dark and long, wet with blood. The guards try to shove her in the same burlap sack Ha-G's torso is in. It doesn't take much effort. The woman is tiny. The size of a twelve-year-old.

Now they handcuff the two sleepy torturers and find a bottle beside them; they hand it to Kamal.

"They have drunk wine, Brother!" One of the guards says.

"That's why they fell asleep!" Sultan says. "Execute them!" That's what the Holy Law says.

"Brother! Have mercy on us!" One of the sleepy torturers pleads. His hair is standing up. "We drank the damn thing to be able to remove the girl's virginity. Neither of us could do it in our right mind, Brother. She was wild, slippery, like a fish. She wouldn't stop biting and kicking. We knew it was the greatest sin to drink alcohol, but we did it for the sake of our job. Our duty. Forgive us, Brother! We may deserve lashes for our stupidity, but nothing more."

"Execute them!" Sultan screams in Ajooza's voice.

"Handcuff this old bastard too!" Kamal orders the guards.

Now Sultan's different personalities act at the same time in chaos and confusion. While Kamal is trying to lift me up, Sultan talks like the good-hearted barber, trying to convince Kamal that he is being manipulated by evil forces.

"My dear sir! My Holiness! Listen to your humble servant! This is not *your* Holy Internal War, this seems to be Doctor Halal's coup d'etat. Don't you know this man, your Holiness? He is the real traitor to our faith and our religion. He is a spy, sir! I can see him standing in the hall, waiting for you to arrest the most humble servant of the Revolution. I spent twenty years of my fucking life in the Damned Monarch's prison. I'm a devotee, a selfless slave. Listen to me, Brother Kamal! You have a good heart and they're using you as a puppet!"

But Kamal doesn't even turn to look at Sultan. He is trying to unwrap my shroud, which has stuck to my clothes and doesn't come off.

Now Sultan pleads like the cunning compromiser, Abasel. "Please! Your Holiness! I'll kiss your feet! I'll become your personal slave!" And a second later, when the guards straightjacket him, his temper changes and he becomes the cruel gardener. "Let me go! Let me go, you bastards! I'm going to call my sons to throw you out of my property! Hey, help! Help!" Now he uses his screechy voice and curses the way Ajooza would, "Motherfuckers! This is a coup d'etat against our Holy Caliph! Fuck you all!" And when they lift him up to prevent him from kicking with his high heels, he becomes Sultan, who, with his thickest voice hollers, "I am Sultan the Asscracker, the longest arm of the Great Octopus. I'm the king!"

The guards squeeze Ajooza's wig into a ball, shove it into Sultan's mouth, and take the many-headed monster away.

The Final Destination

"Well, little brother, didn't I tell you just save your soul and I would come and take you out?" Kamal smiles, lifts me up with the white sheet still rolled around me and lies me carefully on the chair like a newborn baby. "A Holy War is going on in El-Deen now; we're purging the corrupt elements. But the bastards, the followers of Ha-G and of Sultan, are fighting back. Early this morning they executed seven Unbreakables. La-Jay wanted them alive. They were in cell four for a long time. The bastards did that to take revenge. This is a real war, brother, and unfortunately the trainees' lives are in danger, too. They'll kill whoever they get their hands on."

"Kamal," I murmur, "Who was the girl? Who was the virgin? A dancer?" I remember my hallucination, the way I journeyed with the transparent girl through the Revolution.

"Don't cry, brother, she wasn't a dancer. She was a teacher. A high school teacher or something. She was arrested not long ago for brainwashing her students against the Holy Republic. May her soul rest in heaven. She died a virgin and in spite of her sins, she's living in heaven now. Don't worry for her. Worry for yourself, brother. You've become so weak—a cry baby!"

"Her name? What was her name?"

"Who knows, brother? If she was a member of a Satanic underground party, she probably had a fake name. Now look who is here!"

I look over Kamal's shoulder and see Doctor Halal entering the room.

"Without my brother's generous help, we couldn't have arrested the old Asscracker and saved you!" Kamal says. "Brother Halal got the warrant of arrest from La-Jay. You owe your life to him, little brother! You do remember the good doctor, don't you?"

I nod and look at Halal through a foggy screen. He smiles at me. His smile reminds me of when I was lying on a gurney in the Clinic and he injected a drug into my veins while lecturing to his invisible colleagues. I was his guinea pig, then and he kept smiling at me. I remember that I yelled at him and called him a traitor. Then during my interrogation, he tip-toed into the room, while Ha-G was out, injected drugs into my vein, encouraging me to dream aloud. I always had a feeling that Halal was more cunning than Ha-G, whose only method was whipping. Is Kamal working for Halal now? Who is Halal working for?

"Brother Kamal told me that you prefer to stay in cell number four, where the Unbreakables are," Doctor Halal says with a pleasant smile. "It sure is the most appropriate place for you. You deserve the title. You are strong and brave. A true son of our county, a real brother. I want to assure you that whatever has happened to you has been a big misunderstanding and this gang of traitors are responsible for all the damages you have suffered." He smiles again, pushes his glasses up and continues. "El-Deen is a Holy University, as our Father, La-Jay believes, not a prison. All we want here is knowledge and all we give is education. I'll do my best to serve this Holy purpose—Education!" He searches around the room and finds what he wants. He picks up Sultan's tape recorder and puts it in his gown's large pocket. "I'll send a doctor to examine you. We have to treat you as soon as possible. Look what this savage has done to you!"

Now Kamal hangs me on his shoulder like old times and walks in the hallway toward cell number four. I whisper in his ear, "Kamal, save your soul! Think about what the Last Holy One said, 'To be able to see straight, without overlooking the twists, turns, and zigzags of reality!'"

But Kamal thinks that I'm hallucinating. He is in a rush to go and fight his Holy Internal War. He keeps assuring me that the complete process of purification won't take that long, and he will get rid of the dangerous elements. Then he praises Halal the way I've never heard him praising anyone—even the Holy Leader, himself.

"Doctor Halal is the most peaceful man I've ever seen, brother," he tells me. "After the Great Leader Himself, Halal is the role model for our nation. Believe me. I'm getting to know him better now. A true believer. But refined, brother. Refined. The way a real man of God must be. He's not crude and cruel like Ha-G and Sultan. He is sensitive and sophisticated.

"Here, brother. At last we reached your final home, the home you sought all the time: cell number four, Hall Twenty—the cell of the Unbreakables. Do you remember what you went through to get here? Kamal the Immortal is a grateful man. You helped me to achieve immortality and I promised to take you here. I won't let you rot in this cell, though. I have a feeling, a premonition, that I'll get more power. All the fucking power!" He clenches his big fist and lowers his voice. "Let me become the Octopus, then I'll set you free, my friend. Free as a dove! Here, take this number. You've got to have a number here."

This is a piece of cardboard, some kind of identification card or a ticket. It says, 20-4-37. Now with the white shroud still hanging on me, soiled with blood and vomit, I step inside a small cell, fully lit by strong fluorescent light. All I see is the blinding light. Everything is blurred. How many inmates are here? Two? Twenty? I can't tell. Kamal pats my shoulder for the last time and locks the door behind me. I lean my back against the iron door and address my invisible comrades, "I'm one of you, friends! An Unbreakable!"

Chapter 7

The Unbreakables

Under nine layers of illusion, whatever the light,
on the face of any object, in the ground itself,
I see your face.
—Rumi

Agha, Ismail, and Shams

Sahar is on the wall with the banner and the flag. I'm in the desert at the ditch—a river now. The crimson water rolls along the bed of stone. Bloody tides hit the rocks, flow and foam. Ali the Bricklayer is raising the wall: swoosh... swoosh... dump! Swoosh... swoosh... dump!

"Sahar, jump down!" I scream. "You'll get buried inside the wall! Throw yourself down!" But the loud roar of the river covers my voice.

"We have a little sister... and she has no breasts..." a voice says.

Sahar stands erect, swinging the flag with one hand, raising the banner with another. Both the flag and the banner are blood-wet, crimson, as if soaked in the river.

The wall is raised. Sahar's feet are mortar, her ankles, hard bricks. I feel the flow of cool, damp mortar in my own veins. Sahar sighs in my head, "Oh! my dancer's feet!"

"What shall we do for our sister... if she be a wall..." a voice says.

I scream, "Sahar, throw yourself down, before it's too late!" But she doesn't hear me; she waves the blood-dripping flag in the stagnant air.

I look at Mount Alborz and call the north wind, "Saba! Come and bring her down!" But the mountain is still and there is no breeze. I try to breath, but either the air is dense, or my lungs have shrunken like old balloons.

"Sahar," I whisper and it's too late. Her olive-colored calves, her thighs all up to her small hips, are part of the wall.

"We have a little sister and she is a wall!" a voice says and makes me weep.

When her breasts become bricks and she is about to lose her arms, she throws the flag and banner down. I try to catch them, but they fall in the

431

river and float away with the tide. I watch them—the flag and the banner—now under the waves of blood, now over, now wrapped around a rock, now unwrapped. They are torn to pieces in the bloody bed; they turn into small, red particles, the same nature as the river, one with the river and lost in it.

I look up. Sahar is the wall. Brick and mortar.

All is left of my sister is a pair of large eyes in the wall, gazing at the desert. But the eyes are alive, shiny stars glitter in the depths of the irises, as if all is not as murky and dark, as hopeless and final, as it looks.

I turn my back to the wall and walk toward the cemetery. A voice, her voice and not hers, echoes in the desert, "I am a wall, and my breasts like the towers." I weep in despair, lost among the graves.

"He's coming to."

"Let me cover him."

I feel a cool, caressing sensation on my chest, a warm and soothing hand on my forehead. Now the warm hand holds my hand, gives it a friendly squeeze. I open my eyes. Two faces bend over me, two masks out of a dream: clean-shaven scalps, lifeless faces on thin wobbling necks. One mask is yellow and wrinkled, with a pair of lentil-colored eyes without eyelashes, blinking fast beneath two pale eyebrows. The other face is dark brown, lined with creases. Under thick, connected eyebrows that form an inevitable frown, a pair of charcoal black eyes, shadowed by thick lashes, look at me piercingly.

The pale mask introduces the dark one. "This is Ismail, Ismail the Baluch. He just covered you with his scarf."

I glance at my chest and find a thin white cloth covering me like a sheet. I realize that I'm lying down on a cot. When I breath, my ribs scream with pain. I hold my breath and now I hear a military march I have heard many times before.

I'm in El-Deen.

"We washed your clothes and the shroud the bastard wrapped you in," Ismail, the dark mask with piercing eyes, says. "They'll dry in a short while. We call this old fellow, Agha—the Master," he pats on the pale man's shoulder, "because he is the chief here. He knows things that even the devil doesn't know. But who knows who he really is!" Ismail says.

"Was," Agha says. "Who he really was."

All this time the man who is called Agha holds my right hand in his. His hand is hot, as if he is burning with fever. Isn't this the same hand I held once in the hallways and once in the interrogation room? Hasn't this hand touched my forehead before?

"I know you," I say. "I used to know you. But I don't remember when."

"Neither do I. And so much the better," Agha says. "Let's not remember when, what, or who. It's not necessary. Oblivion, oh, sweet oblivion!" he sings.

"Come now! Don't start singing your oblivion song again," Ismail says. "I'm a man of the mountains. I know who I am, why I'm here, and when they brought me. I have all the answers for myself. I'm here in this cell because I helped some young people cross the border of the country and I refuse to tell these Godless bastards who they were. I refuse to tell them anything!"

"Ismail claims that he hasn't lost his memory," Agha says. "He is a stubborn Baluch. I have lost mine, and he has lost his," he points to the left wall. "This man is Shams. I have named him Shams—the Sufi's beloved. 'Shams' means sun. Are you familiar with literature, my friend?" But he doesn't wait for my answer. He goes on, "Shams cannot talk. Or maybe he can, but has decided not to. He barely eats anything. Murmurs his lines, all day and night."

I look at Shams, lying on the floor, against the wall, staring at a vague spot on the ceiling with one eye open. The other eye is closed. Blind? His lips move, saying something. The open eye is sunken, deep in the sockets, framed by a purple circle. The man's thick lips are purple too. His bumpy head is shaved. A noisy march on TV covers Shams' voice. But when the noise stops for a few seconds, I hear him murmuring, "What shall we do for our sister... if she be a wall." This voice was in my dream. Sahar was on top of the wall. She became the wall. I was in the desert, desperate. I headed toward the graveyard. All this comes to my mind in a sudden flash. I close my eyes and say, "I dreamed."

"You'll tell us your dream tonight. If you want to," Agha says. "Every night, after dinner, we chat. Ismail tells real stories—or stories that he claims to be real—and I make his stories into pure fiction. Sometimes we play a game. We make a story together. Now you'll dream for us. I'm sure Ismail will turn your dreams into real incidents so that I can create a fiction out of them.

Our triangle is perfect. And Shams of course. His lines will be the refrains of our narrative."

"You see, here we talk a lot," Agha goes on, "we don't have anything else to do. Every now and then, they take us to the Black Box, the Clinic, another interrogation, next door to Sultan's barbershop, or to the Community Center. They give us a massage for a change, or lock us up in the Hothouse. We don't talk about all this. We stick to our own stories."

"Once in a while, there is the Cleaning Up Operation," Ismail says. "You need to know about this, brother. It can happen to any of us. At any moment," Ismail says.

"You are Unbreakables!" I murmur, realizing exactly where I am.

"You too!" Agha squeezes my hand. "Welcome to cell number four. Yesterday we were ten. They executed seven of us. Three are left. With you, we're four."

"They come and go," Ismail says. "The Unbreakables. God only knows how many people we've seen here. There was a time when we were thirty inmates in this little room. We slept on our sides, like Sardines in a can. Still there was not enough room. I remember a few inmates volunteered to stand up all night and sleep later, during the day."

"I don't remember this, Ismail!" Agha says.

"You don't? It was a while ago."

"A while?" Agha asks with genuine surprise. His small eyes become larger. "I don't know how long a while is. It can be only a few days, or many years. Who knows? We mark the days by Shams' repertoire. One day is Solomon Day, the other day is Sufi Day. On Solomon Day, Shams recites the Song of Songs, on Sufi Day he chants Rumi's quatrains. Today is a Solomon Day. You see, we don't mark the days by the prison's lentil soup and rice pudding, which they claim they alternate. Because I'm sure they don't always alternate. To confuse us about the days, they feed us lentil soup for a couple a days and rice pudding the third day. Rice pudding again and again, and then lentil soup." Agha says all this and stares at me. Confused.

"We could mark the days by the TV programs," Ismail says. " But we have covered the screen so as not to see their shitty faces."

I glance at the TV set hanging from the ceiling at the right corner of the cell. A gray shirt covers the screen.

"We can't do anything about the sound," Ismail explains. "It doesn't have a switch. Many inmates have gone crazy because of this constant noise. We call it Satan's Box. Satan's Box has broken some of the Unbreakables!"

"Neither can we mark the days by the executions," Agha says, still staring at a spot above my head, "which happen frequently behind this wall. Because they don't always schedule them early mornings; they kill people any time of the day. Once it was sunset."

"How did you know it was sunset?" Ismail asks.

"Because Shams got to the point where the poet says, 'I sought him, but I found him not...'" He sighs, squeezes my hand, and his mask like face stretches into a big smile. "Do you know your name, son?" He asks gently.

"No," I say. "I got close to it at one point in Sultan's room, but then I lost it again."

"That's all right! It comes with Unbreakability. We all push the memories back. Except Ismail, of course, who is an exception!"

"I'm not an exception!" Ismail protests. "I'm a man of desert, duststorm, horseback, and gun! I don't forget! I cannot forget!" He gets up, stretches himself and moves his long arms in the air for exercise. He is tall and slim. I picture him with thick beard and black moustache, wearing a Baluchi turban, riding on a horse.

Agha joins him in the exercise. He is short and stooped, gray from head to foot. I feel that I've seen him all my life. Didn't he used to wear a suit three sizes larger than him and ride an old bicycle? But that old man barely talked; this one is eloquent. Agha's pants are large too. He keeps pulling them up. While exercising, his small gray head wobbles on his body. He looks like an old bird with all the feathers shaved. A bald, clawless bird.

Even in the ugly gray pajamas, Ismail is handsome. He looks erect and proud. But he is not rough. I sense a hidden source, a mysterious fountain somewhere inside his body that can make him cry all the waters of the world. I've seen him breaking into sobs in the past. Not for himself, for someone he loved.

Now, they both touch their toes with fingertips and stretch their backs. They hop and open their legs, hop and close their legs. I remember my dead friend Ilych, when he exercised. I sigh and feel the human mortality deep in the marrow of my bones. Was it just two or three days ago that Ilych and I ate, talked, and slept in cell eleven? He told me the story of Turniphead and taught me how to pray without knowing the words. I'll become attached to these people too. Then they'll die.

I close my eyes and wish for death. I'm not capable anymore of knowing people, loving them, and losing them forever. I have a feeling that I've lost Kamal too. I'll never walk in the corridors with him. But who knows? Is there any law governing all this? I may walk in the hallways again. I may find someone who has been lost. The only definite thing is death. The dead will never come back to life. This is the law. Sahar, if alive, may be found again; if dead, she's gone forever.

"I sought him, but found I him not..." Shams recites.

The poet must have been after a dead one, I think. If the beloved was alive, he would've found him.

Dinner Around the White Scarf

We sit cross-legged on the floor around Ismail's white scarf, now serving as our tablecloth. Shams doesn't join us. He cannot sit. His spine is damaged. In Sultan's room, they hung him from the ceiling for too long. He cannot use the cot either. He has to lie down on the hard floor all the time. Ismail and Agha feed him and help him to sit on the toilet. He screams with pain when he sits for a short time.

A guard opens the door and slides a tray in. No one can see his face. I notice a large gold ring on his index finger with a carnelian stone, sacred words carved on it. The tray contains four plastic bowls of lentil soup.

I can't stay cross-legged. My feet are bandaged and I have a tight wrap around my waist too. When I breath or swallow, a sharp pain pierces my chest and back. Agha tells me that tonight is my second night in cell number four. I've been sleeping for more than twenty-four hours. Doctor Halal himself came to the cell and treated me. When Halal's name is mentioned, I ask if a tall guard was with him. He says no.

I'm an Unbreakable now. Achieved my goal, reached my destination, my final home. Now I want more. I want to get out. Clean. As an Unbreakable. What if Kamal succeeds in his coup? Will he set me free? What if Doctor Halal is controlling Kamal and won't let him contact me?

Agha talks with his gentle voice. I miss most of what he says.

"—the noblemen used to sit on the stage. Can you believe this, Ismail?

Right where the actors were acting."

"But I've never seen a stage, brother," Ismail says. "I can't picture what you're saying." He takes a big sip of his soup.

"Yes you have seen one, Ismail, in the Community Center. We were together, don't you remember? We watched that lousy show, the Holy One and the Caliph and so on and so forth, remember?"

"Oh, that!"

"But bear in mind that that stage was an arena stage. The stage I'm talking about is a proscenium." Agha tilts the bowl and takes the last sip of the watery soup, cleaning his lips with the back of his hand.

"Make your point, brother. So what? The noblemen sat on the stage and watched the show—" Ismail says impatiently.

"You don't let me finish, Ismail. My point is that the ordinary people stood in the hall. Get me? Stood!"

"Well, in my village, whenever there is a Holy Show, they put the best cushioned chairs for the mayor and the mullah, right where the actors are acting, and the rest of the people stand around. It's the same thing, isn't it?" Ismail says, smacking his tongue and licking the inside of his bowl.

"You gave me an excellent subject to study, Ismail. I appreciate this. A comparative study," Agha says. "Now I'll be busy for the next few days. I'm going to ask you more questions about these village shows. I only wish I had paper and pen."

"Have you been a university professor?" I ask Agha.

"Oh, no. I don't think so. Absolutely not," he says, rubbing his bald head absentmindedly.

"Tonight he talks about stage," Ismail says, "Tomorrow he'll interpret the Bible, the night after, he'll read something by heart in a weird language. Only God knows who this man is. The devil himself? But even if he's the devil, I love him and I'm his disciple!" He laughs and shakes his head.

"Okay, it's our chat time now," Agha announces. He claps his hands as if calling for attention in his class. "Ismail, go ahead and feed our friend. Shams sleeps after his dinner. He sleeps early and wakes up very early. Tomorrow we have a Sufi Day. We'll wake up with this line: 'Late by myself, in the boat of myself—' it's a strange line. Isn't it? Our body as a boat. Just imagine! And late... and alone..." He stares at me, completely lost, as if he's fallen in a deep black hole. He searches for something in his head; he cannot remember.

He gives up. Now he continues, "Ismail and I sit here and chat until the Satan's Box plays the last anthem. These days are the days of their anniversary, they celebrate how they dismembered the people's Revolution. They kill one zillion sheep and one zillion cows and eat all day and night. They play their stupid anthem one zillion times a day. It's hard to figure which one is the last anthem—probably the one they finally shut up after— but only for a short time. Sometimes Ismail and I talk until morning and when Shams wakes up with his song, we realize that we have confused the last anthem. But who cares? We take a nap during the day, or several naps. Days are long. We get tired of talking too."

"Now what, Master?" Ismail asks. He has finished feeding Shams and is wrapping the white cloth that served as my sheet and tablecloth around his bare head. He ties it twice, makes a big knot above his ear, and leaves the corners hanging down, Baluchi style. In contrast to the white turban, Ismail's eyes glow like black gems.

I look at Ismail with admiration; I read the lines of his face, memorizing him. But perhaps I have already memorized them before and I'm just recalling. Now I notice the picture of a green peacock embroidered on the corner of Ismail's scarf. Cold sweat wets my armpits, bubbling on my forehead. My mouth dries up, my tongue feels heavy and sticks to the roof of my mouth.

"What are you staring at?" Ismail asks.

"Your scarf!" I mumble. "It belonged to my great-grandmother, and—"

"And what?" Ismail asks.

"I'm not sure. I'm confused. Maybe I've dreamed about this scarf. Maybe I've never seen it in real life—"

"It's very possible that you've seen it on Ismail before," Agha says. "You may have been in this cell many times, my friend. You don't remember; Ismail doesn't remember either. Because of so many times lying in the Black Box. We tend not to talk about the Box, but that's where all our memories go." He pauses and then continues absentmindedly, "I've put a theory together, listen!" He hugs his knees and squeezes himself into a gray ball. "What if there is a circular movement here?" With his index finger he draws a circle in the air. "I mean what if they've designed this tour to drive us out of our minds. I'm not talking about anything supernatural. Do you follow me?"

I nod. But I'm not quite sure what he means.

"The Black Box, the hallways, the cell. The Box, the hallways, the cell. A full circle. But each time you go to the Box, you lose part of your memory. At the end you're empty. Blank. Then they may stop the tour." He glances at Shams.

"But he's not blank," I protest. "He remembers all these—"

"—lines of poetry. These are all he remembers," Agha interrupts me. "These are what he repeats to himself each time he is locked up in the Box. And yet, they keep him here; they don't send him to the Psychiatric Wing," he says.

"Do you think he belongs there?" I ask.

"I don't know. Oftentimes I wonder where the boundary is and how one defines it." He stares at me. "They might be waiting for him to forget his last lines."

"He won't!" Ismail says angrily.

"By reciting them day and night he's resisting, struggling." Agha says, looking at Shams. "I pay close attention every day to see if he's missing some lines."

"Has he missed?" I ask.

"He has. Like an old tape that gradually goes blank. There are some gaps."

There is silence for a long moment, then Agha starts again. "Without the Black Box, the tour would be bearable. You don't put a live human being in a coffin, do you? They didn't do this in medieval times. The Inquisition."

"First I close my eyes," Ismail murmurs and closes his eyes. "I know it's stupid. What difference does it make? If your eyes are open or closed? It's total darkness." He looks at me, his chestnut brown face suddenly ashen.

"Are you sure you want to talk about this, Ismail?" Agha asks.

"Yes. Let me talk about it, Master. Now that you brought it up, I want to talk about it. "I'm in the Box. It's the size of a coffin, with tiny holes on the lid. They don't want me to suffocate. My hands are on my chest. I feel my heartbeats. I close my eyes and pray. I whisper all the prayers I've ever learned. 'In the Name of God, the Compassionate, the Merciful!... I seek refuge in the Lord of Daybreak from the mischief of His Creation; from the mischief of the night when she spreads her darkness; from the mischief of conjuring witches...' When I'm through, I start all over. I concentrate on him. Allah. Because if I think about something else, anything, I'll feel my legs, my arms, my head, and I'll need to move them. But can I move them? No. For how long? As long as they wish. Or maybe they'll forget me altogether. Who cares?"

Ismail wipes his sweat off. His long hands shake.

"Then the needs. I wet myself—I pray to Allah—I cry—I pray—I vomit and swallow it back—I vomit again, I try not to swallow it—I cough—I pray, 'the mischief of His Creation—the mischief of night—' I seek refuge in you, God. You are the Compassionate, the Merciful! But He doesn't hear me. Take me, Allah! I cry. But he doesn't take me. My heart beats. Beats and beats. It can beat forever. I pray for death. For sleep. A long one. But I stay awake. Alive and awake. In a dark coffin. Now I forget my prayers and just repeat his name, 'Allah! Allah! Allah!' But he is not there. He is nowhere."

Ismail covers his eyes with his scarf. He weeps.

Shams is asleep. He mumbles something in his dream. The words of his endless poems. But jumbled in confusion.

"Okay, cheer up now!" Agha jumps on his feet. "Enough of this gloom! We're under this blinding light. The TV is on. The sound of the War. We have enough space to move in and even to exercise. We have a toilet right here. To pee. A sink—a real luxury! A cot, in case we want to lie down. We have each other. We can talk or not talk. We're free to sleep or not sleep. Spit in the toilet and flush, spit and not flush. Or not spit at all. We can somersault, do acrobatics. We can tell a story, make one, mix a real one with a made up one. We're free to act out our stories, dramatize them. We can make long stories and memorize them. Or, we can forget them all. In short, we are free! We have enough sanity and we're not alone. Now let me tell you an anecdote!"

Pacing up and down the cell, Agha starts his anecdote. He almost acts out the scene. His body becomes light and flexible, like a young actor's. "This psychiatrist has a patient who believes he is a bone. Yes, a big piece of old bone." He opens his arms wide to show the size of the bone. "The doctor treats his patient for a long time and finally one day he asks him, 'Do you still think that you're a bone?' 'No, doctor, I'm not a bone anymore. I'm a human being now.' 'Great! Excellent!' The doctor pats his patient on the shoulder, 'You are cured. I'll go to my office to sign up your papers. You can go home.' But the moment the doctor leaves the room, the patient hollers and screams and runs around the room." Now Agha runs around the cell, acting as the patient. "The doctor opens the door and says, 'Didn't you say you're not a bone anymore?' The patient pants and answers, 'Yes, But the dogs don't know that. They're chasing me!'" Agha laughs at his own joke. His heavy head wobbles, his face flushes crimson. Ismail raises his head and smiles faintly. He has heard this before.

Aroose

Under the blinding light, Agha is fast asleep. Tonight is his turn to sleep on the cot. He has covered his eyes with a piece of rag and curled up like a baby. His hands rest between his thighs. He snores. Ismail sits at the right wall, under the hanging TV. He has covered his face with the white scarf. I can see the green peacock. I lie down on a blanket in the middle of the cell. I've rolled Sultan's white shroud, now washed and dried, into a pillow. The toilet bowl is right above my head. I can't sleep. The odor bothers me. I move further back—closer to the cot. Now Agha blows his breath into my face. I'm sleepless. The incandescent light, the never-dying light of the fluorescent bulbs drive me crazy. I miss a black blindfold around my eyes. Kamal's scarf.

Shams mumbles meaningless words. His legs jerk. His face twitches. I crawl toward Ismail and sit beside him, watching him for a while.

"Ismail!" I whisper. I know he is not asleep. "I need to talk to you."

He removes the scarf, looking at me. "Humm?" he inquires. His eyebrows tangle.

"Did I wake you up, or—"

"I was on my horse. On Soluch. We were on top of Mount Solomon, looking at the dry valley. I was debating whether to pass the border and find her, or not," he says and stares at me. "I frequently passed the border, you know. The eastern border. I was a smuggler."

"You were?"

"All my life. Opium. Then it happened that I smuggled people. This one was not for money. At first it was, but then it wasn't."

"Ismail, where did you find this scarf?" I touch the embroidered peacock with the tip of my finger, barely, as if it's about to fly away. "Since I've seen it, I feel confused. Where did you find this?"

"I didn't find it. It was a present. Aroose gave it to me." He sits up now, leaning back against the wall. "Aroose is the lady I was just thinking about. I was thinking about all those days that I sat on the horse, looking down at the valley, debating whether to pass the border and find her, or not. But then what? Just to see her one more time?" He sighs. "I never knew her name. So, I called her Aroose—bride. Forty-nine hours and forty-five minutes. This is the time I spent with my bride."

"Where?" I ask, without thinking how private this memory for Ismail can be. "Where, Ismail? Trust me. I won't tell anyone."

"Oh, everybody knows this. I've told my story to my cellmates many times. It's a legend now. Agha has already made several 'fictions' with it. They know too." He glances up at the TV set. "The bastards know. And that's why I'm here. But I don't know Aroose's real name. They don't believe me. They want the real name."

"Who was she, Ismail? This is important to me. I can't tell you how. It's a long story, very long. I've forgotten most of it. But if you tell me who Aroose was, I may remember something."

"An old friend of mine, a Baluch who had gone to the capital to become a factory worker, found me a juicy job, as he called it. This fellow Baluch was a former tenant of this old man. A very old man who was called Doctor. The doctor lived in an old house in a run-down neighborhood very close to where we are now. When I went there for the deal, the doctor took me up on the roof of his old house, pointed his finger to the north, where the top of a white building showed among tall trees, and said, 'This is El-Deen, my friend, the central prison. I've already lost two dear ones to the monster and I don't want to lose more.' Then he took me downstairs to a small room that looked like a storage room with black curtains all around. He said he took films out of his camera there, that's why the curtains where black. Then he locked the door behind us and talked to me."

I hold my breath and listen. I'm in the dark room, smelling wet papers, onions, paper money, the old wood of the ancient abacus. Sahar is breathing beside me.

"The old doctor asked me if I was willing to make some money. I said, why not? What was the deal? He said that I had to take someone over the border of the country—her life was in danger. There were two, a woman and a child. He said if they take the woman to El-Deen, they'll take the child too. He said they torture the female prisoners in front of their children. To break them.

He said they raise the children to become torturers. And all this time his old voice was shaking and his crooked fingers were trembling. I looked at his dark face—wrinkled and full of the tiny holes of smallpox. I liked him. He had lived a long life.

"We negotiated the money, and I accepted the deal. He went to another storage room, a smaller one, where his money was hanging in small purses from the ceiling. He laughed and said that was to protect his bills from the rats. He gave me a down payment. He promised the rest when the passengers were safe in a neighboring country.

"We planned to disguise the lady as a Baluchi bride, in a long native dress. I would travel with her as her husband. I'd take her to the mountains, where we would stay in the shepherd's hut (a friend of mine) and wait for an opportunity to pass the border. The problem was her baby. A one-and-a-half year-old. Still sucking the breast.

"But everything went well. She acted as my wife for forty-nine hours and forty-five minutes." Ismail stops.

"What did she look like?"

"To me?"

"To you."

"She was small. A little wild thing. Didn't know fear. She was fast. Wrapped the baby on her back and walked through the desert with me. She walked faster than me, almost jumped over the ditches, like a deer or something. This was a minefield, brother—I had to ask her all the time to be more cautious. To pass the border, she dressed like a man. Looked like a little boy, her hair tucked in a hat. She had thick dark hair. I saw how she made it into braids and hid them in a hat. She wrapped this white scarf around her neck. When I led her to the other side, and she was safe, when it was time to say good-bye, she gave me this scarf. She wrapped it around my neck with her own hands and kissed me. Here on this spot." Ismail points to his cheek. "No woman had ever kissed me there. Not even my wife." He says this and tears bubble in his eyes.

"I sat on Soluch," Ismail goes on, "on the peak of Mount Solomon, so many dawns, thinking about Aroose, debating whether I should cross the border and find her again. Find her for what? Just to see her one more time. But I never did. I lost her forever."

Above us the TV plays the anthem—the last anthem, or one of the many anthems before the last one of the day: "The enemy must know that we are the roaring sea—." Ismail and I sit facing each other—I, gazing at his dark irises searching for more, and he, stealing his eyes from me, sealing his lips. In this strange game of hide and seek, we remain quiet for a long while.

"Are you satisfied?" He asks finally.

"Yes. Thank you."

"Do you know her?"

"No."

"Her husband was already arrested. They were after her. I never knew what she had done. We never talked about those things. That little boy took most of our time. He had a funny name, Saba. She said it was the wind's name. She said the only reason she was convinced to leave the country was to find a safe place for her son."

I wish I could withdraw from Ismail, creep into a corner and live with what I know. I want to put the pieces together. She has returned. Not as a dancer. As an activist. She married. There, or here. A little baby. Saba. The Revolution. The husband arrested. She was convinced to cross the border. By Grandfather. Who else? Now she is somewhere safe. All this is enough for the rest of my life. But now Ismail wants to talk more.

"Then after Aroose, I helped more people across. I imagined that they were all her friends and I was doing this for her. I didn't take money from them. By the way, I went to the old doctor and returned his down-payment. He couldn't understand why."

"You fell in love with her, Ismail."

"In forty-nine hours and forty-five minutes?"

"It can happen in an instant, brother."

"I had a wife. Aroose had a husband."

"This can happen too."

"I don't know if it is called love. But I think about her. Every single day of my life. Here, in El-Deen. I imagine her husband. I think that he must be somewhere close to me. This gives me strength. He can't be an ordinary prisoner—Aroose's husband. He must be one of the Unbreakables. So, I study every single man who comes here. Is this him? No, it can't be. He is too old for her. Is this him? No, he is not handsome enough. I live with her, brother. This is the secret of my survival in El-Deen."

"I know what you mean."

"I could be a happy man. Content. Even here in El-Deen, living with her image, if one thing wouldn't torment me, wouldn't pierce my heart like a hot needle."

"What is piercing your heart, Ismail?"

"The thought that she might have returned. Got arrested."

"Why should she return?"

"Many did. They stayed outside the country for a while, then came back to fight again. She might have left her baby somewhere safe and come back. She told me that she had good friends in foreign lands. She didn't look like a woman who would give up the struggle, live in peace and forget about her country. Besides, her husband was in prison. This worries me."

"Did she ever mention anyone else? Someone she was looking for?"

"No. I have memorized everything she said in that short period of forty-nine hours and forty-five minutes. She didn't say she was looking for anyone."

"The things that she didn't say were all that mattered, Ismail. You memorized the wrong things. I'm sure she was looking for someone. She came back from abroad to find him and if she returned from her safe place back to the belly of the monster, it was to search for him."

"Didn't you say you didn't know her?" Ismail is confused.

"I don't know her. What I'm saying applies to all of us. What we say is not what matters. What matters is what we don't talk about."

The Chat

"Late by myself, in the boat of myself—" Shams recites.

A Sufi Day begins. But dawn doesn't bring peace here. War noises attack us from the Satan's Box—above. The rattles of machine guns, explosion of rockets, bombs, frantic voice of the reporter, gasping and announcing a new victory for the Army of God. The angry anthem and the slogans—"Rush to the Holy Battlefields, where the Last Holy One, the Absent One, rewards you with the Holy Water of Immortality!" And the prayers and endless military marches, shower us, flog us. All from the Satan's Box. Above.

I miss a quiet cell. A blindfold and cool cement.

And I feel rage. Wasn't this my goal, my desire, my quest to become

Unbreakable and stay in cell number four? Then why do I want to be somewhere else? Jealousy has disturbed my equilibrium. I feel jealous like a young lad with only the shadow of a mustache above his lips. A boy in love with a schoolgirl. This adolescent jealousy is below me. Despicable. It's chewing me from within. I'm jealous of the man Sahar has married. The man she was worried for and might have returned to from her safe place only because he was (or still is) locked up in El-Deen. Am I not locked up? Does she know this at all? I feel abandoned. Betrayed. But then I comfort myself by the thought that she might have kept her most precious secret, her real worry, hidden from Ismail.

Agha strolls most of the day. He and Ismail don't talk much. They talk when there is something to say, to share. Agha walks from where Shams and I are sitting to the opposite wall where the sink is, and back again. Ten steps total. I count it while he walks. Ismail sits on the cot, lies down, gets up, and exercises. Sits on the floor under the hanging TV, gets up, and sits down again. He washes his face, dries it with his scarf, and lies down again. Restless. Now they sit together, Ismail and Agha. Agha begins a subject he has been thinking about. They discuss.

"Was the Revolution an immediate need, Ismail? Inevitable?"

"It was," Ismail says in a serious tone, "otherwise it wouldn't have happened."

"I think you make sense, Ismail. The clash between the bourgeois comprador and the national bourgeoisie, on the one hand, and the situation of the proletariat, the peasants, and the urban petty bourgeoisie on the other, which resulted in severe, protracted economic crisis, and the lower standard of living, the ability of the clerical leadership to consolidate its power—" He goes on and on. Ismail grasps what he can and forgets the rest.

Now they keep quiet. Agha thinks and strolls and they chat some more. Sometimes Ismail starts, in his own way, his own story.

"I'm on top of Mount Solomon. On Soluch. Looking at the dry valley and the border—the ditch. It's dawn. The mountain air is as fresh and cool as spring water. I debate. Should I go and find her? I may endanger her—it's selfish. Let her be. I don't go. I never go. I repeat this, Master, repeat this all day and night. Because I don't want to forget."

"You're doing the right thing, Ismail." Agha tells him. "If this keeps you alive, do it. We have to stay alive. Who knows? Huh? What if people rise

446

again? What if they hang the bastards by their turbans on all the telephone posts? What if they open the gates and let us out? You can never know what people can do. Did you see how they opened the gate of El-Deen, once? Did you see what they did to the monarch?"

"But you never know when they're going to do it. When?" Ismail asks. "Maybe thirty years from now when we're all ashes and bones behind this wall. It seems to me, Master, that people endure and endure, to the point where they can't endure anymore. Then they explode. They're enduring now."

"A mass movement needs organization," Agha mumbles.

"Under nine layers of illusion—in the ground itself, I see your face," Shams says.

The Story

At the sunset of the same Sufi Day, they shoot seven bullets behind the wall. Shams has reached this line: "The spring we're looking for is somewhere in this murkiness."

It's lentil soup again, like yesterday. Or was it two days ago? We eat in silence. Ismail feeds Shams and wraps the white scarf around his head like a turban. Without any introduction, clapping, or calling our attention, Agha starts. Ismail and I sit, all ears. Shams breaths heavily, falling deeper and deeper into a dark hole. An old sheikh on TV sings the prayer of sunset. He has a warm voice.

"The old man had lived alone all his life." Agha pauses, rubs his chin and looks at the wall, where a small barred window could have been. "He'd lived alone, except for two short intervals. Once when he was very young, he worked in the gas city, and lived in the rose city with a woman whose hair smelled of lotus. And once when he was much older, in his dark apartment he lived with a young lad who took refuge with him to recover from a loss. But the man had lived alone for most of his life. Now for the third time he was going to live with someone. But he knew this would be shorter than the previous ones." Agha stops and looks at me. "I want you to continue my story. This is a game. Say as much as it flows, when it becomes an effort, stop. You can pass your turn too. Now, go on!"

447

"This was after the girl had passed the murky water and stayed in the foreign lands," I continue. "This was after she had come back home to find the young lad. Which she didn't. Because no one knew where he was except the old uncle. But why didn't the uncle write to him, letting him know that she was finally back? Who knows? Maybe the uncle did write and the letter got lost. Maybe he did, but the young man had already left the town. Anyway, the girl went to live with her uncle because she was running away. She needed a shelter. A baby was in her arms." I stop.

Ismail speaks: "And all this time, Ismail was on Soluch, on top of Mount Solomon, looking at the dry valley, knowing that a day not too far from then, he was going to lead the young woman to the other side of the border and stay alone and miserable the rest of his life." Ismail stops.

"She came," Agha says still staring at the windowless wall. "A baby in her arms. The uncle gave them the dark room with a window to the brick wall. Did he have a sunny room? That was the only room in the dingy place. She stayed there many days and nights. The old uncle brought her food and sometimes something for the boy. A rattle, or a plastic doll to teeth on. A toy car. She read all day. She said her uncle's books smelled of lotus.

I resume: "And this was long after the young man had stayed there with his uncle and had read the same books and smelled the scent of lotus. She somehow knew this. Did she ever ask the uncle, 'Hasn't he lived here before? I can feel it. I can feel him. Hasn't he?' There is no way to know. To know whether she ever asked this or not. But she thought about the young man all the time. Especially when she sang a lullaby, put her little boy to sleep, and drew the thick curtain back, just a crack. She remembered him when she saw the wall. A tall brick wall. Oh, how many times had they both seen this wall? In reality. In their dreams. In play-games. In make-believe. In front of the wall, they had taken an oath to kill the monster. She closed her eyes, holding her breath like when they were little, and heard, swoosh, swoosh, dump! Swoosh, swoosh, dump! She smiled, although the wall was thick, tall, and impassible and she was hidden behind it. Why was she hiding? Because she didn't want to end up against the wall. If she did, with four hot bullets they'd pierce her heart." I stop.

Ismail takes over: "All this time, Ismail was on Soluch, on top of Mount Solomon, looking at the valley, thinking. He had the premonition that one day he was going to take her to the other side and stay alone and miserable the rest of his life. He knew her already, although he had never seen her before. He had named her Aroose—'bride.' But Ismail had a wife, an old sickly wife who couldn't bear a son for him. He seldom went to his wife. She lived somewhere in their remote village, behind the mountain, tending their small herd of sheep. He had even forgotten how rough and calloused the skin of her hands was because of the mountain winds, and how deep the creases were on her sun-burned face. Now all he knew and saw in his vision was the girl, his bride for forty-nine hours and forty-five minutes. He was waiting for someone to call him and tell him something about her." Ismail stops.

"The old uncle was on his bike one day," Agha continues, "the way he had been most of his life. He biked and thought. Biked and looked at the people and thought. People said his brain had gone soft after witnessing the fall of all the revolutions, from living like a hermit all his life. But he knew well that this wasn't true. These days, he just biked around the block to see if his house was safe.

"The Revolution was living its last days. It was a giant being dismembered, limb by limb. But something was still left of it. The old man pulled to a corner and watched it passing: the Revolution, lame, panting, waving the blood-soaked flags in the sky, passed. The old man waved to it. It waved back, with tired arms. Now he saw an army of Black Flaggers, buttons ripped open, approaching. They came with their shaved heads, bloody mouths, striking their chests with chains, cracking their heads open with scimitars, chanting: 'One party, Party of God! One leader, chosen by God!' They reached the tired giant and cut off another limb with their butcher knives. The giant sighed, moaned and collapsed. But it was still alive.

"The next day, while biking around the block to see if the girl was safe up there in the dark apartment, the old man saw the noble giant. He saw it day after day after day, each day more feeble, missing more limbs. Until one day, he saw that just a head was left of the Revolution. The head was big and bloody, rolling and screaming along the street: 'I'm your Revolution! I'm still alive!' The Black Flaggers showered it with hot bullets. Blood gushed out. The Revolution's head shrunk and wrinkled like an old rotten pomegranate at the bottom of a garbage can." Agha stops.

I take over: "All this time, while the Revolution was being dismembered and sacrificed out there, the young man was aging in the endless hallways of El-Deen for the crime of carrying the banner and the flag. He journeyed from the Black Box to the cell, from the cell to the Box, stopping at different chambers. He dreamed and daydreamed of bringing her back to life. And all this time she never knew that her twin was locked up, trapped where no one could ever come out. And this was when the giant was being martyred and people had no strength anymore to kill the bloody watch-dog and open the heavy gate."

"This Baluch," Ismail clears his throat and continues, "who had gone to the city to become a factory worker called Ismail once. They met in a caravanserai outside a village. Over hot tea and water-pipe, he told Ismail about his former landlord in the city, an old doctor who was looking for someone trustworthy. 'What for?' Ismail asked, his heart pounding, because he knew what the whole thing was about. He had a premonition. Or had he lived the same life before? 'The doctor wants a smuggler to pass his grand-daughter to the other side of the border,' the Baluch worker said. Ismail headed toward the capital, the tea still steaming on the wooden table of the caravanserai." Ismail stops.

"Now in the old uncle's apartment," Agha starts, "there was light. The silence of solitude had been broken with giggles and innocent cries for food. Cough and sneeze and burp! The young mother tickled the chubby boy. They both laughed until tears rolled down their eyes. She was a joy when she was with her boy. They both sat on the floor, on the old man's dirty mat and yelled, 'Saba... Saba... Saba... lift the carpet!' Now she made wind sounds, 'Hoooooo... ' And both mother and son clung to the old rug, pretending it was floating in the sky. The old man sat and watched them, a smile on his face, tears in his eyes. How could he ever lose them?" Agha stops.

"In this chamber and that," I continue, "in the melting heat and freezing cold, under the lashes of the cable whip, on the gurney, strapped on a chair, he dreamed of himself and his twin on the Turkman carpet."

"She was small," Ismail says. "Up to Ismail's chest. Her eyes were big and wet with an unusual luster, as if she had tears in her eyes. Her black irises reflected the sunshine, the moonlight, a bulb, a candle, anything luminous. Ismail thought stars twinkled in her eyes. He told her so. She said she knew."

"They came one day," Agha pauses, a long pause, as if he doesn't want to go on. But he continues, "The grandfather and the smuggler. They came to take her and the baby. To take her across the border where they could be safe. The old uncle held the baby while the girl changed into a long heavy dress. She veiled herself, but not with a dark one. With blue gauze and satin. She became a Baluchi bride. The smuggler had brought the most beautiful native dress for his forty-nine-hour bride. When they went down to sit in the car, the old man stayed up in the apartment, behind the window. He didn't wave. The little boy, Saba, kept looking up from the car, searching for him." Agha stops.

"And in the chambers, on the gurney, strapped to a barber's chair, he dreamed of her," I say.

"Ismail was speechless," Ismail takes over. "He was mute all the way from the capital city to the border town. He hadn't seen such a woman before. She talked to him without bending her head, or lowering her lids. She talked, staring into Ismail's eyes. She talked as if Ismail were her friend, her equal. When she didn't talk, she opened a book between the folds of her massive skirt. Ismail warned her that the book could cause problem and she had to get rid of it. 'Why?' she wanted to know. 'It's a story book—it has nothing to do with politics.' 'Baluchi women cannot read story books,' Ismail told her. 'They cannot read any book.' So they got rid of the book and she talked instead the rest of the long trip. Ismail was drowned in the dark waters of her eyes."

"All that remained in the old man's dark apartment was a rubber rattle, half-chewed. It made a sad, lonely sound," Agha says.

"'Is she here in El-Deen?' the young man asked himself, searching for her eyes in the dark auditorium. 'Is she in El-Deen?' He studied the female voices, the passing veiled figures on TV screens. 'Is this her?' He tormented himself more than Sultan tormented him when he saw a woman hanging from her ankles behind an opaque screen. 'Is this her?'" Here I stop.

Ismail resumes: "When she didn't talk to Ismail, she talked to Saba. Grown-up talk. The child looked at her lips, picking the words. He listened and repeated. She told him, 'When we walk in the desert and it's dark, you just lay your head on my shoulder. You don't make a noise. If you make a noise, the bad men will come. Uncle Ismail is with us. Taking care of us. His horse Soluch is strong, almost magical, like Rakhsh, Rostam's horse. They will protect us. But we must not talk, or cry, or make any noise.' The little boy listened to the very end, staring at his mother's lips, where the words came out."

451

"All that remained for the old uncle was a rattle," Agha says.

"'Why did she leave when she left?' the young man thought whenever he could think. 'Can one separate herself from herself?'" I say.

"At the border, the travelers slept on a ragged bamboo spread in the shepherd's hut," Ismail says. "The shepherd's hut was right at the first ditch. Aroose slept with her baby and the shepherd's wife. Ismail slept further away, but where he could see her. Before dawn, she woke Ismail up. *She* woke him up! She was all dressed in boy's clothes, ready to cross the border. Ismail had overslept. He was dreaming of himself on Soluch, on top of Mount Solomon, looking at the dry valley and the ditch, regretting her loss. He had dreamed the future. She was in her boy's clothes now, but her hair was down to her waist. While Ismail was laying a saddle on Soluch, she sat on a rock in front of the hut and brushed her hair. She made a long braid, wrapped it snake-like behind her neck, and hid it in a hat. She hung her white scarf around her neck. Brushing Soluch's rough black hair, Ismail watched her from the corner of his eyes." Ismail stops.

"One day the old man pulled his bike to a corner and watched," Agha says this and pauses as if watching something. "The guards surrounded his place. They chased the people away from the sidewalk. They hit an old woman who sold flowers. He saw his books fly out of the window, wings open, landing on the cement. The rose petals, little yellow notes, scented pages, all turned to powder before reaching the ground. They took the rattle with them." Agha stops.

"'She must have returned for me,' the young man thought. 'She had made an oath with me, at the wall of El-Deen. To be here together when the Revolution comes. It came and she returned to find me.'" I stop here.

"Ismail sat her on Soluch. The sleeping baby was on her back. Ismail held the horse's leash. They stepped on the minefield. She whispered to Ismail, 'I can't sit on a horse. Once I fell off a horse. I'm afraid. I want to walk.' There was no time to waste. They had to cross the border before dawn. Ismail took her down. The boy woke up, finding himself on his mother's back, with Ismail and a black horse in the total darkness of the desert. He remembered what his mother had told him; he lay his cheek on her shoulder, but his large eyes remained wide open until the end. They walked in silence. She was further ahead of Ismail now, jumping over the thorn bushes like a deer," Ismail says.

"The old uncle stayed at his brother's place for a day or two," Agha says. "His brother's wife, the fortune-teller, hid him behind the beaded curtain of her fortune-telling room. Was there anywhere else for him? The guards knew that too. They pulled him out from behind the screen and took him to El-Deen. They shook the rattle in his face. The lonely sound stayed in his ears forever," Agha says and stops.

"She left him, yes. But she came back for him." I continue. "She left again. Was forced to leave, yes. But she may have come back again. For him." I stop.

"The last ditch, the widest, was the border," Ismail says. "They crossed and the sun came up. The boy lifted his head and pulled his mother's hat off and giggled. Her braid fell down, loose on her breast. She pulled off the white scarf, which was wrapped around her neck, lifted herself up on her toes to reach Ismail, and looped the scarf around his neck. She leashed the rough man forever. Kissed his cheek, as if he were her friend, her equal, not Ismail the smuggler, the man of the mountains." Ismail stops. His voice breaks.

"The old uncle circled in El-Deen," Agha says. "From the Black Box to the cell, from the cell to the Box. He forgot. Bit by bit. He forgot all, except for the sound of the rattle." Agha stops.

"He can feel her," I add. "Sometimes somewhere very close. As if he can stretch his arm and reach her."

"Every dawn, Ismail rode Soluch on top of Mount Solomon, debating whether to go to the other side and see her or not. He never did," Ismail says.

"Dark oblivion filled the old man's head like a thick substance. The sound of the rattle died," Agha says.

"She must be somewhere near. He can feel it. She came back for him. For him," I say.

"And then it happened that they arrested Ismail while he was smuggling more people. They took him to El-Deen where he circles between the Black Box and the cell, the cell and the Black box. But he hasn't lost his memory. He remembers. And all that he says are real accounts of his life." Ismail stops.

"Dark oblivion," Agha says, closing his eyes.

"She is here, for him," I murmur.

"Ismail remembers." Ismail ends the story.

In Ismail's Absence

The next day, a Solomon Day, when the muezzin calls the believers to midday prayer, and Shams murmurs, "Come with me from Lebanon, my bride—," two hooded guards enter the cell. They handcuff and blindfold Ismail, leash him, and take him away. In the last instant, before leaving, Ismail unwraps his white turban and throws it to me.

We sit motionless, Agha and I, for a long time. I wear the scarf around my neck. I feed Shams. Agha doesn't talk much. He doesn't share his thoughts with me, the way he did with Ismail. He paces up and down, from wall to wall. Not a word.

I watch Agha's shrunken body, his small, heavy head, wobbling on his neck. I watch him pacing the cell. Could this man be Uncle Yahya? Our Uncle knew a lot, but he never talked. He lived like a shadow, a gray shadow on a bike. This old man is gray too, but with a strong presence. He talks. He has a sense of humor, he can act and entertain, even be a clown. If this is Uncle Yahya, El-Deen has changed him. Now he is thinking of Ismail, his old friend. Ismail was scared of the Black Box.

Finally the old man invites me to exercise with him. We move our arms and legs rather dutifully and stop soon. We don't feel like doing more. I sit. He paces up and down again.

The usual NHRT programs have stopped. The internal news is on. I listen carefully to find out if there is any mention of a coup.

"The Great Leader of the Holy Revolution," the announcer says, "in the glorious ceremonies of the anniversary of the Holy Revolution, honored three Revolutionary Devotees by adding the title of 'Holy' to their previous titles. These selfless sons of the Revolution have worked day and night to purify the God Almighty's Republic of the Satanic influences. The first soldier of the Faith to be honored and titled is Brother La-Jay, the Father of the University of El-Deen, the Gate of Paradise. Now he is the Holy Father of the University. The second Brother is Doctor Halal, the Healer of the El-Deenians, now to be known as the Holy Healer of the El-Deenians. The third Brother honored and titled by our Great Leader is Brother Kamal, the Revolutionary Devotee, now the Holy Revolutionary Devotee—"

Lying on the cot, I try to put this hypothesis together: Kamal climbed the ladder (with the help of Doctor Halal, who himself is guided by the foreign advisors), reached the top of the pyramid where La-Jay is, proved his devotion and unearthed the corruption of former Ha-G the Shit Mouth and Sultan the Asscracker. He presented himself as the most capable Revolutionary Guard. Halal supported him. La-Jay nominated him for the designation of "Holiness"—a big deal for a small devotee like Kamal. He is "Holy" now.

So my friend is up there. The Loony, the Immortal. But in the news there is no mention of his immortality. He must have kept this secret for later. He doesn't want to intimidate Brother La-Jay. First he needs to establish himself. But I'm sure his party, the Holy Revolutionary Party of the Immortals, has secret meetings in the dark corridors and abandoned cells. Kamal won't give up. He believes that he has a mission. He wants to purify the Republic. His starting point is El-Deen.

Oh, Brother Kamal, my old friend, seize the power and let me out. Now that Sahar has left the country with her baby, Saba, I want to get out, roam the world and search for her. Get the power and a long train of titles, Brother. Make haste!

"Make haste, my beloved/ And be like a gazelle/ or a young stag/ Upon the mountains of spices," Shams murmurs.

A Solomon Day ends.

Brother Hamid

Sufi and Solomon come and go. Ismail is still absent. Today they drag in a blindfolded man. He is tall and square, wearing the black shirt of the devotees. His soles bleed. The cable whip has shredded his flesh. He sits on the toilet, holds his head between his hands, and sobs. Agha washes his feet and offers him the cot. There, he falls asleep.

"This smells," Agha whispers to me. "But it's a good smell. They're torturing their own guards. They'll kill one another down to the last person and then we'll get out of here." His gray eyes sparkle for the first time since they have taken Ismail away.

The sleeping guard moans and sobs in his dream. Agha talks to me. Fast. Agitated. His gestures are quick. He is restless and incoherent. What if his old heart stops beating?

"If we get out soon, it will still be winter. I know it's winter, because of the anniversary of the Revolution. The air will be sweet and dry. It will taste like ice cream." He chuckles and goes on. "I'll buy an ice cream cone and lick it in the cold air. I'll travel. You know what I mean? Travel. All the reading is not half the seeing. I want to stand in the main square of a remote city and stare at the thousand-year-old, tall minaret to figure out how the mosaic artist has laid the blue and green tiles together and created this unique turquoise. I'll feed the pigeons in the courtyard of a mosque. I'll live at least ten more years..."

"In the city of Raz there is a cul-de-sac by the name of Safa," I interrupt him. "There is a house at the end of the narrow cul-de-sac, orange blossoms hang over the walls."

Agha stares at me for a long moment. "Are we playing the story game, or am I trying to plan my future?"

"I'm sorry, Agha. Go on. I won't talk anymore."

"Where was I? Aha... I'll go there... to this remote city—to Raz. It's strange. I'd forgotten its name and now—. I have lived there. In my youth. I'm remembering strange things. It's scary. Details. All because of the possibility of going out. What does this mean? Are we suppressing our memories because there is no hope of getting out? And a glimpse of hope brings them back again?" He rubs his chin, holds his forehead and sits on the toilet, thinking. After a long pause he says, "This has happened to me before. Remembering."

The guard wakes up, sits and looks around. He doesn't know where he is.

"They call me Agha," Agha introduces himself, "Although I don't think I deserve this title. The man lying against the wall is Shams. He deserves his name. He rises early and sets early, as the sun does. And this young man— oh God, we haven't named you yet, have we?" He looks at me.

"No, sir. I guess we didn't have enough time to name me!"

Agha laughs. "It's ridiculous! Let's name you, then. Wow! To name a person. A person who has had a name all his life and then has lost it for a long while. This is a special occasion. No, I don't want to do it now. Let's wait for our friend Ismail. You've been nameless all this time, wait a little while more—a day or two."

Agha's forehead is red. He gasps and talks, fast and excited. All because of this guard. He hopes that the guards are destroying each other.

"What's your name, Brother?" He asks the young man.

"Hamid."

"Brother Hamid, welcome to the cell of the Unbreakables. I hope you know where you are!" Agha asks.

"I know. The cell of the blasphemers, unbelievers, rotten reds, Godless bastards. This is the way they're torturing me. This is worse than their cable whip, their Hothouse and Freezer," he says, turning his head to the wall, sulking.

"Oh, now I see. Your sin must have been too big then. They've locked you up with the blasphemers and atheists. Did you insult the Great Leader?"

The guard shakes his head. No.

"Did you neglect your prayers?"

He shakes his head.

"Did you disobey your superiors?"

He shakes his head.

"Did you talk to a woman?"

He shakes his head.

"Did you shave your beard?"

He shakes his head.

"Did you wear a short sleeve shirt?"

He doesn't respond to this.

"Well, I don't see why they've brought you here, then," Agha says.

"I said there was a Thirteenth Holy One, the Immortal One—" he mumbles, his back still turned to us.

"Ah! Heresy! That's a huge sin, my son." Agha plays with Brother Hamid. "Who is he? I mean this Thirteenth One? Is he around?"

"He is here, in El-Deen."

"No!" Agha acts as if he is shocked. "In El-Deen?"

"Yes. He is the first human immortal. The first one who drank the Holy Water of Immortality from the sacred hands of the Absent One."

"Was the Absent One present, then?" Agha asks.

"He was here, in the Psychiatric Wing. The bastard Ha-G locked up the Promised One with the lunatics. But a young, brave Brother, a true Revolutionary Devotee, dreamed about him, found him in the Psychiatric Wing, and received the honor of drinking the Holy Water of Immortality. He became Holy. Even the Great Leader has given him the title of Holy."

"And he became the Thirteenth One?" Agha asks.

"We have no doubt about it," the guard says.

"Who is 'we?'" Agha asks.

"The Holy Revolutionary Party of the Immortals. His followers. We're his devotees. We have no doubt that he has a mission in this world. Although he is working with Brother La-Jay now, he is not secure. The gang of Ha-G and Sultan are still active. Look what they've done to me! To me! The devotee of the Revolution, a hero of the Holy War!" He weeps.

"If your Thirteenth Holy One is one of the authorities now, then why are you worried for him?" Agha tries to draw more information out of the weeping guard.

"There are traitors among us. Spies. They must have informed the authorities that I've said Brother Kamal is the Thirteenth Holy One."

"Brother Kamal?" Agha asks.

"The Holy Revolutionary Devotee, that's the title the Great Leader has given him."

"I wonder if I've seen him before—" Agha rubs his chin.

"I don't care what is going to happen to me. I'm worried for him, for the Holy Kamal."

"Didn't you say he is immortal?" Agha asks.

Hamid answers Agha's question with another one: "How can he be the Thirteenth Holy One and not be immortal?"

"Are you immortal too?"

"How can I be a member of the Party of Immortals and not be immortal?" Brother Hamid asks again, now looking at Agha.

"Then, what do you have to fear? How can they harm you and your Holy One?"

"They can't kill us, but they can banish us. What can we do elsewhere? We want to be here. This is our Holy Battlefield. This is where our World Revolution begins."

"Aha!" Agha says, then keeps quiet.

The young man lies down again, turns his back to us and stays motionless.

A minute later Agha calls me to the toilet seat where he is sitting and contemplating. I squat at his foot; he whispers to me, "These fanatic assholes are after something that is objectively confirmable! By evidence and reason.

458

Since their Holy Ones are not capable of doing anything while residing in the Heaven of God, the bastards create a new Holy One, a visible one, a tangible one, here in the battlefields! Reality is 'matter' my friend, isn't it? And they lock people up, torture, and execute them for saying the same thing!" He chuckles, then becomes serious and sinks into deep thought.

Shams murmurs: "When I die, lay out the corpse/ You may want to kiss my lips/ Just beginning to decay. Don't be frightened/ if I open my eyes... "

I'm the Wall

I'm on top of the wall holding the flag in one hand, the banner in another. I'm making a speech, addressing the millions, "I'm a gauger, a sailor... I seek the storm—" But I have no voice. Below in the murky ocean of oil, the dark gray tides rise up. People try to swim. They kick their legs, struggle with their arms, but high tides swallow them. They become buried under the dark foam. Now a head comes up and disappears, now a torso sinks. Forever.

Black Flaggers hold gigantic barrels at the shore. All the greasy liquid flows into the barrels. The ocean dries up and becomes a desert. The men close the barrels and load them in a ship. They raise a black flag on top of a post.

The desert is vacant, deserted.

As the wall rises, I still wave my flag and raise my banner. I hear the familiar sound of swoosh, swoosh, dump! Swoosh, swoosh, dump! My feet feel wet and cool. I look at them, and they are mortar.

Someone calls me from far away, "Jump down! Jump! Before it's too late!"

I look at the desert and see Sahar. She is wearing men's clothes, a baby resting on her back. A cap covers her hair; the white scarf wraps around her neck.

"Jump down before it's too late!" She calls again. But the wall rises fast. My knees are brick, my thighs mortar. My hips are brick, my waist, mortar. My heart is a brick.

I cast my eyes down to see her. She talks to the child, "Saba, go and bring him down!" She unwraps the boy and throws him up in the air like a light ball. The baby floats, rises to sit on top of the wall and tries to pull me out of the wall. Now I'm brick and mortar up to my neck. The child pulls my head, kicks the hard wall with his little fists, struggling to take me out. In vain. I'm all brick and mortar. I'm the wall. My eyes stay alive though. I blink. Saba touches my eyes with his little fingers to make sure that there is life in them, then he flies back to his mother.

Beneath me, Sahar spreads the white scarf on the dirt and lies down on her side. Her boy rests beside her, sucking her full breast. She stares at me, at my dry blinking eyes. We stay like this forever, looking at each other.

The blast of a single shot opens my eyes. After a few seconds, another one—muffled. These are bullets from a revolver. A different execution.

Shams says, "They smote me, they wounded me/ The keepers of the walls took my mantle from me."

I look at the cot. Hamid, the Revolutionary Devotee, hero of the Holy War, is not there. Agha is sitting on the toilet staring at me. The TV plays the anthem, "Anja, anja... Za, za, za—" The choir of the Revolutionary Sisters screams.

"They took him in the middle of the night," Agha says, pointing to the empty cot. "It's him they just shot."

I want to say something, but I can't. I've lost myself in my confused dream. I look at Agha, with dry blinking eyes.

"Shams is going blank," Agha says. "He skipped a long part of his song today. He is forgetting." He keeps quiet for a long moment and then adds, "Ismail is not back."

I'm still lost, listening to Agha, but I cannot talk. I hold the white scarf in my arms like it is a living thing.

"I slept just a few hours at the beginning of the night," Agha says. "I dreamed. I forgot all, except one thing."

A repentant is confessing on TV. This is El-Deen's morning program.

"I was a materialist by ideology," the repentant says. I would like to see his face, but it's hidden behind the gray shirt Ismail has hung over the screen. The voice continues: "I didn't believe in God. To me, reality was matter and objectively confirmable, by evidence and reason. Matter to me was the basic content of existence. I believed in scientific investigations and the rationally demonstrable conclusions—"

"I dreamed about the sound of the rattle," Agha says. "I heard it again."

"The University has changed me," the repentant continues. "Now I believe in a truth higher than that yielded by reason. And this truth is attainable only through faith. Faith in the Creator, His prophet, the representatives of the prophet and the Holy Ones, and finally, faith in the Holy Revolution and the Holy War. I'm at peace now. Grateful for my Holy Father, La-Jay, the head of the University of El-Deen, the Gate of Paradise!"

"I'm a wall," Shams says and keeps quiet.

Agha crawls on the cement floor, reaches Shams, and shakes him, "Hey, son! Shams, my friend! I won't let you forget. You have to sing your songs from the beginning to the end everyday. You're our calender, our clock, our sun and moon, Shams! Do you hear me? You just skipped several stanzas. 'I'm a wall' comes toward sunset—it's not noon yet. Shams! I'm talking to you!" He slaps him on both cheeks. Shams breaks into sobs. Agha lays Shams' head on his own chest and lets him cry. "Cry son, cry! It's a good sign. An excellent sign. Cry!"

I cover my face in Sahar's white scarf to inhale her ancient scent, now mixed with Ismail's lost odor.

Faction Fights

Ismail comes, lies down on the cot, and falls asleep. His blue-gray pajamas are soiled with dry vomit, urine, and excrement. Agha sits by the cot, studies Ismail's face, and sighs.

"He is back, but I'm not sure how much of him is left."

All day Shams recites broken lines. Long silences fall in between; half of a stanza follows. By the end of the day, he mixes Solomon and the Sufi: "I'm a rose of Sharon... Somewhere in the murkiness... "

Ismail awakes, takes his pajamas off, washes them and lets them dry flat on the cement floor. He wears the sleeveless gray shirt hanging on the TV set. He squats in his corner without a word.

There is a roundtable debate on TV. Since the screen is uncovered, I see three turbaned men and two bearded, bare-headed men sitting around a table. They talk fervently, interrupting each other and even yelling at one another.

"—As I said before, the people have decided not to be intimidated by these labels. Call us Fascists if you like—" One of the bearded men says.

461

The second bearded man, who is wearing round spectacles interrupts him. "Is this something to be proud of? Monopolizing is a reactionary attitude. How can you—"

"Stop using foreign terminology, Brother. Use the words of God. It's as simple as this: we have decided to close down the offices of all those organizations who do not follow the line of the Party of God!"

"People are grumbling," the third man, a clergy, says. "If their grumblings become serious complaints and complaints become opposition, we'll face a catastrophe—"

"Do we intend to rule this country or not?" the first speaker asks. "Yes, or no? Do we intend to spread the word of God or not? Had we not outlawed those corrupt parties and set up the hanging poles to punish their leaders, we wouldn't be here now. Open your eyes, Brothers! Democracy is a Western notion; throw it out of your heads! Get rid of the West and East!" He wipes his sweaty face with a big checkered kerchief.

"To hell with both West and East. I'm talking about the principles here," the spectacled man says. "Closing down the religious organizations is against the ideals of our Holy Republic—"

"Let people choose—"

"We're all devotees of the Republic, Brothers—"

"—Certain amount of freedom is—"

"Instead of crying for democracy, cry for faith, Brother! We want to spread our Faith all over the world, don't we?"

"By what means? Persecution of the believers?"

"Those who cry for democracy are pursuing the wrong path. We do not consider them believers—"

"This is outrageous!"

"Unheard of—"

The program is interrupted by a military march. Now the march is interrupted by static and deafening scratchy sounds. Everything goes off the air. Silence.

"Let them eat each other," Agha says. "The sooner, the better. If sooner, I'll be alive. I'll lick an ice cream cone, in the cool air of winter. I'll travel. To the south. Raz!"

What will I do if they eat each other up? I sit against the wall, next to

Shams's bumpy head, and daydream. I'm not as optimistic as Agha is. I know that they won't eat each other up. Or if they do, they'll do it at such a slow speed, that we will perish here. Still, I play with the thought. What else is here for me to do? I have no pains to think about and worry myself over. My pains and aches have stopped. My soles have grown new skin. They are as pink and fresh as a baby's feet. I eat. A little, but enough to stay alive. I move my body several times a day. They haven't beaten me up or drugged me since I've come to this cell. Maybe Kamal is protecting me, hasn't forgotten me.

If the Holy Republicans eat one another quickly and people open El-Deen's gates, I'll go and find Sahar. Like a dervish, I'll take a lantern and walk around the world in search of her. I'll grow old this way. I'll lose my clothes and shoes. I'll become a naked dervish with long gray hair and a long gray beard, searching for my other half. With a lantern in the dark.

The Sin of Dervish Ali

Two guards open the iron gate, push and prod a dervish in. He stumbles and falls at the foot of the cot. The old man is almost naked, only a dirty cloth wrapped around his waist. They haven't shaved his long hair and long beard yet. He smells of the outdoors. The odor is so sharp and so different than the familiar smells of our cell that my stomach cramps. Agha and I help the dervish to lie down on the cot. They have whipped him with a cable. His soles bleed.

"How did you get yourself in trouble, old man?" Agha asks him teasingly.

"They took me all the way here from the city of Raz. In a black windowless car." He murmurs and moans. I know that his soles are stinging.

"Did you insult the authorities?" Agha asks.

"No, son."

"Did you foretell the Republic's gloomy future in your book of ghazals?"

"No son."

"Did you talk to a woman?"

The dervish shakes his head.

"Did you drink wine?"

He shakes his head.

"You didn't say there was no God, did you, Dervish?" Agha asks playfully.

"I didn't say there was no God, son. I said there was. They asked me, 'Where is He?' I knew that I should not say, 'He is in me' as Mansour the Quiltmaker said, and they chopped him to pieces. I'm not Mansour, I'm Dervish Ali, a poor, weak dervish. So my answer was silence."

"They asked you, 'Where is God?' and your answer was silence?"

Dervish Ali nods. "They asked me many times and my silence was many folded. They wanted me to say that he was in the Holy Balcony of the Great Leader. But I couldn't lie. Because he is not there. He has never been there and will not be. Ever." He closes his eyes.

Dervish Ali sleeps. We watch him. Agha touches his forehead many times to see if he is still alive. He is very old. I look at his blue eyelids, his white lashes, the twitches of many creases around his eyes.

Time doesn't move anymore. We don't have Solomon Day and Sufi Day. Today is today and tomorrow is today. Always is today. Shams is quiet and the TV is dead. The silence in our cell has many layers, like the dervish's silence. But Ismail breaks it soon.

Ismail's Illusion

Agha and I sit in the center of the cell, eating our rice pudding quietly. Ismail is at his corner, eating alone. He has been eating alone since his return from the Box. Now we hear him talking, as if to himself, but to us.

"We made a story one night. Before they took me away. When we made that story I didn't end it the way I should have—"

Agha and I move to Ismail's corner and sit opposite him. Agha is excited that Ismail is talking.

"Tell me, my friend. Tell me what your real ending is. You can always change it if you want."

"But my stories are real. I've lived them. I've told you this before, haven't I?"

"You've told me, my friend. I trust you. Your stories are real. But still you can change the ending if you like," Agha says.

"When she left, Soluch and I climbed the mountain. I sat on the horse

464

and watched the dry valley—the desert and the ditches. I vaguely saw the last ditch, the widest of all—the border. I debated with myself: to cross, to go to the other land, and search for her, or not? I decided to go. And I did," Ismail says. There is a sudden sparkle in his sunken eyes.

"So you did, Ismail," Agha says thoughtfully.

"I did," he says.

"Tell us, Ismail! Did you find her in that foreign land?" I ask him, hoping that Ismail did finally find her.

"I walked along the dirt road of that border town. A ruin of a town. I passed the fallen walls, heaps of dust and broken bricks—people's houses before the war. I walked through the vacant alleys. I saw corpses half-devoured by the hyenas a long time ago. Their eyes empty sockets, eaten by greedy crows. I tripped over the bones—piles of them, sometimes. I covered my face with this white scarf so that I wouldn't inhale the odor of decay. I reached a house. A big mansion, but old and half-ruined, the only house in the town.

"The gate was open. I entered and noticed that there was not one single leaf of grass anywhere. The yard was a desert. Dust had covered the tiled floor. A dry well was covered with a tin lid in a corner. I was thirsty, but here was no water. I entered the building. In a long hallway, there were three rooms on the right and three on the left. The doors were swinging open. But no one was there. The rooms were all elaborately furnished. Elaborate for a small town at a remote border. Cushioned chairs, chestnut tables, large carpets, glass cabinets and so on. But a thick dust covered them all. I saw a game of chess, half-played on a small table, warriors buried under the dust. The last room on the left was a bedroom. A bed was waiting for me. It was a tall bed, up to my waist when I stood, with a thick mattress on it. I was tired, so I rested on the bed and covered my face with Aroose's white scarf. Soon I fell asleep."

Ismail talks as if he is hypnotized. There is no soul in his voice. A dark contagious chill enters my bones. Shams recites a line after a long silence. It's a Sufi verse and a Solomon line, mixed: "Today, like every other day, we wake up empty and frightened... Upon the mountain of spices..."

"I felt a breeze on my face," Ismail continues. "I felt someone removing the scarf, kissing my right cheek. I saw her face in my dream. Her wet eyes. Her long braids. Then I tried to wake myself up. 'Ismail doesn't dream,'

I told myself in my dream. 'To dream will be Ismail's ruin, Ismail's end. Ismail lives a real life,' I told myself. So I tried hard to remove her vision and awake myself. But my body was as heavy as Mount Solomon. I couldn't move it. I told myself, 'Ismail, if you can't move your body, at least open your eyes and see who is removing your scarf, blowing onto your face.' And with much effort I did. I opened my heavy eyelids and saw him. It wasn't her, the mother, it was him, the son." Ismail sighs and remains quiet for a long moment.

Agha sits cross-legged, resting his right elbow on his right knee, holding his broad forehead in his wide hand, immersed in Ismail's story. He needs this long moment to roam around the vacant house, enter the bedroom, look at the tall bed and find Ismail lying on it, a child sitting on his chest.

"The little wind-boy was sitting on my chest, blowing onto my face," Ismail continues. "I felt his weight on my body. I asked him, 'Saba, where is your mother?' This is the first thing I asked him, for the fear that the fiend child would disappear. 'My mother is gone,' he said. 'Gone where?' I asked. 'Gone to the other side of the ditch, where we came from.' 'Gone without you?' I asked. 'Without me. She left me here to live with the good Colonel and his wife. I'll be safe here, my mother said.' I looked at Saba's round face, fat cheeks, large black eyes, and dark curly hair, and I doubted he was a human child. He was much larger than a two-year-old. A two-year-old could never climb that tall bed. But it was him and I believed him and trusted him. I rose and wrapped the scarf around my head to leave. 'Where are you going, Uncle Ismail?' the boy asked. 'To find your mother,' I answered. 'You'll never find her,' the boy said. 'Stay here with me. The Colonel's wife has a long table full of foods and sherbets. Stay, Uncle, stay!'

"But I left. I passed the vacant alleys, ruins of houses, heaps of bones and fallen minarets. I passed the ditches and returned to the top of Mount Solomon where my horse, Soluch, was waiting for me. I sat on Soluch and looked at the dry desert for the last time. There was no reason anymore to climb up the mountain and look at the valley. Aroose was not on the other side, she was here. So I went to the village, to the caravanserai, to drink a glass of hot tea, eat a bite of bread and head toward the capital city to find her in the crowd of millions. But this is when they came for me." Ismail pauses and dries his sweaty forehead.

"They were many. All in black shirts. Some of them were carrying black flags.

466

They all had machine guns. They surrounded the caravanserai as if I were armed or had an army with me. They blindfolded and handcuffed me, pulling me into a black van. They drove to the capital city. It took twenty hours to get here; I was in darkness all that time. I was hungry and thirsty and the cold muzzles of their guns were on my chest.

"Soluch stayed at the door of the caravanserai. I knew that the native Baluchs, my cousins, would take care of him. I was not worried for the horse, I was worried for Aroose. I had a feeling that she was here in El-Deen. Yes, this was where she was. This is where she is. And I know that before long, I'll see her."

Agha and I move back and leave Ismail alone.

"Ismail has divorced from reality," Agha whispers to me. "He lives in illusion. The Black Box did this."

Agha and Dervish Ali Debate

Dervish Ali wakes up, sits on the bed and looks around. His old watery eyes stay on me.

"Did you find it, son?" he asks.

"Find what?"

"What you've been looking for—years ago, when I first met you at the poet's tomb, in Raz."

"I don't remember you, Dervish. But it's true. I've been searching."

"Did you find it?" he asks.

"No," I answer.

"I haven't found it either. And this is my end. Maybe there is only one search: wandering itself. Maybe there is nothing ahead. Maybe the miracle of Jesus is the man himself, not what he said or did. Maybe the cure of pain is pain. Maybe the one who is lost is inside us. Maybe there's no place like that anywhere in the world."

"Maybe," I say.

"It depends," Agha says from the toilet seat, where he is sitting and listening to us. "Can you endure the Holy Republic, Dervish?" He points to the TV set, which has resumed its programs with a hysterical report of recent victories in the Holy War.

"Can I endure them?" the old man repeats Agha's question.

"Can you?" Agha asks again.

"No," the dervish says.

"So you can't plunge into yourself and stay safe and secure. Can you?"

The dervish doesn't answer.

"Let the flood flow and take the whole world with it. I'm safe in my shelter. This is your philosophy. Isn't it, Dervish Ali?" Agha says.

The dervish is quiet.

"The miracle of Jesus is what he said and did," Agha paces up and down the cell, moving his arms as if teaching in a classroom. "I may not be the beloved you're seeking, your 'truth,' your 'Hagh,' but I'm alive, am I not? Don't you feel compassion for me?"

The dervish is silent.

"What if they tear me apart in front of your eyes? Will you come out of your shell to stop them? Will you scream for help, at least? Will you cry? Will you be able to stay safe and happy after what you witnessed?"

No answer.

"What you were searching for all your life, Dervish, is here, in this cell. Your spring is in this murkiness. Don't plunge into that deep nothingness; come out and look at us. We may die together and there is no truth after that." He grabs his red forehead and bends, thinking.

The dervish stays mute.

Teimoor, the Child-Soldier

Two hooded guards push a boy in the cell and close the iron gate behind him with a bang. He is thirteen, thin and wiry. His ribs show through his naked skin. He stumbles and falls in the middle of the cell. They haven't shaved his hair. His long, dark, bushy hair makes his head big and heavy on the stick of his body.

"They must be very busy these days," Agha says, helping the boy to get up. "They must be arresting people and locking them up without even having time to shave their heads or give them the circular tour."

I look at the boy's face—black and blue with bruises, swollen on the right side. If he had less hair and was paler in the face, he could be the twin brother of Saboor the Servant.

468

"Who are you?" Agha asks with a genuine surprise. "Is this a children's prison now? Who are you, son?"

"Teimoor."

"Teimoor what?" Agha asks.

"Teimoor the Water Carrier. But this was before I became a soldier. In the battlefields they called me Teimoor the Soldier."

"Tell me how you became a soldier, son. Lie down on this sheet and tell me the whole thing."

"They came to our village and took all the boys who were over ten in a van. They told our parents that they were taking us where the Last Holy One, the Absent One, would appear and bless us. We could go back home, or stay with Him."

"And your parents let them take you?

"They took me by force. My mother cried. My father prayed that I wouldn't stay with the Holy One."

"Did you see Him?" Agha asks.

"Who?"

"The Holy One."

"Oh, yes, sir, I saw him all right. One night in the Holy Battlefield, they showed us a light on a horse, approaching our camp. That was Him. When the horse got very close to us, the light was so blinding that we closed our eyes. We never saw the Holy One's features."

"And He blessed you—" Agha says.

"Yes, sir."

"How come you didn't go back home?"

"Because I didn't fight."

"How come?"

"I couldn't. I tried hard, but I couldn't shoot. They taught me how to shoot, but still I couldn't push the trigger. I couldn't eat or sleep either. I wanted to be home and help my father on the farm, to sell water in our village."

"And they brought you here to teach you a lesson," Agha concludes.

"I guess."

"You haven't said bad things about the Holy Revolution?" Agha asks.

"No, sir."

"You haven't insulted your superiors, by any chance?"

"No, sir."

"You didn't forget to pray, huh?"

"No, sir. I prayed more than anyone else in the battlefield."

"So they brought you here because you couldn't fight?"

"Yes, sir."

"Okay, lie down and rest. I'll put a wet cloth on your bruises. You'll be all right. They'll set you free one of these days. Don't worry."

"Sir!" Teimoor calls Agha.

"What is it, son?"

"Do you think they'll let me become the water carrier of the prison?"

"I don't think they have such a position here," Agha says, turning on the tap. "Look! We're in the Capital city; there is running water everywhere. Even in El-Deen. You have to go back home, where people need your help."

Kamal the Tree Frog

While Dervish Ali and Teimoor are asleep and Ismail stares at the opposite wall, Agha lays Shams' head on his lap, whispering to him, practicing his lines.

"Shams, listen to me, I want you to repeat after me. Do you hear me?"

Shams is motionless. His bad eye is closed, his good eye stares at the ceiling.

Agha reads the Sufi's quatrains from the beginning. After each quatrain, he stops and waits for Shams to repeat. Shams repeats finally, but faintly. I notice his lips moving. No voice.

"Late, by myself, in the boat of myself/ No light and no land anywhere," Agha says. His voice mixes with Dervish's moans.

Teimoor wakes up and crawls toward Ismail. Before long, Ismail breaks his silence and talks to the boy.

Now on TV, the report of the Holy War ends and El-Deen's internal programs start. The gray sleeveless shirt is not covering the screen anymore. Dervish is wearing it. I lie down at the foot of the cot and watch the old tomb, the symbol of El-Deen's programs. The tomb fades away and Kamal's broad face fills the screen.

"Brothers and Sisters! El-Deenians!" Kamal addresses the prisoners. He

470

looks much better than the last time I saw him. His face is full, his head freshly shaved, his beard trimmed, his black shirt buttoned up to his neck, pressing his double-chin, forcing it to overlap the collar. "My name is Kamal the Immortal, your Holy Revolutionary Devotee, the servant of the Great Leader of the Holy Revolution, the server of the Holy Republic. I'm addressing you as the special representative of our Holy Father, La-Jay, the head of the University of El-Deen: the Gate of Paradise. I have an announcement for you. Let us raise our arms to the Heavens and thank the God Almighty for helping us to fulfill our Holy Cultural Revolution in El-Deen.

"Yes, a Cultural Revolution took place and I congratulate the members of the Headquarters and the selfless staff." Now Kamal speaks agitatedly, something I've never heard before. I can't help wondering whether this is real excitement or he is using one of his acting techniques. "Brothers and Sisters!" He goes on, "In these glorious days of the anniversary of our Holy Republic, we celebrate the birth of our new University! The unfaithful, the hypocrites, the spies of the West and East, the cynics, the imbeciles, the suspicious elements who had crept like reptiles into the ranks of the revolutionaries are now purged. They're all shot or hanged. El-Deen is clean, pure, and Holy as heaven itself.

"I, Kamal the Immortal, the Holy Revolutionary Devotee, the right hand of our Holy Father, La-Jay, assure you that freedom and equality, brotherhood and benevolence is the slogan of the Headquarters now. I'm going to give you some practical examples of the revolutionary changes which are taking place in El-Deen's day to day life." Now he reads from a paper:

"One—From now on, the sisters who are under training will have equal rights with the brothers. Their rooms and their facilities will be as comfortable and their guard-companions will all be as friendly and merciful as the brothers'. The sisters with newborn babies will visit their babies three times a day for breastfeeding.

"Two—Sultan's room, the bloody barbershop, as named by the El-Deenians, will be closed forever. Instead, a pleasantly furnished conversation room will replace it. I, myself, will show up frequently in the room to converse with the brothers. My wife, Sister Najiba, will talk to the sisters.

"Three—The menu will change. More nutritious items will be added.

"Four— Regular medical check-ups will be provided. Brother Doctor Halal, the Holy Healer of El-Deen and his hard working team will visit the patients regularly.

"Five—Soap will be provided for all the underground rooms.

"Six—Religious education will be provided for the cells of Hall Twenty. This will be offered in the form of private tutoring sessions. These brothers and sisters will have a last chance to purify their ideology, repent, and join the ranks of the repentants and enjoy the comforts of the sixth floor.

"There are more changes to come," Kamal says with a pleasant smile. "This is an ongoing revolution! Brothers and Sisters, support your staff by following the rules. Further announcements will be made this evening. Tune to your Headquarters. We're the Holy Faculty of your University, at your service. May God and the Holy Ones lead you to the path of Faith! Amen." He vanishes. A military march plays over a black flag, waving in the wind.

"We are the mirror as well as the face in it—" Agha says.

"We are pain, and what cures pain, both," Shams continues.

"Dervish!" I shake the old man. "Dervish Ali, wake up, I need to talk to you."

The old man doesn't move. Agha keeps reciting the quatrains. He reads a line, Shams continues the stanza, remembering his lines. Ismail and Teimoor are in a remote village beyond Mount Alborz, at the shore of the Caspian Sea. They talk about trout fishing.

I feel alone. I need to talk. I'm tired of watching my cellmates and listening to them. I don't remember anything of my past. Sahar even fades away from my mind and when she appears, she casts a pale shadow, as if she is present and not present.

Kamal has changed again. I saw it and I have no doubt. He is one of them now. But wasn't he one of them from the beginning? At one stage of our journey he went through something like a change. I noticed different traits in him: Ilych's influence, my influence. Now he is close to La-Jay and Halal. He is turning into them. Kamal, the Tree Frog! That's what I name you, brother. You change to green sitting on a leaf, and to brown on a tree trunk!

And your World Revolution, brother, your Holy Internal War, your cleansing mission—all are reduced to this petty reform. Yes this a reform, brother, not a revolution. Don't fool me! Soup and soap, private tutor instead of torturer, and conversation, not interrogation. Ah, Kamal, how frail you are! Just remembering you kneeling down on the cold cement, weeping your eyes out because you denied the Last Holy One, makes me vomit. How unreliable, how unstable, how capricious you are! You loony, you bastard, you worthless color-changing tree frog!

The One-Armed Ayatollah

Late, after Shams falls asleep, after Agha, Ismail, and Teimoor get tired of talking about hunting leopards in the jungles of the north, after the old dervish's lingering in silence and sinking into the abyss of a dark dream, late, when the last anthem ends, they bring in a one-armed Ayatollah. He still wears his black robe, but one of the sleeves is empty. They have taken his turban from him. He is bald. His beard is salt and pepper. He limps a few steps to the right and left. Then he sits in the middle of the cell. There is no wall left to lean against. They haven't whipped him, but there are purple bruises on his wrinkled neck.

"Where is the House of God, son?" he asks me.

"There!" I point to the TV set.

He kneels on the hard floor and bows, facing the TV, murmuring his prayers. He raises one arm to the ceiling and looks up as if he is seeing the cloudless sky. He doesn't have a rosary, nor a sacred stone. His forehead each time touches the cold cement.

"Say that there is no god except the God—"

A quick snapshot of a scene flashes in my head, then everything goes dark: a boy and a girl bend over the railings watching the Holy Procession. A one armed sheikh runs to reach the procession, his four wives gasp and run behind him, carrying his slippers. The twins laugh with delight, even though on the day of the Holy Mourning, laughter is forbidden.

Conversation With Shams, 1

Shams is quiet. His verses don't mark the days. But it must be a new day now, I can feel it. Some of us are up, pacing up and down. I wake up and find myself in a crowded cell. Dervish Ali, the boy, and the Ayatollah were not in my dream, they were real. The Ayatollah has problems sitting on the toilet, emptying himself in front of everybody. Agha tries to convince him that there is no other way here. Either this, or in his pants.

"We'll turn our heads away and you'll have more privacy, sir," Agha says. "Believe me, just the first time is difficult, then you get used to it. We have washed each other's shit here." He laughs.

"I surrender myself to the Almighty!" The Ayatollah says and farts.

The dervish sits on the cot, staring at Agha. It's impossible to penetrate his mind.

Ismail and the boy, Teimoor, are still sleeping. Side by side. Father and a son.

Shams is mute. All of Agha's work was in vain. He awoke quietly, opened one eye and stared at the ceiling. Motionless.

"Talk to Shams," Agha tells me. "We shouldn't let him fade away. Talk about whatever you want. Just go, sit with him and talk."

I lay down next to Shams and hold my head on my palm, looking at his profile. His bad eye is on my side; his good eye stares at the ceiling. His nose is straight, shapely—a Roman nose. I picture him with dark curly hair, a pair of black piercing eyes behind thin-rimmed glasses. I picture him standing up, his body erect. A chill runs through my veins. This man must have been tall and handsome, filled with verses from head to foot. A poet himself, or a teacher of poetry. This man, such a man, could have stolen a young woman's heart.

"Shams, you know me, don't you? If you know me wink with your left eye."

Shams doesn't wink.

"That's all right. I don't have poems by heart, but I can tell you stories perhaps. You know, Shams, before they brought me to this cell, I knew more about myself than now. In the last room, in Sultan's, I remembered plenty. Do you think they drug us here? I mean in this cell?"

Shams is mute.

"This Ayatollah. Let me start with him. Because he is here in front of my eyes and cannot disappear—the way my memories do. This old man reminds me of a sheikh in our neighborhood who had one arm and limped. He lived in the last house in the row of match-box houses at the end of New

Spring Street. First he had two wives, and then, four. Sahar and I hated him. He hated us. He hated our whole family. Our grandfather the most. Our grandfather had changed religions several times and didn't have one in the end.

"The Sheikh called the Black Flaggers. It was a New Year's day. They arrested my sister and took her to El-Deen for dancing the fire dance. But, wait—this can not be true. This must be a dream. When Sahar danced the fire dance, she was a little girl and there were no Black Flaggers then. It was Monarch's time. The Monarch had different kinds of guards. They wouldn't have minded people dancing. They would only arrest people if they were against the Monarchy. The Monarch himself had a group of dancers, the Royal Court's Dance Company. Our mother wanted my sister to become a dancer—a member of that company. Sahar practiced for years and became a dancer. She fulfilled our mother's wish. Then she left the country to become even a better dancer, to become the star of the company—I don't know the rest—there is a missing link. She never wrote. No one ever went to see what happened to her. I was in Raz, then—

"Did she return? As a dancer? Or something else? Ismail tells a story about her. In Ismail's story she doesn't seem to be a dancer anymore. She is more like a revolutionary. Her husband is in prison. She is in danger. Did you hear Ismail's story? No. You were asleep. In Agha's story, she is not a dancer either. Agha's story matches Ismail's. Do you think they have practiced it together before I came here? But you were asleep all through it and you can't help.

"How is it to go blank, Shams? Is it gradual? Or sudden? Am I becoming like you?

"You used to wake up early, with, 'Late by myself in the boat of myself—' on Sufi Days and 'Let him kiss me with the kisses of his mouth—' on Solomon Days. What happened, Shams? I miss your poems. Sing, Shams, sing for me. It's as if you're singing them for me. It's as if these lines are written for me. I know you feel the same way, or felt the same way when you used to sing them. Agha too. He feels the same. And Ismail. Love is in all of us. What I feel is what Dervish feels and what Agha feels. Although Dervish and Agha are the either side of a coin. Truth is one. Do you get me? I'm not really very good at expressing myself. To tell you the truth, I don't have much education. I'm sure that you used to be a

475

knowledgeable man. I like to think that you were a poet, who taught literature. Who else could recite all these lines by heart? And probably many more which you've forgotten now. I don't mean that I've never read before. I've read books. But without guidance. I'm self-educated. I read mostly when I lived with my Uncle Yahya.

"Uncle Yahya was the uncle who rode the bike. Everybody thought he was crazy, but he wasn't. He biked all day long and then sat in his dark room, contemplating, reflecting on what he had seen or heard in the streets. In his youth he was an oil-worker, a union organizer in the city of Raz. He was a self-educated revolutionary. This Agha somehow reminds me of him. He is him and he is not him. Uncle Yahya was passive, shy. Agha is bold and energetic. Look at him now, arguing with Dervish and Ayatollah at the same time!

"Hey, Shams, Shams—I like to talk to you. I'd never enjoyed talking to anyone like this before. Not even to Loony Kamal, when he was still a friend. Kamal is nothing to me. Some time I'll talk to you about him. You help me remember myself. Lately, I've been confused and empty. Distanced. Thank you, my friend. Now if you heard all that I said wink with your good eye."

Shams's open eye stays open.

The Former Poet Laureate

Now Agha sits with Shams, recites the lines, and has him repeat. Shams' lips move, but I'm not sure if he is repeating. The Ayatollah sleeps on the cot. Dervish Ali, Teimoor, and Ismail are cramped against the right wall. They are quiet, each plunged into himself. I lie down at the foot of Ayatollah's cot and listen to him hissing regularly like a machine.

Is he Sheikh Ahmad? Why not? Let's assume that Sheikh Ahmad climbed the theological ladder and became an Ayatollah. This is possible. At the beginning of the Revolution, he had a respectable governmental position. But later he found himself in the wrong faction. Before he had time to shift to the right faction, they arrested him and brought him here. Why has he aged so much?

While I'm busy creating the Ayatollah's biography, the guards open the iron gate and push a half-naked beggar in. A dirty rag is covering his body. He is a skeleton of a man, ribs sticking out of his dark skin. His knees buckle under him. He melts onto the floor. I look at his long bony face, hair down to his shoulders, long, kinky beard and restless rolling eyes. I notice a pale red bandana around his head. I recognize my uncle.

"Uncle Massi!" I get close to him, ready to open my arms.

"My name is Massi-Alla Nadim El-Omat. I'm the poet Laureate of the Holy Republic," he says aggressively.

"But Uncle—" I mumble.

"I'm nobody's Uncle. They've made a mistake bringing me here. The whole thing is a misunderstanding. I'm the Great Leader's sole companion: Massi-Alla Nadim—" and he repeats his long name again.

I leave him alone, and sit in a corner, watching him. He is the same Uncle Massi, with his Messiah face. A bit older than before. I remember that I saw him on TV reciting his ode, praising the Leader. He is not lying about being the Poet Laureate of the Republic. But what happened to him? Now I try to put his story together:

Our crazy uncle claimed to be the poet-prophet all his life. He even took part in the First Revolt when Sahar and I were eight or nine. All the participants of that revolt were arrested, except Uncle, Sheikh Ahmad, and Salman the Brainless. But Uncle lost his beloved wife, Mariam the Big Mole.

Years later, the Revolution happened and soon Uncle realized that he could not be the poet-prophet anymore. The winners of the Revolution already had a prophet and a big one too. He might even have put himself in trouble by claiming to be a prophet. The Republic lacked a poet, Uncle thought. So, cunningly, he assumed a very humble role: a poor poet who admired the Republic and its Great Leader. He wrote long odes, praising the Leader and the Holy Revolution in quatrains. Local religious newspapers published his poems. Or maybe he just recited them in the public squares and bazaars. The guards took the news to the sheikhs, the sheikhs to the Ayatollahs, and the Ayatollahs to the Great Leader.

They took Uncle Massi to the Leader's headquarters. The Leader felt very much pleased listening to Uncle's long odes, praising him and the Faith. He made Uncle the Poet Laureate of the Republic and Uncle lived safely and comfortably in the Great Leader's house for a period. He sat in the Holy Balcony on the Leader's right side, but slightly behind him, and waved to the pilgrims and worshipers with a stiff hand, exactly as the Leader waved.

Now this caused immense envy among the sheikhs, Ayatollahs, and all ranks of bearded men with or without a turban who buzzed like hungry flies around the Holy One's house. They wanted to get rid of this crazy man who was now allowed to wear the Leader's robes. They whispered among themselves, what if the crazy poet wears a turban one of these days? The Leader's turban? This is most dangerous for the Republic.

They also worried about the possibility of the Great Leader disinheriting his son and announcing the crazy poet as his successor. The Faith would fall, and the World Revolution would die in its cradle, the bearded men said. So they tried to destroy Uncle Massi.

But the Leader really loved our uncle. Uncle was his only companion. For a while, the Leader had not set foot into his wife's chamber or talked intimately with his sons. He was bitter with everybody. He thought that nobody cared about the Holy Revolution and the Faith. All the buzzing flies worried about was what they could take from the Revolution. Massi-Alla, the Leader thought, was the only faithful who didn't want anything for himself. He was content with his long rolls of paper and his feather pen. And the Leader loved him for his dignity.

This is what the enemies did: they dug out Uncle's family history and found out that Massi-Alla's father was a faithless quack. His mother had died long ago as a crazy beggar in one the Precipices of Oblivion. One of his sisters had married an activist. This activist brother-in-law had gone mad in El-Deen at the time of the Damn Monarch. The same sister later mingled with the monarchists in the Alleys of Heaven where she ran a beauty salon. In this salon, she and her corrupt friends gambled and partied every night. But worst of all was this: Massi-Alla's nephew and niece, the twins, were confined to El-Deen as enemies of the Faith and the Holy Revolution.

They reported the corruptions of this family to the Leader to blur His Holiness' mind. Nothing could have changed the Great Leader's love and affection to hatred and rage except for this report of pleasure seekers, unbelievers, and atheists. They arrested Uncle Massi while he was enjoying his evening walk in the Great Leader's rose garden, taking notes for the new ode he had to recite at the opening ceremony of the anniversary of the Revolution. They pushed him into the black van. He wept and pleaded, repented of sins he hadn't committed. But they didn't take him to the sixth floor where the repentants were. They wanted to get rid of him, so they took him to Hall Twenty, cell number four, the cell of the Unbreakables.

Now Uncle whispers something under his lips, fingering a carnelian rosary. They haven't taken his rosary from him. Maybe it was a gift from the Great Leader.

I approach him and squat next to him, watching his dry, stony face. "Uncle, don't you remember me? The twins? Sahar—and I—"

Uncle Massi turns his back to me, showing his annoyance by raising his voice, praying in Arabic.

I don't attempt to talk to him anymore. Either he doesn't recognize me, or denies me with the hope that he can go out and join the Great Leader.

At lunch time, we sit in factions. The Ayatollah and Uncle Massi eat together on the cot. They chat, pray, and exchange Arabic words from the Holy Book. Ismail, Teimoor, and Agha eat around the white scarf. I stay with Shams and feed him. Dervish Ali doesn't eat.

We sleep in the same fashion, in factions. Ayatollah takes the cot (although he is not wounded and he is younger than the dervish); Uncle sleeps at the foot of Ayatollah's cot. They chat, pray, take turns fingering and kissing the sacred rosary; they whisper Arabic until late.

When his good eye is open, I talk to Shams. When it's closed, I close my eyes and try to sleep. Ismail and Teimoor sleep side by side, talking about village life, comparing Teimoor's northern village by the sea to Ismail's eastern one in the folds of Mount Solomon. They talk about horses. Ismail tells his young companion long stories about Soluch, his brave, old horse. Agha lies down close to the toilet bowl without complaining. Dervish Ali doesn't sleep.

Conversation With Shams, 2

"Once I was a gauger in the city of Raz," I whisper into Shams' right ear. His left eye is open. "This rhythmic hiss of Ayatollah's snore reminds me of the hissing sounds of the machines. I walked all through the night on huge tanks. The oil ran under my feet like a river trapped in a pipe. I could feel it and hear its tiny tides, hitting the metal walls of the tank. The sky above me was as dark as the ocean below. But suddenly, hundreds of torches lit the black field; the sky turned red. The glare flickered on and off, on and off, like a warning sign.

"Nights—many nights—walking up and down the tank, I called her name in the hissing hum of the machines. I said, 'Sahar, come back! It's getting close now. Very close. The day that I'll shut the gauges is approaching. Look at the warning lights!' I knew that the Revolution was coming. We were preparing for it in the old man's bookstore.

"It's strange that I'm remembering all this. Is this our last night, Shams? I've heard that whenever the Unbreakables' cell fills with prisoners, another Cleaning Up Operation happens. But isn't it better to die? Agha would argue with me. He is eternally hopeful. The old man of Raz who had a bookstore full of people was like that. Agha reminds me of him. They are one and they are not.

"Shams, is this our last night?"

Shams' good eye is closed.

I crawl to where Uncle Massi is sleeping. I sit up next to him and look down at his face. His calloused, sun-burned skin has gone pale in the Great Leader's mansion. I smell rose-water on his skin. The red bandana, now a ragged cloth, is tied around his forehead. Mariam the Big Mole's belt has faded and lost its scent. In the TV program when he was still a Poet Laureate, Uncle wore a sheikh's robe. They must have taken the robe back and given him back his rags.

"Uncle Massi," I whisper. "Crazy Uncle Massi! Goodnight!"

Seven Bullets

Sixteen hooded guards invade the cell, two for each of us. They handcuff and push us out. The cold muzzles of their guns touch our temples. They drag Shams like an empty sack behind them. They hit the dervish in the mouth. He keeps murmuring.

They take us to the courtyard. "Ah!" I tell myself. "This is outside. Finally I'm outside and this is the end." The first thing we all do is to look at the sky. It's the strangest blue, the darkest of all. The Wall of the Almighty rises up to this gloom. I've seen this wall many times in my life. It has dark holes in it. Many. Bullet holes. Some of the blood stains on the wall have darkened, some are still fresh. Crimson red. I feel a creeping chill in my feet. I look down at the courtyard's cement floor. We are standing in a pool of blood.

But they don't line us up. Instead, they push and prod us into a van. We sit in two rows, facing each other. The hooded guards sit between us, guns aimed at our temples. The van moves. There is no window, no way to see outside, so they don't blindfold us. One of us weeps. This must be the child.

Where are they taking us? A different prison? Somewhere in the middle of a desert to kill us? But why? Why not kill us at the Wall of the Almighty? I blink to be able to see Agha's face. Maybe I can read something in his wise eyes. Maybe he will smile and make me feel better. But the darkness is deep. I hear heavy breathing, the hissing sound of Ayatollah's nostrils. He doesn't dare pray. Dervish Ali mumbles something and they smack him. The child weeps. They let him weep. But Ismail, hand-cuffed, cannot wrap his arm around the boy's bony shoulders.

The road is bumpy. The van bounces up and down. What is outside? How does it look? I feel an unbearable urge to see outside. The van stops. The guards open the door and push us out. They hit and prod us and pierce our shoulders with the muzzles of their guns. We find ourselves in a vast blue desert. Nothing grows here, not even thorn bushes. Flat dirt spreads endlessly, and the sky is close to the earth. This is the end of the earth, I think, where there is nothing and you confuse the sky with the ground. The same strange, luminous blue of the heavens reflects in the soft sand.

But there is a wall here too. It stands alone. Behind it the desert continues. This is a brick wall, the exact twin of the Wall of the Almighty. On this one, there are no holes or blood stains. They push us to the wall. We stand facing it. I smell fresh mortar; this wall is a new one.

Shams cannot stand. He slips and falls down. The guards slap him. Ismail says, "He cannot stand!" and one of the guards backhands Ismail on the mouth. His ring's big carnelian stone, carved with the picture of the Great Leader, tears Ismail's lip.

The guards finally believe that Shams is not able to stand. They order Ismail and Agha to hold him up from both sides. Teimoor is crying, loud and infantile. He talks in his native language. The Ayatollah prays loud, his voice shaking, "Be witnessed that there is no god except the God!" He has no fear anymore. Death is coming, taking him to heaven, where all the prophets and Holy Ones await his arrival. There will be a feast in the seventh garden of heaven for his homecoming. The dishes of heavenly fruits, the meats and sherbets, will all be waiting for him. He is too old for the Hoories—the beautiful long haired angels, but he can watch and admire them, when they serve him and wash his earthly wounds.

Uncle Massi shouts, "Enough of this now! I'm your poet-prophet, bastards! Fuck you! Fuck your fake revolution!" A guard rams his mouth with his gun butt. Massi vomits blood. His teeth come off in a red, thick foam, running down his beard.

The guards move away from us. They are behind us, preparing their guns. In a few seconds of total silence, when all of us are holding our breaths, I hear the swoosh sound: swoosh, swoosh... dump! Swoosh, swoosh... dump! I raise my head, slightly, so that the guards won't notice me, to see if Ali the Bricklayer, Ali the Wall Raiser, is up there laying brick on top of brick. He is. I see him—small as an insect. I whisper, "Sahar can you see him?" The guards' guns click, but instead of the sounds of the bullets, I hear Dervish Ali screaming, "I found the answer! I found it! I'm the Hagh!" In a strange frenzy, he rips his white robe off and dances nakedly, repeating, "Hagh, Hagh, Hagh, Hagh—" One of the guards shouts, "Fire!" Agha, holding Shams with his right hand, raises his left fist up and screams, "Death to the Satanic Republic! All Power to the People!"

They fire.

I whisper again, "Sahar—" I want this to be the last word on my lips.

But the guns are not machine guns. They are regular shot guns and they fire in a strange way. One bullet at a time. I count them. They fire seven bullets. I look to my right: Teimoor is the first one in the row; Ismail, the second; Shams, the third; Agha, the fourth. They are all on the ground. They roll in the dust, blood foaming and bubbling out of their mouths. I look to my left: the naked dervish, Uncle Massi, and the Ayatollah are on the ground, jerking with the last convulsions.

I'm on my feet. I turn back and look at the guards. They laugh behind their paper masks, cleaning the muzzles of their guns. They take me to the black van and only one of them sits with me. The van coughs, bumps up and down, and runs through the desert. I beat the black iron walls of the van, screaming, "Let me die too! Don't take me back to El-Deen! Please!" My guard pulls his hood up and winks at me. He is Kamal, Loony Kamal. The Immortal.

Grief

I open my eyes into Agha's lashless gray eyes. They are shadowed. He is sitting beside me, watching my face. I look around and find Ismail sitting against the opposite wall, knees folded into his chest, head rested on his knees. Shams is lying down in his usual place. One eye open. They're alive, I think. But, where are the others?

"When they shot the bullets, your face twitched in your sleep," Agha says.

"Seven?"

"That's right. Seven," he says.

"One bullet for each? What if they don't die?" I ask him, as if he has all the answers.

"Some time, long after the last anthem, they took the four of them. They said La-Jay has ordered not to waste more than one bullet each. They were not worth more."

"Teimoor, too?"

"Yes."

"My Uncle?"

"And the old dervish."

"Even the Ayatollah?"

"Oh, yes!"

I look at Ismail. Agha follows my gaze. He is not going to recover anymore, I think. He had found a son. A flower in this murkiness.

Agha nods, as if reading my mind.

For a long time we stay quiet, but the babble and rattle from the Satan's Box kills the silence. Now Agha paces up and down restlessly and finally speaks.

"We have no way other than forgetting. We need to travel back in time. To where four of us were here and no one had come. Can we do this, my friend?" He addresses Ismail. "We have to survive."

"That's how you lose your memory, Master. You want to wipe the pain out. This is not the first time we knew people. But you manage to forget. I don't like this. Let me grieve."

"It will weaken you, Ismail. It will break your back!"

"I can't forget the child. When they took him, his hair stood up. All his hair—like he'd been struck by thunder." Ismail breaks into sobs, hiding his face in Sahar's scarf.

"Let's mourn then. Let's weaken our morale. Let's do what they want!" Agha sulks and sits on the toilet. He holds his chin, seals his lips.

Pain, the Cure of Pain

I stay empty for a long time. Days and nights. There is no way to tell how long. Agha pleads with me to help him work with Shams. He says we need to talk to him, help him to stay alive. But I can't. It pains me to disappoint the old man. It pains me to let Shams fade away. But the lights have burned out in me. I'm all dark within. Maybe only one weak, twinkling candle still flickers somewhere in my chest. A vague hope.

So I sit and do not turn my eyes. Not even a fragment of the past is left in me. The ceaseless noise of the TV does not remind me of anything or anyone. Kamal appears on the screen frequently. But I don't care. He addresses the "faithful students," announces new changes, talks about the reform. New toilet bowls, disinfectant, larger paper cups, frequent visits by the guard-companions. He has changed some of El-Deen's terminology. The prison keepers and the torturers, who were called trainers, are "educators" now. Special torturers and brain-washers are "private tutors;" the inmates who were called trainees before are now simply "students," the repentants, "faithseekers," the guards, "guard-companions;" doctors are "healers" and so on. As I sit and listen to the accounts of this genius reform, the weak candle close to my heart goes dim.

I eat my rice pudding and lentil soup alternatively. I go to sleep, empty myself and do the same things over and over again. I see Agha as if he is at the end of a long tunnel. He feeds Shams. Pulls him up. Takes him to the toilet. Helps him lie down. Lays Shams' head on his lap. Recites the stanzas one after the other, loudly. Waits for him to repeat. Shams repeats sometimes, murmuring in a low voice. He doesn't repeat most of the time.

Ismail keeps mourning, head on his knees, or lying down on the cot, the scarf covering his face.

Two guards open the gate. They are not the ones who bring the food. They're not masked. One of them reads out of a paper.

"Is anyone by the name of Teimoor, here?"

"Not anymore," Agha answers.

"What do you mean by 'not anymore,' you old wizard! Any of you called Teimoor?" He repeats.

Ismail raises his head and looks at the guards. His piercing eyes dig hot holes in them.

"Are you Teimoor?" the guard asks.

"No," Ismail says. "They shot him a while ago."

"Shit!" the guard says.

"What's the matter?" his friend asks.

"They shouldn't have shot him. He is released. This is an order from Holy Kamal. Giving the boy another chance to fight at the Holy Front," the guard says.

"Well, he is with the Almighty now. If he wasn't a sinner, he is definitely with Him. Let's go before the Holy Show starts," the second guard says. They leave, slamming the iron gate. We hear the metallic echo in the empty hallway.

Ismail groans like a wounded lion, then he jumps up to his feet, raises his long arms, looking at the ceiling as if he is on Mount Solomon, raising his arms to the sky. "Plague on you, destroyers of life!" he screams, shaking his fists at the ceiling. This doesn't satisfy him. He punches into the hard wall. "A burning curse on you, offspring of Satan!" He spits on the iron gate. "You child-killers! Bastards, Godless barbarians! You criminals! Creators of hell on earth! Baser, uglier, meaner than worms. I smash you under my feet!" He stamps his feet and smashes invisible worms on the floor. "You blood-sucking worms. Not snakes, but worms. Worthless worms! The blood of our children sucked up by worms! Worms! Worms! I smash them under my feet. Like this: Ah, ah, ah, ah!" He stamps the floor, killing the imaginary worms.

This way Ismail breaks his silence. A new pain cures the old one. And a new pain in my body breaks my silence too. I press the flat of my hand under my abdomen, moaning and repeating what the dervish once said, "Maybe the cure of pain is pain."

Ismail believes that I have a stone in my bladder. He tells a story about one of his villagers who screamed with pain and agony, pressing the same spot under his belly. When the wise great-grandfather, the advisor of the village, prescribed water for his pain, people laughed and whispered that the

485

old man had lost his wits. But water cured the sick man. It washed the stone out of his body, cleaned his bladder.

So Ismail takes me to the sink, forcing me to drink. He repeats this many times a day. But Agha is not sure this will be enough. He believes that I have to ask for a doctor. This must be an infection, Agha says. The fear of going out of the cell and lying on a gurney in the Clinic prevents me from saying anything to the guards. What if they take me out and make me walk in the long hallways again? I won't be able to walk with such pain. Or what if they make a mistake and take me to a torture chamber, or the Black Box?

I squat on the floor and let my burning urine drip in my pants. I bite my lips hard and rock myself, moaning like a wounded animal. This way we all forget our loss.

The Silent Clock

Ismail has moved me under the sink. Every five minutes, he lifts me up, cups his two broad hands under the running water, and orders me to drink. I bend and drink from the large fountain of Ismail's hands as if this is the water of life. I drink until my belly swells. After a few days the dagger stops piercing my bladder. I lie down at Shams's side, exhausted.

Shams is withering away. He doesn't murmur. The only sign showing that he is still alive is his one eye. He opens it in the morning and shuts it at night. Shams, our silent clock.

"Shams," I call him. "Let's talk. We haven't talked for a long time. The last time was the night before the execution. Do you remember how crowded our cell was? All of them are gone now. Good for them. They wouldn't be able to survive. But the boy. He had a chance to go to the front again and this time, who knows? He might have become a hero, returned to his village as a proud young veteran, grown up, married, raised children. He had a chance to die old.

"What is the purpose of all this, Shams?" I continue. "Leave our mother's wombs, grow up, work, make a family, follow the same old path, the same worn out road everybody else has followed before? To follow, to suffer, to grow old and die? Do you get me, my friend? What else is there? Something beyond this. My sister and I felt this early in our childhood. This vanity.

We wanted to do something. Something brave, different, something that would change the old order of things. Why was Faithland so dark and smelly, we asked. Who decided that Zahra should wash the people's filth from sunrise to sundown all year round? Who put our father behind bars for trying to change the old order of things?

"We dreamed about breaking the huge gate of El-Deen and taking our father and other prisoners out. El-Deen was the monster that we wanted to grow up and challenge.

"But I wasn't the fighter, Shams. If it weren't for her, I would have plunged deep into myself and hid there like a little dervish. I was the old part, she was the young. I was the cold part, she, the hot. I was shadow, she was light. I was night, she was dawn. I was moon, she, the sun. But her fire always warmed my soul. She's been gone for a long time, but I still feel her warmth.

"Do I make sense? You follow me? I carry love in my cold heart," I say, striking myself on the chest. "Shams! Hey—don't close your good eye!"

Agha's Revision

Before I drift and pass the blurred line—the entrance to the realm of dreams—Agha shakes my shoulders.

"Get up, son, get up!" He goes to Ismail and shakes him too. "Ismail, sorry brother, but I have to wake you up. Hey, Ismail!"

Agha is red in the face. His broad forehead and his scalp—now covered with a thin layer of snow white hair—are blushing. His blood pressure must have risen suddenly.

We sit in the middle of the cell, Ismail rubbing his sleepy eyes.

"This might be just another night and one thousand more nights may follow," Agha says. "But what if this is the last? Or the last night for one of us?" He rubs his forehead.

"Is that all, Master?" Ismail asks.

"No, my friend. This is not all." But he hesitates.

"What is bothering you, brother?" Ismail asks softly. "It's so fucking easy to forget to care for you," Ismail says guiltily. "Damn me, the selfish brute that I am. Day in and day out, I haven't even asked you how you are, haven't taken your pulse to see if your blood pressure is all right! Damn me!"

"Stop Ismail! I didn't wake you to feel sorry for me. I'm fine. It's just a thought, maybe even a dream. I guess I dreamed our story. I want to change my ending."

"Oh!" Ismail laughs, showing his big white teeth. "Go on, brother, change it the way it suits you. We sit here all ears. Isn't that right my friend?" he asks me.

"Change it, Agha!" I urge him. "Change your ending. The night is long and the story is all yours."

"She came with the baby and the cold silence broke in the old man's house," Agha says, staring at the windowless wall. "The laughter was loud, the screams were of joy, and the cry was for food. The old man's apartment was filled with life. The girl brushed her long hair, sitting cross-legged on the old man's bed. The little boy ran toward him, as if he were going to fall and break his head, but the old man opened his arms and held the child just before he fell. He threw him up and enjoyed the baby's shriek of fear and then his pleasure. The mother sang. The baby sang the same song with his funny voice. The old ragged rug flew." He stops.

"So when the day came that the smuggler was supposed to come and take the mother and child away," Agha continues, "the old man changed the plan and his destiny changed with it. He asked the girl not to cross the border. She might never be able to return. She might suffer the rest of her life. 'Don't you have a lost one here?' the old man asked her. She said she had. She knew where her husband was, but she didn't know her brother's whereabouts. The old man said that he had written to her brother at the break of the Revolution that his sister was back. But the young man had already left the city of Raz. He never saw the letter.

"'Let's go to Raz, then,' the old man urged the girl. 'Let's go to the old house at the end of the shady cul-de-sac. Let's stay there with Naz-Gol, the lady of the house. No one can find us there. We can live there as long as the Republic survives. And your brother may show up. That place is his home.'"

"In Naz-Gol's house," I hear myself continuing Agha's story, "the young woman found a trunk, gold-rimmed with turquoise flowers adorning the black surface, a lock hanging on it. Naz-Gol said this was his trunk, the brother's, and now the sister could have it. The old woman gave her a small key hanging on a thin gold chain from her neck. The girl opened the trunk.

There she found Grand-Lady's Turkman carpet.

"She spread it out on the porch the way her brother used to. She sat on the carpet, facing the orange blossoms on the wall and one single rose bush with strange blossoms—all colors in one. Naz-Gol washed and scrubbed the blue fountain, letting the water jet out and reach the blue sky. The Uncle, Naz-Gol, the young mother, and the child sat around the carpet's peacock when the sun set and listened to the splash of the water and the flap of the sparrows' wings. Sparrows had returned to the small yard to build their old nests."

Ismail joins in: "Ismail stood on top of Mount Solomon each dawn, waiting for a messenger to come and bring him the news of a woman who needed his help. The messenger never came. The ditches down in the dry valley stayed there waiting. No one jumped over them like a deer; no one passed them to leave her land behind."

"As it is in the old stories," Agha sighs, "one ends up happy, one ends up sad, one gains, the other loses. The winner's happiness is the loser's grief. The old man became happy. What more did he want? The ancient scent of lotus rising from Naz-Gol's long braids under his nose, Saba's laughter, the sound of life in his ears, the sight of beauty, the graceful peak of youth, his view. What else did he want?

"Naz-Gol brought him fresh brewed tea in a china pot and he looked at his old books, which had been locked in Naz-Gol's trunk for so long. He glanced at the yard now and then, watching the boy. The boy ran, chasing his mother who hid behind the rose bush, then leaped out with a happy cry. The boy laughed and fell in the fountain. The mother threw herself in the water, wading with her son. The old man smiled and told himself, 'If your end is close, Uncle, and you have to die soon, die now, you'll never be happier than this.'"

"The young mother asked thousands of questions of Naz-Gol," I continue. "What did my brother do all day? Did he plant this rose bush here? Where did he walk to work? Where is this refinery he used to work for? Take me there!"

"The old man and Naz-Gol took her to the refinery. But just once. She was not supposed to go out. The Black Flaggers were sitting in their vans at every intersection. Naz-Gol said, 'This is the Gas Alley. And this two-story mud and clay building, now whitewashed and flagged, is where the prostitutes' hovels once were. The guards stoned the wretched women and imprisoned them. They painted the place, called it 'the Marriage House.' They say there are more than a hundred women in this house. They bring starving young girls here. Virgins, mostly. Men come, pay some cash to a sheikh and he recites the prayer of the temporary marriage. The men go up to the rooms and spend time with their half-hour or one-hour wives. Some of these women are the ones who used to live in the hovels before the Revolution. They either survived the stoning, or were released from prison, and have their old jobs back. These older women teach the virgins their skills to prepare them for the temporary marriages.'

"Naz-Gol sighed, a sigh of grief, and continued, 'And here on your left, opposite the Marriage House, on top of that tank, is where your brother used to walk all night. He walked on the ocean of oil, as he used to call it.'

"'What was he?' The girl asked.

"'A gauger,' said Naz-Gol.

"'You know, my dear,' the old man said, putting one arm on her shoulder, and stretching out the other, pointing to the black tank. 'A gauger is a sailor; he has the rudder in his hands. He leads the ship. He turns the gauges off. Oil stops flowing into the tanks.'

"'Tanks?' the young woman asked.

"'Tanks, which take the oil to the barrels, which go to the ships, which leave our seas, heading toward the foreign lands—'

"'We always sought the storm,' the sister said. One thousand images of the past passed through her head."

"So Ismail never knew her," Ismail says. "The premonition was not a premonition, after all. It was a glimpse of hope, that he would find love in his barren life. Dawn after dawn, he rode Soluch, downhill, alone, to the old caravanserai to see if a messenger had brought him a message. No. No one was waiting for Ismail the Baluch."

"I pass," Agha says. "I'm content."

"In El-Deen, the young man opened his arms to pain," I say, "He waited for death. His twin was in Raz, safe with her son. Let the beheaders chop off his limbs, he thought. He danced the joy dance in a frenzy of love. The lover was alive, the fire was tall, burning in his chest. 'I'm It!' he screamed, when they took him to the wall. They spent only one bullet on him, but it pierced the heart, right where life pulsed. He died painlessly.

Blood didn't foam out of his mouth. He didn't wet his pants. His eyes didn't bulge out. Only a red circle stained his white shirt. The circle grew and grew and turned his shirt into a soaking wet flag. 'Can you see this?' he whispered to his sister before he died."

"The old man died in peace," Agha says. "One sunset, between the tea and the sparrows returning to their nest, Naz-Gol closed his eyelids. They buried him in the Rose Cemetery, near the tomb of the bard, the melancholic sufi poet. A tall weeping willow hung over the old man's grave. He rested in eternal shade," Agha ends, sighing with relief.

"Ismail never possessed a white scarf, a green peacock embroidered on one corner. He never helped the revolutionaries, never got arrested, never circled in El-Deen, never became Unbreakable and lost his memory. In an endless dusk, he rode to his remote village behind the back of the many-folded slopes of Mount Solomon. He found his house, his old wife, and his goats. Ismail the Baluch, Ismail the smuggler, Ismail the brave, became Ismail the Shepherd, Ismail the Tame. He tended his goats and grew old. His back stooped. His brave horse Soluch aged and became fat and lazy. Ismail stopped taking him out of the village. Ismail stayed barren, childless, loveless, until his end.

"But sometimes, in the dark depths of Ismail's dreams, there appeared a young woman in men's clothing, who ran over the ditches in the minefield like a deer, her baby on her back. On such nights, Ismail awoke, lit a candle, and stared at the flickering flame until dawn."

A Man with a Black Hood

I open my eyes and see a hooded man sitting in our cell. His hood is a black sack, covering him down to his waist. He sees through two holes, breathes through one hole. His black sleeved arms hang from two holes on the either side of the sack. They end in black-gloved hands. He wears black slacks, no boots. His huge boots, tall and polished, sit at the iron door. The man's feet are the largest I've ever seen. He sits on the floor next to the sink, doing nothing. He folds his knees halfway and awkwardly into his belly. His legs are too thick.

With the hooded man in the cell, we cannot talk anymore. We resume our daily life in total silence. We feed and clean Shams, but we don't talk to him. We uncover the TV screen and sit in front of it motionless, pretending to watch. This man, if a guard, or a repentant, is here to observe us. To see who is going crazy, who is rebellious, who is depressed. To report all this. If we talk to Shams, the black-hooded man will report that he is barely alive and they should get rid of him. This is what I think. He is here to observe.

Agha and I talk with our eyes. Agha is good at this. He can even laugh with his eyes. When he laughs, the wrinkles around his gray eyes move upward and form two fans. When he is sad, the corners fall down. Then he looks like a dying dog. Ever since he changed the end of his story, he is in a good mood. Like a young man, he exercises and takes care of Shams. He does more than Ismail does. He hums something these days. Because of the hooded man he doesn't hum aloud, but I recognize the song. I've heard it somewhere. As a child I've heard it. It's the rebel saying farewell to his lover: "Kiss me—kiss me for the last time—I'm going toward my fate. In the midst of the storm, I'm wandering with the boatmen—We sacrificed our lives—that's why we can't keep our promises—"

In his floppy gray pajamas, Agha moves around the cell like a housewife, tidying up, mopping the cement floor, washing the sheets. He washes, dries, and folds my shroud, the one Sultan wrapped me in when he jumped on my chest. He washes and dries Ismail's white scarf. He sticks his hand inside the toilet bowl and cleans it, humming the rebel's song.

Since Agha has changed the end of his story, Ismail sits in a corner sulking. He is depressed again. The presence of the unwelcome stranger gives him a good excuse not to communicate. He stops doing his daily exercises.

At the end of each day, after the soup and the last anthem, the hooded man lies down and sleeps, but we don't hear him snoring. What if he is awake, still watching us? Waiting for us to talk? Now he snores, his snore sounding like real nasal congestion. I crawl toward Ismail, whispering into his ear:

"Ismail, make the end of your story the way you want. It should end the way you wish. Do this and you'll feel better. I don't see why you should end up as a tame shepherd. Go back to the top of the mountains and straighten your stooped back!"

He smiles at me. The first smile in a long time. His pearl-white teeth show.

Flawless teeth. "Yessir!" He whispers and salutes me. "I'll go back to the mountain. The village doesn't suit me." He pauses and adds, "Now that I know where Aroose lives, I'll saddle Soluch and gallop with the speed of wind! I'll seek her and find her!"

This is the last thing I hear from Ismail the Baluch.

The Last Dance

With the sound of a soft lamentation wafting down from the TV, I open my eyes. My heart freezes; I stop breathing for a long moment. A hand is on my shoulder. I turn my head and see the black-sacked head blocking the light. He motions to me with his gloved forefinger, meaning, get up. I stand on my shaky legs. He calls Agha, Ismail, and Shams the same way—without a sound. He wears his heavy boots and tucks his pants in. Now I notice that he is very tall. He lines us up in the cell. He knows that Shams cannot stand. He lifts him up, hangs him on his right shoulder, like an old coat. We follow the tall hooded man down the empty hallway. No other guard shows up to help him. He is not armed or if he is, the gun is concealed.

Walking behind him, I listen to hear his key chain rattling in his pocket. But he is holding Shams' ankles tightly, pressing them against his right pocket. The chain doesn't hop.

We pass Sultan's room. I look at the tall iron doors of Hall Twenty and I wonder if other cells are empty. We reach the end of the hall. On the right, another hall opens its mouth; on the left there is a door. We are all barefoot on the cold black cement. We have to stand for a moment and wait for the hooded man to open the door. He pulls his key chain out of his pocket, but I can't see what it looks like. He opens the door. We follow him out.

I've been here before, here in this courtyard, not long ago. I raise my head and look at the sky. It's still dark—a black ceiling over the yard. Now I see the wall. The same wall with bullet marks on it. Dark stains of old blood. Some circle shaped, some dried up while running down, forming tear shapes. At the right side of the courtyard there is a tall post, a black flag hanging from it. Although there is no breeze, the flag is stretched, as if starched, or made of cardboard.

The hooded man doesn't lead us to the wall. He stops us ten steps away

493

from the wall, showing us soundlessly to stand where normally the guards stand. There are white marks on the floor. Each of us stands on a mark, lined up facing the wall. The hooded man is still holding Shams, trying to make him stand on his white mark. But Shams melts, his legs made of dough. Now eight guards appear out of nowhere. Two for each of us. The man with the black hood gives orders without a sound.

Two guards approach me. One hands me a machine gun and helps me to hold it the right way. He goes behind me, embraces me, holds my arms, and makes sure that my finger is on the trigger. I look like a student of target practice. This is a class. This man is teaching me how to shoot.

The second guard stands on my left side. He is a short man. My height. He points the muzzle of his revolver at my temple. From the corner of my eyes, I look at Agha, who is at my right. Two guards are doing the same thing to him. He turns his head to look at me. The corners of his gray eyes are hanging. A dying dog.

We stay in this awkward position for a long moment. My arms tire. The guard holding me from behind breathes heavily, his warm breath brushing my neck. He smells of grease—the cold grease of leftover meat. Now he places his forefinger over mine on the trigger.

They bring a few sacks in the courtyard. I count them. Seven burlap sacks. They are heavy and the guards carrying them on their shoulders are bent under the weight. They are potato sacks. But when they dump them on the cement, the sacks move and wriggle. The guards place them at the wall in a row.

The potato sacks are tied at the top with a piece of blonde rope. They keep wriggling; now I hear faint moaning. Suddenly a strange whining fills the quiet courtyard. It comes from of the sacks. Like a sound you hear after an earthquake from the people buried alive.

The hooded man steps back and stands under the black flag. He lifts his arms up, looking at the dark sky. He prays. Now he finally shouts something, but I can't make it out. The sacks continue moving and wriggling. One of them, the last one on the left, the one directly opposite me, stretches one arm up. I see a small burlap fist.

The hooded man lifts his right arm up to the level of his shoulder. Now he looks up at the tall wall of El-Deen as if expecting something from the white monster. The last signal, maybe. The signal comes. The hooded man brings his arm down and I hear the rattle of machine guns. Our machine guns.

The guard on my left hasn't shot me in my temple. I'm alive. So this means that I've pressed the trigger. With or without the help of the finger over my finger.

At the wall, the brown sacks are soaking wet with blood. Small wet circles expand fast, growing bigger, eating up the burlap. Some sacks don't move anymore. One or two move faintly. One of them, the one opposite me, the one with a fist in it, moves frantically. I imagine a human-sized fish in a dark net. The wounded fish pushes the walls of the sack from inside, trying to tear it up.

At last the rope loosens, unties, and a head pops out. A shaved head. Yellowish. Small. Now a figure pops out, as tall as a child in a long white gown, dotted with many red spots. The figure stands erect for a second, raises one arm to make a fist, looking at us. All four of us.

This is a small woman. Her large eyes have unusual shine. Either she smiles, or I think that she does. She walks a few tiny steps on her toes, away from the wall, toward us, and falls. Slow and melting. On the cement, not on the burlap sack. The way she falls is like the end of a dance, improvised on the spot with a sudden flash of inspiration. Her white gown spreads around her like a bride's. The small red dots expand and become a pool of blood.

Dawn comes. The black sky turns pale blue. Somewhere not far from here, the sun stretches itself up from inside the bosom of Alborz, as if from the depth of a deep dark well. The hooded man takes us back to our cell. "Chee, chee, chee—" Now he walks fast and I hear his key chain rattling in his pocket. The sound of thousands of chains hitting bare shoulders and chests. He walks ahead in the long hallway and we follow him behind.

At the cell, he opens the iron gate, leads Agha and Ismail in and slams the door. I notice that Shams is left in the courtyard, lying on the cold cement. Now the man pulls a long black scarf out of his pocket, ties it around my neck, and holds the end like a leash. He takes his black hood off, throwing it away. He walks ahead of me, pulling me behind. His key chain rattles.

495

from Lebanon

Samarakand

by Amin Maalouf
trans. by Russell Harris

Winner of the Prix des Maisons de la Presse

"[An] accomplished novel by one of the best European voices to have emerged in the last decade."

—*Kirkus Reviews*

"Remarkable... Maalouf has written an extraordinary book."

—*The Independent (London)*

ISBN 1-56656-200-7 · $35.00 hb
ISBN 1-56656-293-7 · $14.95 pb · 312 pages

---

from Lebanon

The Gardens of Light

by Amin Maalouf
trans. by Dorthy S. Blair

"A compelling tale... the poignant story of a man born before his time... the character of Mani is carefully and warmly drawn..."

—*Times Literary Supplement (London)*

"Maalouf is as eloquent as ever... [He] weaves tapestries of intrigue that illuminate a broader historical moment... Maalouf, in his engaging prose, goes a considerable way towards restoring Mani to us."

—*The Times (London)*

ISBN 1-56656-247-3 · $25.00 hb
ISBN 1-56656-248-4 · $15.00 pb · 272 pages

from Turkey

Cages on Opposite Shores

by Janet Berkok Shami

"The affirmative power of this work is graced with subtlety and simplicity."

—*Publishers Weekly*

Set in Istanbul, this novel tells the story of Meral, a modern-day Turkish woman searching for identity and renewal after leaving her husband of 11 years and realizing for the first time her part-Armenian heritage.

ISBN 1-56656-165-5 · $24.95 hb
ISBN 1-56656-157-4 · $11.95 pb · 256 pages

---

from Serbia

The Dawning

by Milka Bajic-Poderegin
trans. by Nadja Poderegin

"A tale of human joy and pain which has the power to stir the heart... *The Dawning* is a jewel of a story, with universal resonance."

—*The Ottowa Citizen*

"Remarkable... a moving portrayal of successive generations of Serbian women."

—*The Spectator (London)*

ISBN 1-56656-198-1 · $29.95 hb
ISBN 1-56656-188-4 · $14.95 pb · 384 pages

from Egypt

War in the Land of Egypt

by Yusuf al-Qa'id

"This haunting 1975 novel (which was banned in Egypt) is set during the 1973 October War... A chorus of superbly differentiated villager's voices chronicles the inescapable fate of ... Marsi, an Everyman (his very name means 'Egyptian') whose exile from his identity reverberates powerfully throughout this subtle study of injustice... A marvelous piece of work."
—*Kirkus Reviews*

ISBN 1-56656-227-9 · $12.95 pb · 192 pages

---

from Palestine

A Balcony Over the Fakihani

by Liyana Badr
trans. by P. Clark with C. Tingley

"An excellent, moving account of the effects of conflict..."
—*Journal of Palestine Studies*

"These novellas effectively represent war and suffering from the point of view of disenfranchised peoples, both Beirutis and Palestinians. Recommended..."

—*Library Journal*

ISBN 1-56656-104-3 · $19.95 hb
ISBN 1-56656-107-8 · $9.95 pb · 128 pages

---

from Lebanon

The Stone of Laughter

by Hoda Barakat
trans. by Sophie Bennett

Winner of the Al-Naqid Award

"This unusual story of Beirut... offers a vividly detailed portrayal of an unfamiliar culture... a gripping story filled with splendidly drawn secondary figures..."

—*Kirkus Reviews*

ISBN 1-56656-197-3 · $29.95 hb
ISBN 1-56656-190-6 · $12.95 pb · 240 pages

---

from Yemen

The Hostage

by Zayd Mutee' Dammaj
trans. by M. Jayyusi and C. Tingley

"The cultural anachronism that was the Imamate of Yemen is artfully captured in *The Hostage*... Dammaj's work vibrantly portrays a real Yemen that is still unknown to many Westerners, even as it is once again torn by revolution. Recommended..."

—*Library Journal*

ISBN 1-56656-146-9 · $24.95 hb
ISBN 1-56656-140-X · $10.95 pb · 168 pages